Raskolnikov was not used to crowds, and, as was said previously, he avoided society of every sort, especially recently. But now all at once he felt a desire to be with other people. Something new seemed to be taking place within him, and with it he felt a sort of thirst for company. (page 13)

"Man grows used to everything, the scoundrel!" (page 29)

"Can it be, can it be, that I will really take an axe, that I will strike her on the head, split her skull open . . . that I will tread in the sticky warm blood, break the lock, steal and tremble; hide, all spattered in the blood . . . with the axe . . . Good God, can it be?" (page 60)

Fear gained more and more mastery over him, especially after this second, quite unexpected murder. (page 80)

At first he thought he was going mad. A dreadful chill came over him; but the chill was from the fever that had begun long before in his sleep. Now he suddenly started shivering violently, so that his teeth chattered and all his limbs were shaking. (page 89)

"You think I am attacking them for talking nonsense? Not a bit! I like them to talk nonsense. That's man's one privilege over all creation. Through error you come to the truth!" (page 194)

Porfiry Petrovich was wearing a dressing-gown, very clean clothing, and trodden-down slippers. He was about thirty-five, short, stout, even corpulent, and clean shaven. He wore his hair cut short and had a large round head which was particularly prominent at the back. His soft, round, rather snub-nosed face was of a sickly yellowish color, but it also had a vigorous and rather ironical expression. It would have been good-natured, except for a look in the eyes, which shone with a watery, sentimental light under almost white, blinking eyelashes. The expression of those eyes was strangely out of keeping with his somewhat womanish figure, and gave it something far more serious than could be guessed at first sight. (page 238)

"Extraordinary men have a right to commit any crime and to transgress the law in any way, just because they are extraordinary." (page 247)

"Legislators and leaders, such as Lycurgus, Solon, Muhammed, Napoleon, and so on, were all without exception criminals, from the very fact that, making a new law, they transgressed the ancient one, handed down from their ancestors and held sacred by the people, and they did not stop short at bloodshed either." (page 247–248)

A minute later Sonia, too, came in with the candle, put down the candlestick and, completely disconcerted, stood before him inexpressibly agitated and apparently frightened by his unexpected visit. The color rushed suddenly to her pale face and tears came into her eyes . . . She felt sick and ashamed and happy, too. (page 301)

"Must I tell her who killed Lizaveta?" (page 385)

"Who is the murderer?" he repeated, as though unable to believe his ears. "You, Rodion Romanovich! You are the murderer," he added almost in a whisper, in a voice of genuine conviction. (page 433)

"You're a gentleman," they used to say. "You shouldn't hack about with an axe; that's not a gentleman's work." (page 517)

CRIME AND PUNISHMENT

Fyodor Dostoevsky

TRANSLATED BY CONSTANCE GARNETT
TRANSLATION REVISED BY JULIYA SALKOVSKAYA AND NICHOLAS RICE

WITH AN INTRODUCTION BY PRISCILLA MEYER
NOTES BY JULIYA SALKOVSKAYA AND NICHOLAS RICE

GEORGE STADE
CONSULTING EDITORIAL DIRECTOR

BARNES & NOBLE CLASSICS
NEW YORK

$\mathcal{B}$

BARNES & NOBLE CLASSICS

NEW YORK

Published by Barnes & Noble Books
122 Fifth Avenue
New York, NY 10011

www.barnesandnoble.com/classics

Dostoevsky's *Prestupleniye i nakazaniye* was originally published in Russian in 1866.
Constance Garnett's translation of *Crime and Punishment* was first published in 1914.

Published in 2007 by Barnes & Noble Classics with new Introduction,
List of Characters, Notes, Biography, Chronology, Inspired By,
Comments & Questions, and For Further Reading.

Introduction, List of Characters, and For Further Reading
Copyright © 2007 by Priscilla Meyer.

Note on Fyodor Dostoevsky, The World of Fyodor Dostoevsky and
Crime and Punishment, Notes, Inspired by *Crime and Punishment*,
Comments & Questions, and revisions to the Constance Garnett
translation by Juliya Salkovskaya and Nicholas Rice
Copyright © 2007 by Barnes & Noble, Inc.

Crime and Punishment
ISBN-13: 978-1-59308-081-5
ISBN-10: 1-59308-081-6
LC Control Number 2004102189

Produced and published in conjunction with:
Fine Creative Media, Inc.
322 Eighth Avenue
New York, NY 10001

Michael J. Fine, President and Publisher

Printed in the United States of America

QM

3   5   7   9   10   8   6   4

FYODOR DOSTOEVSKY

Fyodor Mikhailovich Dostoevsky was born in Moscow on October 30, 1821. His mother died when he was fifteen, and his father, a former army surgeon, sent him and his older brother, Mikhail, to preparatory school in St. Petersburg. Fyodor continued his education at the St. Petersburg Academy of Military Engineers and graduated as a lieutenant in 1843. After serving as a military engineer for a short time, and inheriting some money from his father's estate, he retired from the army and decided instead to devote himself to writing.

Dostoevsky won immediate recognition with the 1846 publication of his first work of fiction, a short novel titled Poor Folk. The important Russian critic Vissarion Grigorievich Belinsky praised his work and introduced him into the literary circles of St. Petersburg. Over the next few years Dostoevsky published several stories, including "The Double" and "White Nights." He also became involved with a progressive group known as the Petrashevsky Circle, headed by the charismatic utopian socialist Mikhail Petrashevsky. In 1849 Tsar Nicholas I ordered the arrest of all the members of the group, including Dostoevsky. He was kept in solitary confinement for eight months while the charges against him were investigated and then, along with other members of Petrashevsky's group, was sentenced to death by firing squad. At the last minute Nicholas commuted the sentence to penal servitude in Siberia for four years, and then service in the Russian Army. This near-execution haunts much of Dostoevsky's subsequent writing.

The ten years Dostoevsky spent in prison and then in exile in Siberia had a profound effect on him. By the time he returned to St. Petersburg in 1859, he had rejected his radical ideas and acquired a new respect for the religious ideas and ideals of the Russian people. He had never been an atheist, but his Christianity was now closer to the Orthodox faith. While in exile he had also married.

Dostoevsky quickly resumed his literary career in St. Petersburg. He and his brother Mikhail founded two journals, Vremia (1861–1863) and Epokha (1864–1865). Dostoevsky published many of his well-known post-Siberian works in these journals, including *The House of the Dead*, an account of his prison experiences, and the dark, complex novella "Notes from Underground."

The next several years of Dostoevsky's life were marked by the deaths of his wife, Maria, and his brother Mikhail. He began to gamble compulsively on his trips abroad, and he suffered from bouts of epilepsy. In 1866, while dictating his novel *The Gambler* to meet a deadline, he met a young stenographer, Anna Snitkina, and the two married a year later. Over the next fifteen years Dostoevsky produced his finest works, including the novels *Crime and Punishment* (1866), *The Idiot* (1868), *The Possessed* (1871–1872), and *The Brothers Karamazov* (1879–1880). His novels are complex psychological studies that examine man's struggle with such elemental issues as good and evil, life and death, belief and reason. Fyodor Mikhailovich Dostoevsky died from a lung hemorrhage on January 28, 1881, in St. Petersburg at the age of fifty-nine.

TABLE OF CONTENTS

The World of Fyodor Dostoevsky and
Crime and Punishment
ix
—

Introduction by Priscilla Meyer
xiii
—

List of Characters
xxxi
—

CRIME AND PUNISHMENT
1
—

Inspired by *Crime and Punishment*
525
—

Comments & Questions
531
—

For Further Reading
537

THE WORLD OF FYODOR DOSTOEVSKY AND CRIME AND PUNISHMENT

1821 Fyodor Mikhailovich Dostoevsky is born on October 30 in Moscow. The second of seven children, he grows up in a middle-class household run by his father, a former army surgeon and strict family man.

1833 Alexander Pushkin's novel in verse *Eugene Onegin* is published.

1836 Pushkin's story "The Queen of Spades" is published.

1837 Fyodor's mother dies. He and his older brother Mikhail are sent to a preparatory school in St. Petersburg.

1838 Dostoevsky begins his tenure at the St. Petersburg Academy of Military Engineers, where he studies until 1843. He becomes acquainted with the works of such writers as Byron, Corneille, Dickens, Goethe, Gogol, Homer, Hugo, Pushkin, Racine, Rousseau, Shakespeare, and Schiller.

1839 Dostoevsky's father is, according to rumor, murdered on his country estate, presumably by his own serfs.

1842 Part 1 of Nikolai Gogol's novel *Dead Souls* is published.

1843 Dostoevsky graduates from the Academy as a lieutenant, but instead of pursuing a career in the army, resolves to dedicate his life to writing.

1844 His first published work appears, a Russian translation of Honoré de Balzac's 1833 novel *Eugénie Grandet*. Dostoevsky begins work on his first novel, *Poor Folk*.

1845 On the basis of *Poor Folk*, Dostoevsky wins the friendship and acclaim of Russia's premier literary critic, Vissarion Grigorievich Belinsky, author of the scathingly critical "Letter to Gogol" (1847).

1846 *Poor Folk* and "The Double" are published. "The Double" is the first work in which Dostoevsky writes about the psychology of the split self. Dostoevsky meets the utopian socialist M. V. Butashevich-Petrashevsky.

1847 Dostoevsky publishes numerous short stories, including "A Weak Heart," "Polzunkov," and "The Landlady."

1848 He publishes the short story "White Nights." The *Communist Manifesto*, by Karl Marx and Friedrich Engels, is published. Revolutions break out in France, Germany, Hungary, Italy, and Poland.

1849 Dostoevsky is arrested for his participation in the socialist Petrashevsky Circle. He first spends eight months in solitary confinement and is then condemned to death by firing squad. Tsar Nicholas I commutes his sentence to penal servitude in Siberia, but orders this to be announced only at the last minute.

1850 Dostoevsky begins his four-year internment at Omsk in western Siberia. His experiences there will influence many of his later works. While imprisoned he abandons the radical ideas of his youth and becomes more deeply religious; his only book in prison is a copy of the Bible.

1852 Part 2 of Gogol's *Dead Souls* is published.

1853 The Crimean War breaks out; the cause is a dispute between Russia and France over the Palestinian holy places.

1854 Still exiled in Siberia, Dostoevsky begins four years of compulsory military service.

1857 He marries the widow Maria Dmitrievna Isaeva.

1859 Dostoevsky and Maria are allowed to return to St. Petersburg.

1861 He and his brother Mikhail establish *Vremia* (Time); this year and the next the journal publishes Dostoevsky's *The House of the Dead*, a work based on his experiences in Siberia.

1862 Dostoevsky travels to England, France, Germany, Italy, and Switzerland, a trip that engenders in him an anti-European outlook. He gambles heavily at resorts abroad, losing money.

1863 Dostoevsky makes a second trip to Europe and arranges to meet Apollinaria Suslova in Paris; he had published a story by her in *Vremia* the previous year. The two have an affair.

1863 The progressive Nikolai Chernyshevsky publishes the utopian novel *What Is to Be Done?*, which Dostoevsky will react against a year later in "Notes from Underground." *Vremia* is banned for printing a potentially subversive article regarding the Polish rebellion.

1864   Dostoevsky and his brother Mikhail establish *Epokha* (Epoch), the short-lived successor to *Vremia*; the journal publishes "Notes from Underground," the first of Dostoevsky's masterworks. Dostoevsky's wife, Maria, dies from tuberculosis. His brother Mikhail dies three months later.

1865   Burdened with debt, Dostoevsky embarks on another failed gambling spree in Europe. He proposes to Apollinaria Suslova without success.

1866   *Crime and Punishment* starts serial publication at the beginning of the year. Dostoevsky interrupts the writing in October in order to work on *The Gambler*, forced to meet the contract deadline for that book in order to retain the rights to his published works, including *Crime and Punishment*. He dictates *The Gambler* to a stenographer, Anna Grigorievna Snitkina, over the course of a month. He and Anna, who is twenty-five years his junior, become romantically involved.

1867   Dostoevsky marries Anna Snitkina; the alliance is one of the most fortunate events of his life. To avoid financial ruin, the two live abroad for the next four years, in Geneva, Florence, Vienna, Prague, and finally Dresden. Dostoevsky's epilepsy worsens. He begins work on his novel *The Idiot*, in which the protagonist is an epileptic. The first three of what will be six volumes of Leo Tolstoy's *War and Peace* appear in print in December, bound in yellow covers.

1868   *The Idiot* is published in installments this year and the next. The fourth volume of *War and Peace* appears in March.

1869   The final volumes of *War and Peace* are published: the fifth in February and the sixth in December.

1871   Dostoevsky and his wife return to St. Petersburg. Serialization of his novel *The Possessed* begins.

1873   Dostoevsky becomes editor of the conservative weekly *Grazhdanin* (The Citizen); "The Diary of a Writer" becomes a regular and popular feature of the weekly.

1875   Tolstoy begins publishing *Anna Karenina*.

1876   *The Diary of a Writer* is published as a monojournal—that is, it is written and edited entirely by Dostoevsky; in it he publishes "The Meek One."

1877 "The Dream of a Ridiculous Man" is published in *The Diary of a Writer*.

1879 Serialization begins in another journal of *The Brothers Karamazov*, widely considered Dostoevsky's greatest novel.

1880 Six months before his death, Dostoevsky delivers his famous speech on Pushkin at the dedication of the Pushkin memorial in Moscow.

1881 Dostoevsky dies from a lung hemorrhage on January 28 in St. Petersburg. His epitaph, also the epigraph to *The Brothers Kara-mazov*, is from the Bible (John 12:24); it reads, "Verily, verily, I say unto you, Except a corn of wheat fall into the ground and die, it abideth alone: but if it die, it bringeth forth much fruit" (King James Version).

1886 German philosopher Friedrich Nietzsche publishes *Beyond Good and Evil*, which was influenced by *The Possessed*.

1912 Constance Garnett begins her translations of the works of Dostoevsky, introducing his writings to the English-reading world.

INTRODUCTION

In Russia prose fiction came into its own in the 1830s, centuries later than in Western Europe. The first Russian work that can be called a novel, Mikhail Lermontov's *A Hero of Our Time*, was published in 1840; Fyodor Dostoevsky's masterpiece of world literature, *Crime and Punishment*, appeared only twenty-six years later—a remarkably compressed development. Dostoevsky was aided by his intense reading of Victor Hugo, Honoré de Balzac, Johann Goethe, and other masters of European literature, while the extraordinarily dramatic events of his life—arrest, imprisonment, a death sentence, four years in a labor camp, exile from the capital—were part of the experiential basis for his thought about the philosophical, social, and religious issues of his time.

Russian censorship restricted discussion of social and political questions, which could be treated only indirectly in prose fiction. Russia was governed by an autocracy; there was no bourgeoisie, and the small educated class was cut off from the rest of the (largely illiterate) population. Serfdom was abolished only in 1861, as part of the reforms effected by Alexander II; his legal reforms introduced trial by jury in criminal cases in 1864. Dostoevsky implicitly comments on the reforms in the investigation, trial, and sentencing of *Crime and Punishment*'s protagonist, Rodion Romanovich Raskolnikov.

Dostoevsky began writing *Crime and Punishment* as the confession of a young criminal. But in November 1865 he found the first-person narrative too constricting, and he burned the entire manuscript and began again in December, completing it a year later. The third-person narrative of the final version creates an interplay between Raskolnikov's consciousness and the narrator's viewpoint: At some points the two are in dialogue with each other; at others the narrator is within Raskolnikov's mind, so much so that he conveys the hero's internal dialogue. On the first page the narrator tells us, "[Raskolnikov] was hopelessly in debt to his landlady and was afraid of meeting her. This was not because he was cowardly and browbeaten, quite the contrary." It is as if in the second sentence Raskolnikov is defending himself against the narrator's charge of cowardice in the first.

Raskolnikov's dual consciousness governs the structure of the entire book. In part one he oscillates between resolving to commit murder and renouncing his vile scheme; in the next five parts he alternates between asserting his right to murder and his anguish at having cut himself off from everyone by his act. These alternations reveal the conflict between Raskolnikov's prideful intellect and his compassionate nature, which we see in his first dream, based on a childhood memory, in which he kisses the muzzle of a poor mare that is being beaten. In part one he twice acts on generous impulses, and each time subsequently disavows his acts with a rational argument: He leaves money on the Marmeladov family's windowsill when he brings the drunken head of the household home, but then thinks, "What a stupid thing I've done . . . they have Sonia and I need it myself" (p. 29); and he tries to help a seduced girl but then suddenly regrets it—"What is it to me?" In another alternation, he renounces his plan to murder the pawnbroker after he dreams of the mare, but then overhears the conversation in Haymarket Square that presents him with a perfect opportunity for his crime.

American readers have seen this duality as a kind of schizophrenia in the psychological sense, and Dostoevsky certainly explores that dimension of human ambivalence. But Russian readers see another aspect crucial to Dostoevsky's concerns: the religious argument present in the smallest details of the novel. Raskolnikov's name, not a common one, is Dostoevsky's invention, based on the Russian word *raskolnik* (schismatic), one who has broken off from the church. The Russian Orthodox Church, which had undergone a schism in the seventeenth century, is a descendant of Greek Orthodoxy. Russians in the nineteenth century distinguished themselves from Western Europeans in part through their Eastern Christianity. They contrasted the more mystical tradition of the Orthodox church to the Western, Roman Catholic one, which they held to be legalistic in the tradition of Roman law and devoid of the spirit of Christian love they considered characteristic of the Russian peasantry, a spirit that united the Russian church and created a national religious community. Raskolnikov's patronymic (the father's name that Russians use in the place of a middle name), Romanovich, suggests that he has cut himself off from Orthodoxy and embraced a Western (Roman) worldview, characterized by faith in reason and a focus on the material world.

This opposition of Russian spiritual values to Western rationalism underlies the duality of Raskolnikov's personality. This conflict was Dostoevsky's deepest concern after his release from prison, at a time when Russian radicals began propagating Western ideas that Dostoevsky believed were based on a false vision of human nature. Raskolnikov is one of the bright young men from the provinces who have come to the capital to attend the university, where he is exposed to discussions of Western theories of economics and politics. These theories are based in a social-scientific approach that studies the material, knowable world using statistics and mathematical calculation—as in, for example, the enlightened self-interest and utilitarianism of Jeremy Bentham (1748–1832) and John Stuart Mill (1806–1873). The author of *Utilitarianism* (1863), Mill considered the goal of social legislation to be to provide "the greatest good for the greatest number," calling it a "felicific calculus." Dostoevsky takes up these ideas through the character of Peter Petrovich Luzhin, Raskolnikov's prospective brother-in-law, who argues for enlightened self-interest: "Up until now, for instance, if I were told, 'love thy neighbor,' what came of it? . . . It meant I had to tear my coat in half to share it with my neighbor and we both were left half naked" (p. 145). Raskolnikov reduces this parody of economic theory to its essence: "If you carry out logically the theory you were advocating just now, it follows that people may be killed" (p. 147)—in other words, that human compassion can be replaced by economic utility and enlightened self-interest. Luzhin, whose name comes from the Russian word for puddle (*luzha*) embodies the economic principle, the primacy of monetary relations in social thought; he provides one of the ideas that influences Raskolnikov's thinking. One of Raskolnikov's initial reasons for his crime is (murkily) associated with the "good" of redistributing the pawnbroker's wealth to the poor.

This dramatic pairing—money, arithmetic, and calculation with their opposite: intuitive, Christian compassion—runs through the novel, and is present in each of its parts. The motifs of *Crime and Punishment*—blood, yellow, water, horses, bells, thresholds, wallpaper, thirty roubles or kopeks, staircases—contain opposites that suggest the deepest level of meaning in the book. Water is both a means of suicide (by drowning in the Neva) and the source of regeneration (the Irtysh River in the Epilogue). Raskolnikov is afraid of the traces of the pawnbroker's blood on his socks but is almost joyful about the spots of Marmeladov's blood on his clothing after he helps Marmeladov from the street to his apartment. Bells can be associated with Raskolnikov's murderous aspect or with the potential for salvation associated with church bells. When Raskolnikov first goes to the pawnbroker's apartment, "he rang the bell of the old woman's flat. The bell gave a faint tinkle as though it were made of tin and not of copper. The little apartments in such houses always have bells that ring like that. He had forgotten the note of that bell, and now its peculiar tinkle seemed to remind him of something" (p. 8). After the murder, he returns at night while the workmen are there: "[He] pulled the bell. The same bell, the same cracked note. He rang it a second and a third time; he listened and remembered. The hideous and agonizingly fearful sensation he had felt then began to come back more and more vividly. He shuddered at every ring" (p. 166). At the first visit, the tone of the bell perhaps reminds him of the tinny sound of village church bells such as he remembers it in his dream; at the second visit, Raskolnikov obsessively evokes the memory of his crime by repeatedly ringing the tinny bell. Later, lying on his bed, he "thought of nothing . . . faces of people he had seen in his childhood or met somewhere once, whom he would never have recalled, the belfry of the church at V., . . . a back staircase quite dark, all sloppy with dirty water and strewn with egg shells, and the Sunday bells floating in from somewhere" (p. 260). Raskolnikov's internal dichotomy is set out through bells: Through them the murder is set in opposition to the saving faith he learned in his village as a child.

The idea of the belfry brings together these two sides of the bell motif in one image. Razumikhin, arguing with Porfiry against a rational, materialist interpretation of how environment determines human nature, parodies socialist logic: "I'll prove to you that your white eyelashes may very well be ascribed to the Church of Ivan the Great's being two hundred and fifty feet high, and I will prove it clearly, exactly, progressively, and even with a Liberal tendency!" (p. 245). The logic of socialists and those spreading the "new ideas" is mocked using the belfry, an emblem of irrational faith. Porfiry unites Raskolnikov's association of bells and murder with the church and the belfry when he says, "I've studied all this morbid psychology in my practice. A man is sometimes tempted to jump out of a window or from a belfry. Just the same with bell-ringing" (p. 329). Porfiry understands the two sides of Raskolnikov's crime: the potentially redemptive function of the belfry juxtaposed to the murdered woman's doorbell.

The Russian word for bell is *kolokol*. The syllable *kol* can be found in Raskolnikov's surname, as well as in the names of two opposed characters: The first, Mikolka, is the peasant who beats the mare in Raskolnikov's dream; he is aligned with Raskolnikov's murderous aspect, and with his going against God (Mikolka does not wear a cross). The second, Nikolai, is the painter who confesses to a crime he didn't commit out of an excess of religious fervor, seeking redemption, as Raskolnikov himself eventually is on the brink of doing. The syllable *kol* thus contains opposed meanings for Raskolnikov. On the one hand, *kolot'* (to chop, to split) is connected to his axe murders, as well as to the idea of the *raskolnik*, the schismatic who splits off from the church. On the other, *kolokol* (bell) relates both to the murders and to the potential redemptive force of the church.

Socialism and Christianity

After the publication of his first book, *Poor Folk*, in 1846, Dostoevsky was welcomed into a leading literary circle led by the critic Vissarion Belinsky, where the utopian socialist ideas of the Frenchmen Henri de Saint-Simon (1760–1825) and Charles Fourier (1772–1837) were discussed. Fourier proposed reorganizing society into phalansteries, communities of 1,600 people, that he thought would reestablish the natural harmony in society and erase the lines between rich and poor. In the 1840s these ideas appeared to be continuous with the ideals of Christianity; Dostoevsky could find in Fourier's phalansteries a Christian transfiguration of the world animated by a love of mankind. He even briefly accepted Belinsky's atheistic materialism that won out over Christian utopianism in the circle's discussions, saying of himself in a letter written from Omsk in the 1850s, "I am a child of the age, a child of unbelief and doubt" (quoted in Mochulsky, *Dostoevsky: His Life and Work*, p. 119–120). Within the circle, Dostoevsky read aloud Belinsky's "Letter to Gogol," which condemns Gogol's *Selected Extracts from a Correspondence with Friends* and contains the thought that the Russian people are "profoundly atheistic." In 1849, for being "freethinking" and for belonging to an associated circle led by Petrashevsky, Dostoevsky was arrested. He spent eight months of solitary incarceration in the Peter and Paul Fortress in St. Petersburg and was sentenced along with his fellow conspirators to be shot by firing squad. Three of Dostoevsky's group were led out blindfolded and had already been tied to posts when at the last minute it was announced that the merciful Tsar Nicholas I had commuted the sentence to hard labor in Siberia; the whole mock execution had been planned by the Tsar himself.

Dostoevsky spent four years in penal servitude as a political criminal living in Omsk among convicts for whom he developed great respect, despite the hostility of the common people to gentry such as Dostoevsky. He describes his prison experience in fictional form in *The House of the Dead* (1862), written after his return to St. Petersburg in 1859. In prison, and during five subsequent years of Siberian exile in Semipalatinsk, Dostoevsky underwent a "regeneration of convictions." Throughout his four years in the barracks, Dostoevsky kept under his pillow a copy of the Gospels that had been given to him by Natalia Dmitrievna Fonvizina, wife of one of the Decembrist rebels exiled to Siberia in 1825, during a stop in Tobolsk on his march to Siberia. As a result of a mental struggle during the years of his imprisonment, he replaced his former acceptance of Belinsky's atheism with the "radiant personality of Christ." Upon leaving prison he wrote to Fonvizina that "if someone were to prove to me that Christ is outside the truth, then I would prefer to remain with Christ than with the truth" (quoted in Mochulsky, p. 152). The struggle between faith and reason is fundamental to Dostoevsky's philosophy.

Dostoevsky was allowed to return to St. Petersburg in December 1859, exactly ten years after he had left. The idealist "men of the 40s" had been succeeded by the "men of the 1860s," who endorsed Western positivist, materialist thought. In 1861 Dostoevsky and his brother Mikhail founded a journal, *Vremia* (*Time*), that attempted to reconcile the opposing camps of the Slavophils (the more conservative, nationalist group who valued the Russian tradition) and the Westernizers (relative liberals who wanted Russia to learn from European culture). In the first (January 1861) issue of *Time*, Dostoevsky described the problems of each position and advocated a "reconciliation of ideas" that would constitute "the Russian idea": "With Westernism we are squeezing into a foreign caftan in spite of the fact that it has long been bursting at every seam, and with Slavophilism we are sharing the poetic illusion of reconstructing Russia according to an ideal view of its ancient manner of life, a view that has been set down in place of a genuine understanding of Russia, some kind of ballet set, pretty, but false and abstract" (quoted in Mochulsky, p. 220). But Russian youth was becoming radicalized. There were student rebellions, the university was closed, and students were imprisoned in the Peter and Paul Fortress. The radical materialist literary critics were applying utilitarian principles to art; their efforts were designed to help men satisfy their wants more rationally, so that they deemed an actual apple more valuable than a painting of an apple because the actual apple can be eaten. Dostoevsky refuted this position, insisting on a focus on man's spiritual nature, which finds sustenance in the aesthetic. As Prince Myshkin says in *The Idiot*, "Beauty will save the world."

In 1862 Dostoevsky went to Europe for the first time. In two and a half months he visited six countries, and he recounted his perceptions in *Winter Notes on Summer Impressions*, which first appeared in *Time* in 1863. He was repelled by the smug well-being of the bourgeoisie, and described London, with its teeming poor and crowds of prostitutes, as Babylon. He saw the Crystal Palace, which had been built for the World's Fair in London in 1851. A new kind of building, constructed of glass and steel, it was widely considered a model of modern technology that would allow the construction of housing for the masses and do away with poverty; as such it was an emblem of Fourier's philosophy that would improve human nature by improving material conditions. However, Dostoevsky saw it as an emblem of the "ant heap," his vision of what man becomes when materialist thought deprives him of free will. In *Notes from the Underground* (1864) he had rejected the idea that the environment determined human behavior, and he continued his argument with materialism in *Crime and Punishment*: Human nature—not the material world or the principle of enlightened self-interest—determines behavior. This is why Dostoevsky has Raskolnikov come perversely close to revealing his secret to the police clerk Zametov; he acts irrationally, against his own self-interest, by hinting at his crime to the police: "And what if it was I?" (p. 160).

Luzhin's young progressive friend Lebeziatnikov—from *lebezit'* (to fawn on someone)—is the purveyor of the so-called "new ideas" circulating in the capital among university students and intellectuals. Dostoevsky's description of their discussions about a commune in the red light district parodies discussions then current among progressives and, in particular, the critic Nikolai Chernyshevsky's book *What Is to Be Done?* (1863), in which a prostitute is rescued from her trade by joining a sewing cooperative.

Dostoevsky argues with German thinkers, too, in *Crime and Punishment*. He alludes to German popularizers of materialist social scientific thought—among them Adolph Wagner, Ludwig Büchner, and Karl Vogt—whose books were being read by the progressive youth of the 1850s and 1860s. Raskolnikov's exposure to their views in St. Petersburg university circles contributes to the theory that leads him to murder. Heavily censored in Russia during the period 1840–1860 (some of them for their "scientific," materialist approach to religion), the German texts are also part of the basis for the "new ideas" that Lebeziatnikov discusses with Luzhin. Dostoevsky further alludes to the German theme with Raskolnikov's old top hat, which is referred to by the name of its German maker, Zimmermann:

> . . . a drunken man who . . . was being taken somewhere in a huge cart dragged by a heavy cart-horse, suddenly shouted at him as he drove past, "Hey there, German hatter" . . . —the young man stopped suddenly and clutched trembling at his hat. It was a tall round one from Zimmermann's, but completely worn out, rusty with age, all torn and bespattered, brimless and bent on one side in a most hideous fashion. Not shame, however, but another feeling akin to terror had overtaken him (p. 7).

Raskolnikov fears that his conspicuous top hat will be remembered and somehow reveal him as the murderer. For Dostoevsky, the Zimmermann reveals Raskolnikov's poverty of spirit; the German hat on Raskolnikov's Russian head suggests that he has imbibed German materialism in St. Petersburg. It also suggests why his friend Razumikhin calls him "a translation"—that is, a Russian imitation of the kind of book, parodied by the title "Is Woman a Human Being?" (p. 111), that Razumikhin generously offers to let him translate from the German in order to earn enough to eat. Razumikhin calls Raskolnikov a "plagiarist" of foreign ideas instead of an "original" (p. 162).

Dostoevsky organizes the cast of characters of *Crime and Punishment* in relation to this conflict between rational materialism and the irrationality of human nature. Raskolnikov builds his theory of the man who dares to transgress in keeping with Western materialist thinking, and the characters surrounding him act as his doubles, displaying aspects of his position.

Razumikhin is the counter-example to Raskolnikov: He lives in abject poverty in St. Petersburg like his friend and fellow student, yet shares none of Raskolnikov's rage at his helplessness or his desire for power. His name comes from *razum* (reason), but in the sense of common sense, reasonableness. The argument that the environment leads Raskolnikov to crime is refuted by Razumikhin's vibrant joy in existence, his generosity to his friend, and his natural compassion. Human nature differentiates the friends, despite their shared material circumstances.

This is all the more clear in the case of Marmeladov's daughter, the prostitute Sonia Marmeladov. Raskolnikov tells her that her situation will drive her to suicide, yet despite everything that should destroy her, she chooses faith in Christ, which allows her not only to sustain her family but to become Raskolnikov's savior as well. Her name is the diminutive form of Sophia, which denotes "divine wisdom" in Greek; her spiritual power is juxtaposed to physical and economic forces and to other forms of earthly power.

Raskolnikov's sister's former employer, Arkady ("Arcadia") Svidrigailov, is Raskolnikov's most complete double. When they meet it is at first unclear both to Raskolnikov and the reader whether Svidrigailov exists in reality or is a figment of Raskolnikov's dream-imagination. Svidrigailov suggests that eternity may be "one little room, like a bathhouse in the country, black and grimy and spiders in every corner" (p. 277). Without a definition of eternity, his existence lacks any moral basis, so that he can commit both evil and benevolent acts with indifference; in this he is perhaps a parody of the concept of the "natural man" of Jean-Jacques Rousseau

(1712–1778). Because his life can have no meaning, he elects to take it "to America" in the form of suicide—a journey from which Sonia can save Raskolnikov because, unlike Svidrigailov, he retains his conscience and compassion from his churchgoing village childhood.

Marmeladov doubles the aspect of Raskolnikov that is at once victim (of poverty) and victimizer (he commits murder). Dostoevsky had originally begun writing a novel called *The Drunkards*; when he abandoned it to write *Crime and Punishment*, he incorporated the tale of the drunkard Marmeladov into Raskolnikov's tale. The identification of the two characters is signaled when Raskolnikov is almost run down by a carriage and whipped by the driver; he is taken for a drunkard when he staggers, delirious, in the street. Marmeladov is a victim of his alcoholism and attendant poverty, while simultaneously victimizing his family with his inability to keep a job.

Russia and France

Russian writers of the nineteenth century, like many others of the period, were consciously creating a new literary tradition, trying to free themselves from the imitation of French language and culture that had shaped the world of the Russian aristocracy from the time of Catherine the Great. Literate Russians, who themselves lived in an imitation of European culture, were painfully aware that Russia's social and cultural level was far lower than that of Western Europe and saw themselves self-consciously through Western European eyes, at once admiring Europe and feeling inferior to it. Russian prose developed in dialogue with the literature of France, where Romantic works at the beginning of the century were followed by a burst of realist prose in the late 1820s.

With the growth of cities and a poor urban class, French literary prose took up the lives of the city poor and the peculiar role of Paris in relation to the provinces; the themes of criminality and the provincial in the city became important. Literary prose became democratized through the growth of a popular press that began publishing four-page weekly inserts (*feuilletons*) containing installments of popular novels by such writers as Eugène Sue, Jules Janin, and Honoré de Balzac. Two major themes were prostitution (the female crime) and murder or demonic ambition (the male crime); the goal in both cases was the redemption of the sinner-criminal. Russians readers and writers followed French literature closely, both in French and in Russian translation, and by the 1830s treatments of the St. Petersburg poor inspired by the French *feuilletons* began to replace Romantic poetry in Russia. Nikolai Gogol's tales of poor St. Petersburg government clerks clearly inspired Dostoevsky's early work, and French novels about prostitutes provided material for Dostoevsky's characterization of Sonia. The French character type of the ambitious young man from the provinces contributes to his portrait of Raskolnikov; the hero of Balzac's *Père Goriot* (1835), Eugène de Rastignac, belongs to this type.

Napoleonism, the Young Man from the Provinces, and the Mandarin

Père Goriot was the first book Dostoevsky recommended to his new bride—his second wife, Anna Grigorievna—four months after he completed *Crime and Punishment*. Immediately after *Père Goriot* appeared in French, it was published in Russian by two different journals. In it, Rastignac is a law student from the provinces who poses a moral question to his friend Bianchon: If he could make his fortune by killing a mandarin living in China without stirring from Paris, would he do it? Dostoevsky's Raskolnikov overhears a student ask an officer a similar question: Would he kill the old pawnbroker in order to use her wealth to aid thousands of struggling young people? Dostoevsky lowers the scene, and Balzac's hypothetical mandarin becomes a greasy-haired St. Petersburg pawnbroker.

The relationship of *Crime and Punishment* to *Père Goriot* centers on the moral question of the superman. The figure of Napoleon—who had conquered Europe, sacrificing more than a million lives, apparently with no pangs of conscience—was revered in France and fascinated Europe. Napoleon's campaigns naturally gave rise to the question of man's right to take human life. Russians in particular experienced Napoleon's army firsthand: Napoleon invaded Russia with 600,000 men, of whom 410,000 perished. Raskolnikov measures himself against Napoleon, an outsider who had risen from humble origins, as one who is emancipated from customary ideas and moral scruples.

In *Père Goriot*, Rastignac's would-be mentor, Jacques Collin, preaches Napoleonism to him: "In every million of this higher livestock, there are perhaps a dozen daredevils who stand above everything, even the law. I am one of them. If you are above the ruck, go straight forward" (p. 110). Collin sees himself as a Napoleon among his fellow thieves.

In the course of *Crime and Punishment*, Raskolnikov gives a series of different reasons for committing murder but finally understands that it is because he wanted to see if he was "above the common ruck." He is ashamed that he is unable to kill even such a "louse" as the pawnbroker without suffering for it horribly. His would-be mentor, Svidrigailov, does in fact attain Raskolnikov's model of superman; he can apparently sacrifice human life without regret. The novel is conceived as a demonstration of the error of their ideas.

The parallels between the casts of characters in *Père Goriot* and *Crime and Punishment* are systematic: In both, young law students from the provinces leave beloved mothers and sisters at home; in the capital they are torn between compassion, whose objects are Goriot and Marmeladov, and immorality, represented by Vautrin and Svidrigailov.

Throughout, Dostoevsky takes what is literal in Balzac and renders it metaphorically, metaphysically. Vautrin plans to go to America to become a slave owner and start a tobacco plantation; Svidrigailov, when he speaks of going to America, is contemplating suicide. Dostoevsky thus presents two variants of false salvation, a literal journey and a figurative journey to the other world.

This pattern governs the many correspondences between the two novels. The heroes' sisters are part of Rastignac's and Raskolnikov's initial motivations for their respective crimes. Each hero, while in the capital, receives a letter from his village home; Rastignac calls his sisters "angels," just as Raskolnikov's mother calls Raskolnikov's sister, Dunia, an angel. Rastignac's mother tells him "Love your aunt; I won't tell you all she's done for you . . . "; Raskolnikov's mother writes, "Love Dunia your sister, Rodia; love her as she loves you and understand that she loves you beyond everything, more than herself" (p. 40). Rastignac's sisters are happy to sacrifice their savings out of their ecstatic love of their brother; Raskolnikov's mother writes that Dunia is prepared to sacrifice her entire life for Raskolnikov by marrying Luzhin, a man she cannot love. Dunia gives her brother not material wealth but selfless love. What is material in Balzac becomes spiritual in Dostoevsky.

Goriot and Marmeladov are similarly obsessed outcasts who are responsible for their own misery. They are guilt-ridden and driven to confession and self-punishment. Dostoevsky's recasting of the material aspect of human motives is particularly striking in his description of Marmeladov's death. Dostoevsky rewrites Père Goriot's deathbed scene, linking it to Marmeladov's with several details—for example, Rastignac and Raskolnikov send for the doctors and provide for the funerals of the fathers; both deathbed scenes are illuminated by a single candle.

More important, while rewriting Balzac's scene Dostoevsky inverts it through the relationship between the fathers and the daughters. Goriot, dying, calls out for his daughters—"Nasie! Fifine!"—but they don't come, while Marmeladov's daughter immediately runs to his bedside, where he cries out "Sonia! Daughter! Forgive me!" (p. 179). Goriot's daughters don't want to compromise their social positions by associating with their father. Marmeladov's daughter, who has already compromised her own social position to maintain him and his second family, comes despite her shame at appearing at Amalia Fiodorovna's apartment:

> Sonia . . . looked about her bewildered, unconscious of everything. She forgot her fourth-hand, gaudy silk dress, so unseemly here with its ridiculous long train, and her immense crinoline that filled up the whole doorway, and her light-colored shoes, and the parasol she brought with her, though it was no use at night, and the absurd round straw hat with its flaring flame-colored feather (p. 177).

Dostoevsky's detailed description of the prostitute's finery that Sonia wears implicitly parodies Balzac's elaborate depictions of Goriot's daughters' clothing, the expense of which contributes to their father's ruin. Balzac's suggestion that Goriot's daughters are simply expensively kept prostitutes is inverted by Dostoevsky's rendition of Sonia. She sacrifices herself out of love for her family, strengthened by her religious faith; her finery is so external to her spiritual nature and love for her family that she is able to forget about it entirely when she runs to her father's deathbed.

This systematic similarity between the two novels highlights the conspicuous point of departure from Dostoevsky's elaborate parallel: the character of Sonia, who is possibly the most important character for Dostoevsky's underlying philosophy in *Crime and Punishment*. In *Père Goriot* her counterpart is Victorine, a devout, pale, "excessively slim" young woman who resembles a medieval statuette and whose eyes "express Christian gentleness and resignation." But Dostoevsky combines Victorine with a stock character from French realist literature of the 1830s, the noble prostitute, to create a collision between opposites: "Sonia was a small thin girl of eighteen with fair hair" (p. 177), "very young, almost like a child . . . with a modest and refined manner" (p. 226), imbued with Christian faith—and a prostitute. Dostoevsky's contrast goes beyond the shock effect to argue with all the French prostitute tales: Unlike the French prostitute stereotype, who usually comes to a gruesome end after some brief success in society, Sonia has found faith, strength, and love through suffering, loving others as herself, and reading the Bible. Dostoevsky gives us two examples of vulnerable females who are not ruined by prostitution, Dunia and Sonia. Faith is Sonia's equivalent of Dunia's pride; Sonia is Dostoevsky's answer to Raskolnikov's reasonable prediction that her young half-sister Polia will go that way, too: Spirit can overcome the environment and material reality. And her faith turns out to be rewarded through the most improbable means. Svidrigailov—the embodiment of faithlessness, cynicism, and amorality, who has himself been implicated in the seduction of a young girl—provides the means for the orphaned Polia's maintenance.

In *Père Goriot*, the diabolic Vautrin proposes that Rastignac marry Victorine to make his fortune: Vautrin will have Victorine's brother killed so that she will inherit millions—the equivalent of killing the mandarin. In *Crime and Punishment*, Dostoevsky recasts the social and monetary "salvation" that is to be attained through murder: Raskolnikov's salvation is brought about not by killing his mandarin, the pawnbroker, as he seems to think it could be, but through his compassion and acceptance of suffering.

The Gospel of John

The character of Sonia is the point at which the French genre of the prostitute with a heart of gold intersects with the detective thriller in the tradition of Eugène Sue, whose descriptions of the underworld appeared in serial novels in French newspapers; through her, Dostoevsky rewrites both genres in order to reject their insistently materialist philosophy. Sonia plays the role of Jesus in the resurrection of Raskolnikov. He asks her to read him "the story of Lazarus," and she tells him it is in "the fourth gospel," the biblical Gospel of John (p. 310). Dostoevsky incorporates the Gospel of John as a hidden system of references in *Crime and Punishment*; indeed the novel may be understood as a kind of modern version of John.

Details along Raskolnikov's path hint at an inverse parallel to the life of Jesus as told by John, for Raskolnikov wants to make himself into a God by giving himself the right to take human life. He commits the sin of which the Jews accuse Jesus when they say, "You, being a man, make yourself God" (John 10:33; English Standard Version). Raskolnikov does this by passing judgment on Aliona Ivanovna, claiming that he benefits mankind by ridding it of the pawnbroker. Jesus, by contrast, says, "I did not come to judge the world but to save the world" (12:47). Jesus prepares a whip from cords in order to chase the money-changers from the temple (2:15–16); Raskolnikov sews his axe-noose and binds his fake pledge with thread, preparing to murder the pawnbroker. Raskolnikov's power over "the whole ant heap" is an arrogant parody of Jesus' "I have overcome the world" (16:33). Dostoevsky has Raskolnikov confuse earthly power (physical force, economic power, the intellect) with moral and spiritual power, as displayed by Raskolnikov's fellow convicts' humility before the frail Sonia.

In John, Capernaum is the administrative center of Galilee. Svidrigailov calls Russia's capital, St. Petersburg, "the administrative center." In St. Petersburg, Svidrigailov lives next door to Sonia, who rents from the Kapernaumovs, themselves reminiscent of the mute and the lame who come to Jesus to be healed. Capernaum is mentioned five times in John (as against seven times total in the three other Gospels of Matthew, Mark, and Luke). The name means "village of consolation," and it is the site of two of Jesus' miracles: He cures an official's son without even seeing him (4:46–54); and he walks on water to Capernaum on the Sea of Galilee (6:16–21). Capernaum, then, is an appropriate association for Sonia. She offers consolation and miracle by reading to Raskolnikov from John at the Kapernau-

movs'. This is the beginning of Raskolnikov's movement toward re-
linquishing his pride in favor of Sonia's faith.

Raskolnikov's evidence at his trial contains further parodic in-
version of Jesus' life. When on the third day the stone is removed
from Jesus' tomb, all that remains of Jesus' earthly self are the
linen cloths, including the one that had been on his head (20:6),
indications of the resurrection of his body. When Raskolnikov's
evidence is investigated, the police turn back the stone in the yard
on Voznesensky ("Ascension") Prospect to find Raskolnikov's
hidden booty and several extremely damaged banknotes. Money
in *Crime and Punishment* is the emblem of earthly power as well as of
compassion; here the booty from the murder rots as the unresur-
rected body rots; money initially signifies power to Raskolnikov,
but Dostoevsky emphasizes with this biblical parallel that it can
represent only earthly power. At the same time, the parallel hints
at the potential, through confession, for resurrection of the spirit.
Raskolnikov's Golgotha comes when he confesses to Nikodim
Fomich, but Raskolnikov has yet to achieve resurrection. Similarly,
in John, it is not the climax of Jesus' tale when Nicodemus gives
Jesus the traditional Jewish burial at the end of chapter 19, or in
20 when Mary finds his body missing from the tomb. Completion
of the miracle of Jesus' resurrection takes place only in chapter
21, when Jesus appears to his disciples.

Dostoevsky's scene of silent recognition at dawn by the shore is
modeled on chapter 21 of John. Raskolnikov has accepted the truth
of Jesus' message as represented by Sonia, just as the disciples recognize, in the midst of their everyday labor, the truth of the miraculous
appearance of their teacher after his crucifixion. John's chapters 20
and 21, like Dostoevsky's scene, bode the "promise of a . . . new view
of life and of his future resurrection" (p. 516). Both epilogues are the
necessary completion of their heroes' sufferings.

As the most mystical Gospel, which nonetheless shows Jesus as
human and part of day-to-day human life, John gives Dostoevsky's
"detective thriller" the deep power it would otherwise lack, despite
the richness of the many literary, philosophical, and journalistic materials that inform it. The omnipresent intonations of John's Gospel
maintain the atmosphere of divine potential throughout the intense
French-inspired naturalism of the novel. Once the reader is sensitized

to the presence of John in the first six books, the epilogue becomes the inevitable and essential completion of the work.

Dostoevsky embeds a rich network of French allusions in his novel in order to refute them with the eternal truth of the Gospel of John. He rewrites the French theme of prostitution in Sonia Marmeladov. Her form of nobility, compassion, and self-sacrifice is modeled on Jesus Christ. Dostoevsky combines the French theme of the young man from the provinces with Balzac's (and others') portrait of the struggle of conscience in a world of waning faith in order to render Raskolnikov's oscillations between Napoleonic ambition and selfless compassion. Dostoevsky casts the police investigator Porfiry as Raskolnikov's spiritual guide, following the model of French detective fiction, and disguises a religious allegory as a suspense tale inspired by the French *feuilleton* novels.

Dostoevsky's tale of murder is a parable for his time, designed to turn his contemporaries away from a false view of the nature of man that was already dominant in the West, one he feared would become predominant in Russia at a point in history when he saw the intellect being enshrined at the expense of the human spirit. In *Crime and Punishment* Dostoevsky uses newspaper articles, French popular novels, and masterpieces of French realism—as well as Russian prose from Pushkin's "Queen of Spades" (1834) to Chernyshevsky's polemical novel—to create a vivid psychological drama. Dostoevsky gives us the painful experience of entering Raskolnikov's world and psyche in order to show us the horrific consequences of the materialist worldview, already prevailing in the West, that he feared was coming to dominate Russian social thought. He grounds his rejection of socialism, utilitarianism, and enlightened self-interest in a religious understanding of human nature, whose compassion and self-sacrifice has its perfect model in Jesus Christ. By bringing readers along Raskolnikov's tortured path, Dostoevsky prepares us to accept John's message and to view the world of St. Petersburg that we have experienced at close range and in vivid realistic detail from a new, and higher, perspective.

Priscilla Meyer received her B.A. from the University of California at Berkeley and her Ph.D. from Princeton University. A professor of Russian language and literature at Wesleyan University, she teaches courses on nineteenth- and twentieth-century prose, the double in literature, and the French and Russian novel, and conducts seminars on Nabokov and Gogol. She has written about and translated the work of the 1960s generation of Soviet writers, including Vasily Aksenov, Yuz Aleshkovsky, and Andrei Bitov; she edited the first collection of Bitov's stories to be translated into English: *Life in Windy Weather*. She wrote *Find What the Sailor Has Hidden*, the first monograph on Nabokov's *Pale Fire*, and has recently completed a book on French sources of the nineteenth-century Russian novel, *How the Russians Read the French*. She is co-editor of four essay collections: *Dostoevsky and Gogol: Texts and Criticism*, *Essays on Gogol: Logos and the Russian Word*, *Nabokov's World*, and *Yuz! Essays in Honor of the 75th Birthday of Yuz Aleshkovsky*. She has published articles in scholarly journals in the United States, the United Kingdom, and Russia on Pushkin, Lermontov, Gogol, Tolstoy, and Nabokov, and on twentieth-century prose.

LIST OF CHARACTERS

Russian middle names, called "patronymics," are derived from the father's first name, with a suffix that indicates the gender of the child. Russian speakers use the first name and patronymic together—for example, Rodion Romanovich—when they want to refer to someone in a formal way. Family members and close friends use diminutives, shortened versions of the first name—for example, Rodia—to refer to one another affectionately. In this list, diminutives and nicknames appear in parentheses after the full names.

RODION ROMANOVICH RASKOLNIKOV (RODIA): The protagonist.

PULCHERIA ALEXANDROVNA RASKOLNIKOV: Raskolnikov's mother.

AVDOTIA ROMANOVNA RASKOLNIKOV (DUNIA): Raskolnikov's sister.

DMITRI PROKOFICH RAZUMIKHIN: Raskolnikov's friend; a poor ex-student.

ALIONA IVANOVNA: The pawnbroker Raskolnikov kills; often referred to as the "old woman."

LIZAVETA IVANOVNA: The half-sister of Aliona Ivanovna; a friend of Sonia.

SEMION ZAHAROVICH MARMELADOV: A government official who is an alcoholic.

KATERINA IVANOVNA MARMELADOV: The wife of Marmeladov; she is afflicted with consumption.

SOFIA SEMIONOVNA MARMELADOV (SONIA): Raskolnikov's beloved; daughter of the Marmeladovs.

POLENKA MARMELADOV (POLIA): The eldest daughter of Katerina Ivanovna from a previous marriage.

LIDA MARMELADOV: The daughter of Katerina Ivanovna from a previous marriage.

KOLIA MARMELADOV: The son of Katerina Ivanovna from a previous marriage.

AMALIA FIODOROVNA LIPPEWECHSEL: The landlady of the Marmeladovs. Her surname is German, but she refers to herself by the Russian-sounding Amalia Ivanovna; to irritate her, Katerina Ivanovna calls her Amalia Ludwigovna, which calls attention to her German origin.

ARKADY IVANOVICH SVIDRIGAILOV: Dunia's former employer.

MARFA PETROVNA SVIDRIGAILOV: The wife of Svidrigailov.

PETER PETROVICH LUZHIN: Dunia's fiancé; a distant relative of Marfa Svidrigailov.

ANDREI SEMIONOVICH LEBEZIATNIKOV: Luzhin's roommate.

ZOSSIMOV: Raskolnikov's doctor; a friend of Dmitri Razumikhin.

NASTASIA PETROVNA: A servant in the house where Raskolnikov lives; she tends to him after the murders.

PRASKOVIA PAVLOVNA ZARNITSYN: Raskolnikov's landlady; Raskolnikov had been engaged to her daughter, who died.

KOCH: With Pestriakov, he discovers the murders.

PESTRIAKOV: With Koch, he discoverers the murders.

PORFIRY PETROVICH: The official investigating the murders.

ILIA PETROVICH: A police official.

NIKODIM FOMICH: The chief of police.

NIKOLAI DEMENTIEV (MIKOLKA): A painter accused of the murders.

AFANASY IVANOVICH VAKHRUSHIN: A merchant; Raskolnikov's mother borrows money from him to send to her son.

F. M. Dostoevsky. Portrait by V. Perov. 1872

RASKOLNIKOV'S PETERSBURG

1. Raskolnikov's room

2. The pawnbroker's room

3. Sonya's room

4. Haymarket Square

5. Place of Svidrigaylov's suicide

6. Tuchkov Bridge

7. Yusupov Gardens

8. St. Isaac's Cathedral

9. Admiralty Square

10. The Winter Palace and the Hermitage

11. The Bourse

12. Academy of Sciences

13. Falconet's statue to Peter the Great

14. St. Peter and St. Paul Fortress

CRIME AND PUNISHMENT

PART ONE

CHAPTER ONE

ON AN EXCEPTIONALLY HOT evening early in July a young man came out of the tiny room which he rented from tenants in S. Place* and walked slowly, as though in hesitation, towards K. Bridge.†

He had successfully avoided meeting his landlady on the stairs. His closet of a room was under the roof of a high, five-floor house and was more like a cupboard than a place in which to live. The landlady who provided him with the room and with dinner and service lived on the floor below, and every time he went out he was obliged to pass her kitchen, the door of which was always open. And each time he passed, the young man had a sick, frightened feeling, which made him grimace and feel ashamed. He was hopelessly in debt to his landlady and was afraid of meeting her.

This was not because he was cowardly and browbeaten, quite the contrary; but for some time past he had been in an overstrained irritable condition, verging on hypochondria. He had become so completely absorbed in himself and isolated from everyone else that he dreaded meeting not only his landlady, but anyone at all. He was crushed by poverty, but even the anxieties of his position had recently ceased to weigh upon him. He had given up attending to matters of practical importance; he had lost all desire to do so. In fact, nothing that any landlady could do held any terror for him. But to be stopped on the stairs, to be forced to listen to her trivial, irrelevant gossip, to pestering demands for payment, threats and complaints, all the while racking his brains for excuses, avoiding the issue, lying—no, he would rather creep down the stairs like a cat and slip out unseen.

However, when he emerged onto the street that evening, he became acutely aware of his fears.

"I want to attempt a thing like that and am frightened by these trifles," he thought, with an odd smile. "Hm . . . yes, everything is in someone's hands and they let it all slip out of cowardice, that's an axiom. It would be interesting to know what it is people are most afraid of. Taking a new step, uttering a new word is what they fear

---

*The Haymarket.
†Kokushkin Bridge.

5

most . . . But I am talking too much. It's because I babble that I do nothing. Or perhaps it is that I babble because I do nothing. I've learned to babble this last month, lying for days on end in my corner thinking . . . just nonsense. Why am I going there now? Am I capable of that? Is that seriously possible? I'm not serious about it at all. It's just a fantasy to amuse myself; a plaything! Yes, maybe it is a plaything."

The heat in the street was terrible: and the airlessness, the bustle, the plaster, the scaffolding, the bricks and the dust all around him, and that special Petersburg stench, so familiar to everyone who is unable to get out of town during the summer—all worked painfully upon the young man's already overwrought nerves. The unbearable stench from the taverns, which are particularly numerous in that part of the town, and the drunken men whom he met continually, although it was a weekday, completed the revolting misery of the picture. An expression of the deepest disgust gleamed for a moment in the young man's refined face. He was, by the way, exceptionally handsome, above average in height, slim, well-built, with beautiful dark eyes and dark brown hair. Soon, though, he sank into deep thought, or more accurately speaking into a complete blankness of mind; he walked along not observing what was around him and not caring to observe it. From time to time, because he used to talk to himself, he would mutter something, a habit to which he had just confessed. At these moments he would become conscious that his ideas were sometimes in a tangle and that he was very weak; for two days he had had almost nothing to eat.

He was so badly dressed that even a man accustomed to shabbiness would have been ashamed to be seen in the street in such rags. In that part of town, however, scarcely any shortcoming in dress would have created surprise. Due to the proximity of the Haymarket, the number of establishments of a certain kind and the overwhelming numbers of craftsmen and workers crowded in these streets and alleys at the center of Petersburg, so many different types of people were to be seen in the streets that no figure, however strange, would have caused surprise. But there was such accumulated spite and contempt in the young man's heart, that, in spite of all the cares of youth, he minded his rags least of all. It was a different matter when he met with acquaintances or with former fellow students, whom, indeed, he disliked meeting at any time. And yet when a drunken man who, for some unknown reason, was being taken somewhere in a huge cart dragged by a heavy cart-horse, suddenly shouted at him as he drove past, "Hey there, German hatter," bellowing at the top of his voice and pointing at him—the young man stopped suddenly and clutched trembling at his hat. It was a tall round one from Zimmermann's,* but completely worn out, rusty with age, all torn and bespattered, brimless and bent on one side in a most hideous fashion. Not shame, however, but another feeling akin to terror had overtaken him.

"I knew it," he muttered in confusion, "I thought so! That's the worst of all! A stupid thing like this, the most trivial detail might spoil the whole plan. Yes, my hat is too noticeable . . . It looks absurd and that makes it noticeable . . . With my rags I ought to wear a cap, any old pancake, but not this grotesque thing. Nobody wears hats like this, it would be noticed a mile off, it would be remembered . . . What matters is that people would remember it, and that would give them a clue. For this business I should be as unnoticeable as possible . . . Trifles, trifles are what matter! It's just such trifles that always ruin everything . . . "

He did not have far to go; he knew indeed how many steps it was from the gate of his house: exactly seven hundred and thirty. He had counted them once when he had been lost in dreams. At the time he had put no faith in those dreams and was only tantalizing himself with their hideous insolence. Now, a month later, he had begun to look upon them differently, and, in spite of the monologues in which he jeered at his own impotence and indecision, he had even, involuntarily as it were, come to regard this "hideous" dream as an exploit to be attempted, although he still did not quite believe in this himself. He was now definitely going for a "rehearsal" of this undertaking of his, and at every step he grew more and more excited.

With a sinking heart and a nervous tremor, he went up to a huge house which on one side looked on to the canal, and on the other into the street. This house was let out in tiny apartments and was inhabited by working people of all kinds—tailors, locksmiths, cooks, Germans of all sorts, girls picking up a living as best they could, petty clerks, etc. There was a continual coming and going through the two

---

*Fashionable men's store in St. Petersburg.

gates and in the two courtyards of the house. Three or four door-
keepers were employed in the building. The young man was very
glad not to meet any of them, and at once slipped unnoticed through
the door on the right, and up the staircase. It was a back staircase,
dark and narrow, but he was familiar with it already, and knew his
way, and he liked all these surroundings: in such darkness even the
most inquisitive eyes were not to be feared.

"If I am so scared now, what would it be if it somehow came to
pass that I were *really going to do it?*" he could not help asking himself
as he reached the fourth floor. There his progress was barred by some
porters who were moving furniture out of an apartment. He knew
that the apartment had been occupied by a German clerk in the civil
service, and his family. This German was moving out then, and so the
fourth floor on this staircase would be vacant except for the old
woman. "That's a good thing anyway," he thought to himself, as he
rang the bell of the old woman's flat. The bell gave a faint tinkle as
though it were made of tin and not of copper. The little apartments
in such houses always have bells that ring like that. He had forgotten
the note of that bell, and now its peculiar tinkle seemed to remind
him of something and to bring it clearly before him . . . He gave a
start, his nerves were terribly overstrained by now. In a little while,
the door was opened a tiny crack: the old woman eyed her visitor
with evident distrust through the crack, and nothing could be seen
but her little eyes, glittering in the darkness. But, seeing a number of
people on the landing, she grew bolder, and opened the door wide.
The young man stepped into the dark entryway, which was partitioned off from the tiny kitchen. The old woman stood facing him in
silence and looking inquiringly at him. She was a diminutive, with-
ered old woman of sixty, with sharp mean eyes and a sharp little
nose. Her colorless, somewhat grizzled hair was thickly smeared with
oil, and she wore no kerchief over it. Round her thin long neck,
which looked like a hen's leg, was knotted some sort of flannel rag,
and, in spite of the heat, there hung flapping on her shoulders a tattered fur cape, yellow with age. The old woman coughed and
groaned at every instant. The young man must have looked at her
with a rather peculiar expression, for a gleam of mistrust came into
her eyes again.

"Raskolnikov, a student, I came here a month ago," the young man made haste to mutter, with a half bow, remembering that he ought to be more polite.

"I remember, sir, I remember quite well your coming here," the old woman said distinctly, still keeping her inquiring eyes on his face.

"And here . . . I am again on the same errand," Raskolnikov continued, a little disconcerted and surprised at the old woman's mistrust. "Perhaps she is always like that though, only I did not notice it the other time," he thought with an uneasy feeling.

The old woman paused, as though hesitating; then stepped to the side, and pointing to the door of the room, she said, letting her visitor pass in front of her:

"Step in, sir."

The little room the young man walked into, with yellow paper on the walls, geraniums and muslin curtains in the windows, was brightly lit up at that moment by the setting sun.

"So the sun will shine like this then too!" flashed as it were by chance through Raskolnikov's mind, and with a rapid glance he scanned everything in the room, trying as far as possible to notice and remember its arrangement. But there was nothing special in the room. The furniture, all very old and made of yellow wood, consisted of a sofa with a huge bent wooden back, an oval table in front of the sofa, a dressing-table with a mirror fixed on it between the windows, chairs along the walls and two or three cheap prints in yellow frames, representing German maidens with birds in their hands—that was all. In the corner a light was burning in front of a small icon. Everything was very clean; the floor and the furniture were brightly polished; everything shone.

"Lizaveta's work," thought the young man. There was not a speck of dust to be seen in the whole apartment.

"It's in the houses of spiteful old widows that one finds such cleanliness," Raskolnikov thought again, and he stole a curious glance at the cotton curtain over the door leading into another tiny room, in which stood the old woman's bed and chest of drawers and into which he had never looked before. These two rooms made up the whole apartment.

"What do you want?" the old woman said severely, coming into the room and, as before, standing in front of him so as to look him straight in the face.

"I've brought something to pawn here," and he drew out of his pocket an old-fashioned flat silver watch, on the back of which was engraved a globe; the chain was of steel.

"But the time is up for your last pledge. The month was up the day before yesterday."

"I will bring you the interest for another month; wait a little."

"That's for me to do as I please, sir, to wait or to sell your pledge at once."

"How much will you give me for the watch, Aliona Ivanovna?"

"You come with such trifles, sir, it's scarcely worth anything. I gave you two rubles last time for your ring and one could buy it quite new at a jeweler's for a ruble and a half."

"Give me four rubles for it, I will redeem it, it was my father's. I will be getting some money soon."

"A ruble and a half, and interest in advance, if you like!"

"A ruble and a half!" cried the young man.

"As you wish"—and the old woman handed him back the watch. The young man took it, and was so angry that he was on the point of going away; but checked himself at once, remembering that there was nowhere else he could go, and that he had had another reason for coming.

"Hand it over," he said roughly.

The old woman fumbled in her pocket for her keys, and disappeared behind the curtain into the other room. The young man, left standing alone in the middle of the room, listened inquisitively, thinking. He could hear her unlocking the chest of drawers.

"It must be the top drawer," he reflected. "So she carries the keys in a pocket on the right. All in one bunch on a steel ring . . . And there's one key there, three times as big as all the others, with deep notches; that can't be the key for the chest of drawers . . . then there must be some other chest or strong-box . . . that's worth knowing. Strong-boxes always have keys like that . . . but how degrading it all is."

The old woman came back.

"Here, sir: as we say ten kopecks the ruble a month, so I must take fifteen kopecks from a ruble and a half for the month in advance. But for the two rubles I lent you before, you owe me now twenty kopecks on the same reckoning in advance. That makes thirty-five kopecks altogether. So I must give you a ruble and fifteen kopecks for the watch. Here it is."

"What! Only a ruble and fifteen kopecks now!"

"Exactly."

The young man did not dispute it and took the money. He looked at the old woman, and was in no hurry to get away, as though there was still something he wanted to say or to do, but he did not himself quite know what.

"I may be bringing you something else in a day or two, Aliona Ivanovna—a valuable thing, silver, a cigarette box, as soon as I get it back from a friend . . . " he broke off in confusion.

"Well, we will talk about it then, sir."

"Goodbye—are you always at home alone, your sister is not here with you?" he asked her as casually as possible as he went out into the passage.

"What business is she of yours, sir?"

"Oh, nothing particular, I simply asked. You are too quick . . . Good-day, Aliona Ivanovna."

Raskolnikov went out in complete confusion. This confusion became more and more intense. As he went down the stairs, he even stopped short, two or three times, as though suddenly struck by some thought. When he was in the street he cried out, "Oh, God, how loathsome it all is! and can I, can I possibly . . . No, it's nonsense, it's absurd!" he added resolutely. "And how could such an atrocious thing come into my head? What filthy things my heart is capable of. Yes, filthy above all, disgusting, loathsome, loathsome!—and for a whole month I've been . . . " But no words, no exclamations, could express his agitation. The feeling of intense repulsion, which had begun to oppress and torture his heart while he was on his way to the old woman, had by now reached such a pitch and had taken such a definite form that he did not know what to do with himself to escape from his wretchedness. He walked along the pavement like a drunken man, oblivious of the passersby, and jostling against them, and only came to his senses when he was in the next street. Looking round, he noticed that he was standing close to a tavern which was entered by steps leading from the pavement to the basement. At that instant two drunken men came out of the door and, abusing and supporting one another, they mounted the steps. Without stopping to think, Raskolnikov went down the steps at once. Until that moment he had never been into a tavern, but now he felt dizzy and was tormented by a burning thirst. He longed for a drink of cold beer, and attributed his sudden weakness to hunger. He sat down at a sticky little table in a dark and dirty corner; ordered some beer, and eagerly drank off the first glassful. At once he felt relief; and his thoughts became clear.

"All that's nonsense," he said hopefully, "and there is nothing in it all to worry about! It's simply physical weakness. Just a glass of beer, a piece of dry bread—and in one moment the brain is stronger, the mind is clearer and the will is firm! Pah, how utterly petty it all is!"

But, though he spat this out so scornfully, he was by now looking cheerful as though he were suddenly set free from a terrible burden: and he gazed round in a friendly way at the people in the room. But even at that moment he had a dim foreboding that this happier frame of mind was also not normal.

There were few people at the time in the tavern. Besides the two drunken men he had met on the steps, a group consisting of about five men, with a girl and a concertina, had gone out at the same time. Their departure left the room quiet and rather empty. The persons remaining were a man who appeared to be an artisan, drunk, but not extremely so, sitting with a beer, and his companion, a huge, stout man with a gray beard, in a short full-skirted coat. He was very drunk and had dozed off on the bench; every now and then, as if in his sleep, he began cracking his fingers, with his arms wide apart and the upper part of his body bouncing about on the bench, while he hummed some meaningless refrain, trying to recall some such lines as these:—

> "His wife a year he stroked and loved
> His wife a—a year he—stroked and loved." —

Or suddenly waking up again:—

> "Walking along the crowded row
> He met the one he used to know."—

But no-one shared his enjoyment: his silent companion looked at all these outbursts with hostility and mistrust. There was another man in the room who looked somewhat like a retired government clerk. He was sitting apart, sipping now and then from his mug and looking round at the company. He, too, appeared to be somewhat excited.

CHAPTER TWO

RASKOLNIKOV WAS NOT USED to crowds, and, as was said previously, he avoided society of every sort, especially recently. But now all at once he felt a desire to be with other people. Something new seemed to be taking place within him, and with it he felt a sort of thirst for company. He was so weary after a whole month of concentrated wretchedness and gloomy excitement that he longed to rest, if only for a moment, in some other world, whatever it might be; and, in spite of the filthiness of the surroundings, he was glad now to stay in the tavern.

The owner of the establishment was in another room, but he frequently came down some steps into the main room, his jaunty, polished boots with red turn-over tops coming into view each time before the rest of him. He wore a full coat and a horribly greasy black satin waistcoat, with no cravat, and his whole face seemed smeared with oil like an iron lock. At the counter stood a boy of about fourteen, and there was another somewhat younger boy who served the customers. On the counter lay some sliced cucumber, some pieces of dried black bread, and some fish chopped up into little pieces, all smelling very bad. It was unbearably humid, and so heavy with the fumes of alcohol that five minutes in such an atmosphere could well cause drunkenness.

We all have chance meetings with people, even with complete strangers, who interest us at first glance, suddenly, before a word is spoken. Such was the impression made on Raskolnikov by the person sitting a little distance from him, who looked like a retired clerk. The young man often recalled this impression afterwards, and even ascribed it to presentiment. He looked repeatedly at the clerk, partly no doubt because the latter was staring persistently at him, obviously anxious to enter into conversation. The clerk looked at the other persons in the room, including the tavern-keeper, as though he were used to their company, and weary of it, showing at the same time a shade of patronizing contempt for them as members of a culture inferior to his own, with whom it would be useless for him to converse. He was over fifty, bald and grizzled, of medium height, and stoutly built. His face, bloated from continual drinking, was of a yellow, even greenish, tinge, with swollen eyelids out of which keen reddish eyes gleamed like little slits. But there was something very strange in him; there was a light in his eyes as though of intense feeling—perhaps there was even a streak of thought and intelligence, but at the same time they gleamed with something like madness. He was wearing an old and hopelessly ragged black dress coat, with all its buttons missing except one, which he had buttoned, evidently wishing to preserve his respectability. A crumpled shirt front covered with spots and stains, protruded from his canvas waistcoat. Like a clerk, he did not have a beard or a moustache, but had been so long unshaven that his chin looked like a stiff grayish brush. And there was also something respectable and official about his manner. But he was restless; he ruffled up his hair and from time to time let his head drop into his hands dejectedly resting his ragged elbows on the stained and sticky table. At last he looked straight at Raskolnikov, and said loudly and resolutely:

"May I venture, dear sir, to engage you in polite conversation? For although your exterior would not command respect, my experience distinguishes in you a man of education and not accustomed to drinking. I have always respected education united with genuine feelings, and I am besides a titular councilor in rank. Marmeladov—that is my name; titular councilor. May I inquire—have you been in the service?"

"No, I am studying," answered the young man, somewhat surprised at the grand style of the speaker and also at being so directly addressed. In spite of the momentary desire he had just been feeling for company of any sort, when he was actually spoken to he felt his habitual irritable uneasiness at any stranger who approached or attempted to approach him.

"A student then, or a former student," cried the clerk. "Just what I thought! I'm a man of experience, immense experience, sir," and he tapped his forehead with his fingers in self-approval. "You've been a student or have attended some learned institution! . . . But allow me . . . " He got up, staggered, took up his jug and glass, and sat down beside the young man, facing him a little sideways. He was drunk, but spoke fluently and boldly, only occasionally losing the thread of his sentences and drawling his words. He pounced upon Raskolnikov as greedily as though he too had not spoken to a soul for a month.

"Dear sir," he began almost with solemnity, "poverty is not a vice, that's a true saying. Yet I know too that drunkenness is not a virtue, and that that's even truer. But destitution, dear sir, destitution is a vice. In poverty you may still retain your innate nobility of soul, but in destitution—never—no-one. For destitution a man is not chased out of human society with a stick, he is swept out with a broom, so as to make it as humiliating as possible; and quite right, too, for in destitution I am the first to humiliate myself. Hence the tavern! Dear sir, a month ago Mr. Lebeziatnikov gave my wife a beating, and my wife is a very different matter from me! Do you understand? Allow me to ask you another question out of simple curiosity: have you ever spent a night on a hay barge, on the Neva?"

"No, I haven't," answered Raskolnikov. "What do you mean?"

"Well, I've just come from one and it's the fifth night . . . " He filled his glass, emptied it and paused. Bits of hay were in fact clinging to his clothes and sticking to his hair. It seemed quite probable that he had not undressed or washed for the last five days. His hands, particularly, were filthy. They were fat and red, with black nails.

His conversation seemed to excite a general though languid interest. The boys at the counter began to snigger. The innkeeper came down from the upper room, apparently on purpose to listen to the "clown" and sat down at a little distance, yawning lazily, but with dignity. Evidently Marmeladov was a familiar figure here, and he had most likely acquired his weakness for high-flown speeches from the habit of frequently entering into conversation with strangers of all sorts in the tavern. This habit develops into a necessity in some drunkards, and especially in those who are looked after strictly and kept in order at home. Hence in the company of other drinkers they try to justify themselves and even if possible obtain respect.

"Clown!" pronounced the innkeeper. "And why don't ya work, why aren't ya at the office, if y'are an official?"

"Why am I not at the office, dear sir," Marmeladov went on, addressing himself exclusively to Raskolnikov, as though it had been he who put that question to him. "Why am I not at the office? Does not my heart ache to think what a useless worm I am? A month ago when Mr. Lebeziatnikov beat my wife with his own hands, and I lay drunk, didn't I suffer? Excuse me, young man, has it ever happened to you . . . hm . . . well, to ask hopelessly for a loan?"

"Yes, it has. But what do you mean by hopelessly?"

"Hopelessly in the fullest sense, when you know beforehand that you will get nothing by it. You know, for instance, beforehand with positive certainty that this man, this most reputable and exemplary citizen, will on no consideration give you money; and indeed I ask you why should he? For he knows of course that I won't pay it back. From compassion? But Mr. Lebeziatnikov who keeps up with modern ideas explained the other day that compassion is forbidden nowadays by science itself, and that that's how it is done now in England, where there is political economy. Why, I ask you, should he give it to me? And knowing beforehand that he won't, you set off to him and . . . "

"Why do you go?" put in Raskolnikov.

"But what if there is no-one, nowhere else one can go! For every man must have somewhere to go. Since there are times when one absolutely must go somewhere! When my own daughter first went out with a yellow ticket,* then I had to go . . . (for my daughter has a yellow ticket)," he added in parenthesis, looking with a certain uneasiness at the young man. "No matter, sir, no matter!" he went on hurriedly and with apparent composure when both the boys at the counter guffawed and even the innkeeper smiled—"No matter, I am not embarrassed by the wagging of their heads; for every one knows everything about it already, and all that is secret will be revealed. And I accept it all, not with contempt, but with humility. So be it! So be it! 'Behold the man!' Excuse me, young man, can you . . . No, to put it more strongly and more distinctly; not *can* you but *dare* you, looking upon me, assert that I am not a pig?"

The young man did not answer a word.

"Well," the orator began again persistently and with even more dignity, after waiting for the laughter in the room to subside. "Well,

---

*Standard identification for registered prostitutes.

so be it, I am a pig, but she is a lady! I have the semblance of a beast, but Katerina Ivanovna, my spouse, is a person of education and an officer's daughter. Granted, granted, I am a scoundrel, but she is a woman of a noble heart, full of sentiments, refined by education. And yet . . . oh, if only she pitied me! Dear sir, dear sir, you know every man ought to have at least one place where people pity him! But Katerina Ivanovna, though she is generous, she is unjust . . . And yet, although I realize that when she pulls my hair she does it merely out of pity—for I repeat without being ashamed, she pulls my hair, young man," he declared with redoubled dignity, hearing the sniggering again—"but, my God, if she would but once . . . But no, no! It's all in vain and it's no use talking! No use talking! For more than once, my wish did come true and more than once she has taken pity on me but . . . such is my trait and I am a beast by nature!"

"Rather!" assented the innkeeper yawning. Marmeladov struck his fist resolutely on the table.

"Such is my trait! Do you know, sir, do you know, I have sold her very stockings for drink? Not her shoes—that would be more or less in the order of things, but her stockings, her stockings I have sold for drink! Her mohair shawl I sold for drink, a present to her long ago, her own property, not mine; and we live in a cold room and she caught cold this winter and has begun coughing and spitting blood too. We have three little children and Katerina Ivanovna is at work from morning till night; she is scrubbing and cleaning and washing the children, for she's been used to cleanliness from childhood. But her chest is weak and she has a tendency to consumption and I feel it! Do you suppose I don't feel it? And the more I drink the more I feel it. That's why I drink, to find sympathy and feeling in drink . . . I drink because I want to suffer profoundly!" And as though in despair he laid his head down on the table.

"Young man," he went on, raising his head again, "in your face I seem to read some kind of sorrow. When you came in I read it, and that was why I addressed you at once. For in unfolding to you the story of my life, I do not wish to make myself a laughing-stock before these idle listeners, who indeed know all about it already, but I am looking for a man of feeling and education. Know then that my wife was educated in a high-class school for the daughters of noblemen, and on leaving she danced the shawl dance before the governor and other personages, for which she was presented with a gold medal and a certificate of merit. The medal . . . well, the medal of course was sold—long ago, hm . . . but the certificate of merit is in her trunk still and not long ago she showed it to our landlady. And although she quarrels with the landlady most continually, yet she wanted to boast to someone or other of her past honors and to tell of the happy days that are gone. I don't condemn her for it, I don't condemn her, for the one thing left her is her memories of the past, and all the rest is dust and ashes! Yes, yes, she is a hot-tempered lady, proud and determined. She scrubs the floors herself and has nothing but black bread to eat, but won't allow herself to be treated with disrespect. That's why she would not overlook Mr. Lebeziatnikov's rudeness to her, and so when he gave her a beating for it, she took to her bed more from the hurt to her feelings than from the blows. She was a widow when I married her, with three children, one smaller than the other. She married her first husband, an infantry officer, for love, and ran away with him from her father's house. She loved her husband very much; but he gave way to cards, wound up in court and with that he died. He used to beat her at the end: and although she didn't let him get away with it, of which I have authentic documentary evidence, to this day she speaks of him with tears and she throws him up to me; and I am glad, I am glad that, though only in imagination, she should think of herself as having once been happy . . . And she was left at his death with three children in a beastly and remote district where I happened to be at the time; and she was left in such hopeless destitution that, although I have seen many ups and downs of all sorts, I am unable to describe it even. Her relations had all abandoned her. And she was proud, too, excessively proud . . . And then, dear sir, and then, I, being at the time a widower, with a daughter of fourteen left me by my first wife, offered her my hand, for I could not bear the sight of such suffering. You can judge the extremity of her calamities, that she, a woman of education and culture and distinguished family, should have consented to be my wife. But she did! Weeping and sobbing and wringing her hands, she married me! For she had nowhere to turn! Do you understand, dear sir, do you understand what it means when you have absolutely nowhere to turn? No, that you don't understand yet . . . And for a whole year, I performed my duties conscientiously and faithfully, and did not touch this" (he tapped the jug with his finger), "for I have feelings. But even so, I could not please her; and then I lost my place too, and that through no fault of mine but through changes in the office; and then I did touch it! . . . It will already be a year and a half ago since we found ourselves at last after many wanderings and numerous calamities in this magnificent capital, adorned with innumerable monuments. Here, too, I obtained a position . . . I obtained it and I lost it again. Do you understand? This time it was through my own fault I lost it: for my trait had come out . . . We have now a corner at Amalia Fiodorovna Lippewechsel's; and what we live upon and what we pay our rent with, I could not say. There are a lot of people living there besides ourselves. A most abominable Sodom . . . hm . . . yes . . . And meanwhile my daughter by my first wife has grown up; and what my daughter has had to put up with from her step-mother whilst she was growing up, I won't speak of. For, though Katerina Ivanovna is full of generous feelings, she is a high-tempered lady, irritable, and will cut you off . . . Yes. But it's no use going over that! Sonia, as you may well imagine, has had no education. I did make an effort four years ago to give her a course of geography and world history, but as I was not very well up in those subjects myself and we had no suitable manuals, and what books we had . . . hm, anyway, we don't have them now, those books, so all our instruction came to an end. We stopped at Cyrus of Persia.* Since she has attained years of maturity, she has read other books of novelistic tendency and recently she had read with great interest a book she got through Mr. Lebeziatnikov, Lewes' Physiology†—do you know it?—and even recounted extracts from it to us: and that's the whole of her education. And now may I venture to address you, dear sir, on my own account with a private question. Do you suppose that a respectable poor girl can earn much by honest work? Not fifteen kopecks a day can she earn, if she is respectable and has no special talent and that without putting her work down for an instant! And what's more, Ivan Ivanich Klopstock the state councilor—have you heard of him?—has not to this day paid her for the half-dozen Holland shirts she made him and drove her

---

*Cyrus the Great (c. 580–c. 529 B.C.), a ruler of the Persian Empire and a staple figure in the classical education of the period.

†*The Physiology of Common Life* (1859–1860), by George Henry Lewes.

away insulted, stamping and calling her names, on the pretext that the shirt collars were not made the right size and were put in askew. And there are the little ones hungry . . . And Katerina Ivanovna walking up and down and wringing her hands, her cheeks flushed red, as they always are in that disease: 'You sponger,' says she, 'living with us, eating and drinking and keeping warm.' And much she gets to eat and drink when there is not a crust for the little ones for three days! I was lying at the time . . . well, what of it! I was lying drunk and I heard my Sonia speaking (she is a meek creature with a gentle little voice . . . fair hair and such a pale, thin little face). She said: 'Katerina Ivanovna, am I really to do a thing like that?' Daria Frantsevna, an evil-minded woman and very well known to the police, had two or three times already tried to get at her through the landlady. 'And why not?' said Katerina Ivanovna with a jeer, 'what's there to save? Some treasure!' But don't blame her, don't blame her, dear sir, don't blame her! She was not in her right mind when she spoke, but driven to distraction by her illness and the crying of the hungry children; and it was said more to wound her than in any precise sense . . . For that's Katerina Ivanovna's character, and when children cry, even from hunger, she starts beating them at once. At six o'clock or so I saw Sonechka get up, put on her kerchief, put on her cape, and go out of the room, and about nine o'clock she came back. She walked straight up to Katerina Ivanovna and she laid thirty rubles on the table before her in silence. She did not utter a word, she did not even look at her, she simply picked up our big green woolen shawl (we all use it, this woolen shawl), put it over her head and face and lay down on the bed with her face to the wall; only her little shoulders and her body kept shuddering . . . And I went on lying there, just as before . . . And then I saw, young man, I saw Katerina Ivanovna, in the same silence go up to Sonechka's little bed; she was on her knees all evening kissing Sonia's feet, and would not get up, and then they both fell asleep in each other's arms . . . together, together . . . yes . . . and I . . . lay drunk."

Marmeladov stopped short, as though his voice had failed him. Then he hurriedly filled his glass, drank, and cleared his throat.

"Since then, sir," he went on after a brief pause—"Since then, due to an unfortunate occurrence and through information given by evil-intentioned persons—in all of which Daria Frantsevna took a leading part on the pretext that she had been treated with too little respect—since then my daughter Sofia Semionovna has been forced to take a yellow ticket, and owing to that she is unable to go on living with us. For our landlady, Amalia Fiodorovna would not hear of it (though she had backed up Daria Frantsevna before) and Mr. Lebeziatnikov too . . . hm . . . All the trouble between him and Katerina Ivanovna was on Sonia's account. At first he was after Sonechka himself and then all of a sudden he got into a huff: 'how,' said he, 'can an enlightened man like me live in the same rooms with a girl like that?' And Katerina Ivanovna would not let it pass, she stood up for her . . . and so that's how it happened. And Sonechka comes to us now, mostly after dark; she comforts Katerina Ivanovna and gives her all she can . . . She has a room at the tailor Kapernaumov, she rents from them; Kapernaumov is a lame man with a cleft palate and all of his numerous family have cleft palates too. And his wife, too, has a cleft palate. They all live in one room, but Sonia has her own, partitioned off . . . Hm . . . yes . . . very poor people and all with cleft palates . . . yes. As soon as I got up in the morning, I put on my rags, lifted up my hands to heaven and set off to his excellency Ivan Afanasyevich. His excellency Ivan Afanasyevich, do you know him? No? Well, then, it's a man of God you don't know. He is wax . . . wax before the face of the Lord; even as wax melteth! . . . He even shed tears when he heard my story. 'Marmeladov, once already you have deceived my expectations . . . I'll take you once more on my own responsibility'—that's what he said, 'remember,' he said, 'and now you can go.' I kissed the dust at his feet—in thought only, for in reality he would not have allowed me to do it, being a statesman and a man of modern political and enlightened ideas. I returned home, and when I announced that I'd been taken back into the service and should receive a salary, heavens, what a to-do there was . . . !"

Marmeladov stopped again in violent excitement. At that moment a whole party of drunkards already drunk came in from the street, and the sounds of a hired concertina and the cracked piping voice of a child of seven singing "The Little Farm" were heard in the entryway. The room was filled with noise. The tavern-keeper and the servants were busy with the newcomers. Marmeladov paying no attention to the new arrivals continued his story. He appeared by now to be extremely weak, but as he became more and more drunk, he became more and more talkative. The recollection of his recent success in getting the position seemed to revive him, and was even reflected in a sort of radiance on his face. Raskolnikov listened attentively.

"That was five weeks ago, sir. Yes . . . As soon as Katerina Ivanovna and Sonechka heard of it, Lord, it was as though I stepped into the kingdom of Heaven. It used to be: you can lie like a beast, nothing but abuse. Now they were walking on tiptoe, hushing the children. 'Semion Zakharovich is tired from his work at the office, he is resting, shh!' They made me coffee before I went to work and boiled cream for me! They began to get real cream for me, do you hear that? And how they managed to scrape together the money for a decent outfit—eleven rubles, fifty kopecks, I can't guess. Boots, cotton shirt-fronts—most magnificent, a uniform, they got it all up in splendid style, for eleven rubles and a half. The first morning I came back from the office I found Katerina Ivanovna had cooked two courses for dinner—soup and salt meat with horse radish—which we had never dreamed of until then. She didn't have any dresses . . . none at all, but she got herself up as though she were going on a visit; and not that she had anything to do it with, they could make everything out of nothing: do the hair nicely, put on a clean collar of some sort, cuffs, and there she was, quite a different person, younger and better looking. Sonechka, my little darling, had only helped with money; 'for the time,' she said, 'it won't do for me to come and see you too often. After dark maybe when no-one can see.' Do you hear, do you hear? I lay down for a nap after dinner and what do you think: though Katerina Ivanovna had quarreled to the last degree with our landlady Amalia Fiodorovna only a week before, she could not resist then asking her in for a cup of coffee. For two hours they were sitting, whispering together. 'Semion Zakharovich is in the service again, now, and receiving a salary,' says she, 'and he went himself to his excellency and his excellency himself came out to him, made all the others wait and led Semion Zakharovich by the hand before everybody into his study.' Do you hear, do you hear? 'To be sure,' says he, 'Semion Zakharovich, remembering your past services,' says he, 'and in spite of your propensity to that foolish weakness, since you promise now and since moreover we've got on badly without you,' (do you hear, do you hear!) 'and so,' says he, 'I rely now on your word as a gentleman.' And all that, let me tell you, she has simply made up for herself, and not simply out of thoughtlessness, for the sake of bragging; no, she believes it all herself, she amuses herself with her own imaginings, upon my word she does! And I don't blame her for it, no, I don't blame her! . . . Six days ago when I brought her my first earnings in full—twenty-three rubles forty kopecks altogether—she called me her little one: little one,' said she, 'my little one.' And when we were by ourselves, you understand? You would not think me a beauty, you would not think much of me as a husband, would you? . . . Well, she pinched my cheek; 'my little one,' she says."

Marmeladov broke off, tried to smile, but suddenly his chin began to twitch. He controlled himself however. The tavern, the degraded appearance of the man, the five nights in the hay barge, and the jug of alcohol, and yet this poignant love for his wife and children bewildered his listener. Raskolnikov listened intently but with a sick sensation. He felt vexed that he had come here.

"Dear sir, dear sir," exclaimed Marmeladov recovering himself— "Oh, sir, perhaps all this seems a laughing matter to you, as it does to others, and perhaps I am only worrying you with the stupidity of all these miserable details of my home life, but it is not a laughing matter to me. For I can feel it all . . . And the whole of that heavenly day of my life and the whole of that evening I passed in fleeting dreams of how I would arrange it all, and how I would dress all the children, and how I would give her rest, and how I would rescue my own daughter from dishonor and restore her to the bosom of her family . . . And a great deal more . . . Quite excusable, sir. Well, then, sir" (Marmeladov suddenly gave a sort of start, raised his head and stared fixedly at his listener) "well, on the very next day after all those dreams, that is to say, exactly five days ago, in the evening, by a cunning trick, like a thief in the night, I stole from Katerina Ivanovna the key of her trunk, took out what was left of my earnings, how much it was I have forgotten, and now look at me, all of you! It's the fifth day since I left home, and they are looking for me there and it's the end of my employment, and my uniform is lying in a tavern on the Egyptian bridge, exchanged for the garments I have on . . . and it's the end of everything!"

Marmeladov struck his forehead with his fist, clenched his teeth, closed his eyes and leaned heavily with his elbow on the table. But a minute later his face suddenly changed and with a certain assumed slyness and affectation of bravado, he glanced at Raskolnikov, laughed and said:

"This morning I went to see Sonia, I went to ask her for a hangover drink! He-he-he!"

"You don't say she gave it to you?" cried one of the newcomers; he shouted the words and went off into a guffaw.

"This very quart was bought with her money," Marmeladov declared, addressing himself exclusively to Raskolnikov. "Thirty kopecks she gave me with her own hands, her last, all she had, as I saw . . . She said nothing, she only looked at me without a word . . . Not on earth, but up there . . . they grieve so over men, they weep, but they don't blame them, they don't blame them! But it hurts more, it hurts more when they don't blame! Thirty kopecks, yes! And maybe she needs them now, eh? What do you think, my dear sir? For now she's got to keep up a clean appearance. It costs money, that clean style, a special one, you know? Do you understand? And there's rouge, too, you see, she must have things; petticoats, starched ones, shoes, too, real jaunty ones to show off her foot when she has to step over a puddle. Do you understand, sir, do you understand what all that cleanliness means? And here I, her own father, here I took thirty kopecks of that money for a drink! And I am drinking it! And I have already drunk it! Come, who will have pity on a man like me, eh? Do you pity me, sir, or not? Tell me, sir, do you pity me or not? He-he-he!"

He would have filled his glass, but there was no drink left. The jug was empty.

"What are you to be pitied for?" shouted the tavern-keeper who was again near them.

Shouts of laughter and even swearing followed. The laughter and the swearing came from those who were listening and also from those who had heard nothing but were simply looking at the figure of the discharged government clerk.

"To be pitied! Why am I to be pitied?" Marmeladov suddenly cried out, standing up with his arm outstretched, positively inspired, as though he had been only waiting for that question.

"Why am I to be pitied, you say? Yes! There's nothing to pity me for! I ought to be crucified, crucified on a cross, not pitied! Crucify, oh judge, crucify, but when you have crucified, take pity on him! And then I myself will go to be crucified, for it's not merry-making I seek but tears and tribulation! . . . Do you suppose, you that sell, that this half-bottle of yours has been sweet to me? It was tribulation I sought at the bottom of it, tears and tribulation, and have tasted it, and have found it; but He will pity us Who has had pity on all men, Who has understood all men and all things, He is the One. He too is the judge. He will come in that day and He will ask: 'Where is the daughter who gave herself for her mean, consumptive step-mother and for the little children of another? Where is the daughter who had pity upon the filthy drunkard, her earthly father, undismayed by his beastliness?' And He will say, 'Come to me! I have already forgiven thee once . . . I have forgiven thee once . . . Thy sins which are many are forgiven thee for thou hast loved much . . . ' And he will forgive my Sonia, He will forgive, I know it . . . I felt it in my heart when I was with her just now! And He will judge and will forgive all, the good and the evil, the wise and the meek . . . And when He has done with all of them, then He will summon us. 'You too come forth,' He will say, 'Come forth ye drunkards, come forth, ye weak ones, come forth, ye children of shame!' And we shall all come forth, without shame and shall stand before him. And He will say unto us, 'Ye are swine, made in the Image of the Beast and with his mark; but come ye also!' And the wise ones and those of understanding will say, 'Oh Lord, why dost Thou receive these men?' And He will say, 'This is why I receive them, oh ye wise, this is why I receive them, oh ye of understanding, that not one of them believed himself to be worthy of this.' And He will hold out His hands to us and we shall fall down before him . . . and we shall weep . . . and we shall understand all things! Then we shall understand everything! . . . and all will understand, Katerina Ivanovna even . . . she will understand . . . Lord, Thy kingdom come!" And he sank down on the bench exhausted and weak, looking at no-one, apparently oblivious of his surroundings and plunged in deep thought. His words had created a certain impression; there was a moment of silence; but soon laughter and swearing were heard again.

"Reasoned it all out!"

"Talked himself silly!"

"A fine clerk he is!"

And so on, and so on.

"Let us go, sir," said Marmeladov suddenly, raising his head and addressing Raskolnikov—"come along with me . . . Kozel's house, looking into the yard. I'm going to Katerina Ivanovna—time I did."

Raskolnikov had for some time been wanting to leave, and he himself had meant to help him. Marmeladov was much weaker on his legs than in his speech and leaned heavily on the young man. They had two or three hundred paces to go. The drunken man was more and more overcome by dismay and confusion as they drew nearer the house.

"It's not Katerina Ivanovna I am afraid of now," he muttered in agitation—"and that she will begin pulling my hair. What does my hair matter! Forget my hair! That's what I say! It will even be better if she does begin pulling it, that's not what I am afraid of . . . it's her eyes I am afraid of . . . yes, her eyes . . . the red on her cheeks, too, frightens me . . . and her breathing too . . . Have you noticed how people with that disease breathe . . . when they are excited? I am afraid of the children's crying, too . . . Because if Sonia has not taken them food . . . I don't know then! I don't know! But blows I am not afraid of . . . Know, sir, that such blows are not a pain to me, but even an enjoyment. For I myself can't manage without it . . . It's better that way. Let her strike me, it relieves her heart . . . it's better that way . . . There is the house. The house of Kozel, the cabinet maker . . . a German, well-off. Lead the way!"

They went in from the yard and up to the fourth floor. The staircase got darker and darker as they went up. It was nearly eleven o'clock and although in summer in Petersburg there is no real night, yet it was quite dark at the top of the stairs.

A grimy little door at the very top of the stairs stood ajar. A very poor-looking room about ten paces long was lit up by a candle-end; the whole of it was visible from the entrance. It was all in disorder, littered up with rags of all sorts, especially children's clothes. Across the furthest corner was stretched a sheet with holes in it. Behind it probably was the bed. There was nothing in the room except two chairs and a very shabby sofa covered with oilcloth, before which stood an old pine kitchen-table, unpainted and uncovered. At the edge of the table stood a smoldering tallow-candle in an iron candlestick. It appeared that the family had a room to themselves, not a corner, but their room was practically a passage. The door leading to

the other rooms, or rather cupboards, into which Amalia Lippewechsel's apartment was divided, stood half open, and there was shouting,
uproar and laughter within. People seemed to be playing cards and
drinking tea there. Words of the most unceremonious kind flew out
from time to time.

Raskolnikov recognized Katerina Ivanovna at once. She was terribly emaciated, a rather tall, slim and graceful woman, with magnificent dark blond hair and indeed with a hectic flush in her cheeks.
She was pacing up and down in her little room, pressing her hands
against her chest; her lips were parched and her breathing came in irregular broken gasps. Her eyes glittered as in fever but looked about
with a harsh immovable stare. And that consumptive and excited face
with the last flickering light of the candle-end playing upon it made
a sickening impression. She seemed to Raskolnikov about thirty years
old and was certainly a strange wife for Marmeladov . . . She had not
heard them and did not notice them coming in. She seemed to be lost
in thought, hearing and seeing nothing. The room was stuffy, but she
had not opened the window; a stench rose from the staircase, but the
door on to the stairs was not closed. From the inner rooms clouds of
tobacco smoke floated in, she kept coughing, but did not close the
door. The youngest child, a girl of six, was asleep, sitting curled up
on the floor with her head against the sofa. A boy a year older stood
crying and shaking in the corner. Probably he had just had a beating.
Beside him stood a girl of nine years old, tall and thin as a matchstick, wearing a worn and ragged shirt with an ancient wool wrap
flung over her bare shoulders, long outgrown and barely reaching
her knees. She stood in the corner next to her little brother, her long
arm, as dry as a matchstick, round her brother's neck. She seemed to
be trying to comfort him, whispering something to him, and doing
all she could to keep him from whimpering again while at the same
time her large dark eyes, which looked larger still from the thinness
of her frightened face, were watching her mother with fear. Marmeladov did not enter the door, but dropped on his knees in the very
doorway, pushing Raskolnikov in front of him. The woman seeing a
stranger stopped absentmindedly facing him, coming to herself for a
moment and apparently wondering what he had come for. But evidently she decided that he was going into the next room, since he
had to pass through hers to get there. Having figured this out and tak-

ing no further notice of him, she walked towards the outer door to close it and uttered a sudden scream on seeing her husband on his knees in the doorway.

"Ah!" she cried out in a frenzy, "he has come back! The criminal! the monster! . . . And where is the money? What's in your pocket, show me! And your clothes are all different! Where are your clothes? Where is the money! speak!"

And she rushed to search him. Marmeladov submissively and obediently held up both arms to facilitate the search. Not a kopeck was there.

"Where's the money?" she cried—"Oh Lord, can he have drunk it all? But there were twelve silver rubles left in the chest!" and suddenly, in a fury, she seized him by the hair and dragged him into the room. Marmeladov helped her efforts by meekly crawling along on his knees.

"And this is enjoyment to me! This does not hurt me, but is actually enjoyment, dear sir," he called out, shaken to and fro by his hair and even once striking the ground with his forehead. The child asleep on the floor woke up, and began to cry. The boy in the corner losing all control began trembling and screaming and rushed to his sister in violent terror, almost in a fit. The eldest girl was shaking like a leaf.

"He's drunk it! He's drunk it all," the poor woman screamed in despair—"and his clothes are gone! And they are hungry, hungry!"— and wringing her hands she pointed to the children. "Oh, accursed life! And you, are you not ashamed?"—she pounced suddenly upon Raskolnikov—"from the tavern! Have you been drinking with him? You have been drinking with him, too! Get out!"

The young man hastened to leave without uttering a word. The inner door, moreover, was thrown wide open and inquisitive faces were peering in. Shameless laughing faces with pipes and cigarettes and heads wearing caps thrust themselves in at the doorway. Further in figures in dressing gowns flung open could be seen, in costumes of unseemly scantiness, some of them with cards in their hands. They were particularly diverted when Marmeladov, dragged about by his hair, shouted that it was enjoyment to him. They even began to come into the room; at last a sinister shrill outcry was heard: this came from Amalia Lippewechsel herself pushing her way forward and trying to restore order in her own way and for the hundredth time to frighten the poor woman by ordering her with coarse abuse to clear out of the room next day. As he went out, Raskolnikov had time to put his hand into his pocket, to snatch up the coppers he had received in exchange for his ruble in the tavern and to lay them unnoticed on the window. Afterwards on the stairs, he changed his mind and wanted to go back.

"What a stupid thing I've done," he thought to himself, "they have Sonia and I need it myself." But reflecting that it would be impossible to take it back now and that in any case he would not have taken it, he dismissed it with a wave of his hand and went back to his room. "Sonia wants rouge too," he said as he walked along the street, and he laughed malignantly—"such cleanliness costs money . . . Hm! And maybe our Sonia herself will be bankrupt today, for there is always a risk, hunting big game . . . digging for gold . . . then they would all be without a crust tomorrow except for my money. Bravo Sonia! What a well they've dug! And they're making the most of it! Yes, they are making the most of it! Got used to it. They've wept a bit and grown used to it. Man grows used to everything, the scoundrel!"

He sank into thought.

"And what if I am wrong," he suddenly cried involuntarily. "What if man is not really a *scoundrel*, man in general, I mean, the whole race of mankind—then all the rest is prejudice, simply artificial terrors and there are no barriers and it's all as it should be."

CHAPTER THREE

HE WOKE UP LATE next day after a troubled sleep. But his sleep had not refreshed him; he woke up bilious, irritable, ill-tempered, and looked with hatred at his room. It was a tiny cupboard of a room about six paces in length. It had a poverty-stricken appearance with its dusty yellow paper peeling off the walls, and the ceiling was so low that a man of just a little more than average height was ill at ease in it and kept feeling every moment that he would knock his head against the ceiling. The furniture was in keeping with the room: there were three old chairs, rather rickety; a painted table in the corner on which lay a few books and notebooks; the dust alone that lay thick upon them showed that they had been long untouched. A big clumsy sofa occupied almost the whole of one wall and half the floor space of the room; it was once covered with chintz, but was now in rags and served Raskolnikov as a bed. Often he went to sleep on it, as he was, without undressing, without sheets, wrapped in his old, shabby student's overcoat, with his head on one little pillow, under which he heaped up all the linen he had, clean and dirty, by way of a bolster. A little table stood in front of the sofa.

It would have been difficult to sink to a lower ebb of slovenliness, but to Raskolnikov in his present state of mind this was even agreeable. He had completely withdrawn from everyone, like a tortoise in its shell, and even the sight of the servant girl who had to wait upon him and looked sometimes into his room made him writhe with nervous irritation. He was in the condition that overtakes some monomaniacs excessively concentrated upon one thing. His landlady had for the last fortnight given up sending him in meals, and he had still not yet thought of expostulating with her, though he went without his dinner. Nastasia, the cook and only servant, was rather pleased at the tenant's mood and had entirely given up sweeping and doing his room, only once a week or so she would stray into his room with a broom. She woke him up now.

"Get up, why are you asleep!" she called to him. "It's past nine, I've brought you some tea; want a cup? You must be starving?"

The tenant opened his eyes, started and recognized Nastasia.

"From the landlady, eh?" he asked, slowly and with a sickly face sitting up on the sofa.

"From the landlady, indeed!"

She set before him her own cracked teapot full of weak and stale tea and laid two yellow lumps of sugar by the side of it.

"Here, Nastasia, take it please," he said, fumbling in his pocket (for he had slept in his clothes) and taking out a handful of coppers—"run and buy me a loaf. And get me a little sausage, the cheapest, at the pork-butcher's."

"The loaf I'll fetch you this very minute, but don't you want some cabbage soup instead of sausage? It's great soup, yesterday's. I saved it for you yesterday, but you came in late. It's fine soup."

When the soup had been brought, and he had started on it, Nastasia sat down beside him on the sofa and began chatting. She was a country peasant-woman and a very talkative one.

"Praskovia Pavlovna wants to complain to the police about you," she said.

He winced.

"To the police? What does she want?"

"You don't pay her money and you won't move out of the room. It's clear what she wants."

"The devil, that's the last straw," he muttered, grinding his teeth, "no, that would not suit me . . . just now. She is a fool," he added aloud. "I'll go and talk to her today."

"Fool she is and no mistake, just as I am. But why, if you are so clever, do you lie here like a sack and have nothing to show for it? One time you used to go out, you say, to teach children. But why is it you do nothing now?"

"I am doing . . . " Raskolnikov began sullenly and reluctantly.

"What are you doing?"

"Work . . . "

"What sort of work?"

"I am thinking," he answered seriously after a pause.

Nastasia burst out laughing. She was given to laughter and when anything amused her, she laughed inaudibly, quivering and shaking all over until she felt ill.

"And have you made much money by your thinking?" she managed to articulate at last.

"One can't go out to give lessons without boots. And who cares."

"Don't spit in a well."

"They pay so little for lessons. What's the use of a few coppers?" he answered, reluctantly, as though replying to his own thought.

"And you want to get a fortune all at once?"

He looked at her strangely.

"Yes, I want a fortune," he answered firmly, after a brief pause.

"Easy, easy, or you'll frighten me! Am I getting you the loaf or not?"

"As you like."

"Ah, I forgot! A letter came for you yesterday when you were out."

"A letter? For me! From whom?"

"I don't know. But I gave three kopecks of my own to the post-man for it. Will you pay me back?"

"Then bring it to me, for God's sake, bring it," cried Raskolnikov greatly excited—"good God!"

A minute later the letter was brought him. Just as he thought: from his mother, from the province of R____.* He even turned pale when he took it. It was a long while since he had received a letter, but another feeling also suddenly stabbed his heart.

"Nastasia, leave me alone, for goodness' sake; here are your three kopecks, but for goodness' sake, make haste and go!"

The letter was quivering in his hand; he did not want to open it in her presence; he wanted to be left alone with this letter. When Nastasia had gone out, he lifted it quickly to his lips and kissed it; then he gazed intently at the address, the small, sloping handwriting, so dear and familiar, of the mother who had once taught him to read and write. He delayed; he even seemed almost afraid of something. At last he opened it; it was a thick heavy letter, weighing over two ounces, two large sheets of note paper were covered with very small handwriting.

"My dear Rodia," wrote his mother—"it's over two months since I last had a talk with you by letter which has distressed me and even kept me awake at night, thinking. But I am sure you will not blame me for my involuntary silence. You know how I love you; you are all we have to look to, Dunia and I, you are our all, our one hope, our one mainstay. What a grief it was to me when I heard that you had given up the university some months ago, for want of means to support yourself and that you had lost your lessons and your other work! How could I help you out of my hundred and twenty rubles a year pension? The fifteen rubles I sent you four months ago I borrowed, as you know, on security of my pension, from Vassily Ivanovich Vakhrushin, our local merchant. He is a kind-hearted man and was a friend of your father's too. But having given him the right to receive the pension, I had to wait till the debt was paid off and that is only just done, so that I've been unable to send you anything all this time. But now, thank God, I believe I will be able to send you something more and in fact we may congratulate ourselves on our good fortune now, of which I hasten to inform you. In

---

*The province of Ryazan, southeast of Moscow.

the first place, would you have guessed, dear Rodia, that your sister has been living with me for the last six weeks and we will not be separated again in the future. Thank God, her sufferings are over, but I will tell you everything in order, so that you may know just how everything has happened and all that we have until now concealed from you. When you wrote to me two months ago that you had heard that Dunia had a great deal of rudeness to put up with in the Svidrigailovs' house, when you wrote that and asked me to tell you all the particulars—what could I write in answer to you? If I had written the whole truth to you, I dare say you would have dropped everything and have come to us, even if you had to walk all the way, for I know your character and your feelings, and you would not let your sister be insulted. I was in despair myself, but what could I do? And, besides, I did not know the whole truth myself then. What made it all so difficult was that Dunia received a hundred rubles in advance when she took the place as governess in their family, on condition of part of her salary being deducted every month, and so it was impossible to quit the position without repaying the debt. This sum (now I can explain it all to you, my dearest Rodia) she took chiefly in order to send you sixty rubles, which you needed so badly then and which you received from us last year. We deceived you then, writing that this money came from Dunechka's savings, but that was not so, and now I tell you all about it, because, thank God, things have suddenly changed for the better, and that you may know how Dunia loves you and what a priceless heart she has. At first indeed Mr. Svidrigailov treated her very rudely and used to make disrespectful and jeering remarks at table . . . But I don't want to go into all those painful details, so as not to worry you for nothing when it is now all over. In short, in spite of the kind and generous behavior of Marfa Petrovna, Mr. Svidrigailov's wife, and all the rest of the household, Dunechka had a very hard time, especially when Mr. Svidrigailov, relapsing into his old regimental habits, was under the influence of alcohol. And how do you think it was all explained later on? Would you believe that the madman had conceived a passion for Dunia from the beginning, but had concealed it under a show of rudeness and contempt. Possibly he was ashamed and horrified himself at his own flighty hopes, considering his years and his being the father of a family; and that made him angry with Dunia. And possibly, too, he simply hoped by his rude and sneering behavior to hide the truth from others. But at last he lost all control and dared to make Dunia an open and vile proposal, promising her all sorts of inducements and offering, besides, to drop everything and take her to another estate of his, or even abroad. You can imagine all she suffered! To leave her situation at once was

impossible not only on account of the money debt, but also to spare the feelings of Marfa Petrovna, whose suspicions would have been aroused; and then
Dunia would have been the cause of a discord in the family. And it would
have meant a terrible scandal for Dunechka too; that would have been inevitable. There were various other reasons owing to which Dunia could not
hope to escape from that awful house for another six weeks. You know
Dunia, of course; you know how clever she is and what a strong will she
has. Dunechka can endure a great deal and even in the most difficult cases
her generous spirit helps her to retain her firmness. She did not even write to
me about everything for fear of upsetting me, although we were constantly
in communication. It all ended very unexpectedly. Marfa Petrovna accidentally overheard her husband imploring Dunia in the garden, and, putting
quite a wrong interpretation on the situation, threw the blame upon her, believing her to be the cause of it all. An awful scene took place between them
on the spot in the garden; Marfa Petrovna went so far as to strike Dunia, refused to hear anything and was shouting at her for a whole hour and then
gave orders that Dunia should be packed off at once to me in a plain peasant's cart, into which they flung all her things, her linen and her clothes, all
pell-mell, without folding it up and packing it. And a heavy shower of rain
came on, too, and Dunia, insulted and put to shame, had to drive with a
peasant in an open cart all the seventeen versts into town. Only think now
what answer could I have sent to the letter I received from you two months
ago and what could I have written? I was in despair; I dared not write to
you the truth because you would have been very unhappy, chagrined and indignant, and yet what could you do? You could only perhaps ruin yourself,
and, besides, Dunechka would not allow it; and I could not fill up my letter
with trifles when my heart was so full of sorrow. For a whole month the
town was full of gossip about this scandal, and it came to the point that
Dunia and I dared not even go to church on account of the contemptuous
looks, whispers, and even remarks made aloud about us. All our acquaintances
avoided us, nobody even bowed to us in the street, and I learnt that some
store assistants and clerks were intending to insult us in a shameful way,
smearing the gates of our house with tar, so that the landlord began to tell
us we must leave. The cause of all this was Marfa Petrovna, who managed to
slander Dunia and throw dirt at her in every family. She knows everyone in
the neighborhood, and that month she was continually coming into the
town, and as she is rather talkative and fond of gossiping about her family
affairs and particularly of complaining to all and each of her husband——

which is not at all right—so in a short time she had spread her story not only in the town, but over the whole surrounding district. It made me ill, but Dunechka was firmer than I was, and if only you could have seen how she endured it all and tried to comfort me and cheer me up! She is an angel! But by God's mercy, our sufferings were cut short: Mr. Svidrigailov returned to his senses and repented and, probably feeling sorry for Dunia, he laid before Marfa Petrovna a complete and unmistakable proof of Dunechka's innocence, in the form of a letter Dunia had been forced to write and give to him, before Marfa Petrovna found them in the garden. This letter, which remained in Mr. Svidrigailov's hands after her departure, she had written to refuse personal explanations and secret meetings, on which he was insisting. In that letter she reproached him with great heat and indignation for the baseness of his behavior in regard to Marfa Petrovna, reminding him that he was the father and head of a family and telling him how vile it was of him to torment and make unhappy a defenseless girl, unhappy enough already. Indeed, dear Rodia, the letter was so nobly and touchingly written that I sobbed when I read it and to this day I cannot read it without tears. Moreover, the evidence of the servants, too, cleared Dunia's reputation; they had seen and known a great deal more than Mr. Svidrigailov had himself supposed—as indeed is always the case with servants. Marfa Petrovna was completely taken aback, and 'again crushed' as she said herself to us, but she was completely convinced of Dunechka's innocence. The very next day, being Sunday, she went straight to the Cathedral, knelt down and prayed with tears to Our Lady to give her strength to bear this new trial and to do her duty. Then she came straight from the Cathedral to us, told us the whole story, wept bitterly and, fully penitent, she embraced Dunia and besought her to forgive her. The same morning without any delay, she went round to all the houses in the town and everywhere, shedding tears, she asserted in the most flattering terms Dunechka's innocence and the nobility of her feelings and her behavior. What was more, she showed and read to every one the letter in Dunechka's own handwriting to Mr. Svidrigailov and even allowed them to take copies of it—which I must say I think was superfluous. In this way she was busy for several days in a row in driving about the whole town, since some people had taken offence that precedence has been given to others, and thus they had to take turns, so that in every house she was expected before she arrived, and everyone knew that on such and such a day Marfa Petrovna would be reading the letter in such and such a place and people assembled for every reading of it, even those who had heard it several times already both in their own houses and in other people's, taking turns. In my opinion a great deal, a very great deal of all this was unnecessary; but that's Marfa Petrovna's character. Anyway she succeeded in completely re-establishing Dunechka's reputation and the whole vileness of this affair rested as an indelible disgrace upon her husband, as the first person to blame, so that I really began to feel sorry for him; it was really treating the madcap too harshly. Dunia was at once asked to give lessons in several families, but she refused. In general everyone suddenly began to treat her with marked respect. All this did much to bring about that unexpected event by which, one may say, all our fate is now transformed. You must know, dear Rodia, that Dunia has a suitor and that she has already consented to marry him, of which I hasten to tell you as soon as possible. And though the matter has been arranged without asking your consent, I think you will not be aggrieved with me or with your sister on that account, for you will see that it would have been impossible for us to wait and put off our decision till we heard from you. And you could not have judged all the facts without being on the spot. This was how it happened. He is already of the rank of a court councilor, Peter Petrovich Luzhin, and is distantly related to Marfa Petrovna, who has been very active in bringing the match about. He began by expressing through her his desire to make our acquaintance, was properly received, drank coffee with us and the very next day he sent us a letter in which he very courteously explained his offer and begged for a speedy and decided answer. He is a very busy man and is in a great hurry to get to Petersburg, so that every moment is precious to him. At first, of course, we were greatly surprised, as it had all happened so quickly and unexpectedly. We thought and deliberated the whole day. He is a well-to-do man, to be depended upon, he has two posts in the government and has already made his fortune. It is true that he is forty-five years old, but he is of a fairly pleasing appearance and might still be thought attractive by women, and he is altogether a very respectable and presentable man, only he seems a little morose and somewhat haughty. But possibly that may only be the impression he makes at first sight. And beware, dear Rodia, when he comes to Petersburg, as he shortly will do, beware of judging him too rashly and heatedly, as your way is, if there is anything you do not like in him at first sight. I say this just in case, although I feel sure that he will make a favorable impression upon you. Moreover, in order to understand any man one must approach gradually and carefully to avoid forming prejudices and mistaken ideas, which are very difficult to correct and remedy afterwards. And Peter Petrovich, judging by many indications, is a thoroughly estimable man. At his first visit, indeed, he told us that he was a practical man, but still he shares, as he expressed it, many of 'the convictions of our most rising generation' and he is an opponent of all prejudices. He said a good deal more, for he seems a little conceited and likes to be listened to, but this is scarcely a vice. I, of course, understood very little of it, but Dunia explained to me that, though he is not a man of great education, he is clever and, it seems, kind. You know your sister's character, Rodia. She is a resolute, sensible, patient and generous girl, but she has an ardent heart, as I know very well. Of course, there is no great love either on his side or on hers, but Dunia, while a clever girl, is also a noble creature, like an angel, and will make it her duty to make her husband happy who on his side will make her happiness his care, of which we have no good reason to doubt, though it must be admitted the matter has been arranged in great haste. Besides he is a man of great prudence and he will see, to be sure, for himself that his own happiness will be the more secure, the happier Dunechka is with him. And as for some defects of character, for some habits and even certain differences of opinion—which indeed are inevitable even in the happiest marriages—Dunechka has said that, as regards all that, she relies on herself, that there is nothing to be uneasy about, and that she is ready to put up with a great deal, if only their future relationship can be an honest and honorable one. He struck me too, for instance, at first, as rather abrupt, but that may well come from his being an outspoken man, and that is no doubt how it is. For instance, at his second visit, after he had received Dunia's consent, in the course of conversation, he declared that before making Dunia's acquaintance, he had made up his mind to marry a girl of good reputation, but without dowry and, above all, one who had experienced poverty, because, as he explained, a man ought not to be indebted to his wife, but that it is better for a wife to look upon her husband as her benefactor. I must add that he expressed it more nicely and politely than I have done, for I have forgotten his actual phrases and only remember the meaning. And, besides, it was obviously not said of design, but slipped out in the heat of conversation, so that he tried afterwards to correct himself and smooth it over, but all the same it did strike me as somewhat rude, and I said so afterwards to Dunia. But Dunia was vexed, and answered that 'words are not deeds,' and that, of course, is perfectly true. Dunechka did not sleep all night before she made up her mind, and, thinking that I was asleep, she got out of bed and was walking up and down the room all night; at last she knelt down before the icon and prayed long and fervently and in the morning she told me that she had decided.

"I have mentioned already that Peter Petrovich is just setting off for Petersburg, where he has a great deal of business, and he wants to open a legal bureau in Petersburg. He has been occupied for many years in conducting various lawsuits and cases, and only the other day he won an important case. He has to be in Petersburg because he has an important case before the Senate. So, Rodia dear, he may be of the greatest use to you, in every way indeed, and Dunia and I have already agreed that from this very day you could definitely enter upon your career and might consider that your future is marked out and assured for you. Oh, if only this comes to pass! This would be such a benefit that we could only look upon it as a providential blessing. Dunia is dreaming of nothing else. We have even ventured already to drop a few words on the subject to Peter Petrovich. He was cautious in his answer, and said that, of course, as he could not get on without a secretary, it would be better to be paying a salary to a relation than to a stranger, if only the former were fit for the duties (as though there could be doubt of your being fit!) but then he expressed doubts whether your studies at the university would leave you time for work at his office. The matter was dropped for the time, but Dunia is thinking of nothing else now. She has been in a sort of fever for the last few days, and has already made a whole plan for your becoming in the future an associate and even a partner in Peter Petrovich's law business, which might well be, seeing that you yourself are a student of law. I am in complete agreement with her, Rodia, and share all her plans and hopes, and think there is every probability of realizing them. And in spite of Peter Petrovich's evasiveness, very natural at present (since he does not know you), Dunia is firmly persuaded that she will gain everything by her good influence over her future husband; this she is sure of. Of course we are careful not to talk of any of these more distant dreams to Peter Petrovich, especially of your becoming his partner. He is a practical man and might take this very coldly, it might all seem to him simply a day dream. Nor has either Dunia or I breathed a word to him of the great hopes we have of his helping us to assist you with money while you are at the university; we have not spoken of it in the first place because it will come to pass of itself, later on, and he himself will no doubt without wasting words offer to do it (as though he could refuse Dunechka that), the more readily since you may by your own efforts become his right hand in the office, and receive this assistance not as a charity, but as a salary earned by your own work. Dunechka wants to arrange it all like this and I quite agree with her. And we have not spoken of our plans for another reason, that is, because I particularly wanted you to feel on an equal footing when you first meet him. When Dunia spoke to him with enthusiasm about you, he answered that one could never judge of a man without seeing him up close, for oneself, and that he would leave it to himself to form his own opinion when he makes your acquaintance. Do you know, my dearest Rodia, I think that perhaps for some reasons (nothing to do with Peter Petrovich though, simply for my own personal, perhaps even old-womanish, whims) I will do better to go on living by myself after the wedding, apart, than with them. I am convinced that he will be generous and delicate enough to invite me and to urge me not to part with my daughter for the future, and if he has said nothing about it until now, it is simply because it has been taken for granted; but I shall refuse. I have noticed more than once in my life that mothers-in-law aren't quite to husbands' liking, and I don't want to be the least bit in anyone's way, and for my own sake, too, would rather be quite independent, so long as I have a crust of bread of my own, and such children as you and Dunechka. If possible, I would settle somewhere near you both, for the most joyful piece of news, dear Rodia, I have kept for the end of my letter: know then, my dear boy, that we may, perhaps, be all together in a very short time and may embrace one another again after a separation of almost three years! It is settled for certain that Dunia and I are to set off for Petersburg, exactly when I don't know, but in any case very, very soon, even possibly in a week. It all depends on Peter Petrovich who will let us know when he has had time to look round him in Petersburg. To suit his own arrangements he is anxious to have the ceremony as soon as possible, even before the fast of Our Lady, if it could be managed, or if that is too soon to be ready, immediately after. Oh, with what happiness I shall press you to my heart! Dunia is all excitement at the joyful thought of seeing you, she said one day in jest that she would be ready to marry Peter Petrovich for that alone. She is an angel! She is not writing anything to you now, and has only told me to write that she has so much, so much to tell you that she is not going to take up her pen now, for a few lines would tell you nothing, and it would only mean upsetting herself; she bids me to send you her love and innumerable kisses. But although we will perhaps be meeting so soon, I will all the same send you as much money as I can in a day or two. Now that everyone has heard that Dunechka is to marry Peter Petrovich, my credit has suddenly improved and I know that Afanasy Ivanovich will trust me now even to seventy-five rubles on the security of my pension, so that perhaps I will be able to send you twenty-five or even thirty rubles. I would send you more, but I am uneasy about our traveling expenses; for though Peter Petrovich has been so kind as to undertake part of the expenses of the journey, that is to say, he has taken upon himself the delivery of our bags and big trunk (through some acquaintances of his, somehow), we must take into account some expenses on our arrival in Petersburg, where we can't be left without any money, at least for the first few days. But we have calculated it all, Dunechka and I, to the last kopeck, and we see that the journey will not cost very much. It is only ninety versts from us to the railway and we have already come to an agreement with a driver we know; and from there Dunechka and I can travel quite comfortably third class. So that I may very likely be able to send to you not twenty-five, but thirty rubles. But enough; I have covered two sheets already and there is no space left for more; our whole history, but so many events have happened! And now, my dearest Rodia, I embrace you and send you a mother's blessing till we meet. Love Dunia your sister, Rodia; love her as she loves you and understand that she loves you beyond everything, more than herself. She is an angel and you, Rodia, you are everything to us—our one hope, our one consolation. If only you are happy, we shall be happy. Do you still say your prayers, Rodia, and believe in the mercy of our Creator and our Redeemer? I am afraid in my heart that you may have been visited by the new fashionable spirit of unbelief. If it is so, I pray for you. Remember, dear boy, how in your childhood, when your father was living, you used to lisp your prayers at my knee, and how happy we all were in those days. Goodbye, or rather, till we meet—I embrace you warmly, warmly, with countless kisses.

"Yours till death,

"PULCHERIA RASKOLNIKOV."—

Almost from the first, while he read the letter, Raskolnikov's face was wet with tears; but when he finished it, his face was pale and distorted and a bitter, wrathful and malignant smile was on his lips. He laid his head down on his threadbare dirty pillow and pondered, pondered a long time. His heart was beating violently, and his thoughts were in a turmoil. At last he felt cramped and stifled in the little yellow room that was like a cupboard or a box. His eyes and his mind craved for space. He took up his hat and went out, this time without dread of meeting anyone; he had forgotten all about that. He turned in the direction of the Vassilyevsky Island, walking along V.

Prospect,* as though hastening on some business, but he walked, as his habit was, without noticing his way, whispering and even speaking aloud to himself, to the astonishment of the passersby. Many of them took him to be drunk.

CHAPTER FOUR

HIS MOTHER'S LETTER HAD been a torture to him. But as regards the chief, the fundamental fact in it, he had felt not one moment's hesitation, even while he was reading the letter. The essential question was settled, and irrevocably settled, in his mind: "Never such a marriage while I am alive, and Mr. Luzhin be damned!" "The thing is perfectly clear," he muttered to himself, with a malignant smile anticipating the triumph of his decision. "No, Mother, no, Dunia, you won't deceive me! And then they apologize for not asking my advice and for making the decision without me! I dare say! They imagine it is arranged now and can't be broken off; but we will see whether it can or not! A magnificent excuse: 'Peter Petrovich is such a busy man, such a busy man that even his wedding has to be rushed, almost express.' No, Dunechka, I see it all and I know what that much is that you want to say to me; and I know too what you were thinking about, when you walked up and down all night, and what your prayers were like before the Holy Mother of Kazan who stands in mother's bedroom. Bitter is the ascent to Golgotha† . . . Hm . . . So it is finally settled; you have determined to marry a rational business man, Avdotia Romanovna, one who has a fortune (has *already* made his fortune, that is so much more solid and impressive), a man who holds two government posts and who shares the ideas of our most rising generation, as mother writes, and who '*seems* to be kind,' as Dunechka herself observes. That *seems* beats everything! And that very Dunechka is marrying that very '*seems*'! Splendid! splendid!

" . . . But I wonder why mother has written to me about 'our

*Voznesensky Prospect.
†The hill where Jesus Christ was crucified.

most rising generation'? Simply as a descriptive touch, or with the idea of predisposing me in favor of Mr. Luzhin? Oh, the cunning of them! I wonder about one other item: how far were they open with one another that day and night and all this time since? Was it all put into *words*, or did both understand that they had the same thing at heart and in their minds, so that there was no need to speak of it aloud, and better not to speak of it. Most likely it was partly like that, from mother's letter it's evident: he struck her as rude, just *a little*, and mother in her simplicity took her observations to Dunia. And she was sure to be vexed and 'answered her angrily.' I should think so! Who would not be furious when it was quite clear without any naive questions and when it was understood that it was useless to discuss it. And why does she write to me, 'love Dunia, Rodia, and she loves you more than herself'? Has she a secret conscience-prick at sacrificing her daughter to her son? 'You are our one comfort, you are everything to us.' Oh, Mother!"

His bitterness grew more and more intense, and if he had happened to meet Mr. Luzhin at the moment, he might have murdered him.

"Hm . . . yes, that's true," he continued, pursuing the whirling ideas that chased each other in his brain, "it is true that 'to get to know a man, one must approach gradually and carefully,' but there is no mistake about Mr. Luzhin. The chief thing is he is 'a man of business and *seems* kind,' that was something, wasn't it, to send the bags and big box for them at his own expense! A kind man, no doubt after that! But his *bride* and her mother are to ride in a peasant's cart covered with matting (I know, I have been driven in it). No matter! It is only ninety versts and then they can 'travel very comfortably, third class,' for a thousand versts! Quite sensible, too. One must cut one's coat according to one's cloth, but what about you, Mr. Luzhin? She is your bride . . . And you couldn't fail to be aware that her mother has to borrow money on her pension for the journey. To be sure it's a matter of transacting business together, a partnership for mutual benefit, with equal shares and, therefore, expenses;—food and drink in common, but pay for your tobacco, as the proverb goes. But here too the business man has got the better of them. The luggage will cost less than their fares and very likely go for nothing. How is it that they don't both see all that, or is it that they don't want to see? And they are pleased, pleased! And to think that this is only the first blossoming, and that the real fruits are to come! For what really matters is not the stinginess, not the tightfistedness, but the *tone* of the whole thing. For that will be the tone after marriage, it's a foretaste of it. And mother too, why is she spending recklessly? What will she have by the time she gets to Petersburg? Three silver rubles or two 'paper ones' as she says . . . that old woman . . . hm. What does she expect to live on in Petersburg afterwards? She has her reasons already for guessing that she could not live with Dunia after the marriage, even at first. The good man has no doubt let it slip on that subject also, made himself clear, though mother is waving the notion aside with both hands: 'I will refuse,' says she. What is she hoping for then? Is she counting on what is left of her hundred and twenty rubles of pension when Afanasy Ivanovich's debt is paid? She knits woolen shawls and embroiders cuffs, ruining her old eyes. And all her shawls don't add more than twenty rubles a year to her hundred and twenty, I know that. So she is building all her hopes on Mr. Luzhin's generosity; 'he will offer it himself, he will press it on me.' You'll have a long wait! That's how it always is with these Schilleresque* noble hearts; till the last moment every goose is a swan with them, till the last moment they hope for good and not ill, and although they have an inkling of the other side of the picture, yet they won't face the truth till they are forced to; the very thought of it makes them shiver; they thrust the truth away with both hands, until the man they deck out in false colors puts a fool's cap on them with his own hands. I wonder whether Mr. Luzhin has any orders of merit; I bet he has the Anna† in his buttonhole and that he puts it on when he goes to dine with contractors or merchants. He'll put it on for his wedding, too! Enough of him, devil take him!

"Well . . . Mother, I don't wonder at, it's like her, God bless her, but how could Dunia? Dunechka, darling, as though I did not know you! You were nearly twenty when I saw you last: I understood you then. Mother writes that 'Dunia can put up with a great deal.' I know that very well. I knew that two years and a half ago, and for the last

---

*Friedrich von Schiller (1759–1805) was a German idealist writer; his "Ode to Joy" provided Beethoven with the text for the final movement of his Ninth Symphony. Dostoevsky loved Schiller in his youth, but his enthusiasm wore off after he was exiled to Siberia.

†Official medal awarded during the Tsarist period.

two and a half years I have been thinking about it, thinking of just that, that 'Dunia can put up with a great deal.' If she could put up with Mr. Svidrigailov and all the rest of it, she certainly can put up with a great deal. And now mother and she have taken it into their heads that she can put up with Mr. Luzhin, who propounds the theory of the superiority of wives raised from destitution and owing everything to their husbands' bounty—who propounds it, too, almost at the first interview. Granted that he 'let it slip,' though he is a rational man (so maybe it was not a slip at all, but he meant to make himself clear as soon as possible), but Dunia, Dunia? She understands the man, of course, but she will have to live with the man. Why! She'd live on black bread and water, she would not sell her soul, she would not barter her moral freedom for comfort; she would not barter it for all Schleswig-Holstein,* much less Mr. Luzhin's money. No, Dunia was not that sort when I knew her and . . . she is still the same, of course! Yes, there's no denying, the Svidrigailovs are a bitter pill! It's hard to spend one's life as a governess in the provinces for two hundred rubles, but I know she would rather be a slave on a plantation or a Latvian with a German master, than degrade her soul, and her moral feeling, by binding herself forever to a man whom she does not respect and with whom she has nothing in common—for her own advantage. And if Mr. Luzhin had been made of pure gold, or one huge diamond, she would never have consented to become his legal concubine. Why is she consenting then? What is this? What's the answer? It's clear enough: for herself, for her comfort, to save her life she would not sell herself, but for someone else she is doing it! For the one she loves, for the one she adores, she will sell herself! That's what it all amounts to; for her brother, for her mother, she will sell herself! She will sell everything! In such cases, we squash our moral feeling if necessary, freedom, peace, conscience even, all, all are brought into the street market. goodbye life! If only these our dear ones may be happy. More than that, we become casuists, we learn to be Jesuitical and for a time maybe we can soothe ourselves, we can persuade ourselves that it is, really is one's duty for a good cause. That's just like us, it's as clear as daylight. It's clear that Rodion Romanovich Raskolnikov

---

*Territory that during the 1860s was disputed by Denmark, Prussia, and Austria.

is the central figure in the business, and no-one else. Oh, yes, she can ensure his happiness, keep him in the university, make him a partner in the office, make his whole future secure; perhaps he may even be a rich man later on, esteemed, respected, and may even end his life a famous man! But mother? Oh, but it's all Rodia, dearest Rodia, her first born! For such a son who would not sacrifice even such a daughter! Oh, loving, over-partial hearts! Why, for his sake we would not shrink even from Sonia's fate. Sonechka, Sonechka Marmeladov, the eternal Sonechka so long as the world lasts. Have you taken the measure of your sacrifice, both of you, have you? Is it right? Can you bear it? Is it any use? Is there sense in it? And let me tell you, Dunechka, Sonechka's life is no worse than life with Mr. Luzhin. 'There can be no question of love,' mother writes. And what if there can be no respect either, if on the contrary there is aversion, contempt, repulsion, what then? Then you will have to 'keep up your appearance,' too. Is that not so? Do you understand, do you, do you, what that cleanliness means? Do you understand that the Luzhin cleanliness is just the same thing as Sonechka's and may be worse, viler, baser, because in your case, Dunechka, it's a bargain for luxuries, after all, but there it's simply a question of starvation. 'It has to be paid for, it has to be paid for, Dunechka, this cleanliness!' And what if it's more than you can bear afterwards, if you regret it? The grief, the misery, the curses, the tears hidden from all the world, for you are not a Marfa Petrovna. And how will your mother feel then? Even now she is uneasy, she is worried, but then, when she sees it all clearly? And I? Yes, indeed, what have you taken me for? I won't have your sacrifice, Dunechka, I won't have it, Mother! It will not be, so long as I am alive, it will not, it will not! I won't accept it!"

He suddenly recollected himself and paused.

"It shall not be? But what are you going to do to prevent it? You'll forbid it? And what right have you? What can you promise them on your side to give you such a right? Your whole life, your whole future, you will devote to them when you have finished your studies and obtained a post? Yes, we have heard all that before, and that's all words, but now? Now something must be done, now, do you understand that? And what are you doing now? You are robbing them. They borrow on their hundred rubles pension. They borrow from the Svidrigailovs. How are you going to save them from the Svidrigailovs, from Afanasy Ivanovich Vakhrushin, oh, future millionaire, oh Zeus who would arrange their lives for them? In another ten years? In another ten years, mother will be blind with knitting shawls, maybe with weeping too. She will be worn to a shadow with fasting; and my sister? Imagine for a moment what may become of your sister in ten years? What may happen to her during those ten years? Have you guessed?"

So he tortured himself, taunting himself with such questions, and finding a kind of enjoyment in it. And yet all these questions were not new ones suddenly confronting him, they were old familiar aches. It was long since they had first begun to grip and rend his heart. Long, long ago his present anguish had its first beginnings; it had waxed and gathered strength, it had matured and concentrated, until it had taken the form of a horrible, wild and fantastic question, which tortured his heart and mind, clamoring insistently for an answer. Now his mother's letter had burst on him like a thunderclap. It was clear that he must not now languish and suffer passively, in thought alone, over questions that appeared insoluble, but that he must do something, do it at once, and do it quickly. He must decide on something no matter what, on anything at all, or . . .

"Or renounce life altogether!" he cried suddenly, in a frenzy— "accept one's lot humbly as it is, once for all and stifle everything in oneself, giving up every right to act, live, and love!"

"Do you understand, dear sir, do you understand what it means when there is absolutely nowhere to go?" Marmeladov's question of the previous day came suddenly into his mind, "for every man must have somewhere to go . . . "

He gave a sudden start; another thought, that he had also had yesterday, flashed through his mind. But he did not start at the thought recurring to him, for he knew, he *had felt beforehand*, that it must 'flash,' he was expecting it; besides it was not only yesterday's thought. The difference was that a month ago, yesterday even, the thought was a mere dream: but now . . . now it appeared not a dream at all, it had taken a new, menacing and completely unfamiliar shape, and he suddenly became aware of this himself . . . He felt a hammering in his head, and eyes were darkened.

He looked round hurriedly, he was searching for something. He wanted to sit down and was looking for a bench; he was walking along K____ Boulevard.* There was a bench about a hundred paces in front of him. He walked towards it as fast he could; but on the way he met with a little adventure which for several minutes absorbed all his attention. Looking for the seat, he had noticed a woman walking some twenty paces in front of him, but at first he took no more notice of her than of other objects that crossed his path. It had happened to him many times already, on the way home, for example, not to notice the road by which he was going, and he was accustomed to walk like that. But there was something so strange about the woman in front of him, so striking even at first sight, that gradually his attention was riveted on her, at first reluctantly and, as it were, resentfully, and then more and more intently. He felt a sudden desire to find out what it was that was so strange about the woman. In the first place, she appeared to be quite a young, and she was walking in the great heat bareheaded and with no parasol or gloves, waving her arms about in an absurd way. She had on a dress of some light silky material, but also put on strangely awry, scarcely fastened, and torn open at the top of the skirt, close to the waist at the back: a great piece was coming apart and hanging loose. A little kerchief was flung about her bare throat, but lay slanting on one side. On top of everything, the girl was walking unsteadily, stumbling and even staggering from side to side. The encounter drew Raskolnikov's whole attention at last. He overtook the girl at the bench, but, on reaching it, she dropped down on it, in the corner; she let her head sink on the back of the bench and closed her eyes, apparently in extreme exhaustion. Looking at her closely, he realized at once that she was completely drunk. It was a strange and shocking sight. He could hardly believe that he was not mistaken. He saw before him the face of an extremely young, fair-haired girl—sixteen, even perhaps only fifteen years old, pretty little face, but flushed and, as it were, swollen. The girl seemed hardly to know what she was doing; she crossed one leg over the other, lifting it indecorously, and showed every sign of being unconscious that she was in the street.

Raskolnikov did not sit down, but he felt unwilling to leave her,

---

*Konnogvardeisky Boulevard.

and stood facing her in perplexity. This boulevard is never much fre-
quented; and now, at two o'clock, in the stifling heat, it was quite deserted. And yet on the further side of the boulevard, about fifteen
paces away, a gentleman was standing on the edge of the pavement;
he, too, would apparently have liked very much to approach the girl
with some purpose of his own. He, too, had probably seen her in the
distance and had followed her, but found Raskolnikov in his way. He
looked angrily at him, though he tried to escape his notice, and stood
impatiently biding his time, till the unwelcome ragamuffin should
have moved away. His intentions were unmistakable. The gentleman
was a fat, thickly-set man, about thirty, full-blooded, with red lips
and a little moustache, and very foppishly dressed. Raskolnikov felt
furious; he had a sudden longing to insult this fat dandy in some way.
He left the girl for a moment and walked towards the gentleman.

"Hey! You Svidrigailov! What do you want here?" he shouted,
clenching his fists and laughing, spluttering with rage.

"What do you mean?" the gentleman asked sternly, frowning
with haughty astonishment.

"Get away, that's what I mean."

"How dare you, you rabble!"

He raised his cane. Raskolnikov rushed at him with his fists,
without reflecting even that the stout gentleman was a match for two
men like himself. But at that instant someone seized him from behind, and a police constable stood between them.

"That's enough, gentlemen, no fighting, please, in a public place.
What do you want? Who are you?" he asked Raskolnikov sternly,
noticing his rags.

Raskolnikov looked at him intently. He had a straight-forward,
sensible, soldierly face, with a gray moustache and whiskers.

"You are just the man I want," Raskolnikov cried, grabbing his
arm. "I am a former student, Raskolnikov . . . You may as well know
that too," he added, addressing the gentleman, "come along, I have
something to show you."

And taking the policeman by the hand he dragged him towards
the bench.

"Look here, hopelessly drunk, and she has just come down the
boulevard. There is no telling who and what she is, but she does not
look like a professional. It's more likely she has been given drink and

deceived somewhere . . . for the first time . . . you understand? And they've put her out into the street like that. Look at the way her dress is torn, look at the way it has been put on: she's been dressed by somebody, she hasn't dressed herself, and dressed by unpracticed hands, by a man's hands; that's evident. And now look there: I don't know that dandy I was going to fight just now, I see him for the first time, but, he, too has seen her on the road, just now, drunk, not knowing what she is doing, and now he is extremely eager to get hold of her, to get her away somewhere while she is in this state . . . that's certain, believe me, I am not wrong. I saw him myself watching her and following her, but I prevented him, and he is just waiting for me to go away. Now he has walked away a little, and is standing still, pretending to roll a cigarette . . . Think—how can we keep her out of his hands, and how are we to get her home?"

The policeman saw it all in a flash. The stout gentleman was easy to understand, he turned to consider the girl. The policeman bent over to examine her more closely, and his face worked with genuine compassion.

"Ah, what a pity!" he said, shaking his head—"why, she is still a child! She has been deceived, that's right. Listen, lady," he began addressing her, "where do you live?" The girl opened her tired and bleary eyes, gazed blankly at the speaker and waved her hand.

"Here," said Raskolnikov feeling in his pocket and finding twenty kopecks, "here, call a cab and tell him to drive her to her address. The only thing is to find out her address!"

"Young lady, young lady!" the policeman began again, taking the money. "I'll fetch you a cab and take you home myself. Where shall I take you, eh? Where do you live?"

"Go away! . . . Won't leave me alone," the girl muttered, and once more waved her hand.

"Ah, ah, how awful! It's shameful, young lady, it's a shame!" He shook his head again, shocked, sympathetic and indignant.

"It's a difficult job," the policeman said to Raskolnikov, and as he did so, he again looked him up and down in a rapid glance. He, too, must have seemed a strange figure to him: dressed in rags and handing him money!

"Did you find her far from here?" he asked him.

"I tell you she was walking in front of me, staggering, just here, in the boulevard. She only just reached the bench and sank down on it."

"Ah, the shameful things that are done in the world nowadays, God have mercy on us! An innocent creature like that, drunk already! She has been deceived, that's a sure thing. See how her dress has been torn too . . . Ah, the vice one sees nowadays! And she probably belongs to gentlefolk too, poor ones maybe . . . There are many like that nowadays. She looks refined, too, as though she were a lady," and he bent over her once more.

Perhaps he had daughters growing up like that, "looking like ladies and refined" with pretensions to gentility and fashion . . .

"The chief thing is," Raskolnikov persisted, "to keep her out of this scoundrel's hands! Why should he too outrage her! It's as clear as day what he is after; ah, the brute, he is not moving off!"

Raskolnikov spoke aloud and pointed to him. The gentleman heard him, and seemed about to fly into a rage again, but thought better of it, and confined himself to a contemptuous look. He then walked slowly another ten paces away and again halted.

"Keep her out of his hands we can," said the constable thoughtfully, "if only she'd tell us where to take her, but as it is . . . Young lady, hey, young lady!" he bent over her once more.

She opened her eyes fully all of a sudden, looked at him intently, as though realizing something, got up from the bench and started walking away in the direction from which she had come. "Ugh! No shame, won't leave me alone!" she said, waving her hand again. She walked quickly, though staggering as before. The dandy followed her, but along another avenue, keeping his eye on her.

"Don't worry, I won't let him have her," the policeman said resolutely, and he set off after them.

"Ah, the vice we see nowadays!" he repeated aloud, sighing.

At that moment something seemed to sting Raskolnikov; in an instant everything turned over inside of him.

"Hey, here!" he shouted after the policeman.

The latter turned round.

"Let it be! What's it to you? Let it go! Let him amuse himself." He pointed at the dandy, "What do you care?"

The policeman was bewildered, and stared at him open-eyed. Raskolnikov laughed.

"Eh!" said the policeman, with a gesture of contempt, and he walked after the dandy and the girl, probably taking Raskolnikov for a madman or something even worse.

"He has carried off my twenty kopecks," Raskolnikov murmured angrily when he was left alone. "Well, let him take as much from the other fellow and let him have the girl and so let it end. And why did I want to interfere? Is it for me to help? Have I any right to help? Let them devour each other alive—what is to me? How did I dare to give him twenty kopecks? Were they mine?"

In spite of those strange words he felt very wretched. He sat down on the deserted bench. His thought strayed aimlessly . . . In fact he found it hard to fix his mind on anything at that moment. He longed to forget himself altogether, to forget everything, and then to wake up and begin anew . . .

"Poor girl!" he said, looking at the empty corner where she had sat—"She will come to her senses and weep, and then her mother will find out . . . She will give her a beating, a horrible, shameful beating and then maybe, throw her out . . . And even if she does not, the Daria Frantsevnas will get wind of it, and the girl will soon be slipping out on the sly here and there. Then right away there will be the hospital (that's always the luck of those girls with respectable mothers, who go wrong on the sly) and then . . . again the hospital . . . drink . . . the taverns . . . and more hospital, in two or three years—a wreck, and her life over at eighteen or nineteen . . . Have not I seen cases like that? And how have they been brought to it? They've all come to it like that. Ugh! But what does it matter? That's as it should be, they tell us. A certain percentage, they tell us, must every year go . . . that way . . . to the devil, I suppose, so that the rest may remain fresh, and not be interfered with. A percentage! What splendid words they have; they are so scientific, so consolatory . . . Once you've said 'percentage,' there's nothing more to worry about. If we had any other word . . . maybe we might feel more uneasy . . . But what if Dunechka were one of the percentage! Of another one if not that one?"

"But where am I going?" he thought suddenly. "Strange, I came out for something. As soon as I had read the letter I came out . . . I was going to Vassilyevsky Island, to Razumikhin. That's what it was . . . now I remember. What for, though? And how is it that the idea of going to Razumikhin flew into my head just now? That's curious."

He wondered at himself. Razumikhin was one of his former

comrades at the university. It was remarkable that Raskolnikov had hardly any friends at the university; he kept aloof from everyone, went to see no-one, and did not welcome anyone who came to see him, and indeed everyone soon turned away from him too. He took no part in the students' gatherings, amusements or conversations. He worked with great intensity without sparing himself, and he was respected for this, but no-one liked him. He was very poor, and there was a sort of haughty pride and reserve about him, as though he were keeping something to himself. He seemed to some of his comrades to look down upon them all as children, as though he were superior in development, knowledge and convictions, as though their convictions and interests were beneath him.

With Razumikhin, though, he had for some reason become friends, or, rather, he was more open and communicative with him. Indeed it was impossible to be on any other terms with Razumikhin. He was an exceptionally good-humored and communicative youth, kind to the point of simplicity, though both depth and dignity lay concealed under that simplicity. The better of his comrades understood this, and all loved him. He was a man of no small intelligence, though he was certainly rather a simpleton at times. He was of striking appearance—tall, thin, black-haired and always badly shaved. He was sometimes rowdy and was reputed to be of great physical strength. One night, when out in a festive company, he had with one blow laid a gigantic policeman on his back. There was no limit to his drinking powers, but he could abstain from drink altogether; he sometimes went too far in his pranks; but he could do without pranks altogether. Another thing striking about Razumikhin, no failure ever distressed him, and it seemed as though no unfavorable circumstances could crush him. He could lodge anywhere, and bear the extremes of cold and hunger. He was very poor, and supported himself entirely on what he could earn by work of one sort or another. He knew of no end of resources by which to get money, through work of course. He spent one whole winter without lighting his stove, and used to declare that he liked it better, because one slept more soundly in the cold. For the present he, too, had been obliged to give up the university, but it was only for a time, and he was working with all his might to save enough to return to his studies again. Raskolnikov had not been to see him for the last four months, and

Razumikhin did not even know his address. About two months before, they had met in the street, but Raskolnikov had turned away and even crossed to the other side so that he might not be observed. And though Razumikhin noticed him, he passed him by, as he did not want to disturb a friend.

CHAPTER FIVE

"OF COURSE, I'VE BEEN meaning lately to go to Razumikhin's to ask for work, to ask him to get me lessons or something . . . " Raskolnikov thought, "but what help can he be to me now? Suppose he gets me lessons, suppose he shares his last kopeck with me, if he has any kopecks, so that I could get some boots and make myself tidy enough to give lessons . . . hm . . . Well and what then? What will I do with the few coppers I earn? That's not what I want now. It's really absurd for me to go to Razumikhin . . . "

The question why he was now going to Razumikhin agitated him even more than he was himself aware; he kept uneasily seeking for some sinister significance in this apparently ordinary action.

"Could I have expected to set it all straight and to find a way out by means of Razumikhin alone?" he asked himself in perplexity.

He pondered and rubbed his forehead, and, strange to say, after long musing, suddenly, as if it were spontaneously and by chance, a very strange thought came into his head.

"Hm . . . to Razumikhin's," he said all at once, calmly, as though he had reached a final determination. "I will go to Razumikhin's of course, but . . . not now. I will go to him . . . on the next day after it, when it will already be over and everything will begin afresh . . . "

And suddenly he realized what he was thinking.

"After it," he shouted, jumping up from the bench, "but is it really going to happen? Is it possible it really will happen?" He left the bench, and went off almost at a run; he meant to turn back, homewards, but the thought of going home suddenly filled him with intense loathing; it was in that hole, in that awful little cupboard of his, that all this had for more than a month now been growing up in him; and he walked on at random.

His nervous shudder had passed into a fever that made him feel shivering; in spite of the heat he felt cold. With a kind of effort he began almost unconsciously, from some inner necessity, to stare at all the objects before him, as though looking for something to distract his attention; but he did not succeed, and kept lapsing every moment into brooding. When with a start he lifted his head again and looked around, he forgot at once what he had just been thinking about and even where he was going. In this way he walked right across Vassilyevsky Island, came out on to the Lesser Neva, crossed the bridge and turned towards the islands. The greenness and freshness were at first restful to his weary eyes used to the dust and lime of the town and the huge houses that hemmed him in and weighed upon him. Here there were no taverns, no stuffiness, no stench. But soon these new pleasant sensations turned into morbid irritability. Sometimes he stood still before a brightly painted summer villa standing among green foliage, he gazed through the fence, he saw in the distance fashionably dressed women on the verandahs and balconies, and children running in the gardens. The flowers especially caught his attention; he gazed at them longer than at anything. He was met, too, by luxurious carriages and by men and women on horseback; he watched them with curious eyes and forgot about them before they had vanished from his sight. Once he stopped and counted his money; he found he had thirty kopecks. "Twenty to the policeman, three to Nastasia for the letter, so I must have given forty-seven or fifty to the Marmeladovs yesterday," he thought, making calculations for some unknown reason, but he soon forgot why he had taken the money out of his pocket. He recalled it on passing an eating-house or tavern, and felt that he was hungry . . . Going into the eatery he drank a glass of vodka and ate a pie of some sort. He finished eating it when he was on the road again. It was a long while since he had taken vodka and it had an effect upon him at once, though he only drank a wine-glassful. His legs felt suddenly heavy and a great drowsiness came upon him. He turned homewards, but reaching Petrovsky Island he stopped completely exhausted, turned off the road into the bushes, sank down upon the grass and instantly fell asleep.

In a morbid condition of the brain, dreams often have an extraordinary distinctiveness, vividness, and extraordinary semblance of reality. At times monstrous images are created, but the setting and the entire process of imagining are so truth-like and filled with details so delicate, so unexpected, but so artistically consistent with the picture as a whole, that the dreamer, were he an artist like Pushkin or Turgenev even, could never have invented them in the waking state. Such sick dreams always remain long in the memory and make a powerful impression on the overwrought and excited nervous system.

Raskolnikov dreamed a frightening dream. He dreamt he was back in his childhood, in their little town. He is a child about seven years old, walking in the countryside with his father on the evening of a holiday. It is a gray and stifling day, the country is exactly as he remembered it; indeed he recalled it far more vividly in his dream than he had done in memory. The little town stands on a level flat as bare as the hand, not a willow near it; only in the far distance, a wood lies, a dark blur on the very edge of the horizon. A few paces beyond the last market garden stands a tavern, a big tavern, which had always aroused in him a feeling of aversion, even of fear, when he walked by it with his father. There was always such a crowd there, such shouting, laughter and swearing, such hideous hoarse singing and often fighting. Drunken and scary mugs were always hanging about the tavern. He used to cling close to his father, trembling all over when he met them. Near the tavern the road becomes a track, always dusty, and the dust is always so black. It is a winding road, and about a hundred paces further on, it turns to the right to the graveyard. In the middle of the graveyard is a stone church with a green cupola where he used to go to mass two or three times a year with his father and mother, when a service was held in memory of his grandmother, who had long been dead, and whom he had never seen. On these occasions they used to take on a white dish tied up in a table napkin a special sort of rice pudding with raisins stuck in it in the shape of a cross. He loved that church, the old-fashioned icons with no setting and the old priest with the shaking head. Near his grandmother's grave, which was marked by a stone, was the little grave of his younger brother who had died at six months old. He did not remember him at all, but he had been told about his little brother, and whenever he visited the graveyard he used religiously and reverently to cross himself and to bow down and kiss the little grave. And now he is dreaming that he is walking with his father past the tavern on the way to the graveyard; he is holding his father's hand and looking with dread at the tavern. A peculiar circumstance attracts his attention: there seems to be some kind of festivity going on here, there are crowds of gaily dressed townspeople, peasant women, their husbands, and riff-raff of all sorts. All are singing, all are drunk, and near the entrance of the tavern there is a cart, but a strange cart. It is one of those big carts usually drawn by heavy cart-horses and laden with casks of wine or other heavy goods. He always liked looking at those great cart-horses, with their long manes, thick legs, and slow even pace, drawing along a perfect mountain with no appearance of effort, as though it were easier going with a load than without it. But now, strange to say, in the shafts of such a cart he sees a thin little sorrel beast, one of those peasants' nags which he had often seen straining their utmost under a heavy load of wood or hay, especially when the wheels were stuck in the mud or in a rut. And the peasants would beat them with whips so cruelly, so cruelly, sometimes even about the nose and eyes, and he felt so sorry, so sorry for them that he almost cried, and his mother always used to take him away from the window. All of a sudden there is a great uproar of shouting, singing and the balalaika, and from the tavern a number of big and very drunken peasants come out, wearing red and blue shirts and coats thrown over their shoulders.

"Get in, get in!" shouts one of them, a young thick-necked peasant with a fleshy face red as a carrot. "I'll take you all, get in!"

But at once there is an outbreak of laughter and exclamations in the crowd.

"Take us all with a beast like that!"

"Why, Mikolka, are you crazy to put a nag like that in such a cart?"

"And this mare is twenty if she is a day, pals!"

"Get in, I'll take you all," Mikolka shouts again, leaping first into the cart, seizing the reins and standing straight up in front. "The bay has gone with Matvey," he shouts from the cart—"and this brute, pals, is just breaking my heart, I could kill her. She's just eating her head off. Get in, I tell you! I'll make her gallop! She'll gallop!" and he picks up the whip, preparing himself with relish to flog the little mare.

"Get in! Come along!" The crowd is laughing. "Do you hear, she'll gallop!"

"Gallop indeed! She has not had a gallop in her for the last ten years!"

"She'll jog along!"

"No being sorry for her, pals, bring a whip each of you, get ready!"

"That's right! Give it to her!"

They all clamber into Mikolka's cart, laughing and making jokes. Six of them get in and there is still room for more. They haul in a fat, rosy-cheeked woman. She is dressed in red cotton, in a pointed, beaded headdress and warm boots; she is cracking nuts and laughing. The crowd round them is laughing too, and really, how could they help laughing? That wretched nag is to drag all the cartload of them at a gallop! Two young lads in the cart get whips ready right away to help Mikolka. With the cry of "Go!" the mare tugs with all her might, but far from galloping, can scarcely move forward; she is struggling with her legs, gasping and shrinking from the blows of the three whips showered upon her like hail. The laughter in the cart and in the crowd is redoubled, but Mikolka flies into a rage and thrashes the mare furiously, with quickened blows, as though he thinks she really can gallop.

"Let me get in, too, pals," shouts a young man in the crowd, his appetite aroused.

"Get in, all get in," cries Mikolka, "she'll pull you all. I'll beat her to death!" And he thrashes and thrashes at the mare, beside himself with fury.

"Father, Father," he cries, "Father, what are they doing? Father, they are beating the poor horse!"

"Come along, come along!" says his father. "They are drunk and foolish, having fun; come away, don't look!" and he tries to lead him away, but he tears himself away from his hand, and, beside himself with horror, runs to the horse. But the poor horse is already in a bad way. She is gasping, pausing, then tugging again and almost falling.

"Beat her to death!" cries Mikolka, "it's come to that. I'll do her in!"

"What are you about, are you a Christian, you devil?" shouts an old man in the crowd.

"Did anyone ever see anything like it? A wretched nag like that pulling such a cartload," adds another.

"You'll kill her!" shouts the third.

"Stay out! It's my property. I do as I like. Get in, more of you! Everyone get in! She'll go at a gallop, I say! . . . "

All of a sudden laughter breaks into a roar and covers everything: the mare, roused by the shower of blows, in her impotence had begun kicking. Even the old man could not help smiling. To think of a wretched little nag like that trying to kick!

Two lads in the crowd snatch up whips and run to the mare to beat her about the ribs, one on each side.

"Lash her in the face, in the eyes, in the eyes," cries Mikolka.

"Give us a song, pals," shouts someone in the cart and everyone in the cart joins in a riotous song, jingling a tambourine and whistling in the refrains. The woman goes on cracking nuts and laughing.

. . . He runs beside the mare, runs in front of her, sees her being whipped across the eyes, right in the eyes! He is crying, his heart is rising, his tears are streaming. One of the men gives him a cut with the whip across the face, he does not feel it. Wringing his hands and screaming, he rushes up to the gray-headed old man with the gray beard, who is shaking his head in disapproval. One woman seizes him by the hand and wants to take him away, but he tears himself from her and runs back to the horse. She is almost at the last gasp, but begins kicking once more.

"I'll teach you to kick," Mikolka shouts ferociously. He throws down the whip, bends forward and picks up from the bottom of the cart a long, thick shaft, takes hold of one end with both hands and with an effort brandishes it over the mare.

"He'll crush her," was shouted round him. "He'll kill her!"

"It's my property," shouts Mikolka and brings the shaft down with a swinging blow. There is a sound of a heavy thud.

"Thrash her, thrash her! What's the matter?" shout voices in the crowd.

And Mikolka swings the shaft a second time and a blow falls a second time on the spine of the luckless mare. She sinks back on her haunches, but lurches forward and tugs forward, tugs with all her force, first on one side and then on the other, trying to move the cart. But the six whips are attacking her in all directions, and the shaft is raised again and falls a third time, then a fourth, with heavy measured blows. Mikolka is furious that he cannot kill her at one blow.

"She's a tough one!" they shout.

"She'll fall in a minute, pals, you'll see, and that's the end of her!" shouts an admiring spectator in the crowd.

"Get an axe, hell! Finish her off," shouts a third.

"Eh, eat the flies! Make way!" Mikolka screams frantically, throws down the shaft, stoops down in the cart and picks up an iron crowbar. "Look out," he shouts, and with all his might deals a stunning blow at his poor mare. The blow crashes down; the mare staggers, sinks back, tries to pull, but the bar falls again with a swinging blow on her back and she falls on the ground as if all four legs had been knocked out from her at once.

"Finish her off," shouts Mikolka and, beside himself, leaps out of the cart. Several young men, also red and drunk, seize anything they come across—whips, sticks, poles, and run to the dying mare. Mikolka stands on one side and begins dealing random blows to her back with the crowbar. The mare stretches out her muzzle, draws a long breath and dies.

"You butchered her!" someone shouts in the crowd.

"Should have galloped!"

"My property!" shouts Mikolka, with bloodshot eyes, brandishing the bar in his hands. He stands as though regretting that he has nothing more to beat.

"No mistake about it, you are not a Christian," many voices are shouting in the crowd.

But the poor boy is already beside himself. He makes his way screaming through the crowd to the sorrel nag, puts his arms round her bleeding dead muzzle and kisses it, kisses the eyes and the lips . . . Then he suddenly jumps up and flies in a frenzy with his little fists out at Mikolka. At that instant his father, who had long been running after him, snatches him up and carries him out of the crowd.

"Come along, come! Let's go home," he says to him.

"Father! Why did they . . . kill . . . the poor horse!" he sobs, but his breath catches and the words come in shrieks from his panting chest.

"They are drunk . . . fooling around . . . it's not our business!" says his father. He puts his arms round his father but he feels choked, choked. He tries to draw a breath, to cry out—and wakes up.

He woke up sweating, gasping for breath, his hair soaked with perspiration, and stood up in terror.

"Thank God, that was only a dream," he said, sitting down under a tree and drawing deep breaths. "But what is it? Is it some fever coming on? Such a hideous dream!"

His whole body felt broken; darkness and confusion were in his soul. He rested his elbows on his knees and put his head in his hands.

"Good God!" he cried, "can it be, can it be, that I will really take an axe, that I will strike her on the head, split her skull open . . . that I will tread in the sticky warm blood, break the lock, steal and tremble; hide, all spattered in the blood . . . with the axe . . . Good God, can it be?"

He was shaking like a leaf as he said this.

"But why am I going on like this?" he continued, sitting up again, as it were in profound amazement. "I knew that I could never bring myself to it, so what have I been torturing myself for till now? Yesterday, yesterday, when I went to make that . . . *experiment*, yesterday I realized completely that I could never bear to do it . . . Why am I going over it again, then? Why have I till now been hesitating? As I came down the stairs yesterday, I said myself that it was base, loathsome, vile, vile . . . the very thought of it made me feel sick *when I wasn't dreaming* and filled me with horror."

"No, I couldn't stand it, I couldn't stand it! Granted, granted that there is no flaw in all that reasoning, that all that I have concluded this last month is clear as day, true as arithmetic . . . My God! Still I couldn't bring myself to it! I couldn't stand it, I couldn't stand it! Why, why then am I still . . . ?"

He rose to his feet, looked round in wonder as though surprised at finding himself in this place, and went towards T____ Bridge.* He was pale, his eyes glowed, he was exhausted in every limb, but he seemed suddenly to breathe more easily. He felt he had already cast off that fearful burden that had so long been weighing upon him, and all at once there was a sense of relief and peace in his soul. "Lord," he prayed, "show me my path—I renounce that accursed . . . dream of mine."

Crossing the bridge, he gazed quietly and calmly at the Neva, at the glowing red sun setting in the glowing sky. In spite of his weakness he was not even conscious of fatigue. It was as though an abscess

---

*Tuchkov Bridge.

that had been forming for a month past in his heart had suddenly broken. Freedom, freedom! He was free now from that spell, that sorcery, that enchantment, that obsession!

Later on, when he recalled that time and all that happened to him during those days, minute by minute, point by point, step by step, he was superstitiously impressed by one circumstance, which though in itself not very exceptional, always seemed to him afterwards the predestined turning-point of his fate. Namely, he could never understand and explain to himself why, when he was tired and worn out, when it would have been more convenient for him to go home by the shortest and most direct way, he had returned by the Haymarket where he had no need to go. It was obviously and quite unnecessarily out of his way, though not much so. It is true that it happened to him dozens of times to return home without noticing what streets he passed through. But why, he was always asking himself, why had such an important, such a decisive and at the same time such an absolutely chance meeting happened in the Haymarket (where he had moreover no reason to go) at the very hour, the very minute of his life when he was just in the very mood and in the very circumstances in which that meeting was able to exert the gravest and most decisive influence on his whole destiny? As though it had been lying in wait for him on purpose!

It was about nine o'clock when he crossed the Haymarket. At the tables and the barrows, at the booths and the stores, all the market people were closing their establishments or clearing away and packing up their wares and, like their customers, were going home. Ragpickers and scroungers of all kinds were crowding round the eateries and especially the taverns in the dirty and stinking courtyards of the Haymarket. Raskolnikov preferred this place and all the neighboring alleys when he wandered aimlessly in the streets. Here his rags did not attract contemptuous attention, and one could walk about in anything without scandalizing people. At the corner of K_____ Alley* a huckster and his wife had two tables set out with ribbons, thread, cotton handkerchiefs, &c. They, too, had got up to go home, but were lingering in conversation with a friend, who had just come up to them. This friend was Lizaveta Ivanovna, or simply, as everyone called

---

*Konny Alley.

her, Lizaveta, the younger sister of the old pawnbroker, Aliona
Ivanovna, whom Raskolnikov had visited the previous day to pawn
his watch and make his experiment . . . He already knew all about Lizaveta and she knew him a little too. She was a single woman of about
thirty-five, tall, clumsy, timid, submissive and almost idiotic. She was
a complete slave to her sister, worked for her day and night, went in
fear and trembling of her, and even suffered beatings from her. She
was standing with a bundle before the huckster and his wife, listening earnestly and doubtfully. They were explaining something to her
especially heatedly. The moment Raskolnikov caught sight of her, he
was overcome by a strange sensation as it were of intense astonishment, though there was nothing astonishing about this meeting.

"You could make up your mind for yourself, Lizaveta Ivanovna,"
the huckster was saying aloud. "Come round tomorrow about seven.
They will be here too."

"Tomorrow?" said Lizaveta slowly and thoughtfully, as though
unable to make up her mind.

"Upon my word, what a fright you are in of Aliona Ivanovna,"
gabbled the huckster's wife, a lively little woman. "I look at you, you
are like some little babe. And she is not your own sister either—nothing but a half sister and what a hand she keeps over you!"

"Just this time don't say a word to Aliona Ivanovna," her husband
interrupted; "that's my advice, but come round to us without asking.
It will be worth your while. Your sister may see for herself later on."

"Should I come?"

"About seven o'clock tomorrow. And they will be here too. You'll
decide for yourself."

"And we'll have tea," added his wife.

"All right, I'll come," said Lizaveta, still pondering, and she
began slowly moving away.

Raskolnikov had just passed and heard no more. He passed softly,
unnoticed, trying not to miss a word. His first amazement turned
gradually to horror, like a shiver running down his spine. He had
learned, he had suddenly and quite unexpectedly learned, that the
next day at seven o'clock Lizaveta, the old woman's sister and only
companion, would be away from home and that therefore at seven
o'clock precisely the old woman would be left alone.

He was only a few steps from his apartment. He went in like a man condemned to death. He thought of nothing and was completely incapable of thinking; but he felt suddenly in his whole being that he had no more freedom of thought, no will, and that everything was suddenly and irrevocably decided.

Certainly, even if he had to wait whole years for a suitable opportunity, his plan in mind, he could not count for sure on a more certain step towards the success of the plan than that which suddenly had just presented itself. In any case, it would have been difficult to find out beforehand and with certainty, with greater exactness and less risk, and without dangerous inquiries and investigations, that next day at such and such a time such and such an old woman, on whose life an attempt was contemplated, would be at home entirely alone.

CHAPTER SIX

LATER ON RASKOLNIKOV HAPPENED to find out why the huckster and his wife had invited Lizaveta. It was a very ordinary matter and there was nothing exceptional about it. A family who had come to the town and been reduced to poverty were selling their household goods and clothes, all women's things. As the things would have fetched little in the market, they were looking for a dealer, and this was Lizaveta's business. She took up commissions, went around on business, and had many clients, as she was very honest and always fixed the best price and stuck to it. She spoke as a rule little and, as we have said already, she was so submissive and timid . . .

But Raskolnikov had become superstitious recently. The traces of superstition remained in him long after, and were almost ineradicable. And in all this he was always afterwards disposed to see something strange and mysterious, as it were the presence of some peculiar influences and coincidences. In the previous winter a student he knew called Pokorev, who had left for Kharkov, had chanced in conversation to give him the address of Aliona Ivanovna, the old pawnbroker, in case he might want to pawn anything. For a long while he did not go to her, for he had lessons and managed to get by somehow. Six weeks ago he had remembered the address; he had two articles that could be pawned: his father's old silver watch and a little gold ring with three red stones, a keepsake from his sister at parting. He decided to take the ring. When he found the old woman he had felt an insurmountable repulsion for her at the first glance, though he knew nothing special about her yet. He got two rubles from her and went into a miserable little tavern on his way home. He asked for tea, sat down and sank into deep thought. A strange idea was pecking at his brain like a chicken in the egg, and very, very much absorbed him.

Almost beside him at the next table there was sitting a student, whom he did not know or remember at all, and with him a young officer. They had played a game of billiards and began drinking tea. Suddenly he heard the student mention to the officer the pawnbroker Aliona Ivanovna and give him her address. This of itself seemed strange to Raskolnikov; he had just come from there and here they were talking about her. By accident, of course, but there he is, unable to shake off a very extraordinary impression, and here someone seems to be speaking expressly for him; the student suddenly begins telling his friend various details about Aliona Ivanovna.

"She is first rate," he said. "You can always get money from her. She is as rich as a Jew, she can give you five thousand at a time but she is not above taking a pledge for a ruble. Lots of our fellows have had dealings with her. But she is an awful old harpy . . . "

And he began describing how spiteful and capricious she was, how if you were only a day late with your interest the pledge was lost; how she gave a quarter of the value of an article and took five and even seven percent a month on it and so on. The student chattered on, saying that she had a sister Lizaveta, whom the repulsive little creature was continually beating, and kept in complete bondage like a small child, though Lizaveta was at least six feet tall . . .

"There's a phenomenon for you," cried the student and he laughed.

They began talking about Lizaveta. The student spoke about her with a peculiar relish and was continually laughing and the officer listened with great interest and asked him to send Lizaveta to do some mending for him. Raskolnikov did not miss a word and learned everything about her right away. Lizaveta was younger than the old woman and was her half-sister, being the child of a different mother. She was already thirty-five. She worked day and night for her sister, and besides doing the cooking and the washing, she did sewing and even hired herself out to wash floors and gave her sister all she earned. She did not dare to accept an order or job of any kind without the old woman's permission. The old woman had already made her will, and Lizaveta knew of it, and by this will she would not get a kopeck; nothing but the movables, chairs and so on; all the money, meanwhile, was left to a monastery in the province of N____,* that prayers might be said for her in perpetuity. Lizaveta was of lower rank than her sister, a collegiate assessor's wife, unmarried and awfully uncouth in appearance, remarkably tall with long feet that looked as if they were bent outwards. She always wore battered goatskin shoes, and kept herself clean. What the student expressed most surprise and amusement about was the fact that Lizaveta was constantly pregnant.

"But you say she is ugly?" observed the officer.

"Yes, she is so dark-skinned and looks like a soldier dressed up, but you know she is not at all ugly. She has such a kind face and eyes. Very much so. And the proof of it is that lots of people are attracted by her. She is such a meek, mild, gentle creature, always willing, willing to do anything. And her smile is really very sweet."

"You seem to find her attractive yourself," laughed the officer.

"Because she's strange. No, I'll tell you what. I could kill that damned old woman and make off with her money, I assure you, without the faintest conscience-prick," the student added hotly. The officer again burst out laughing while Raskolnikov shuddered. How strange it was!

"Listen, I want to ask you a serious question," the student said heatedly. "I was joking of course, but look here; on one side we have a stupid, senseless, worthless, spiteful, ailing old woman, not simply useless but doing actual harm, who herself has no idea what she is living for, and who will die in a day or two in any case. You understand? You understand?"

"Yes, yes, I understand," answered the officer, watching his excited companion attentively.

"Well, listen then. On the other hand, fresh young lives thrown away in vain for lack of support—and by thousands, on every side! A hundred, a thousand good deeds and undertakings could be done

*The province of Novgorod, south of St. Petersburg.

and helped on that old woman's money, which will be buried in a monastery! Hundreds, thousands perhaps, might be set on the right path; dozens of families saved from destitution, from corruption, from ruin, from vice, from venereal wards—and all with her money. Kill her, take her money and with the help of it devote yourself to the service of humanity and the common good. What do you think, would not one tiny crime be wiped out by thousands of good deeds? For one life thousands would be saved from corruption and decay. One death, and a hundred lives in exchange—it's simple arithmetic! Besides, what value has the life of that sickly, stupid, ill-natured old woman in the balance of existence! No more than the life of a louse, of a cockroach, less in fact because the old woman is doing harm. She is wearing out the lives of others; the other day she bit Lizaveta's finger out of spite; it almost had to be amputated!"

"Of course she does not deserve to live," remarked the officer, "but there it is, it's nature."

"Oh, well, brother, but we have to correct and direct nature, and, but for that, we'll drown in an ocean of prejudice. But for that, there would never have been a single great man. They talk of duty, conscience—I don't want to say anything against duty and conscience; but the point is what do we mean by them. Wait, I have another question to ask you. Listen!"

"No, you wait, I'll ask you a question. Listen!"

"Well?"

"You are talking and speechifying away, but tell me, would you kill the old woman *yourself* or not?"

"Of course not! I was only arguing the justice of it . . . It's nothing to do with me . . . "

"But I think, if you would not do it yourself, then there's no justice in it! Let's have another game!"

Raskolnikov was extremely agitated. Of course, it was all very ordinary and very frequent youthful talk and thought, such as he had often heard before, only in different forms and on different themes. But why had he happened to hear just such a discussion and such ideas at the very moment when his own brain was just conceiving . . . *the very same ideas?* And why, just at the moment when he had brought away the embryo of his idea from the old woman had he happened upon a conversation about her? This coincidence always seemed strange to him. This trivial talk in a tavern had an immense influence on him as the action developed further; as though there had really been in it something preordained, some guiding hint . . .

*   *   *   *

When he returned from the Haymarket he flung himself on the sofa and sat for a whole hour without stirring. Meanwhile it got dark; he had no candle and, indeed, it did not occur to him to light up. He could never recollect whether he had been thinking about anything at that time. At last he was conscious of his former fever and shivering, and he realized with relief that he could lie down on the sofa. Soon heavy, leaden sleep came over him, as though crushing him.

He slept an extraordinarily long time and without dreaming. Nastasia, coming into his room at ten o'clock the next morning, had a hard time waking him. She brought him tea and bread. The tea was again the second brew and again in her own tea-pot.

"My goodness, how he sleeps!" she cried indignantly. "Sleeping and sleeping!"

He got up with an effort. His head ached, he stood up, took a turn in his little room and sank back on the sofa again.

"Going to sleep again," cried Nastasia. "Are you ill, eh?"

He made no reply.

"Do you want some tea?"

"Later," he said with an effort, closing his eyes again and turning to the wall.

Nastasia stood over him.

"Perhaps he really is ill," she said, turned and went out. She came in again at two o'clock with soup. He was lying as before. The tea stood untouched. Nastasia felt positively offended and began angrily rousing him.

"Why are you lying like a log?" she shouted, looking at him with repulsion.

He got up, and sat down again, but said nothing and stared at the floor.

"Are you ill or not?" asked Nastasia and again received no answer. "You'd better go out and get a breath of air," she said after a pause. "Will you eat it or not?"

"Later," he said weakly. "You can go."

And he motioned her out.

She remained a little longer, looked at him with compassion and went out.

A few minutes later, he raised his eyes and looked for a long while at the tea and the soup. Then he took the bread, took up a spoon and began to eat.

He ate a little, three or four spoonfuls, without appetite, as it were, mechanically. His head ached less. After his meal he stretched himself on the sofa again, but now he could not sleep; he lay without stirring, with his face in the pillow. He was haunted by day-dreams and such strange daydreams; in one, that kept recurring, he imagined that he was in Africa, in Egypt, in some sort of oasis. The caravan is resting, the camels are peacefully lying down; the palms stand all around in a complete circle; everyone is eating dinner. But he is drinking water straight from a spring which flows gurgling close by. And it is so cool, and such wonderful, wonderful, blue, cold water is running among the colored stones and over the clean sand which glistens here and there like gold . . . Suddenly he heard a clock strike. He started, roused himself, raised his head, looked out of the window, and seeing how late it was, suddenly jumped up wide awake as though someone had pulled him off the sofa. He crept on tiptoe to the door, stealthily opened it and began listening on the staircase. His heart beat terribly. But all was quiet on the stairs as if everyone was asleep . . . It seemed to him strange and monstrous that he could have slept in such forgetfulness from the previous day and had done nothing, had prepared nothing yet . . . And meanwhile perhaps it had struck six. And his drowsiness and stupefaction were followed by an extraordinary, feverish, as it were, distracted, haste. But the preparations to be made were few. He concentrated all his energies on think-ing of everything and forgetting nothing; and his heart kept beating and thumping so that he could hardly breathe. First he had to make a noose and sew it into his overcoat—a work of a moment. He rum-maged under his pillow and picked out amongst the linen stuffed away under it, a completely worn out old unwashed shirt. From its rags he tore a long strip, a couple of inches wide and about sixteen inches long. He folded this strip in two, took off his wide, sturdy summer overcoat of some thick cotton material (his only outer garment) and began sewing the two ends of the rag on the inside, under the left armhole. His hands shook as he sewed, but he prevailed, and so well that nothing showed on the outside when he put the coat on again. He had got the needle and thread ready long before and they lay on his table in a piece of paper. As for the noose, it was a very ingenious device of his own; the noose was intended for the axe. He couldn't very well carry the axe through the street in his hands. And if hidden under his coat he would still have had to support it with his hand, which would have been noticeable. Now he had only to put the head of the axe in the noose, and it would hang quietly under his arm on the inside. Putting his hand in his coat pocket, he could hold the end of the handle all the way, so that it did not swing; and as the coat was very full, a regular sack in fact, it could not be seen from outside that he was holding something with the hand that was in the pocket. This noose, too, he had designed two weeks before.

When he had finished with this, he thrust his hand into a little opening between his "Turkish" sofa and the floor, fumbled in the left corner and pulled out the *pledge*, which he had got ready long before and hidden there. This pledge was, however, not a pledge at all, but only a smoothly planed piece of wood the size and thickness of a silver cigarette case. He picked up this piece of wood in one of his wanderings in a courtyard where there was some sort of a workshop. Afterwards he had added to the wood a thin smooth piece of iron, some fragment, probably, which he had also picked up at the same time in the street. Putting the iron piece, which was a little smaller, on the piece of wood, he fastened them very firmly, crossing and recrossing the thread round them; then wrapped them carefully and daintily in clean white paper and tied up the parcel so that it would be very difficult to untie it. This was in order to divert the attention of the old woman for a time, while she was trying to undo the knot, and so to gain a moment. The iron strip was added to give weight, so that the woman might not immediately guess that the "thing" was made of wood. All this had been stored by him beforehand under the sofa. He had only just got the pledge out when suddenly he heard someone shouting in the yard:

"It struck six long ago!"

"Long ago! My God!"

He rushed to the door, listened, grabbed his hat and began to descend his thirteen steps cautiously, noiselessly, like a cat. He had still the most important thing to do—to steal the axe from the kitchen. That the deed must be done with an axe he had decided long ago. He had also a pocket pruning-knife, but he could not rely on the knife and still less on his own strength, and so resolved finally on the axe. We may note in passing, one peculiarity in regard to all the final resolutions taken by him in the matter; they had one strange characteristic: the more final they were, the more hideous and the more absurd they at once became in his eyes. In spite of all his agonizing inward struggle, he never for a single instant all that time could believe in the carrying out of his plans.

And, indeed, if it had ever happened that everything to the least point could have been considered and finally settled, and no uncertainty of any kind had remained, he would, it seems, have renounced it all as something absurd, monstrous and impossible. But a whole heap of unsettled points and uncertainties remained. As for getting the axe, that trifling business cost him no anxiety, for nothing could be easier. Nastasia was continually out of the house, especially in the evenings; she would run in to the neighbors' apartments or to a store, and always left the door ajar. It was the one thing the landlady was always scolding her about. And so when the time came, he would only have to go quietly into the kitchen and to take the axe, and an hour later (when everything was over) go in and put it back again. But there were doubtful points too. Supposing he returned an hour later to put it back, and Nastasia had come back and was on the spot. He would of course have to go by and wait till she went out again. But supposing she were in the meantime to miss the axe, start looking, make an outcry—that would mean suspicion or at least grounds for suspicion.

But those were all trifles which he had not even begun to consider, and indeed he had no time. He was thinking of the chief point, and put off trifling details, until he *could believe in it all*. But that seemed utterly unattainable. So it seemed to him at least. He could not imagine, for instance, that he would sometime stop thinking, get up and simply go there . . . Even his recent *experiment* (i.e., his visit with the intention of conducting a final survey of the place) was simply *an attempt at an experiment*, far from being the real thing, as though one should say "come, let us go and try it—why dream about it!"—and at once he had broken down and had run away cursing, furious with himself. Meanwhile it would seem, as regards the moral question, that his analysis was complete; his casuistry had become keen as a razor, and he could no longer find conscious objections in himself. But in the end he simply ceased to believe himself, and doggedly, slavishly sought arguments in all directions, fumbling for them, as though someone were forcing and drawing him to it. This last day, however, which had come so unexpectedly deciding everything at once, had an almost completely mechanical effect on him, as though someone took him by the hand and started pulling with unnatural force, irresistibly, blindly, without his objections. It was as though a part of his clothing had gotten caught in the wheel of a machine, and he was being drawn into it.

At first—long before, in fact—he had been extremely occupied by a single question; why are almost all crimes so badly concealed and so easily detected, and why do almost all criminals leave such obvious traces? He had come gradually to many different and curious conclusions, and in his opinion the chief reason lay not so much in the material impossibility of concealing the crime, as in the criminal himself. Almost every criminal is subject to a failure of will and reasoning power by a childish and phenomenal heedlessness, at the very instant when reason and caution are most essential. It was his conviction that this eclipse of reason and failure of will power attacked a man like a disease, developed gradually and reached its highest point just before the perpetration of the crime, continued with equal violence at the moment of the crime and for longer or shorter time after, according to the individual case, and then passed off like any other disease. The question whether the disease gives rise to the crime, or whether the crime, due to its own peculiar nature, is always accompanied by something like a disease, he did not yet feel able to decide.

When he reached these conclusions, he decided that in his own case there could not be such morbid reversals, that his reason and will would remain unimpaired at the time of carrying out his design, for the simple reason that his design was "not a crime . . . " We will omit all the process by means of which he arrived at this last conclusion; we have run too far ahead already . . . We may add only that the practical, purely material difficulties of the affair occupied an altogether secondary position in his mind. "So long as one keeps all

one's will power and reason to deal with them, they will all be overcome at the time when once one has familiarized oneself with the
minutest details of the business . . . " But the business wouldn't begin.
His final decisions were what he continued to trust least, and when
the hour struck, it all turned out quite differently, as it were accidentally and even unexpectedly.

One trifling circumstance upset his calculations, before he had
even left the staircase. When he reached the landlady's kitchen, wide
open as usual, he glanced cautiously in to see whether, in Nastasia's
absence, the landlady herself was there, or if not, whether the door
to her own room was closed, so that she might not peep out when
he went in for the axe. To his amazement, however, he suddenly saw
that Nastasia was not only at home in the kitchen this time, but was
even occupied there, taking linen out of a basket and hanging it on a
line! Seeing him, she stopped hanging the clothes, turned to him and
stared at him all the time he was passing. He turned away his eyes,
and walked past as though he noticed nothing. But it was the end of
everything: there was no axe! He was overwhelmed.

"What made me think," he reflected, as he went under the gateway, "what made me think that she would be sure not to be at home
at that moment! Why, why, why did I assume this so certainly?"

He was crushed and even humiliated. He could have laughed at
himself in his anger . . . A dull animal rage boiled within him.

He stood hesitating in the gateway. To go into the street, to go for a
walk for appearance sake was revolting; to go back to his room, even
more revolting. "And what a chance I have lost forever!" he muttered,
standing aimlessly in the gateway, just opposite the porter's little dark
room, which was also open. Suddenly he started. From the porter's
room, two paces away from him, something shining under the bench
to the right caught his eye . . . He looked about him—nobody. He approached the room on tiptoe, went down two steps into it and in a faint
voice called the porter. "Yes, not at home! Somewhere near though, in
the yard, for the door is wide open." He dashed to the axe (it was an
axe) and pulled it out from under the bench, where it lay between two
chunks of wood; at once before going out, he secured it in the noose,
thrust both hands into his pockets and went out of the room; no-one
had noticed him! "When reason fails, the devil helps!" he thought with
a strange grin. This incident raised his spirits extraordinarily.

He walked along quietly and sedately, without hurry, to avoid awakening suspicion. He scarcely looked at the passersby, even tried to escape looking at their faces at all, and to be as little noticeable as possible. Suddenly he thought of his hat. "Good heavens! I had the money the day before yesterday and did not get a cap to wear instead!" A curse rose from the bottom of his soul.

Glancing out of the corner of his eye into a store, he saw by a clock on the wall that it was ten minutes past seven. He had to hurry up and at the same time to make a detour, so as to approach the house round about, from the other side . . .

When he had happened to imagine all this beforehand, he had sometimes thought that he would be very much afraid. But he was not very much afraid now, not afraid at all, in fact. His mind was even occupied by irrelevant matters, but by nothing for long. As he passed the Yusupov Garden, he was deeply absorbed in considering the building of great fountains, and of their refreshing effect on the atmosphere in all the squares. Little by little he arrived at the conviction that if the summer garden were extended to all of the Mars Field, and perhaps even joined to the garden of the Mikhailovsky Palace, it would be a splendid thing and a great benefit to the town. Then he suddenly became interested in the question why in all great towns men are not simply driven by necessity, but in some peculiar way inclined to live in those parts of the town where there are no gardens nor fountains; where there is filth and stench and all sorts of nastiness. Then his own walks through the Haymarket came back to his mind, and for a moment he woke up to reality. "What nonsense!" he thought, "better think of nothing at all!"

"So probably men led to execution clutch mentally at every object that meets them on the way," flashed through his mind, but simply flashed, like lightning; he himself quickly extinguished this thought . . . And by now he was near; here was the house, here was the gate. Suddenly a clock somewhere struck once. "What! can it be half-past seven? Impossible, it must be fast!"

Luckily for him, everything went well again at the gates. What's more, at that very moment, as though on purpose, a huge cart of hay had just driven in at the gate, completely screening him as he passed under the gateway, and the cart had scarcely had time to drive through into the yard, before he had slipped in a flash to the right.

On the other side of the cart he could hear several voices shouting and quarrelling; but no-one noticed him and no-one passed him. Many windows looking into that huge quadrangular yard were open at that moment, but he did not raise his head—he did not have the strength. The staircase leading to the old woman's room was close by, just on the right of the gateway. He was already on the stairs . . .

Catching his breath, pressing his hand against his throbbing heart, and once more feeling for the axe and setting it straight, he began softly and cautiously ascending the stairs, listening every minute. But the stairs, too, were quite deserted at that time; all the doors were shut; he met no-one after all. It is true that one apartment on the first floor was wide open and painters were at work in it, but they did not glance at him. He stood still, thought a minute and went on. "Of course it would be better if they had not been here, but . . . it's two floors above them."

And there was the fourth floor, here was the door, here was the apartment opposite, the empty one. On the third floor, the apartment underneath the old woman's was apparently empty also; the visiting card nailed on the door had been torn off—they had moved out! . . . He was out of breath. For one instant the thought flashed through his mind "Should I leave?" But he made no answer and began listening at the old woman's door: a dead silence. Then he listened again on the staircase, listened long and intently . . . then looked about him for the last time, pulled himself together, drew himself up, and once more tried the axe in the noose. "Am I very pale?" he wondered. "Am I too agitated? She is mistrustful . . . Had I better wait a little longer . . . till my heart stops thumping?"

But his heart would not stop thumping. On the contrary, as though on purpose, it throbbed more and more and more . . . He could stand it no longer, slowly put out his hand to the bell and rang. Half a minute later he rang again, more loudly.

No answer. To go on ringing was useless and out of place. The old woman was, of course, at home, but she was suspicious and alone. He had some knowledge of her habits . . . and once more he put his ear to the door. Either his senses were peculiarly keen (which it is difficult to suppose), or the sound was really very distinct, but at any rate he suddenly heard something like the cautious touch of a hand on the lock and the rustle of a skirt at the very door. Someone was standing quietly close to the lock and just as he was doing on the outside was stealthily listening within, and also, it seemed, had her ear to the door . . . He moved a little on purpose and muttered something aloud so as not to give the impression that he was hiding, then rang a third time, but quietly, soberly and without impatience. Recalling it afterwards, that moment stood out in his mind vividly, distinctly, forever; he could not make out how he had had such cunning, especially since his mind was as it were clouded at moments and he was almost unconscious of his body . . . An instant later he heard the latch unfastened.

CHAPTER SEVEN

THE DOOR WAS AS before opened a tiny crack, and again two sharp and suspicious eyes stared at him out of the darkness. Then Raskolnikov lost his head and nearly made a great mistake.

Fearing the old woman would be frightened by their being alone, and not hoping that the sight of him would disarm her suspicions, he took hold of the door and pulled it towards him to prevent the old woman from attempting to shut it again. Seeing this she did not pull the door back, but she did not let go the handle, either, so that he almost dragged her out with it on to the stairs. Seeing that she was standing in the doorway not allowing him to pass, he advanced straight upon her. She stepped back in alarm, tried to say something, but seemed unable to speak and stared with open eyes at him.

"Good evening, Aliona Ivanovna," he began, trying to speak as casually as possible, but his voice would not obey him, it broke and shook. "I have come . . . I have brought something . . . but we'd better go over here . . . to the light . . . "

And leaving her, he walked straight into the room uninvited. The old woman ran after him; her tongue was loosened.

"Good heavens! What are you doing here? Who are you? What do you want?"

"Why, Aliona Ivanovna, you know me . . . Raskolnikov . . . here, I brought you the pledge I promised the other day . . . " and he held out the pledge.

The old woman glanced for a moment at the pledge, but at once stared in the eyes of her uninvited visitor. She looked intently, maliciously and mistrustfully. A minute passed; he even thought he saw something like a sneer in her eyes, as though she had already guessed everything. He felt that he was losing his head, that he was almost frightened, so frightened that if she were to look like that and not say a word for another half minute, he would have run away from her.

"Why do you look at me as though you didn't recognize me?" he said suddenly, also with malice. "Take it if you like, if not I'll go elsewhere, I am in a hurry."

He had not even thought of saying this; it was just suddenly said of itself. The old woman recovered herself, and her visitor's resolute tone evidently set her at ease.

"But why, sir, all of a sudden . . . What is it?" she asked, looking at the pledge.

"The silver cigarette case; I spoke of it last time, you know."

She held out her hand.

"But why are you so pale somehow? And your hands are trembling too! Have you been bathing, or what?"

"Fever," he answered abruptly. "You can't help getting pale . . . if you've nothing to eat," he added, with difficulty articulating the words.

His strength was failing him again. But his answer sounded like the truth; the old woman took the pledge.

"What is it?" she asked once more, scanning Raskolnikov intently, and weighing the pledge in her hand.

"A thing . . . cigarette case . . . Silver . . . Look at it."

"It does not seem somehow like silver . . . How he has wrapped it up!"

Trying to untie the string and turning to the window, to the light (all her windows were shut, in spite of the stifling heat), she left him altogether for several seconds and stood with her back to him. He unbuttoned his coat and freed the axe from the noose, but did not yet take it out altogether, simply holding it in his right hand under the coat. His hands were terribly weak, he himself felt them every moment growing more numb and more wooden. He was afraid he would let the axe slip and fall . . . Suddenly his head seemed to spin.

"But what has he tied it up like this for?" the old woman cried with vexation and moved towards him.

He had not an instant more to lose. He pulled the axe out completely, swung it with both arms, scarcely conscious of himself, and almost without effort, almost mechanically, brought the blunt side down on her head. He seemed not to use his own strength in this. But as soon as he had once brought the axe down, strength was born in him.

The old woman was as always bareheaded. Her thin, light hair, streaked with gray, thickly smeared with grease, was plaited in a rat's tail and fastened by a broken horn comb which stood out on the nape of her neck. As she was so short, the blow fell on the very top of her skull. She cried out, but very faintly, and suddenly sank all of a heap on the floor, though still managing to raise her hands to her head. In one hand she still held "the pledge." Then with all his strength he dealt her another and another blow with the blunt side, and on the same spot. The blood gushed as from an overturned glass, the body fell back. He stepped back, let it fall, and at once bent over her face; she was already dead. Her eyes seemed to be starting out of their sockets, the forehead and the whole face were drawn and contorted convulsively.

He laid the axe on the ground near the dead body and felt at once in her pocket (trying to not get smeared with the streaming blood)—the same right hand pocket from which she had taken the key on his last visit. He was in full possession of his faculties, free from confusion or giddiness, but his hands were still trembling. He remembered afterwards that he had been particularly cautious and careful, trying all the time not to get stained . . . He pulled out the keys at once, they were all, as before, in one bunch on a steel ring. He ran at once into the bedroom with them. It was a very small room with a whole shrine of holy images. Against the other wall stood a big bed, very clean and covered with a silk patchwork wadded quilt. Against a third wall was a chest of drawers. Strange to say, as soon as he began to fit the keys into the chest, as soon as he heard their jingling, a convulsive shudder passed over him. He suddenly felt tempted again to give it all up and go away. But that was only for an instant; it was too late to go back. He even smiled at himself, when suddenly another alarming idea occurred to his mind. He suddenly fancied that the old woman might be still alive and might recover her senses. Leaving the keys in the chest, he ran back to the body, snatched up the axe and lifted it once more over the old woman, but did not bring it down. There was no doubt that she was dead. Bending down and examining her again more closely, he saw clearly that the skull was broken and even battered in on one side. He was about to feel it with his finger, but drew back his hand and indeed it was evident without that. Meanwhile there was a whole pool of blood. All of a sudden he noticed a string on her neck; he tugged at it, but the string was strong and did not snap and besides, it was soaked with blood. He tried to pull it out from the front of the dress, but something held it and prevented its coming. In his impatience he raised the axe again to hack at the string from above, right on the body, but did not dare, and with difficulty, smearing his hands and the axe in the blood, after two minutes' hurried effort, he cut the string and took it off without touching the body with the axe; he was not mistaken—it was a purse. On the string were two crosses, one of Cyprus wood and one of copper, and an enameled icon, and with them a small greasy suede purse with a steel rim and ring. The purse was stuffed very full; Raskolnikov thrust it in his pocket without looking at it, flung the crosses on the old woman's chest and rushed back into the bedroom, this time taking the axe with him.

He was in a terrible hurry, he snatched the keys, and began trying them again. But he was unsuccessful. They would not fit in the locks. It was not so much that his hands were shaking, but that he kept making mistakes; though he saw, for instance, that a key was not the right one and would not fit, still he tried to put it in. Suddenly he remembered and realized that the big key with the deep notches, which was hanging there with the small keys, could not possibly belong to the chest of drawers (on his last visit this had struck him), but to some strong-box, and that everything perhaps was hidden in that box. He abandoned the chest of drawers, and at once felt under the bedstead, knowing that old women usually keep boxes under their beds. And so it was; there was a good-sized box under the bed, at least a yard in length, with an arched lid covered with red leather and studded with steel nails. The notched key fit at once and unlocked it. At the top, under a white sheet, was a coat of thick red silk cloth lined with hare skin; under it was a silk dress, then a shawl and it seemed as though there was nothing below but clothes. The first thing he did was to wipe his blood-stained hands on the thick red silk. "It's red, and on red blood will be less noticeable," the thought passed through his mind; then he suddenly came to. "Good God, am I going out of my mind?" he thought with terror.

But no sooner did he touch the clothes than a gold watch slipped from under the fur coat. He started turning everything over. And in fact there were various articles made of gold among the clothes—probably all pledges, unredeemed or waiting to be redeemed—bracelets, chains, earrings, pins and such. Some were in cases, others simply wrapped in newspaper, carefully and exactly folded, in double sheets, and tied round with tape. Losing not a moment, he began stuffing the pockets of his trousers and overcoat without examining or opening the parcels and cases; but he didn't get to take many . . .

He suddenly heard steps in the room where the old woman lay. He stopped short and was still as death. But all was quiet, so he must have been imagining things. All of a sudden he distinctly heard a faint cry, as though someone had uttered a low broken moan. Then again dead silence for a minute or two. He sat squatting on his heels by the box and waited holding his breath, then suddenly jumped up, seized the axe and ran out of the bedroom.

In the middle of the room stood Lizaveta with a big bundle in her arms. She was gazing in stupefaction at her murdered sister, white as a sheet and seeming not to have the strength to cry out. Seeing him run out of the bedroom, she began faintly quivering all over, like a leaf, a shudder ran down her face; she lifted her hand, opened her mouth, but still did not scream. She began slowly backing away from him into the corner, staring intently, persistently at him, but still uttered no sound, as though she could not get breath to scream. He rushed at her with the axe; her mouth twitched piteously, as one sees babies' mouths, when they begin to be frightened, stare intently at what frightens them and are on the point of screaming. And this hapless Lizaveta was so simple and had been so thoroughly scared and browbeaten that she did not even raise a hand to protect her face, though that was the most necessary and natural action at the moment, for the axe was raised over her face. She only lifted her empty left hand ever so slightly, still far from her face, slowly holding it out before her as though motioning him away. The axe fell with the sharp edge just on the skull and split at one blow all the top of the head. She collapsed at once. Raskolnikov completely lost control of himself, snatched up her bundle, dropped it again and ran into the entryway.

Fear gained more and more mastery over him, especially after this second, quite unexpected murder. He longed to run away from the place as fast as possible. And if at that moment he had been capable of seeing and reasoning more correctly, if he had been able to realize all the difficulties of his position, the hopelessness, the hideousness and the absurdity of it, if he could have understood how many obstacles and, perhaps, villainies he had still to overcome or to commit, to get out of that place and to make his way home, it is very possible that he would have abandoned everything, and would have gone to give himself up, and not from fear for himself, but from simple horror and loathing of what he had done. The feeling of loathing especially surged up within him and grew stronger every minute. Not for anything in the world would he now have gone to the strong-box or even into the room.

But a sort of blankness, even dreaminess had begun by degrees to take possession of him; at moments he forgot himself, or rather, forgot what was of importance, and caught at trifles. Glancing, however, into the kitchen and seeing a bucket half full of water on a bench, he did realize that he needed to wash his hands and the axe. His hands were sticky with blood. He dropped the axe with the blade in the water, snatched a piece of soap that lay in a broken saucer on the window, and began washing his hands right there in the bucket. When they were clean, he took out the axe, washed the blade and spent a long time, about three minutes, washing the wood where there were spots of blood, even rubbing them with soap. Then he wiped it all with some linen that was hanging to dry on a line in the kitchen and then he spent a long time attentively examining the axe at the window. There was no trace left on it, only the wood was still damp. He carefully hung the axe in the noose under his coat. Then as far as was possible, in the dim light in the kitchen, he looked over his overcoat, his trousers and his boots. At the first glance there seemed to be nothing but stains on the boots. He wetted the rag and rubbed the boots. But he knew he was not looking thoroughly, that there might be something quite noticeable that he was overlooking. He stood in the middle of the room, lost in thought. A dark agonizing thought rose in his mind—the thought that he was going mad and that at that moment he was incapable of reasoning, of protecting himself, that he ought perhaps to be doing something utterly different from what he was now doing. "Good God!" he muttered "I must run, run," and he rushed into the entryway. But here a shock of terror awaited him such as he had never of course known before.

He stood and gazed and could not believe his eyes: the door, the outer door from the stairs, the one at which he had not long before waited and rung, was standing unlocked and at least six inches open. No lock, no bolt, all the time, all that time! The old woman had not shut it after him perhaps as a precaution. But, good God! Why, he had seen Lizaveta afterwards! And how could he, how could he have failed to reflect that she must have come in somehow! She could not have come through the wall!

He dashed to the door and fastened the latch.

"But no, the wrong thing again. I must get away, get away . . . "

He unfastened the latch, opened the door and began listening on the staircase.

He listened a long time. Somewhere far away, probably in the gateway, two voices were loudly and shrilly shouting, quarrelling and scolding. "What are they yelling about?" He waited patiently. At last everything was still, as though suddenly cut off; they had separated. He was meaning to go out, but suddenly, on the floor below, a door was noisily opened and someone began going downstairs humming a tune. "How is it they all make such a noise!" flashed through his mind. Once more he closed the door and waited. At last everything was still, not a soul was stirring. He was just taking a step towards the stairs when he heard fresh footsteps.

The steps sounded very far off, at the very bottom of the stairs, but he remembered quite clearly and distinctly that from the first sound he began for some reason to suspect that this was someone coming there, to the fourth floor, to the old woman. Why? Were the sounds somehow peculiar, significant? The steps were heavy, even and unhurried. Now he had passed the first floor, now he was mounting higher, it was growing more and more distinct! He could hear his heavy breathing. And now the third storey had been reached. Coming here! And it seemed to him all at once that he was turned to stone, that it was like a dream in which one is being pursued, nearly caught and will be killed, and is rooted to the spot and cannot even move one's arms.

At last when the unknown was mounting to the fourth floor, he suddenly started, and succeeded in slipping neatly and quickly back into the flat and closing the door behind him. Then he took the hook and softly, noiselessly, fixed it in the catch. Instinct helped him. When he had done this, he crouched holding his breath, by the door. The unknown visitor was by now also at the door. They were now standing opposite one another, as he had just before been standing with the old woman, when the door divided them and he was listening.

The visitor panted several times. "He must be a big, fat man," thought Raskolnikov, squeezing the axe in his hand. It seemed like a dream. The visitor took hold of the bell and rang loudly.

As soon as the tin bell tinkled, Raskolnikov seemed to be aware of something moving in the room. For some seconds he listened quite seriously. The unknown rang again, waited and suddenly tugged violently and impatiently at the handle of the door. Raskolnikov gazed in horror at the hook shaking in its fastening, and in blank terror expected every minute that the fastening would be pulled out. It certainly did seem possible, so violently was he shaking it. He was tempted to hold the fastening, but he might be aware of it. Dizziness came over him again. "I shall fall down!" flashed through his mind, but the unknown began to speak and he recovered himself at once.

"What's up? Are they asleep or murdered? D-damn them!" he bawled in a thick voice, "Hey, Aliona Ivanovna, old witch! Lizaveta Ivanovna, hey, my beauty! Open the door! Damn them! Are they asleep or what?"

And again, enraged, he tugged with all his might a dozen times at the bell. He must certainly be a man of authority and an intimate acquaintance.

At this moment light hurried steps were heard not far off, on the stairs. Someone else was approaching. Raskolnikov had not heard them at first.

"You don't say there's no-one at home," the newcomer cried in a cheerful, ringing voice, addressing the first visitor, who still went on pulling the bell. "Good evening, Koch."

"From his voice he must be quite young," thought Raskolnikov.

"Who the hell can tell? I've almost broken the lock," answered Koch. "But how do you come to know me?"

"Why! The day before yesterday I beat you three times in a row at billiards at Gambrinus'."

"Oh!"

"So they are not at home? That's strange. It's pretty stupid though. Where could the old woman have gone? I've come on business."

"Yes; and I have business with her, too."

"Well, what can we do? Go back, I suppose! And I was hoping to get some money!" cried the young man.

"We must give up, of course, but what did she fix this time for? The old witch fixed the time for me to come herself. It's out of my way. And where the devil she can have got to, I can't make out. She sits here from year's end to year's end, the old hag; her legs are bad and yet here all of a sudden she is out for a walk!"

"Hadn't we better ask the porter?"

"What?"

"Where she's gone and when she'll be back."

"Hm . . . Damn it all! . . . We might ask . . . But you know she never does go anywhere."

And he once more tugged at the door-handle.

"Damn it all. There's nothing to be done, we must go!"

"Stay!" cried the young man suddenly. "Do you see how the door shakes if you pull it?"

"Well?"

"That shows it's not locked, but fastened with the hook! Do you hear how the hook clanks?"

"Well?"

"Why, don't you see? That proves that one of them is at home. If they were all out, they would have locked the door from the outside with the key and not with the hook from inside. There, do you hear how the hook is clanking? To fasten the hook on the inside they must be at home, don't you see. So there they are sitting inside and aren't opening the door!"

"Well! And so they must be!" cried Koch, astonished. "What are they doing in there!" And he began furiously shaking the door.

"Stay!" cried the young man again. "Don't pull at it! There must be something wrong . . . Here, you've been ringing and pulling at the door and still they don't open! So either they've both fainted or . . . "

"What?"

"I tell you what. Let's go fetch the porter, let him wake them up."

"All right."

Both of them went down.

"Stop. You stay here while I run down for the porter."

"What for?"

"Well, you'd better."

"All right."

"I'm studying law, you see! It's evident, e-vi-dent there's something wrong here!" the young man cried hotly, and he ran downstairs.

Koch remained. Once more he softly touched the bell which gave one tinkle, then gently, as though reflecting and looking about him, began touching the door-handle pulling it and letting it go to make sure once more that it was only fastened by the hook. Then puffing and panting he bent down and began looking at the keyhole; but the key was in the lock on the inside and so nothing could be seen.

Raskolnikov stood keeping tight hold of the axe. He was in a sort of delirium. He was even getting ready to fight when they came in. While they were knocking and talking together, the idea several times occurred to him to end it all at once and shout to them through the door. Now and then he was tempted to swear at them, to jeer at them, while they could not open the door! "Just hurry up!" was the thought that flashed through his mind.

"But what the devil is he about? . . . " Time was passing, one minute, and another—no-one came. Koch began to be restless.

"What the hell?" he cried suddenly and in impatience deserting his sentry duty, he, too, went down, hurrying and thumping his heavy boots on the stairs. The steps died away.

"God! What should I do?"

Raskolnikov unfastened the hook, opened the door—there was no sound. Abruptly, without any thought at all, he went out, closing the door as thoroughly as he could, and went downstairs.

He had gone down three flights when he suddenly heard a loud voice below—where could he go! There was nowhere to hide. He was just going back to the flat.

"Hey there! Catch the brute!"

Somebody dashed out of a flat below, shouting, and rather fell than ran down the stairs, bawling at the top of his voice.

"Mitka! Mitka! Mitka! Mitka! Mitka! Damn him!"

The shout ended in a shriek; the last sounds came from the yard; all was still. But at the same instant several men talking loud and fast began noisily mounting the stairs. There were three or four of them. He distinguished the ringing voice of the young man. "Them!"

Filled with despair he went straight to meet them, feeling "come what may!" If they stopped him—all was lost; if they let him pass—all was lost too; they would remember him. They were approaching; they were only a flight away from him—and, suddenly, salvation! A few steps from him on the right there was an empty flat with the door wide open, the flat on the second floor where the painters had been at work, and which, as though for his benefit, they had just left. It was they, no doubt, who had just run down, shouting. The floor had only just been painted, in the middle of the room stood a pail and a broken pot with paint and brushes. In one instant he had whisked in at the open door and hidden behind the wall and just in the nick of time; they had already reached the landing. Then they turned and went on up to the fourth floor, talking loudly. He waited, went out on tiptoe and ran down the stairs.

No-one was on the stairs or in the gateway. He passed quickly through the gateway and turned to the left into the street.

He knew, he knew perfectly well that at that moment they were at the flat, that they were greatly astonished at finding it unlocked, as the door had just been fastened, that by now they were looking at the bodies, that before another minute had passed they would guess and eventually realize that the murderer had just been there, and had succeeded in hiding somewhere, slipping by them and escaping. They would guess most likely that he had been in the empty flat while they were going upstairs. And meanwhile he dared not speed up too much, though the next turning was still nearly a hundred yards away. "Should he slip through some gateway and wait somewhere in an unknown street? No, hopeless! Should he fling away the axe? Should he take a cab? Hopeless, hopeless!"

At last he reached the turning. He turned down it more dead than alive. Here he was halfway to safety, and here he understood it;

it was less risky because there was a great crowd of people, and he was lost in it like a grain of sand. But everything he had suffered had so weakened him that he could scarcely move. Perspiration ran down him in drops, his neck was all wet. "My God, he's been at it!" someone shouted at him when he came out on the canal bank.

He was only dimly conscious of himself now, and the farther he went the worse it was. He remembered, however, that when he came out onto the canal bank, he was alarmed at finding few people there and at being more conspicuous, and he had thought of turning back. Though he was almost falling from fatigue, he went a long way round so as to get home from a different direction.

He was not fully conscious when he passed through the gateway of his house; he was already on the staircase before he remembered the axe. And yet he had a very grave problem before him, to put it back and to escape observation as far as possible in doing so. He was of course incapable of reflecting that it might perhaps be far better not to put the axe back at all, but to drop it later on in somebody's yard. But it all turned out beautifully: the door of the porter's room was closed but not locked, so it seemed most likely that the porter was at home. But he had lost his powers of reflection so completely that he walked straight to the door and opened it. If the porter had asked him "What do you want?" he would perhaps have simply handed him the axe. But again the porter was not at home, and he succeeded in putting the axe back under the bench, and even covering it with the chunk of wood just as before. He met no-one, not a soul, on the way to his room; the landlady's door was shut. When he was in his room, he flung himself on the sofa just as he was—he did not sleep, but sank into blank forgetfulness. If anyone had come into his room then, he would have jumped up at once and screamed. Scraps and shreds of thoughts were simply swarming in his brain, but he could not catch at one, he could not rest on one, in spite of all his efforts . . .

PART TWO

CHAPTER ONE

HE LAY LIKE THAT for a very long time. Now and then he seemed to wake up, and at such moments he became conscious that it was far into the night, but it did not occur to him to get up. At last he noticed that it was already dawn. He was lying on his back, still dazed from his recent oblivion. Fearful, despairing cries rose shrilly from the street, sounds which he heard every night under his window after two o'clock; now they woke him up.

"Ah! The drunkards are coming out of the taverns," he thought, "it's past two o'clock," and at once he leaped up, as though someone had pulled him from the sofa.

"What! Past two o'clock!"

He sat down on the sofa—and instantly remembered everything! All at once, in a flash, he remembered everything.

At first he thought he was going mad. A dreadful chill came over him; but the chill was from the fever that had begun long before in his sleep. Now he suddenly started shivering violently, so that his teeth chattered and all his limbs were shaking. He opened the door and began listening; everyone in the house was asleep. With amazement he gazed at himself and everything in the room around him, wondering how he could have come in the night before without fastening the door and have flung himself on the sofa without undressing, without even taking his hat off. It had fallen off and was lying on the floor near his pillow.

"If someone had come in, what would they have thought? That I'm drunk but . . . "

He rushed to the window. There was enough light for him to begin hurriedly checking himself all over from head to foot, all his clothes: were there no traces? But there was no use doing it like that; shivering with cold, he began taking off everything and looking himself over again. He turned everything over to the last threads and rags and, mistrusting himself, went through his search three times.

But there seemed to be nothing, no trace, except in one place, where some thick drops of congealed blood were clinging to the frayed edge of his trousers. He picked up a big pocket knife and cut off the frayed threads. There seemed to be nothing more.

Suddenly he remembered that the purse and the things he had

taken out of the old woman's box were still in his pockets! He had not thought until then of taking them out and hiding them! He had not even thought of them while he was examining his clothes! What next? Instantly he rushed to take them out and fling them on the table. When he had pulled out everything and turned the pocket inside out to be sure there was nothing left, he carried the whole heap to the corner. The paper had come off the bottom of the wall and hung there in tatters. He began stuffing all the things into the hole under the paper. "They're in! All out of sight, and the purse too!" he thought gleefully, getting up and gazing blankly at the hole which bulged out more than ever. Suddenly he shuddered all over with horror. "My God!" he whispered in despair. "What's the matter with me? Are they hidden? Is that the way to hide things?"

He had not counted on having trinkets to hide. He had only thought of money, and so he had not prepared a hiding-place.

"But now, now, what am I pleased about?" he thought, "Is that hiding things? My reason's deserting me—it's as simple as that!"

He sat down on the sofa in exhaustion and was at once shaken by another unbearable fit of shivering. Mechanically he drew from a chair beside him his old student's winter coat, which was still warm though almost in rags, covered himself up with it and once more sank into drowsiness and delirium. He lost consciousness.

Not more than five minutes had passed when he jumped up a second time, and at once pounced in a frenzy on his clothes again.

"How could I go to sleep again with nothing done? Yes, yes; I haven't taken the noose off the armhole! I forgot it, forgot a thing like that! Such a piece of evidence!"

He pulled off the noose, hurriedly cut it to pieces and threw the bits among his linen under the pillow.

"Pieces of torn linen couldn't arouse suspicion, whatever happened; I think not, I think not—anyway!" he repeated, standing in the middle of the room, and with painful concentration he started gazing about him again, at the floor and everywhere, trying to make sure he had not forgotten anything. The conviction that all his faculties were failing him, even his memory and his most basic powers of reflection, began to be an insufferable torture.

"Surely it isn't beginning already? Surely it isn't my punishment coming upon me? It is!"

The frayed rags he had cut off his trousers were actually lying on the floor in the middle of the room, where anyone coming in would see them!

"What is the matter with me!" he cried again, distraught.

Then a strange idea entered his head; that, perhaps, all his clothes were covered with blood, that, perhaps, there were many stains, but that he did not see them, did not notice them because his perceptions were failing, were going to pieces . . . his reason was clouded . . . Suddenly he remembered that there had been blood on the purse too. "Ah! Then there must be blood on the pocket too, because I put the wet purse in my pocket!"

In a flash he had turned the pocket inside out and, yes! There were traces, stains on the lining of the pocket!

"So my reason has not quite deserted me, so I still have some kind of memory and common sense, since I guessed it myself," he thought triumphantly, with a deep sigh of relief. "It's simply the weakness of fever, a moment's delirium," and he tore the whole lining out of the left pocket of his trousers. At that instant the sunlight fell on his left boot; on the sock which poked out from the boot he thought there were traces! He flung off his boots—"traces! The tip of the sock was soaked with blood"; he must have unwarily stepped into that pool . . . "But what am I to do with this now? Where am I to put the sock and rags and pocket?"

He gathered them all up in his hands and stood in the middle of the room.

"In the stove? But they would search the stove first. Burn them? But what can I burn them with? There aren't even any matches. No, better go out and throw it all away somewhere. Yes, better throw it away," he repeated, sitting down on the sofa again, "and straightaway, immediately, without delay . . . "

But his head sank on the pillow instead. Again the unbearable icy shivering came over him; again he drew his coat over him.

And for a long while, for some hours, he was haunted by the impulse to "go off somewhere at once, this minute, and fling it all away, just so it's out of sight and done with, at once, at once!" Several times he tried to rise from the sofa but could not.

He was properly woken at last by a violent knocking on his door.

"Open the door, are you dead or alive? He keeps sleeping here!"

Fyodor Dostoevsky

shouted Nastasia, banging with her fist on the door. "For days on end he's been snoring here like a dog! A dog he is too. Open it, come on! It's past ten."

"Maybe he's not at home," said a man's voice.

"Ha! That's the porter's voice . . . What does he want?"

He jumped up and sat on the sofa. Even the beating of his heart was painful.

"Then who can have latched the door?" retorted Nastasia.

"He's taken to bolting himself in! As if he were worth stealing! Open it, you idiot, wake up!"

"What do they want? Why the porter? They've found me out. Resist or open? Come what may! . . . "

He half rose, stooped forward and unlatched the door.

His room was so small that he could undo the latch without leaving the bed. Yes; the porter and Nastasia were standing there.

Nastasia stared at him in a strange way. He glanced with a defiant and desperate air at the porter, who without a word held out a gray folded paper sealed with wax.

"A notice from the office," he announced, as he gave him the paper.

"From what office?"

"A summons to the police office, of course. You know which office."

"To the police? . . . What for? . . . "

"How can I tell? You're sent for, so you go."

The man looked at him attentively, looked round the room and turned to go away.

"He's seriously ill!" observed Nastasia, not taking her eyes off him. The porter turned his head for a moment. "He's been in a fever since yesterday," she added.

Raskolnikov made no response and held the paper in his hands, without opening it. "Don't get up then," Nastasia went on compassionately, seeing that he was letting his feet down from the sofa. "You're ill, so don't go; there's no hurry. What have you got there?"

He looked; in his right hand he held the shreds he had cut from his trousers, the sock, and the rags of the pocket. So he had been asleep with them in his hand. When he reflected on it afterwards, he remembered that, half waking up in his fever, he had grasped all this tightly in his hand and fallen asleep again.

"Look at the rags he's collected and sleeps with, as though he's got treasure in his hands . . . "

And Nastasia went off into her hysterical giggle.

Instantly he thrust them all under his overcoat and fixed his eyes intently upon her. Far as he was from being capable of rational reflection at that moment, he felt that no-one would behave like that with a person who was going to be arrested. "But . . . the police?"

"You'd better have some tea! Yes? I'll bring it, there's some left."

"No . . . I'm going; I'll go at once," he muttered, getting on to his feet.

"Why, you'll never get downstairs!"

"Yes, I'll go."

"As you wish."

She followed the porter out.

At once he rushed to the light to examine the sock and the rags.

"There are stains, but not very noticeable; all covered with dirt, and rubbed and discolored. No-one who wasn't suspicious could distinguish anything. Nastasia couldn't have noticed from a distance, thank God!" Then with a tremor he broke the seal of the notice and began reading; he spent a long time reading it before he understood. It was an ordinary summons from the district police station to appear that day at half past nine at the office of the district superintendent.

"But when has such a thing happened? I never have anything to do with the police! And why just today?" he thought in agonizing bewilderment. "Good God, just get it over with as soon as possible!"

He was flinging himself on his knees to pray, but broke into laughter—not at the idea of prayer, but at himself.

He began to dress himself hurriedly. "If I'm lost, I'm lost, I don't care! Shall I put the sock on?" he suddenly wondered. "It will get even dustier and the traces will be gone."

But no sooner had he put it on than he pulled it off again in loathing and horror. He pulled it off, but reflecting that he had no other socks, he picked it up and put it on again—and again he laughed.

"That's all conventional, that's all relative, just a way of looking at it," he thought in a flash, but only on the surface of his mind, while he was shuddering all over. "There, I've got it on! I've actually managed to get it on!"

But his laughter was quickly followed by despair.

"No, it's too much for me . . . " he thought. His legs shook. "Fear," he muttered. His head swam and ached with fever. "It's a trick! They want to decoy me and confuse me about everything," he mused, as he went out onto the stairs. "The worst of it is I'm almost light-headed . . . I may blurt out something stupid . . . "

On the stairs he remembered that he was leaving all the things just as they were in the hole in the wall, "and, very likely, it's on purpose to search when I'm out," he thought, and stopped short. But he was possessed by such despair, such cynicism of misery, if that is what it could be called, that with a wave of his hand he went on. "Just to get it over with!"

In the street the heat was unbearable again; not a drop of rain had fallen. Again, dust, bricks and mortar, again, the stench from the stores and taverns, again the drunken men, the Finnish street-sellers and half-broken-down cabs. The sun shone straight in his eyes, so that it hurt him to look out of them, and he felt his head spinning— as a person in a fever is apt to feel when they come out into the street on a bright sunny day.

When he reached the turning into the street, in agonizing terror he looked down it . . . at the house . . . and at once turned his eyes away.

"If they question me, perhaps I'll just tell them everything," he thought, as he neared the police station.

The police station was about a quarter of a mile off. It had recently been moved to new rooms on the fourth floor of a new house. He had been once for a moment in the old office, but long ago. Turning in at the gateway, he saw on the right a flight of stairs which a peasant was mounting with a book in his hand. "A house-porter, no doubt; so then, the office is here," and he began climbing the stairs in case. He did not want to ask anyone any questions.

"I'll go in, fall on my knees, and confess everything . . . " he thought as he reached the fourth floor.

The staircase was steep, narrow and all sloppy with dirty water. The kitchens of the apartments opened onto the stairs and stood open almost the whole day. There was a terrible smell and heat. The staircase was crowded with porters going up and down with their books under their arms, policemen, and people of all sorts and both sexes. The door of the office, too, stood wide open. Peasants stood waiting inside. There, too, the heat was stifling and there was a sickening smell of fresh paint and stale oil from the newly decorated rooms.

After waiting a little, he decided to move forward into the next room. All the rooms were small and low-ceilinged. A terrible impatience drew him on and on. No-one paid attention to him. In the second room some clerks sat writing, dressed hardly better than he was—a rather strange-looking set. He went up to one of them.

"What is it?"

He showed him the notice he had received.

"You're a student?" the man asked, glancing at the notice.

"Yes, a former student."

The clerk looked at him, but without any interest. He was a particularly untidy person with a fixed expression in his eye.

"There would be no use trying to get anything out of him because he has no interest in anything," thought Raskolnikov.

"Go in there to the head clerk," said the clerk, pointing towards the furthest room.

He went into the room, the fourth in order; it was a small room and packed full of people, who were rather better dressed than in the outer rooms. Among them were two ladies. One, dressed in cheap mourning clothes, sat at the table opposite the chief clerk, writing something at his dictation. The other, a very stout, buxom woman with a purplish-red, blotchy face, excessively smartly dressed with a brooch on her bosom as big as a saucer, was standing on one side, apparently waiting for something. Raskolnikov thrust his notice at the head clerk. The latter glanced at it, said, "Wait a minute," and went on attending to the lady in mourning.

He breathed more freely. "It can't be that!"

By degrees he began to regain confidence, he kept urging himself to have courage and be calm.

"Some foolishness, some insignificant carelessness, and I may betray myself! Hm . . . it's a pity there's no air here," he added, "it's stifling . . . It makes your head dizzier than ever . . . and your mind too . . . "

He was conscious of a terrible inner turmoil. He was afraid of losing his self-control; he tried to catch at something and fix his mind on it, something entirely irrelevant, but he could not succeed at all. Yet the head clerk greatly interested him; he kept hoping to see through him and guess something from his face.

He was a very young man, about twenty-two, with a dark mobile face that looked older than its years. He was fashionably dressed and effeminate, with his hair parted in the middle, well combed and greased, and wore a number of rings on his well-scrubbed fingers and a gold chain on his waistcoat. He said a couple of words in French to a foreigner who was in the room and said them fairly correctly.

"Luise Ivanovna, you can sit down," he said casually to the cheerfully dressed, purple-faced lady, who was still standing as if she were not venturing to sit down, though there was a chair beside her.

"*Ich danke*,"* said the latter, and softly, with a rustle of silk she sank into the chair. Her light blue dress trimmed with white lace floated about the table like an air-balloon and filled almost half the room. She smelt of scent. But she was obviously embarrassed at filling half the room and smelling so strongly of scent; and though her smile was impudent as well as cringing, it betrayed evident uneasiness.

The lady in mourning had done at last and got up. All at once, with some noise, an officer walked in very jauntily, with a peculiar swing of his shoulders at each step. He tossed his cockaded cap on the table and sat down in an easy-chair. The small lady really skipped from her seat when she saw him, and started curtsying in a sort of ecstasy; but the officer did not take the slightest notice of her, and she did not venture to sit down again in his presence. He was the assistant superintendent. He had a reddish moustache that stood out horizontally on each side of his face, with extremely small features that expressed nothing much except insolence. He looked sideways and rather indignantly at Raskolnikov; he was so badly dressed, and in spite of his humiliating position, his bearing was by no means in keeping with his clothes. Raskolnikov had unwarily fixed a very long and direct look at him, and he felt offended.

"What do you want?" he shouted, apparently astonished that

---

*I thank you (German).

such a ragged person was not annihilated by the majesty of his gaze.

"I was summoned . . . by a notice . . . " Raskolnikov faltered.

"For the recovery of money due, from the student," the head clerk interfered hurriedly, tearing himself from his papers. "Here!" and he flung Raskolnikov a document and pointed out the place. "Read that!"

"Money? What money?" thought Raskolnikov, "but . . . then . . . it's definitely not that."

And he trembled with joy. He felt sudden intense indescribable relief. A load was lifted from his back.

"And what time were you asked to appear, sir?" shouted the assistant superintendent, seeming for some unknown reason to be more and more aggrieved. "You were told to come at nine, and now it's twelve!"

"The notice was only brought to me a quarter of an hour ago," Raskolnikov answered loudly over his shoulder. To his own surprise, he too grew suddenly angry and found a certain pleasure in it. "And it's enough that I've come here ill with fever."

"Please stop shouting!"

"I'm not shouting, I'm speaking very quietly, it's you who are shouting at me. I'm a student: I don't let anyone shout at me."

The assistant superintendent was so furious that for the first minute he could only splutter inarticulately. He leaped up from his seat.

"Be silent! You are in a government office. Don't be impudent, sir!"

"You're in a government office, too," cried Raskolnikov, "and you're smoking a cigarette as well as shouting, so you are showing disrespect to all of us."

He felt an indescribable satisfaction at having said this.

The head clerk looked at him with a smile. The angry assistant superintendent was obviously confused.

"That's not your business!" he shouted at last with unnatural loudness. "Kindly make the declaration demanded of you. Show him, Alexander Grigorievich. There is a complaint against you! You don't pay your debts! Who's the disrespectful one around here!"

But Raskolnikov was not listening now; he had eagerly clutched at the paper in order to find an explanation. He read it once, and a second time, and still did not understand.

"What is this?" he asked the head clerk.

"It is for the recovery of money on an I.O.U., a writ. You must either pay it, with all expenses, costs and so on, or give a written declaration as to when you can pay it and at the same time an undertaking not to leave the capital without payment, nor to sell or conceal your property. The creditor is at liberty to sell your property, and proceed against you according to the law."

"But I . . . am not in debt to anyone!"

"That's not our business. Here, an I.O.U. for a hundred and fifteen rubles, legally attested, and due for payment, has been brought us for recovery, given by you to the widow of the assessor Zarnitsyn, nine months ago, and paid by the widow Zarnitsyn to a Mr. Chebarov. That is why we have summoned you."

"But she is my landlady!"

"And what if she is your landlady?"

The head clerk looked at him with a patronizing smile of compassion, and at the same time with a certain triumph, like he would at a novice under fire for the first time—as though he was about to say: "Well, how do you feel now?" But what did he care now for an I.O.U., for a writ of recovery! Was that worth worrying about now, was it even worth his attention! He stood, he read, he listened, he answered, he even asked questions himself, but he did it all mechanically. The triumphant sense of security, of deliverance from overwhelming danger—that was what filled his whole soul that moment without thought for the future, without analysis, without suppositions or surmises, without doubts and without questioning. It was an instant of full, direct, purely instinctive joy. But at that very moment something like a thunderstorm took place in the office. The assistant superintendent, still shaken by Raskolnikov's disrespect, still fuming and obviously anxious to keep up his wounded dignity, pounced on the unfortunate lady, who had been gazing at him ever since he came in with an exceedingly silly smile.

"And you!" he shouted suddenly at the top of his voice. (The lady in mourning had left the office.) "What was going on at your house last night? Eh! Yet another scandal, you're a disgrace to the whole street. Fighting and drinking again. Do you want to end up in jail? I have warned you ten times over that I would not let you off the eleventh! And here you are again, again, you . . . you! . . . "

The paper fell out of Raskolnikov's hands, and he looked wildly at the smart lady who was being so unceremoniously treated. But he soon saw what it meant, and at once began to find some real amusement in the scandal. He listened with such pleasure that he longed to laugh and laugh . . . all his nerves were on edge.

"Ilia Petrovich!" the head clerk began anxiously, but stopped short, for he knew from experience that the enraged assistant could not be stopped except by force.

As for the smart lady, at first she trembled before the storm. But strange to say, the more numerous and violent the terms of abuse became, the more likeable she looked, and the more seductive the smiles she lavished on the terrible assistant. She moved uneasily, and curtsied incessantly, waiting impatiently for a chance of putting in her word; and at last she found it.

"There was no noise or fighting in my house, Mr. Captain," she pattered all at once, like peas dropping, speaking Russian confidently, though with a strong German accent, "and no scandal, and his honor came drunk, and it's the whole truth I am telling, Mr. Captain, and I am not to blame . . . Mine is an honorable house, Mr. Captain, and honorable behavior, Mr. Captain, and I always, always dislike any scandal myself. But he came so tipsy, and asked for three bottles again, and then he lifted up one leg, and began playing the piano with one foot, and that is not at all right in an honorable house, and he *ganz** broke the piano, and it was very bad manners indeed and I said so. And he picked up a bottle and began hitting everyone with it. And then I called the porter, and Karl came, and he took Karl and hit him in the eye; and he hit Henriette in the eye, too, and gave me five slaps on the cheek. And it was so ungentlemanly in an honorable house, Mr. Captain, and I screamed. And he opened the window over the canal, and stood in the window, squealing like a little pig; it was a disgrace. The idea of squealing like a little pig at the window into the street! And Karl pulled him away from the window by his coat, and it is true, Mr. Captain, he tore *sein Rock*.† And

---

*Completely (German).
†His coat (German).

then he shouted that *man muss* pay him* fifteen rubles damages. And
I did pay him, Mr. Captain, five rubles for *sein Rock*. And he is an ungentlemanly visitor and caused all the scandal. 'I will show you up,'
he said, 'because I can write to all the papers about you.' "

"So he was an author?"

"Yes, Mr. Captain, and what an ungentlemanly visitor in an honorable house . . . "

"Now then! Enough! I have told you already . . . "

"Ilia Petrovich!" the head clerk repeated significantly.

The assistant glanced rapidly at him; the head clerk shook his
head slightly.

" . . . So I'm telling you again, Mrs. Luise Ivanovna, and I'm
telling you for the last time," the assistant went on. "If there is one
more scandal in your honorable house, I will put you in the lock-up,
as it is called in polite society. Do you hear? So a literary man, an author took five rubles for his coat-tail in an 'honorable house'? A nice
lot, these authors!"

And he cast a contemptuous glance at Raskolnikov. "There was a
scandal the other day in a restaurant, too. An author had eaten his
dinner and would not pay; 'I'll write a satire about you,' he says. And
there was another of them on a steamer last week who used the most
disgraceful language to the respectable family of a civil councilor, his
wife and daughter. And there was one of them turned out of a con-
fectioner's store the other day. They are like that, authors, literary
men, students, town-criers . . . Pah! You get along! I shall look in on
you myself one day. Then you had better be careful! Do you hear?"

With hasty submissiveness, Luise Ivanovna started curtsying to
everyone, and then curtsied herself to the door. But at the door, she
stumbled backwards against a good-looking officer with a fresh,
open face and splendid thick fair whiskers. This was the superintendent of the district himself, Nikodim Fomich. Luise Ivanovna
made haste to curtsy almost to the ground, and with dainty little
steps, she fluttered out of the office.

"Again thunder and lightning—a hurricane!" said Nikodim
Fomich to Ilia Petrovich in a civil and friendly tone. "You are aroused
again, you are fuming again! I heard it on the stairs!"

---

*He must be paid (German and English).

"Well, what's it matter!" Ilia Petrovich drawled with gentlemanly indifference; and he walked with some papers to another table, with a jaunty swing of his shoulders at each step. "Here, if you will glance over this: an author, or a student, has been one at least, does not pay his debts, has given an I.O.U., won't clear out of his room, and complaints are constantly being lodged against him, and here he has made a protest against my smoking in his presence! He behaves like a hooligan himself; just take a look. That's him over there: attractive, isn't he?"

"Poverty is not a vice, my friend, but we know you go off like powder, you can't bear any disagreements, you probably took offense at something and went too far yourself," continued Nikodim Fomich, turning affably to Raskolnikov. "But you were wrong there; he is a wonderful person, I assure you, but explosive, explosive! He gets hot, fires up, boils over, and no stopping him! And then it's all over! And at the bottom he's a heart of gold! His nickname in the regiment was the Explosive Lieutenant . . . "

"And what a regiment it was, too," cried Ilia Petrovich, happy with all this friendly chat, although he was still sulking.

All at once, Raskolnikov had a desire to say something exceptionally pleasant to them all. "Excuse me, Captain," he began easily, suddenly addressing Nikodim Fomich, "look at it from my point of view . . . I apologize if I have been badly behaved. I am a poor student, sick and shattered" ("shattered" was the word he used) "by poverty. I am not studying, because I cannot keep myself now, but I shall get money . . . I have a mother and sister in the province of X. They will send it to me, and I will pay. My landlady is a good-hearted woman, but she is so angry at my having lost my lessons, and not paying her for the last four months, that she does not even send up my dinner . . . and I don't understand this I.O.U. at all. She is asking me to pay her what is on this I.O.U. How can I pay her? Judge for yourselves! . . . "

"But that is not our business, you know," the head clerk was observing.

"Yes, yes. I entirely agree with you. But let me explain . . . " Raskolnikov put in again, still addressing Nikodim Fomich, but trying his best to address Ilia Petrovich as well, though the latter persistently appeared to be rummaging among his papers and to be contemptuously oblivious of him. "Allow me to explain that I have been living with her for nearly three years and at first . . . at first . . . why should I not confess it, at the very beginning I promised to marry her daughter, it was a verbal promise, freely given . . . she was a girl . . . indeed, I liked her, though I was not in love with her . . . a youthful affair, in fact . . . that is, I mean to say, that my landlady gave me credit freely in those days, and I led a life of . . . I paid very little attention . . . "

"Nobody asks you for these personal details, sir, we can't waste our time on this," Ilia Petrovich interrupted roughly and with a note of triumph; but Raskolnikov stopped him hotly, though he suddenly found it extremely difficult to speak.

"But excuse me, excuse me. It is for me to explain . . . how it all happened . . . In my turn . . . though I agree with you . . . it is unnecessary. But a year ago, the girl died of typhus. I remained lodging there as before, and when my landlady moved into her present quarters, she said to me . . . and in a friendly way . . . that she had complete trust in me, but still, would I not give her an I.O.U. for one hundred and fifteen rubles, all the debt I owed her? She said if only I gave her that, she would trust me again, as much as I liked, and that she would never, never—those were her own words—make use of that I.O.U. until I could pay it myself . . . and now, when I have lost my lessons and have nothing to eat, she takes action against me. What am I to say to that?"

"All these affecting details are no business of ours," Ilia Petrovich interrupted rudely. "You must give a written undertaking but as for your love affairs and all these tragic events, we have nothing to do with that."

"Come now . . . you are harsh," muttered Nikodim Fomich, sitting down at the table and also beginning to write. He looked a little ashamed.

"Write!" said the head clerk to Raskolnikov.

"Write what?" the latter asked, gruffly.

"I will dictate to you."

Raskolnikov thought that the head clerk treated him more casually and contemptuously after his speech, but strangely enough he suddenly felt completely indifferent to anyone's opinion, and this revulsion took place in a flash, in an instant. If he had cared to think a little, he would have been amazed, in fact, that he could have talked to them like that a minute before, forcing his feelings on them. And where had those feelings come from? Now if the whole room had been filled, not with police officers, but with those nearest and dearest to him, he would not have found one human word for them, so empty was his heart. A gloomy sensation of agonizing, eternal solitude and remoteness took conscious form in his soul. It was not the meanness of his sentimental outburst before Ilia Petrovich nor the meanness of the latter's triumph over him that had caused this sudden revulsion in his heart. What should he do now with his own baseness, with all these petty vanities, officers, German women, debts, police offices? If he had been sentenced to be burnt at that moment, he would not have stirred, would hardly have heard the sentence to the end. Something was happening to him, something entirely new, sudden and unknown. It was not that he understood, but he felt clearly with all the intensity of sensation that he could no longer appeal to these people in the police office with sentimental outbursts, or with anything whatsoever; and that if they had been his own brothers and sisters and not police officers, it would have been utterly out of the question to appeal to them in any circumstance of life. He had never experienced such a strange and awful sensation. And what was most agonizing was that it was more a sensation than a conception or idea, a direct sensation, the most agonizing of all the sensations he had known in his life.

The head clerk began dictating to him the usual form of declaration, that he could not pay, that he undertook to do so at a future date, that he would not leave the town or sell his property, and so on.

"But you can't write, you can hardly hold the pen," observed the head clerk, looking with curiosity at Raskolnikov. "Are you ill?"

"Yes, I am dizzy. Go on!"

"That's all. Sign it."

The head clerk took the paper, and turned to attend to the others.

Raskolnikov gave back the pen; but instead of getting up and going away, he put his elbows on the table and pressed his head in his hands. He felt as if a nail were being driven into his skull. A strange idea suddenly occurred to him—to get up at once, to go up to Nikodim Fomich, and tell him everything that had happened yesterday, and then to go with him to his lodgings and to show him the things in the hole in the corner. The impulse was so strong that he got up from his seat to carry it out. "Hadn't I better think a minute?" flashed through his mind. "No, better cast off the burden without thinking." But all at once he stood still, rooted to the spot. Nikodim Fomich was talking eagerly to Ilia Petrovich, and the words reached him:

"It's impossible, they'll both be released. To begin with, the whole story contradicts itself. Why should they have called the porter, if it had been their doing? To inform against themselves? Or as a blind? No, that would be too cunning! Besides, Pestriakov, the student, was seen at the gate by both the porters and a woman as he went in. He was walking with three friends, who left him only at the gate, and he asked the porters to direct him, in the presence of his friends. Now, would he have asked his way if he had been going with a purpose like that? As for Koch, he spent half an hour at the silversmith's below, before he went up to the old woman, and he left him at exactly a quarter to eight. Now just consider . . . "

"But, excuse me, how do you explain this contradiction? They state themselves that they knocked and the door was locked; yet three minutes later when they went up with the porter, it turned out the door was unfastened."

"That's just it; the murderer must have been there and bolted himself in; and they'd have caught him for certain if Koch had not been an ass and gone to look for the porter too. He must have seized the interval to get downstairs and slip by them somehow. Koch keeps crossing himself and saying: "If I had been there, he would have jumped out and killed me with his axe.' He is going to have a thanksgiving service—ha, ha!"

"And no-one saw the murderer?"

"They might well have not seen him; the house is a real Noah's Ark," said the head clerk, who was listening.

"It's clear, it's clear," Nikodim Fomich repeated hotly.

"No, it is anything but clear," Ilia Petrovich maintained.

Raskolnikov picked up his hat and walked towards the door, but he did not reach it . . .

When he regained consciousness, he found himself sitting in a chair, supported by someone on the right, while someone else was standing on the left, holding a yellowish glass filled with yellow water, and Nikodim Fomich standing before him, looking intently at him. He got up from the chair.

"What's this? Are you ill?" Nikodim Fomich asked, rather sharply.

"He could hardly hold his pen when he was signing," said the head clerk, settling back in his place and taking up his work again.

"Have you been ill long?" cried Ilia Petrovich from his place, where he, too, was looking through papers. He had, of course, come to look at the sick man when he fainted, but retired at once when he recovered.

"Since yesterday," muttered Raskolnikov in reply.

"Did you go out yesterday?"

"Yes."

"Though you were ill?"

"Yes."

"At what time?"

"About seven."

"And where did you go, may I ask?"

"Along the street."

"Short and clear."

Raskolnikov, white as a handkerchief, had answered sharply, jerkily, without dropping his black feverish eyes before Ilia Petrovich's stare.

"He can scarcely stand upright. And you . . . " Nikodim Fomich was beginning.

"No matter," Ilia Petrovich pronounced in a strange voice.

Nikodim Fomich would have made some further protest, but glancing at the head clerk who was looking very hard at him, he did not speak. There was a strange silence suddenly.

"Very well, then," concluded Ilia Petrovich, "we will not keep you."

Raskolnikov went out. He caught the sound of eager conversation on his departure, and above the rest rose the questioning voice of Nikodim Fomich. In the street, his faintness passed completely.

"A search—there will be a search at once," he repeated to himself, hurrying home. "The brutes! They suspect me."

His former terror completely mastered him once more.

CHAPTER TWO

"AND WHAT IF THERE has been a search already? What if I find them in my room?"

But here was his room. Nothing and no-one in it. No-one had peeped in. Even Nastasia had not touched it. But, Lord! how could he have left all those things in the hole?

He rushed to the corner, slipped his hand under the paper, pulled the things out and lined his pockets with them. There were eight articles in all, two little boxes with earrings or something of the sort—he hardly looked to see—then four small leather cases. There was a chain, too, just wrapped in newspaper and something else in newspaper that looked like a decoration . . . He put them all in the different pockets of his overcoat and the remaining pocket of his trousers, trying to conceal them as much as possible. He took the purse too. Then he went out of his room, leaving the door open. He walked quickly and resolutely, and though he felt shattered, he had his senses about him. He was afraid they would pursue him, he was afraid that in another half-hour, another quarter of an hour perhaps, instructions would be issued for them to pursue him, and so at all costs, he must hide every trace before then. He must clear everything up while he still had some strength, some reasoning power left . . . Where was he to go?

That had long been settled. "Fling them into the canal, and all traces hidden in the water, the whole thing would be over." That was what he had decided during the night of his delirium when several times he had had the impulse to get up and go away, to hurry up and get rid of it all. But getting rid of it turned out to be a very difficult task. He wandered along the bank of the Ekaterinsky Canal for half an hour or more and looked several times at the steps running down to the water, but he could not think of carrying out his plan; either rafts stood at the steps' edge, and women were washing clothes on them, or boats were moored there, and people were swarming everywhere. Moreover he could be seen and noticed from the banks on all sides; it would look suspicious for someone to go down on purpose, stop, and throw something into the water. And what if the boxes were to float instead of sinking? And, of course, they would. Even as it was, everyone he met seemed to stare and look round, as if they had nothing to do but to watch him. "Why is it, or is it my imagination?" he thought.

At last the thought struck him that it might be better to go to the Neva. There were not so many people there, he would be less well observed, and it would be more convenient in every way—above all, it was further off. He wondered how he could have been wandering for a good half hour, worried and anxious in this dangerous part of town without thinking of it before. And that half hour he had lost over an irrational plan, simply because he had thought of it in delirium! He had become extremely absent and forgetful and he was aware of it. He must finish it quickly.

He walked towards the Neva along V____ Prospect, but on the way another idea struck him. "Why to the Neva? Would it not be better to go somewhere far off, to the Islands again, and hide the things there in some solitary place, in a wood or under a bush, and mark the spot, perhaps?" And though he felt incapable of clear judgment, the idea seemed to him a good one. But he was not destined to go there. For coming out of V____ Prospect towards the square, he saw on the left a passage leading between two blank walls to a courtyard. On the right-hand side, the blank unwhitewashed wall of a four-storied house stretched far into the court; on the left, a wooden hoarding ran parallel to it for twenty paces into the courtyard and then turned sharply to the left. Here was a deserted fenced-off place where rubbish of various sorts was lying. At the end of the courtyard, the corner of a low, seedy stone shed, apparently part of some workshop, peeped from behind the hoarding. It was probably a carriage builder's or carpenter's shed; the whole place from the entrance was black with coal dust. Here would be the place to throw it, he thought. Not seeing anyone in the yard, he slipped in and at once saw a sink near the gate, such as is often put in yards where there are many workmen or cabdrivers; and on the hoarding above had been scribbled in chalk the age-old joke, "Standing here strictly forbidden." This was all for the better, because there would be nothing suspicious about him going in. "Here I could throw it all in a heap and get away!"

Looking round once more, with his hand already in his pocket, he noticed against the outer wall, between the entrance and the sink, a big uncut stone, weighing perhaps sixty pounds. The other side of the wall was a street. He could hear passersby, always numerous in that part, but he could not be seen from the entrance, unless someone came in from the street, which might well happen, in fact, so he needed to hurry.

He bent down over the stone, seized the top of it firmly in both hands and, using all his strength, turned it over. Under the stone was a small hollow in the ground, and he immediately emptied his pocket into it. The purse lay at the top, and yet the hollow was not filled up. Then he seized the stone again and with one twist turned it back, so that it was in the same position again, though it stood a touch higher. But he scraped the earth around it and pressed it at the edges with his foot. Nothing could be noticed.

Then he went out, and turned into the square. Again an intense, almost unbearable joy overwhelmed him for an instant, as it had in the police office. "I have buried my tracks! And who, who can think of looking under that stone? It has been lying there most likely ever since the house was built, and will lie as many years more. And if it were found, who would think of me? It is all over! No clue!" And he laughed. Yes, he remembered that he began laughing a thin, nervous noiseless laugh, and went on laughing all the time he was crossing the square. But when he reached the K____ Boulevard where two days before he had come upon that girl, his laughter suddenly ceased. Other ideas crept into his mind. He felt all at once that it would be loathsome to pass that seat on which he had sat and pondered after the girl had gone, and that it would be hateful, too, to meet that whiskered policeman to whom he had given the twenty kopecks: "Damn him!"

He walked, looking around him angrily and distractedly. All his ideas now seemed to be circling round some single point, and he felt that there really was such a point, and that now, now, he was left facing that point—and for the first time, in fact, during the last two months.

"Curse it all!" he thought suddenly, in a fit of uncontrollable fury. "If it's begun, then it's begun. Damn the new life! Lord, how stupid it is! . . . And what lies I told today! How despicably I fawned on that wretched Ilia Petrovich! But that is all stupidity! What do I care for them all, and the fact that I fawned on them! It's not that at all! It's not that at all!"

Suddenly he stopped; an utterly unexpected and extremely simple new question perplexed and bitterly confounded him.

"If all this has really been done deliberately and not idiotically, if I really had a certain and definite object, how is it that I didn't even glance into the purse and don't know what I had there, that purse for which I have undergone these agonies and have deliberately undertaken this base, filthy, degrading business? And here I wanted to throw into the water the purse together with all the things which I had not seen either . . . how's that?"

Yes, that was true, that was all true. Yet he had known it all before, and it was not a new question for him, even when it was decided in the night without hesitation and consideration, as though that was how it must be, as though it could not possibly be otherwise . . . Yes, he had known it all, and understood it all; surely it had all been settled even yesterday at the moment when he was bending over the box and pulling the jewel-cases out of it . . . Yes, that's the way it was.

"It's because I'm very ill," he decided grimly at last, "I've been worrying and irritating myself, and I don't know what I'm doing . . . Yesterday and the day before yesterday and all this time I've been worrying myself . . . I'll get well and I shan't worry . . . But what if I don't get well at all? Good God, how sick I am of it all!"

He walked on without resting. He had a terrible longing for some distraction, but he did not know what to do, what to attempt. A new overwhelming sensation was gaining more and more mastery over him every moment; it was an immeasurable, almost physical repulsion for everything surrounding him, a stubborn, malignant feeling of hatred. All who met him were loathsome to him—he loathed their faces, their movements, their gestures. If anyone had addressed him, he felt that he might have spat at them or bitten them . . .

He stopped suddenly on coming out onto the bank of the Little Neva, near the bridge to Vassilyevsky Island. "But he lives here, in that house," he thought, "but it's not as if I've not come to Razumikhin of my own accord! Here it is, the same thing over again . . . I wonder, though; have I come on purpose or have I simply got here by chance? Never mind, I said the day before yesterday that I would go and see him the day after, so I will! Besides, I really cannot go any further now."

He went up to Razumikhin's room on the fifth floor.

The latter was at home in his little room, busily writing at the time, and he opened the door himself. It was four months since they had seen each other. Razumikhin was sitting in a ragged dressing-gown, with slippers on his bare feet, untidy, unshaven and unwashed. His face showed surprise.

"Is it you?" he cried. He looked his comrade up and down; then after a brief pause, he whistled. "As hard up as all that! My friend, you've cut me out!" he added, looking at Raskolnikov's rags. "Come and sit down, you look tired."

And when he had sunk down on the American leather sofa, which was in an even worse condition than his own, Razumikhin saw at once that his visitor was ill.

"Hey, you're seriously ill, do you know that?" He began feeling his pulse. Raskolnikov pulled his hand away.

"Never mind," he said, "I have come for this; I have no lessons . . . I wanted . . . but I don't want lessons . . . "

"My God! You're delirious!" Razumikhin remarked, watching him carefully.

"No, I am not."

Raskolnikov got up from the sofa. As he had mounted the stairs to Razumikhin's, he had not realized that he would be meeting his friend face to face. Now, in a flash, he knew that what he was least of all disposed for at that moment was to be face to face with anyone in the world. He almost choked with rage at himself as soon as he crossed Razumikhin's threshold.

"Goodbye," he said abruptly, and walked to the door.

"Stop, stop! You're behaving very strangely."

"I don't want to," said the other, again pulling away his hand.

"Then why in God's name have you come? Are you mad, or what? This is . . . almost insulting! I won't let you go like that."

"Well, then, I came to you because I know no-one but you who could help . . . to begin with . . . because you are kinder than any-one—clever, I mean, and can judge . . . and now I see that I want nothing. Do you hear? Nothing at all . . . no-one's services . . . no-one's sympathy. I am by myself . . . alone. Come on, that's enough. Leave me alone."

"Stay a minute, you idiot! You are a total madman. Do what you like for all I care. I have no lessons, do you see, and I don't care about that, but there's a bookseller, Kheruvimov, and he's what I've replaced my lessons with. I wouldn't exchange him for five of them. He's doing some kind of publishing, and issuing natural science manuals, and what a circulation they have! Even the titles are worth the money! You always told me I was a fool, but, my God, there are greater fools than I am! Now he is setting up for being advanced, not that he has any understanding of anything, but, of course, I encourage him. Here are two signatures of the German text—in my opinion, the crudest charlatanism; it discusses the question, 'Is woman a human being?' and, of course, triumphantly proves that she is. Kheruvimov is going to bring out this work as a contribution to the question of women; I am translating it; he will expand these two and a half signatures into six, we shall make up a gorgeous title half a page long and bring it out at half a ruble. It will do! He pays me six rubles per signature, it works out to fifteen rubles for the job, and I've had six already in advance. When we have finished this, we are going to begin a translation about whales, and then some of the dullest scandals out of the second part of "The Confessions" we have marked for translation; somebody has told Kheruvimov that Rousseau was a kind of Radishchev.* You can be sure I don't contradict him, damn him! Well, would you like to do the second signature of 'Is woman a human being?' If you would, take the German and pens and paper—all those are provided—and take three rubles; for as I have had six rubles in advance on the whole thing, three rubles come to you for your share. And when you have finished the signature there will be another three rubles for you. And please don't think I am doing you a service; quite the contrary, as soon as you came in, I saw how you could help me; to start with, I am bad at spelling, and secondly, I am sometimes totally lost when I read German, so I make it up as I go along for the most part. The only comfort is that it's bound to be a change for the better. Though who can tell, maybe it's sometimes for the worse. Will you take it?"

Raskolnikov took the German sheets in silence, took the three rubles and, without a word, went out. Razumikhin gazed after him in astonishment. But when Raskolnikov was in the next street, he

---

*French philosopher Jean-Jacques Rousseau (1712–1778) included many controversial revelations about his private life in his memoir The Confessions. Such contemporary French thought was an important influence on Russian polemicist Alexander Radishchev (1749–1802), who was exiled by Catherine the Great and later committed suicide. The "somebody" here is Dostoevsky's contemporary Nikolai Chernyshevsky (1828–1889), a socialist and a novelist.

Fyodor Dostoevsky

turned back, mounted the stairs to Razumikhin's again and laying on the table the German article and the three rubles, went out again, still without uttering a word.

"Are you raving, or what?" Razumikhin shouted, roused to fury at last. "What farce is this? You'll drive me crazy too . . . what did you come to see me for, damn you?"

"I don't want . . . translation," muttered Raskolnikov from the stairs.

"Then what on earth do you want?" shouted Razumikhin from above.

Raskolnikov continued descending the staircase in silence.

"Hey! Where are you living?"

No answer.

"Well, then, go to hell!"

But Raskolnikov was already stepping out into the street. On the Nikolaevsky Bridge he was roused to full consciousness again by an unpleasant incident. A coachman, after shouting at him two or three times, gave him a violent lash on the back with his whip, for having almost fallen under his horses' hoofs. The lash so infuriated him that he dashed away to the railing (for some unknown reason he had been walking right in the middle of the bridge in the traffic). He angrily clenched and ground his teeth. He heard laughter, of course.

"Serves him right!"

"A pickpocket, I'd say."

"Pretending to be drunk, and getting under the wheels on purpose; and you have to answer for him."

"It's a regular profession, that's what it is."

But while he stood at the railing, still looking angry and bewildered at the retreating carriage and rubbing his back, he suddenly felt someone thrust money into his hand. He looked. It was an elderly woman in a shawl and goatskin shoes, with a girl, probably her daughter, wearing a hat, and carrying a green parasol.

"Take it, my good man, in Christ's name."

He took it, and they passed by. It was a twenty kopeck piece. From his dress and appearance they might well have taken him for a beggar asking for donations in the streets, and the gift of the twenty kopecks he doubtless owed to the blow, which made them feel sorry for him.

He closed his hand on the twenty kopecks, walked on for ten paces, and turned facing the Neva, looking towards the palace. The sky was cloudless and the water was almost bright blue, which is so rare in the Neva. The dome of the cathedral, which is seen at its best from the bridge about twenty paces from the chapel, glittered in the sunlight, and in the pure air every ornament on it could be clearly distinguished. The pain from the lash eased off, and Raskolnikov forgot about it; one uneasy and not quite definite idea now occupied him completely. He stood still, and gazed long and intently into the distance; this spot was especially familiar to him. When he was attending the university, he had hundreds of times— generally on his way home—stood still on this spot, gazed at this truly magnificent spectacle and almost always marveled at a vague and mysterious emotion it aroused in him. It left him strangely cold; for him, this gorgeous picture was blank and lifeless. He wondered every time at his somber and enigmatic impression and, mistrusting himself, put off finding an explanation for it. He vividly recalled those old doubts and perplexities, and it seemed to him that it was no mere chance that he recalled them now. It struck him as strange and grotesque that he should have stopped at the same spot as before, as though he actually imagined he could think the same thoughts, be interested in the same theories and pictures that had interested him . . . so short a time ago. He felt it almost amusing, and yet it wrung his heart. Deep down, hidden far away out of sight all that seemed to him now—all his old past, his old thoughts, his old problems and theories, his old impressions and that picture and himself and all, all . . . He felt as though he were flying upwards, and everything were vanishing from his sight. Making an unconscious movement with his hand, he suddenly became aware of the piece of money in his fist. He opened his hand, stared at the coin, and with a sweep his arm flung it into the water; then he turned and went home. It seemed to him, he had cut himself off from every one and from everything at that moment.

Evening was coming on when he reached home, so he must have been walking for about six hours. How and where he came back he did not remember. Undressing, and quivering like an overdriven horse, he lay down on the sofa, drew his overcoat over him, and at once sank into oblivion . . .

It was dusk when he was woken by a fearful scream. God, what a scream! He had never heard such unnatural sounds, such howling, wailing, grinding, tears, blows and curses.

He could never have imagined such brutality, such frenzy. In terror he sat up in bed, almost swooning with agony. But the fighting, wailing and cursing grew louder and louder. And then to his intense amazement he caught the voice of his landlady. She was howling, shrieking and wailing, rapidly, hurriedly, incoherently, so that he could not make out what she was talking about; she was pleading, no doubt, not to be beaten, as she was being mercilessly beaten on the stairs. The voice of her assailant was so horrible with spite and rage that it was almost a croak; but he, too, was saying something, and just as quickly and indistinctly, hurrying and spluttering. All at once Raskolnikov trembled; he recognized the voice—it was the voice of Ilia Petrovich. Ilia Petrovich here and beating the landlady! He is kicking her, banging her head against the steps—that's clear, he could tell that from the sounds, from the cries and the thuds. What's happening, has the world turned upside down? He could hear people running in crowds from all the floors and staircases; he heard voices, exclamations, knocking, doors banging. "But why, why, and how could it be?" he repeated, thinking seriously that he had gone mad. But no, he heard it too distinctly! And then they would come to him next, "for no doubt . . . it's all about that . . . about yesterday . . . My God!" He would have fastened his door with the latch, but he could not lift his hand . . . besides, it would be useless. Terror gripped his heart like ice, tortured him and numbed him . . . But at last all this uproar, after continuing for about ten minutes, gradually began to subside. The landlady was moaning and groaning; Ilia Petrovich was still uttering threats and curses . . . But at last he, too, seemed to be silent, and now he could not be heard. "Can he have gone away? Good Lord!" Yes, and now the landlady is going too, still weeping and moaning . . .

And then her door slammed . . . Now the crowd was going from the stairs to their rooms, exclaiming, disputing, calling to one another, raising their voices to a shout, dropping them to a whisper. There must have been huge numbers of them—almost all the inmates of the block. "But, good God, how could it be! And why, why had he come here!"

Raskolnikov sank worn out on the sofa, but could not close his eyes. He lay for half an hour in such anguish, such intolerably infinite terror as he had never experienced before. Suddenly a bright light flashed into his room. Nastasia came in with a candle and a plate of soup. Looking at him carefully and making sure that he was not asleep, she set the candle on the table and began to lay out what she had brought—bread, salt, a plate, a spoon.

"You've eaten nothing since yesterday, I bet. You've been trudging about all day, and you're shaking with fever."

"Nastasia . . . what were they beating the landlady for?"

She looked intently at him.

"Who beat the landlady?"

"Just now . . . half an hour ago, Ilia Petrovich, the assistant-superintendent, on the stairs . . . Why was he maltreating her like that, and . . . why was he here?"

Nastasia scrutinized him, silent and frowning, and her scrutiny lasted a long time. He felt uneasy, even frightened at her searching eyes.

"Nastasia, why aren't you saying anything?" he said timidly at last in a weak voice.

"It's the blood," she answered at last softly, as though speaking to herself.

"Blood? What blood?" he muttered, growing white and turning towards the wall.

Nastasia still looked at him without speaking.

"Nobody has been beating the landlady," she declared at last in a firm, resolute voice.

He gazed at her, hardly able to breathe.

"I heard it myself . . . I was not asleep . . . I was sitting up," he said still more timidly. "I listened for a long while. The assistant-superintendent came . . . Everyone ran out on to the stairs from all the apartments."

"No-one has been here. That's the blood crying in your ears. When there's no outlet for it and it gets clotted, you start imagining things . . . Will you eat something?"

He made no answer. Nastasia still stood over him, watching him.

"Give me something to drink . . . Nastasia."

She went downstairs and returned with a white earthenware jug of water. He remembered only swallowing one sip of the cold water and spilling some on his neck. Then he sank into oblivion.

CHAPTER THREE

HE WAS NOT COMPLETELY unconscious, however, all the time he was ill; he was in a feverish state, sometimes delirious, sometimes half conscious. He remembered a great deal afterwards. Sometimes it seemed as though there were a number of people around him; they wanted to take him away somewhere, there was a great deal of squabbling and discussing about him. Then he would be alone in the room; they had all gone away afraid of him, and only now and then opened the door a crack to look at him; they threatened him, plotted something together, laughed, and mocked him. He remembered Nastasia often at his bedside; he distinguished another person, too, whom he seemed to know very well, though he could not remember who they were, and this upset him, even made him cry. Sometimes he imagined he had been lying there a month; at other times it all seemed part of the same day. But of that—of that he had no recollection, and yet every minute he felt that he had forgotten something he ought to remember. He worried and tormented himself trying to remember, moaned, flew into a rage, or sank into awful, intolerable terror. Then he struggled to get up, would have run away, but someone always prevented him by force, and he sank back into impotence and forgetfulness. At last he returned to complete consciousness.

It happened at ten o'clock in the morning. On fine days the sun shone into the room at that hour, throwing a streak of light on the right wall and the corner near the door. Nastasia was standing beside him with another person, a complete stranger, who was looking at him very inquisitively. He was a young man with a beard, wearing a full, short-waisted coat, and looked like a messenger. The landlady was peeping in at the half-opened door. Raskolnikov sat up.

"Who is this, Nastasia?" he asked, pointing to the young man.

"He's himself again!" she said.

"He's himself," echoed the man.

Concluding that he had returned to his senses, the landlady closed the door and disappeared. She was always shy and dreaded conversations or discussions. She was a woman of forty, not at all bad-looking, fat and buxom, with black eyes and eyebrows, good-natured from fatness and laziness, and absurdly bashful.

"Who . . . are you?" he went on, addressing the man. But at that moment the door was flung open, and, stooping a little, as he was so tall, Razumikhin came in.

"What a cabin it is!" he cried. "I am always knocking my head. You call this an apartment! So you are conscious, my friend? I've just heard the news from Pashenka."

"He has just come to," said Nastasia.

"Just come to," echoed the man again, with a smile.

"And who are you?" Razumikhin asked, suddenly addressing him. "My name is Vrazumikhin, at your service; not Razumikhin, as I am always called, but Vrazumikhin, a student and gentleman; and he is my friend. And who are you?"

"I am the messenger from our office, from the merchant Shelopaev, and I've come on business."

"Please sit down." Razumikhin seated himself on the other side of the table. "It's a good thing you've come to, my friend," he went on to Raskolnikov. "For the last four days you have scarcely eaten or drunk anything. We had to give you tea in spoonfuls. I brought Zossimov to see you twice. You remember Zossimov? He examined you carefully and said at once it was nothing serious—something seemed to have gone to your head. Some nervous nonsense, the result of bad feeding, he says you have not had enough beer and radish, but it's nothing much, it will pass and you will be all right. Zossimov is first-rate! He is making a real name for himself. Come, then, I won't keep you," he said, addressing the man again. "Will you explain what you want? You must know, Rodia, this is the second time they have sent from the office; but it was another man last time, and I talked to him. Who was it who came before?"

"That was the day before yesterday, I would venture, if you please, sir. That was Alexey Semionovich; he is in our office, too."

"He was more intelligent than you, don't you think so?"

"Yes, indeed, sir, he's weightier than I am."

"Fine; go on."

"At your mother's request, through Afanasy Ivanovich Vakhrushin, of whom I presume you have heard more than once, a gift has been sent to you from our office," the man began, addressing Raskolnikov. "If you are in an intelligible condition, I've thirty-five rubles to give to you, as Semion Semionovich has received from Afanasy Ivanovich at your mother's request instructions to that effect, as on previous occasions. Do you know him, sir?"

"Yes, I remember . . . Vakhrushin," Raskolnikov said dreamily.

"You hear that, he knows Vakhrushin," cried Razumikhin. "He is in 'an intelligible condition'! And I see you are an intelligent man too. Well, it's always pleasant to hear words of wisdom."

"That's the gentleman, Vakhrushin, Afanasy Ivanovich. And at your mother's request—she has sent you a gift once before in the same manner, through him—he did not refuse this time either, and sent instructions to Semion Semionovich some days since to hand you thirty-five rubles in the hope of better things to come."

"That 'hoping for better things to come' is the best thing you've said, though 'your mother' isn't bad either. Come on then, what do you think? Is he fully conscious?"

"That's all right. If he can just sign this little paper."

"He can scrawl his name. Have you got the book?"

"Yes, here's the book."

"Give it to me. Here, Rodia, sit up. I'll hold you. Take the pen and scribble 'Raskolnikov' for him. At the moment, my friend, money is sweeter to us than treacle."

"I don't want it," said Raskolnikov, pushing away the pen.

"Not want it?"

"I won't sign it."

"How the devil can you do without signing it?"

"I don't want . . . the money."

"Don't want the money! Come on, that's nonsense, I'll be a witness to that. Don't worry, he's just on his travels again. But that's pretty common with him anyway . . . You are a man of judgment and we will take him in hand, that is, more simply, take his hand and he will sign it. Here."

"But I can come another time."

"No, no. Why should we trouble you? You are a man of judgment . . . Now, Rodia, don't keep your visitor, you can see that he's waiting," and he made ready to hold Raskolnikov's hand in earnest.

"Stop, I'll do it alone," said the latter, taking the pen and signing his name.

The messenger took out the money and went away.

"Bravo! And now, brother, are you hungry?"

"Yes," answered Raskolnikov.

"Is there any soup?"

"Some of yesterday's," answered Nastasia, who was still standing there.

"With potatoes and rice in it?"

"Yes."

"I know it by heart. Bring us soup and tea."

"I will."

Raskolnikov observed all this with profound astonishment and a dull, unreasoning terror. He made up his mind to keep quiet and see what would happen. "I don't think I'm feverish; I think it's all real," he pondered.

In a couple of minutes Nastasia returned with the soup, and announced that the tea would soon be ready. With the soup she brought two spoons, two plates, salt, pepper, mustard for the beef, and so on. The table was set as it had not been for a long time. The cloth was clean.

"It would not be amiss, Nastasia, if Praskovia Pavlovna were to send us up a couple of bottles of beer. We could empty them."

"You don't stop, do you," muttered Nastasia, and she left to carry out his orders.

Raskolnikov still gazed wildly with strained attention. Meanwhile Razumikhin sat down on the sofa beside him, as clumsily as a bear put his left arm round Raskolnikov's head, although he was able to sit up, and with his right hand gave him a spoonful of soup, blowing on it so it would not burn him. But the soup was only just warm. Raskolnikov swallowed one spoonful greedily, then a second, then a third. But after giving him a few more spoonfuls of soup, Razumikhin suddenly stopped, and said that he must ask Zossimov whether he ought to have more.

Nastasia came in with two bottles of beer.

"And will you have tea?"

"Yes."

"Come on, Nastasia, bring some tea; tea we can attempt without the faculty. But here is the beer!" He moved back to his chair, pulled the soup and meat in front of him, and began eating as though he had not touched food for three days.

"I must tell you, Rodia, I dine like this here every day now," he mumbled with his mouth full of beef, "and it's all Pashenka, your dear little landlady, who sees to that; she loves to do anything for me. I don't ask for it, but, of course, I don't object. And here's Nastasia with the tea. She's a quick girl. Nastasia, my dear, won't you have some beer?"

"No way!"

"A cup of tea, then?"

"A cup of tea, maybe."

"Pour it out. Stop, I'll pour it out myself. Sit down."

He poured out two cups, left his dinner, and sat on the sofa again. As before, he put his left arm round the sick man's head, raised him up and gave him tea in spoonfuls, again blowing each spoonful steadily and earnestly, as though this process was the principal and most effective means towards his friend's recovery. Raskolnikov said nothing and made no resistance, though he felt strong enough to sit up on the sofa without support and could not only have held a cup or a spoon, but maybe even walked about. But in a moment of some strange, almost animal cunning he dreamt up the idea of hiding his strength and lying low for a time, pretending if necessary that he was not yet in full possession of his faculties, and meanwhile listening to find out what was going on. Yet he could not overcome his sense of repugnance. After sipping a dozen spoonfuls of tea, he suddenly released his head, pushed the spoon away capriciously, and sank back on the pillow. There were actually real pillows under his head now, down pillows in clean cases, he observed that, too, and took note of it.

"Pashenka must give us some raspberry jam today to make him some raspberry tea," said Razumikhin, going back to his chair and attacking his soup and beer again.

"And where is she going to get raspberries for you?" asked Nastasia, balancing a saucer on her five outspread fingers and sipping tea through a lump of sugar.

"She'll get it at the store, my dear. You see, Rodia, all sorts of things have been happening while you have been laid up. When you went off in that terrible way without leaving your address, I felt so angry that I resolved to find you and punish you. I set to work that very day. How I ran about making inquiries for you! This apartment of yours I had forgotten, though I never remembered it, indeed, because I did not know it; and as for your old lodgings, I could only remember it was at the Five Corners, Kharlamov's house. I kept trying to find that Kharlamov's house, and afterwards it turned out that it was not Kharlamov's, but Buch's. How confusing sounds get sometimes! So I lost my temper, and I went on the off chance to the address bureau the next day, and just imagine, in two minutes they looked you up! Your name is down there."

"My name!"

"I should think so; and yet they couldn't find a General Kobelev while I was there. Well, it's a long story. But as soon as I did land on this place, I soon got to learn about all your affairs—all of them, all of them, my friend, I know everything; Nastasia here will tell you. I made the acquaintance of Nikodim Fomich and Ilia Petrovich, and the house-porter and Mr. Zametov, Alexander Grigorievich, the head clerk in the police office, and, last, but not least, of Pashenka; Nastasia here knows . . . "

"He's got round her," Nastasia murmured, smiling slyly.

"Why don't you put sugar in your tea, Nastasia Nikiforovna?"

"You are a one!" Nastasia cried suddenly, going off into a giggle. "I'm not Nikiforovna, I'm Petrovna," she added suddenly, recovering from her mirth.

"I'll make a note of it. Well, my friend, to cut a long story short, I was going in for a real explosion here to uproot all the bad influences in the neighborhood, but Pashenka won the day. I had not expected to find her so . . . headstrong. So, what do you think?"

Raskolnikov did not speak, but he still kept his eyes fixed upon him, full of anxiety.

"And all that could be wished, indeed, in every respect," Razumikhin went on, not at all embarrassed by his silence.

"You're so cunning!" Nastasia shrieked again. This conversation gave her unspeakable delight.

"It's a pity, my friend, that you did not set to work in the right way at first. You ought to have approached her differently. She is, so to speak, a pretty inexplicable character. But we will talk about her character later ... How could you let things come to such a pass that she gave up sending you your dinner? And that I.O.U.? You must have been mad to sign an I.O.U. And that promise of marriage when her daughter, Natalia Yegorovna, was alive? ... I know all about it! But I see that's a delicate matter and I am an idiot; sorry. But, talking of idiocy, do you know Praskovia Pavlovna is not nearly as idiotic as you would think at first sight?"

"No," mumbled Raskolnikov, looking away, but feeling that it was better to keep up the conversation.

"She isn't, is she?" cried Razumikhin, delighted to get an answer out of him. "But she's not very clever either, eh? She's essentially, essentially an inexplicable character! I'm sometimes entirely at a loss, I assure you ... She must be forty; she says she's thirty-six, and of course she has every right to say so. But I swear I think highly of her intellectually, simply from the metaphysical point of view; there is a sort of symbolism between us, a sort of algebra or what not! I don't understand it! Well, that's all nonsense. Only, seeing as you are not a student now and have lost your lessons and your clothes, and that because of the young lady's death she has no need to treat you as a relation, she suddenly took fright; and as you hid in your den and dropped all your old relations with her, she planned to get rid of you. And she's been cherishing that design for a long time, but she was sorry to lose the I.O.U. because you assured her yourself that your mother would pay."

"It was base of me to say that ... My mother herself is almost a beggar ... and I told a lie to keep my room ... and be fed," Raskolnikov said loudly and distinctly.

"Yes, you did very sensibly. But the worst of it is that at that point Mr. Chebarov turns up, a business man. Pashenka would never have thought of doing anything on her own account, she is too retiring; but the business man is by no means retiring, and first thing he puts the question, 'Is there any hope of realizing the I.O.U.?' Answer: there is, because he has a mother who would save her Rodia with her hundred and twenty-five rubles pension, if she has to starve herself; and a sister, too, who would go into slavery for his sake. That's what he was counting on ... Why do you start? I know all the ins and outs of your affairs now, my friend—it's not for nothing that you were so open with Pashenka when you were her prospective son-in-law, and I say all this as a friend . . . But I tell you what it is; an honest and sensitive man is open; and a business man 'listens and goes on eating you up.' Well, then she gave the I.O.U. as payment to this Chebarov, and without hesitation he made a formal demand for payment. When I heard of all this I wanted to blow him up, too, to clear my conscience, but by that time Pashenka and I were getting along beautifully, and I insisted on stopping the whole affair, telling him that you would pay. I went security for you, brother. Do you understand? We called Chebarov, flung him ten rubles and got the I.O.U. back from him, and here I have the honor of presenting it to you. She trusts your word now. Here, take it, you see I have torn it."

Razumikhin put the note on the table. Raskolnikov looked at him and turned to the wall without uttering a word. Even Razumikhin felt a twinge.

"I see, my friend," he said a moment later, "that I've been playing the fool again. I thought my chatter would keep you amused, and I think all I've done is made you angry."

"Was it you I didn't recognize when I was delirious?" Raskolnikov asked, after a moment's pause without turning his head.

"Yes, and you flew into a rage about it, especially when I brought Zametov one day."

"Zametov? The head clerk? What for?" Raskolnikov turned round quickly and fixed his eyes on Razumikhin.

"What's the matter with you? . . . What are you upset about? He wanted to meet you because I talked to him a lot about you . . . How could I have found out so much except from him? He's wonderful, my friend, he's great . . . in his own way, of course. Now we are friends—see each other almost every day. I have just moved into this part of town. I've been with him to Luise Ivanovna once or twice . . . Do you remember Luise, Luise Ivanovna?

"Did I say anything when I was delirious?"

"I'd say you did! You were beside yourself."

"What did I rave about?"

"What next? What did you rave about? What people do rave about . . . Well, my friend, I can't waste time. I must do some work." He got up from the table and took up his cap.

"What did I rave about?"

"How he keeps on! Are you afraid of having let out some secret? Don't worry yourself; you said nothing about a countess. But you said a lot about a bulldog, and about earrings and chains, and about Krestovsky Island, and some porter, and Nikodim Fomich and Ilia Petrovich, the assistant superintendent. And another thing that was of special interest to you was your own sock. You whined, 'Give me my sock.' Zametov hunted all about your room for your socks, and with his own scented, ring-bedecked fingers he gave you the rag. And only then were you comforted, and for the next twenty-four hours you held the wretched thing in your hand; we could not get it from you. It is most likely somewhere under your quilt at this moment. And then you asked so piteously for some fringe for your trousers. We tried to find out what sort of fringe, but we couldn't make it out. Now, business! Here are thirty-five rubles; I'll take ten of them, and I shall give you an account of them in an hour or two. I will let Zossimov know at the same time, though he ought to have been here long ago, it's nearly twelve. And you, Nastasia, look in pretty often while I am away, to see whether he wants a drink or anything else. And I will tell Pashenka what she needs to do myself. Goodbye!"

"He calls her Pashenka! Ah, he's a clever one!" said Nastasia as he went out; then she opened the door and stood listening, but could not resist running downstairs after him. She was very eager to hear what he would say to the landlady. She was evidently quite fascinated by Razumikhin.

No sooner had she left the room than the sick man flung off the bedclothes and leapt out of bed like a madman. With burning, twitching impatience he had waited for them to be gone so that he might set to work. But to what work? Now, as though to spite him, it eluded him.

"Good God, just tell me one thing: do they know about it or not? What if they know and they're just pretending, mocking me while I'm laid up, and then they'll come in and tell me that they found out long ago and that they have only . . . What should I do now? That's what I forgot; it's as if I did it on purpose—forgot it all at once, I remembered a minute ago."

He stood in the middle of the room and gazed in miserable bewilderment around him; he walked to the door, opened it, listened; but that was not what he wanted. Suddenly, as though recalling something, he rushed to the corner where there was a hole under the paper, began examining it, put his hand into the hole, fumbled—but that was not it. He went to the stove, opened it and began rummaging in the ashes; the frayed edges of his trousers and the rags cut off his pocket were lying there just as he had thrown them. No-one had looked, then! Then he remembered the sock which Razumikhin had just been telling him about. Yes, there it lay on the sofa under the quilt, but it was so covered with dust and grime that Zametov could not have seen anything on it.

"Bah, Zametov! The police office! And why did they send for me? Where's the notice? Bah! I'm mixing it up; that was then. I looked at my sock then, too, but now . . . now I've been ill. But what did Zametov come for? Why did Razumikhin bring him?" he muttered, helplessly sitting on the sofa again. "What does it mean? Am I still delirious, or is it real? I believe it is real . . . Ah, I remember, I must escape! Escape fast. Yes, I must, I must escape! Yes . . . but where? And where are my clothes? I haven't got any boots. They've taken them away! They've hidden them! I understand! Ah, here's my coat—they didn't take that! And here's money on the table, thank God! And here's the I.O.U. . . . I'll take the money and go and rent another place to stay. They won't find me! . . . Yes, but the address bureau? They'll find me, Razumikhin will find me. Better escape altogether . . . far away . . . to America, and let them do their worst! And take the I.O.U. . . . it'd be of use to me there . . . What else shall I take? They think I am ill! They don't know that I can walk, ha-ha-ha! I could see by their eyes that they know all about it! If only I could get downstairs! And what if they have put someone on guard there—policemen! What's this tea? Ah, and here is some beer left, half a bottle, cold!"

He snatched up the bottle, which still contained a glassful of beer, and gulped it down with relish, as though quenching a flame in his chest. But in a minute the beer had gone to his head, and a faint and even pleasant shiver ran down his spine. He lay down and pulled the quilt over him. His sick and incoherent thoughts grew more and more disconnected, and soon a light, pleasant drowsiness came upon him. With a sense of comfort he nestled his head in the pillow, wrapped more closely about him the soft, wadded quilt which had replaced the old, ragged overcoat, sighed softly and sank into a deep, sound, refreshing sleep.

He woke up, hearing someone come in. He opened his eyes and saw Razumikhin standing in the doorway, uncertain whether to come in or not. Raskolnikov sat up quickly on the sofa and gazed at him, as though trying to recall something.

"Ah, you are not asleep! Here I am! Nastasia, bring in the parcel!" Razumikhin shouted down the stairs. "You shall have the account immediately."

"What time is it?" asked Raskolnikov, looking round uneasily.

"Yes, you had a fine sleep, my friend, it's almost evening; it will be six o'clock soon. You've slept more than six hours."

"My God! Have I?"

"And why not? It'll do you good. What's the hurry? Do you have a date? We've got all eternity before us. I've been waiting for the last three hours for you; I've been up twice and found you asleep. I called on Zossimov twice; he wasn't in. It doesn't matter, he'll turn up. And I've been out on my own business, too. You know I've been moving today, moving with my uncle. I have an uncle living with me now. But that's unimportant, let's get down to business. Give me the parcel, Nastasia. We'll open it immediately. And how do you feel now, my friend?"

"I am quite well, I am not ill. Razumikhin, have you been here long?"

"I tell you I've been waiting for the last three hours."

"No, before."

"How do you mean?"

"How long have you been coming here?"

"I told you all about it this morning. Don't you remember?"

Raskolnikov pondered. The morning seemed like a dream to him. He could not remember alone, and looked inquiringly at Razumikhin.

"Hm!" said the latter, "he has forgotten. I suspected then that you were not quite yourself. Now you are better for your sleep . . . You really look much better. First rate! Well, to business. Look here."

He began untying the bundle, which evidently interested him.

"Believe me, my friend, this is something especially close to my heart. We've got to make a man of you. Let's start from the top. Do you see this cap?" he said, taking out of the bundle a fairly good, though cheap, and ordinary cap. "Let me try it on."

"In a moment, afterwards," said Raskolnikov, waving it off.

"Come on, Rodia, don't oppose it, afterwards will be too late; and I shan't sleep all night, because I guessed your size without measuring it. Just right!" he cried triumphantly, fitting it on, "just your size! A proper head-covering is the most important item of clothing and a recommendation in its own way. Tolstiakov, a friend of mine, is always obliged to take off his pudding basin when he goes into any public place where other people wear their hats or caps. People think he does it out of slavish politeness, but it's simply because he's ashamed of his bird's nest; he gets embarrassed so easily! Look, Nastasia, here are two specimens of headgear: this Palmerston"*—he took from the corner Raskolnikov's old, battered hat, which for some unknown reason, he called a Palmerston—"or this jewel! Guess the price, Rodia! Nastasia, what do you suppose I paid for it?" he said, turning to her, seeing that Raskolnikov did not speak.

"Twenty kopecks, no more, I'd say," answered Nastasia.

"Twenty kopecks, silly!" he cried, offended. "Why, nowadays it would cost you more than that—eighty kopecks! And even then only if it's been worn. And it's bought on condition that when's it's worn out, they will give you another next year. I swear! Well, now let us pass to the United States of America, as they called them at school. I'm proud of these trousers, I can tell you" and he exhibited to Raskolnikov a pair of light, summer trousers made of a gray woolen material. "No holes, no spots, and quite respectable, although a little worn; and a waistcoat to match, pretty fashionable at the moment. And when it's worn it really improves, it gets softer, smoother . . . You see, Rodia, the way I see it, the great thing for getting on in the world is always to keep to the seasons; if you don't insist on having asparagus in January, you keep your money in your purse! and it's the same with this purchase. It's summer now, so I've been buying summer things—warmer materials will be wanted for autumn, so you will have to throw these away in any case . . . especially as they will be done for by then due to their own lack of sturdiness if not your higher standard of luxury. Come on, give them a price! What do you say? Two rubles twenty-five kopecks! And remember the conditions:

---

*British statesman Lord Henry Palmerston (1784–1865) served two terms as prime minister and three as foreign secretary.

if you wear these out, you will have another suit for nothing! They only do business on that system at Fediaev's; if you've bought a thing once, you're satisfied for life, and you'll never go there again of your own free will. Now for the boots. What do you say? You can see that they're a bit worn, but they'll last a couple of months because it's foreign work and foreign leather; the secretary of the English Embassy sold them last week—he had only worn them six days, but he was very short of cash. Price—a ruble and a half. A bargain?"

"But maybe they won't fit," observed Nastasia.

"Won't fit? Just look!" and he pulled out of his pocket Raskolnikov's old, broken boot, stiffly coated with dry mud. "I didn't go empty-handed—they took the size from this monster. We all did our best. And as for your linen, your landlady has seen to that. Here, to begin with, are three shirts made of hemp, but they've got a fashionable front . . . So, eighty kopecks for the cap, two rubles twenty-five kopecks for the suit—together that's three rubles five kopecks—a ruble and a half for the boots—you see they're pretty good—and that makes four rubles fifty-five kopecks; five rubles for the underclothes—they were bought in the lot—which makes exactly nine rubles fifty-five kopecks. Forty-five kopecks change in coppers. Will you take it? Come on, Rodia, you've got a new set of clothes, because your overcoat will do, and it's even got a style of its own. That comes from getting your clothes from Sharmer's!* As for your socks and other things, I'll leave them to you; we've got twenty-five rubles left. And as for Pashenka and paying for your lodging, don't you worry. I tell you, she'll trust you for anything. And now, my friend, let me change your clothes; I'm sure you'll throw off your illness with your shirt."

"Let me be! I don't want to!" Raskolnikov waved him off. He had listened with disgust to Razumikhin's efforts to be playful about his purchases.

"Come, brother, don't tell me I've been trudging around for nothing," Razumikhin insisted. "Nastasia, don't be shy, help me— that's it," and in spite of Raskolnikov's resistance he dressed him. The latter sank back on the pillows and for a minute or two said nothing.

"It will be a long time before I get rid of them," he thought.

---

*Fashionable menswear store in St. Petersburg.

"What money was all that bought with?" he asked at last, gazing at the wall.

"Money? Your own, what the messenger brought from Vakhrushin, your mother sent it. Have you forgotten that, too?"

"I remember now," said Raskolnikov after a long, sullen silence. Razumikhin looked at him, frowning and uneasy.

The door opened and a tall, stout man whose appearance seemed familiar to Raskolnikov came in.

"Zossimov! At last!" cried Razumikhin, delighted.

CHAPTER FOUR

ZOSSIMOV WAS A TALL, fat man with a puffy, colorless, clean-shaven face and straight flaxen hair. He wore glasses and a big gold ring on his fat finger. He was twenty-seven. He was wearing a fashionable light gray loose coat and light summer trousers, and everything about him was loose, fashionable and tidy and able, his clothes were faultless and his watch-chain was massive. In behavior he was slow and almost indifferent, and at the same time studiously free and easy; he made efforts to conceal his self-importance, but it was always too obvious. All his acquaintances found him tedious, but said he was clever at his work.

"I've been to your apartment twice today, my friend. You see, he's come to," cried Razumikhin.

"I see, I see; and how do we feel now, eh?" said Zossimov to Raskolnikov, watching him carefully and, sitting down at the foot of the sofa, he settled himself as comfortably as he could.

"He's still down," Razumikhin went on. "We've just changed his linen and he almost cried."

"That's very natural; you might have put it off if he didn't want you to . . . His pulse is excellent. Is your head still aching, eh?"

"I'm fine, I'm perfectly fine!" Raskolnikov declared positively and irritably. He raised himself on the sofa and looked at them with glittering eyes, but sank back on to the pillow at once and turned to the wall. Zossimov watched him intently.

"Very good . . . He's doing all right," he said lazily. "Has he eaten anything?"

They told him, and asked what he could have.

"He can have anything . . . soup, tea . . . you mustn't give him mushrooms and cucumbers, of course; he'd better not have meat either, and . . . but no need to tell you that!" Razumikhin and he looked at each other. "No more medicine or anything. I'll look at him again tomorrow. Maybe even today . . . but never mind . . . "

"Tomorrow evening I shall take him for a walk," said Razumikhin. "We are going to the Yusupov Garden* and then to the Crystal Palace."†

"I wouldn't disturb him tomorrow at all, but I don't know . . . a little, maybe . . . but we'll see."

"Ah, what a nuisance! I've got a house-warming party tonight; it's just round the corner. Couldn't he come? He could lie on the sofa. Are you coming?" Razumikhin said to Zossimov. "Don't forget, you promised."

"All right, only a lot later. What are you going to do?"

"Oh, nothing—tea, vodka, herrings. There'll be a pie . . . just our friends."

"And who?"

"All neighbors here, almost all new friends, except my old uncle, and he is new too—he only arrived in Petersburg yesterday to see to some business of his. We meet once every five years."

"What does he do?"

"He's been stagnating all his life as a district postmaster; he gets a little pension. He is sixty-five—not worth talking about . . . But I am fond of him. Porfiry Petrovich, the head of the Investigation Department here . . . But you know him."

"Is he a relation of yours, too?"

"A very distant one. But why are you scowling? Because you quarreled once, won't you come then?"

---

*One of the main public gardens along the Neva River in St. Petersburg.

†Inexpensive restaurant in St. Petersburg that was named for the glass and steel building in London built for the great exposition of 1851, which became a model of utopian hope for modern solutions to poverty, and thus of rational approaches to social thought.

"I don't care a damn for him."

"So much the better. Well, there'll be some students, a teacher, a government clerk, a musician, an officer and Zametov."

"Do tell me, please, what you or he"—Zossimov nodded at Raskolnikov—"can have in common with this Zametov?"

"Oh, you particular gentleman! Principles! You work by principles like you work by springs; you won't bother turning round on your own account. If a person is nice, that's the only principle I go on. Zametov is a wonderful person."

"Though he does take bribes."

"Well, he does! and what of it? I don't care if he does take bribes," Razumikhin cried with unnatural irritability. "I don't praise him for taking bribes. I only say he is a nice man in his own way! But if you look at men in all ways—are there many good ones left? I'm sure I wouldn't be worth a baked onion myself . . . perhaps with you thrown in."

"That's too little; I'd give two for you."

"And I wouldn't give more than one for you. No more of your jokes! Zametov's no more than a boy. I can pull his hair and draw him, not repel him. You'll never improve a man by repelling him, especially a boy. You have to be twice as careful with a boy. Oh, you tedious progressives! You don't understand. You harm yourselves running another person down . . . But if you want to know, we really have something in common."

"I'd like to know what."

"It's all about a house-painter . . . We are getting him out of a mess! Though indeed there's nothing to fear now. The matter is absolutely self-evident. We only put on steam."

"A painter?"

"Why, haven't I told you about it? I only told you the beginning then about the murder of the old pawnbroker-woman. Well, the painter is mixed up in it . . . "

"Oh, I heard about that murder before and was rather interested in it . . . partly . . . for one reason . . . I read about it in the papers, too . . . "

"Lizaveta was also murdered," Nastasia blurted out, suddenly addressing Raskolnikov. She remained in the room all the time, standing by the door listening.

"Lizaveta," murmured Raskolnikov hardly audibly.

"Lizaveta, the one who sold old clothes. Didn't you know her? She used to come here. She mended a shirt for you, too."

Raskolnikov turned to the wall where in the dirty, yellow paper he picked out one clumsy, white flower with brown lines on it and began examining how many petals there were in it, how many scallops in the petals and how many lines on them. He felt his arms and legs as lifeless as though they had been cut off. He did not attempt to move, but stared obstinately at the flower.

"But what about the painter?" Zossimov interrupted Nastasia's chatter with marked displeasure. She sighed and was silent.

"He was accused of the murder," Razumikhin went on hotly.

"Was there evidence against him then?"

"Evidence against him! Evidence that was no evidence, and that's what we have to prove. It was just as they pinned it on those other two, Koch and Pestriakov, at first. Pah! how stupidly it's all done, it makes me sick, though it's not my business! Pestriakov may be coming to-night . . . By the way, Rodia, you've heard about all of this already; it happened before you were ill, the day before you fainted at the police office while they were talking about it."

Zossimov looked curiously at Raskolnikov. He did not stir.

"But I say, Razumikhin, I wonder at you. What a busybody you are!" Zossimov observed.

"Maybe I am, but we will get him off anyway," shouted Razumikhin, bringing his fist down on the table. "What's the most offensive is not their lying—one can always forgive lying—lying is a wonderful thing, it gets you closer to the truth—what is offensive is that they lie and worship their own lying . . . I respect Porfiry, but . . . What threw them out at first? The door was locked, and when they came back with the porter it was open. So it followed that Koch and Pestriakov were the murderers—that was their logic!"

"But don't excite yourself; they just detained them, they couldn't help it . . . And, by the way, I've met that man Koch. Didn't he buy unredeemed pledges from the old woman?"

"Yes, he is a swindler. He buys up bad debts, too. He makes a profession out of it. But enough of him! Do you know what makes me angry? It's their sickening, rotten, petrified routine . . . And this case might be a means of introducing a new method. You can show from the psychological data alone how to track down the real man. 'We have facts,' they say. But facts aren't everything—at least half the business lies in how you interpret them!"

"Can you interpret them, then?"

"Anyway, you can't hold your tongue when you have a feeling, a tangible feeling that you might be able to help if only . . . Do you know the details of the case?"

"I am waiting to hear about the painter."

"Oh, yes! Well, here's the story. Early on the third day after the murder, when they were still dangling Koch and Pestriakov—though they accounted for every step they took and it was absolutely obvious—an unexpected fact turned up. A peasant called Dushkin, who keeps a liquor store facing the house, brought a jeweler's case containing some gold earrings to the police office, and told them a long story. 'The day before yesterday, just after eight o'clock'—remember the day and the time!—'a traveling house-painter, Nikolai, who had been in to see me already that day, brought me this box of gold earrings and stones, and asked me to give him two rubles for them. When I asked him where he got them, he said that he picked them up in the street. I did not ask him anything more.' I am telling you Dushkin's story. 'I gave him a note'—a ruble, he meant—'for I thought if he did not pawn it with me he would with someone else. It would all come to the same thing—he'd spend it on drink, so it had better be with me. The further you hide it the quicker you will find it, and if anything turns up, if I hear any rumors, I'll take it to the police.' Of course, that's all nonsense; I know this Dushkin, he lies like a horse, he's a pawnbroker and a receiver of stolen goods, and he did not cheat Nikolai out of a thirty-ruble trinket in order to give it to the police. He was just afraid. But anyway, back to Dushkin's story. 'I've known this peasant, Nikolai Dementiev, since he was a child; he comes from the same province and district of Zaraisk, we are both Ryazan men. And though Nikolai isn't a drunkard, he drinks, and I knew he had a job in that house, painting work with Dmitri, who comes from the same village too. As soon as he got the ruble he spent it, had a couple of glasses, took his change and went out. But I did not see Dmitri with him then. And the next day

I heard that someone had murdered Aliona Ivanovna and her sister, Lizaveta Ivanovna, with an axe. I knew them, and I felt suspicious about the earrings at once, because I knew the murdered woman lent money on pledges. I went to the house, and began to make careful inquiries without saying a word to anyone. First of all I asked, "Is Nikolai here?" Dmitri told me that Nikolai had gone off on a binge; he had come home at dawn drunk, stayed in the house about ten minutes and went out again. Dmitri didn't see him again and is still finishing the job alone. And their job is on the same staircase as the murder, on the second floor. When I heard all that I didn't say a word to anyone'—that's Dushkin's tale—'but I found out what I could about the murder, and went home feeling as suspicious as ever. And at eight o'clock this morning'—that was the third day, you understand—'I saw Nikolai coming in, not sober, though not that drunk—he could understand what was said to him. He sat down on the bench and didn't speak. There was only one stranger in the bar and a man I knew asleep on a bench and our two boys. "Have you seen Dmitri?" I said. "No, I haven't," he said. "And you've not been here either?" "Not since the day before yesterday," he said. "And where did you sleep last night?" "In Peski, with the Kolomensky men." "And where did you get those earrings?" I asked. "I found them in the street," and the way he said it was a little strange; he didn't look at me. "Did you hear what happened that very evening, that very hour, on that same staircase?" I said. "No," he said, "I didn't," and all the while he was listening, his eyes were staring out of his head and he turned as white as chalk. I told him all about it and he took his hat and began getting up. I wanted to keep him. "Wait a bit, Nikolai," said I, "won't you have a drink?" And I signed to the boy to hold the door, and I came out from behind the bar; but he darted out and down the street to the turning at a run. I haven't seen him since. Then my doubts were over—he did it, as clear as could be . . . ' "

"I should think so," said Zossimov.

"Wait! Hear the end. Of course they sought high and low for Nikolai; they detained Dushkin and searched his house; Dmitri, too, was arrested; the Kolomensky men also were turned inside out. And the day before yesterday they arrested Nikolai in a tavern at the end of the town. He had gone there, taken the silver cross off his neck and asked for a drink for it. They gave it to him. A few minutes afterwards the woman went to the cowshed, and through a crack in the wall she saw in the stable adjoining he had made a noose of his sash from the beam, stood on a block of wood, and was trying to put his neck in the noose. The woman screeched her hardest; people ran in. 'So that's what you are up to!' 'Take me,' he says, 'to such-and-such a police officer; I'll confess everything.' Well, they took him to that police station—that is here—with a suitable escort. So they asked him this and that, how old he is, 'twenty-two,' and so on. To the question, 'When you were working with Dmitri, didn't you see anyone on the staircase at such-and-such a time?'—his reply was: 'Sure, folks may have gone up and down, but I didn't notice them.' 'And didn't you hear anything, any noise, and so on?' 'We heard nothing special.' 'And did you hear, Nikolai, that on the same day Widow So-and-so and her sister were murdered and robbed?' 'I never knew a thing about it. The first I heard of it was from Afanasy Pavlovich the day before yesterday.' 'And where did you find the earrings?' 'I found them on the pavement.' 'Why didn't you go to work with Dmitri the other day?' 'Because I was drinking.' 'And where were you drinking?' 'Oh, in such-and-such a place.' 'Why did you run away from Dushkin's?' 'Because I was very frightened.' 'What were you frightened of?' 'That I'd be accused.' 'How could you be frightened, if you felt free from guilt?' Now, Zossimov, you may not believe me, that question was put literally in those words. I know it for a fact, it was repeated to me exactly! What do you say to that?"

"Well, anyway, there's the evidence."

"I'm not talking about the evidence now, I am talking about that question, about their own idea of themselves. Well, so they squeezed and squeezed him and he confessed: 'I didn't find it in the street, I found it in the apartment where I was painting with Dmitri.' 'And how was that?' 'Dmitri and I were painting there all day, and we were just getting ready to go, and Dmitri took a brush and painted my face, and he ran off and I after him. I ran after him, shouting my hardest, and at the bottom of the stairs I ran straight into the porter and some gentlemen—and how many gentlemen were there I don't remember. And the porter swore at me, and the other porter swore, too, and the porter's wife came out, and swore at us, too; and a gentleman came into the entry with a lady, and he swore at us, too, because Dmitri and I were lying right in the way. I got hold of Dmitri's hair and knocked him down and began punching him. And Dmitri, too, caught me by the hair and began punching me. But we didn't do any of it because we were angry, but in a friendly way, for fun. And then Dmitri escaped and ran into the street, and I ran after him; but I didn't catch him, so I went back to the apartment alone; I had to clear up my things. I began putting them together, expecting Dmitri to come, and there in the passage, in the corner by the door, I stepped on the box. I saw it lying there wrapped up in paper. I took off the paper, saw some little hooks, undid them, and in the box were the earrings . . . ' "

"Behind the door? Lying behind the door? Behind the door?" Raskolnikov cried suddenly, staring with a blank look of terror at Razumikhin, and he slowly sat up on the sofa, leaning on his hand.

"Yes . . . why? What's the matter? What's wrong?" Razumikhin, too, got up from his seat.

"Nothing," Raskolnikov answered faintly, turning to the wall. Everyone was silent for a while.

"He must have woken up from a dream," Razumikhin said at last, looking inquiringly at Zossimov. The latter shook his head slightly.

"Well, go on," said Zossimov. "What next?"

"What next? As soon as he saw the earrings, forgetting Dmitri and everything, he took up his cap and ran to Dushkin and, as we know, got a ruble from him. He told a lie saying he found them in the street, and went off drinking. He keeps repeating his old story about the murder: 'I knew nothing about it, never heard of it until the day before yesterday.' 'And why didn't you come to the police until now?' 'I was frightened.' 'And why did you try to hang your-self?' 'Because I was anxious.' 'Why were you anxious?' 'In case I was accused of it.' Well, that's the whole story. And now what do you suppose they deduced from that?"

"But there's no supposing. There's a clue, such as it is, a fact. You wouldn't have your painter set free?"

"Now they've just taken him for the murderer. They haven't a shadow of a doubt."

"That's nonsense. You're overexcited. But what about the ear-rings? You must admit that, if on the very same day and hour earrings from the old woman's box have come into Nikolai's hands, they must have got there somehow. It means a lot in a case like that."

"How did they get there? How did they get there?" cried Razumikhin. "How can you, a doctor, whose duty it is to study man and who has more opportunity than anyone else for studying human nature—how can you fail to see the character of the man in the whole story? Don't you see at once that the answers he gave in the cross-examination are the holy truth? They came into his hand precisely as he has told us—he stepped on the box and picked it up."

"The holy truth! But didn't he own up to telling a lie at first?"

"Listen to me, pay attention. The porter and Koch and Pestriakov and the other porter and the wife of the first porter and the woman who was sitting in the porter's lodge and the man Kryukov, who had just got out of a cab and went in the entryway with a lady on his arm, that is eight or ten witnesses, agree that Nikolai had Dmitri on the ground, was lying on him beating him, while Dmitri hung on to his hair, beating him, too. They lay right in the way, blocking the road. They were sworn at on all sides while they 'like children' (in the witnesses' own words) were falling over one another, squealing, fighting and laughing with the funniest faces, and, chasing one another like children, they ran into the street. Now take careful note. The bodies upstairs were warm, you understand, warm when they found them! If they, or Nikolai alone, had murdered them and broken open the boxes, or simply taken part in the robbery, let me ask you one question: do their state of mind, their squeals and giggles and childish scuffling at the gate fit in with axes, bloodshed, fiendish cunning and robbery? They'd just killed them, not five or ten minutes before, the bodies were still warm, and at once, leaving the apartment open, knowing that people would go there at once, flinging away their booty, they rolled about like children, laughing and attracting general attention. And there are a dozen witnesses to swear to it!"

"Of course it is strange! It's even impossible, but . . . "

"No, my friend, no buts. And if the fact that the earrings were found in Nikolai's hands on the same day and at the same hour as the murder constitutes an important piece of circumstantial evidence against him—although the explanation given by him deals with it and doesn't count seriously against him—you must take into consideration the facts which prove him innocent, especially as they are facts that cannot be denied. And do you suppose, from the character of our legal system, that they will accept, or that they are in a position to accept, this fact—resting simply on a psychological impossibility—as irrefutable and conclusively breaking down the circumstantial evidence for the prosecution? No, they won't accept it, they definitely won't, because they found the jewel-case and the man tried to hang himself, 'which he couldn't have done if he hadn't felt guilty.' That's the point, that's what excites me, you must understand!"

"Oh, I see you are excited! Wait a bit. I forgot to ask you; what proof is there that the box came from the old woman?"

"That's been proved," said Razumikhin with apparent reluctance, frowning. "Koch recognized the jewel-case and gave the name of the owner, who proved conclusively that it was his."

"That's bad. Now another point. Did anyone see Nikolai at the time that Koch and Pestriakov were going upstairs at first, and is there no evidence about that?"

"Nobody did see him," Razumikhin answered with vexation. "That's the worst thing about it. Even Koch and Pestriakov didn't notice them on their way upstairs, though in fact their evidence could not have been worth much. They said they saw the apartment was open, and that there must be work going on in it, but they took no special notice and could not remember whether there actually were men at work in it."

"Hm! . . . So the only evidence for the defense is that they were beating one another and laughing. That's a bold assumption, but . . . How do you explain the facts yourself?"

"How do I explain them? What is there to explain? It's clear. At any rate, the direction in which explanation is to be sought is clear, and the jewel-case points to it. The real murderer dropped those earrings. The murderer was upstairs, locked in, when Koch and Pestriakov knocked at the door. Koch, like an ass, didn't stay at the door; so the murderer popped out and ran down, too, because he had no other way of escape. He hid from Koch, Pestriakov and the porter in the apartment when Nikolai and Dmitri had just run out of it. He stopped there while the porter and others were going upstairs, waited until they were out of hearing and then went calmly downstairs at the very minute when Dmitri and Nikolai ran out into the street and there was no-one in the entryway; maybe he was seen, but not noticed. There are lots of people going in and out. He must have dropped the earrings out of his pocket when he stood behind the door, and didn't notice he'd dropped them, because he had other things to think of. The jewel-case is conclusive proof that he did stand there . . . That's how I explain it."

"Too clever! No, my friend, you're too clever. That beats everything."

"But, why, why?"

"Why, because everything fits too well . . . it's too melodramatic."

"A-ah!" Razumikhin was exclaiming, but at that moment the door opened and a stranger walked in.

CHAPTER FIVE

HE WAS CLEARLY NO longer a young man: he looked stiff and portly and had a cautious, sour expression on his face. He began by stopping short in the doorway, staring around himself with offensive and undisguised astonishment, as though asking himself what kind of a place he had come to. Mistrustfully pretending to be alarmed and almost affronted, he scanned Raskolnikov's low and narrow "cabin." With the same amazement he gazed at Raskolnikov, who lay undressed, disheveled, unwashed, on his miserable dirty sofa, staring at him fixedly. Then with the same deliberation he scrutinized the improper, untidy figure and unshaven face of Razumikhin, who looked him boldly and inquiringly in the face without rising from his seat. A constrained silence lasted for a couple of minutes, and then, as expected, some scene-shifting occurred. Reflecting, probably from certain fairly unmistakable signs, that he would get nothing in this "cabin" by attempting to overawe them, the gentleman softened somewhat, and civilly, though with some severity, emphasizing every syllable of his question, addressed Zossimov:

"Rodion Romanovich Raskolnikov, a student, or former student?"

Zossimov made a slight movement, and would have answered if Razumikhin had not anticipated him.

"Here he is lying on the sofa! What do you want?"

This familiar "what do you want" seemed to cut the ground

from under the feet of the pompous gentleman. He was turning to Razumikhin, but checked himself in time and turned to Zossimov again.

"This is Raskolnikov," mumbled Zossimov, nodding towards him. Then he yawned long and hard, opening his mouth as wide as possible, lazily put his hand into his waistcoat-pocket, pulled out a huge gold watch in a round hunter's case, opened it, looked at it and slowly and lazily put it back.

Raskolnikov himself lay without speaking, on his back, gazing persistently at the stranger, though without any understanding. Now that his face was turned away from the strange flower on the wallpaper, it was extremely pale, with a look of anguish, as though he had just undergone an agonizing operation or just been taken from the rack. But the newcomer gradually began to arouse his attention, then his wonder, then suspicion and even alarm. When Zossimov said "This is Raskolnikov," he jumped up quickly, sat on the sofa and with an almost defiant, but weak and breaking, voice articulated:

"Yes, I am Raskolnikov! What do you want?"

The visitor scrutinized him and pronounced impressively:

"Peter Petrovich Luzhin. I believe I have reason to hope that my name is not wholly unknown to you?"

But Raskolnikov, who had expected something quite different, gazed blankly and dreamily at him, making no reply, as though he was hearing the name of Peter Petrovich for the first time.

"Is it possible that you can up until now have received no information?" asked Peter Petrovich, somewhat confused.

In reply Raskolnikov sank languidly back on the pillow, put his hands behind his head and gazed at the ceiling. A look of dismay came into Luzhin's face. Zossimov and Razumikhin stared at him more inquisitively than ever, and at last he showed unmistakable signs of embarrassment.

"I had presumed and calculated," he faltered, "that a letter posted more than ten days, if not a fortnight ago . . . "

"Why are you standing in the doorway?" Razumikhin interrupted suddenly. "If you've got something to say, sit down. You and Nastasia are so crowded. Nastasia, make room for him. Here's a chair, thread your way in!"

He moved his chair back from the table, made a little space between the table and his knees, and waited in a rather cramped position for the visitor to "thread his way in." The minute was chosen so that it was impossible to refuse, and the visitor squeezed his way through, hurrying and stumbling. Reaching the chair, he sat down, looking suspiciously at Razumikhin.

"There's no need to be nervous," the latter blurted out. "Rodia has been ill for the last five days and delirious for three, but now he is recovering and has got an appetite. This is his doctor, who has just had a look at him. I am a colleague of Rodia's, like him, formerly a student, and now I am nursing him; so don't take any notice of us, just carry on with your business."

"Thank you. But shall I not disturb the invalid by my presence and conversation?" Peter Petrovich asked of Zossimov.

"N-no," mumbled Zossimov; "you may amuse him." He yawned again.

"He has been conscious a long time, since the morning," went on Razumikhin, whose familiarity seemed so much like unaffected good-nature that Peter Petrovich began to be more cheerful, partly, perhaps, because this shabby and insolent person had introduced himself as a student.

"Your mother," began Luzhin.

"Hm!" Razumikhin cleared his throat loudly. Luzhin looked at him inquiringly.

"That's all right, go on."

Luzhin shrugged his shoulders.

"Your mother had commenced a letter to you while I was sojourning in her neighborhood. On my arrival here I purposely allowed a few days to elapse before coming to see you, in order that I might be fully assured that you were in full possession of the news; but now, to my astonishment . . . "

"I know, I know!" Raskolnikov cried suddenly with impatient vexation. "So you're the fiancé? I know, and that's enough!"

There was no doubt that Peter Petrovich was offended this time, but he said nothing. He made a violent effort to understand what it all meant. There was a moment's silence.

Meanwhile Raskolnikov, who had turned a little towards him when he answered, began suddenly staring at him again with marked curiosity, as though he had not had a good look at him yet, or as though something new had struck him; he rose from his pillow on purpose to stare at him. There certainly was something peculiar in Peter Petrovich's whole appearance, something which seemed to justify the title of "fiancé" which had so unfortunately been applied to him. In the first place, it was evident, far too evident, actually, that Peter Petrovich had eagerly used his few days in the capital to buy himself a new set of clothes in which to greet his fiancée—which was in fact an entirely innocent, permissible thing to do. Even his slightly complacent consciousness of the improvement in his appearance might have been forgiven in such circumstances, given that Peter Petrovich had just got engaged. All his clothes were fresh from the tailor's and fine for the occasion, except for the fact that they were too new and too distinctly appropriate. Even the stylish new round hat had the same significance. Peter Petrovich treated it too respectfully and held it too carefully in his hands. The exquisite pair of lavender gloves, real Louvain, told the same tale, if only because he did not wear them and just carried them in his hand for show. Light, youthful colors were the dominant feature of Peter Petrovich's dress. He wore a charming fawn-colored summer jacket, light thin trousers, a waistcoat of the same fine new cloth, a cravat made of the lightest cambric with pink stripes on it—and the best thing about it was that it all suited Peter Petrovich. His very fresh and even handsome face always looked younger than forty-five, his real age. His dark, lambchop whiskers made a beautiful setting on both sides, growing thickly about his shining, clean-shaven chin. Although his hair was touched here and there with gray and had been combed and curled at a hairdresser's, it did not give him a stupid appearance, as curled hair usually does, by inevitably suggesting a German on his wedding-day. If there really was something unpleasant and repulsive in his pretty good-looking and imposing face, it was caused by a completely different factor. After he had disrespectfully scanned Mr. Luzhin, Raskolnikov smiled wickedly, sank back on the pillow and stared at the ceiling as before.

But Mr. Luzhin hardened his heart and seemed to determine to take no notice of their oddities.

"I feel the greatest regret at finding you in this situation," he began, again breaking the silence with an effort. "If I had been aware of your illness I should have come earlier. But you know what business is. I have, too, a very important legal affair in the Senate, not to mention other preoccupations which you may well conjecture. I am expecting your mother and sister any minute."

Raskolnikov made a movement and seemed about to speak; his face showed some excitement. Peter Petrovich paused, waited, but as nothing followed, he went on:

" . . . Any minute. I have found an apartment for when they arrive."

"Where?" asked Raskolnikov weakly.

"Very near here, in Bakaleyev's house."

"That's in Voskresensky," put in Razumikhin. "There are two floors there which are let by a merchant called Yushin; I've been there."

"Yes, rooms . . . "

"A disgusting place—filthy, stinking and, what's more, dubious. Things have happened there, and there are all sorts of queer people living there. And I went there to investigate a scandal. It's cheap, though . . . "

"I could not, of course, find out so much about it, as I am a stranger in Petersburg myself," Peter Petrovich replied sulkily. "However, the two rooms are extremely clean, and as it is going to be for such a short time . . . I have already found a permanent, that is, our future apartment," he said, addressing Raskolnikov, "and I am having it done up. And meanwhile I myself have been crammed into a room with my friend Andrei Semionovich Lebeziatnikov, in Madame Lippewechsel's apartment; it was he who told me about Bakaleyev's house, too . . . "

"Lebeziatnikov?" said Raskolnikov slowly, as if remembering something.

"Yes, Andrei Semionovich Lebeziatnikov, a clerk in the Ministry. Do you know him?"

"Yes . . . no," Raskolnikov answered.

"I apologize, I imagined that was the case from your inquiry. I was once his guardian . . . A very nice young man, and a progressive as well. I like to meet young people: you can learn new things from them." Luzhin looked round hopefully at them all.

"How do you mean?" asked Razumikhin.

"In the most serious and essential matters," Peter Petrovich replied, as though delighted by the question. "You see, it's ten years since I visited Petersburg. All the novelties, reforms, ideas have reached us in the provinces, but to see it all more clearly one must be in Petersburg. And in my opinion you observe and learn most by watching the younger generation. And I confess I am delighted . . . "

"At what?"

"Your question is a broad one. I may be mistaken, but I think I find clearer views, more, as it were, criticism, more practicality . . . "

"That's true," Zossimov let drop.

"Nonsense! There's no practicality." Razumikhin flew at him. "Practicality is a difficult thing to find; it does not drop down from heaven. And for the last two hundred years we have been divorced from all practical life. Ideas, if you like, are fermenting," he said to Peter Petrovich, "and desire for good exists, though it's in a childish form, and honesty you may find, although there are people who hijack it. Anyway, there's no practicality. Practicality has to have some kind of experience behind it."

"I don't agree with you," Peter Petrovich replied, with evident enjoyment. "Of course, people do get carried away and make mistakes, but you must be indulgent of that; those mistakes are merely evidence of enthusiasm for the cause and of an abnormal external environment. If little has been done, then there hasn't been the time, let alone the means. It's my personal view, if you would like to know, that something has been accomplished already. New and valuable ideas, new and valuable works are circulating instead of our dreamy old romantic authors. Literature is taking on a more mature form, many unjust prejudices have been rooted up and turned into ridicule . . . In a word, we have cut ourselves off irreversibly from the past, and that, to my thinking, is a great thing . . . "

"He's learnt it by heart to show off," Raskolnikov pronounced suddenly.

"What?" asked Peter Petrovich, not catching his words; but he received no reply.

"That's all true," Zossimov hastily remarked.

"Isn't it so?" Peter Petrovich went on, giving Zossimov a friendly glance. "You must admit," he went on, addressing Razumikhin with a shade of triumph and superiority—he almost added "young man"—

"that there has been an advance or, as they say now, progress in the name of science and economic truth . . . "

"A commonplace."

"No, not a commonplace! Up until now, for instance, if I were told, 'love thy neighbor,' what came of it?" Peter Petrovich went on, perhaps too hastily. "It meant I had to tear my coat in half to share it with my neighbor and we both were left half naked. As the Russian proverb says, 'catch several hares and you won't catch one.' Science now tells us, love yourself above everyone else, for everything in the world relies on self-interest. You love yourself and manage your own affairs properly and your coat remains whole. Economic truth adds that the better private affairs are organized in society—the more whole coats, so to speak—the firmer its foundations and the better organized common welfare shall be. Therefore, in acquiring wealth solely and exclusively for myself, I am acquiring, so to speak, for everyone, and helping to get my neighbor a little more than a torn coat; and that is not because of my private, personal liberality, but because of a general advance. The idea is simple, but unhappily it has been a long time reaching us because we have been hindered by idealism and sentimentality. And yet very little intelligence is needed to perceive it . . . "

"Excuse me, I've very little intelligence myself," Razumikhin cut in sharply, "so let's drop it. I began this discussion with a purpose, but I've grown so sick during the last three years of chattering to amuse myself, of constantly pouring forth commonplaces, which are always the same, that I blush even when other people talk like that. You are in a hurry, no doubt, to exhibit your acquirements; and I don't blame you, it's forgivable. I only wanted to find out what sort of man you are, because so many unscrupulous people have got hold of the progressive cause recently and have distorted it in their own interests to such an extent that the whole cause has been dragged through the mire. That's enough!"

"Excuse me, sir," said Luzhin, offended, and speaking with excessive dignity. "Do you mean to suggest so improperly that I too . . . "

"Oh, sir . . . how could I? . . . Come on, that's enough," Razumikhin concluded, and he turned abruptly to Zossimov to continue their previous conversation.

Peter Petrovich was sensible enough to accept this denial. He made up his mind to take leave in another minute or two.

"I trust our acquaintance," he said, addressing Raskolnikov, "may, upon your recovery and in view of the circumstances, become closer . . . Above all, I hope you return to health . . . "

Raskolnikov did not even turn his head. Peter Petrovich began getting up from his chair.

"One of her customers must have killed her," Zossimov declared.

"Not a doubt," replied Razumikhin. "Porfiry hasn't given me his opinion, but he's examining everyone who left pledges with her."

"Examining them?" Raskolnikov asked aloud.

"Yes. What then?"

"Nothing."

"How does he get hold of them?" asked Zossimov.

"Koch has put forward some of their names, other names are on the wrappers of the pledges and some have come forward themselves."

"It must have been a cunning, experienced criminal! The boldness of it! The coolness!"

"That's just what it wasn't!" interposed Razumikhin. "That's what throws you all off the scent. I don't think he's cunning or experienced; this was probably his first crime! Assuming the criminal planned it all out doesn't work. Suppose he's inexperienced: it's clear that the only thing which saved him was chance—and chance can do anything. Perhaps he didn't even foresee any obstacles! What did he do? He took jewels worth ten or twenty rubles, stuffed his pockets with them, ransacked the old woman's trunk, her rags—and they found fifteen hundred rubles, besides notes, in a box in the top drawer of the chest! He didn't know how to rob anyone; he could only carry out the murder. It was his first crime, I'm telling you, his first crime; he lost his head. He got off because he was lucky, not because he was experienced!"

"You are talking about the murder of the old pawnbroker, I believe?" Peter Petrovich put in, addressing Zossimov. He was standing, hat and gloves in hand, but before departing he felt disposed to throw off a few more intellectual phrases. He was evidently anxious to make a favorable impression and his vanity overcame his good sense.

"Yes. You've heard about it?"

"Oh, yes, being in the neighborhood."

"Do you know the details?"

"I can't say that; but there's another circumstance which interests me about the case—the whole question, so to say. Not to speak of the fact that crime has been greatly on the increase among the lower classes during the last five years, not to speak of the cases of robbery and arson everywhere—what strikes me as the strangest thing is that even on the upper rungs of the social ladder crime is increasing proportionately. In one place you hear about a student robbing the mail on the high road; in another place high-class people forge false banknotes; in Moscow a whole gang has recently been caught forging lottery tickets, and one of the ringleaders was a lecturer in universal history; then one of our diplomats abroad was murdered for some obscure motive of gain . . . And if this old woman, the pawnbroker, has been murdered by member of the higher classes—peasants, after all, don't pawn gold trinkets—how are we to explain this demoralization of the civilized part of our society?"

"There have been many economic changes," put in Zossimov.

"How can we explain it?" Razumikhin caught him up. "Perhaps it's happening because we are totally impractical."

"How do you mean?"

"How did your lecturer in Moscow reply when he was asked why he was forging notes? 'Everybody is getting rich one way or another, so I want to hurry up and get rich too.' I don't remember the exact words, but the upshot was that he wants money for nothing, without waiting or working! We've got used to having everything ready-made for us, from walking on crutches to chewing our food. Then the great moment* arrived, and everyone showed their true colors."—

"But morality? And, so to speak, principles . . . "

"But why do you worry about it?" Raskolnikov interposed suddenly. "It's in accordance with your theory!"

"In accordance with my theory?"

"Well, if you carry out logically the theory you were advocating just now, it follows that people may be killed . . . "

"My God!" cried Luzhin.

---

*Reference to Tsar Alexander II's emancipation of the serfs in 1861; previously, serfs in Russia were treated as slaves.

"No, that's not true," put in Zossimov.

Raskolnikov lay with a white face and twitching upper lip, breathing painfully.

"There's a measure in all things," Luzhin continued with an air of superiority. "Economic ideas are not an incitement to murder, and you only have to suppose . . . "

"And is it true," Raskolnikov interposed once more suddenly, again in a voice quivering with fury and delight in insulting him, "is it true that you told your fiancée . . . within an hour of her acceptance, that what pleased you most . . . was that she was a beggar . . . because it was better to raise a wife from poverty, so that you could have complete control over her, and reproach her because she is dependent on your charitable donations?"

"My God," Luzhin cried furiously and irritably, crimson with confusion, "you have entirely distorted my words! Excuse me, allow me to assure you that the report which has reached you or, rather, has been conveyed to you, has no foundation in the truth, and I . . . suspect who . . . in a word . . . this arrow . . . in a word, your mother . . . . She seemed to me in other things, with all her excellent qualities, a little high-flown and romantic . . . But I was a thousand miles from thinking that she would misunderstand and misrepresent things so willfully . . . And in fact . . . in fact . . . "

"I tell you what," cried Raskolnikov, raising himself on his pillow and fixing his piercing, glittering eyes upon him, "I tell you what."

"What?" Luzhin stood still, waiting with a defiant and offended face. Silence lasted for some seconds.

"If ever again . . . you dare to mention a single word . . . about my mother . . . I shall send you flying down the stairs!"

"What's the matter with you?" cried Razumikhin.

"So that's how it is?" Luzhin turned pale and bit his lip. "Let me tell you, sir," he began deliberately, making the greatest possible effort to restrain himself but breathing hard, "from the moment I set eyes on you, I could see that you disliked me, but I remained here on purpose to find out more. I could forgive a great deal in a sick man and a connection, but you . . . never after this . . . "

"I am not ill," cried Raskolnikov.

"So much the worse . . . "

"Go to hell!"

But Luzhin was already leaving without finishing his speech, squeezing between the table and the chair; Razumikhin got up this time to let him past. Without glancing at anyone, and not even nodding to Zossimov, who had for some time been making signs to him to leave the sick man alone, he went out, lifting his hat to the level of his shoulders to avoid crushing it as he stooped to go out of the door. And even the curve of his spine indicated the horrible insult he had received.

"How could you—how could you!" Razumikhin said, shaking his head in perplexity.

"Leave me alone—leave me alone, all of you!" Raskolnikov shouted in a frenzy. "Will you ever stop tormenting me? I am not afraid of you! I am not afraid of anyone, anyone now! Get away from me! I want to be alone, alone, alone!"

"Come along," said Zossimov, nodding to Razumikhin.

"But we can't leave him like this!"

"Come along," Zossimov repeated insistently, and he went out. Razumikhin thought a minute and ran to overtake him.

"It might be worse not to obey him," said Zossimov on the stairs. "He mustn't be irritated."

"What's the matter with him?"

"If only he could get some favorable shock, that's what would do it! At first he was better . . . You know he has got something on his mind! Some fixed idea weighing on him . . . he must have!"

"Perhaps it's that man, Peter Petrovich. From his conversation it seems he is going to marry his sister, and that he had received a letter about it just before his illness . . . "

"Yes, damn it! He may have completely wrecked the case. But have you noticed, he doesn't take any interest in anything, he doesn't respond to anything except one point he seems excited about—the murder?"

"Yes, yes," Razumikhin agreed, "I noticed that, too. He is interested, frightened. It gave him a shock on the day he was ill in the police office; he fainted."

"Tell me more about that this evening and I'll tell you something afterwards. He interests me a lot! In half an hour I'll go and see him again . . . There'll be no inflammation though."

"Thanks! And I'll wait with Pashenka in the meanwhile and keep watch over him through Nastasia . . . "

Raskolnikov, left alone, looked with impatience and misery at Nastasia, but she stayed.

"Don't you want some tea now?" she asked.

"Later! I am sleepy! Leave me be."

He turned abruptly to the wall, and Nastasia went out.

CHAPTER SIX

BUT AS SOON AS she went out, he got up, latched the door, undid the parcel which Razumikhin had brought in that evening and started dressing. Curiously, he seemed all at once to have become perfectly calm—not a trace of his recent delirium, nor of the panic that had haunted him of late. It was the first moment of a strange and sudden peace. His movements were precise and definite; there was even a firm purpose to them. "Today, today," he muttered to himself. He understood that he was still weak, but his intense spiritual concentration gave him strength and self-confidence. He hoped, moreover, that he would not fall down in the street. When he had dressed in entirely new clothes, he looked at the money lying on the table, and after a moment's thought put it in his pocket. It was twenty-five rubles. He also took all of the copper change from the ten rubles spent by Razumikhin on the clothes. Then he softly unlatched the door, went out, slipped downstairs and glanced in at the open kitchen door. Nastasia was standing with her back to him, blowing up the landlady's samovar. She heard nothing. Who would have dreamed that he would go out? A minute later he was in the street.

It was nearly eight o'clock; the sun was setting. It was as stifling as before, but he eagerly drank in the stinking, dusty town air. His head felt very dizzy; a sort of savage energy gleamed suddenly in his feverish eyes and in his wasted, pale yellow face. He did not know and did not think where he was going; he had one thought alone, "that all this must be ended today, once and for all, immediately, that he would not return home without it, because he would not go on living like that." How, what to put an end to? He had no idea; he did not even want to think about it. He drove away thought; thought tortured him. All he knew, all he felt was that everything must be changed "one way or another," he repeated with desperate and immovable self-confidence and determination.

Out of old habit he took a walk in the direction of the Haymarket. A dark-haired young man with a barrel organ was standing in the road in front of a little store and was grinding out a very sentimental song. He was with a fifteen-year-old girl, who stood on the pavement in front of him. She was dressed up in a crinoline, a mantle and a straw hat with a flame-colored feather in it, all very old and shabby. In a strong and reasonably pleasant voice, cracked and coarsened by street music, she was singing in hope of getting a copper from the store. Raskolnikov joined two or three listeners, took out a five kopeck piece and put it in the girl's hand. She broke off abruptly on a sentimental high note, shouted sharply to the organ grinder "Come on," and both moved on to the next store.

"Do you like street music?" said Raskolnikov, addressing a middle-aged man standing idly by him. The man looked at him, startled and curious.

"I love to hear singing accompanied by a street organ," said Raskolnikov, and his manner seemed strangely out of keeping with the subject—"I like it on cold, dark, damp autumn evenings—they must be damp—when all the passersby have pale green, sickly faces, or better still when wet snow is falling straight down, when there's no wind—you know what I mean?—and the street lamps shine through it . . . "

"I don't know . . . Excuse me . . . " muttered the stranger, frightened by the question and Raskolnikov's strange manner, and he crossed over to the other side of the street.

Raskolnikov walked straight on and came out at the corner of the Haymarket, where the salesman and his wife had talked with Lizaveta; but they were not there now. Recognizing the place, he stopped, looked round and addressed a young fellow in a red shirt who stood gaping before a corn chandler's store.

"Isn't there a man who keeps a booth with his wife at this corner?"

"All sorts of people keep booths here," answered the young man, glancing at Raskolnikov with a superior air.

"What's his name?"

"What he was christened."

"Aren't you a Zaraisky man, too? Which province?"

The young man looked at Raskolnikov again.

"It's not a province, your Excellency, it's a district. Kindly forgive me, your Excellency!"

"Is that a tavern at the top there?"

"Yes, it's an eating-house and there's a billiard-room and you'll find princesses there too . . . La-la!"

Raskolnikov crossed the square. In that corner there was a dense crowd of peasants. He pushed his way into the thickest part of it, looking at the faces. He felt an inexplicable inclination to enter into conversation with people. But the peasants took no notice of him; they were all shouting in groups. He stood and thought a little and took a turning to the right in the direction of V.

He had often crossed that little street which turns at an angle, leading from the market-place to Sadovy Street. Recently he had often felt drawn to wander about this district when he felt depressed, so that he might feel even more so.

Now he walked along, thinking of nothing. On the bend there is a large block of buildings, entirely let out to liquor stores and eating-houses; women were continually running in and out, bare-headed and in their indoor clothes. Here and there they gathered in groups, on the pavement, especially around the entrances to various festive establishments on the lower floors. From one of these a loud din, sounds of singing, the tinkling of a guitar and shouts of merriment, floated into the street. A crowd of women were thronging round the door; some were sitting on the steps, others on the pavement, others were standing talking. A drunken soldier, smoking a cigarette, was walking near them in the road, swearing; he seemed to be trying to find his way somewhere, but had forgotten where. One beggar was quarrelling with another, and a man, dead drunk, was lying right across the road. Raskolnikov joined the throng of women, who were talking in husky voices. They were bare-headed and wore cotton dresses and goatskin shoes. There were women of forty and some not more than seventeen; almost all had blackened eyes.

He felt strangely attracted by the singing and all the noise and uproar in the saloon below . . . Someone could be heard dancing frantically inside, marking time with his heels to the sounds of the guitar and of a thin falsetto voice singing a jaunty air. He listened intently, gloomily and dreamily, bending down at the entrance and peeping inquisitively in from the pavement.—

"Oh, my handsome soldier

Don't beat me for nothing,"—

trilled the thin voice of the singer. Raskolnikov felt a great desire to make out what he was singing, as though everything depended on that.

"Shall I go in?" he thought. "They're laughing. Because they're drinking. Shall I get drunk?"

"Won't you come in?" one of the women asked him. Her voice was still musical and less thick than the others, she was young and not repulsive—the only one of the group.

"She's pretty," he said, drawing himself up and looking at her.

She smiled, much pleased at the compliment.

"You're very nice looking yourself," she said.

"Isn't he thin though!" observed another woman in a deep bass. "Have you just come out of a hospital?"

"They're all generals' daughters, it seems, but they have all snub noses," interposed a tipsy peasant with a sly smile on his face, wearing a loose coat. "See how jolly they are."

"Go along with you!"

"I'll go, sweetie!"

And he darted down into the saloon below. Raskolnikov moved on.

"Hey, sir," the girl shouted after him.

"What is it?"

She hesitated.

"I'll always be pleased to spend an hour with you, kind gentleman, but now I feel shy. Give me six kopecks for a drink, there's a nice young man!"

Raskolnikov gave her what came first—fifteen kopecks.

"Ah, what a good-natured gentleman!"

"What's your name?"

"Ask for Duclida."

"Well, that's too much," one of the women observed, shaking her head at Duclida. "I don't know how you can ask like that. I believe I should drop with shame . . . "

Raskolnikov looked curiously at the speaker. She was a pock-marked wench of thirty, covered with bruises, with her upper lip swollen. She made her criticism quietly and earnestly. "Where is it," thought Raskolnikov. "Where is it I've read that someone condemned to death says or thinks, an hour before his death, that if he had to live on some high rock, on such a narrow ledge that he'd only got room to stand, with the ocean, everlasting darkness, everlasting solitude, everlasting tempest around him, if he had to remain standing on a square yard of space all his life, a thousand years, eternity, it were better to live like that than to die at once! Only to live, to live and live! Life, whatever it may be! . . . How true it is! Good God, how true! Man is a vile creature! . . . And vile is he who calls man vile for that," he added a moment later.

He went into another street. "Bah, the Crystal Palace! Razumikhin was just talking about the Crystal Palace. But what the hell did I want? Yes, the newspapers . . . Zossimov said he'd read it in the papers. Have you got a copy of the papers?" he asked, going into a very spacious and definitely clean restaurant, consisting of several rooms, which were however rather empty. Two or three people were drinking tea, and in a room further away were four men drinking champagne. Raskolnikov thought that Zametov was one of them, but he could not be sure at that distance. "What if it is!" he thought.

"Will you have vodka?" asked the waiter.

"Give me some tea and bring me the papers, the old ones for the last five days and I'll give you something."

"Yes, sir, here's today's. No vodka?"

The old newspapers and the tea were brought. Raskolnikov sat down and began to look through them.

"Oh, damn . . . these are the items of intelligence. An accident on a staircase, spontaneous combustion of a storekeeper from alcohol, a fire in Peski . . . a fire in the Petersburg quarter . . . another fire in the Petersburg quarter . . . and another fire in the Petersburg quarter . . . Ah, here it is!" He found at last what he was seeking and began to read it. The lines danced before his eyes, but he read it all and began eagerly seeking later additions in the following numbers. His hands shook with nervous impatience as he turned the sheets. Suddenly someone sat down beside him at his table. He looked up, it was the head clerk Zametov, looking just the same, with the rings on his fin-

gers and the watch-chain, with the curly, black hair, parted and po-
maded, with the smart waistcoat, shabby coat and dubious dress. He
was in a good mood; at least, he was smiling very merrily and good-
humoredly. His dark face was rather flushed from the champagne he
had drunk.

"What, you here?" he began in surprise, speaking as though he'd
known him all his life. "Razumikhin told me only yesterday you were
unconscious. How strange! Did you know I've been to see you?"

Raskolnikov knew he would come up to him. He laid aside the
papers and turned to Zametov. There was a smile on his lips, and a
new shade of irritable impatience was apparent in it.

"I know you have," he answered. "I've heard. You looked for my
sock . . . And you know Razumikhin has lost his heart to you? He says
you've been with him to Luise Ivanovna's, you know the woman you
tried to befriend, for whom you winked to the Explosive Lieutenant
and he wouldn't understand. Do you remember? How could he fail
to understand—it was quite clear, wasn't it?"

"What a hothead he is!"

"The explosive one?"

"No, your friend Razumikhin."

"You must have a jolly life, Mr. Zametov; free entry to the best
places. Who's been pouring champagne into you just now?"

"We've just been . . . having a drink together . . . You talk about
pouring it into me!"

"As a fee! You profit by everything!" Raskolnikov laughed, "it's
all right, my friend," he added, slapping Zametov on the shoulder.
"I'm not saying that because I'm angry, but in a friendly way, for
sport, as that workman of yours said when he was scuffling with
Dmitri, in the case of the old woman . . . "

"How do you know about it?"

"Perhaps I know more about it than you do."

"How strange you are . . . you must still be very unwell. You
shouldn't have come out."

"Oh, do I seem strange to you?"

"Yes. What are you doing, reading the papers?"

"Yes."

"There's a lot about the fires."

"No, I'm not reading about the fires." Here he looked mysteriously at Zametov; his lips were twisted again in a mocking smile. "No, I am not reading about the fires," he went on, winking at Zametov. "But confess now, my friend, you're pretty anxious to know what I am reading about?"

"I am not in the least. Mayn't I ask a question? Why do you keep on . . . ?"

"Listen, you are a man of culture and education?"

"I was in the sixth class at the gymnasium," said Zametov with some dignity.

"Sixth class! Ah, my little sparrow! With your parting and your rings—you're a lucky man. God, what a charming lad!" Here Raskolnikov broke into a nervous laugh right in Zametov's face. The latter drew back, more amazed than offended.

"Pah, how strange you are!" Zametov repeated very seriously. "I can't help thinking you are still delirious."

"I am delirious? You are lying, my sparrow! So I am strange? You find me curious, do you?"

"Yes, curious."

"Shall I tell you what I was reading about, what I was looking for? See what a lot of papers I've made them bring me. Suspicious?"

"Well, what is it?"

"You prick up your ears?"

"How do you mean—prick up my ears?"

"I'll explain that afterwards, but now, my friend, I declare to you . . . no, better 'I confess' . . . No, that's not right either; 'I make a deposition and you take it.' I depose that I was reading, that I was looking and searching . . . " he screwed up his eyes and paused. "I was searching—and came here on purpose to do it—for news of the murder of the old pawnbroker woman," he articulated at last, almost in a whisper, bringing his face extremely close to Zametov's. Zametov looked at him steadily, without moving or drawing his face away. What struck Zametov afterwards as the strangest part of it all was that silence followed for exactly a minute, and that they gazed at one another all the while.

"What if you have been reading about it?" he cried at last, perplexed and impatient. "That's no business of mine! What of it?"

"The same old woman," Raskolnikov went on in the same whisper, paying no attention to Zametov's explanation, "who you were talking about in the police office, you remember, when I fainted. Well, do you understand now?"

"What do you mean? Understand . . . what?" Zametov brought out, almost alarmed.

Raskolnikov's set and earnest face was suddenly transformed, and he suddenly went off into the same nervous laugh as before, as though utterly unable to restrain himself. And in a flash he recalled with extraordinary vividness of sensation a moment in the recent past, that moment when he stood with the axe behind the door, while the latch trembled and the men outside swore and shook it, and he had a sudden desire to shout at them, to swear at them, to put out his tongue at them, to mock them, to laugh, and laugh, and laugh!

"You are either mad, or . . . " began Zametov, and he broke off, as though stunned by the idea that had suddenly flashed into his mind.

"Or? Or what? What? Come, tell me!"

"Nothing," said Zametov, getting angry, "it's all nonsense!"

Both were silent. After his sudden fit of laughter Raskolnikov became suddenly thoughtful and melancholy. He put his elbow on the table and leaned his head on his hand. He seemed to have completely forgotten Zametov. The silence lasted for some time.

"Why don't you drink your tea? It's getting cold," said Zametov.

"What! Tea? Oh, yes . . . " Raskolnikov sipped the glass, put a morsel of bread in his mouth and, suddenly looking at Zametov, seemed to remember everything and pulled himself together. At the same moment his face resumed its original mocking expression. He went on drinking tea.

"There have been many of these crimes recently," said Zametov. "Only the other day I read in the Moscow News that a whole gang of false coiners had been caught in Moscow. It was a real club. They used to forge tickets!"

"Oh, but that was a long time ago! I read about it a month ago," Raskolnikov answered calmly. "So you think they're criminals?" he added smiling.

"Of course they're criminals."

"Them? They are children, simpletons, not criminals! Fifty people meeting for a purpose like that—what an idea! Three would be too many, and then they want to have more faith in one another than in themselves! One of them just has to blab when he's drunk and it all collapses. Simpletons! They engaged untrustworthy people to change the notes—what a thing to trust to a casual stranger! Well, let us suppose that these simpletons succeed and each makes a million, and what follows for the rest of their lives? Each is dependent on the others for the rest of his life! Better hang yourself at once! And they didn't know how to change the notes either; the man who changed the notes took five thousand rubles, and his hands trembled. He counted the first four thousand, but did not count the fifth thousand—he was in such a hurry to get the money into his pocket and run away. Of course he roused suspicion. And the whole thing came to a crash through one fool! Is it possible?"

"That his hands trembled?" observed Zametov, "yes, that's quite possible. That I feel quite sure is possible. Sometimes people can't stand things."

"Can't stand that?"

"Could you stand it then? No, I couldn't. For the sake of a hundred rubles, to face such a terrible experience! To go with false notes into a bank where it's their business to spot that sort of thing! No, I wouldn't have the nerve to do it. Would you?"

Raskolnikov had an intense desire again to stick his tongue out. Shivers kept running down his spine.

"I would do it differently," Raskolnikov began. "This is how I would change the notes: I'd count the first thousand three or four times backwards and forwards, look at every note and then start on the second thousand; I'd count that halfway through and then hold some fifty ruble note to the light, then turn it, then hold it to the light again—to see whether it was a good one. 'I'm afraid,' I would say. 'A relation of mine lost twenty-five rubles the other day because of a false note,' and then I'd tell them the whole story. And after I began counting the third, 'no, excuse me,' I would say, 'I think I made a mistake in the seventh hundred in that second thousand, I am not sure.' And so I would give up the third thousand and go back to the second and so on to the end. And when I had finished, I'd pick out one from the fifth and one from the second thousand and take them again to the light and ask again 'change them, please,' and put the clerk into such a stew that he would not know how to get rid of me.

When I'd finished and had gone out, I'd come back, 'No, excuse me,' and ask for some explanation. That's how I'd do it."

"Pah, what terrible things you say!" said Zametov, laughing. "But all that is only talk. When it came down to doing it you'd make a slip. I believe that even an experienced, desperate man cannot always count on himself, much less you and I. To take an example closer to home—that old woman who was murdered in our district. The murderer seems to have been a desperate man, he risked everything in open daylight, was saved by a miracle—but his hands shook, too. He didn't manage to rob the place, he couldn't stand it. That was clear from the . . . "

Raskolnikov seemed offended.

"Clear? Why don't you catch him then?" he shouted at Zametov mockingly.

"Well, they will catch him."

"Who? You? Do you think you could catch him? You've got a tough job on your hands! A great point for you is whether someone is spending money or not. If someone has no money and suddenly starts spending, they must be guilty. Any child can mislead you."

"The fact is they always do that, though," answered Zametov. "A man will commit a clever murder, risk his life and then at once go drinking in a tavern. They are caught spending money, they are not all as cunning as you are. You wouldn't go to a tavern, of course?"

Raskolnikov frowned and looked steadily at Zametov.

"You seem to enjoy the subject and would like to know how I would behave in that case, too?" he asked with displeasure.

"I would like to," Zametov answered firmly and seriously. His words and looks were becoming a little too earnest.

"Very much?"

"Very much!"

"All right then. This is how I would behave," Raskolnikov began, again bringing his face close to Zametov's, again staring at him and speaking in a whisper; the latter started shuddering. "This is what I would have done. I would have taken the money and jewels, I would have walked out of there and have gone straight to some deserted place with fences round it and scarcely anyone to be seen, some kitchen garden or place of that sort. I would have found beforehand some stone weighing a hundredweight or more which had been lying in the corner from the time the house was built. I would lift that stone—there would be sure to be a hollow under it, and I would put the jewels and money in that hole. Then I'd roll the stone back so that it would look as before, would press it down with my foot and walk away. And for a year or two, three maybe, I wouldn't touch it. And, well, they could search! There'd be no trace."

"You are a madman," said Zametov, and for some reason he too spoke in a whisper, and moved away from Raskolnikov, whose eyes were glittering. He had turned extremely pale and his upper lip was twitching and quivering. He bent down as close as possible to Zametov, and his lips began to move without uttering a word. This lasted for half a minute; he knew what he was doing, but could not restrain himself. The terrible word trembled on his lips, like the latch on that door; in another moment it will break out, in another moment he will let it go, he will speak out.

"And what if it was I who murdered the old woman and Lizaveta?" he said suddenly and—realized what he had done.

Zametov looked wildly at him and turned white as the tablecloth. His face had a contorted smile on it.

"But is it possible?" he brought out faintly. Raskolnikov looked angrily at him.

"Own up, you believed it, yes, you did?"

"Not at all, I believe it less than ever now," Zametov cried hastily.

"I've caught my sparrow! So you did believe it before, if now you believe it less than ever?"

"Not at all," cried Zametov, obviously embarrassed. "Have you been frightening me to lead up to this?"

"You don't believe it then? What were you talking about behind my back when I went out of the police office? And why did the Explosive Lieutenant question me after I fainted? Hey, there," he shouted to the waiter, getting up and taking his cap, "how much?"

"Thirty kopecks," the latter replied, running up.

"And there is twenty kopecks for vodka. See what a lot of money!" he held out his shaking hand to Zametov with notes in it. "Red notes and blue, twenty-five rubles. Where did I get them? And where did my new clothes come from? You know I hadn't a kopeck. You've cross-examined my landlady, I'll be bound . . . Well, that's that! We've talked enough! Goodbye!"

He went out, trembling all over from a sort of wild hysterical sensation, in which there was an element of unbearable ecstasy. Yet he was gloomy and horribly tired. His face was twisted as if he had just had a fit. His fatigue increased rapidly. Any shock, any irritating sensation stimulated and revived his energies at once, but his strength failed just as quickly when the stimulus was removed.

Zametov, left alone, sat for a long time in the same place, deep in thought. Raskolnikov had unwittingly worked a revolution in his brain on a certain point and had made up his mind for him conclusively.

"Ilia Petrovich is a blockhead," he decided.

Raskolnikov had hardly opened the door of the restaurant when he bumped into Razumikhin on the steps. They did not see each other until they almost knocked against each other. For a moment they stood looking each other up and down. Razumikhin was greatly astounded, then anger, real anger gleamed fiercely in his eyes.

"So here you are!" he shouted at the top of his voice—"you ran away from your bed! And here I've been looking for you under the sofa! We went up to the garret. I almost beat Nastasia because of you. And here he is after all. Rodia! What is the meaning of it? Tell me the whole truth! Confess! Do you hear?"

"It means that I'm sick to death of all of you and I want to be alone," Raskolnikov answered calmly.

"Alone? When you are not able to walk, when your face is as white as a sheet and you are gasping for breath! Idiot! . . . What have you been doing in the Crystal Palace? Tell me now!"

"Let me go!" said Raskolnikov and tried to pass him. This was too much for Razumikhin; he gripped him firmly by the shoulder.

"Let you go? You dare tell me to let you go? Do you know what I'll do with you? I'll pick you up, tie you up in a bundle, carry you home under my arm and lock you up!"

"Listen, Razumikhin," Raskolnikov began quietly, apparently calm, "can't you see that I don't want your benevolence? A strange desire you have to shower benefits on a man who . . . curses them, who feels them to be a burden, in fact! Why did you seek me out at the beginning of my illness? Maybe I was very happy to die. Didn't I tell you plainly enough today that you were torturing me, that I was . . . sick of you! You seem to want to torture people! I assure you that all of this is seriously hindering my recovery, because it's continually irritating me. You saw Zossimov went away just now to avoid irritating me. You leave me alone too, for goodness' sake! What right do you have to keep me by force? Can't you see that I am in possession of all my faculties now? How can I persuade you not to persecute me with your kindness? I may be ungrateful, I may be mean, but just let me be, for God's sake, let me be! Let me be, let me be!"

He began calmly, gloating beforehand over the venomous phrases he was about to utter, but finished, panting for breath, in a frenzy, as he had been with Luzhin.

Razumikhin stood a moment, thought and let his hand drop.

"Well, go to hell then," he said gently and thoughtfully. "Stay here," he roared, as Raskolnikov was about to move. "Listen to me. Let me tell you, that you are all a set of babbling, posing idiots! If you've got any little trouble you brood over it like a hen over an egg. And you are plagiarists even in that! There isn't a sign of independent life in you! You're made of spermaceti ointment and you've got lymph in your veins instead of blood. I don't trust any of you! When anything happens the first thing all of you do is fail to behave like human beings! Stop!" he cried with redoubled fury, noticing that Raskolnikov was again making a movement, "hear me out! You know I'm having a house-warming this evening, I dare say they've arrived by now, but I left my uncle there—I just ran in—to receive the guests. And if you weren't a fool, a common fool, a perfect fool, if you were an original instead of a translation . . . you see, Rodia, I recognize you're a clever fellow, but you're a fool! And if you weren't a fool you'd come round to me this evening instead of wearing out your boots in the street! Since you've gone out, there's no help for it! I'd give you a snug easy chair, my landlady has one . . . a cup of tea, company . . . Or you could lie on the sofa—in any case, you would be with us . . . Zossimov will be there too. Will you come?"

"No."

"R-rubbish!" Razumikhin shouted, his patience lost. "How do you know? You can't answer for yourself! You don't know anything about it . . . Thousands of times I've fought tooth and nail with people and run back to them afterwards . . . You feel ashamed and go back to them! So remember, Potchinkov's house on the third storey . . . "

"Razumikhin, you'd let anybody beat you from sheer benevolence."

"Beat? Whom? Me? I'd twist his nose off at the idea of it! Potchinkov's house, 47, Babushkin's apartment . . . "

"I shan't come, Razumikhin." Raskolnikov turned and walked away.

"I bet you will," Razumikhin shouted after him. "I refuse to know you if you don't! Stop, hey, is Zametov in there?"

"Yes."

"Did you see him?"

"Yes."

"Talked to him?"

"Yes."

"What about? Damn you, don't tell me then. Potchinkov's house, 47, Babushkin's apartment, remember!"

Raskolnikov walked on and turned the corner into Sadovy Street. Razumikhin looked after him thoughtfully. Then with a wave of his hand he went into the house but stopped short of the stairs.

"Damn it," he went on almost aloud. "He talked sensibly but yet . . . I am a fool! As if madmen didn't talk sensibly! And this was just what Zossimov seemed afraid of." He struck his finger on his forehead. "What if . . . how could I let him go off alone? He may drown himself . . . Ah, what a blunder! I can't." And he ran back to overtake Raskolnikov, but there was no trace of him. With a curse he returned swiftly to the Crystal Palace to question Zametov.

Raskolnikov walked straight to X____ Bridge, stood in the middle and, leaning both elbows on the rail, stared into the distance. On parting with Razumikhin, he felt so much weaker that he could scarcely reach it. He longed to sit or lie down somewhere in the street. Bending over the water, he gazed mechanically at the last pink flush of the sunset, at the row of houses growing dark in the gathering twilight, at one distant attic window on the left bank, flashing as though on fire in the last rays of the setting sun, at the darkening water of the canal, and the water seemed to catch his attention. At last red circles flashed before his eyes, the houses seemed to be moving, the passersby, the canal banks, the carriages all danced before his eyes. Suddenly he started, saved again perhaps from fainting by an uncanny and hideous sight. He became aware of someone standing to his right; he looked and saw a tall woman with a kerchief on her head, with a long, yellow, wasted face and red sunken eyes. She was looking straight at him, but she obviously saw nothing and recognized no-one. Suddenly she leaned her right hand on the parapet, lifted her right leg over the railing, then her left and threw herself into the canal. The filthy water parted and swallowed up its victim for a moment, but an instant later the drowning woman floated to the surface, moving slowly with the current, her head and legs in the water, her skirt billowing like a balloon over her back.

"A woman drowning! A woman drowning!" shouted dozens of voices; people ran up, both banks were thronged with spectators, on the bridge people crowded around Raskolnikov, pressing up behind him.

"Mercy! It's our Afrosinia!" a woman cried tearfully close by. "Mercy! Save her! Good people, pull her out!"

"A boat, a boat" was shouted in the crowd. But there was no need of a boat; a policeman ran down the steps to the canal, threw off his overcoat and his boots and rushed into the water. It was easy to reach her; she floated within a couple of yards of the steps, he caught hold of her clothes with his right hand and with his left seized a pole which a comrade held out to him; the drowning woman was pulled out at once. They laid her on the granite pavement of the embankment. She soon recovered consciousness, raised her head, sat up and began sneezing and coughing, stupidly wiping her wet dress with her hands. She said nothing.

"She's drunk out of her senses," the same woman's voice wailed at her side. "Out of her senses. The other day she tried to hang herself, we cut her down. I ran out to the store just now, left my little girl to look after her—and here she is, in trouble again! A neighbor, we live close by, the second house from the end, over there . . . "

The crowd broke up. The police still remained around the woman, someone mentioned the police station . . . Raskolnikov looked on with a strange sensation of indifference and apathy. He felt disgusted. "No, that's loathsome . . . water . . . it's not good enough," he muttered to himself. "Nothing will come of it," he added, "no use to wait. What about the police office . . . ? And why isn't Zametov at the police office? The police office is open until ten o'clock . . . " He turned his back to the railing and looked about him.

"Very well then!" he said resolutely; he moved from the bridge and walked in the direction of the police office. His heart felt hollow and empty. He did not want to think. Even his depression had passed, there was not a trace now of the energy with which he had set out "to make an end of it all." Complete apathy had succeeded it.

"Well, it's a way out of it," he thought, walking slowly and listlessly along the canal bank. "Anyway I'll put an end to it, because I want to . . . But is it a way out? What does it matter! There'll be the square yard of space—ha! But what an end! Is it really the end? Shall I tell them or not? Ah . . . damn! How tired I am! If I could find somewhere to sit or lie down soon! What I am most ashamed of is the fact that it's so stupid. But I don't care about that either! What idiotic ideas come into my head."

To reach the police office he had to go straight forward and take the second turning to the left. It was only a few yards away. But at the first turning he stopped and, after a minute's thought, turned into a side street and went two streets out of his way, possibly without any purpose, or possibly to delay a minute and gain time. He walked, looking at the ground; suddenly someone seemed to whisper in his ear. He lifted his head and saw that he was standing at the gate of the house. He had not passed it, he had not been near it since that evening. An overwhelming inexplicable prompting drew him on. He went into the house, passed through the gateway, then into the first entrance on the right, and began mounting the familiar staircase to the fourth floor. The narrow, steep stairway was very dark. He stopped at each landing and looked round him with curiosity; on the first landing the framework of the window had been taken out. "That wasn't how it was then," he thought. Here was the apartment on the second floor where Nikolai and Dmitri had been working. "It's shut up and the door's newly painted. So they're going to rent it." Then the third floor and the fourth. "Here!" He was perplexed to find the door of the apartment wide open. There were men there, he could hear voices; he had not expected that. After brief hesitation he mounted the last stairs and went into the apartment. It, too, was being done up; there were workmen in it. This seemed to amaze him; he somehow thought he would find everything as he left it, even perhaps the corpses in the same place on the floor. And now, bare walls, no furniture; it seemed strange. He walked to the window and sat down on the window sill. There were two workmen, both young men, but one much younger than the other. They were papering the walls with a new white paper covered with lilac flowers, instead of the dirty old yellow one. Raskolnikov for some reason felt horribly annoyed by this. He looked at the new paper with dislike, as though he felt sorry to have it all changed. The workmen had obviously stayed beyond their time and now they were hurriedly rolling up their paper and getting ready to go home. They took no notice of Raskolnikov; they were talking. Raskolnikov folded his arms and listened.

"She came to me in the morning," said the elder to the younger, "very early, all dressed up. 'Why are you preening yourself?' I said. 'I'm ready to do anything to please you, Tit Vassilich!' That's one way of going about it! She was dressed up like a real fashion book!"

"What's a fashion book?" the younger one asked. He obviously regarded the other as an authority.

"A fashion book is a lot of pictures, colored, and they come to the tailors here every Saturday, by post from abroad, to show people how to dress, men as well as women. They're pictures. The men are usually wearing fur coats and as for the ladies' fluffy stuff, they're beyond anything you can imagine."

"There's nothing you can't find in Petersburg," the younger cried enthusiastically, "except father and mother, there's everything!"

"Except them, there's everything to be found, my friend," the elder declared pompously.

Raskolnikov got up and walked into the other room where the strong box, the bed, and the chest of drawers had been; the room seemed to him very tiny without furniture in it. The paper was the same; the paper in the corner showed where the case of icons had stood. He looked at it and went to the window. The elder workman looked at him sideways.

"What do you want?" he asked suddenly.

Instead of answering Raskolnikov went into the passage and pulled the bell. The same bell, the same cracked note. He rang it a second and a third time; he listened and remembered. The hideous and agonizingly fearful sensation he had felt then began to come back more and more vividly. He shuddered at every ring and it gave him more and more satisfaction.

"Well, what do you want? Who are you?" the workman shouted, going out to him. Raskolnikov went inside again.

"I want to rent an apartment," he said. "I am looking round."

"Night's not the time to look at the rooms! You ought to come up with the porter."

"The floors have been washed, will they be painted?" Raskolnikov went on. "Is there no blood?"

"What blood?"

"The old woman and her sister were murdered here. There was a real pool there."

"But who are you?" the workman cried, uneasy.

"Who am I?"

"Yes."

"You want to know? Come to the police station, I'll tell you."

The workmen looked at him in amazement.

"It's time for us to go, we are late. Come on, Alyoshka. We've got to lock up," said the elder workman.

"Very well then, come along," said Raskolnikov indifferently, and going out first, he went slowly downstairs. "Hey, porter," he cried in the gateway.

At the entrance several people were standing, staring at the passersby; the two porters, a peasant woman, a man in a long coat and a few others. Raskolnikov went straight up to them.

"What do you want?" asked one of the porters.

"Have you been to the police office?"

"I've just been there. What do you want?"

"Is it open?"

"Of course."

"Is the assistant there?"

"He was there for a while. What do you want?"

Raskolnikov made no reply, but stood beside them lost in thought.

"He's been to look at the apartment," said the elder workman, coming forward.

"Which apartment?"

"Where we're at work. 'Why have you washed away the blood?' he says. 'There has been a murder here,' he says, 'and I've come to take it.' And he began ringing at the bell, all but broke it. 'Come to the police station,' says he. 'I'll tell you everything there.' He wouldn't leave us."

The porter looked at Raskolnikov, frowning and perplexed.

"Who are you?" he shouted as impressively as he could.

"I am Rodion Romanovich Raskolnikov, a former student, I live in Shil's house, not far from here, apartment Number 14, ask the porter, he knows me." Raskolnikov said all this in a lazy, dreamy voice, not turning round, but looking intently into the darkening street.

"Why have you been to the apartment?"

"To look at it."

"What is there to look at?"

"Take him straight to the police station," the man in the long coat jerked in abruptly.

Raskolnikov looked intently at him over his shoulder and said in the same slow, lazy tone, "Come along."

"Yes, take him," the man went on more confidently. "Why was he going into that, what's in his mind?"

"He's not drunk, but God knows what's the matter with him," muttered the workman.

"But what do you want?" the porter shouted again, beginning to get angry in earnest. "Why are you hanging about?"

"Are you afraid of the police station then?" said Raskolnikov jeeringly.

"What do you mean, afraid of it? Why are you hanging around?"

"He's a rogue!" shouted the peasant woman.

"Why waste time talking to him?" cried the other porter, a huge peasant in a full open coat with keys on his belt. "Get out of here! He's causing trouble. Get out of here!"

And seizing Raskolnikov by the shoulder he flung him into the street. He lurched forward, but recovered his footing, looked at the spectators in silence and walked away.

"He's strange!" observed the workman.

"There are strange people about nowadays," said the woman.

"All the same, you should have taken him to the police station," said the man in the long coat.

"Better have nothing to do with him," decided the big porter. "A real troublemaker! Just what he wants, but once you take him up, you won't get rid of him . . . We know the sort!"

"Shall I go there or not?" thought Raskolnikov, standing in the middle of the crossroads, and he looked around him, as though expecting a decisive word from someone. But no sound came, everything was dead and silent like the stones on which he walked, dead to him, to him alone . . . All at once at the end of the street, two hundred yards away, in the gathering dusk, he saw a crowd and heard people talking and shouting. In the middle of the crowd stood a carriage . . . A light gleamed in the middle of the street. "What is it?" Raskolnikov turned to the right and went up to the crowd. He seemed to clutch at everything and smiled coldly when he recognized it. He had decided to go to the police station; soon, it would be over.

CHAPTER SEVEN

AN ELEGANT CARRIAGE STOOD in the middle of the road with a pair of hot gray horses; there was no-one in it, and the coachman had got off his box and was standing nearby; the horses were being held by the bridle . . . A mass of people had gathered round, with policemen standing in front of them. One of them held a lighted lantern which he was turning on something lying close to the wheels. Everyone was talking, shouting, exclaiming; the coachman seemed to be at a loss and kept repeating:

"What a misfortune! Lord, what a misfortune!"

Raskolnikov pushed his way in as far as he could, and succeeded at last in seeing the object of the commotion and interest. On the ground a man who had been run over lay apparently unconscious and covered in blood; he was very badly dressed, but not like a workman. Blood was flowing from his head and face; his face was crushed, mutilated and disfigured. He was evidently badly injured.

"Lord have mercy!" wailed the coachman, "what more could I do? If I'd been driving fast or if I hadn't shouted to him—but I was going quietly, I wasn't hurrying! Everybody could see I was going along just like everybody else. People who are drunk can't walk straight, we all know that . . . I saw him crossing the street, staggering and falling almost. I shouted again and a second and a third time, then I held the horses in, but he fell straight under their feet! Either he did it on purpose or he was very drunk . . . The horses are young and take fright pretty easily . . . they started, he screamed . . . that made them worse. That's how it happened!"

"That's just how it was," a voice in the crowd confirmed.

"He shouted, that's true, he shouted three times," another voice declared.

"Three times it was, we all heard it," shouted a third.

But the coachman was not very distressed and frightened. It was evident that the carriage belonged to a rich and important person who was waiting for it somewhere; the police, of course, were anxious to avoid upsetting his arrangements. All they had to do was to take the injured man to the police station and the hospital. No-one knew his name.

Meanwhile Raskolnikov had squeezed in and stooped closer over him. The lantern suddenly lit up the unfortunate man's face. He recognized him.

"I know him! I know him!" he shouted, pushing to the front. "It's a government clerk retired from the service, Marmeladov. He lives close by in Kozel's house . . . Hurry up and get a doctor! I will pay, look." He pulled money out of his pocket and showed it to the policeman. He was violently excited.

The police were glad that they had found out who the man was. Raskolnikov gave his own name and address, and, as earnestly as if it had been his father, he asked the police to carry the unconscious Marmeladov to his apartment at once.

"Just here, three houses away," he said eagerly, "the house belongs to Kozel, a rich German. He was going home, no doubt drunk. I know him, he is a drunkard. He has a family there, a wife, children, he has one daughter . . . It will take time to take him to the hospital, and there is sure to be a doctor in the house. I'll pay, I'll pay! At least he will be looked after at home . . . they will help him at once. But he'll die before you get him to the hospital." He managed to slip something unseen into the policeman's hand. But the thing was straightforward and legitimate, and in any case help was closer here. They lifted the injured man; people volunteered to help.

Kozel's house was thirty yards away. Raskolnikov walked behind, carefully holding Marmeladov's head and showing the way.

"This way, this way! We must take him upstairs head first. Turn round! I'll pay, I'll make it worth your while," he muttered.

Katerina Ivanovna had just begun to walk to and fro in her little room from the window to the stove and back again, with her arms folded across her chest, talking to herself and coughing; she used to do this whenever she had a moment to spare. Recently she had begun to talk more than ever to her eldest girl, Polenka, a child of ten, who, though there was much she did not understand, understood very well that her mother needed her, and so always watched her with her big clever eyes and did her utmost to appear to understand. This time Polenka was undressing her little brother, who had been unwell all day and was going to bed. The boy was waiting for her to take off his shirt, which had to be washed at night. He was sitting straight and motionless on a chair, with a silent, serious face, with his legs stretched out straight before him, heels together and toes turned out.

He was listening to what his mother was saying to his sister, sitting perfectly still with pouting lips and wide-open eyes, just like all good little boys have to sit when they are undressed to go to bed. A little girl, even younger, dressed literally in rags, stood at the screen, waiting for her turn. The door on to the stairs was open to relieve them a little from the clouds of tobacco smoke which floated in from the other rooms and brought on long terrible fits of coughing in the poor, tubercular woman. Katerina Ivanovna seemed to have grown even thinner during that week and the hectic flush on her face was brighter than ever.

"You wouldn't believe, you can't imagine, Polenka," she said, walking about the room, "what a happy luxurious life we had in my papa's house and how this drunkard has brought me, and will bring you all, to ruin! Father was a civil colonel and only a step from being a governor; everyone who came to see him said, 'We look upon you, Ivan Mikhailovich, as our governor!' When I . . . when . . . " she coughed violently, "oh, cursed life," she cried, clearing her throat and pressing her hands to her breast, "when I . . . when at the last ball . . . at the marshal's . . . Princess Bezzemelny saw me—she was the one who gave me the blessing when your father and I were married, Polenka—she asked at once, 'Isn't that the pretty girl who did the shawl dance at the end?' (You must mend that tear, you must take your needle and darn it as I showed you, or tomorrow—cough,

cough, cough—he will make the hole bigger," she articulated with
effort.) "Prince Shchegolskoy, a kammerjunker, had just come from
Petersburg then . . . he danced the mazurka with me and wanted to
make me an offer next day; but I thanked him in flattering expressions and told him that my heart had long been another's. That other
was your father, Polia; Father was extremely angry . . . Is the water
ready? Give me the shirt, and the stockings! Lida," she said to the
youngest one, "you must manage without your shirt tonight . . . and
lay your stockings out with it . . . I'll wash them together . . . How
come that drunken vagabond hasn't come back yet? He's worn his
shirt so much it looks like a dishcloth, he's torn it to rags! I'd do it all
together, so I don't have to work two nights running! Oh, God!
(Cough, cough, cough, cough!) Again! What's this?" she cried, noticing a crowd in the passage and the men who were pushing into her
room, carrying a burden. "What is it? What are they bringing? Lord
have mercy!"

"Where should we put him?" asked the policeman, looking
round when Marmeladov, unconscious and covered with blood, had
been carried in.

"On the sofa! Put him straight on the sofa, with his head this
way," Raskolnikov showed him.

"Run over in the road! Drunk!" someone shouted in the passage.

Katerina Ivanovna stood, turning white and gasping for breath.
The children were terrified. Little Lida screamed, rushed to Polenka
and clutched at her, trembling all over.

Having laid Marmeladov down, Raskolnikov flew to Katerina
Ivanovna.

"For God's sake be calm, don't be frightened!" he said, speaking
quickly, "he was crossing the road and was run over by a carriage,
don't be frightened, he will come to, I told them to bring him
here . . . I've been here already, you remember? He will come to; I'll
pay!"

"He's done it this time!" Katerina Ivanovna cried despairingly
and she rushed to her husband.

Raskolnikov noticed at once that she was not one of those
women who swoon easily. She instantly placed a pillow under the
luckless man's head, which no-one had thought of, and began undressing and examining him. She kept her head, forgetting herself,

biting her trembling lips and stifling the screams which were ready to break from her.

Raskolnikov meanwhile induced someone to run for a doctor. There was a doctor, it appeared, next door but one.

"I've sent for a doctor," he kept assuring Katerina Ivanovna, "don't worry, I'll pay. Haven't you got any water? . . . and give me a napkin or a towel, anything, as quick as you can . . . He is injured, but not killed, believe me . . . We'll see what the doctor says!"

Katerina Ivanovna ran to the window; there, on a broken chair in the corner, a large earthenware basin full of water had been standing, ready for her to wash her children's and her husband's clothing that night. Katerina Ivanovna did the washing at night at least twice a week, if not more frequently than that. The family had sunk so low that they had practically no change of clothes, and Katerina Ivanovna could not stand this absence of cleanliness and, rather than see dirt in the house, she preferred to wear herself out at night, working beyond her strength when the rest were asleep, so as to get the wet clothes hung on a line and dry by the morning. She took up the basin of water at Raskolnikov's request, but almost fell down with her burden. But the latter had already succeeded in finding a towel, wetted it and begun washing the blood off Marmeladov's face.

Katerina Ivanovna stood by, breathing painfully and pressing her hands to her chest. She was in need of attention herself. Raskolnikov began to realize that he might have made a mistake in having the injured man brought here. The policeman, too, stood there in hesitation.

"Polenka," cried Katerina Ivanovna, "run to Sonia's, hurry. If you don't find her at home, tell her that her father has been run over and that she must come here at once . . . when she comes in. Run, Polenka! There, put on the shawl."

"Run your fastest!" cried the little boy on the chair suddenly, after which he relapsed into the same dumb rigidity, with round eyes, his heels thrust forward and his toes spread out.

Meanwhile the room had become so full of people that you could not have dropped a pin. The policemen left, all except one, who remained for a while, trying to drive out the people who came in from the stairs. Almost all Madame Lippewechsel's lodgers had streamed in from the inner rooms of the apartment; at first they were squeezed together in the doorway, but afterwards they overflowed into the room. Katerina Ivanovna flew into a fury.

"You might let him die in peace, at least," she shouted at the crowd, "is it a spectacle for you to gape at? With cigarettes! (Cough, cough, cough!) You might as well keep your hats on . . . And there is one in his hat! . . . Get away! You should respect the dead, at least!"

Her cough choked her—but her reproaches were not entirely fruitless. They evidently stood in some awe of Katerina Ivanovna. The lodgers, one after another, squeezed back into the doorway with that strange inner feeling of satisfaction which may be observed during a sudden accident, even in those nearest and dearest to the victim, from which no-one alive is exempt, even despite the sincerest sympathy and compassion.

Voices outside were heard, however, talking about the hospital and saying that they'd no business to make a disturbance here.

"No business to die!" cried Katerina Ivanovna, and she was rushing to the door to vent her wrath upon them, but in the doorway came face to face with Madame Lippewechsel who had only just heard of the accident and ran in to restore order. She was a particularly argumentative and irresponsible German.

"Ah, my God!" she cried, clasping her hands, "your husband drunken horses have trampled! To the hospital with him! I am the landlady!"

"Amalia Ludwigovna, please think about what you are saying," Katerina Ivanovna began in a superior tone of voice (she always adopted a superior tone with the landlady so that the landlady might "remember her place in society". Even now, she could not deny herself this satisfaction). "Amalia Ludwigovna . . . "

"I have you once before told that you to call me Amalia Ludwigovna may not dare; I am Amalia Ivanovna."

"You are not Amalia Ivanovna, you are Amalia Ludwigovna, and since I am not one of your despicable flatterers like Mr. Lebeziatnikov, who's laughing behind the door at the moment" (a laugh and a shout of "they're at it again" was in fact audible at the door), "I shall always call you Amalia Ludwigovna, though I fail to understand why you dislike that name. You can see for yourself what has happened to Semion Zakharovich; he is dying. I beg you to close that door at once and let no-one in. Let him at least die in peace! Or I warn you the

Governor-General himself shall be informed of your conduct tomorrow. The prince knew me as a girl; he remembers Semion Zakharovich well and has often given him generous donations. Everyone knows that Semion Zakharovich had many friends and protectors, whom he abandoned himself from an honorable pride, knowing his unfortunate weakness, but now" (she pointed to Raskolnikov) "a generous young man has come to our assistance, who has wealth and connections and whom Semion Zakharovich has known since he was a child. You may rest assured, Amalia Ludwigovna . . . "

All this was uttered with extreme rapidity, getting quicker and quicker, but a cough suddenly cut short Katerina Ivanovna's eloquence. At that instant the dying man recovered consciousness and uttered a groan; she ran to him. The injured man opened his eyes and without recognition or understanding gazed at Raskolnikov who was bending over him. He drew deep, slow, painful breaths; blood oozed at the corners of his mouth and drops of perspiration came out on his forehead. Not recognizing Raskolnikov, he began looking round uneasily. Katerina Ivanovna looked at him with a sad but stern face, and tears trickled from her eyes.

"My God! His whole chest is crushed! How he is bleeding," she said in despair. "We must take off his clothes. Turn a little, Semion Zakharovich, if you can," she shouted to him.

Marmeladov recognized her.

"A priest," he articulated huskily.

Katerina Ivanovna walked to the window, laid her head against the window frame and exclaimed in despair:

"Oh, wretched life!"

"A priest," the dying man said again after a moment's silence.

"They've gone for him," Katerina Ivanovna shouted to him; he obeyed her and fell silent. With sad and timid eyes he looked for her; she returned and stood by his pillow. He seemed a little more eased, but not for long.

Soon his eyes rested on little Lida, his favorite, who was shaking in the corner as though she were in a fit and staring at him with her wondering childish eyes.

"A-ah," he signed towards her uneasily. He wanted to say something.

"What now?" shouted Katerina Ivanovna.

"Barefoot, barefoot!" he muttered, indicating with frenzied eyes the child's bare feet.

"Be quiet," Katerina Ivanovna shouted irritably, "you know why she is barefoot."

"Thank God, the doctor," exclaimed Raskolnikov, relieved.

The doctor came in, a precise little old man, a German, looking about him mistrustfully; he went up to the sick man, took his pulse, carefully felt his head and with the help of Katerina Ivanovna he unbuttoned the blood-stained shirt, and bared the injured man's chest. It was gashed, crushed and fractured, several ribs on the right side were broken. On the left side, just over the heart, was a large, sinister-looking yellowish-black bruise—a cruel kick from the horse's hoof. The doctor frowned. The policeman told him that he was caught in the wheel and turned round with it for thirty yards on the road.

"It's wonderful that he has recovered consciousness," the doctor whispered softly to Raskolnikov.

"What do you think?" he asked.

"He will die immediately."

"Is there really no hope?"

"Not even the slightest! He is at the last gasp . . . His head is badly injured, too . . . Hm . . . I could bleed him if you like, but . . . it would be useless. He is bound to die within the next five or ten minutes."

"Better bleed him then."

"If you like . . . But I warn you it will be perfectly useless."

At that moment other steps were heard; the crowd in the passage parted, and the priest, a little, gray old man, appeared in the doorway bearing the sacrament. A policeman had gone to look for him at the time of the accident. The doctor changed places with him, exchanging glances with him. Raskolnikov begged the doctor to remain a little while. He shrugged his shoulders and remained.

Everyone stepped back. The confession was soon over. The dying man probably understood little; he could only utter indistinct broken sounds. Katerina Ivanovna took little Lida, lifted the boy from the chair, knelt down in the corner by the stove and made the children kneel in front of her. The little girl was still trembling; but the boy, kneeling on his little bare knees, lifted his hand rhythmically, crossing himself with precision and bowed down, touching the floor with his forehead, which seemed to afford him special satisfaction. Katerina Ivanovna bit her lips and held back her tears; she prayed, too, pulling the boy's shirt straight now and then, and managed to cover the girl's bare shoulders with a kerchief, which she took from the chest without rising from her knees or ceasing to pray. Meanwhile the door from the inner rooms was opened inquisitively again. In the passage the crowd of spectators from all the apartments on the staircase grew denser and denser, but they did not venture beyond the threshold. A single candle-end lit up the scene.

At that moment Polenka forced her way through the crowd at the door. She came in panting from running so fast, took off her kerchief, looked for her mother, went up to her and said, "She's coming, I met her in the street." Her mother made her kneel beside her.

Timidly and noiselessly a young girl made her way through the crowd, and her appearance in that room was strange, in the midst of want, rags, death and despair. She too was in rags, her clothing was all made of the cheapest material, but decked out in gutter finery of a special kind, unmistakably betraying its shameful purpose. Sonia stopped short in the doorway and looked about her bewildered, unconscious of everything. She forgot her fourth-hand, gaudy silk dress, so unseemly here with its ridiculous long train, and her immense crinoline that filled up the whole doorway, and her light-colored shoes, and the parasol she brought with her, though it was no use at night, and the absurd round straw hat with its flaring flame-colored feather. Under this flirtatiously tilted hat was a pale, frightened little face with lips parted and eyes staring in terror. Sonia was a small thin girl of eighteen with fair hair, rather pretty, with wonderful blue eyes. She looked intently at the bed and the priest; she too was out of breath from running. At last whispers, some words in the crowd probably, reached her. She looked down and took a step forward into the room, still keeping close to the door.

The service was over. Katerina Ivanovna went up to her husband again. The priest stepped back and turned to say a few words of advice and consolation to Katerina Ivanovna as he was leaving.

"What am I to do with these?" she interrupted sharply and irritably, pointing to the little ones.

"God is merciful; look for help to the Most High," the priest began.

"Ah! He is merciful, but not to us."

"That's a sin, a sin, madam," observed the priest, shaking his head.

"And isn't that a sin?" cried Katerina Ivanovna, pointing to the dying man.

"Perhaps those who have involuntarily caused the accident will agree to compensate you, at least for the loss of his earnings."

"You don't understand!" cried Katerina Ivanovna angrily waving her hand. "And why should they compensate me? Why, he was drunk and threw himself under the horses! What earnings? He brought us in nothing but misery. He drank everything away, the drunkard! He robbed us to get drink, he wasted their lives and mine for drink! And thank God he's dying! One less to keep!"

"You must forgive in the hour of death, that's a sin, madam, such feelings are a great sin."

Katerina Ivanovna was busy with the dying man; she was giving him water, wiping the blood and sweat from his head, setting his pillow straight, and had only turned now and then for a moment to address the priest. Now she flew at him almost in a frenzy.

"Ah, Father! That's words and only words! Forgive! If he'd not been run over, he'd have come home today drunk and his only shirt dirty and in rags and he'd have fallen asleep like a log, and I would have been drenching and rinsing until dawn, washing his rags and the children's and then drying them by the window and as soon as it was daylight I would have been darning them. That's how I spend my nights! . . . What's the use of talking of forgiveness! I have forgiven enough as it is!"

A terrible hollow cough interrupted her words. She put her handkerchief to her lips and showed it to the priest, pressing her other hand to her aching chest. The handkerchief was covered with blood. The priest bowed his head and said nothing.

Marmeladov was in the middle of the final agony; he did not take his eyes off the face of Katerina Ivanovna, who was bending over him again. He kept trying to say something to her; he began moving his tongue with difficulty and articulating indistinctly, but Katerina Ivanovna, understanding that he wanted to ask her forgiveness, called peremptorily to him:

"Be silent! No need! I know what you want to say!" And the sick man was silent, but at the same instant his wandering eyes strayed to the doorway and he saw Sonia.

Until then he had not noticed her: she was standing in the shadow in a corner.

"Who's that? Who's that?" he said suddenly in a thick gasping voice, in agitation, turning his eyes in horror towards the door where his daughter was standing, and trying to sit up.

"Lie down! Lie do-own!" cried Katerina Ivanovna.

With unnatural strength he had succeeded in propping himself on his elbow. He looked wildly and fixedly for some time on his daughter, as though he did not realize her. He had never seen her dressed like that before. Suddenly he recognized her, crushed and ashamed in her humiliation and gaudy clothes, meekly awaiting her turn to say goodbye to her dying father. His face showed intense suffering.

"Sonia! Daughter! Forgive me!" he cried, and he tried to hold out his hand to her, but losing his balance, he fell off the sofa, face downwards on the floor. They rushed to pick him up, they put him on the sofa; but he was dying. Sonia with a faint cry ran up, embraced him and stayed there motionless. He died in her arms.

"He's got what he wanted," Katerina Ivanovna cried, seeing her husband's dead body. "Well, what's to be done now? How am I to bury him! What can I give them tomorrow to eat?"

Raskolnikov went up to Katerina Ivanovna.

"Katerina Ivanovna," he began, "last week your husband told me about his entire life and circumstances . . . Believe me, he spoke about you passionately and with the deepest of respect. From that evening, when I learnt how devoted he was to you all and how he loved and respected you especially, Katerina Ivanovna, in spite of his unfortunate weakness, from that evening we became friends . . . Allow me now . . . to do something . . . to repay my debt to my dead friend. Here are twenty rubles I think—and if that can be of any assistance to you, then . . . I . . . in short, I will come again, I will be sure to come again . . . I shall, perhaps, come again tomorrow . . . Goodbye!"

And he went quickly out of the room, squeezing his way through the crowd to the stairs. But in the crowd he suddenly jostled against Nikodim Fomich, who had heard of the accident and had come to give instructions in person. They had not met since the scene at the police station, but Nikodim Fomich knew him instantly.

"Ah, is that you?" he asked him.

"He's dead," answered Raskolnikov. "The doctor and the priest have been, all as it should have been. Don't worry the poor lady too much, she is tubercular as it is. Try and cheer her up, if possible . . . you are a kind-hearted man, I know . . . " he added with a smile, looking straight in his face.

"But you are spattered with blood," observed Nikodim Fomich, noticing in the lamplight some fresh stains on Raskolnikov's waistcoat.

"Yes . . . I'm covered with blood," Raskolnikov said with a peculiar air; then he smiled, nodded and went downstairs.

He walked down slowly and deliberately, feverish but not conscious of it, entirely absorbed in a new overwhelming sensation of life and strength that surged up suddenly within him. This sensation might be compared to that of a man condemned to death who has suddenly been pardoned. Halfway down the staircase he was overtaken by the priest on his way home; Raskolnikov let him pass, exchanging a silent greeting with him. He was just descending the last steps when he heard rapid footsteps behind him. Someone overtook him; it was Polenka. She was running after him, calling "Wait! Wait!"

He turned round. She was at the bottom of the staircase and stopped short a step above him. A dim light came in from the yard. Raskolnikov could distinguish the child's thin but pretty little face, looking at him with a bright childish smile. She had run after him with a message which she was evidently glad to give.

"Tell me, what is your name? . . . Where do you live?" she said hurriedly in a breathless voice.

He laid both hands on her shoulders and looked at her in a sort of ecstasy. It was such a joy to him to look at her, he could not have said why.

"Who sent you?"

"My sister Sonia sent me," answered the girl, smiling still more brightly.

"I knew it was your sister Sonia who sent you."

"Mother sent me, too . . . when Sonia was sending me, Mother came up, too, and said 'Run fast, Polenka.' "

"Do you love Sonia?"

"I love her more than anyone," Polenka answered with a peculiar earnestness, and her smile became graver.

"And will you love me?"

By way of answer he saw the little girl's face approaching him, her full lips naively held out to kiss him. Suddenly her arms as thin as sticks held him tightly, her head rested on his shoulder and the little girl wept softly, pressing her face against him.

"I am sorry for Father," she said a moment later, raising her tear-stained face and brushing away the tears with her hands. "It's nothing but unhappiness now," she added suddenly with that peculiarly sedate air which children try hard to assume when they want to speak like adults.

"Did your father love you?"

"He loved Lida the most," she went on very seriously without a smile, exactly like an adult, "he loved her because she is little and because she is sick, too. And he always used to bring her presents. But he taught us to read and me grammar and scripture, too," she added with dignity. "And Mother never used to say anything, but we knew that she liked it and father knew it, too. And Mother wants to teach me French, because it's time I started on my education."

"And do you know your prayers?"

"Of course we do! We knew them long ago. I say my prayers to myself because I am a big girl now, but Kolia and Lida say them aloud with Mother. First they repeat the 'Ave Maria' and then another prayer: 'Lord, forgive and bless our sister Sonia,' and then another, 'Lord, forgive and bless our second father.' Our elder father is dead and this is another one, but we do pray for the other as well."

"Polenka, my name is Rodion. Pray for me sometimes, too. 'And Thy servant Rodion,' nothing more."

"I'll pray for you all the rest of my life," the little girl declared hotly, and suddenly smiling again she rushed at him and hugged him warmly once more.

Raskolnikov told her his name and address and promised to be sure to come next day. The child went away quite enchanted with him. It was past ten when he came out into the street. In five minutes he was standing on the bridge at the spot where the woman had jumped in.

"Enough," he pronounced resolutely and triumphantly. "I've

done with imaginary terrors and phantoms! Life is real! Haven't I lived just now? My life has not yet died with that old woman! The Kingdom of Heaven to her—and now leave me in peace! Now for the reign of reason and light . . . and of will, and of strength . . . and now we will see! We will try our strength!" he added defiantly, as though challenging some power of darkness. "And I was ready to consent to live in a square of space!

"I am very weak at this moment, but . . . I believe my illness is all over. I knew it would be over when I went out. By the way, Potchinkov's house is only a few steps away. I certainly must go to Razumikhin's even if it were not close by . . . let him win his bet! Let us give him some satisfaction, too—no matter! Strength, strength is what you need, you can get nothing without it, and strength must be won by strength: that's what they don't know," he added proudly and self-confidently as he walked with flagging footsteps from the bridge. Pride and self-confidence grew continually stronger in him; he was becoming a different man every minute. What had worked this revolution inside him? He did not know himself; like a man clutching at straws, he suddenly felt that he, too, "could live, that there was still life for him, that his life had not died with the old woman." Perhaps he hurried his conclusion too much, but he did not think of that.

"But I did ask her to remember 'Thy servant Rodion' in her prayers," the idea struck him. "Well, that was . . . in case of emergency," he added and laughed himself at his boyish sally. He was in the best of spirits.

He easily found Razumikhin; the new lodger was already known at Potchinkov's and the porter at once showed him the way. Halfway upstairs he could hear the noise and animated conversation of a big gathering of people. The door was wide open on the stairs; he could hear exclamations and discussion. Razumikhin's room was fairly large; the company consisted of fifteen people. Raskolnikov stopped in the entry, where two of the landlady's servants were busy behind a screen with two samovars, bottles, plates and dishes of pie and savories brought up from the landlady's kitchen. Raskolnikov sent in for Razumikhin. He ran out delighted. At first glance it was apparent that he had had a great deal to drink and, though no amount of liquor could make Razumikhin drunk, this time he was noticeably affected by it.

"Listen," Raskolnikov said quickly, "I've only just come to tell you you've won your bet and that no-one really knows what may happen to him. I can't come in; I am so weak that I shall fall down immediately. And so good evening and goodbye! Come and see me tomorrow."

"Do you know what? I'll see you home. If you say you're weak yourself, you must . . . "

"And your visitors? Who is the curly-headed one who has just peeped out?"

"Him? Goodness only knows! Some friend of my uncle's, I expect, or perhaps he has come without being invited . . . I'll leave uncle with them, he is an invaluable person, pity I can't introduce you to him now. But confound them all now! They won't notice me, and I need a little fresh air, because you've come just in the nick of time—another two minutes and I would have come to blows! They are talking such a lot of wild stuff . . . you simply can't imagine what people will say! Though why shouldn't you imagine? Don't we talk nonsense ourselves? And let them . . . that's the way to learn not to! . . . Wait a minute, I'll fetch Zossimov."

Zossimov pounced upon Raskolnikov almost greedily; he showed a special interest in him. Soon his face brightened.

"You must go to bed at once," he pronounced, examining the patient as far as he could, "and take something for the night. Will you take it? I got it ready some time ago . . . a powder."

"Two, if you like," answered Raskolnikov. The powder was taken at once.

"It's a good thing you are taking him home," observed Zossimov to Razumikhin. "We shall see how he is tomorrow, today he's not at all bad—a considerable change since the afternoon. Live and learn . . . "

"Do you know what Zossimov whispered to me when we were coming out?" Razumikhin blurted out, as soon as they were in the street. "I won't tell you everything, my friend, because they are such idiots. Zossimov told me to talk freely to you on the way and get you to talk freely to me, and afterwards I am to tell him about it, for he's got a notion in his head that you are . . . mad or close to it. Just imagine! Firstly, you've three times the brains he has; secondly, if you aren't mad, you needn't care that he's got such a wild idea; and,

thirdly, that piece of beef whose specialty is surgery has gone mad on
mental diseases, and what's brought him to this conclusion about
you was your conversation today with Zametov."

"Zametov told you all about it?"

"Yes, and he did well. Now I understand what it all means and
so does Zametov . . . Well, the fact is, Rodia . . . the point is . . . I am
a little drunk now . . . But that's . . . no matter . . . the point is that
this idea . . . you understand?—was just being hatched in their
brains . . . you understand? That is, no-one dared say it aloud, because
the idea is too absurd and especially since the arrest of that painter,
that bubble's burst and gone for ever. But why are they such fools? I
gave Zametov a bit of a thrashing at the time—that's between ourselves, brother; please don't tell anyone you know about it; I've noticed he is a ticklish subject; it was at Luise Ivanovna's. But today,
today it's all cleared up. That Ilia Petrovich is at the bottom of it! He
took advantage of the fact that you fainted at the police station, but
he is ashamed of it himself now; I know that . . . "

Raskolnikov listened greedily. Razumikhin was drunk enough to
talk too freely.

"I fainted then because it was so close and because of the smell
of paint," said Raskolnikov.

"No need to explain that! And it wasn't just the paint: the fever
had been coming on for a month; Zossimov testifies to that! But how
crushed that boy is now, you wouldn't believe! 'I am not worth his
little finger,' he says. Yours, he means. He has good feelings at times,
brother. But the lesson, the lesson you gave him today in the Crystal
Palace, that was too good for anything! You frightened him at first,
you know, he nearly went into convulsions! You almost convinced
him again of the truth of all that disgusting nonsense, and then you
suddenly—put out your tongue at him: 'There now, what do you
make of it?' It was perfect! He is crushed, annihilated now! It was
masterly, my God, it's what they deserve! Ah, that I wasn't there! He
was really hoping to see you. Porfiry wants to meet you as well . . . "

"Ah! . . . he too . . . but why did they put me down as mad?"

"Oh, not mad. I must have said too much, my friend . . . What
struck him, you see, was that that was the only subject that seemed
to interest you; now it's clear why it did interest you; knowing all the
circumstances . . . and how it irritated you and worked in with your

illness . . . I am a little drunk, brother, only, damn him, he has some idea of his own . . . I tell you, he's mad on mental diseases. But don't pay any attention to him . . . "

For half a minute both were silent.

"Listen, Razumikhin," began Raskolnikov, "I wanted to tell you: I've just been at a death-bed, a clerk who died . . . I gave them all my money . . . and besides I've just been kissed by someone who, if I had killed anyone, would just the same . . . in fact I saw someone else there . . . with a flame-colored feather . . . but I am talking nonsense; I am very weak, support me . . . we shall be at the stairs soon . . . "

"What's the matter? What's the matter with you?" Razumikhin asked anxiously.

"I am a little giddy, but that's not the point, I am so sad, so sad . . . like a woman. Look, what's that? Look, look!"

"What is it?"

"Don't you see? A light in my room, you see? Through the crack . . . "

They were already at the foot of the last flight of stairs, at the level of the landlady's door, and they could, as a fact, see from below that there was a light in Raskolnikov's room.

"That's strange! Maybe it's Nastasia," observed Razumikhin.

"She's never in my room at this time and she must have been in bed long ago, but . . . I don't care! Goodbye!"

"What do you mean? I'm coming with you, we'll come in together!"

"I know we are going in together, but I want to shake hands here and say goodbye to you here. So give me your hand, goodbye!"

"What's the matter with you, Rodia?"

"Nothing . . . come along . . . you shall be my witness."

They began mounting the stairs, and the idea struck Razumikhin that perhaps Zossimov might be right after all. "Ah, I've upset him with my chatter!" he muttered to himself.

When they reached the door they heard voices in the room.

"What is it?" cried Razumikhin. Raskolnikov was the first to open the door; he flung it wide and stood still in the doorway, dumbfounded.

His mother and sister were sitting on his sofa and had been waiting an hour and a half for him. Why had he never expected them, never even thought of them, though it had been repeated to him that they had started, were on their way and would arrive immediately? They had spent that hour and a half plying Nastasia with questions. She was standing in front of them and had told them everything by now. They were beside themselves with alarm when they heard how he "ran away" today when he was ill and, as they understood from her story, delirious! "Lord Almighty, what's happened to him?" For that hour and a half both of them had been weeping with anguish.

A cry of joy, of ecstasy, greeted Raskolnikov when he came in. Both rushed to him. But he stood there like a dead man; a sudden intolerable sensation struck him like a thunderbolt. He did not lift his arms to embrace them, he could not. His mother and sister clasped him in their arms, kissed him, laughed and cried. He took a step, tottered and fell to the ground, fainting.

Anxiety, cries of horror, moans . . . Razumikhin who was standing in the doorway flew into the room, seized the sick man in his strong arms and in a moment had him on the sofa.

"It's nothing, nothing!" he cried to the mother and sister—"he's just fainting, it's all right! Only just now the doctor said he was much better, said he was perfectly fine! Water! Look, he is coming to, he is all right again!"

And seizing Dunia by the arm and almost dislocating it, he made her bend down to see that "he is all right again." The mother and sister gazed at him with emotion and gratitude, as if he were their Providence. They had already heard from Nastasia about everything that had been done for their Rodia during his illness, by this "very competent young man," as Pulcheria Alexandrovna Raskolnikov called him that evening in conversation with Dunia.

PART THREE

CHAPTER ONE

RASKOLNIKOV GOT UP AND sat down on the sofa. He waved his hand weakly at Razumikhin to cut short the flow of warm and incoherent consolations he was addressing to his mother and sister, took them both by the hand and for a minute or two gazed from one to the other without speaking. His mother was alarmed by his expression. It revealed an agonizingly poignant emotion, and at the same time something immobile, almost insane. Pulcheria Alexandrovna began to cry.

Avdotia Romanovna was pale; her hand trembled in her brother's.

"Go home . . . with him," he said in a broken voice, pointing to Razumikhin, "goodbye until tomorrow; tomorrow everything . . . Is it long since you arrived?"

"This evening, Rodia," answered Pulcheria Alexandrovna, "the train was awfully late. But, Rodia, nothing would induce me to leave you now! I will spend the night here, near you . . . "

"Don't torture me!" he said with a gesture of irritation.

"I will stay with him," cried Razumikhin, "I won't leave him for a moment. Damn all my visitors! Let them rage to their hearts' content! My uncle can keep an eye on them."

"How, how can I thank you!" Pulcheria Alexandrovna was beginning, once more pressing Razumikhin's hands, but Raskolnikov interrupted her again.

"I can't have it! I can't have it!" he repeated irritably, "don't worry me! Enough, go away . . . I can't stand it!"

"Come, mamma, come out of the room at least for a minute," Dunia whispered in dismay; "we are distressing him, that's obvious."

"Can't I look at him after three years?" wept Pulcheria Alexandrovna.

"Hold on," he stopped them again, "you keep interrupting me, and my ideas get muddled . . . Have you seen Luzhin?"

"No, Rodia, but he already knows about our arrival. We have heard, Rodia, that Peter Petrovich was kind enough to visit you today," Pulcheria Alexandrovna added somewhat timidly.

"Yes . . . he was so kind . . . Dunia, I promised Luzhin I'd throw him downstairs and told him to go to hell . . . "

"Rodia, what are you saying! Surely, you don't mean to tell

us . . . " Pulcheria Alexandrovna began in alarm, but she stopped, looking at Dunia.

Avdotia Romanovna was looking attentively at her brother, waiting for what would come next. Both of them had heard of the quarrel from Nastasia, so far as she had succeeded in understanding and reporting it, and were in painful perplexity and suspense.

"Dunia," Raskolnikov continued with an effort, "I don't want that marriage, so at the first opportunity tomorrow you must refuse Luzhin, so we will never hear his name again."

"Good Heavens!" cried Pulcheria Alexandrovna.

"Brother, think what you are saying!" Avdotia Romanovna began impetuously, but immediately checked herself. "You are not fit to talk now, perhaps; you are tired," she added gently.

"You think I am delirious? No . . . You are marrying Luzhin for my sake. But I won't accept the sacrifice. And so write a letter before tomorrow, to refuse him . . . Let me read it in the morning and that will be the end of it!"

"I can't do that!" the girl cried, offended, "what right do you have . . . "

"Dunia, you're rushing things, be quiet, tomorrow . . . Don't you see . . . " the mother interposed in dismay. "We'd better go!"

"He is raving," Razumikhin cried drunkenly, "or how would he dare! Tomorrow all this nonsense will be over . . . today he certainly did drive him away. That's true. And Luzhin got angry, too . . . He made speeches here, wanted to show off his learning and he went out crest-fallen . . . "

"Then it's true?" cried Pulcheria Alexandrovna.

"Goodbye until tomorrow, brother," said Dunia compassionately. "Let us go, Mother . . . goodbye, Rodia."

"Do you hear, sister," he repeated after them, making a last effort, "I am not delirious; this marriage is—scandalous. Let me be mean, but you mustn't . . . one is enough . . . and though I am mean, I wouldn't own such a sister. It's me or Luzhin! Go now . . . "

"But you're out of your mind! Despot!" roared Razumikhin; but Raskolnikov did not and perhaps could not answer. He lay down on the sofa, and turned to the wall, utterly exhausted. Avdotia Romanovna looked with interest at Razumikhin; her black eyes flashed. Razumikhin started at her glance.

Pulcheria Alexandrovna stood overwhelmed.

"Nothing would induce me to go," she whispered in despair to Razumikhin. "I will stay somewhere here . . . escort Dunia home."

"You'll spoil everything," Razumikhin answered in the same whisper, losing patience—"come out onto the stairs, anyway. Nastasia, get us a light! I'm telling you," he went on in a half whisper on the stairs—"that he was almost beating the doctor and me this afternoon! Do you understand? Even the doctor! Even he gave way and left him, so as not to irritate him. I remained downstairs on guard, but he dressed at once and slipped off. And he will slip off again if you irritate him, at this time of night, and will do himself harm . . . "

"What are you saying?"

"And Avdotia Romanovna can't possibly be left in those lodgings without you. Just think where you are staying! That blackguard Peter Petrovich couldn't find you better lodgings . . . But you know I've had a little to drink, and that's what makes me . . . swear; don't pay any attention . . . "

"But I'll go to the landlady here," Pulcheria Alexandrovna insisted, "I'll ask her to find some corner for Dunia and me for the night. I can't leave him like that, I can't!"

This conversation took place on the landing right in front of the landlady's door. Nastasia lighted them from a step below. Razumikhin was extraordinarily excited. Half an hour earlier, while he was bringing Raskolnikov home, he had indeed talked too freely, but he was aware of it himself, and his head was clear in spite of the vast quantities of drink which he had consumed. Now he was in a state bordering on ecstasy, and all that he had drunk seemed to fly to his head with redoubled effect. He stood with the two ladies, seizing both by their hands, persuading them, and reasoning through his plans with astonishing clarity, and at almost every word he uttered, probably to emphasize his arguments, he squeezed their hands painfully, as if in a vise. He stared at Avdotia Romanovna without the least regard for good manners. They sometimes pulled their hands out of his huge bony paws, but far from noticing what was the matter, he drew them closer towards him. If they'd told him to jump head foremost from the staircase, he would have done it without thought or hesitation in their service. Though Pulcheria Alexandrovna felt that the young man was really too eccentric and pinched her hand too much, in her anxiety over her Rodia she looked on his presence as providential and was unwilling to notice all his peculiarities. But though Avdotia Romanovna shared her anxiety, and was not of timorous disposition, she could not see the glowing light in his eyes without wonder and almost alarm. It was only the unbounded confidence inspired by Nastasia's account of her brother's strange friend which prevented her from trying to run away from him and persuading her mother to do the same. She realized, too, that even running away was perhaps impossible now. Ten minutes later, however, she was considerably reassured; it was characteristic of Razumikhin that he showed his true nature at once, whatever mood he might be in, so that people quickly saw the sort of man they had to deal with.

"You can't go to the landlady, that's perfect nonsense!" he cried. "If you stay, though you are his mother, you'll drive him into a frenzy, and then God knows what will happen! Listen, I'll tell you what I'll do: Nastasia will stay with him now, and I'll walk you both home, you can't be in the streets alone; Petersburg is an awful place in that respect . . . But no matter! Then I'll run straight back here and a quarter of an hour later, on my word of honor, I'll bring you news of how he is, whether he is asleep, and all that. Then, listen! Then I'll run home in an instant—I've got a lot of friends there, all drunk— I'll fetch Zossimov—that's the doctor who is looking after him, he's there, too, but he's not drunk—he's not drunk, he's never drunk! I'll drag him to Rodia, and then to you, so you'll get two reports within the hour—from the doctor, you understand, from the doctor himself, that's a very different thing from my account of him! If there's anything wrong, I swear I'll bring you here myself, but, if it's all right, you go to bed. And I'll spend the night here, in the passage, he won't hear me, and I'll tell Zossimov to sleep at the landlady's, to be at hand. Which is better for him: you or the doctor? So come home then! But the landlady is out of the question; it's all right for me, but it's out of the question for you: she wouldn't take you, because she's . . . because she's a fool . . . She'd be jealous on my account of Avdotia Romanovna, and of you too if you want to know . . . of Avdotia Romanovna certainly. She is an absolutely, absolutely inexplicable character! But I am a fool, too! . . . No matter! Come along! Do you trust me? Come on, do you trust me or not?"

"Let's go, Mother," said Avdotia Romanovna, "he will certainly do what he has promised. He has saved Rodia already, and if the doctor really will agree to spend the night here, what could be better?"

"You see, you . . . you . . . understand me, because you are an angel!" Razumikhin cried in ecstasy, "let us go! Nastasia! Fly upstairs and sit with him with a light; I'll come in a quarter of an hour."

Though Pulcheria Alexandrovna was not entirely convinced, she made no further resistance. Razumikhin gave an arm to each of them and took them down the stairs. He still made her uneasy: although he was competent and good-natured, was he capable of carrying out his promise? He seemed to be in such a state . . .

"Ah, so you think I'm in such a state!" Razumikhin broke in upon her thoughts, guessing them, as he strolled along the pavement with huge steps, such that the two ladies could hardly keep up with him, a fact he did not observe, however. "Nonsense! That is . . . I am drunk like a fool, but that's not it; I am not drunk from wine. It's seeing you that has turned my head . . . But don't mind me! Don't take any notice: I'm talking nonsense, I'm not worthy of you . . . I am utterly unworthy of you! The minute I've taken you home, I'll pour a couple of bucketfuls of water over my head in the gutter here, and then I shall be all right . . . If only you knew how I love you both! Don't laugh, and don't be angry! You can be angry with anyone, but not with me! I am his friend, and therefore I am your friend, too, I want to be . . . I had a presentiment . . . Last year there was a moment . . . though it wasn't a presentiment really, for you seem to have fallen from heaven. And I expect I shan't sleep all night . . . Zossimov was afraid a little time ago that he would go mad . . . that's why he mustn't be irritated."

"What do you say?" cried the mother.

"Did the doctor really say that?" asked Avdotia Romanovna, alarmed.

"Yes, but it's not so, not a bit of it. He gave him some medicine, a powder, I saw it, and then your coming here . . . Ah! It would have been better if you had come tomorrow. It's a good thing we went away. And in an hour Zossimov himself will tell you about everything. He isn't drunk! And I shan't be drunk . . . And what made me get so tight? Because they got me into an argument, damn them! I've sworn never to argue! They talk such trash! I almost started a fight! I've left my uncle to keep an eye over them. Would you believe, they insist on complete absence of individualism and that's just what they relish! Not to be themselves, to be as unlike themselves as they can. That's what they regard as the highest point of progress. If only their nonsense were their own, but as it is . . . "

"Listen!" Pulcheria Alexandrovna interrupted timidly, but it only added fuel to the flames.

"What do you think?" shouted Razumikhin, louder than ever, "you think I am attacking them for talking nonsense? Not a bit! I like them to talk nonsense. That's man's one privilege over all creation. Through error you come to the truth! I am a man because I err! You never reach any truth without making fourteen mistakes and very likely a hundred and fourteen. And a fine thing, too, in its way; but we can't even make mistakes on our own account! Talk nonsense, but talk your own nonsense, and I'll kiss you for it. To go wrong in your own way is better than to go right in someone else's. In the first case you're a human being, in the second you're no better than a bird. Truth won't escape you, but life can be cramped. There have been examples. And what are we doing now? In science, development, thought, invention, ideals, aims, liberalism, judgment, experience and everything, everything, everything, we are still in the preparatory class at school. We prefer to live on other people's ideas, it's what we are used to! Am I right, am I right?" cried Razumikhin, pressing and shaking the two ladies' hands.

"Oh, mercy, I do not know," cried poor Pulcheria Alexandrovna.

"Yes, yes . . . though I don't agree with you about everything," added Avdotia Romanovna earnestly and at once cried out because he squeezed her hand so painfully.

"Yes, you say yes . . . well after that you . . . you . . . " he cried in a transport, "you are a fount of goodness, purity, sense . . . and perfection. Give me your hand . . . you give me yours, too! I want to kiss your hands here at once, on my knees . . . " and he fell on his knees on the pavement, fortunately at that time deserted.

"Leave off, I beg you, what are you doing?" Pulcheria Alexandrovna cried, greatly distressed.

"Get up, get up!" said Dunia laughing, though she, too, was upset.

"Not for anything until you let me kiss your hands! That's it! Enough! I get up and we'll go on! I am a luckless fool, I am unwor-

thy of you and I'm drunk . . . and I am ashamed . . . I am not worthy
to love you, but to pay homage to you is the duty of every man who
is not a perfect beast! And I've paid homage . . . Here are your lodgings, and for that alone Rodia was right in driving your Peter Petrovich away . . . How dare he! how dare he put you in such lodgings!
It's a scandal! Do you know the sort of people they take in here? And
you his betrothed! You are his betrothed? Yes, well, then, I'll tell you,
your fiancé is a scoundrel."

"Excuse me, Mr. Razumikhin, you are forgetting . . . " Pulcheria
Alexandrovna was beginning.

"Yes, yes, you are right, I did forget myself, I am ashamed of it,"
Razumikhin made haste to apologize. "But . . . but you can't be angry
with me for speaking like that! I'm speaking sincerely and not because . . . hm, hm! That would be disgraceful; in fact not because I'm
in . . . hm! Well, anyway I won't say why, I daren't . . . But we all saw
today when he came in that that man is not of our sort. Not because
he had his hair curled at the barber's, not because he was in such a
hurry to show off his intelligence, but because he is a spy, a specula-
tor, because he is a cheapskate and a moron. That's obvious. Do you
think he's clever? No, he is a fool, a fool. And is he a match for you?
Good heavens! Do you see, ladies?" he stopped suddenly on the way
upstairs to their rooms, "though all my friends there are drunk, yet
they are all honest, and though we do talk a lot of trash, and I do too,
yet we shall talk our way to the truth at last, for we are on the right
path, while Peter Petrovich . . . is not on the right path. Though I've
been calling them all sorts of names just now, I do respect them
all . . . though I don't respect Zametov, I like him, because he is a
puppy, and that ox Zossimov, because he is an honest man and knows
his work. But enough, it's all said and forgiven. Is it forgiven? Well,
then, let's go on. I know this corridor, I've been here, there was a
scandal here at Number 3 . . . Where are you here? Which number?
Eight? Well, lock yourselves in for the night, then. Don't let anybody
in. In a quarter of an hour I'll come back with news, and half an hour
later I'll bring Zossimov, you'll see! Goodbye, I'll run."

"Good heavens, Dunia, what is going to happen?" said Pulcheria
Alexandrovna, addressing her daughter with anxiety and dismay.

"Don't worry yourself, Mother," said Dunia, taking off her hat
and cape. "God has sent this man to help us, even though he has

come from a drinking party. I'm sure we can depend on him. And everything he's done for Rodia . . . "

"Ah, Dunia, goodness knows whether he will come! How could I bring myself to leave Rodia? . . . And how different, how different I had thought our meeting would be! How sullen he was, it was as if he wasn't pleased to see us . . . "

Tears came into her eyes.

"No, it's not that, Mother. You didn't see, you were crying all the time. He is suffering from a serious illness—that's the reason."

"Ah, that illness! What will happen, what will happen? And the way he talked to you, Dunia!" said the mother, looking timidly at her daughter, trying to read her thoughts and already half consoled by the fact that Dunia was standing up for her brother, which meant that she had already forgiven him. "I am sure he will have a different opinion about the whole thing tomorrow," she added, probing her further.

"And I am sure that he will say the same tomorrow . . . about that," Avdotia Romanovna said finally. And, of course, there was no going beyond that, for this was a point which Pulcheria Alexandrovna was afraid to discuss. Dunia went up and kissed her mother. The latter warmly embraced her without speaking. Then she sat down to wait anxiously for Razumikhin's return, timidly watching her daughter who walked up and down the room with her arms folded, lost in thought. This walking up and down when she was thinking was a habit of Avdotia Romanovna's and the mother was always afraid to break in on her daughter's mood at such moments.

Razumikhin, of course, was ridiculous in his sudden drunken infatuation for Avdotia Romanovna. Yet apart from his eccentric condition, many people would have thought it justified if they had seen Avdotia Romanovna, especially at that moment when she was walking to and fro with her arms folded, pensive and melancholy. Avdotia Romanovna was remarkably good looking; she was tall, strikingly well-proportioned, strong and self-reliant—the latter quality was apparent in every gesture, though it did not in the least detract from the grace and softness of her movements. In her face she resembled her brother, but she might be described as really beautiful. Her hair was dark brown, a little lighter than her brother's; there was a proud light in her almost black eyes and yet at times a look of extraordinary kindness. She was pale, but it was a healthy pallor; her face was radiant with freshness and vigor. Her mouth was rather small; the full red lower lip projected a little as did her chin; it was the only irregularity in her beautiful face, but it gave it a peculiarly individual and almost haughty expression. Her face was always more serious and thoughtful than gay; but how well smiles, how well youthful, lighthearted, irresponsible laughter suited her face! It was natural enough that a warm, open, simple-hearted, honest giant like Razumikhin, who had never seen anyone like her and was not quite sober at the time, should lose his head immediately. Besides, as chance would have it, he saw Dunia for the first time transfigured by her love for her brother and her joy at meeting him. Afterwards he saw her lower lip quiver with indignation at her brother's insolent, cruel and ungrateful words—and his fate was sealed.

He had spoken the truth, moreover, when he blurted out in his drunken talk on the stairs that Praskovia Pavlovna, Raskolnikov's eccentric landlady, would be jealous of Pulcheria Alexandrovna as well as of Avdotia Romanovna on his account. Although Pulcheria Alexandrovna was forty-three, her face still retained traces of her former beauty; she looked much younger than her age, in fact, which is almost always the case with women who retain serenity of spirit, sensitiveness and pure sincere warmth of heart into old age. We may add in parenthesis that to preserve all this is the only means of retaining beauty into old age. Her hair had begun to grow gray and thin, there had long been little crow's foot wrinkles round her eyes, her cheeks were hollow and sunken from anxiety and grief, and yet it was a handsome face. She was Dunia over again, twenty years older, but without the projecting underlip. Pulcheria Alexandrovna was emotional, but not sentimental, timid and yielding, but only to a certain point. She could give way and accept a great deal even of what was contrary to her convictions, but there was a certain barrier fixed by honesty, principle and the deepest convictions which nothing would induce her to cross.

Exactly twenty minutes after Razumikhin's departure, there came two subdued but hurried knocks at the door: he had come back.

"I won't come in, I haven't got time," he said right after he opened the door. "He's sleeping like a baby, soundly, quietly, and God grant he may sleep ten hours. Nastasia's with him; I told her not to leave until I came. Now I am fetching Zossimov, he will tell you what's going on and then you'd better get some rest; I can see you're too tired to do anything . . . "

And he ran off down the corridor.

"What a competent and . . . devoted young man!" cried Pulcheria Alexandrovna, overjoyed.

"He seems wonderful!" Avdotia Romanovna replied with some warmth, resuming her walk up and down the room.

It was nearly an hour later when they heard footsteps in the corridor and another knock at the door. Both women waited this time completely relying on Razumikhin's promise; he actually had succeeded in bringing Zossimov. Zossimov had agreed at once to desert the drinking party to go to Raskolnikov's, but he came reluctantly and with the greatest suspicion to see the ladies, mistrusting Razumikhin in his exhilarated condition. But his vanity was at once reassured and flattered; he saw that they were really depending on his expert opinion. He stayed just ten minutes and succeeded in completely convincing and comforting Pulcheria Alexandrovna. He spoke with real sympathy, but with the reserve and extreme seriousness of a young doctor at an important consultation. He did not utter a word on any other subject and did not display the slightest desire to enter into more personal relations with the two ladies. Taking note of Avdotia Romanovna's dazzling beauty, he endeavored not to notice her at all during his visit and addressed himself solely to Pulcheria Alexandrovna. All this gave him extraordinary inward satisfaction. He said he thought that the invalid's condition was currently satisfactory. According to his observations the patient's illness was due partly to his unfortunate material circumstances during the last few months, but it had also a moral origin, "was so to speak the product of several material and moral influences, anxieties, apprehensions, troubles, certain ideas . . . and so on." Noticing stealthily that Avdotia Romanovna was following his words with close attention, Zossimov allowed himself to enlarge on this theme. When Pulcheria Alexandrovna anxiously and timidly inquired about "some suspicion of insanity," he replied with a composed and candid smile that his words had been exaggerated; that certainly the patient had some fixed idea, something approaching a monomania—he, Zossimov, was now studying this interesting branch of medicine—but that it must be recalled that until today the patient had been in delirium and . . . and that no doubt the presence of his family would have a favorable effect on his recovery and distract his mind, "if only all fresh shocks can be avoided," he added significantly. Then he got up, took leave with an impressive and friendly bow, while blessings, warm gratitude, and requests were showered upon him, and Avdotia Romanovna spontaneously offered her hand to him. He went out exceedingly pleased with his visit and still more so with himself.

"We'll talk tomorrow; go to bed at once!" Razumikhin said in conclusion, following Zossimov out. "I'll be with you tomorrow morning as early as possible with my report."

"That's a fetching little girl, Avdotia Romanovna," remarked Zossimov, almost licking his lips as they both came out into the street.

"Fetching? You said fetching?" roared Razumikhin and he flew at Zossimov and seized him by the throat. "If you dare . . . Do you understand? Do you understand?" he shouted, shaking him by the collar and squeezing him against the wall. "Do you hear?"

"Let me go, you drunken devil," said Zossimov, struggling, and when he had let him go, he stared at him and went off into a sudden fit of laughter. Razumikhin stood facing him in gloomy and earnest reflection.

"Of course, I am an idiot," he observed, somber as a storm cloud, "but still . . . you are another."

"No, my friend, not 'another' at all. I'm not dreaming of any such stupidity."

They walked along in silence and only when they were close to Raskolnikov's lodgings, Razumikhin broke the silence in considerable anxiety.

"Listen," he said, "you're a wonderful person, but among your other failings, you play loose, and dirty too. You're a feeble, nervous wretch, a mass of caprice, you're getting fat and lazy and can't deny yourself anything—which is dirty because it leads on straight into dirt. You've let yourself get so slack that I don't know how you manage to be a good, even a devoted doctor. You—a doctor—sleep on a feather bed and get up at night for your patients! In another three or four years you won't even get up for your patients . . . But damn it, that's not the point! . . . You are going to spend tonight in the landlady's apartment here. (I've had my work cut out persuading her!)

And I'll be in the kitchen. So here's a chance for you to get to know
her better . . . It's not what you think! There's not a trace of anything
like that, my friend . . . !"

"But I don't think!"

"Here you have modesty, brother, silence, bashfulness, a savage
virtue . . . and yet she's sighing and melting like wax, simply melting! Save me from her, by all that's unholy! She's so overwhelming . . .
I'll repay you, I'll do anything . . . "

Zossimov laughed more violently than ever.

"Well, you are smitten! But what am I to do with her?"

"It won't be much trouble, I assure you. Talk any rot you like to
her, as long as you sit by her and talk. You're a doctor, too; try curing
her of something. I swear you won't regret it. She has a piano, and
you know, I strum a little. I have a song there, a genuine Russian one:
'I shed hot tears.' She likes the genuine article—and well, it all began
with that song; now you're a regular performer, a master, a Rubinstein* . . . I assure you, you won't regret it!"

"But have you made her some promise? Something signed? A
promise of marriage, perhaps?"

"Nothing, nothing, absolutely nothing of the kind! Besides, she
is not like that at all . . . Chebarov tried that . . . "

"Well, then, drop her!"

"But I can't drop her like that!"

"Why can't you?"

"Well, I can't, that's all about it! There's an element of attraction
here, brother."

"Then why have you fascinated her?"

"I haven't fascinated her; perhaps, I was fascinated myself in my
idiocy. But she won't care whether it's you or I, so long as somebody
sits beside her, sighing . . . I can't explain it, my friend . . . look here,
you are good at mathematics, and working at it now . . . start teaching her integral calculus; I swear, I'm not joking, I'm serious, it'll be
all the same to her. She will gaze at you and sigh all year long. I talked
to her once for two days straight about the Prussian House of Lords
(you've got to talk about something)—she just sighed and sweated!

---

*The Rubinstein brothers, Anton and Nikolai, were two of the finest Russian pianists
of the nineteenth century.

And you can't talk about love—she gets shy around hysterics—but just let her see you can't tear yourself away—that's enough. It's really quite comfortable; you feel at home pretty quickly, you can read, sit, lie about, write. You can even try a kiss, if you're careful."

"But what do I want with her?"

"Don't you understand? You're made for each other! I have often been reminded of you! . . . You'll come to it in the end! So does it matter whether it's sooner or later? There's the featherbed element here, brother,—ah! and not only that! There's an attraction here— here you have the end of the world, an anchorage, a quiet haven, the navel of the earth, the three fishes that are the foundation of the world, the essence of pancakes, of fish-pies, of the evening samovar, of soft sighs and warm shawls, and hot stoves to sleep on—as snug as though you were dead, and yet you're alive—the advantages of both at once! Well, damn it, brother, what nonsense I'm talking, it's bedtime! Listen. I sometimes wake up at night; so I'll go in and look at him. But there's no need, it's all right. Don't worry; if you like, you might just look in once. But if you notice anything, delirium or fever—wake me. But there can't be . . . "

CHAPTER TWO

RAZUMIKHIN WOKE UP NEXT morning at eight o'clock, troubled and serious. He found himself confronted with many new and unforeseen difficulties. He had never expected that he would ever wake up feeling like that. He remembered every detail of the previous day and he knew that a perfectly novel experience had happened to him, that he had received an impression unlike anything he had known before. At the same time he recognized clearly that the dream which had fired his imagination was hopelessly unattainable—so unattainable that he felt ashamed of it, and he moved on quickly to the other more practical cares and difficulties bequeathed him by that "thrice accursed yesterday."

The most awful memory of the previous day was the way he had shown how "base and mean" he was, not only because he had been

drunk, but because he had taken advantage of the young girl's position to abuse her fiancé in his stupid jealousy, knowing nothing of
their mutual relations and obligations and next to nothing of the man
himself. And what right did he have to criticize him in that hasty and
unguarded way? Who had asked for his opinion! Was it thinkable that
a girl like Avdotia Romanovna would be marrying an unworthy man
for money? So there must be something else to him. The lodgings?
But after all how could he know anything about the character of the
lodgings? He was furnishing an apartment . . . Pah, how despicable it
all was! And what justification was it that he was drunk? A stupid excuse like that was even more degrading! In wine is truth, and the
truth had all come out, "that is, all the uncleanness of his coarse and
envious heart!" And would such a dream ever be permissible to him,
Razumikhin? What was he compared to a girl like that—he, the
drunken noisy braggart of last night? "Was it possible to imagine
such an absurd and cynical juxtaposition?" Razumikhin blushed desperately at the very idea and suddenly the recollection forced itself
vividly upon him of how he had said last night on the stairs that the
landlady would be jealous of Avdotia Romanovna . . . that was simply
intolerable. He brought his fist down heavily on the kitchen stove,
hurt his hand and sent one of the bricks flying.

"Of course," he muttered to himself a minute later with a feeling of self-abasement, "of course, all these bad deeds can never be
wiped out or smoothed over . . . and so it's useless even to think of
it, and I must go to them in silence and do my duty . . . in silence,
too . . . and not ask forgiveness, and say nothing . . . now all is lost!"

And yet as he dressed he examined his clothing more carefully
than usual. He hadn't got another suit—if he had, perhaps he
wouldn't have put it on. "I would have made a point of not putting
it on." But in any case he could not remain a dirty cynic; he had no
right to offend the feelings of others, especially when they needed his
help and kept asking him to see them. He brushed his clothes carefully. His dress was always decent; in that respect he was especially
clean.

He washed carefully that morning—he got some soap from Nastasia—he washed his hair, his neck, and especially his hands. When it
came to the question of whether or not to shave his stubby chin
(Praskovia Pavlovna had excellent razors that had been left by her late

husband), the question was angrily answered in the negative. "Let it stay as it is! What if they think that I shaved on purpose to . . . ? They would definitely think so! Not on any account!"

"And . . . the worst of it was he was so coarse, so dirty, his manners came straight from the drinking-house; and . . . and even admitting that he knew he had some of the essentials of a gentleman . . . what was there to be proud of about that? Everyone ought to be a gentleman and more than that . . . and all the same" (he remembered) "he, too, had done little things . . . not exactly dishonest, and yet . . . and what thoughts he sometimes had; hm . . . and to set all that beside Avdotia Romanovna! Damn it! So be it! Well, he'd make a point then of having dirty, greasy, drinking-house manners and he wouldn't care! He'd be worse!"

He was engaged in these monologues when Zossimov, who had spent the night in Praskovia Pavlovna's parlor, came in.

He was going home and was in a hurry to look at the invalid first. Razumikhin informed him that Raskolnikov was sleeping like a dormouse. Zossimov gave orders for them not to wake him and promised to see him again at about eleven.

"If he's still at home," he added. "Damn it! If you can't control your patients, how can you cure them! Do you know whether he will go to them, or whether they are coming here?"

"They're coming, I think," said Razumikhin, understanding the point of the question, "and no doubt they'll discuss their family affairs. I'll be off. You, as the doctor, have more right to be here than I do."

"But I am not a father confessor; I shall come and go away; I've plenty to do besides looking after them."

"One thing worries me," interposed Razumikhin, frowning. "On the way home I talked a lot of drunken nonsense to him . . . all sorts of things . . . including that you were afraid that he . . . might go mad."

"You told the ladies so, too."

"I know it was stupid! You can beat me if you like! Did you seriously think so?"

"Nonsense, how could I! You described him yourself as a monomaniac when you fetched me to take a look at him . . . and we added fuel to the fire yesterday, you did, that is, with your story about the

painter; it was a nice conversation, given that it was a point he might
have been particularly crazy about! If only I'd known what happened
at the police station and that some wretch . . . had insulted him with
his suspiciousness! Hm . . . I would not have allowed that conversation yesterday. These monomaniacs will make a mountain out of a
molehill . . . and see their fantasies as solid realities . . . As far as I remember, it was Zametov's story that in my opinion cleared up half
the mystery. I know one case in which a hypochondriac, a man of
forty, cut the throat of a little boy of eight, because he couldn't endure the jokes he made every day at table! And in this case his rags,
the insolent police officer, the fever and this suspicion! All that working on a man half frantic with hypochondria, and with his morbidly
exceptional vanity! That may well have been the starting-point of illness. Anyway, it can all go to hell! . . . And, by the way, that Zametov
is certainly pleasant, but hm . . . he shouldn't have told us that last
night. He is a real chatterbox!"

"But who did he tell it to? You and me?"

"And Porfiry."

"What does that matter?"

"And, by the way, do you have any influence over them, his
mother and sister? Tell them to be more careful with him today . . . "

"They'll get on all right!" Razumikhin answered reluctantly.

"Why is he so set against this Luzhin? A man with money and
she doesn't seem to dislike him . . . and they haven't got a penny, I
suppose?"

"But what business is it of yours?" Razumikhin cried with annoyance. "How can I tell whether they've got any money? Ask them
yourself and perhaps you'll find out . . . "

"God, what an idiot you are sometimes! Last night's wine hasn't
worn off yet . . . Goodbye; thank your Praskovia Pavlovna from me
for my night's lodging. She locked herself in, made no reply to my
greeting through the door; she was up at seven o'clock, the samovar
was taken in to her from the kitchen. I was not granted a personal interview . . . "

At nine o'clock precisely Razumikhin reached the lodgings at
Bakaleyev's house. Both ladies were waiting for him with nervous impatience. They had got up at seven o'clock or earlier. He entered looking as black as night, bowed awkwardly and was at once furious with

himself for it. He had reckoned without his host: Pulcheria Alexandrovna rushed at him, seized him by both hands and was almost kissing them. He glanced timidly at Avdotia Romanovna, but at that moment her proud face bore an expression of such gratitude and friendliness, such complete and unexpected respect (instead of sneering looks and badly-disguised contempt), that it threw him into greater confusion than if he had been met with abuse. Fortunately there was a subject for conversation, and he was quick to snatch at it.

When she heard that everything was going well and that Rodia had not yet woken up, Pulcheria Alexandrovna announced that she was glad, because "there was something which she absolutely had to discuss beforehand." Then followed an inquiry about breakfast and an invitation to have it with them; they had waited for him before they started. Avdotia Romanovna rang the bell: it was answered by a ragged dirty waiter, and they asked him to bring tea which was served at last, but in such a dirty and disorderly way that the ladies were ashamed. Razumikhin vigorously attacked the lodgings, but, remembering Luzhin, stopped in embarrassment and was greatly relieved by Pulcheria Alexandrovna's questions, which showered in a continual stream upon him.

He talked for three quarters of an hour, being constantly interrupted by their questions, and succeeded in describing to them all the most important facts he knew of the last year of Raskolnikov's life, concluding with a circumstantial account of his illness. However, he omitted many things which were better omitted, including the scene at the police station with all its consequences. They listened eagerly to his story; but when he thought he had finished and satisfied his listeners, he realized that they reckoned he had hardly begun.

"Tell me, tell me! What do you think . . . ? Excuse me, I still don't know your name!" Pulcheria Alexandrovna put in quickly.

"Dmitri Prokofich."

"I should like very, very much to know, Dmitri Prokofich . . . how he looks . . . on things in general now, that is, how can I explain, what are his likes and dislikes? Is he always so irritable? Tell me, if you can, what hopes and, so to speak, dreams do you think he has? What influences him now? In other words, I would like . . . "

"Mother, how can he answer all that at once?" observed Dunia.

"Good heavens, I had not expected to find him in the least like this, Dmitri Prokofich!"

"Naturally," answered Razumikhin. "I have no mother, but my uncle comes every year and almost every time he can scarcely recognize me, even in appearance, though he is a clever man; and your three years' separation means a great deal. What can I tell you? I have known Rodion for a year and a half; he is gloomy, proud and disdainful, and recently—although perhaps he's been like this for a while—he has become suspicious and almost absorbed in his fantasies. He has a noble nature and a kind heart. He does not like showing his feelings and would rather do a cruel thing than open his heart freely. Sometimes, though, he is not at all morbid, just cold and inhumanly callous; it's as though he were alternating between two characters. Sometimes he is extremely reserved! He says he is so busy that everything gets in his way, and yet he lies in bed doing nothing. He doesn't jeer at things, not because he hasn't got the intelligence, but as though he hasn't got the time to waste on such unimportant issues. He never listens to what people say to him. He is never interested in what interests other people at any given moment. He thinks very highly of himself and perhaps he is right. Well, what more? I think your arrival will have a very beneficial influence on him."

"God grant it may," cried Pulcheria Alexandrovna, upset by Razumikhin's account of her Rodia.

And Razumikhin ventured to look more boldly at Avdotia Romanovna at last. He glanced at her often while he was talking, but only for a moment and looked away again at once. Avdotia Romanovna sat at the table, listening attentively, then got up again and began walking to and fro with her arms folded and her lips compressed, occasionally putting in a question, without stopping her walk. She had the same habit of not listening to what was said. She was wearing a dress of thin dark stuff and she had a white transparent scarf round her neck. Razumikhin soon detected signs of extreme poverty in their belongings. Had Avdotia Romanovna been dressed like a queen, he felt that he would not be afraid of her, but perhaps just because she was poorly dressed and that he noticed all the misery of her surroundings, his heart was filled with dread and he began to be afraid of every word he uttered, every gesture he made, which was very trying for a man who already felt diffident.

"You've told us many interesting things about my brother's character . . . and have told it impartially. I am glad. I thought that you were too uncritically devoted to him," observed Avdotia Romanovna with a smile. "I think you are right that he needs a woman's care," she added thoughtfully.

"I didn't say so; but I suppose you are probably right, only . . . "

"What?"

"He loves no-one and perhaps he never will," Razumikhin declared decisively.

"You mean he is not capable of love?"

"Do you know, Avdotia Romanovna, you are awfully like your brother, in every way, in fact!" he blurted out suddenly to his own surprise, but remembering at once what he had just said about her brother, he turned as red as a crab and was overcome with confusion. Avdotia Romanovna couldn't help laughing when she looked at him.

"You may both be mistaken about Rodia," Pulcheria Alexandrovna remarked, slightly offended. "I am not talking about our current difficulties, Dunia. What Peter Petrovich writes in this letter and what you and I have supposed may be mistaken, but you can't imagine, Dmitri Prokofich, how moody and, so to speak, capricious he is. I could never depend on what he would do when he was only fifteen. And I am sure that he might do something now that nobody else would think of doing . . . Well, for instance, do you know how a year and a half ago he astounded me and gave me a shock that nearly killed me, when he had the idea of marrying that girl—what was her name—his landlady's daughter?"

"Did you hear about that affair?" asked Avdotia Romanovna.

"Do you suppose—" Pulcheria Alexandrovna continued warmly. "Do you suppose that my tears, my pleas, my illness, my possible death from grief, our poverty would have made him pause? No, he would calmly have disregarded all obstacles. And yet it isn't that he doesn't love us!"

"He has never spoken a word about that to me," Razumikhin answered cautiously. "But I did hear something from Praskovia Pavlovna herself, though she is by no means a gossip. And what I heard certainly was rather strange."

"And what did you hear?" both the ladies asked at once.

"Well, nothing very special. I only learned that the marriage, which only failed to take place through the girl's death, was not at all to Praskovia Pavlovna's liking. They say, too, the girl was not at all pretty, in fact I am told positively ugly . . . and such an invalid . . . and also strange. But she seems to have had some good qualities. She must have had some good qualities or it's quite inexplicable . . . She had no money either and he wouldn't have taken her money into account . . . But it's always difficult to judge with these things."

"I am sure she was a good girl," Avdotia Romanovna observed briefly.

"God forgive me, I simply rejoiced at her death. Though I don't know which of them would have caused more misery to the other— he to her or she to him," Pulcheria Alexandrovna concluded. Then she began questioning him tentatively about the scene on the previous day with Luzhin, hesitating and continually glancing at Dunia, obviously to the latter's annoyance. This incident evidently made her more uneasy, perhaps even more disturbed, than all the rest. Razumikhin described it in detail again, but this time he added his own conclusions: he openly blamed Raskolnikov for intentionally insulting Peter Petrovich and did not attempt to excuse him because of his illness.

"He had planned it before his illness," he added.

"I think so, too," Pulcheria Alexandrovna agreed with a dejected air. But she was very surprised to hear Razumikhin express himself so carefully and even respectfully when he was discussing Peter Petrovich. Avdotia Romanovna, too, was struck by it.

"So this is your opinion of Peter Petrovich?" Pulcheria Alexandrovna could not resist asking.

"I can have no other opinion of your daughter's future husband," Razumikhin answered firmly and with warmth, "and I don't say it simply from vulgar politeness, but because . . . simply because Avdotia Romanovna has of her own free will decided to accept this man. If I spoke so rudely of him last night, it was because I was disgustingly drunk and . . . mad besides; yes, mad, crazy, I lost my head completely . . . and this morning I am ashamed of it."

He crimsoned and stopped speaking. Avdotia Romanovna flushed, but did not break the silence. She had not uttered a word from the moment they started talking about Luzhin.

Without her support Pulcheria Alexandrovna obviously did not know what to do. At last, faltering and continually glancing at her daughter, she confessed that she was extremely worried by one thing in particular.

"You see, Dmitri Prokofich," she began. "Can I be open with Dmitri Prokofich, Dunia?"

"Of course, Mother," said Avdotia Romanovna emphatically.

"This is what it is," she began quickly, as though a weight had been lifted from her mind because she was finally allowed to talk about her troubles. "Very early this morning we got a note from Peter Petrovich in reply to our letter announcing our arrival. He promised to meet us at the station; instead, he sent a servant to bring us the address of these lodgings and to show us the way; and he sent a message that he would be here himself this morning. But this morning this note came from him. You'd better read it yourself; there is one point in it which worries me very much . . . you will soon see what that is, and . . . tell me frankly what you think, Dmitri Prokofich! You know Rodia's character better than anyone and no-one can advise us better than you can. Dunia, I should tell you, made her decision at once, but I still don't feel sure how to act and I . . . I've been waiting for your opinion."

Razumikhin opened the note, which was dated the previous evening, and read as follows:—

"DEAR MADAM, Pulcheria Alexandrovna, I have the honor to inform you that owing to unforeseen obstacles I was rendered unable to meet you at the railway station; I sent a very competent person with the same object in view. I likewise shall be deprived of the honor of an interview with you tomorrow morning by business in the Senate that does not admit of delay, and also that I may not intrude on your family circle while you are meeting your son, and Avdotia Romanovna her brother. I shall have the honor of visiting you and paying you my respects at your lodgings not later than tomorrow evening at eight o'clock precisely, and herewith I venture to present my earnest and, I may add, imperative request that Rodion Romanovich may not be present at our interview—as he offered me a gross and unprecedented assault on the occasion of my visit to him in his illness yesterday, and, moreover, since I desire from you personally an indispensable explanation of a certain point, about which I wish to have your own opinion. I have the honor to inform you, in anticipation, that if, in spite of my request, I meet Rodion Romanovich, I shall be compelled to withdraw immediately and then *you have only yourself to blame. I write on the assumption that Rodion Romanovich, who appeared so ill when I visited, suddenly recovered two hours later and may visit you also. I was confirmed in that belief by witnessing him with my own eyes in the residence of a drunken man who was run over and has since died; he gave twenty-five rubles to his daughter, a young woman of notorious behavior, under the pretext of contributing to the funeral, which gravely surprised me knowing what pains you took to raise that sum. I hereby give my special regards to your estimable daughter, Avdotia Romanovna, and I beg you to accept the respectful homage of*

"Your humble servant,
"P. LUZHIN."—

"What am I to do now, Dmitri Prokofich?" began Pulcheria Alexandrovna, almost weeping. "How can I ask Rodia not to come? Yesterday he insisted so earnestly that we should refuse Peter Petrovich and now we are ordered not to invite Rodia! He will come on purpose if he knows, and . . . what will happen then?"

"Act on Avdotia Romanovna's decision," Razumikhin answered calmly at once.

"Oh, dear! She says . . . goodness knows what she says, she hasn't explained it! She says that it would be best, at least, not that it would be best, but that it's absolutely necessary that Rodia should make a point of being here at eight o'clock and that they must meet . . . I didn't even want to show him the letter, I wanted to prevent him from coming somehow, with your help . . . because he is so irritable . . . Besides I don't understand about that drunkard who died and that daughter, and how he could have given that daughter all the money . . . which . . . "

"For which you sacrificed so much," put in Avdotia Romanovna.

"He was not himself yesterday," Razumikhin said thoughtfully, "if you only knew what he was up to in a restaurant yesterday, though there was sense in it too . . . Hm! He did say something, as we were going home yesterday evening, about a dead man and a girl, but I didn't understand a word . . . But last night, I myself . . . "

"The best thing, Mother, would be for us to go to see him ourselves and there we will definitely understand at once what we should do. Besides, it's getting late—my goodness, it's past ten," she cried, looking at a splendid gold enameled watch which hung round her neck on a thin Venetian chain and looked entirely out of keeping with the rest of her dress. "A present from her fiancé," Razumikhin thought.

"We must be off, Dunia, we must be off," her mother cried in a flutter. "He will think we are still angry after yesterday if we get there so late. Lord have mercy!"

While she said this she was hurriedly putting on her hat and mantle; Dunia, too, put on her things. Her gloves, Razumikhin noticed, were not only shabby but had holes in them, and yet this evident poverty gave the two ladies an air of special dignity which is always found in people who know how to wear poor clothes. Razumikhin looked reverently at Dunia and felt proud of escorting her. "The queen who mended her stockings in prison,"* he thought, "must have looked every inch a queen and even more of a queen than at sumptuous banquets and celebrations."

"My God," exclaimed Pulcheria Alexandrovna, "little did I think that I should ever fear seeing my son, my darling, darling Rodia! I am afraid, Dmitri Prokofich," she added, glancing at him timidly.

"Don't be afraid, Mother," said Dunia, kissing her, "it's better to trust him."

"Oh, dear, I trust him, but I haven't slept all night," exclaimed the poor woman.

They came out into the street.

"Do you know, Dunia, when I dozed a little this morning I dreamed of Marfa Petrovna . . . she was all in white . . . she came up to me, took my hand, and shook her head at me, but so sternly, as though she were blaming me . . . Is that a good omen? Oh, dear! Didn't you know, Dmitri Prokofich, that Marfa Petrovna died?"

"No, I didn't know; who is Marfa Petrovna?"

"She died suddenly; just think . . . "

"Afterwards, mamma," put in Dunia. "He doesn't know who Marfa Petrovna is."

"Ah, you don't know? And I was thinking that you knew all about us. Forgive me, Dmitri Prokofich, I don't know what I've been

---

*Marie Antoinette, wife of French king Louis XVI; in 1793, during the French Revolution, the two were captured and beheaded.

thinking about for these past few days. I'm treating you as our providence, so I took it for granted that you knew all about us. I look on
you as a relation . . . Don't be angry with me for saying so. Dear me,
what's the matter with your right hand? Have you knocked it?"

"Yes, I bruised it," muttered Razumikhin, overjoyed.

"I sometimes speak too much from the heart, and Dunia finds
fault with me . . . But, dear me, what a cupboard he lives in! I wonder whether he is awake? Does this woman, his landlady, think it's a
proper room? Listen, you say he doesn't like to show his feelings, so
perhaps I'll annoy him with my . . . weaknesses? Please advise me,
Dmitri Prokofich, how should I treat him? I feel so distracted."

"Don't question him too much about anything if you see him
frown! Don't ask him too much about his health; he doesn't like that."

"Ah, Dmitri Prokofich, how hard it is to be a mother! Ah, here
are the stairs . . . What an awful staircase!"

"Mother, you're so pale, don't make yourself upset," said Dunia,
caressing her. Then with flashing eyes she added, "He ought to be
happy to see you, and you're tormenting yourself so badly."

"Wait, I'll look in and see whether he has woken up."

The ladies slowly followed Razumikhin, who went on in front of
them, and when they reached the landlady's door on the fourth floor,
they noticed that her door was open a tiny crack and that two keen
black eyes were watching them from the darkness inside. When their
eyes met, the door was suddenly shut with such a slam that Pulcheria
Alexandrovna almost cried out.

CHAPTER THREE

"HE'S DOING WELL, REALLY well!" Zossimov shouted cheerfully as
they came in.

He had arrived ten minutes earlier and was sitting in the same
place as before, on the sofa. Raskolnikov was sitting in the opposite
corner, fully dressed and more carefully washed and combed than he
had been for some time. The room was immediately crowded, yet
Nastasia managed to follow the visitors in and stayed to listen.

Raskolnikov was actually almost better again compared to his condition the day before, but he was still pale, listless and somber. He looked like a wounded man or someone who has undergone terrible physical pain. His eyebrows were knitted, his lips compressed, his eyes feverish. When he spoke, he said little and did so reluctantly, as though he were performing a duty; his movements were restless.

He only needed a sling on his arm or a bandage on his finger to complete the impression of a man with a painful abscess or a broken bone. The pale, somber face lit up for a moment when his mother and sister entered, but this only gave it a look of more intense suffering instead of its listless dejection. The light soon died away, but the look of suffering remained, and Zossimov, watching and studying his patient with all the passion of a young doctor beginning to practice, noticed no joy in him at the arrival of his mother and sister, but a sort of bitter, hidden determination to bear another hour or two of inevitable torture. He saw later that almost every word of their conversation seemed to touch on some sore place and irritate it. But at the same time he marveled at the restraint and self-control of a patient who the previous day had, like a monomaniac, become frenzied at the slightest word.

"Yes, I can see myself that I am almost well," said Raskolnikov, giving his mother and sister a welcoming kiss which made Pulcheria Alexandrovna radiant at once. "And I'm not just saying this like I did yesterday," he said, addressing Razumikhin with a friendly handshake.

"Yes, I'm actually surprised at him today," began Zossimov, delighted that the ladies had arrived, since he had not even managed to keep up a conversation with his patient for ten minutes. "In another three or four days, if he goes on like this, he will be just as before, that is, as he was a month ago, or two . . . or perhaps even three. It's been coming on for a long time . . . yes? Own up, wasn't it maybe your own fault?" he added, with a tentative smile, as though still afraid of irritating him.

"Maybe," answered Raskolnikov coldly.

"I'd say," continued Zossimov, evidently enjoying himself, "that your complete recovery depends on yourself alone. Now that we can talk, I'd like to remind you that it is essential to avoid the elementary, so to speak, fundamental causes which tend to produce your morbid condition. In that case, you will be cured; if not, it will go from bad to worse. I don't know what these fundamental causes are, but you should. You're an intelligent man, of course, you must have observed yourself. I reckon the first stage of your derangement coincided with you leaving the university. You mustn't be left without an occupation, so work and a definite aim set in front of you might, I imagine, be very beneficial."

"Yes, yes; you are absolutely right . . . I'll hurry up and get back to the university, and then everything will go smoothly . . . "

Zossimov, who had started giving him advice partly to make an impact on the ladies, was certainly a little mystified when he glanced at his patient and noticed an unmistakably mocking expression on his face. However, it only lasted for an instant. Pulcheria Alexandrovna began to thank Zossimov at once, especially for his visit to their apartment the previous night.

"What! He saw you last night?" Raskolnikov asked, as though startled. "Then you haven't slept either after your journey."

"Rodia, that was only until two o'clock. Dunia and I never go to bed before two at home."

"I don't know how to thank him either," Raskolnikov went on suddenly frowning and looking down. "Aside from the question of payment—sorry for referring to it" (he turned to Zossimov)—"I really don't know what I have done to deserve such special attention from you! I just don't understand it . . . and . . . and . . . in fact, it weighs upon me because I don't understand it. I'm telling you honestly."

"Don't be annoyed." Zossimov forced himself to laugh. "Assume that you are my first patient—well—people like me who are just starting to practice love our first patients as if they were our children, and some almost fall in love with them. And, of course, I don't have a lot of patients."

"Let alone him," added Raskolnikov, pointing to Razumikhin, "though he has had nothing from me either but insults and trouble."

"What nonsense! You're in a sentimental mood today, aren't you?" shouted Razumikhin.

If he had looked more carefully he would have seen that there was no trace of sentimentality in him—the opposite, in fact. But Avdotia Romanovna noticed. She was intently and uneasily watching her brother.

"As for you, Mother, I don't know how to begin," he went on, as though repeating a lesson learned by heart. "It's only today that I've begun to realize just how upset you must have been here yesterday, waiting for me to come back."

When he said this, he suddenly held out his hand to his sister, smiling without a word. But in this smile there was a flash of real feeling. Dunia caught it at once, and warmly pressed his hand, overjoyed and thankful. It was the first time he had spoken to her since their argument the previous day. The mother's face lighted up with ecstatic happiness at the sight of this conclusive unspoken reconciliation. "Yes, that's what I love him for," Razumikhin, exaggerating it all, muttered to himself, with a vigorous turn in his chair. "He has these movements."

"And how well he does it all," the mother was thinking to herself. "What generous impulses he has, and how simply, how delicately he put an end to all the misunderstandings with his sister—just by holding out his hand at the right minute and looking at her like that . . . And what handsome eyes he has, and how handsome his whole face is! . . . He is even better looking than Dunia . . . But, my goodness, what a suit—how terribly he's dressed! . . . Vasia, the messenger boy in Afanasy Ivanovich's store, is better dressed! I could rush at him and hug him . . . weep over him—but I'm afraid . . . Oh dear, he's so strange! He's talking kindly, but I'm afraid! Why, what am I afraid of? . . . "

"Oh, Rodia, you wouldn't believe," she began suddenly, hastily answering his words to her, "how unhappy Dunia and I were yesterday! Now that it's all over and done with and we are truly happy again—I can tell you. Can you imagine—we ran here almost straight from the train to embrace you and that woman—ah, here she is! Good morning, Nastasia! . . . She told us at once that you were lying in a high fever and had just run away from the doctor in delirium, and they were looking for you in the streets. You can't imagine how we felt! I couldn't help thinking about the tragic end of Lieutenant Potanchikov, a friend of your father's—you won't remember him, Rodia—who ran out in the same way in a high fever and fell into the well in the courtyard and they couldn't pull him out until next day. Of course, we exaggerated things. We were about to rush off and find Peter Petrovich to ask him to help . . . Because we were alone, totally alone," she said mournfully and stopped short, suddenly, remembering it was still pretty dangerous to speak about Peter Petrovich, although "we are truly happy again."

"Yes, yes . . . Of course it's very annoying . . . " Raskolnikov muttered in reply, but in such a preoccupied and inattentive way that Dunia gazed at him, perplexed.

"What else was it I wanted to say," he went on, trying to remember. "Oh, yes; mother, and Dunia, you too, don't think I didn't mean to come and see you today and just waited for you to come first."

"What are you saying, Rodia?" cried Pulcheria Alexandrovna. She too was surprised.

"Is he answering us as a duty?" Dunia wondered. "Is he being reconciled and asking for our forgiveness as though he were performing a ritual or repeating a lesson?"

"I've only just woken up, and I wanted to come and see you, but I was delayed because of my clothes; I forgot yesterday to ask her . . . Nastasia . . . to wash out the blood . . . I've only just dressed."

"Blood! What blood?" Pulcheria Alexandrovna asked in alarm.

"Oh, nothing—don't worry. It was when I was wandering about yesterday, when I was delirious, I met a man who had been run over . . . a clerk . . . "

"Delirious? But you remember everything!" Razumikhin interrupted.

"That's true," Raskolnikov answered with special carefulness. "I remember everything down to the last detail, and yet—why I did that and went there and said that, I can't explain."

"A familiar phenomenon," Zossimov interrupted, "actions are sometimes performed in a masterly and remarkably cunning way, while the motive for the actions is deranged and dependent on various morbid impressions—it's like a dream."

"Maybe it's really a good thing that he thinks I'm almost mad," thought Raskolnikov.

"But people in perfect health act in the same way as well," observed Dunia, looking uneasily at Zossimov.

"There is some truth in your observation," the latter replied. "In that sense we certainly all resemble madmen quite often, but with the slight difference that the deranged are even madder, because we have to draw the line somewhere. It's true that a normal man hardly even exists. It's hard to find one in a dozen—perhaps even one in a hundred thousand."

At the word "madmen," carelessly dropped by Zossimov in his chatter about his favorite subject, everyone frowned.

Raskolnikov seemed not to pay any attention to them and sat there plunged in thought, with a strange smile on his pale lips. He was still meditating on something.

"Well, what about the man who was run over? I interrupted you!" Razumikhin shouted swiftly.

"What?" Raskolnikov seemed to wake up. "Oh . . . I got spattered with blood when I was helping them carry him to his apartment. By the way, Mother, I did an unforgivable thing yesterday. I was literally out of my mind. I gave away all the money you sent me . . . to his wife for the funeral. She's a widow now, tubercular, poor lady . . . three little children, starving . . . nothing in the house . . . there's a daughter, too . . . perhaps you'd have given it yourself if you'd seen them. But I had no right to do it, I admit, especially as I knew how you needed the money yourself. To help others you've got to have the right to do it, or else you've just got to accept it." He laughed, "That's right, isn't it, Dunia?"

"No, it's not," answered Dunia firmly.

"Pah! You have ideals too," he muttered, looking at her almost with hatred, and smiling sarcastically. "I ought to have thought about that . . . Well, that's praiseworthy, and it's better for you . . . and if you reach a line you won't cross, you'll be unhappy . . . and if you cross it, maybe you'll be even unhappier . . . But that's all nonsense," he added irritably, annoyed that he got carried away. "I only meant to ask mother to forgive me," he concluded, shortly and abruptly.

"That's enough, Rodia, I'm sure that everything you do is very good," said his mother, delighted.

"Don't be too sure," he answered, twisting his mouth into a smile.

A silence followed. There was a constraint in all this conversation, and in the silence, and in the reconciliation, and in the forgiveness, and everyone felt it.

"It is as though they were afraid of me," Raskolnikov was thinking to himself, looking sideways at his mother and sister. Pulcheria Alexandrovna definitely grew more timid the longer she kept silent.

"Yet when they were gone I seemed to love them so much," flashed through his mind.

"Do you know, Rodia, Marfa Petrovna is dead," Pulcheria Alexandrovna suddenly blurted out.

"What Marfa Petrovna?"

"Lord have mercy on us—Marfa Petrovna Svidrigailov. I wrote you so much about her."

"A-a-h! Yes, I remember . . . So she's dead! Really?" he roused himself suddenly, as if waking up. "What did she die of?"

"Just imagine, she died so suddenly," Pulcheria Alexandrovna answered hurriedly, encouraged by his curiosity. "On the same day I sent you that letter! Would you believe it, that terrible man seems to have been the cause of her death. They say he used to beat her horribly."

"Why, were they on such bad terms?" he asked, addressing his sister.

"No, not at all; exactly the opposite. With her, he was always very patient, even considerate. In fact, all those seven years of their married life he gave way to her, often too much, in fact. All of a sudden he seemed to have lost his patience."

"Then he couldn't have been so nasty if he controlled himself for seven years? You seem to be defending him, Dunia?"

"No, no, he's a terrible man! I can't imagine anything more disgusting!" Dunia answered, almost with a shudder, wrinkling up her brows and sinking into thought.

"It happened in the morning," Pulcheria Alexandrovna went on hurriedly. "And immediately afterwards she ordered the horses to be harnessed to drive to the town immediately after dinner. She always used to drive to the town in cases like that. They said she ate a really good dinner . . . "

"After the beating?"

"That was always her . . . habit; and immediately after dinner, so she wasn't late setting out, she went to the bathhouse . . . You see, she was having some bath treatment. They have a cold spring there, and she used to bathe in it regularly every day, and no sooner did she get into the water when she suddenly had a stroke!"

"I should think so," said Zossimov.

"And did he beat her badly?"

"What does that matter!" put in Dunia.

"Hmm! Mother, I don't know why you want to tell us gossip like that," said Raskolnikov irritably, almost in spite of himself.

"My dear, I don't know what to talk about," Pulcheria Alexandrovna said.

"Why, are you all afraid of me?" he asked, with a constrained smile.

"That's definitely true," said Dunia, looking directly and sternly at her brother. "Mother was crossing herself with terror as she came up the stairs."

His face worked, as though in convulsion.

"What are you saying, Dunia! Don't be angry, please, Rodia . . . Why did you say that, Dunia?" Pulcheria Alexandrovna began, overwhelmed. "You see, coming here, I was dreaming all the way, in the train, how we would meet, how we would talk over everything together . . . And I was so happy, I didn't notice the journey! But what am I saying? I am happy now . . . You shouldn't, Dunia . . . I am happy now—just to see you, Rodia . . . "

"Shsh, Mother," he muttered in confusion, not looking at her, but pressing her hand. "We shall have time to talk freely about everything!"

As he said this, he was suddenly overwhelmed with confusion and turned pale. Again that awful sensation he had known of late passed with deadly chill over his soul. Again it became suddenly plain and perceptible to him that he had just told a terrible lie: that now he would never be able to talk freely about everything, that never again would he be able to talk freely about anything to anyone. The anguish of this thought was such that for a moment he almost forgot himself. He got up from his seat, and not looking at anyone walked towards the door.

"What are you doing?" cried Razumikhin, clutching him by the arm.

He sat down again, and began looking around him in silence. They were all looking at him, perplexed.

"But what are you all so silent about?" he shouted, suddenly and entirely unexpectedly. "Say something! What's the use of sitting like this? Come on, speak! Let's talk . . . We meet and sit in silence . . . Come on, anything!"

"Thank God; I was afraid the same thing as yesterday was beginning again," said Pulcheria Alexandrovna, crossing herself.

"What's the matter, Rodia?" asked Avdotia Romanovna, distrustfully.

"Oh, nothing! I remembered something," he answered, and suddenly laughed.

"Well, if you remembered something; that's all right! . . . I was beginning to think . . . " muttered Zossimov, getting up from the sofa. "It is time for me to be off. I will look in again perhaps . . . if I can . . . " He made his bows, and went out.

"What an excellent man!" observed Pulcheria Alexandrovna.

"Yes, excellent, splendid, well-educated, intelligent," Raskolnikov began, suddenly speaking with surprising rapidity, and a liveliness he had not shown until then. "I can't remember where I met him before my illness . . . I think I met him somewhere— . . . And this is a good man, too," he nodded at Razumikhin. "Do you like him, Dunia?" he asked her; and suddenly, for some unknown reason, laughed.

"Very much," answered Dunia.

"Pah! What a pig you are," Razumikhin protested, blushing in terrible embarrassment, and he got up from his chair. Pulcheria Alexandrovna smiled faintly, but Raskolnikov laughed out loud.

"Where are you off to?"

"I must go."

"You don't need to go at all. Stay. Zossimov has gone, so you must. Don't go. What's the time? Is it twelve o'clock? What a pretty watch you've got, Dunia. But why are you all silent again? I'm doing all the talking."

"It was a present from Marfa Petrovna," answered Dunia.

"And a very expensive one!" added Pulcheria Alexandrovna.

"A-ah! What a big one! Hardly like a lady's."

"I like that sort," said Dunia.

"So it is not a present from her fiancé," thought Razumikhin, and was senselessly delighted.

"I thought it was a present from Luzhin," observed Raskolnikov.

"No, he has not given Dunia any presents yet."

"A-ah! Do you remember, Mother, when I was in love and I wanted to get married?" he said suddenly, looking at his mother, who was confused by the sudden change of subject and the way he spoke about it.

"Oh yes, my dear."

Pulcheria Alexandrovna exchanged glances with Dunia and Razumikhin.

"Hmm, yes. What can I tell you? Actually, I don't remember much. She was such a sickly girl," he went on, growing dreamy and looking down again. "A real invalid. She was fond of giving to the poor, and was always dreaming of being a nun, and once she burst into tears when she started talking to me about it. Yes, yes, I remember. I remember very well. She was an ugly little thing. I really don't know what drew me to her then—I think it was because she was always ill. If she had been lame or hunchback, I think I would have liked her even more," he smiled dreamily. "Yes, it was a sort of a spring delirium."

"No, it wasn't just a spring delirium," said Dunia, with warm feeling.

He gave his sister a strained, intent look, but did not hear or did not understand her words. Then, completely lost in thought, he got up, went up to his mother, kissed her, went back to his place and sat down.

"You love her even now?" said Pulcheria Alexandrovna, touched.

"Her? Now? Oh, yes . . . You ask about her? No . . . somehow it all seems like it's in another world . . . and so long ago. And in fact everything happening here seems far away somehow." He looked attentively at them. "You now . . . I seem to be looking at you from a thousand miles away . . . but, Lord knows why we are talking about that! And what's the use of asking about it," he added with annoyance and, biting his nails, he fell into a dreamy silence again.

"What a wretched apartment you have, Rodia! It's like a tomb," said Pulcheria Alexandrovna, suddenly breaking the oppressive silence. "I am sure it's half because of your room here that you have become so melancholy."

"My room," he answered, listlessly. "Yes, the room had a great deal to do with it . . . I thought that, too . . . If only you knew, though, what a strange thing you said just now, Mother," he said, laughing strangely.

A little more, and their companionship, this mother and sister, with him after three years' absence, this intimate tone of conversation,

in the face of the utter impossibility of really speaking about anything—everything would have been beyond his power of endurance.
But there was one urgent matter which must be settled one way or another that day—he had decided when he woke up. Now he was glad
he had remembered it, because now he had a means of escape.

"Listen, Dunia," he began, gravely and dryly, "of course I asked
you to forgive me yesterday, but I think I ought to tell you again that
I'm not backing down from my decision. It's me or Luzhin. If I'm a
bad person, you mustn't be; one is enough. If you marry Luzhin, I
shall immediately stop treating you as my sister."

"Rodia, Rodia! It is the same as yesterday again," Pulcheria
Alexandrovna cried, mournfully. "And why do you call yourself a bad
person? I can't bear it. Yesterday you said the same thing."

"Rodia," Dunia answered firmly and with the same dryness.
"You're making a mistake. I thought it over last night, and I discovered what it was. It's all because you seem to think I am sacrificing
myself to someone for someone else. That's not the case at all. I'm
just marrying for my own sake, because things are hard for me.
Though, of course, I shall be glad if I manage to be useful to my family. But that's not the chief motive for my decision . . . "

"She's lying," he thought to himself, biting his nails vindictively.
"What a proud person she is! She won't even admit she wants to do
it out of charity! Too high and mighty! What terrible people! They
even love as if they hate . . . And how I . . . hate them all!"

"In fact," continued Dunia, "I'm marrying Peter Petrovich because I have decided to choose the lesser of two evils. I intend to do
everything he asks me to do honestly, so I'm not deceiving him . . .
Why did you smile just now?" She, too, flushed, and there was a
gleam of anger in her eyes.

"Everything?" he asked, with a malignant grin.

"Within certain limits. Both the manner and form of Peter Petrovich's courtship showed me at once what he wanted. He may, of
course, think too highly of himself, but I hope he respects me, too . . .
Why are you laughing again?"

"And why are you blushing again? You're lying, Dunia. You're
lying on purpose, just because of your feminine obstinacy, just to hold
your own against me . . . You can't respect Luzhin. I've seen him and
talked to him. So you're selling yourself for money, and so in any case

you're behaving badly, and I'm at least glad that you can blush about it."

"It's not true. I'm not lying," cried Dunia, losing her temper. "I wouldn't marry him if I weren't satisfied that he respects me and thinks highly of me. I wouldn't marry him if I weren't absolutely satisfied that I can respect him. Fortunately, I've had convincing proof of it today . . . and a marriage like that's not cheap, as you say it is! And even if you were right, if I really had decided to behave badly, isn't it merciless of you to speak to me like that? Why do you demand I have a heroism that maybe you don't have either? It's dictatorial; it's tyrannical. If I ruin anyone, then I'll only be ruining myself . . . I'm not committing a murder. Why are you looking at me like that? Why are you so pale? Rodia, darling, what's the matter?"

"Lord have mercy! You made him faint," cried Pulcheria Alexandrovna.

"No, no, nonsense! It's nothing. A little dizziness—not fainting. You've got fainting on the brain. Hmm, yes, what was I saying? Oh, yes. In what way will you get convincing proof today that you can respect him, and that he . . . respects you, you said earlier. I think that's what you said?"

"Mother, show Rodia Peter Petrovich's letter," said Dunia.

With trembling hands, Pulcheria Alexandrovna gave him the letter. He took it with great interest, but, before opening it, he suddenly looked with a sort of amazement at Dunia.

"It is strange," he said, slowly, as though struck by a new idea. "What am I making such a fuss for? What is it all about? Marry who you like!"

He said this almost to himself, but said it aloud, and looked for some time at his sister, as though he were puzzled. He opened the letter at last, still with the same look of strange amazement on his face. Then, slowly and attentively, he started reading, and read it through twice. Pulcheria Alexandrovna showed particular anxiety, and in fact everyone expected something strange to happen.

"What surprises me," he began, after a short pause, handing the letter to his mother, but not addressing anyone in particular, "is that he is a businessman, a lawyer, that his conversation is definitely pretentious, and yet he writes such an uneducated letter."

They were all astonished. They had expected something totally different.

"But they all write like that, you know," Razumikhin observed, abruptly.

"Have you read it?"

"Yes."

"We showed him, Rodia. We . . . consulted him just now," Pulcheria Alexandrovna began, embarrassed.

"That's just the jargon of the courts," Razumikhin put in. "Legal documents have always been written like that."

"Legal? Yes, it's just legal—business language—not entirely uneducated, and not quite educated—business language!"

"Peter Petrovich makes no secret of the fact that he had a cheap education; in fact, he is proud of having made his own way," Avdotia Romanovna observed, a little offended by her brother's tone.

"Well, if he's proud of it, he has reason to be, I don't deny it. You seem to be offended, sister, that I only made such a frivolous criticism of the letter; you think that I talk about such unimportant matters in order to annoy you on purpose. It's exactly the opposite: a stylistic observation occurred to me which is definitely not irrelevant given the way things stand at the moment. There's one expression, 'blame yourselves,' which has been put in very significantly and clearly, and there's also a threat that he'll leave at once if I'm present. That threat to leave is equivalent to a threat to abandon you both if you are disobedient, and to abandon you now after summoning you to Petersburg. Well, what do you think? Can one resent such an expression from Luzhin, as we should if he" (he pointed to Razumikhin) "had written it, or Zossimov, or one of us?"

"N-no," answered Dunia, with more animation. "I saw clearly that it was too naively expressed, and that perhaps he doesn't know how to write well . . . that's a fair criticism, Rodia. I didn't expect, in fact . . . "

"It is expressed in a legal style, and maybe it sounds coarser than he intended. But I must disillusion you a little. There is one expression in the letter, one slander about me, and a pretty despicable one at that. I gave the money last night to the widow, a tubercular woman in serious difficulties, and not 'under the pretext of contributing to the funeral,' but simply to pay for the funeral, and not to the daughter—a young woman, as he writes, of notorious behavior (whom I saw last night for the first time in my life)—but to the widow. In all this I think he has been suspiciously hasty to slander me and to make us disagree. It is expressed again in legal jargon, that is to say, with too obvious a display of the aim, and with a very naive eagerness. He is an intelligent man, but to act sensibly, intelligence is not enough. It all shows him up for who he really is and . . . I don't think he has any great respect for you. I'm telling you this just to warn you, because I sincerely wish for your own good . . . "

Dunia did not reply. Her decision had been taken. She was just waiting to see what would happen that evening.

"Then what have you decided, Rodia?" asked Pulcheria Alexandrovna, who was more uneasy than ever at the sudden new businesslike tone of his talk.

"What decision?"

"You see Peter Petrovich writes that you mustn't be with us this evening, and that he will go away if you come. So will you . . . come?"

"That, of course, is not for me to decide, but for you first and foremost, if you are not offended by such a request; and secondly, by Dunia, if she, too, is not offended. I will do what you think best," he added dryly.

"Dunia has already decided, and I fully agree with her," Pulcheria Alexandrovna hastened to declare.

"I decided to urge you, Rodia, to be with us at this interview," said Dunia. "Will you come?"

"Yes."

"I will ask you too to be with us at eight o'clock," she said, addressing Razumikhin. "Mother, I am inviting him, too."

"Quite right, Dunia. Well, since you have decided," added Pulcheria Alexandrovna, "so be it. I shall feel easier myself. I do not like concealment and deception. Better for us to have the whole truth, whether Peter Petrovich is angry or not!"

CHAPTER FOUR

AT THAT MOMENT THE door was softly opened, and a young girl walked into the room, looking timidly around her. Everyone turned

towards her with surprise and curiosity. At first sight, Raskolnikov did
not recognize her. It was Sofia Semionovna Marmeladov. He had seen
her yesterday for the first time, but at such a moment, in such surroundings and in such clothing, that his memory retained a very different image of her. Now she was a modestly and poorly-dressed
young girl, very young, almost like a child, in fact, with a modest and
refined manner, with a candid but somewhat frightened-looking
face. She was wearing a very plain indoor dress and a shabby old-
fashioned hat, but she was still carrying a parasol. Unexpectedly finding the room full of people, she was not so much embarrassed as
completely overwhelmed with shyness, like a little child. She was
even about to retreat. "Oh . . . it's you!" said Raskolnikov, extremely
astonished, and he, too, was confused. He at once recollected that his
mother and sister knew through Luzhin's letter of "some young
woman of notorious behavior." He had only just been protesting
against Luzhin's slander and declaring that he had seen the girl last
night for the first time, and suddenly she had walked in. He remembered, too, that he had not protested against the expression "of notorious behavior." All this passed vaguely and fleetingly through his
brain, but looking at her more intently, he saw that the humiliated
creature was so humiliated that he felt suddenly sorry for her. When
she made a movement to retreat in terror, it sent a pang to his heart.

"I did not expect you," he said, hurriedly, with a look that made
her stop. "Please sit down. You come, no doubt, from Katerina
Ivanovna. Allow me—not there. Sit here . . . "

At Sonia's entrance, Razumikhin, who had been sitting on one of
Raskolnikov's three chairs, close to the door, got up to allow her to
enter. Raskolnikov had at first shown her the place on the sofa where
Zossimov had been sitting, but feeling that the sofa he used as a bed
was a little too intimate, he hurriedly motioned her to Razumikhin's
chair.

"You sit here," he said to Razumikhin, putting him on the sofa.

Sonia sat down, almost shaking with terror, and looked timidly
at the two ladies. It was evidently almost inconceivable to herself that
she could sit down beside them. At the thought of it, she was so
frightened that she hurriedly got up again, and in utter confusion addressed Raskolnikov.

"I . . . I . . . have come for one minute. Forgive me for disturbing you," she began falteringly. "I came from Katerina Ivanovna's, and she had no-one to send. Katerina Ivanovna told me to beg you . . . to be at the service . . . in the morning . . . at Mitrofanievsky . . . and then . . . to us . . . to her . . . to do her the honor . . . she told me to beg you . . . " Sonia stammered and ceased speaking.

"I will try, certainly, for certain," answered Raskolnikov. He, too, stood up, and he, too, faltered and could not finish his sentence. "Please sit down," he said, suddenly. "I want to talk to you. Maybe you're in a hurry, but please spare me two minutes," and he drew up a chair for her.

Sonia sat down again, and again timidly she took a hurried, frightened look at the two ladies, and dropped her eyes. Raskolnikov's pale face flushed, a shudder passed over him, his eyes glowed.

"Mother," he said, firmly and insistently, "this is Sofia Semi-onovna Marmeladov, the daughter of the unfortunate Mr. Marme-ladov who was run over yesterday in front of me, the man who I was just telling you about."

Pulcheria Alexandrovna glanced at Sonia, and screwed up her eyes a little. In spite of her embarrassment before Rodia's urgent and challenging gaze, she could not deny herself that satisfaction. Dunia gazed gravely and intently into the poor girl's face, and scrutinized her, perplexed. Sonia, hearing herself introduced, tried to raise her eyes again, but was more embarrassed than ever.

"I wanted to ask you," said Raskolnikov, hastily, "how things were arranged yesterday. You weren't bothered by the police, for instance?"

"No, that was all right . . . it was too evident, the cause of death . . . they didn't bother us . . . only the lodgers are angry."

"Why?"

"Because the body has remained there for so long. You see, it is hot now. So today they will carry it to the cemetery, into the chapel, until tomorrow. At first Katerina Ivanovna was unwilling, but now she sees herself that it's necessary . . . "

"Today, then?"

"She wanted to ask you to do us the honor of being in the church tomorrow for the service and then to come to the funeral lunch."

"She is giving a funeral lunch?"

"Yes . . . just a little . . . She told me to thank you very much for helping us yesterday. If it weren't for you, we would have had nothing for the funeral."

All at once her lips and chin began trembling, but, with an effort, she controlled herself, looking down again.

During the conversation, Raskolnikov watched her carefully. She had a thin, very thin, pale little face, rather irregular and angular, with a sharp little nose and chin. She could not have been called pretty, but her blue eyes were so clear, and when they lit up there was such a kindliness and simplicity in her expression that one could not help being attracted. Her face, and her whole figure in fact, had another peculiar characteristic. In spite of the fact that she was eighteen years old, she looked almost like a little girl—almost like a child. And in some of her gestures this childishness seemed almost absurd.

"But has Katerina Ivanovna been able to manage with such a small amount of money? Does she even intend to have a funeral lunch?" Raskolnikov asked, persistently keeping up the conversation.

"The coffin will be plain, of course . . . and everything will be plain, so it won't cost much. Katerina Ivanovna and I have worked it all out so there'll be enough left . . . and Katerina Ivanovna was very anxious that's how it should be. You know we can't . . . it's a comfort to her . . . she is like that, you know . . . "

"I understand, I understand . . . of course . . . why are you looking at my room like that? My mother has just said it looks like a tomb."

"You gave us everything yesterday," Sonia said suddenly, in reply, in a loud rapid whisper; and again she looked down in confusion. Her lips and chin were trembling once more. She had been struck at once by Raskolnikov's poor surroundings, and now these words broke out spontaneously. A silence followed. There was a light in Dunia's eyes, and even Pulcheria Alexandrovna looked kindly at Sonia.

"Rodia," she said, getting up, "we shall have dinner together, of course. Come on, Dunia . . . And, Rodia, you had better go for a little walk, and then rest and lie down before you come to see us . . . I am afraid we have exhausted you . . . "

"Yes, yes, I'll come," he answered, getting up fussily. "But I have something to see to."

"But surely you're going to have dinner together?" cried Razumikhin, looking in surprise at Raskolnikov. "What do you mean?"

"Yes, yes, I'm coming . . . of course, of course! And you stay a minute. You don't want him just now, do you, Mother? Or maybe I'm taking him from you?"

"Oh, no, no. And please, Dmitri Prokofich, will you have dinner with us?"

"Please do," added Dunia.

Razumikhin bowed, absolutely radiant. For a moment, they were all strangely embarrassed.

"Goodbye, Rodia, that is, until we meet: I don't like saying goodbye. Goodbye, Nastasia. Ah, I have said goodbye again."

Pulcheria Alexandrovna meant to say goodbye to Sonia, too; but it somehow failed to come off, and she went in a flutter out of the room.

But Avdotia Romanovna seemed to wait her turn, and following her mother out, gave Sonia an attentive, courteous bow. Sonia, in confusion, gave a hurried, frightened curtsy. There was a look of poignant discomfort in her face, as though Avdotia Romanovna's courtesy and attention were oppressive and painful to her.

"Dunia, goodbye," called Raskolnikov, in the passage. "Give me your hand."

"Why, I did give it to you. Have you forgotten?" said Dunia, turning warmly and awkwardly to him.

"Never mind, give it to me again." And he squeezed her fingers warmly.

Dunia smiled, flushed, pulled her hand away, and went off happy.

"Come, that's wonderful," he said to Sonia, going back and looking brightly at her. "God give peace to the dead; the living still have to live. That's right, isn't it?"

Sonia looked surprised at the sudden brightness of his face. He looked at her for some moments in silence. The whole history of the dead father floated in his memory at those moments . . .

"Goodness, Dunia," Pulcheria Alexandrovna began, as soon as they were in the street, "I really feel relieved myself at coming away—more at ease. How little did I think yesterday in the train that was something I could ever be glad about!"

"I'm telling you again, Mother, he is still very ill. Don't you see it? Perhaps worrying about us upset him. We must be patient, and there is a lot that can be forgiven."

"Well, you weren't very patient!" Pulcheria Alexandrovna caught her up, hotly and jealously. "Do you know, Dunia, I was looking at you two. You are the very portrait of him, and not so much in face as in soul. You are both melancholy, both gloomy and hot-tempered, both proud and both generous . . . Surely he can't be an egoist, Dunia. Eh? When I think of what is in store for us this evening, my heart sinks!"

"Don't be uneasy, Mother. What will be will be."

"Dunia, just think what a position we are in! What if Peter Petrovich breaks it off?" poor Pulcheria Alexandrovna blurted out, incautiously.

"He won't be worth much if he does," answered Dunia, sharply and contemptuously.

"We did well to leave," Pulcheria Alexandrovna hurriedly broke in. "He was in a hurry about some business or other. If he gets out and has a breath of fresh air . . . it is horribly close in his room . . . But where can you get a breath of fresh air here? Even the streets here feel like shut-up rooms. Goodness! What a town! . . . Stay . . . this side . . . they will crush you—they're carrying something. It is a piano they have got . . . look how they are pushing . . . I am very much afraid of that young woman, too."

"What young woman, Mother?

"That Sofia Semionovna, who was there just now."

"Why?"

"I have a presentiment, Dunia. Well, believe it or not, as soon as she came in, that very minute, I felt that she was the chief cause of the problem . . . "

"Nothing of the sort!" cried Dunia, in vexation. "What nonsense, with your presentiments, Mother! He only first met her the evening before, and he did not recognize her when she came in."

"Well, you will see . . . She worries me; but you will see, you will see! I was so frightened. She was gazing at me with those eyes. I could scarcely sit still in my chair when he began introducing her, do you remember? It seems so strange, but Peter Petrovich writes like that about her, and he introduces her to us—to you! So he must think a great deal of her."

"People will write anything. We were talked about and written about, too. Have you forgotten? I am sure that she's a good girl and that it's all nonsense."

"God grant it may be!"

"And Peter Petrovich is a despicable slanderer," Dunia snapped out, suddenly.

Pulcheria Alexandrovna was crushed; the conversation was not resumed.—

"I will tell you what I want with you," said Raskolnikov, drawing Razumikhin to the window.

"Then I will tell Katerina Ivanovna that you are coming," Sonia said hurriedly, preparing to depart.

"One moment, Sofia Semionovna. We have no secrets. You are not in our way. I want to have another word or two with you. Listen!" he turned suddenly to Razumikhin again. "You know that . . . what's his name . . . Porfiry Petrovich?"

"I should think so! He's a relation. Why?" added Razumikhin, with interest.

"Isn't he managing that case . . . you know about that murder? . . . You were talking about it yesterday."

"Yes . . . well?" Razumikhin's eyes opened wide.

"He was asking about people who had pawned things, and I have some pledges there, too—trinkets—a ring my sister gave me as a keepsake when I left home, and my father's silver watch—they are only worth five or six rubles altogether . . . but I value them. So what should I do now? I do not want to lose the things, especially the watch. I was trembling just now in case my mother would ask to look at it, when we were talking about Dunia's watch. It's the only thing of my father's left. She'd be ill if it were lost. You know what women are like. So tell me what to do. I know I ought to have given notice at the police station, but would it not be better to go straight to Porfiry? What do you think? We might get it over with more quickly. You see, Mother may ask for it before dinner."

"Certainly not to the police station. We should see Porfiry," Razumikhin shouted in extraordinary excitement. "I'm so happy about that! Let's go now. It's a couple of steps. We'll definitely be able find him."

"Good, let's go."

"And he will be very, very pleased to meet you. I have often talked to him about you; I was speaking to him about you yesterday. Let's go. So you knew the old woman? So that's it! It's all turning out wonderfully . . . Oh, yes, Sofia Ivanovna . . . "

"Sofia Semionovna," corrected Raskolnikov. "Sofia Semionovna, this is my friend Razumikhin. He's a good person."

"If you have to go now," Sonia was beginning, not looking at Razumikhin at all, and even more embarrassed.

"Let's go," Raskolnikov decided. "I'll visit you today, Sofia Semionovna. Just tell me where you live."

He was not exactly uneasy, but he seemed hurried and avoided her eyes. Sonia gave him her address, and blushed as she did so. They all went out together.

"Don't you lock up?" asked Razumikhin, following him onto the stairs.

"Never," answered Raskolnikov. "I've been meaning to buy a lock for the last two years. People who don't need any locks are happy," he said, laughing, to Sonia. They stood still in the gateway.

"Do you go right here, Sofia Semionovna? How did you find me, by the way?" he added, as though he wanted to say something different. He wanted to look at her soft clear eyes, but this was not easy.

"You gave your address to Polenka yesterday."

"Polenka? Oh, yes; Polenka, that's the little girl. She's your sister? Did I give her the address?"

"Why, had you forgotten?"

"No, I remember."

"I'd heard my father mention you . . . only I did not know your name, and he did not know it. And now I came . . . and as I had learnt your name, I asked today, 'Where does Mr. Raskolnikov live?' I did not know you only had a room too . . . Goodbye, I will tell Katerina Ivanovna."

She was extremely glad to escape at last; she went away looking down, hurrying to get out of sight as soon as possible, to walk the twenty steps to the turning on the right and to be at last alone, and then moving rapidly along, looking at no-one, noticing nothing, to think, to remember, to meditate on every word, every detail. Never, never had she felt anything like this. Dimly and unconsciously a whole new world was opening in front of her. She remembered suddenly that Raskolnikov meant to come to see her that day, perhaps at once!

"Only not today, please, not today!" she kept muttering with a sinking heart, as though entreating someone, like a frightened child. "Mercy! To see me . . . to that room . . . he will find . . . oh, dear!"

She was incapable at that instant of noticing the stranger who was watching her and following at her heels. He had accompanied her from the gateway. At the moment when Razumikhin, Raskolnikov and she were standing still as they said goodbye on the pavement, this gentleman, who was just passing, started when he heard Sonia's words: "and I asked where Mr. Raskolnikov lived?" He cast a rapid but attentive glance at all three of them, especially at Raskolnikov, to whom Sonia was speaking; then looked back and noted the house. All this was done in an instant as he passed, and trying not to betray his interest, he walked on more slowly as though he were waiting for something. He was waiting for Sonia; he saw that they were leaving, and that Sonia was going back home.

"Home? Where? I've seen that face somewhere," he thought. "I must find out."

At the turning he crossed over, looked round, and saw Sonia coming the same way without noticing anything. She turned the corner. He followed her on the other side. After about fifty paces he crossed over again, overtook her and kept two or three yards behind her.

He was a man of about fifty, rather tall and thickly set, with broad high shoulders which made him look as if he stooped a little. He wore good, fashionable clothes, and looked like he had some kind of standing in society. He carried a handsome cane, which he tapped on the pavement every step he took; his gloves were spotless. He had a broad, rather pleasant face with high cheek-bones and a fresh color not often seen in Petersburg. His flaxen hair was still thick, and only touched here and there with gray, and his thick square beard was even lighter than his hair. His eyes were blue and had a cold and thoughtful look; his lips were crimson. He was a remarkably well-preserved man and looked much younger than his years.

When Sonia came out on the canal bank, they were the only two people on the pavement. He noticed that she was dreamy and lost in her thoughts. On reaching the house where she lodged, Sonia turned in at the gate; he followed her, seeming rather surprised. In the courtyard she turned to the right corner. "Bah!" muttered the unknown gentleman, and mounted the stairs behind her. Only then did Sonia notice him. She reached the third storey, turned down the passage, and rang at No. 9. On the door was inscribed in chalk, "Kapernau-mov, Tailor." "Bah!" the stranger repeated again, wondering at the strange coincidence, and he rang next door, at No. 8. The doors were two or three yards apart.

"You lodge at Kapernaumov's," he said, looking at Sonia and laugh-ing. "He altered a waistcoat for me yesterday. I am staying close by here at Madame Resslich's. How odd!" Sonia looked at him attentively.

"We are neighbors," he went on gaily. "I only came to town the day before yesterday. Anyway, goodbye for now."

Sonia made no reply; the door opened and she slipped in. She felt for some reason ashamed and uneasy.

On the way to Porfiry's, Razumikhin was obviously excited.

"That's wonderful, my friend," he repeated several times, "I'm glad! I'm glad!"

"What are you glad about?" Raskolnikov thought to himself.

"I didn't know you pledged things at the old woman's as well. And . . . was it long ago? I mean, was it long since you were there?"

"What a simple-hearted fool he is!"

"When was it?" Raskolnikov stopped still to recollect. "Two or three days before her death, it must have been. But I am not going to redeem the things now," he put in with a sort of hurried and con-spicuous concern about his possessions. "I've not more than a silver ruble left . . . after last night's accursed delirium!"

He laid special emphasis on the delirium.

"Yes, yes," Razumikhin hastened to agree—with what was not clear. "Then that's why you . . . were struck . . . partly . . . you know in your delirium you kept mentioning some rings or chains! Yes, yes . . . that's clear, it's all clear now."

"My God! The idea must have really spread far. This man will go to the stake for me, and now he's delighted that we cleared up the fact that I mentioned rings when I was delirious! What a hold the idea must have on all of them!"

"Shall we find him?" he asked suddenly.

"Oh, yes," Razumikhin answered quickly. "He's a nice person, you'll see, my friend. Pretty clumsy—that's to say, he has real manners, but I mean clumsy in a different sense. He's intelligent, very intelligent, in fact, but he has his own range of ideas . . . He is incredulous, skeptical, cynical . . . he likes to impose on people, or rather to make fun of them. His method is old, circumstantial . . . But he understands his work . . . thoroughly . . . Last year he cleared up a murder case the police had hardly a clue about. He is very, very anxious to meet you."

"On what grounds is he so anxious?"

"Oh, it's not exactly . . . you see, since you've been ill I happen to have mentioned you several times . . . So, when he heard about you . . . about the fact that you were a law student and that you were unable to finish your studies, he said, 'What a pity!' And so I concluded . . . from everything together, not only that; yesterday, Zametov . . . you know, Rodia, I talked some nonsense on the way home to you yesterday, when I was drunk . . . I'm afraid, my friend, that you will exaggerate it, you see."

"What? That they think I am a madman? Maybe they are right," he said with a constrained smile.

"Yes, yes . . . I mean, no! . . . But everything I said (and there was something else too) was all nonsense, drunken nonsense."

"But why are you apologizing? I am so sick of it all!" Raskolnikov cried with exaggerated irritability. It was partly false, however.

"I know, I know, I understand. Believe me, I understand. I'm ashamed to talk about it."

"If you're ashamed to talk about it, then don't."

Both were silent. Razumikhin was more than ecstatic and Raskolnikov perceived it with repulsion. He was alarmed, too, by what Razumikhin had just said about Porfiry.

"I shall have to put on a show for him too," he thought, with a beating heart, and he turned white, "and do it naturally. But the most natural thing would be to do nothing at all. Carefully do nothing at all! No, carefully would not be natural again . . . Oh, well, we'll see how it turns out . . . We'll see . . . right now. Is it a good thing to go or not? The butterfly flies to the light. My heart is beating, that's what's bad!"

"In this gray house," said Razumikhin.

"The most important thing is, does Porfiry know that I was at the old hag's apartment yesterday . . . and did he ask about the blood? I must find that out immediately, as soon as I go in, find out from his face; otherwise . . . I'll find out, if it destroys me."

"I was wondering, my friend," he said suddenly, addressing Razumikhin with a sly smile, "I've been noticing all day that you seem to be strangely excited. Isn't that so?"

"Excited? Not at all," said Razumikhin, deeply embarrassed.

"Yes, my friend, I can tell you, it's noticeable. You sat on your chair in a way I've never seen you sit, on the edge somehow, and you seemed to be wriggling all the time. You kept jumping up for no reason. One moment you were angry, and the next your face looked like candy. You even blushed; especially when you were invited to dinner, you blushed terribly."

"Nothing of the sort, nonsense! What do you mean?"

"But why are you wriggling out of it, like a schoolboy? My God, he's blushing again."

"What a pig you are!"

"But why are you so shamefaced about it? Romeo! Stay, I'll tell of you today. Ha-ha-ha! I'll make mother laugh, and someone else, too . . . "

"Listen, listen, listen, this is serious . . . What next, you fiend!" Razumikhin was utterly overwhelmed, turning cold with horror. "What will you tell them? Come on . . . God, what a pig you are!"

"You are like a summer rose. And if only you knew how it suits you; a Romeo over six foot high! And how you've washed today— you even cleaned your nails! That's unheard of! I think you've even got grease on your hair! Bend down."

"Pig!"

Raskolnikov laughed as though he could not restrain himself, and Razumikhin also started to laugh; soon they were entering Porfiry Petrovich's apartment. This is what Raskolnikov wanted: from inside they could be heard laughing as they came in through the passage.

"Not a word here or I'll . . . brain you!" Razumikhin whispered furiously, seizing Raskolnikov by the shoulder.

CHAPTER FIVE

RASKOLNIKOV WAS ALREADY ENTERING the room. He came in looking as though he would have the utmost difficulty not to burst out laughing again. Behind him Razumikhin strode in gawky and awkward, shamefaced and red as a peony, with an utterly crestfallen and ferocious expression. His face and figure really were ridiculous at that moment and amply justified Raskolnikov's laughter. Raskolnikov, without waiting for an introduction, bowed to Porfiry Petrovich, who stood in the middle of the room looking inquiringly at them. He held out his hand to shake Porfiry's, still apparently making desperate efforts to subdue his mirth and utter a few words to introduce himself. But he had no sooner succeeded in assuming a serious air and muttering something when he suddenly glanced again at Razumikhin, as if by accident, and could no longer control himself: his stifled laughter broke out the more irresistibly the more he tried to restrain it. The extraordinary ferocity with which Razumikhin received this "spontaneous" mirth gave the whole scene the appearance of the most natural playfulness. Razumikhin strengthened this impression as if on purpose.

"Idiot! You fiend," he roared, waving his arm which at once struck a little round table with an empty tea-glass on it. Everything was sent flying and crashing.

"But why break chairs, gentlemen? You know it's a loss to the Crown," Porfiry Petrovich quoted gaily.*

Raskolnikov was still laughing, with his hand in Porfiry Petrovich's, but anxious not to overdo it, waited for the right moment to put a natural end to it. Razumikhin, completely confused by upsetting the table and smashing the glass, gazed gloomily at the fragments, swore and turned sharply to the window where he stood looking out with his back to the company with a fierce frown, seeing nothing. Porfiry Petrovich laughed and was ready to go on laughing, but was obviously looking for explanations. Zametov had been sitting in the corner, but he got up when the visitors came in and was standing in expectation with a smile on his lips, though he looked with surprise and even it seemed incredulity at the whole scene and at Raskolnikov with a certain embarrassment. Zametov's unexpected presence struck Raskolnikov unpleasantly.

---

*From Nikolai Gogol's play The Government Inspector (1836); Gogol was a favorite author of Dostoevsky.

"I've got to consider that," he thought. "Excuse me, please," he began, affecting extreme embarrassment. "Raskolnikov."

"Not at all, very pleasant to see you . . . and how pleasantly you've come in . . . Won't he even say good morning?" Porfiry Petrovich nodded at Razumikhin.

"I swear I have no idea why he is in such a rage with me. I only told him as we came along that he was like Romeo . . . and proved it. And that was all, I think!"

"Pig!" Razumikhin spat out, without turning round.

"There must have been very serious grounds for it, if he is so furious at the word," Porfiry laughed.

"Oh, you sharp lawyer! . . . Damn you all!" snapped Razumikhin, and suddenly bursting out laughing himself, he went up to Porfiry with a more cheerful face as though nothing had happened. "That'll do! We are all fools. Now, to business. This is my friend Rodion Romanovich Raskolnikov; firstly, he has heard of you and wants to meet you, and secondly, he has a little matter to settle with you. Bah! Zametov, what brought you here? Have you met before? Have you known each other long?"

"What does this mean?" thought Raskolnikov uneasily.

Zametov seemed taken aback, but not very much so.

"It was at your rooms we met yesterday," he said easily.

"Then I've been spared the trouble. All last week he was begging me to introduce him to you. Porfiry and you have sniffed each other out without me. Where is your tobacco?"

Porfiry Petrovich was wearing a dressing-gown, very clean clothing, and trodden-down slippers. He was about thirty-five, short, stout, even corpulent, and clean shaven. He wore his hair cut short and had a large round head which was particularly prominent at the back. His soft, round, rather snub-nosed face was of a sickly yellowish color, but it also had a vigorous and rather ironical expression. It would have been good-natured, except for a look in the eyes, which shone with a watery, sentimental light under almost white, blinking eyelashes. The expression of those eyes was strangely out of keeping with his somewhat womanish figure, and gave it something far more serious than could be guessed at first sight.

As soon as Porfiry Petrovich heard that his visitor had a little matter to settle with him, he begged him to sit down on the sofa and sat down himself on the other end, waiting for him to explain his business, with that careful and over-serious attention which is at once oppressive and embarrassing, especially to a stranger, and especially if what you are discussing is in your opinion of far too little importance for such exceptional solemnity. But in brief and coherent phrases Raskolnikov explained his business clearly and exactly, and was so satisfied with himself that he even succeeded in taking a good look at Porfiry. Porfiry Petrovich did not once take his eyes off him. Razumikhin, sitting opposite at the same table, listened warmly and impatiently, looking from one to the other every moment with rather excessive interest.

"Fool," Raskolnikov swore to himself.

"You have to give information to the police," Porfiry replied, with a most businesslike air, "that having learnt of this incident, that is of the murder, you beg to inform the lawyer in charge of the case that such and such things belong to you, and that you wish to redeem them . . . or . . . but they will write to you."

"That's just the point, that at the moment," Raskolnikov tried his best to pretend to be embarrassed, "I don't quite have the funds . . . and even this tiny sum is beyond me . . . For the moment, you see, I only wanted to declare that the things are mine, and that when I have money . . . "

"That doesn't matter," answered Porfiry Petrovich, receiving his explanation of his financial position coldly, "but you can, if you prefer, write straight to me, to say, that having been informed of the matter, and claiming such and such as your property, you would like . . . "

"On an ordinary sheet of paper?" Raskolnikov interrupted eagerly, again interested in the financial side of the question.

"Oh, the most ordinary," and suddenly Porfiry Petrovich looked with obvious irony at him, screwing up his eyes as if he were winking at him. But perhaps it was Raskolnikov's imagination, since it all lasted for just a moment. There was certainly something of the sort, Raskolnikov could have sworn he winked at him, God knows why.

"He knows," flashed through his mind like lightning.

"Sorry for troubling you about something so unimportant," he went on, a little confused, "the things are only worth five rubles, but I prize them because of the people who gave them to me, and I have to say that I was alarmed when I heard . . . "

"That's why you were so struck when I mentioned to Zossimov that Porfiry was asking about anyone who had pledges!" Razumikhin put in with obvious intention.

This was really unbearable. Raskolnikov could not help glancing at him with a flash of vindictive anger in his black eyes, but immediately reverted to his previous demeanor.

"You seem to be laughing at me, my friend?" he said to him, with convincing mock irritability. "I probably do seem to you to be absurdly anxious about such trash; but you shouldn't think I'm selfish or grasping: these two things are anything but trash as far as I'm concerned. I told you just now that the silver watch, though it's not worth a kopeck, is the only thing left us of my father's. You may laugh at me, but my mother is here," he turned suddenly to Porfiry, "and if she knew," he turned again hurriedly to Razumikhin, carefully making his voice tremble, "that the watch was lost, she would be in despair! You know what women are like!"

"Not a bit of it! I didn't mean that at all! Exactly the opposite!" shouted Razumikhin distressed.

"Was it right? Was it natural? Did I overdo it?" Raskolnikov asked himself in a tremor. "Why did I say that about women?"

"Oh, your mother is with you?" Porfiry Petrovich inquired.

"Yes."

"When did she come?"

"Last night."

Porfiry paused as though reflecting.

"Your things would not in any case be lost," he went on calmly and coldly. "I have been expecting you here for some time."

And as though that was a matter of no importance, he carefully offered the ash-tray to Razumikhin, who was ruthlessly scattering cigarette ash over the carpet. Raskolnikov shuddered, but Porfiry did not seem to be looking at him, and was still concerned with Razumikhin's cigarette.

"What? Expecting him? Why, did you know that he had pledges there?" cried Razumikhin.

Porfiry Petrovich addressed himself to Raskolnikov.

"Your things, the ring and the watch, were wrapped up together, and on the paper your name was legibly written in pencil, together with the date on which you left them with her . . . "

"How observant you are!" Raskolnikov smiled awkwardly, doing his very utmost to look him straight in the face, but he failed, and suddenly added:

"I say that because I suppose there were a quite a few pledges . . . that it must be difficult to remember them all . . . But you remember them all so clearly, and . . . and . . . "

"Stupid! Feeble!" he thought. "Why did I add that?"

"But we know all who had pledges, and you are the only one who hasn't come forward," Porfiry answered with hardly perceptible irony.

"I haven't been very well."

"I heard that too. I heard, in fact, that you were in great distress about something. You look pale still."

"I am not pale at all . . . No, I am well again," Raskolnikov snapped out rudely and angrily, completely changing his tone. His anger was mounting, he could not repress it. "And in this angry mood I'll give myself away," flashed through his mind again. "Why are they torturing me?"

"Not very well!" Razumikhin caught him up. "What next! He was unconscious and delirious all yesterday. Would you believe, Porfiry, as soon as our backs were turned, he got dressed, though he could hardly stand, and gave us the slip and went off on a spree somewhere till midnight, delirious all the time! Would you believe it! Extraordinary!"

"Delirious? Really?" Porfiry shook his head in a womanish way.

"Nonsense! Don't you believe it! But you don't believe it anyway," Raskolnikov let slip in his anger. But Porfiry Petrovich did not seem to catch those strange words.

"But how could you have gone out if you hadn't been delirious?" Razumikhin got hot suddenly. "What did you go out for? What was the point? And why behind our backs? Were you thinking clearly when you did it? Now that all the danger is over I can talk about it openly."

"I was totally fed up with them yesterday." Raskolnikov addressed Porfiry suddenly with a smile of insolent defiance, "I ran away from them to take lodgings where they wouldn't find me, and took a lot of money with me. Mr. Zametov there saw it. Mr. Zametov, was I in my right mind or was I delirious yesterday? Settle our dispute."

He could have strangled Zametov at that moment, so hateful were his expression and his silence to him.

"In my opinion you talked sensibly and even skillfully, but you were extremely irritable," Zametov pronounced dryly.

"And Nikodim Fomich was telling me today," put in Porfiry Petrovich, "that he met you very late last night in the apartment of a man who had been run over."

"And there," said Razumikhin, "weren't you mad then? You gave your last penny to the widow for the funeral. If you wanted to help, give fifteen or twenty even, but keep three rubles for yourself at least, but he flung away all twenty-five at once!"

"Maybe I found some money somewhere and you know nothing about it? So that's why I was liberal yesterday . . . Mr. Zametov knows I found something! Excuse us, please, for disturbing you for half an hour with such unimportant matters," he said turning to Porfiry Petrovich, with trembling lips. "We are boring you, aren't we?"

"Oh no, quite the contrary, quite the contrary! If only you knew how you interest me! It's interesting to look on and listen . . . and I am really glad you have come forward at last."

"But could you give us some tea! My throat's dry," cried Razumikhin.

"Great idea! Perhaps we will all keep you company. Wouldn't you like . . . something more essential before tea?"

"Oh, stop it!"

Porfiry Petrovich went out to order tea.

Raskolnikov's thoughts were in a whirl. He was absolutely fed up.

"The worst of it is they don't try to hide it; they don't even stand on ceremony! And how if you didn't know me at all, did you come to talk to Nikodim Fomich about me? So they didn't care to hide that they are tracking me like a pack of dogs. They simply spit in my face." He was shaking with rage. "Come on, strike me openly, don't play with me like a cat with a mouse. It's hardly fair, Porfiry Petrovich, but perhaps I won't allow it! I'll get up and throw the whole truth in your ugly faces, and you'll see how much I hate you." He could hardly breathe. "And what if it's just my imagination? What if I'm making a mistake, getting angry through inexperience and failing to keep up my wretched part? Perhaps it's all unintentional. All their phrases are the usual ones, but there's something about them . . . Whatever you say, there's something. Why did he say it so bluntly—'With her'? Why did Zametov add that I was talking 'skillfully'? Why are they speaking in that tone? Yes, the tone . . . Razumikhin is sitting here, why doesn't he see anything? That innocent blockhead never sees anything! Feverish again! Did Porfiry wink at me just now? Of course it's nonsense! What could he wink for? Are they trying to upset my nerves or are they teasing me? Either it's my imagination or they know! Even Zametov is rude . . . Is Zametov rude? Zametov has changed his mind. I predicted he'd change his mind! He's at home here; it's my first visit. Porfiry doesn't treat him like a visitor: he sits with his back to him. They're as thick as thieves over me, there's no doubt about it! No doubt they were talking about me before we came. Do they know about the apartment? If only they'd hurry up! When I said that I ran away to take an apartment he let it pass . . . I put that in cleverly about an apartment, it may come in useful later . . . Delirious . . . ha-ha-ha! He knows all about last night! He didn't know about my mother's arrival! The hag had written the date on in pencil! You're wrong, you won't catch me! There are no facts . . . it's all supposition! You produce facts! Even the apartment isn't a fact, it's a delirium. I know what to say to them . . . Do they know about the apartment? I won't go without finding out. What did I come for? But maybe the fact that I'm angry now is a fact! I'm an idiot for getting so irritable! Perhaps that's right; to play the invalid . . . He's feeling for a way in. He'll try to catch me out. Why did I come?"

All this flashed like lightning through his mind.

Porfiry Petrovich returned quickly. He suddenly became more jovial.

"Your party yesterday, my friend, has left my head rather . . . And I am completely out of shape," he began in quite a different tone, laughing to Razumikhin.

"Was it interesting? I left you yesterday at the most interesting point. Who got the best of it?"

"Oh, no-one, of course. They got on to everlasting questions, floated off into space."

"Rodia, just imagine what we got on to yesterday. Whether there is such a thing as crime. I told you that we talked our heads off."

"What's strange about that? It's an everyday social question," Raskolnikov answered casually.

"The question wasn't put quite like that," observed Porfiry.

"Not quite, that's true," Razumikhin agreed at once, getting warm and hurried as usual. "Listen, Rodion, and tell us your opinion, I want to hear it. I was fighting tooth and nail with them and wanted you to help me. I told them you were coming . . . It began with the socialist doctrine. You know their doctrine; crime is a protest against the abnormality of the social organization* and nothing more, nothing; no other causes admitted! . . . "

"You are wrong there," cried Porfiry Petrovich; he was noticeably excited and kept laughing as he looked at Razumikhin, which made him more excited than ever.

"Nothing is admitted," Razumikhin interrupted with heat.

"I'm not wrong. I'll show you their pamphlets. Everything with them is 'the influence of the environment,' and nothing else. Their favorite phrase! From which it follows that, if society is normally organized, crime will instantly cease to exist, since there will be nothing to protest against and all men will become righteous in an instant. Human nature is not taken into account, it is excluded, it's not supposed to exist! They don't recognize that humanity has developed by a living historical process and will eventually become normal; they believe that a social system that has come out of some mathematical brain is going to organize all of humanity at once and make it just and sinless in an instant, quicker than any living process! That's why they instinctively dislike history, 'nothing but ugliness and stupidity in it,' and they explain it all as stupidity! That's why they dislike the living process of life; they don't want a living soul! The living soul demands life, the soul won't obey the rules of mechanics, the soul is an object of suspicion, the soul is backward! But what they want, though it smells of death and can be made of rubber, is at least not alive, has no will, is servile and won't revolt! And it comes in the end to their reducing everything to the building of walls and the planning of rooms and passages in a commune! The commune is ready, but human nature isn't ready for the commune— it needs life, it hasn't completed its vital process, it's too soon for the graveyard! You can't skip over nature by logic. Logic presupposes

---

*Dostoevksy's contemporary Nikolai Chernyshevsky, a socialist, discussed this view in his novel *What Is to Be Done?* (1863).

three possibilities, but there are millions! Cut away a million, and reduce it all to a question of comfort! That's the easiest solution to the
problem! It's seductively clear and you mustn't think about it. That's
the great thing, you mustn't think! The whole secret of life in two
pages of print!"

"Now he is off, beating the drum! Catch hold of him, do!"
laughed Porfiry. "Can you imagine," he turned to Raskolnikov, "six
people holding forth like that last night, in one room, with punch as
a preliminary! No, my friend, you are wrong, environment accounts
for a great deal in crime, I can tell you."

"Oh, I know it does, but just tell me: a man of forty rapes a child
of ten; was it environment that drove him to it?"

"Well, strictly speaking, it did," Porfiry observed with notewor-
thy gravity; "a crime of that nature may be very well ascribed to the
influence of the environment."

Razumikhin was almost in a frenzy. "Oh, if you like," he roared.
"I'll prove to you that your white eyelashes may very well be ascribed
to the Church of Ivan the Great's being two hundred and fifty feet
high, and I will prove it clearly, exactly, progressively, and even with
a Liberal tendency! I will! Do you want to bet on it?"

"Done! Let's hear, please, how he will prove it!"

"He is always humbugging, confound him," cried Razumikhin,
jumping up and gesticulating. "What's the use of talking to you! He
does all that on purpose; you don't know him, Rodion! He took their
side yesterday, simply to make fools of them. And the things he said
yesterday! And they were delighted! He can keep it up for a fortnight
together. Last year he persuaded us that he was going into a
monastery: he stuck to it for two months. Not long ago he took it
into his head to declare he was going to get married, that he had
everything ready for the wedding. He ordered new clothes indeed. We
all began to congratulate him. There was no bride, nothing, all pure
fantasy!"

"Ah, you are wrong! I got the clothes before. It was the new
clothes in fact that made me think of taking you in."

"Are you such a good liar?" Raskolnikov asked carelessly.

"You wouldn't have supposed it? Just wait, I'll take you in, too.
Ha-ha-ha! No, I'll tell you the truth. All these questions about crime,
environment, children, remind me of an article of yours which in-

terested me at the time. 'On Crime' . . . or something of the sort, I forget the title, I read it with pleasure two months ago in the Periodical Review."

"My article? In the Periodical Review?" Raskolnikov asked in astonishment. "I certainly did write an article about a book six months ago when I left the university, but I sent it to the Weekly Review."

"But it came out in the Periodical."

"And the Weekly Review ceased to exist, so that's why it wasn't printed at the time."

"That's true; but when it ceased to exist, the Weekly Review was amalgamated with the Periodical, and so your article appeared two months ago in the latter. Didn't you know?"

Raskolnikov had not known.

"Why, you might get some money out of them for the article! What a strange person you are! You lead such a solitary life that you know nothing of matters that concern you directly. It's a fact, I assure you."

"Bravo, Rodia! I knew nothing about it either!" cried Razumikhin. "I'll run today to the reading-room and ask for the number. Two months ago? What was the date? It doesn't matter though, I'll find it. Think of not telling us!"

"How did you find out that the article was mine? It's only signed with an initial."

"I only found out by chance, the other day. Through the editor; I know him . . . I was very interested."

"It analyzed, if I remember, the psychology of a criminal before and after the crime."

"Yes, and you maintained that the perpetration of a crime is always accompanied by illness. Very, very original, but . . . it was not that part of your article that interested me so much, but an idea at the end of the article which unfortunately you just suggested without working it out clearly. There is, if you remember, a suggestion that there are certain persons who can . . . that is, not precisely are able to, but have a perfect right to commit breaches of morality and crimes, and that the law is not for them."

Raskolnikov smiled at the exaggerated and intentional distortion of his idea.

"What? What do you mean? A right to crime? But not because of the influence of their environment?" Razumikhin inquired with some alarm even.

"No, not exactly because of it," answered Porfiry. "In his article all men are divided into 'ordinary' and 'extraordinary.'* Ordinary men have to live in submission, have no right to transgress the law, because, don't you see, they are ordinary. But extraordinary men have a right to commit any crime and to transgress the law in any way, just because they are extraordinary. That was your idea, if I am not mistaken?"

"What do you mean? That can't be right?" Razumikhin muttered in bewilderment.

Raskolnikov smiled again. He saw the point at once, and knew where they wanted to drive him. He decided to take up the challenge.

"That wasn't quite what I said," he began simply and modestly. "But I admit that you have stated it almost correctly; perhaps even perfectly." (It almost gave him pleasure to admit this.) "The only difference is that I don't contend that extraordinary people are always bound to commit breaches of morals, as you call it. In fact, I doubt whether such an argument could be published. I simply hinted that an 'extraordinary' man has the right . . . that is not an official right, but an inner right to decide in his own conscience to overstep . . . certain obstacles, and only in case it is essential for the practical fulfillment of his idea (sometimes, perhaps, of benefit to the whole of humanity). You say that my article isn't definite; I am ready to make it as clear as I can. Perhaps I am right in thinking you want me to; very well. I maintain that if the discoveries of Kepler and Newton could not have been made known except by sacrificing the lives of one, a dozen, a hundred, or more people, Newton would have had the right, would in fact have been duty bound . . . to eliminate a dozen or a hundred men for the sake of making his discoveries known to the whole of humanity. But it does not follow from that that Newton had a right to murder people right and left and to steal every day in the market. Then, I remember, I maintain in my article that all . . . well, legislators and leaders, such as Lycurgus, Solon,†

---

*Opinion expounded by Napoleon III (1808–1873) in his history of Julius Caesar.
†Ancient Greek lawgivers: Lycurgus (seventh century B.C.?) was a perhaps legendary Spartan, Solon (c.630–c.560 B.C.) a historical Athenian.

Muhammed, Napoleon, and so on, were all without exception criminals, from the very fact that, making a new law, they transgressed the
ancient one, handed down from their ancestors and held sacred by
the people, and they did not stop short at bloodshed either, if that
bloodshed—often of innocent persons fighting bravely in defense of
ancient law—were of use to their cause. It's remarkable, in fact, that
the majority, in fact, of these benefactors and leaders of humanity
were guilty of terrible carnage. In short, I maintain that all great people or even people who are slightly uncommon, that is to say capable of producing some new idea, must by nature be criminals—more
or less, of course. Otherwise it's hard for them to get out of the common rut; and to remain in the common rut is what they can't submit
to, from their very nature again, and to my mind they ought not, in
fact, to submit to it. You see that there is nothing particularly new in
all that. The same thing has been printed and read a thousand times
before. As for my division of people into ordinary and extraordinary,
I acknowledge that it's somewhat arbitrary, but I don't insist upon
exact numbers. I only believe in my leading idea that men are in general divided by a law of nature into two categories, inferior (ordinary), that is, so to say, material that serves only to reproduce its kind,
and men who have the gift or the talent to produce something new.
There are, of course, innumerable sub-divisions, but the distinguish-
ing features of both categories are fairly well marked. The first category, generally speaking, contains men who are conservative in
temperament and law-abiding; they live under control and love to be
controlled. To my thinking it is their duty to be controlled, because
that's their vocation, and there is nothing humiliating in it for them.
The second category transgresses the law; they are destroyers or disposed to destruction according to their capacities. The crimes of
these men are of course relative and varied; for the most part they
seek in very varied ways the destruction of the present for the sake of
the better. But if such people are forced for the sake of their ideas to
step over a corpse or wade through blood they can, I maintain, find
within themselves, in their conscience, a justification for wading
through blood—which, you should note, depends on the idea and its
dimensions. It's only in that sense I speak of their right to crime in
my article (you remember it began with the legal question). There's
no need for such anxiety, however; the masses will scarcely ever

admit this right, they punish them or hang them (more or less), and in doing so quite justly fulfill their conservative vocation. But the same masses set these criminals on a pedestal in the next generation and worship them (more or less). The first category is always the man of the present, the second the man of the future. The first preserve the world and people it, the second move the world and lead it to its goal. Each class has an equal right to exist. In fact, all have equal rights with me—and I hope eternal war flourishes—until the New Jerusalem, of course!"

"Then you believe in the New Jerusalem, do you?"

"I do," Raskolnikov answered firmly; as he said these words and during the whole tirade which preceded them he kept his eyes on one spot on the carpet.

"And . . . and do you believe in God? Excuse my curiosity."

"I do," repeated Raskolnikov, raising his eyes to Porfiry.

"And . . . do you believe that Lazarus rose from the dead?"

"I . . . I do. Why do you ask all this?"

"You believe it literally?"

"Literally."

"You don't say so . . . I asked because I was curious. Excuse me. But let us go back to the question; they are not always executed. Some, on the contrary . . . "

"Triumph in their lifetime? Oh, yes, some attain their ends in this life, and then . . . "

"They begin executing other people?"

"If it's necessary; indeed, for the most part they do. Your remark is very witty."

"Thank you. But tell me this: how do you distinguish those extraordinary people from the ordinary ones? Are there signs at their birth? I feel there ought to be more exactitude, more external definition. Excuse the natural anxiety of a practical law-abiding citizen, but couldn't they adopt a special uniform, for instance, couldn't they wear something, be branded in some way? For you know if confusion arises and a member of one category imagines that he belongs to the other, begins to 'eliminate obstacles,' as you so happily expressed it, then . . . "

"Oh, that very often happens! That remark is wittier than the other."

"Thank you."

"No reason to; but take note that the mistake can only arise in the first category, that is among the ordinary people (as I perhaps unfortunately called them). In spite of their predisposition to obedience very many of them, through a playfulness of nature, sometimes vouchsafed even to the cow, like to imagine themselves advanced people, 'destroyers,' and to push themselves into the 'new movement,' and quite sincerely at that. Meanwhile the really new people are very often unobserved by them, or even despised as reactionaries of groveling tendencies. But I don't think there is any considerable danger here, and you really needn't be uneasy; they never go very far. Of course, they might have a thrashing sometimes for letting their imagination run away with them and to teach them their place, but no more; in fact, even this isn't necessary as they chastise themselves, because they are very conscientious: some perform this service for one another and others chastise themselves with their own hands . . . They will impose various public acts of penitence upon themselves with a beautiful and edifying effect; in fact, you've nothing to be uneasy about . . . It's a law of nature."

"Well, you have certainly set my mind more at rest on that score; but there's another thing worries me. Tell me, please, are there many people who have the right to kill others, these extraordinary people? I am ready to bow down to them, of course, but you must admit it's alarming if there are a great many of them, eh?"

"Oh, you needn't worry about that either," Raskolnikov went on in the same tone. "People with new ideas, people with the faintest capacity for saying something new, are extremely few in number, extraordinarily so in fact. One thing only is clear, that the appearance of all these grades and sub-divisions of men must follow with unfailing regularity some law of nature. That law, of course, is unknown at present, but I am convinced that it exists, and one day may become known. The vast mass of mankind is mere material, and only exists in order by some great effort, by some mysterious process, by some crossing of races and stocks, to bring into the world at last perhaps one man out of a thousand with a spark of independence. One in ten thousand perhaps—I speak roughly, approximately—is born with some independence, and with still greater independence one in a hundred thousand. The man of genius is one of millions, and the great geniuses, the crown of humanity, appear on earth perhaps one in many thousand millions. In fact I have not peeped into the retort in which all this takes place. But there certainly is and must be a definite law, it cannot be a matter of chance."

"Why, are you both joking?" Razumikhin cried at last. "There you sit, making fun of one another. Are you serious, Rodia?"

Raskolnikov raised his pale and almost mournful face and made no reply. And the unconcealed, persistent, nervous, and discourteous sarcasm of Porfiry seemed strange to Razumikhin beside that quiet and mournful face.

"Well, my friend, if you're really serious . . . You're right, of course, in saying that it's not new, that it's like what we've read and heard a thousand times already; but what is really original in all this, and is exclusively your own, to my horror, is that you permit bloodshed in the name of conscience, and, excuse my saying so, with such fanaticism . . . That, I take it, is the point of your article. But that permission of bloodshed by conscience is to my mind . . . more terrible than the official, legal permission of bloodshed . . . "

"You are quite right, it is more terrible," Porfiry agreed.

"Yes, you must have exaggerated! There is some mistake, I shall read it. You can't think that! I shall read it."

"All that is not in the article, there's only a hint of it," said Raskolnikov.

"Yes, yes." Porfiry couldn't sit still. "Your attitude to crime is pretty clear to me now, but . . . excuse me for my impertinence (I am really ashamed to be worrying you like this), you see, you've removed my anxiety as to the two grades getting mixed, but . . . there are various practical possibilities that make me uneasy! What if some man or youth imagines that he is a Lycurgus or Muhammed—a future one of course—and suppose he begins to remove all obstacles . . . He has some great enterprise before him and needs money for it . . . and tries to get it . . . do you see?"

Zametov gave a sudden guffaw in his corner. Raskolnikov did not even raise his eyes to him.

"I must admit," he went on calmly, "that such cases must certainly arise. The vain and foolish are particularly apt to fall into that snare; young people especially."

"Yes, you see. Well then?"

"What then?" Raskolnikov smiled in reply; "that's not my fault. So it is and so it always will be. He said just now" (he nodded at Razumikhin) "that I permit bloodshed. Society is too well protected by prisons, banishment, criminal investigators, penal servitude. There's no need to be uneasy. You have but to catch the thief."

"And what if we do catch him?"

"Then he gets what he deserves."

"You are certainly logical. But what of his conscience?"

"Why do you care about that?"

"Simply from humanity."

"If he has a conscience he will suffer for his mistake. That will be his punishment—as well as the prison."

"But the real geniuses," asked Razumikhin frowning, "those who have the right to murder? Oughtn't they to suffer at all even for the blood they've shed?"

"Why the word 'ought'? It's not a matter of permission or prohibition. He will suffer if he is sorry for his victim. Pain and suffering are always inevitable for a large intelligence and a deep heart. The really great men must, I think, have great sadness on earth," he added dreamily, not in the tone of the conversation.

He raised his eyes, looked earnestly at them all, smiled, and took his cap. He was too quiet by comparison with his manner at his entrance, and he felt this. Everyone got up.

"Well, you may abuse me, be angry with me if you like," Porfiry Petrovich began again, "but I can't resist. Allow me one little question (I know I am troubling you). There is just one little notion I want to express, simply that I may not forget it."

"Very good, tell me your little notion," Raskolnikov stood waiting, pale and grave before him.

"Well, you see . . . I really don't know how to express it properly . . . It's a playful, psychological idea . . . When you were writing your article, surely you couldn't have helped, he-he, fancying yourself . . . just a little, an 'extraordinary' man, uttering a new word in your sense . . . That's so, isn't it?"

"Quite possibly," Raskolnikov answered contemptuously.

Razumikhin made a movement.

"And, if so, could you bring yourself in case of worldly difficulties and hardship or for some service to humanity—to overstep obstacles? . . . For instance, to rob and murder?"

And again he winked with his left eye, and laughed noiselessly just as before.

"If I did I certainly wouldn't tell you," Raskolnikov answered with defiant and proud contempt.

"No, I was only interested because of your article, from a literary point of view . . . "

"God, how obvious and insolent that is," Raskolnikov thought with repulsion.

"Allow me to observe," he answered dryly, "that I don't consider myself a Muhammed or a Napoleon, nor any person of that kind, and not being one of them I cannot tell you how I would act."

"Oh, come, don't we all consider ourselves Napoleons now in Russia?" Porfiry Petrovich said with alarming familiarity.

Something peculiar betrayed itself in the very intonation of his voice.

"Perhaps it was one of these future Napoleons who did for Aliona Ivanovna last week?" Zametov blurted out from the corner.

Raskolnikov did not speak, but looked firmly and intently at Porfiry. Razumikhin was scowling gloomily. He seemed before this to be noticing something. He looked angrily around. There was a minute of gloomy silence. Raskolnikov turned to go.

"Are you going already?" Porfiry said amiably, holding out his hand with excessive politeness. "Very, very pleased to meet you. As for your request, have no uneasiness, write just as I told you, or, better still, come to me there yourself in a day or two . . . tomorrow, indeed. I shall be there at eleven o'clock for certain. We'll arrange it all; we'll have a talk. As one of the last to be there, you might perhaps be able to tell us something," he added with a most good-natured expression.

"You want to cross-examine me officially in due form?" Raskolnikov asked sharply.

"Why? For the moment, that's unnecessary. You misunderstand me. I lose no opportunity, you see, and . . . I've talked to everyone who had pledges . . . I obtained evidence from some of them, and you are the last . . . Yes, by the way," he cried, seemingly suddenly delighted, "I just remember, what was I thinking of?" he turned to

Razumikhin, "you were talking my ears off about that Nikolai . . . of course, I know, I know very well," he turned to Raskolnikov, "that the man is innocent, but what can you do? We had to trouble Dmitri too . . . This is the point, this is all I wanted to ask: when you went up the stairs it was past seven, wasn't it?"

"Yes," answered Raskolnikov, with an unpleasant sensation at the very moment he spoke that he need not have said it.

"Then when you went upstairs between seven and eight, didn't you see in an apartment that stood open on a second storey, do you remember, two workmen or at least one of them? They were painting there, didn't you notice them? It's very, very important for them."

"Painters? No, I didn't see them," Raskolnikov answered slowly, as though ransacking his memory, while at the same instant he was racking every nerve, almost swooning with anxiety to guess as quickly as possible where the trap lay and not to overlook anything. "No, I didn't see them, and I don't think I noticed an apartment like that open . . . But on the fourth floor" (he had mastered the trap now and was triumphant) "I remember now that someone was moving out of the apartment opposite Aliona Ivanovna's . . . I remember . . . I remember it clearly. Some porters were carrying out a sofa and they squeezed me against the wall. But painters . . . no, I don't remember that there were any painters, and I don't think that there was an apartment open anywhere, no, there wasn't."

"What do you mean?" Razumikhin shouted suddenly, as though he had reflected and realized. "Why, it was on the day of the murder the painters were at work, and he was there three days before? What are you asking?"

"Goodness! I've got it all mixed up!" Porfiry slapped himself on the forehead. "Damn this business, it's doing my head in!" he said to Raskolnikov, somewhat apologetically. "It would be such a great thing for us to find out whether anyone had seen them between seven and eight at the apartment, so I fancied you could perhaps have told us something . . . I got it all muddled."

"Then you should be more careful," Razumikhin observed grimly.

The last words were uttered in the passage. Porfiry Petrovich saw them to the door with excessive politeness.

They went out into the street gloomy and sullen, and for some steps they did not say a word. Raskolnikov drew a deep breath.

CHAPTER SIX

"I DON'T BELIEVE IT, I can't believe it!" repeated Razumikhin, trying in perplexity to refute Raskolnikov's arguments.

They were by now approaching Bakaleyev's lodgings, where Pulcheria Alexandrovna and Dunia had been expecting them a long while. Razumikhin kept stopping on the way in the heat of discussion, confused and excited by the very fact that they were for the first time speaking openly about it.

"Don't believe it, then!" answered Raskolnikov, with a cold, careless smile. "You were noticing nothing as usual, but I was weighing every word."

"You are suspicious. That is why you weighed their words . . . hm . . . certainly, I agree, Porfiry's tone was rather strange, and still more that wretch Zametov! . . . You are right, there was something about him—but why? Why?"

"He has changed his mind since last night."

"Quite the contrary! If they had that brainless idea, they would do their best to hide it, and conceal their cards, in order to catch you afterwards . . . But it was all impudent and careless."

"If they had had facts—I mean, real facts—or at least grounds for suspicion, then they would certainly have tried to hide their game, in the hope of getting more (they would have made a search long ago anyway). But they haven't got any facts, not a single one. It's all a mirage—all ambiguous. Just a floating idea. So they try to throw me with impudence. And perhaps he was irritated at having no facts, and blurted it out in vexation—or perhaps he has a plan . . . he seems like an intelligent man. Perhaps he wanted to frighten me by pretending to know. They have a psychology of their own, my friend. But it's so revolting to explain it all; let's stop."

"And it's insulting, insulting! I understand you. But . . . since we have spoken openly now (and it is an excellent thing that we have at last, I'm glad) I will now admit frankly that I noticed it in them long ago, this idea. Just a hint, of course—an insinuation—but why even an insinuation? How dare they? What grounds do they have? If only you knew how furious I've been. Think about it! Just because a poor student, unhinged by poverty and hypochondria, on the eve of a severe delirious illness (note that), suspicious, vain, proud, who has not seen a soul to speak to for six months, in rags and in boots without soles, has to face some wretched policemen and put up with their insolence; and the unexpected debt thrust under his nose, the I.O.U. presented by Chebarov, the new paint, thirty degrees and a stifling atmosphere, a crowd of people, a conversation about the murder of a person whose apartment he had been at just before, and all that on an empty stomach—he might well have a fainting fit! And that, that is what they base it all on! Damn them! I understand how annoying it is, but if I were you, Rodia, I would laugh at them, or better still, spit in their ugly faces, and spit a dozen times in all directions. I'd hit out in all directions, neatly too, and put an end to it. Damn them! Don't be downhearted. How shameful it all is!"

"He really has put it well, though," Raskolnikov thought.

"Damn them? But the cross-examination again, tomorrow?" he said with bitterness. "Must I really start explaining things to them? I feel annoyed as it is that I started speaking to Zametov yesterday in the restaurant . . . "

"Damn it! I will go myself to Porfiry. I will squeeze it out of him, as one of the family: he must let me know the ins and outs of it all! And as for Zametov . . . "

"At last he sees through him!" thought Raskolnikov.

"Stop!" cried Razumikhin, seizing him by the shoulder again. "Stop! You were wrong. I have thought it out. You're wrong! How was that a trap? You say that the question about the workmen was a trap. But if you had done that, could you have said you had seen them painting the apartment . . . and the workmen? On the contrary, you would have seen nothing, even if you had seen it. Who would produce evidence against himself?"

"If I had done that thing, I should certainly have said that I had seen the workmen and the apartment." Raskolnikov answered, with reluctance and obvious disgust.

"But why speak against yourself?"

"Because only peasants, or the most inexperienced novices deny everything flatly at examinations. If a man is undeveloped and inexperienced, he will certainly try to admit all the external facts that can't be avoided, but seek other explanations of them, introduce some special, unexpected turn that will lend them another meaning and put them in another light. Porfiry might well reckon that I should be sure to answer so, and say I had seen them to give an air of truth, and then make some explanation."

"But he would have told you at once, that the workmen could not have been there two days before, and that therefore you must have been there on the day of the murder at eight o'clock. And so he would have caught you over a detail."

"Yes, that is what he was reckoning on, that I should not have time to reflect, and should be in a hurry to make the most likely answer, and so would forget that the workmen could not have been there two days before."

"But how could you forget it?"

"Nothing easier. It is in just such stupid things that clever people are most easily caught. The more cunning a man is, the less he suspects that he will be caught out in a simple trap. The more cunning a man is, the simpler the trap he must be caught in. Porfiry is not as much of a fool as you think . . . "

"He is a knave then, if that is so!"

Raskolnikov could not help laughing. But at the very moment, he was struck by the strangeness of his own frankness, and the eagerness with which he had made this explanation, though he had kept up all the preceding conversation with gloomy repulsion, obviously with a motive, from necessity.

"I am getting a relish for certain aspects!" he thought to himself. But almost at the same instant, he became suddenly uneasy, as though an unexpected and alarming idea had occurred to him. His uneasiness kept on increasing. They had just reached the entrance to Bakaleyev's.

"Go in alone!" said Raskolnikov suddenly. "I'll be back soon."

"Where are you going? We've just got here."

"I can't help it . . . I will come back in half an hour. Tell them."

"Say what you like, I will come with you."

"So you want to torture me too!" he screamed, with such bitter irritation, such despair in his eyes that Razumikhin's hands dropped. He stood for some time on the steps, looking gloomily at Raskolnikov striding rapidly away in the direction of his lodging. At last, gritting his teeth and clenching his fist, he swore he would squeeze Porfiry like a lemon that very day, and went up the stairs to reassure Pulcheria Alexandrovna, who was by now alarmed at their long absence.

When Raskolnikov got home, his hair was soaked with sweat and he was breathing heavily. He went rapidly up the stairs, walked into his unlocked room and at once fastened the latch. Then in senseless terror he rushed to the corner, to that hole under the paper where he had put the thing; put his hand in, and for some minutes felt carefully in the hole, in every crack and fold of the paper. Finding nothing, he got up and drew a deep breath. As he was reaching the steps of Bakaleyev's, he suddenly thought that something, a chain, a stud or even a bit of paper in which they had been wrapped with the old woman's handwriting on it, might somehow have slipped out and been lost in some crack, and then might suddenly turn up as unexpected, conclusive evidence against him.

He stood as if were lost in thought, and a strange, humiliated, half senseless smile strayed on his lips. He took his cap at last and went quietly out of the room. His ideas were all tangled. He went dreamily through the gateway.

"Here he is," shouted a loud voice.

He raised his head.

The porter was standing at the door of his little room and was pointing him out to a short man who looked like an artisan, wearing a long coat and a waistcoat, and looking at a distance remarkably like a woman. He stooped, and his head in a greasy cap hung forward. From his wrinkled flabby face he looked over fifty; his little eyes were lost in fat and they looked out grimly, sternly and discontentedly.

"What is it?" Raskolnikov asked, going up to the porter.

The man stole a look at him from under his brows and he looked at him attentively, deliberately; then he turned slowly and went out of the gate into the street without saying a word.

"What is it?" cried Raskolnikov.

"He was asking whether a student lived here, mentioned your name and who you lodged with. I saw you coming and pointed you out and he went away. Seems strange to me."

The porter also seemed fairly puzzled, but not excessively so, and after wondering about it for a moment he turned and went back to his room.

Raskolnikov ran after the stranger, and at once caught sight of him walking along the other side of the street with the same even, deliberate step, his eyes fixed on the ground, as if he were meditating. He soon overtook him, but kept walking behind him for some time. At last, moving level with him, he looked at his face. The man noticed him at once, looked at him quickly, but dropped his eyes again; and so they walked for a minute side by side without uttering a word.

"You were asking for me . . . at the porter's?" Raskolnikov said at last, but in a strangely quiet voice.

The man didn't answer; he didn't even look at him. Again they were both silent.

"Why did you . . . come and ask for me . . . and say nothing . . . Why?"

Raskolnikov's voice broke and he seemed unable to articulate the words clearly.

The man raised his eyes this time and turned a gloomy sinister look at Raskolnikov.

"Murderer!" he said suddenly in a quiet but clear and distinct voice.

Raskolnikov went on walking beside him. His legs felt suddenly weak, a cold shiver ran down his spine, and his heart seemed to stand still for a moment, then suddenly began throbbing as though it were set free. So they walked for about a hundred paces, side by side in silence.

The man did not look at him.

"What do you mean . . . what is . . . Who's a murderer?" muttered Raskolnikov hardly audibly.

"You are a murderer," the man answered still more articulately and emphatically, with a smile of triumphant hatred, and again he looked straight into Raskolnikov's pale face and stricken eyes.

They had just reached the crossroads. The man turned to the left without looking behind him. Raskolnikov remained standing, gazing after him. He saw him turn round fifty paces away and look back at him still standing there. Raskolnikov could not see clearly, but he imagined that he was again smiling the same smile of cold hatred and triumph.

With slow faltering steps, with shaking knees, Raskolnikov made his way back to his little garret, feeling chilled all over. He took off his cap and put it on the table, and for ten minutes he stood without moving. Then he sank exhausted on the sofa and with a weak moan of pain he stretched himself out on it. So he lay for half an hour.

He thought of nothing. Some thoughts or fragments of thoughts, some images without order or coherence floated before his mind— faces of people he had seen in his childhood or met somewhere once, whom he would never have recalled, the belfry of the church at V., the billiard table in a restaurant and some officers playing billiards, the smell of cigars in some underground tobacco store, a tavern room, a back staircase quite dark, all sloppy with dirty water and strewn with egg shells, and the Sunday bells floating in from somewhere . . . The images followed one another, whirling like a hurricane. Some of them he liked and tried to clutch at, but they faded and all the while there was an oppressive feeling inside him, but it was not overwhelming, sometimes it was even pleasant . . . The slight shivering still persisted, but that too was an almost pleasant sensation.

He heard the hurried footsteps of Razumikhin; he closed his eyes and pretended to be asleep. Razumikhin opened the door and stood for some time in the doorway as though hesitating, then he stepped softly into the room and went cautiously to the sofa. Raskolnikov heard Nastasia's whisper:

"Don't disturb him! Let him sleep. He can have his dinner later."

"Fine," answered Razumikhin. Both withdrew carefully and closed the door. Another half hour passed. Raskolnikov opened his eyes, turned on his back again, clasping his hands behind his head.

"Who is he? Who is that man who sprang out of the earth? Where was he, what did he see? He saw it all, that's clear. Where was he then? And where did he see it from? Why has he only now sprung out of the earth? And how could he see it? Is it possible? Hm . . . " continued Raskolnikov, turning cold and shivering, "and the jewel case Nikolai found behind the door—was that possible? A clue? You miss an infinitesimal line and you can build it into a pyramid of evidence! A fly flew by and saw it! Is it possible?" He felt with sudden loathing how weak, how physically weak he had become. "I ought to have known it," he thought with a bitter smile. "And how dared I, knowing myself, knowing how I would be, take up an axe and shed blood! I ought to have known beforehand . . . Ah, but I did know!" he whispered in despair. At times he came to a standstill at some thought.

"No, those men are not made like that. The real Master to whom all is permitted storms Toulon, makes a massacre in Paris, forgets an army in Egypt, wastes half a million men in the Moscow expedition and gets off with a jest at Vilna. And altars are set up to him after his death, and so everything is permitted. No, such people, it seems, are made not of flesh but of bronze!"

One sudden irrelevant idea almost made him laugh. Napoleon, the pyramids, Waterloo, and a wretched skinny old woman, a pawn-broker with a red trunk under her bed—it's a nice hash for Porfiry Petrovich to digest! How can they digest it! It's too inartistic. "A Napoleon creeping under an old woman's bed! Ugh, how loath-some!"

At moments he felt he was raving. He sank into a state of fever-ish excitement. "The old woman doesn't matter," he thought, hotly and incoherently. "The old woman was a mistake perhaps, but she isn't what matters! The old woman was just an illness . . . I was in a hurry to overstep . . . I didn't kill a human being, but a principle! I killed the principle, but I didn't overstep, I stopped on this side . . . I was only capable of killing. And it seems I wasn't even capable of that . . . Principle? Why was that fool Razumikhin abusing the socialists? They are industrious, commercial people; 'universal happiness' is their case. No, life is only given to me once and I shall never have it again; I don't want to wait for 'universal happiness.' I want to live myself, or else better not live at all. I simply couldn't pass by my mother starving, keeping my trouble in my pocket while I waited for 'universal happiness.' I am putting my little brick into universal hap-piness and so my heart is at peace. Ha-ha! Why have you let me slip? I only live once, I too want . . . God, esthetically I'm a louse and noth-ing else," he added suddenly, laughing like a madman. "Yes, I'm def-initely a louse," he went on, clutching at the idea, gloating over it and playing with it with vindictive pleasure. "In the first place, because I can reason that I am one, and secondly, because for a month past I have been troubling benevolent Providence, calling it to witness that I didn't do it for my own fleshly lusts, but with a grand and noble object—ha-ha! Thirdly, because I aimed to carry it out as justly as possible, weighing, measuring and calculating. Of all the lice I picked out the most useless one and proposed to take from her only as much as I needed for the first step, no more, no less (so the rest would have gone to a monastery, according to her will, ha-ha!). And the thing which really shows that I am a louse," he added, grinding his teeth, "is that I am perhaps viler and more loathsome than the louse I killed, and I felt beforehand that I would tell myself so after I killed her. Can anything be compared with the horror of that! The vulgarity! The abjectness! I understand the 'prophet' with his saber, on his steed: Allah commands and 'trembling' creation must obey! The 'prophet' is right, he is right when he sets a battery across the street and blows up the innocent and the guilty without explaining! It's for you to obey, trembling creation, and not to have desires, that's not for you! . . . I shall never, never forgive the old woman!"

His hair was soaked with sweat, his quivering lips were parched, his eyes were fixed on the ceiling.

"Mother, sister—how I loved them! Why do I hate them now? Yes, I hate them, I feel a physical hatred for them, I can't bear to have them near me . . . I went up to my mother and kissed her, I remember . . . To embrace her and think if she only knew . . . shall I tell her then? That's just what I might do . . . She must be the same as I am," he added, straining himself to think, as it were struggling with delirium. "Ah, how I hate the old woman now! I feel I would kill her again if she came to life! Poor Lizaveta! Why did she come in? . . . It's strange though, why is it I scarcely ever think of her, as though I hadn't killed her! Lizaveta! Sonia! Poor gentle things, with gentle eyes . . . Dear women! Why don't they weep? Why don't they moan? They give up everything . . . their eyes are soft and gentle . . . Sonia, Sonia! Gentle Sonia!"

He lost consciousness; it seemed strange to him that he didn't remember how he got into the street. It was late in the evening. The twilight had fallen and the full moon was shining more and more brightly; but there was a peculiar breathlessness in the air. There were crowds of people in the street; workmen and business people were making their way home; other people had come out for a walk; there was a smell of mortar, dust and stagnant water. Raskolnikov walked along, mournful and anxious; he was definitely aware of having come out with a purpose, of having to do something in a hurry, but what it was he had forgotten. Suddenly he stood still and saw a man standing on the other side of the street, beckoning to him. He crossed over, but at once the man turned and walked away with his head hanging, as though he had made no sign to him. "Hold on, did he really beckon?" Raskolnikov wondered, but he tried to overtake him. When he was within ten paces he recognized him and was frightened; it was the same man with stooping shoulders in the long coat. Raskolnikov followed him at a distance; his heart was beating; they went down a turning; the man still did not look round. "Does he know I am following him?" thought Raskolnikov. The man went into the gateway of a big house. Raskolnikov hastened to the gate and looked in to see whether he would look round and make a sign to him. In the courtyard the man did turn round and again seemed to beckon him. Raskolnikov at once followed him into the yard, but the man was gone. He must have gone up the first staircase. Raskolnikov rushed after him. He heard slow measured steps two flights above. The staircase seemed strangely familiar. He reached the window on the first floor; the moon shone through the panes with a melancholy and mysterious light; then he reached the second floor. Bah! This is the apartment where the painters were at work . . . but how was it he did not recognize it at once? The steps of the man above had died away. "So he must have stopped or hidden somewhere." He reached the third floor, should he go on? There was a stillness that was dreadful . . . But he went on. The sound of his own footsteps scared and frightened him. How dark it was! The man must be hiding in some corner here. Ah! the apartment was standing wide open, he hesitated and went in. It was very dark and empty in the passage, as though everything had been removed; he crept on tiptoe into the parlor which was flooded with moonlight. Everything there was as before, the chairs, the looking-glass, the yellow sofa and the pictures in the frames. A huge, round, copper-red moon looked in at the windows. "It's the moon that makes it so still, weaving some mystery," thought Raskolnikov. He stood and waited, waited a long while, and the more silent the moonlight, the more violently his heart beat, until it grew painful. And still the same hush. Suddenly he heard a momentary sharp crack like the snapping of a splinter and all was still again. A fly flew up suddenly and struck the window pane with a plaintive buzz. At that moment he noticed in the corner between the window and the little cupboard something like a cloak hanging on the wall. "Why is that cloak there?" he thought, "it wasn't there before . . . " He went up to it quietly and felt that there was someone hiding behind it. He cautiously moved the cloak and saw, sitting on a chair in the corner, the old woman bent double so that he couldn't see her face; but it was she. He stood over her. "She is afraid," he thought. He stealthily took the axe from the noose and struck her one blow, then another on the skull. But strange to say she did not stir, as though she were made of wood. He was frightened, bent down nearer and tried to look at her; but she, too, bent her head lower. He bent right down to the ground and peeped up into her face from below—he peeped and turned cold with horror: the old woman was sitting and laughing, shaking with noiseless laughter, doing her best to prevent him hearing it. Suddenly he imagined that the door from the bedroom was ajar and that there was laughter and whispering inside. He was overcome with frenzy and he began hitting the old woman on the head with all his strength, but at every blow of the axe the laughter and whispering from the bedroom grew louder and the old woman was actually shaking with amusement. He was rushing away, but the passage was full of people, the doors of the apartments stood open and on the landing, on the stairs and everywhere below there were people, rows of heads, all looking, but huddled together in silence and expectation. Something gripped his heart, his legs were rooted to the spot, they would not move . . . He tried to scream and woke up.

He drew a deep breath—but his dream seemed to persist strangely: his door was flung open and a man whom he had never seen stood in the doorway watching him intently.

Raskolnikov had hardly opened his eyes and he instantly closed them again. He lay on his back without stirring.

"Is it still a dream?" he wondered and again raised his eyelids almost imperceptibly; the stranger was standing in the same place, still watching him.

He stepped cautiously into the room, carefully closing the door after him, went up to the table, paused a moment, still keeping his eyes on Raskolnikov and noiselessly seated himself on the chair by the sofa; he put his hat on the floor beside him and leaned his hands on his cane and his chin on his hands. It was evident that he was prepared to wait indefinitely. As far as Raskolnikov could make out from his stolen glances, he was stout, with a full, fair, almost whitish beard.

Ten minutes passed. It was still light, but dusk was just falling. There was a complete stillness in the room. Not a sound came from the stairs. Only a big fly buzzed and fluttered against the window pane. Finally, it became unbearable. Raskolnikov suddenly got up and sat on the sofa.

"Come, tell me what you want."

"I knew you weren't asleep, just pretending," the stranger answered oddly, laughing calmly. "Arkady Ivanovich Svidrigailov, allow me to introduce myself . . . "

PART FOUR

CHAPTER ONE

"CAN THIS BE STILL a dream?" Raskolnikov thought once more.

He looked carefully and suspiciously at the unexpected visitor.

"Svidrigailov! What nonsense! It can't be!" he said at last aloud in bewilderment.

His visitor did not seem at all surprised at this exclamation.

"I've come to you for two reasons. Firstly, I wanted to meet you personally, as I have already heard a great deal about you that is interesting and flattering; secondly, I dearly hope that you may not refuse to assist me in a matter which directly concerns the welfare of your sister, Avdotia Romanovna. Without your support she might not let me come near her now, since she is prejudiced against me, but with your help I think I . . . "

"You think wrongly," interrupted Raskolnikov.

"They only arrived yesterday, didn't they?"

Raskolnikov made no reply.

"It was yesterday, I know. I only arrived myself the day before. Well, let me tell you, Rodion Romanovich, I don't consider it necessary to justify myself; but I would be grateful if you could explain to me what was particularly criminal about how I behaved in all this, speaking without prejudice, with common sense?"

Raskolnikov continued to look at him in silence.

"That in my own house I persecuted a defenseless girl and 'insulted her with my appalling proposals'—is that it? (I am anticipating you.) But you've only to assume that I, too, am a man *et nihil humanum* . . . * in a word, that I am capable of being attracted and falling in love (which does not depend on our will), then everything can be explained in the most natural manner. The question is, am I a monster, or am I myself a victim? And what if I am a victim? In proposing to the object of my passion to elope with me to America or Switzerland, I may have cherished the deepest respect for her and may have thought that I was promoting our mutual happiness! Rea-

---

*Quote from *Heauton timoroumenos* (*The Self-Tormentor;* 163 B.C.), by Terence, a Roman comic dramatist; the Latin words translate as "and nothing human."

son is the slave of passion, you know; why, probably, I was doing more harm to myself than anyone!"

"But that's not the point," Raskolnikov interrupted with disgust. "It's simply that whether you are right or wrong, we dislike you. We don't want to have anything to do with you. We will show you the door. Get out!"

Svidrigailov broke into a sudden laugh.

"But you're . . . but I can't get round you," he said, laughing in the frankest way. "I was hoping to get round you, but you took up the right line at once!"

"But you are trying to get round me still!"

"What of it? What of it?" cried Svidrigailov, laughing openly. "But this is what the French call *bonne guerre*,* and the most innocent form of deception! . . . But still you have interrupted me; one way or another, I repeat again: there would never have been any unpleasantness except for what happened in the garden. Marfa Petrovna . . . "

"You've got rid of Marfa Petrovna, too, so they say?" Raskolnikov interrupted rudely.

"Oh, you've heard that, too, then? You'd be sure to, though . . . But as for your question, I really don't know what to say, though my own conscience is quite at rest on that score. Don't suppose that I am in any apprehension about it. All was regular and in order; the medical inquiry diagnosed apoplexy due to bathing immediately after a heavy dinner and a bottle of wine, and indeed it could have proved nothing else. But I'll tell you what I have been thinking to myself recently, on my way here in the train, especially: didn't I contribute to that whole . . . calamity, morally, in a way, by my irritation or something of the sort. But I came to the conclusion that that, too, was out of the question."

Raskolnikov laughed.

"I'm amazed you trouble yourself about it!"

"But what are you laughing at? Only consider, I struck her just twice with a whip—there were no marks even . . . don't regard me as a cynic, please; I am perfectly aware how atrocious it was of me; but I know for certain, too, that Marfa Petrovna was very likely pleased at my warmth, so to speak. The story of your sister had been wrung out

---

*Honest warfare (French).

to the last drop; for the last three days Marfa Petrovna had been forced to sit at home; she had nothing to show herself with in the town. Besides, she had bored them so much with that letter (you heard about her reading the letter). And all of a sudden those two whiplashes fell from heaven! Her first act was to order the carriage to be got out . . . Not to speak of the fact that there are cases when women are very, very glad to be insulted in spite of all their show of indignation. There are instances of it with everyone; human beings in general, indeed, greatly love to be insulted, have you noticed that? But it's particularly so with women. You might even say it's their only amusement."

At one time Raskolnikov thought of getting up and walking out and thus drawing their interview to a close. But some curiosity and even a sort of carefulness made him linger for a moment.

"Are you fond of fighting?" he asked casually.

"No, not very," Svidrigailov answered, calmly. "And Marfa Petrovna and I scarcely ever fought. We lived very harmoniously, and she was always pleased with me. I only used the whip twice in all our seven years (not counting a third occasion, which was really very ambiguous). The first time was two months after our marriage, immediately after we arrived in the country, and the last time was the one we were just speaking about. Did you suppose I was such a monster, such a reactionary, such a slave driver? Ha, ha! By the way, do you remember, Rodion Romanovich, how a few years ago, in those days of kindly publicity, a nobleman, I've forgotten his name, was put to shame everywhere, in all the papers, for having thrashed a German woman in the railway train. You remember? It was in those days, the same year I believe, that the 'disgraceful action of the Age' took place (you know, 'The Egyptian Nights,'* that public reading, you remember? The dark eyes, you know! Ah, the golden days of our youth, where are they now?).† Well, as for the gentleman who thrashed the German, I feel no sympathy with him, because after all what need is there for sympathy? But I must say that there are sometimes such provoking 'Germans' that I don't believe there is a progressive who could quite answer for himself. No-one looked at the subject from

---

*Reference to a controversial reading of Russian writer Alexander Pushkin's *Egyptian Nights* (1835) at a public event several years previously. The work describes a man's gift at improvising poetry.

†Distorted quote from Pushkin's verse novel *Evgeny Onegin* (1833).

that point of view then, but that's the truly humane point of view, I assure you."

After saying this, Svidrigailov broke into a sudden laugh again. Raskolnikov saw clearly that this was a man with a firm purpose in his mind who was able to keep it to himself.

"I expect you've not talked to anyone for several days?" he asked.

"Scarcely anyone. I suppose you are wondering at how adaptable a man I am?"

"No, I am only wondering at the fact that you are too adaptable."

"Because I am not offended at the rudeness of your questions? Is that it? But why take offence? As you asked, so I answered," he replied, with a surprising expression of simplicity. "You know, there's hardly anything I take interest in," he went on, as it were dreamily, "especially now, I've nothing to do . . . You are entirely free to imagine though that I am making up to you with a motive, particularly as I told you I want to see your sister about something. But I'll confess frankly, I am very bored. The last three days especially, so I am delighted to see you . . . Don't be angry, Rodion Romanovich, but you seem somehow to be very strange yourself. Say what you like, there's something wrong with you, and now, too . . . not this very minute, I mean, but now, generally . . . Well, well, I won't, I won't, don't scowl! I am not as much of a bear, you know, as you think."

Raskolnikov looked gloomily at him.

"You're not a bear, perhaps, at all," he said. "In fact, I think you're a man of very good breeding, or at least know how on occasion to behave like one."

"I am not particularly interested in anyone's opinion," Svidrigailov answered, dryly and even with a shade of pride, "and therefore why not be vulgar at times when vulgarity is such a convenient cloak for our climate . . . and especially if you are naturally inclined that way," he added, laughing again.

"But I've heard you have many friends here. You are, as they say, 'not without connections.' What can you want from me, then, unless you have some special purpose?"

"That's true that I have friends here," Svidrigailov admitted, not responding to the main point. "I've met some already. I've been lounging about for the last three days, and I've seen them, or they've seen me. That's a matter of course. I'm well dressed, I'm not consid-

ered poor. The emancipation of the serfs hasn't affected me: my property consists mainly of forests and water meadows. The revenue has
not fallen off; but . . . I am not going to see them, I was sick of them
long ago. I've been here three days and have called on no-one . . .
What a town it is! How has it come into existence among us, tell me
that? A town of officials and students of all sorts. Yes, there's a great
deal I didn't notice when I was here eight years ago, kicking up my
heels . . . My only hope now is in anatomy, by God, it is!"

"Anatomy?"

"But as for these clubs, Dussauts,* parades, or progress, indeed,
may be—well, all that can go on without me," he went on, again
without noticing the question. "Besides, who wants to be a card-
cheat?"

"Why, have you been a card-cheat then?"

"How could I help being? There was a regular set of us, men of
the best society, eight years ago; we had a fine time. And all men of
breeding, you know, poets, men of property. And in fact as a rule in
Russian society, the best manners are found among those who've
been thrashed, have you noticed that? I've deteriorated in the country. But I did get into prison for debt, because of a mean Greek from
Nezhin.† Then Marfa Petrovna turned up; she bargained with him
and bought me off for thirty thousand silver pieces (I owed seventy
thousand). We were united in lawful wedlock and she bore me off
into the country like a treasure. You know she was five years older
than I. She was very fond of me. For seven years I never left the country. And take note that all my life she held a document over me, the
I.O.U. for thirty thousand rubles, so if I were to choose to complain
about anything I would be trapped at once! And she would have done
it! Women find nothing incompatible in that."

"If it hadn't been for that, would you have given her the slip?"

"I don't know what to say. It was scarcely the document that restrained me. I didn't want to go anywhere else. Marfa Petrovna herself invited me to go abroad, seeing I was bored, but I've been abroad
before; I always felt sick there. For no reason, but the sunrise, the bay
of Naples, the sea—you look at them and it makes you sad. What's

---

*Dussauts was a restaurant in St. Petersburg.
†Region near Kiev.

most revolting is that you really get sad! No, it's better at home. Here at least you blame others for everything and excuse yourself. I should have gone perhaps on an expedition to the North Pole, because I take wine badly and hate drinking, and there's nothing left but wine. I've tried it. But I've been told Berg* is going up in a large balloon next Sunday from the Yusupov Garden and will take up passengers at a fee. Is it true?"

"Why, would you go up?"

"I . . . No, oh, no," muttered Svidrigailov, really seeming to be deep in thought.

"What does he mean? Is he serious?" Raskolnikov wondered.

"No, the document didn't restrain me," Svidrigailov went on, meditatively. "It was my own doing, not leaving the country, and nearly a year ago Marfa Petrovna gave me back the document on my name day and made me a present of a considerable sum of money, too. She had a fortune, you know. 'You see how I trust you, Arkady Ivanovich'—that was actually her expression. You don't believe she used it? But do you know I managed the estate quite decently, they know me in the neighborhood. I ordered books, too. Marfa Petrovna approved at first, but afterwards she was afraid that I was over-studying."

"You seem to be missing Marfa Petrovna very much?"

"Missing her? Perhaps. Really, perhaps I am. And, by the way, do you believe in ghosts?"

"What ghosts?"

"Why, ordinary ghosts."

"Do you believe in them?"

"Perhaps not, to please you . . . I wouldn't say no exactly."

"Do you see them, then?"

Svidrigailov looked at him rather oddly.

"Marfa Petrovna is pleased to visit me," he said, twisting his mouth into a strange smile.

"What do you mean, 'she is pleased to visit you'?"

"She has been three times. I saw her first on the very day of the funeral, an hour after she was buried. It was the day before I left to come here. The second time was the day before yesterday, at day-

---

*Petersburg entrepreneur.

break, on the journey at the station of Malaia Vishera,* and the third time was two hours ago in the room where I am staying. I was alone."

"Were you awake?"

"Absolutely. I was wide awake every time. She comes, speaks to me for a minute and goes out at the door—always at the door. I can almost hear her."

"What made me think that something of the sort must be happening to you?" Raskolnikov said suddenly.

At the same moment he was surprised at having said it. He was extremely excited.

"What! Did you think so?" Svidrigailov asked in astonishment. "Did you really? Didn't I say that there was something in common between us?"

"You never said so!" Raskolnikov cried sharply and with heat.

"Didn't I?"

"No!"

"I thought I did. When I came in and saw you lying with your eyes shut, pretending, I said to myself at once, 'here's the man.'"

"What do you mean by 'the man'? What are you talking about?" cried Raskolnikov.

"What do I mean? I really don't know . . ." Svidrigailov muttered ingenuously, as though he, too, were puzzled.

For a minute they were silent. They stared in each other's faces.

"That's all nonsense!" Raskolnikov shouted with vexation. "What does she say when she comes to you?"

"She! Would you believe it, she talks of the silliest trifles and—man is a strange creature—it makes me angry. The first time she came in (I was tired you know: the funeral service, the funeral ceremony, the lunch afterwards. At last I was left alone in my study. I lit a cigar and began to think), she came in at the door. 'You've been so busy today, Arkady Ivanovich, you've forgotten to wind the dining room clock,' she said. All those seven years I've wound that clock every week, and if I forgot it she would always remind me. The next day I set off on my way here. I got out at the station at daybreak; I'd been asleep, tired out, with my eyes half open, I was drinking some coffee. I looked up and there was suddenly Marfa

---

*Town on the railroad line from Moscow to St. Petersburg.

Petrovna sitting beside me with a pack of cards in her hands. 'Shall I tell your fortune for the journey, Arkady Ivanovich?' She was a great one for telling fortunes. I shall never forgive myself for not asking her to. I ran away in a fright, and, besides, the bell rang. I was sitting today, feeling very heavy after a miserable dinner from a café; I was sitting smoking, and all of a sudden Marfa Petrovna appeared again. She came in very smart in a new green silk dress with a long train. 'Hello, Arkady Ivanovich! How do you like my dress? Aniska couldn't make one like this.' (Aniska was a dressmaker in the country, one of our former serf girls who had been trained in Moscow, a pretty wench.) She stood turning round before me. I looked at the dress, and then I looked carefully, very carefully, at her face. 'I'm surprised you bother to come to me about such unimportant matters, Marfa Petrovna.' 'Good gracious, you won't let anyone disturb you about anything!' To tease her I said, 'I want to get married, Marfa Petrovna.' 'That's just like you, Arkady Ivanovich; it does you very little credit to come looking for a bride when you've hardly buried your wife. And if you could make a good choice, at least, but I know it won't be for your happiness or hers, you will only be a laughing-stock to all good people.' Then she went out and her train seemed to rustle. Isn't it nonsense?"

"But perhaps you are lying?" Raskolnikov put in.

"I rarely lie," answered Svidrigailov thoughtfully, apparently not noticing the rudeness of the question.

"And in the past, have you ever seen ghosts before?"

"Y-yes, I have seen them, but only once in my life, six years ago. I had a serf, Filka; just after his burial I called out forgetfully, 'Filka, my pipe!' He came in and went to the cupboard where my pipes were. I sat still and thought, 'He is doing it to take revenge on me,' because we had a violent quarrel just before his death. 'How dare you come in with a hole in your elbow,' I said. 'Go away, you fool!' He turned and went out, and never came again. I didn't tell Marfa Petrovna at the time. I wanted to have a service sung for him, but I was ashamed."

"You should go to a doctor."

"I know I am not well, without your telling me, though I don't know what's wrong; I believe I am five times as strong as you are. I didn't ask you whether you believe that ghosts can be seen, but whether you believe that they exist."

"No, I won't believe it!" Raskolnikov cried, with real anger.

"What do people generally say?" muttered Svidrigailov, as though speaking to himself, looking aside and bowing his head: "They say, 'You are ill, so what appears to you is only unreal fantasy.' But that's not strictly logical. I agree that ghosts only appear to the sick, but that only proves that they are unable to appear except to the sick, not that they don't exist."

"Nothing of the sort," Raskolnikov insisted irritably.

"No? You don't think so?" Svidrigailov went on, looking at him deliberately. "But what do you say to this argument (come on, help me with it): ghosts are as it were shreds and fragments of other worlds, the beginning of them. A man in health has, of course, no reason to see them, because he is above all a man of this earth and is bound for the sake of completeness and order to live only in this life. But as soon as he is ill, as soon as the normal earthly order of the organism is broken, he begins to realize the possibility of another world; and the more seriously ill he is, the closer becomes his contact with that other world, so that as soon as the man dies he steps straight into that world. I thought of that long ago. If you believe in a future life, you could believe in that, too."

"I don't believe in a future life," said Raskolnikov.

Svidrigailov sat lost in thought.

"And what if there are only spiders there, or something of that sort," he said suddenly.

"He is a madman," thought Raskolnikov.

"We always imagine eternity as something beyond our conception, something vast, vast! But why must it be vast? Instead of all that, what if it's one little room, like a bathhouse in the country, black and grimy and spiders in every corner, and that's all eternity is? I sometimes imagine it like that."

"Can it be you can imagine nothing more just and comforting than that?" Raskolnikov cried, with a feeling of anguish.

"More just? And how can we tell, perhaps that is just, and, do you know, it's what I would certainly have made it," answered Svidrigailov, with a vague smile.

This horrible answer sent a cold chill through Raskolnikov.

Svidrigailov raised his head, looked at him, and suddenly started laughing.

"Only think," he cried, "half an hour ago we had never seen each other, we regarded each other as enemies; there is a matter unsettled between us; we've thrown it aside, and away we've gone into the abstract! Wasn't I right in saying that we were birds of a feather?"

"Please allow me," Raskolnikov went on irritably, "to ask you to explain why you have honored me with your visit . . . and . . . and I am in a hurry, I have no time to waste. I want to go out."

"By all means, by all means. Your sister, Avdotia Romanovna, is going to be married to Mr. Luzhin, Peter Petrovich?"

"Can you stop asking questions about my sister and mentioning her name? I can't understand how you dare say her name in my presence, if you really are Svidrigailov."

"But I've come here to speak about her; how can I avoid mentioning her?"

"Very good, speak, but be quick about it."

"I am sure that you must have formed your own opinion of this Mr. Luzhin, who is a connection of mine through my wife, if you have only seen him for half an hour, or heard any facts about him. He is no match for Avdotia Romanovna. I believe Avdotia Romanovna is sacrificing herself generously and imprudently for the sake of . . . for the sake of her family. I imagined from all I had heard of you that you would be very glad if the engagement could be broken off without sacrificing any material advantages. Now I know you personally, I am convinced of it."

"All this is very naive . . . excuse me, I should have said insolent on your part," said Raskolnikov.

"You mean to say that I am seeking my own ends. Don't be uneasy, Rodion Romanovich, if I were working for my own advantage, I would not have spoken out so directly. I am not quite a fool. I will confess something psychologically curious about that: just now, defending my love for Avdotia Romanovna, I said I was myself the victim. Well, let me tell you that I've no feeling of love now, not the slightest, so that I wonder myself indeed, because I really did feel something . . . "

"Through idleness and depravity," Raskolnikov put in.

"I certainly am idle and depraved, but your sister has such qualities that even I could not help being impressed by them. But that's all nonsense, as I see myself now."

"Have you seen that long?"

"I began to be aware of it before, but was only perfectly sure of it the day before yesterday, almost at the moment I arrived in Petersburg. I still imagined in Moscow, though, that I was coming to try to get Avdotia Romanovna's hand and to cut out Mr. Luzhin."

"Excuse me for interrupting you; please be brief and tell me why you've come to visit. I am in a hurry, I want to go out . . . "

"With the greatest of pleasure. On arriving here and deciding to make a certain . . . journey, I would like to make some necessary preliminary arrangements. I left my children with an aunt; they are well provided for; and they have no need of me personally. And a nice father I'd make, too! I have taken nothing but what Marfa Petrovna gave me a year ago. That's enough for me. Excuse me, I am just coming to the point. Before the journey, which may come off, I want to settle Mr. Luzhin, too. It's not that I hate him so much, but it was because of him that I quarreled with Marfa Petrovna when I learned that she had served up this marriage. I would now like to see Avdotia Romanovna through your mediation and, if you like, in your presence, to explain to her that in the first place she will never gain anything but harm from Mr. Luzhin. Then begging her pardon for all past unpleasantness, to make her a present of ten thousand rubles and so assist the rupture with Mr. Luzhin, a rupture to which I believe she is herself not disinclined, if she could find some way of achieving it."

"You're absolutely insane," cried Raskolnikov, not so much angered as astonished. "How dare you talk like that!"

"I knew you would scream at me; but in the first place, though I am not rich, this ten thousand rubles is perfectly free; I have absolutely no need for it. If Avdotia Romanovna does not accept it, I shall waste it in some more foolish way. That's the first thing. Secondly, my conscience is perfectly at ease; I am not making the offer with any ulterior motive. You may not believe it, but in the end Avdotia Romanovna and you will know. The point is that I did actually cause your sister, whom I greatly respect, some trouble and unpleasantness, and so, sincerely regretting it, I want—not to compensate, not to repay her for the unpleasantness, but simply to do something to her advantage, to show that I am not, after all, privileged to do nothing but harm. If there were a millionth fraction of self-interest in my offer, I should not have made it so openly; and I should not have offered her ten thousand only, when five weeks ago I offered her more. Besides, I may, perhaps, very soon marry a young lady, and that alone ought to prevent suspicion of any design on Avdotia Romanovna. In conclusion, let me say that in marrying Mr. Luzhin, she is taking money just the same, only from another man. Don't be angry, Rodion Romanovich, think it over coolly and quietly."

Svidrigailov himself was extremely cool and quiet when he was saying this.

"Please don't say anything else," said Raskolnikov. "In any case, this is unforgivably insolent."

"Not in the least. Then a man may do nothing but harm to his neighbor in this world, and is prevented from doing the tiniest bit of good by trivial conventional formalities. That's absurd. If I died, for instance, and left that sum to your sister in my will, surely she wouldn't refuse it?"

"Very likely she would."

"Oh, no, she would not. If you refuse it, so be it, though ten thousand rubles is a wonderful thing to have on occasion. In any case, please repeat what I have said to Avdotia Romanovna."

"No, I won't."

"In that case, Rodion Romanovich, I shall be obliged to try and see her myself and worry her by doing so."

"And if I do tell her, will you not try to see her?"

"I don't really know what to say. I would like very much to see her once more."

"Don't hope for it."

"I'm sorry. But you don't know me. Perhaps we may become better friends."

"You think we may become friends?"

"And why not?" Svidrigailov said, smiling. He stood up and took his hat. "I didn't really intend to disturb you and I came here without thinking I would . . . though I was very struck by your face this morning."

"Where did you see me this morning?" Raskolnikov asked uneasily.

"I saw you by chance . . . I kept thinking we have something in common . . . But don't be uneasy. I am not intrusive; I used to get on all right with card-cheats, and I never bored Prince Svirbey, a great nobleman who is a distant relation of mine, and I could write about Raphael's Madonna in Madam Prilukov's album, and I never left Marfa Petrovna's side for seven years, and I used to stay the night at Viazemsky's house in the Haymarket in the old days, and I may go up in a balloon with Berg, perhaps."

"All right, all right. Are you setting off soon on your travels?"

"What travels?"

"On that 'journey'; you mentioned it yourself."

"A journey? Oh, yes. I did mention a journey. Well, that's a broad topic . . . if only you knew what you are asking," he added, and gave a sudden, loud, short laugh. "Perhaps I'll get married instead of the journey. They're making a match for me."

"Here?"

"Yes."

"How have you had time for that?"

"But I am very anxious to see Avdotia Romanovna once. Please. Well, goodbye for now. Oh, yes, I've forgotten something. Tell your sister, Rodion Romanovich, that Marfa Petrovna remembered her in her will and left her three thousand rubles. That's absolutely certain. Marfa Petrovna arranged it a week before her death, and it was done in my presence. Avdotia Romanovna will be able to receive the money in two or three weeks."

"Are you telling the truth?"

"Yes, tell her. Well, I am at your service. I am staying close by."

As he went out, Svidrigailov ran into Razumikhin in the doorway.

CHAPTER TWO

IT WAS NEARLY EIGHT o'clock. The two young men hurried to Bakaleyev's, to arrive before Luzhin.

"Who was that?" asked Razumikhin, as soon as they were in the street.

"It was Svidrigailov, that landowner whose house my sister was insulted in when she was their governess. She was turned out by his wife, Marfa Petrovna, because he kept persecuting her with his 'attention'. This Marfa Petrovna begged Dunia's forgiveness afterwards, and she's just died suddenly. That was the woman we were talking about this morning. I don't know why I'm afraid of him. He came here at once after his wife's funeral. He is very strange, and he is determined to do something . . . We must protect Dunia from him . . . that's what I wanted to tell you."

"Protect her! What can he do to harm Avdotia Romanovna? Thank you, Rodia, for telling me about it . . . We will, we will protect her. Where does he live?"

"I don't know."

"Why didn't you ask? What a pity! I'll find out, though."

"Did you see him?" asked Raskolnikov after a pause.

"Yes, I took notice of him, I took careful notice of him."

"You did really see him? You saw him clearly?" Raskolnikov insisted.

"Yes, I remember him perfectly, I would recognize him in a crowd of a thousand; I have a good memory for faces."

They were silent again.

"Hm! . . . that's all right," muttered Raskolnikov. "Do you know, I imagined . . . I keep thinking that it may have been a hallucination."

"What do you mean? I don't understand."

"Well, you all say," Raskolnikov went on, twisting his mouth into a smile, "that I'm mad. I thought just now that perhaps I really am mad, and that I just saw a ghost."

"What do you mean?"

"Why, who can tell? Perhaps I am really mad, and perhaps everything that happens these days is just my imagination."

"Ah, Rodia, you have been upset again! . . . But what did he say, what did he come for?"

Raskolnikov did not answer. Razumikhin thought for a minute.

"Now let me tell you my story," he began, "I came to you, you were asleep. Then we had dinner and then I went to Porfiry's, Zametov was still with him. I tried to start, but it was no use. I couldn't speak in the right way. They don't seem to understand and can't understand, but they aren't even slightly ashamed of themselves. I drew Porfiry to the window, and began talking to him, but it was still no use. He looked away and I looked away. At last I shook my fist in his ugly face, and told him as a cousin I'd brain him. He just looked at me, I cursed and left. That was all. It was very stupid. I didn't say a word to Zametov. But, you see, I thought I'd made a mess of it, but as I went downstairs a brilliant idea struck me: why should we bother? Of course, if you were in any danger or anything, but why should you care? You shouldn't care about them at all. We shall have a laugh at them afterwards, and if I were in your place I'd mystify them more than ever. How ashamed they'll be afterwards! Damn them! We can thrash them afterwards, so let's laugh at them now!"

"Definitely," answered Raskolnikov. "But what will you say to-morrow?" he thought to himself. Strangely enough, until that moment it had never occurred to him to wonder what Razumikhin would think when he knew. As he was thinking, Raskolnikov looked at him. Razumikhin's account of his visit to Porfiry held very little interest for him; so much had come and gone since then.

In the corridor they found Luzhin; he had arrived punctually at eight, and was looking for the number, so all three went in together without greeting or looking at one another. The young men walked in first, while Peter Petrovich, in order to preserve his good manners, lingered a little in the passage, taking off his coat. Pulcheria Alexandrovna came forward at once to greet him in the doorway; Dunia was welcoming her brother. Peter Petrovich walked in and quite amiably, though with even greater dignity, bowed to the ladies. He looked, however, as though he were a little offended and could not yet recover his composure. Pulcheria Alexandrovna, who also seemed a little embarrassed, quickly made them all sit down at the round table where a samovar was boiling. Dunia and Luzhin were facing one another on opposite sides of the table. Razumikhin and Raskolnikov were facing Pulcheria Alexandrovna, Razumikhin was next to Luzhin and Raskolnikov was beside his sister.

A moment's silence followed. Peter Petrovich deliberately drew out a cambric handkerchief stinking of scent and blew his nose with an air of a kindly man who felt offended and had decided to insist on an explanation. In the passage an idea had occurred to him to keep on his overcoat and walk away, and so give the two ladies a sharp and emphatic lesson and make them feel the seriousness of the situation. But he could not bring himself to do this. Besides, he could not stand uncertainty and he wanted an explanation: if his request had been so openly disobeyed, there was something behind it, and in that case it was better to find it out beforehand; it was his task to punish them and there would always be time for that.

"I trust you had a good journey," he asked Pulcheria Alexandrovna officially.

"Oh, very, Peter Petrovich."

"I am pleased to hear it. And Avdotia Romanovna is not overly tired either?"

"I am young and strong, I don't get tired, but it was a great strain for mother," answered Dunia.

"That's unavoidable; our national railways are of terrible length. 'Mother Russia,' as they say, is a vast country . . . In spite of all my desire to do so, I was unable to meet you yesterday. But I trust everything passed off without any inconvenience?"

"Oh, no, Peter Petrovich, it was all terribly disheartening," Pulcheria Alexandrovna declared hurriedly in a strange tone of voice, "and if Dmitri Prokofich had not been sent to us, I really believe by God Himself, we would have been totally lost. Here, he is! Dmitri Prokofich Razumikhin," she added, introducing him to Luzhin.

"I had the pleasure . . . yesterday," muttered Peter Petrovich with a hostile sideways glance at Razumikhin; then he scowled and fell silent.

Peter Petrovich belonged to that class of people who on the surface are very polite in society, who make a great point of behaving properly, but who are completely disconcerted when they are contradicted about anything, and become more like sacks of flour than elegant, lively people of society. Again everyone was silent; Raskolnikov was obstinately mute, Avdotia Romanovna was unwilling to start the conversation again too soon. Razumikhin had nothing to say, so Pulcheria Alexandrovna was anxious again.

"Marfa Petrovna is dead, have you heard?" she began having recourse to her leading item of conversation.

"Yes, I heard so. I was immediately informed, and I have come to tell you that Arkady Ivanovich Svidrigailov set off in haste for Petersburg immediately after his wife's funeral. So at least I have excellent grounds for believing it."

"To Petersburg? Here?" Dunia asked in alarm and looked at her mother.

"Yes, and doubtlessly not without some kind of intention, bearing in mind how swiftly he left, and all the preceding circumstances."

"Goodness! Won't he leave Dunia in peace even here?" cried Pulcheria Alexandrovna.

"I imagine that neither you nor Avdotia Romanovna has any grounds for uneasiness, unless, of course, you wish to communicate with him. As far as I am concerned, I am going to watch out for him; I am currently trying to find out where he is staying."

"Oh, Peter Petrovich, you would not believe what a fright you have given me," Pulcheria Alexandrovna went on. "I've only seen him twice, but I thought he was terrible, terrible! I am convinced that he was the cause of Marfa Petrovna's death."

"It's impossible to be certain about that. I have precise information. I do not dispute that he may have accelerated the course of events by the moral influence, so to say, of the offence; but as to his general conduct and moral characteristics, I agree with you. I do not know whether he is well off now, and precisely what Marfa Petrovna left him; this will be known to me within a very short period; but no doubt here in Petersburg, if he has any financial resources, he will lapse at once into his old habits. He is the most vicious, depraved specimen of that particular type. I have considerable reason to believe that Marfa Petrovna, who was unfortunate enough to fall in love with him and to pay his debts eight years ago, was also of service to him in another way. Solely by her exertions and sacrifices, a criminal charge, involving an element of fantastic and homicidal brutality for which he might well have been sentenced to Siberia, was hushed up. That's the sort of man he is, if you care to know."

"Good heavens!" cried Pulcheria Alexandrovna. Raskolnikov listened attentively.

"Are you speaking the truth when you say that you have good evidence of this?" Dunia asked sternly and emphatically.

"I only repeat what I was told in secret by Marfa Petrovna. I must observe that from the legal point of view the case was far from clear. There was, and I believe still is, living here a woman called Resslich, a foreigner, who lent small sums of money at interest, and did other commissions, and with this woman Svidrigailov had for a long while close and mysterious relations. She had a relation, a niece I believe, living with her, a deaf and dumb girl fifteen years of age, or perhaps not more than fourteen. Resslich hated this girl, and grudged her every crust; she used to beat her mercilessly. One day the girl was found hanging in the garret. At the inquest the verdict was suicide. After the usual proceedings the matter ended, but, later on, information was given that the child had been . . . cruelly outraged by Svidrigailov. It is true, this was not clearly established, the information was given by another German woman of notorious character whose word could not be trusted; no statement was actually made to the police, thanks to Marfa Petrovna's money and efforts; it did not get beyond gossip. And yet the story is a very significant one. You heard, no doubt, Avdotia Romanovna, when you were with them the story of the servant Philip who died of ill treatment he received six years ago, before the abolition of serfdom."

"I heard on the contrary that this Philip hanged himself."

"That is true, but what drove him, or rather perhaps disposed him, to suicide, was the systematic persecution and severity of Mr. Svidrigailov."

"I don't know that," answered Dunia, dryly. "I only heard a strange story that Philip was some type of hypochondriac, a sort of domestic philosopher, the servants used to say, 'he read himself silly,' and that he hanged himself partly because of Mr. Svidrigailov's mockery of him and not the injuries he inflicted. When I was there he behaved well to the servants, and they were actually fond of him, though they certainly did blame him for Philip's death."

"I notice, Avdotia Romanovna, that you seem disposed to undertake his defense all of a sudden," Luzhin observed, twisting his lips into an ambiguous smile, "there's no doubt that he is an astute man, and charming where ladies are concerned, of which Marfa Petrovna, who has died so strangely, is a terrible example. My only desire has been to be of service to you and your mother with my advice, in view of the renewed efforts which may certainly be anticipated from him. For my part it's my firm conviction that he will end up in debtor's prison again. Marfa Petrovna had not the slightest intention of leaving him anything substantial, given his children's interests, and, if she left him anything, it would only be the slightest means on which to get by, something insignificant, which would not last a year for a man of his habits."

"Peter Petrovich, I beg you," said Dunia, "don't say anything else about Mr. Svidrigailov. It makes me miserable."

"He has just been to see me," said Raskolnikov, breaking his silence for the first time.

There were exclamations from everyone, and they all turned to him. Even Peter Petrovich's interest was aroused.

"An hour and a half ago, he came in when I was asleep, woke me up, and introduced himself," Raskolnikov continued. "He was fairly cheerful and at ease, and hopes that we shall become friends. He is particularly anxious by the way, Dunia, to arrange an interview with you, at which he asked me to be present. He has a proposition to make to you, and he told me about it. He told me, too, that a week before her death Marfa Petrovna left you three thousand rubles in her will, Dunia, and that you will receive the money very soon."

"Thank God!" cried Pulcheria Alexandrovna, crossing herself. "Pray for her soul, Dunia!"

"It's a fact!" broke from Luzhin.

"Tell us, what more?" Dunia urged Raskolnikov.

"Then he said that he wasn't rich and all the estate was left to his children who are now with an aunt, then that he was staying somewhere not far from me, but where, I don't know, I didn't ask . . . "

"But what, what is this proposition he wants to make to Dunia?" cried Pulcheria Alexandrovna in a fright. "Did he tell you?"

"Yes."

"What was it?"

"I'll tell you afterwards."

Raskolnikov ceased speaking and turned his attention to his tea. Peter Petrovich looked at his watch.

"I am compelled to keep a business engagement, and so I shall not be in your way," he added with an air of some pique and he began getting up.

"Don't go, Peter Petrovich," said Dunia, "you intended to spend the evening here. Besides, you wrote yourself that you wanted to sort something out with mother."

"Precisely so, Avdotia Romanovna," Peter Petrovich answered impressively, sitting down again, but still holding his hat. "I certainly desired to sort out a very important point with you and your mother, whom I respect so highly. But as your brother cannot speak openly in my presence about Mr. Svidrigailov's proposals, I, too, do not desire and am not able to speak openly . . . in the presence of others . . . about certain matters of the greatest importance. Moreover, my most insistent and urgent request has been disregarded . . . "

Assuming an aggrieved air, Luzhin lapsed into dignified silence.

"Your request that my brother should not be present at our meeting was disregarded solely because I wanted to disregard it," said Dunia. "You wrote that you had been insulted by my brother; I think you must explain this at once, and you must be reconciled. And if Rodia really has insulted you, then he should and will apologize."

Peter Petrovich took a stronger line.

"There are insults, Avdotia Romanovna, which no goodwill can make us forget. There is a line in everything which it is dangerous to overstep; and when it has been overstepped, there is no return."

"That wasn't quite what I was talking about, Peter Petrovich," Dunia interrupted with some impatience. "Please understand that our whole future now depends on whether all this can be explained and set right as soon as possible. I am telling you frankly, from the start, that I cannot look at it in any other light, and if you have the slightest regard for me, this business must end today, however hard that may be. I repeat that if my brother is to blame he will ask your forgiveness."

"I am surprised that you put the question like that," said Luzhin, getting more and more irritated. "Respecting and, so to say, adoring you, I may at the same time, very well indeed, be able to dislike a member of your family. Though I lay claim to the happiness of your hand in marriage, I cannot accept duties incompatible with . . . "

"Ah, don't be so ready to take offence, Peter Petrovich," Dunia interrupted with feeling, "and be the sensible and generous man I have always considered, and wish to consider, you to be. I've given you a great promise; I am engaged to you. Trust me in this matter and, believe me, I shall be capable of judging impartially. My assuming the part of judge is as much a surprise for my brother as for you. When I insisted that he came to our interview today after your letter, I told him nothing about what I meant to do. You must understand that, if you are not reconciled, I must choose between you—it must be either you or he. That is how the question rests on your side and on his. I don't want to be mistaken in my choice, and I must not be.

For your sake I must break off with my brother, for my brother's sake I must break off with you. I can find out for certain now whether he is behaving like a brother to me and, as a matter of fact, I would like to; and I can also find out whether I am dear to you, whether you respect me, whether you are the husband for me."

"Avdotia Romanovna," Luzhin declared in an offended tone, "your words have too many implications for me; moreover, they are offensive in view of the position I have the honor to occupy in relation to you. To say nothing of your strange and offensive behavior in setting me on a level with an insolent boy, you admit the possibility of breaking your promise to me. You say 'you or he,' thereby showing how unimportant I am to you . . . I cannot let this pass considering the relationship and . . . the obligations existing between us."

"What!" cried Dunia, flushing. "I set your interest beside everything that has up until now been most precious in my life, what has made up the whole of my life, and here you are offended because I haven't sufficiently taken you into account!"

Raskolnikov smiled sarcastically, Razumikhin fidgeted, but Peter Petrovich did not accept her rebuke; on the contrary, at every word he became more persistent and irritable, as though he relished it.

"Love for the future partner of your life, for your husband, ought to outweigh your love for your brother," he pronounced sententiously, "and in any case I cannot be put on the same level . . . Although I said so emphatically that I would not speak openly in your brother's presence, nevertheless I now intend to ask your dear mother for a necessary explanation on a point of which is extremely important to my dignity. Your son," he turned to Pulcheria Alexandrovna, "yesterday in the presence of Mr. Razsudkin (or . . . I think that's it? excuse me I have forgotten your surname," he bowed politely to Razumikhin) "insulted me by misrepresenting the idea I expressed to you in a private conversation over coffee, that is, that marriage to a poor girl who has had her fair share of troubles is more advantageous from the conjugal point of view than a marriage to a girl who has lived in luxury, since it is more profitable for the moral character. Your son intentionally exaggerated the significance of my words and made them ridiculous, accusing me of malicious intentions, and, as far as I could see, relied on your correspondence with him. I shall consider myself happy, Pulcheria Alexandrovna, if you could convince me of the opposite conclusion and thus considerately reassure me. Please let me know in what terms precisely you repeated my words in your letter to Rodion Romanovich."

"I don't remember," faltered Pulcheria Alexandrovna. "I repeated them as I understood them. I don't know how Rodia repeated them to you, perhaps he exaggerated."

"He could not have exaggerated them unless you gave him good cause."

"Peter Petrovich," Pulcheria Alexandrovna declared with dignity, "the proof that Dunia and I did not take your words in a very bad sense is the fact that we are here."

"Good, Mother," said Dunia approvingly.

"Then this is my fault again," said Luzhin, aggrieved.

"Well, Peter Petrovich, you keep blaming Rodion, but you your-self have just written something false about him," Pulcheria Alexan-drovna added, gaining courage.

"I don't remember writing anything false."

"You wrote," Raskolnikov said sharply, not turning to Luzhin, "that I gave money yesterday not to the widow of the man who was killed, as was the case, but to his daughter (whom I had never seen until yesterday). You wrote this to cause a rift between me and my family, and so you added coarse expressions about the conduct of a girl whom you don't know. That is all the meanest sort of slander."

"Excuse me, sir," said Luzhin, quivering with fury. "I enlarged upon your qualities and conduct in my letter solely in response to your sister's and mother's inquiries about how I found you and what impression you made on me. As for what you've referred to in my letter, be so good as to point out one word of falsehood, show, that is, that you didn't throw away your money, and that there are not worthless persons in that family, however unfortunate."

"To my thinking, you with all your virtues are not worth the lit-tle finger of that unfortunate girl at whom you choose to throw stones."

"Would you go so far then as to let her associate with your mother and sister?"

"I have done so already, if you care to know. I made her sit down today with mother and Dunia."

"Rodia!" cried Pulcheria Alexandrovna. Dunia crimsoned, Razumikhin knitted his brows. Luzhin smiled with lofty sarcasm.

"You may see for yourself, Avdotia Romanovna," he said, "whether it is possible for us to agree. I hope now that this question has been dealt with once and for all. I will withdraw in order not to hinder the pleasures of family intimacy and the discussion of secrets." He got up from his chair and took his hat. "But before I withdraw, I would like to request that in future I may be spared similar meetings and, so to say, compromises. I appeal particularly to you, my dearest Pulcheria Alexandrovna, on this subject, as my letter was addressed to you and no-one else."

Pulcheria Alexandrovna was a little offended.

"You seem to think we are completely under your authority, Peter Petrovich. Dunia has told you the reason she disregarded your desire, she had the best intentions. You even write as though you were giving me orders. Should we consider every desire of yours an order? Let me tell you on the contrary that you ought to show particular sensitivity and consideration for us now, because we have thrown up everything and have come here relying on you, and so we are in any case in a sense in your hands."

"That is not quite true, Pulcheria Alexandrovna, especially at the moment, when news has come of Marfa Petrovna's legacy, which seems indeed very timely, judging from the new tone which you are taking with me," he added sarcastically.

"Judging from that remark, we may certainly assume that you were counting on our helplessness," Dunia observed irritably.

"But now in any case I cannot count on it, and I am particularly unwilling to hinder your discussion of Arkady Ivanovich Svidrigailov's secret proposals, which he has entrusted to your brother and which, I perceive, interest you greatly, perhaps even favorably."

"Good heavens!" cried Pulcheria Alexandrovna.

Razumikhin could not sit still on his chair.

"Aren't you ashamed now, Dunia?" asked Raskolnikov.

"I am ashamed, Rodia," said Dunia. "Peter Petrovich, get out," she turned to him, white with anger.

Peter Petrovich had apparently not expected this type of conclusion. He had too much confidence in himself, in his power and in the helplessness of his victims. He could not believe it even now. He turned pale, and his lips quivered.

"Avdotia Romanovna, if I go out of this door now, after such a dismissal, then you can be sure I will never come back. Consider what you are doing. My word is unshakeable."

"What insolence!" cried Dunia, springing up from her seat. "I don't want you to come back again."

"What! So that's how it stands!" cried Luzhin, entirely unable to believe in the disagreement to the last, and now totally at a loss. "So that's how it stands! Do you realize, Avdotia Romanovna, that I can protest?"

"What right do you have to speak to her like that?" Pulcheria Alexandrovna intervened hotly. "And what can you protest about? What rights do you have? Should I give Dunia to a man like you? Go away, leave us alone! We are to blame for having agreed to the wrong course of action, and I above all . . . "

"But you have bound me, Pulcheria Alexandrovna," Luzhin stormed in a frenzy, "by your promise, and now you deny it and . . . besides . . . I have been led on account of that into expenses . . . "

This last complaint was so characteristic of Peter Petrovich, that Raskolnikov, pale with anger and with the effort of restraining it, could not help breaking into laughter. But Pulcheria Alexandrovna was furious.

"Expenses? What expenses? Are you talking about our trunk? But the conductor brought it for nothing for you. Mercy on us, we have bound you! What are you thinking about, Peter Petrovich, it was you who bound us, hand and foot, not we!"

"Enough, Mother, no more please," Avdotia Romanovna begged them. "Peter Petrovich, please go!"

"I am going, but one last word," he said, quite unable to control himself. "Your mother seems to have entirely forgotten that I made up my mind to take you, so to speak, after the gossip of the town had spread all over the district in regard to your reputation. Disregarding public opinion for your sake and reinstating your reputation, I certainly might well count on a fitting return and might in fact look for gratitude on your part. And my eyes have only now been opened! I see myself that I may have acted very, very recklessly in disregarding the universal verdict . . . "

"Does the fellow want his head smashed?" cried Razumikhin, jumping up.

"You are a mean and spiteful man!" cried Dunia.

"Not a word! Not a movement!" cried Raskolnikov, holding Razumikhin back; then going close up to Luzhin, "Kindly leave the room!" he said quietly and distinctly, "and not a word more or . . ."

Peter Petrovich gazed at him for some seconds with a pale face distorted by anger, then he turned and left; and rarely has any man carried away in his heart such vindictive hatred as he felt against Raskolnikov. Him, and him alone, he blamed for everything. It is worth noting that as he went downstairs he still imagined that his case was perhaps not entirely lost, and that, so far as the ladies were concerned, all might "very well indeed" be set right again.

CHAPTER THREE

THE FACT WAS THAT up to the last moment he had never expected such an ending; he had been overbearing to the last degree, never dreaming that two destitute and defenseless women could escape from his control. This conviction was strengthened by his vanity and conceit, a conceit which he took to the point of excess. Peter Petrovich, who had made his way up from insignificance, was morbidly given to self-admiration, had the highest opinion of his intelligence and capacities, and sometimes even gloated in solitude over his reflection in the mirror. But what he loved and valued above all was the money he had amassed by his work, and by all sorts of devices: that money made him the equal of all who had been his superiors.

When he had bitterly reminded Dunia that he had decided to take her in spite of various evil reports, Peter Petrovich had spoken with perfect sincerity and had, indeed, felt genuinely indignant at such "black ingratitude." And yet, when he made Dunia his offer, he was fully aware of the groundlessness of all the gossip. The story had been contradicted in every quarter by Marfa Petrovna and was by then distrusted among all the townspeople, who were warm in Dunia's defense. And he would not have denied that he knew all that at the time. Yet he still thought highly of his own resolution in lifting Dunia to his level and regarded it as something heroic. In speaking of it to Dunia, he had let out the secret feeling he cherished and admired, and he could not understand that others should fail to admire it too. He had called on Raskolnikov with the feelings of a benefactor who is about to reap the fruits of his good deeds and to hear pleasing flattery. And as he went downstairs now, he considered himself undeservedly injured and unrecognized.

Dunia was simply essential to him; to do without her was unthinkable. For many years he had voluptuous dreams of marriage, but he had gone on waiting and amassing money. He brooded with relish, in profound secret, over the image of a girl—virtuous, poor (she must be poor), very young, very pretty, well-born and well-educated, very timid, one who had suffered much, and was completely humbled before him, one who would all her life look on him as her savior, worship him, admire him and only him. How many scenes, how many amorous episodes he had imagined on this seductive and playful theme, when his work was over! And, behold, the dream of so many years was all but realized; the beauty and education of Avdotia Romanovna had impressed him; her helpless position had been a great allurement; in her he had found even more than he dreamed of. Here was a girl of pride, character, virtue, of education and breeding superior to his own (he felt that), and this creature would be slavishly grateful all her life for his heroic condescension, and would humble herself in the dust before him, and he would have absolute, unbounded power over her! . . . Not long before, he had also, after long reflection and hesitation, made an important change in his career and was now entering into a wider circle of business. With this change his cherished dreams of rising into a higher class of society seemed likely to be realized . . . He was, in fact, determined to try his fortune in Petersburg. He knew that women could do a very great deal. The fascination of a charming, virtuous, highly educated woman might make things easier for him, might do wonders in attracting people to him, throwing an aura round him, and now everything was in ruins! This sudden horrible rupture affected him like a clap of thunder; it was like a hideous joke, an absurdity. He had only been a tiny bit masterful, had not even time to speak out, had simply made a joke, got carried away—and it had ended so seriously. And, of course, too, he did love Dunia in his own way; he already possessed her in his dreams—and all at once! No! The next day, the very next day, it must all be set right, smoothed over, settled. Above all he must crush that conceited brat who was the cause of it all. With a sick feeling he could not help remembering Razumikhin too, but, he soon reassured himself on that score; as though a man like that could be put on a level with him! The person he really dreaded in earnest was Svidri-gailov . . . He had, in short, a great deal to attend to . . . —

"No, I, I am more to blame than anyone!" said Dunia, kissing and embracing her mother. "I was tempted by his money, but I swear, Rodia, I had no idea he was such an evil man. If I had seen through him before, nothing would have tempted me! Don't blame me, Rodia!"

"God has delivered us! God has delivered us!" Pulcheria Alexan-drovna muttered, but half consciously, as though scarcely able to re-alize what had happened.

They were all relieved, and in five minutes they were laughing. Only now and then Dunia turned white and frowned, remembering what had happened. Pulcheria Alexandrovna was surprised to find that she, too, was glad: she had only that morning thought rupture with Luzhin a terrible misfortune. Razumikhin was delighted. He did not yet dare to express his joy fully, but he was in a fever of excitement as though a ton-weight had fallen off his heart. Now he had the right to devote his life to them, to serve them . . . Anything might happen now! But he felt afraid to think of further possibilities and dared not let his imagination range. But Raskolnikov sat still in the same place, almost sullen and indifferent. Though he had been the most insistent on get-ting rid of Luzhin, he seemed now the least concerned at what had happened. Dunia could not help thinking that he was still angry with her, and Pulcheria Alexandrovna watched him timidly.

"What did Svidrigailov say to you?" said Dunia, approaching him.

"Yes, yes!" cried Pulcheria Alexandrovna.

Raskolnikov raised his head.

"He wants to make you a present of ten thousand rubles and he wishes to see you once in my presence."

"See her! On no account!" cried Pulcheria Alexandrovna. "And how dare he offer her money!"

Then Raskolnikov repeated (rather dryly) his conversation with

Svidrigailov, omitting his account of Marfa Petrovna's ghost, wishing to avoid all unnecessary talk.

"How did you reply?" asked Dunia.

"At first I said I would not take any message to you. Then he said that he would do his worst to obtain an interview with you without my help. He assured me that his passion for you was a passing infatuation, now he has no feeling for you. He doesn't want you to marry Luzhin . . . All in all, he was rather muddled."

"How do you explain what he said, Rodia? How did he strike you?"

"I have to say, I don't quite understand him. He offers you ten thousand, and yet he says he's not well off. He says he's going away, and in ten minutes he forgets he's said it. Then he says he's going to get married and has already decided on the girl . . . No doubt he has a motive, and probably a bad one. But it's odd that he should be so clumsy about it if he had any designs against you . . . Of course, I refused this money on your behalf, once for all. All in all, I thought he was rather strange . . . One might almost assume he was mad. But I may be mistaken; he may just be pretending. The death of Marfa Petrovna seems to have made a great impact on him."

"God rest her soul," exclaimed Pulcheria Alexandrovna. "I shall always, always pray for her! Where would we be now, Dunia, without this three thousand! It's as though it'd fallen from heaven! Why, Rodia, this morning we had only three rubles in our pocket and Dunia and I were just planning to pawn her watch in order to avoid borrowing from that man until he offered us help."

Dunia seemed strangely impressed by Svidrigailov's offer. She still stood meditating.

"He has got some terrible plan," she said in a half whisper to herself, almost shuddering.

Raskolnikov noticed this slightly hysterical terror.

"I imagine I shall have to see him more than once again," he said to Dunia.

"We will watch him! I will track him down!" cried Razumikhin, vigorously. "I won't lose sight of him. Rodia has given me permission. He said to me himself just now, 'Take care of my sister.' Will you give me permission, too, Avdotia Romanovna?"

Dunia smiled and held out her hand, but the look of anxiety did not leave her face. Pulcheria Alexandrovna gazed at her timidly, but the three thousand rubles had obviously had a soothing effect on her.

A quarter of an hour later, they were all engaged in a lively conversation. Even Raskolnikov listened attentively for some time, though he did not talk. Razumikhin was speaking.

"And why, why should you go away?" he flowed on ecstatically. "And what would you do in a little town? The great thing is, you are all here together and you need one another—you do need one another, believe me. For a time, anyway . . . Take me on as your partner and I assure you we'll plan a brilliant enterprise. Listen! I'll explain it all in detail to you, the whole project! It all flashed into my head this morning, before anything had happened . . . This is it: I have an uncle, I must introduce him to you (he's a very obliging, respectable old man). This uncle has got a thousand rubles, and he lives on his pension and has no need of the money. For the last two years he has been bothering me to borrow it from him and pay him six per cent interest. I know what that means; he simply wants to help me. Last year I had no need of it, but this year I resolved to borrow it as soon as he arrived. Then you lend me another thousand of your three and we have enough for a start, so we'll go into partnership, and what are we going to do?"

Then Razumikhin began to unfold his project, and he explained at length that almost all our publishers and booksellers know nothing at all about what they are selling, and for that reason they are usually bad publishers, and that any decent publications pay as a rule and gain a profit, sometimes a considerable one. Razumikhin had in fact been dreaming of setting up as a publisher. For the last two years he had been working in publishers' offices, and knew three European languages well, though he had told Raskolnikov six days before that he was "weak" in German in order to persuade him to take half his translation and half the payment for it. He had told a lie, then, and Raskolnikov knew he was lying.

"Why, why should we let our chance slip when we have one of the chief means of success—money of our own!" cried Razumikhin warmly. "Of course there will be a lot of work, but we will work, you, Avdotia Romanovna, I, Rodion . . . You get an excellent profit on some books nowadays! And the great point of the business is that we shall know just what needs to be translated, and we shall be translating, publishing and learning all at once. I can be of use because I have experience. For nearly two years I've been busying about among the publishers, and now I know every detail of their business. You don't need to be a saint to make pots, believe me! And why, why should we let our chance slip! I know—and I kept the secret—two or three books which you might get a hundred rubles for, even if you just thought of translating and publishing them. I wouldn't take five hundred even for the idea of one of them. So what do you think? If I were to tell a publisher, I dare say he'd hesitate—they are such blockheads! And as for the business side, printing, paper, selling, you entrust that to me, I know my way about. We'll begin in a small way and go on to a large. In any case it will get us our living and we shall get a return on our capital."

Dunia's eyes shone.

"I like what you are saying, Dmitri Prokofich!" she said.

"I know nothing about it, of course," put in Pulcheria Alexandrovna, "it may be a good idea, but again, God knows. It's new and untried. Of course, we must stay here at least for a time." She looked at Rodia.

"What do you think, brother?" said Dunia.

"I think he's got a very good idea," he answered. "Of course, it's too soon to dream of a publishing firm, but we certainly might bring out five or six books and be sure of success. I know of one book myself which would be sure to go well. And as for whether he's able to manage it, there's no doubt about that either. He knows the business . . . But we can talk it over later . . . "

"Hurrah!" cried Razumikhin. "Now, wait, there's an apartment here in this house, belonging to the same owner. It's a special apartment; it doesn't connect to these lodgings. It's furnished, moderate rent, three rooms. Suppose you take them to begin with. I'll pawn your watch tomorrow and bring you the money, and everything can be arranged then. You can all live together, and Rodia will be with you. But, Rodia, where are you off to?"

"What, Rodia, you are going already?" Pulcheria Alexandrovna asked in dismay.

"At a moment like this?" cried Razumikhin.

Dunia looked at her brother in wonder and disbelief. He held his cap in his hand, he was preparing to leave them.

"One would think you were burying me or saying goodbye for ever," he said somewhat oddly. He tried to smile, but it did not come out as a smile. "But who knows, maybe it is the last time we shall see each other . . . " he let slip accidentally. It was what he was thinking, and somehow he uttered it aloud.

"What is the matter with you?" cried his mother.

"Where are you going, Rodia?" asked Dunia rather strangely.

"Oh, I'm absolutely obliged to . . . " he answered vaguely, as though he were hesitating about what he was going to say. But there was a look of sharp determination in his white face.

"I meant to say . . . as I was coming here . . . I meant to tell you, Mother, and you, Dunia, that it would be better for us to part for a time. I'm unwell, I'm not at peace . . . I'll come afterwards, I'll come of my own accord . . . whenever possible, I'll remember you and love you . . . Leave me, leave me alone. I decided this beforehand . . . I'm absolutely set on it. Whatever may happen to me, whether I come to ruin or not, I want to be alone. Forget me altogether, it's better. Don't ask after me. When I can, I'll come of my own accord or . . . I'll send for you. Perhaps it will all come back, but now if you love me, give me up . . . or else I shall begin to hate you, I feel it . . . Goodbye!"

"Good God!" cried Pulcheria Alexandrovna. Both his mother and his sister were extremely alarmed. Razumikhin was also.

"Rodia, Rodia, let us be reconciled! Let us be as before!" cried his poor mother.

He turned slowly to the door and slowly went out of the room. Dunia overtook him.

"Rodia, what are you doing to her?" she whispered, her eyes flashing with indignation.

He looked dully at her.

"No matter, I will come . . . I'm coming," he muttered in an undertone, as though he was not fully conscious of what he was saying, and he went out of the room.

"Wicked, heartless egoist!" cried Dunia.

"He is insane, but not heartless. He is mad! Don't you see? It's heartless of you to say it!" Razumikhin whispered in her ear, squeezing her hand tightly. "I shall be back immediately," he shouted to their horror-stricken mother, and he ran out of the room.

Raskolnikov was waiting for him at the end of the passage.

"I knew you would run after me," he said. "Go back to them—be with them . . . be with them tomorrow and always . . . I . . . perhaps I shall come . . . if I can. Goodbye."

And without holding out his hand he walked away.

"But where are you going? What are you doing? What's the matter with you? How can you go on like this?" Razumikhin muttered, at his wits' end.

Raskolnikov stopped once more.

"For the last time, never ask me about anything. I have nothing to tell you. Don't come to see me. Maybe I'll come here . . . Leave me, but don't leave them. Do you understand me?"

It was dark in the corridor, they were standing near the lamp. For a minute they were looking at one another in silence. Razumikhin remembered that minute all his life. Raskolnikov's burning and intent eyes grew more penetrating every moment, piercing into his soul, into his consciousness. Suddenly Razumikhin started. Something strange, as it were, passed between them . . . Some idea, some hint as it were, slipped, something awful, hideous, and suddenly understood on both sides . . . Razumikhin turned pale.

"Do you understand now?" said Raskolnikov, his face twitching nervously. "Go back, go to them," he said suddenly, and turning quickly, he went out of the house.

I will not attempt to describe how Razumikhin went back to the ladies, how he soothed them, how he protested that Rodia needed rest in his illness, protested that Rodia was sure to come, that he would come every day, that he was very, very upset, that he must not be irritated, that he, Razumikhin, would watch over him, would get him a doctor, the best doctor, a consultation . . . In fact from that evening onwards Razumikhin took his place with them as a son and as a brother.

CHAPTER FOUR

RASKOLNIKOV WENT STRAIGHT TO the house on the canal bank where Sonia lived. It was an old green house three floors high. He found the porter, who gave him vague directions as to where to find Kapernaumov the tailor. Having found the entrance to the dark and narrow staircase in the corner of the courtyard, he went up to the second floor and came out into a gallery that ran round the whole second storey over the yard. While he was wandering in the darkness, uncertain where to turn for Kapernaumov's door, a door opened three paces from him; he mechanically took hold of it.

"Who's there?" a woman's voice asked uneasily.

"It's me . . . come to see you," answered Raskolnikov and he walked into the tiny entryway.

On a broken chair stood a candle in a battered copper candlestick.

"It's you! My goodness!" cried Sonia weakly, and she stood rooted to the spot.

"Which is your room? This way?" and Raskolnikov, trying not to look at her, hurried in.

A minute later Sonia, too, came in with the candle, put down the candlestick and, completely disconcerted, stood before him inexpressibly agitated and apparently frightened by his unexpected visit. The color rushed suddenly to her pale face and tears came into her eyes . . . She felt sick and ashamed and happy, too . . . Raskolnikov turned away quickly and sat on a chair by the table. He scanned the room in a rapid glance.

It was a large but extremely low-ceilinged room, the only one let by the Kapernaumovs, to whose rooms a closed door led in the wall on the left. In the opposite side on the right-hand wall was another door, which was always kept locked. That led to the next apartment, which formed a separate lodging. Sonia's room looked like a barn; it was a very irregular quadrangle, giving it a grotesque appearance. A wall with three windows looking out on to the canal ran on a slant so that one corner formed a very acute angle, and it was difficult to see in it without very strong light. The other corner was disproportionately obtuse. There was scarcely any furniture in the big room: in the corner on the right was a bedstead, beside it, nearest the door, was a chair. A plain, deal table covered by a blue cloth stood against the same wall, close to the door into the other apartment. Two rush-seated chairs stood by the table. On the opposite wall near the acute angle stood a small plain wooden chest of drawers looking, as it were, lost in a desert. That was all there was in the room. The yellow, scratched and shabby wall-paper was black in the corners. It must have been damp and full of fumes in the winter. There was every sign of poverty; even the bedstead had no curtain.

Sonia looked in silence at her visitor, who was so attentively and unceremoniously scrutinizing her room, and at last even began to tremble with terror, as though she were standing before her judge and the arbiter of her destinies.

"I am late . . . eleven, isn't it?" he asked, still not lifting his eyes.

"Yes," muttered Sonia, "oh, yes, it is," she added, hastily, as though it was her means of escape. "My landlady's clock has just struck . . . I heard it myself . . . "

"I've come to you for the last time," Raskolnikov went on gloomily, although this was the first time. "Perhaps I may not see you again . . . "

"Are you . . . going away?"

"I don't know . . . tomorrow . . . "

"Then you are not coming to Katerina Ivanovna's tomorrow?" Sonia's voice shook.

"I don't know. I shall know tomorrow morning . . . Never mind that: I've come to say one word . . . "

He raised his brooding eyes to her and suddenly noticed that he was sitting down while she had been standing before him.

"Why are you standing? Sit down," he said in a changed voice, gentle and friendly.

She sat down. He looked kindly and almost compassionately at her.

"How thin you are! What a hand! Quite transparent, like a dead hand."

He took her hand. Sonia smiled faintly.

"I have always been like that," she said.

"Even when you lived at home?"

"Yes."

"Of course you were," he added abruptly and the expression of his face and the sound of his voice changed again suddenly.

He looked round him once more.

"You rent this room from the Kapernaumovs?"

"Yes . . . "

"They live there, through that door?"

"Yes . . . They have another room like this."

"All in one room?"

"Yes."

"I would be afraid in your room at night," he observed gloomily.

"They are very good people, very kind," answered Sonia, who still seemed bewildered, "and all the furniture, everything . . . everything is theirs. And they are very kind and the children, too, often come to see me."

"They all stammer, don't they?"

"Yes . . . He stammers and he's lame. And his wife, too . . . It's not exactly that she stammers, but she can't speak plainly. She is a very kind woman. And he used to be a house serf. And there are seven children . . . and it's only the eldest one that stammers and the others are simply ill . . . but they don't stammer . . . But where did you hear about them?" she added with some surprise.

"Your father told me, then. He told me all about you . . . And how you went out at six o'clock and came back at nine and how Katerina Ivanovna knelt down by your bed."

Sonia was confused.

"I thought I saw him today," she whispered hesitatingly.

"Who?"

"My father. I was walking in the street, out there at the corner, at about ten o'clock and he seemed to be walking in front. It looked just like him. I wanted to go to Katerina Ivanovna . . . "

"You were walking in the streets?"

"Yes," Sonia whispered abruptly, again overcome with confusion and looking down.

"Katerina Ivanovna used to beat you, I daresay?"

"Oh no, what are you saying? No!" Sonia looked at him almost with dismay.

"You love her, then?"

"Love her? Of course!" said Sonia with plaintive emphasis, and she clasped her hands in distress. "Ah, you don't . . . If you only knew! You see, she is just like a child . . . Her mind is entirely unhinged, you see . . . from sorrow. And how clever she used to be . . . how generous . . . how kind! Ah, you don't understand, you don't understand!"

Sonia said this as though in despair, wringing her hands in excitement and distress. Her pale cheeks flushed, there was a look of anguish in her eyes. It was clear that she was stirred to the depths, that she was longing to speak, to champion, to express something. A sort of insatiable compassion, if you could call it that, was reflected in every feature of her face.

"Beat me! How can you? Good heavens, beat me! And if she did beat me, what then? What of it? You know nothing, nothing about it . . . She is so unhappy . . . ah, how unhappy! And ill . . . She is seeking righteousness, she is pure. She has such faith that there must be righteousness everywhere and she expects it . . . And if you were to torture her, she wouldn't do wrong. She doesn't see that it's impossible for people to be righteous and she is angry at it. Like a child, like a child. She is good!"

"And what will happen to you?"

Sonia looked at him inquiringly.

"They are left on your hands, you see. They were all on your hands before, though . . . And your father came to you to beg for drink. Well, how will it be now?"

"I don't know," Sonia articulated mournfully.

"Will they stay there?"

"I don't know . . . They are in debt for the lodging, but the landlady, I hear, said today that she wanted to get rid of them, and Katerina Ivanovna says that she won't stay another minute."

"How has she come to be so bold? She relies on you?"

"Oh, no, don't talk like that . . . We are one, we live as if we were one." Sonia was agitated again and even angry, as though a canary or some other little bird were to be angry. "And what could she do? What, what could she do?" she persisted, getting hot and excited. "And how she cried today! Her mind is unhinged, haven't you noticed it? One minute she is worrying like a child that everything will be right tomorrow, the lunch and all that . . . Then she is wringing her hands, spitting blood, weeping, and all at once she will begin knocking her head against the wall, in despair. Then she will be comforted again. She builds all her hopes on you; she says that you will help her now and that she will borrow a little money somewhere and go to her native town with me and set up a boarding school for the daughters of gentlemen and take me to superintend it, and we will begin a new splendid life. And she kisses and hugs me, comforts me, and you know she has such faith, such faith in these dreams of hers!

You can't contradict her. And all day long she has been washing, cleaning, mending. She dragged the wash tub into the room with her feeble hands and sank on the bed, gasping for breath. We went this morning to a store to buy shoes for Polenka and Lida as theirs are completely worn out. Only the money we brought wasn't enough, not nearly enough. And she picked out such lovely little boots, because she has taste, you don't know. And there in the store she burst out crying in front of the assistants because she hadn't enough . . . Ah, it was sad to see her . . . "

"Well, after that I can understand why you live like this," Raskolnikov said with a bitter smile.

"And aren't you sorry for them? Aren't you sorry?" Sonia flew at him again. "Why, I know, you gave your last penny yourself, though you'd seen nothing of it, and if you'd seen everything, oh dear! And how often, how often I've brought her to tears! Only last week! Yes, I! Only a week before his death. I was cruel! And how often I've done it! Ah, I've been wretched at the thought of it all day!"

Sonia wrung her hands as she spoke at the pain of remembering it.

"You were cruel?"

"Yes, I—I. I went to see them," she went on, weeping, "and my father said, 'Read me something, Sonia, my head hurts, read to me, here's a book.' He had a book he had got from Andrei Semionovich Lebeziatnikov, he lives there, he always used to get hold of such strange books. And I said, 'I can't stay,' because I didn't want to read, and I'd gone in mainly to show Katerina Ivanovna some collars. Lizaveta, the salesgirl, sold me some collars and cuffs cheap, pretty, new, embroidered ones. Katerina Ivanovna liked them very much; she put them on and looked at herself in the glass and was delighted with them. 'Make me a present out of them, Sonia,' she said, 'please do.' 'Please do,' she said, she wanted them so much. And when could she wear them? They just reminded her of her old happy days. She looked at herself in the glass, admired herself, and she has no clothes at all, no things of her own, hasn't had all these years! And she never asks anyone for anything; she is proud, she'd sooner give away everything. And these she asked for, she liked them so much. And I was sorry to give them. 'What use are they to you, Katerina Ivanovna?' I said. I spoke like that to her, I shouldn't have said it! She gave me such a look. And she was so upset, so upset that I refused her. And it was so sad to see . . . And she wasn't upset because of the collars, but because I refused, I saw that. Ah, if only I could bring it all back, change it, take back those words! Ah, if I . . . but it's nothing to you!"

"Did you know Lizaveta, the salesgirl?"

"Yes . . . Did you know her?" Sonia asked with some surprise.

"Katerina Ivanovna is tubercular, seriously tubercular; soon she will be dead," said Raskolnikov after a pause, without answering her question.

"Oh, no, no, no!"

And Sonia unconsciously clutched both his hands, as though imploring for her not to be.

"But it will be better if she does die."

"No, not better, not better at all!" Sonia unconsciously repeated in dismay.

"And the children? What can you do except take them to live with you?"

"Oh, I don't know," cried Sonia, almost in despair, and she put her hands to her head.

It was evident that the idea had very often occurred to her before and he had only raised it again.

"And, what, if even now, while Katerina Ivanovna is alive, you get ill and are taken to the hospital, what will happen then?" he persisted pitilessly.

"How can you? That can't happen!"

And Sonia's face was tortured with terror.

"Can't happen?" Raskolnikov went on with a harsh smile. "You're not insured against it, are you? What will happen to them then? They'll be in the street, all of them, she'll cough and beg and knock her head against some wall, as she did today, and the children will cry . . . Then she will fall down, be taken to the police station and to the hospital, she will die, and the children . . . "

"Oh, no . . . God will not let it be!" broke at last from Sonia's overburdened body.

She listened, looking imploringly at him, dumbly clasping her hands as if she were begging him for something, as though it all depended on him.

Raskolnikov got up and began to walk around the room. A

minute passed. Sonia was standing with her hands and her head hanging in terrible dejection.

"And can't you save? Put something aside for a rainy day?" he asked, stopping suddenly before her.

"No," whispered Sonia.

"Of course not. Have you tried?" he added almost ironically.

"Yes."

"And it didn't come off! Of course not! No need to ask."

And again he paced the room. Another minute passed.

"You don't get money every day?"

Sonia was more confused than ever and color rushed into her face again.

"No," she whispered with a painful effort.

"It will be the same with Polenka, no doubt," he said suddenly.

"No, no! It can't be, no!" Sonia cried aloud in desperation, as though she had been stabbed. "God would not allow anything so awful!"

"He lets others come to it."

"No, no! God will protect her, God!" she repeated beside herself.

"But, perhaps, there is no God at all," Raskolnikov answered with a sort of malignance, laughed and looked at her.

Sonia's face suddenly changed; a tremor passed over it. She looked at him with unutterable reproach, tried to say something, but could not speak and broke into bitter, bitter sobs, hiding her face in her hands.

"You say Katerina Ivanovna's mind is unhinged; your own mind is unhinged," he said after a brief silence.

Five minutes passed. He still paced up and down the room in silence, not looking at her. At last he went up to her; his eyes glittered. He put his two hands on her shoulders and looked straight into her tearful face. His eyes were hard, feverish and piercing, his lips were twitching. All at once he bent down quickly and dropping to the ground, kissed her foot. Sonia drew back from him as from a madman. He certainly looked like a madman.

"What are you doing to me?" she muttered, turning pale, and a sudden anguish clutched at her heart.

He stood up at once.

"I did not bow down to you, I bowed down to all the suffering of humanity," he said wildly and walked away to the window. "Listen," he added, turning to her a minute later. "I said just now to an insolent man that he was not worth your little finger . . . and that I did my sister an honor by making her sit with you."

"Ach, you said that to them! And in her presence?" cried Sonia, frightened. "Sit down with me! An honor! But I'm . . . dishonorable . . . Ah, why did you say that?"

"It was not because of your dishonor and your sin I said that of you, but because of your great suffering. But you are a great sinner, that's true," he added almost solemnly, "and your worst sin is that you have destroyed and betrayed yourself for nothing. Isn't that terrible? Isn't it terrible that you are living in this filth which you loathe so much, and at the same time you know yourself (you've only got to open your eyes) that you are not helping anyone by it, not saving anyone from anything! Tell me," he went on almost in a frenzy, "how this shame and degradation can exist in you side by side with other, opposite, holy feelings? It would be better, a thousand times better and wiser to leap into the water and end it all!"

"But what would become of them?" Sonia asked faintly, gazing at him with eyes of anguish, but not seeming surprised at his suggestion.

Raskolnikov looked strangely at her. He read it all in her face; so she must have had that thought already, perhaps many times, and earnestly she had thought out in her despair how to end it and so earnestly, that now she scarcely wondered at his suggestion. She had not even noticed the cruelty of his words. (The significance of his reproaches and his peculiar attitude to her shame she had, of course, not noticed either, and that, too, was clear to him.) But he saw how monstrously the thought of her disgraceful, shameful position was torturing her and had long tortured her. "What, what," he thought, "could have hindered her from putting an end to it?" Only then he realized what those poor little orphan children and that pitiful half-crazy Katerina Ivanovna, tubercular and knocking her head against the wall, meant for Sonia.

But, nevertheless, it was clear to him again that with her character and the amount of education she had after all received, she could not in any case remain the way she was. He was still confronted by the question of how could she have remained so long in that position without going out of her mind, since she could not bring herself to jump into the water? Of course he knew that Sonia's position was an exceptional case, though unhappily not unique and not infrequent, in fact; but her exceptional nature, her tinge of education, her previous life might, one would have thought, have killed her at the first step on that revolting path. What held her up—surely not depravity? All that infamy had obviously only touched her mechanically, not one drop of real depravity had penetrated to her heart; he saw that. He saw through her as she stood before him . . .

"There are three ways before her," he thought, "the canal, the madhouse, or . . . at last to sink into depravity which obscures the mind and turns the heart to stone."

The last idea was the most revolting, but he was a skeptic, he was young, abstract, and therefore cruel, and so he could not help believing that the last way was the most likely.

"But can it be true?" he cried to himself. "Can that creature, who has still preserved the purity of her spirit, be consciously drawn at last into that sink of filth and iniquity? Can the process already have begun? Can it be that she has only been able to bear it until now, because vice has begun to be less loathsome to her? No, no, that cannot be!" he cried, as Sonia had just before. "No, what has kept her from the canal until now is the idea of sin and they, the children . . . And if she has not gone out of her mind . . . but who says she has not gone out of her mind? Is she in her senses? Can people talk, can people reason as she does? How can she sit on the edge of the abyss of loathsomeness into which she is slipping and refuse to listen when she is told about the dangers which face her? Does she expect a miracle? No doubt she does. Doesn't that all mean madness?"

He stopped obstinately at that thought. In fact, he liked that explanation better than any other. He began looking more intently at her.

"So you pray to God a great deal, Sonia?" he asked her.

Sonia did not speak; he stood beside her waiting for an answer.

"What would I be without God?" she whispered rapidly, forcibly, glancing at him with suddenly flashing eyes, and squeezing his hand.

"Ah, so that is it!" he thought.

"And what does God do for you?" he asked, probing her further.

Sonia was silent a long while, as though she could not answer. Her weak chest kept heaving with emotion.

"Be silent! Don't ask! You don't deserve!" she cried suddenly, looking sternly and angrily at him.

"That's it, that's it," he repeated to himself.

"He does everything," she whispered quickly, looking down again.

"That's the way out! That's the explanation," he decided, scrutinizing her with eager curiosity, with a new, strange, almost morbid feeling. He gazed at that pale, thin, irregular, angular little face, those soft blue eyes, which could flash with such fire, such stern energy, that little body still shaking with indignation and anger—and it all seemed to him more and more strange, almost impossible. "She's a religious maniac!" he repeated to himself.

There was a book lying on the chest of drawers. He had noticed it every time he paced up and down the room. Now he took it up and looked at it. It was the New Testament in the Russian translation. It was bound in leather, old and worn.

"Where did you get that?" he called to her across the room.

She was still standing in the same place, three steps from the table.

"It was brought to me," she answered, as if unwillingly, not looking at him.

"Who brought it?"

"Lizaveta, I asked her for it."

"Lizaveta! Strange!" he thought.

Everything about Sonia seemed to him stranger and more wonderful every moment. He carried the book to the candle and began to turn over the pages.

"Where is the story of Lazarus?" he asked suddenly.

Sonia looked obstinately at the ground and would not answer. She was standing sideways to the table.

"Where is the raising of Lazarus? Find it for me, Sonia."

She stole a glance at him.

"You are not looking in the right place . . . It's in the fourth gospel," she whispered sternly, without looking at him.

"Find it and read it to me," he said. He sat down with his elbow on the table, leaned his head on his hand and looked away sullenly, prepared to listen.

"In three weeks' time they'll welcome me to the madhouse! I shall be there if I am not in a worse place," he muttered to himself.

Sonia heard Raskolnikov's request distrustfully and moved hesitatingly to the table. She took the book, however.

"Haven't you read it?" she asked, looking up at him across the table.

Her voice became sterner and sterner.

"Long ago . . . When I was at school. Read it!"

"And haven't you heard it in church?"

"I . . . haven't been. Do you often go?"

"N-no," whispered Sonia.

Raskolnikov smiled.

"I understand . . . And you won't go to your father's funeral tomorrow?"

"Yes, I shall. I was at church last week, too . . . I had a requiem service."

"For whom?"

"For Lizaveta. She was killed with an axe."

His nerves were more and more strained. His head began to go round.

"Were you friends with Lizaveta?"

"Yes . . . She was good . . . she used to come . . . not often . . . she couldn't . . . We used to read together and . . . talk. She will see God."

The last phrase sounded strange in his ears. And here was something new again: the mysterious meetings with Lizaveta and both of them—religious maniacs.

"I shall be a religious maniac myself soon! It's infectious!"

"Read!" he cried irritably and insistently.

Sonia still hesitated. Her heart was throbbing. She hardly dared to read to him. He looked almost with exasperation at the "unhappy lunatic."

"What for? You don't believe? . . . " she whispered softly and as it were breathlessly.

"Read! I want you to," he persisted. "You used to read to Lizaveta."

Sonia opened the book and found the place. Her hands were shaking, her voice failed her. Twice she tried to begin and could not bring out the first syllable.

"Now a certain man was sick named Lazarus of Bethany . . . " she forced herself at last to read, but at the third word her voice broke like an overstrained string. There was a catch in her breath.

Raskolnikov saw in part why Sonia could not bring herself to read to him and the more he saw this, the more roughly and irritably he insisted on her doing so. He understood only too well how painful it was for her to betray and unveil all that was her own. He understood that these feelings really were her secret treasure, which she had kept perhaps for years, perhaps from childhood, while she lived with an unhappy father and a distracted stepmother crazed by grief, in the midst of starving children and unseemly abuse and reproaches. But at the same time he knew now and knew for certain that, although it filled her with dread and suffering, yet she had a tormenting desire to read and to read to him that he might hear it, and to read now whatever might come of it! . . . He read this in her eyes, he could see it in her intense emotion. She mastered herself, controlled the spasm in her throat and went on reading the eleventh chapter of St. John. She went on to the nineteenth verse:

"And many of the Jews came to Martha and Mary to comfort them concerning their brother.

"Then Martha as soon as she heard that Jesus was coming went and met Him: but Mary sat still in the house.

"Then said Martha unto Jesus, Lord, if Thou hadst been here, my brother had not died.

"But I know that even now whatsoever Thou wilt ask of God, God will give it Thee . . . "

Then she stopped again with a shamefaced feeling that her voice would quiver and break again.

"Jesus said unto her, thy brother shall rise again.

"Martha saith unto Him, I know that he shall rise again in the resurrection, at the last day.

"Jesus said unto her, I am the resurrection and the life: he that believeth in Me though he were dead, yet shall he live.

"And whosoever liveth and believeth in Me shall never die. Believest thou this?

"She saith unto Him,"

(And drawing a painful breath, Sonia read distinctly and forcibly as though she were making a public confession of faith.)

"Yea, Lord: I believe that Thou art the Christ, the Son of God Which should come into the world."

She stopped and looked up quickly at him, but controlling herself went on reading. Raskolnikov sat without moving, his elbows on the table and his eyes turned away. She read to the thirty-second verse.

"Then when Mary was come where Jesus was and saw Him, she fell down at His feet, saying unto Him, Lord if Thou hadst been here, my brother had not died.

"When Jesus therefore saw her weeping, and the Jews also weeping which came with her, He groaned in the spirit and was troubled,

"And said, Where have ye laid him? They said unto Him, Lord, come and see.

"Jesus wept.

"Then said the Jews, behold how He loved him!

"And some of them said, could not this Man which opened the eyes of the blind, have caused that even this man should not have died?"

Raskolnikov turned and looked at her with emotion. Yes, he had known it! She was trembling in a real physical fever. He had expected it. She was getting near the story of the greatest miracle and a feeling of immense triumph came over her. Her voice rang out like a bell; triumph and joy gave it power. The lines danced before her eyes, but she knew what she was reading by heart. At the last verse "Could not this Man which opened the eyes of the blind . . . " dropping her voice she passionately reproduced the doubt, the reproach and censure of the blind disbelieving Jews, who in another moment would fall at His feet as though struck by thunder, sobbing and believing . . . "And he, he, too, is blinded and unbelieving, he, too, will hear, he, too, will believe, yes, yes! At once, now," was what she was dreaming, and she was quivering with happy anticipation.

"Jesus therefore again groaning in Himself cometh to the grave. It was a cave, and a stone lay upon it.

"Jesus said, Take ye away the stone. Martha, the sister of him that was dead, saith unto Him, Lord by this time he stinketh: for he hath been dead four days."

She laid emphasis on the word "four."

"Jesus saith unto her, Said I not unto thee that if thou wouldest believe, thou shouldest see the glory of God?

"Then they took away the stone from the place where the dead was laid. And Jesus lifted up His eyes and said, Father, I thank Thee that Thou hast heard Me.

"And I know that Thou hearest Me always; but because of the people which stand by I said it, that they may believe that Thou hast sent Me.

"And when He thus had spoken, He cried with a loud voice, Lazarus, come forth.

"And he that was dead came forth."

(She read loudly, cold and trembling with ecstasy, as though she were seeing it before her eyes.)

"Bound hand and foot with graveclothes; and his face was bound about with a napkin. Jesus saith unto them, Loose him and let him go.

"Then many of the Jews which came to Mary and had seen the things which Jesus did believed in Him."

She could read no more, closed the book and got up from her chair quickly.

"That is all about the raising of Lazarus," she whispered severely and abruptly, and turning away she stood motionless, not daring to raise her eyes to him. She still trembled feverishly. The candle-end was flickering out in the battered candlestick, dimly lighting up in the poverty-stricken room the murderer and the harlot who had so strangely been reading together the eternal book. Five minutes or more passed.

"I came to speak of something," Raskolnikov said aloud, frowning. He got up and went to Sonia. She lifted her eyes to him in silence. His face was particularly stern and there was a sort of savage determination in it.

"I have abandoned my family today," he said, "my mother and sister. I am not going to see them. I've broken with them completely."

"What for?" asked Sonia amazed. Her recent meeting with his mother and sister had left a great impression which she could not analyze. She heard his news almost with horror.

"I have only you now," he added. "Let us go together . . . I've come to you, we are both accursed, let us go our way together!"

His eyes glittered "as though he were mad," Sonia thought, in her turn.

"Go where?" she asked in alarm and she involuntarily stepped back.

"How do I know? I only know it's the same road, I know that and nothing more. It's the same goal!"

She looked at him and understood nothing. She knew only that he was terribly, infinitely unhappy.

"No-one of them will understand, if you tell them, but I have understood. I need you, that is why I have come to you."

"I don't understand," whispered Sonia.

"You'll understand later. Haven't you done the same? You, too, have overstepped your boundaries . . . have had the strength to overstep them. You have laid hands on yourself, you have destroyed a life . . . your own (it's all the same!). You might have lived in spirit and understanding, but you'll end in the Haymarket . . . But you won't be able to stand it, and if you remain alone you'll go out of your mind like me. You are like a mad creature already. So we must go together on the same road! Let us go!"

"What for? What's all this for?" said Sonia, strangely and violently agitated by his words.

"What for? Because you can't remain like this, that's why! You must look things straight in the face at last, and not weep like a child and cry that God won't allow it. What will happen, if you really are taken to the hospital tomorrow? She is mad and tubercular, she'll die soon, and the children? Do you mean to tell me Polenka won't come to grief? Haven't you seen children here at the street corners sent out by their mothers to beg? I've found out where those mothers live and what surroundings they live in. Children can't remain children there! At seven the child is vicious and a thief. Yet children, you know, are the image of Christ: 'theirs is the kingdom of Heaven.' He bade us honor and love them, they are the humanity of the future . . . "

"What's to be done, what's to be done?" repeated Sonia, weeping hysterically and wringing her hands.

"What's to be done? Break what must be broken, once and for all, that's all, and take the suffering on yourself. What, you don't understand? You'll understand later . . . Freedom and power, and above all, power! Over all trembling creation, the whole ant heap! . . . That's the goal, remember that! That's my farewell message. Perhaps it's the last time I shall speak to you. If I don't come tomorrow, you'll hear of it all, and then remember these words. And some day later on, in years to come, you'll understand perhaps what they meant. If I come tomorrow, I'll tell you who killed Lizaveta . . . goodbye."

Sonia started with terror.

"Why, do you know who killed her?" she asked, chilled with horror, looking wildly at him.

"I know and will tell . . . you, only you. I have chosen you. I'm not coming to you to ask forgiveness, but simply to tell you. I chose you long ago to hear this, when your father talked about you and when Lizaveta was alive, I thought of it. Goodbye, don't shake hands. Until tomorrow!"

He went out. Sonia gazed at him as she would at a madman. But she herself felt as if she were insane and knew it. Her head was whirling.

"My goodness, how does he know who killed Lizaveta? What did those words mean? It's awful!" But at the same time the idea did not enter her head, not for a moment! "Oh, he must be terribly unhappy! . . . He has abandoned his mother and sister . . . What for? What has happened? And what did he have in mind? What did he say to her? He had kissed her foot and said . . . said (yes, he had said it clearly) that he could not live without her . . . Oh, merciful heavens!"

Sonia spent the whole night feverish and delirious. She jumped up from time to time, wept and wrung her hands, then sank again into feverish sleep and dreamt of Polenka, Katerina Ivanovna and Lizaveta, of reading the gospel and him . . . him with pale face, with burning eyes . . . kissing her feet, weeping.

On the other side of the door on the right, which divided Sonia's room from Madame Resslich's apartment, was a room which long stood empty. A card was fixed on the gate and a notice stuck in the windows over the canal advertising it to let. Sonia had long been accustomed to the room being uninhabited. But all that time Mr. Svidrigailov had been standing, listening at the door of the empty room. When Raskolnikov went out he stood still, thought a moment, went on tiptoe to his own room which adjoined the empty one, brought a chair and noiselessly carried it to the door that led to Sonia's room. The conversation had struck him as interesting and remarkable, and he had greatly enjoyed it—so much so that he brought a chair that he might not in the future, tomorrow, for instance, have to endure the inconvenience of standing a whole hour, but would be able listen in comfort.

CHAPTER FIVE

WHEN NEXT MORNING AT eleven o'clock punctually Raskolnikov went into the department of the investigation of criminal causes and sent his name in to Porfiry Petrovich, he was surprised at being kept waiting so long: it was at least ten minutes before he was summoned. He had expected that they would pounce upon him. But he stood in the waiting-room, and people, who apparently had nothing to do with him, were continually passing to and fro before him. In the next room which looked like an office, several clerks were sitting writing and obviously they had no notion who or what Raskolnikov might be. He looked uneasily and suspiciously about him to see whether there was not some guard, some mysterious watch being kept on him to prevent his escape. But there was nothing of the sort: he saw only the faces of clerks absorbed in petty details, then other people, none of whom seemed to have any business with him. He could go where he liked for all they cared. The conviction grew stronger in him that if that enigmatic man yesterday, that phantom who had sprung out of the earth, had seen everything, they would not have let him stand and wait like that. And would they have waited until he chose to appear at eleven? Either the man had not yet given information, or . . . or he simply knew nothing, had seen nothing (and how could he have seen anything?) and so everything that had happened to him the day before was again a phantom exaggerated by his sick and overstrained imagination. This thought had begun to grow strong the day before, in the midst of all his alarm and despair. Thinking it all over now and preparing for a fresh conflict, he was suddenly aware that he was trembling—and he felt a rush of indignation at the thought that he was trembling with fear at facing that hateful Porfiry Petrovich. What he dreaded above all was meeting that man again; he hated him with an intense, unmitigated hatred and was afraid his hatred might betray him. His indignation was such that he stopped trembling at once; he prepared to go in with a cold and arrogant bearing and vowed to himself to keep as silent as possible, to watch and listen and for once at least to control his overstrained nerves. At that moment he was summoned to Porfiry Petrovich.

He found Porfiry Petrovich alone in his study. His study was a room, neither large nor small, furnished with a large writing-table that stood before a sofa which was upholstered in checked material, a bureau, a bookcase in the corner and several chairs—all government furniture, made of polished yellow wood. In the furthest wall there was a closed door, beyond which there were, no doubt, other rooms. On Raskolnikov's entrance Porfiry Petrovich had immediately closed the door through which he had come in and they remained alone. He met his visitor with an apparently genial and good-tempered air, and it was only after a few minutes that Raskolnikov saw signs of a certain awkwardness in him, as though he had been thrown off guard or caught in the middle of something very secret.

"Ah, my friend! Here you are . . . in our domain . . . " began Porfiry, holding out both hands to him. "Come on, sit down, my boy . . . or perhaps you don't like to be called 'my friend' and 'my boy!'— *tout court?** Please don't think it's too informal . . . Here, on the sofa."

Raskolnikov sat down, keeping his eyes fixed on him. "In our domain," the apologies for being so informal, the French phrase "*tout court*" were all characteristic signs.

"He held out both hands to me, but he did not give me one— he drew it back in time," struck him suspiciously. Both were watching each other, but when their eyes met, quick as lightning they looked away.

"I brought you this paper . . . about the watch. Here it is. Is it all right or shall I copy it again?"

"What? A paper? Yes, yes, don't be uneasy, it's all right," Porfiry Petrovich said as though in a hurry, and after he had said it he took the paper and looked at it. "Yes, it's all right. Nothing more is needed," he declared with the same rapidity and he laid the paper on the table.

A minute later when he was talking of something else he took it from the table and put it on his bureau.

"I believe you said yesterday you would like to question me . . . formally . . . about my acquaintance with the murdered woman?" Raskolnikov was beginning again. "Why did I put in 'I believe'" passed through his mind in a flash. "Why am I so uneasy at having put in that 'I believe'?" came in a second flash. And he suddenly felt that his uneasiness at the mere contact with Porfiry, at the first words, at

---

*Should I stop (French)?

the first looks, had grown in an instant to monstrous proportions, and that this was fearfully dangerous. His nerves were quivering, his emotion was increasing. "It's bad, it's bad! I shall say too much again."

"Yes, yes, yes! There's no hurry, there's no hurry," muttered Porfiry Petrovich, moving to and fro about the table without any apparent aim, making dashes as it were towards the window, the bureau and the table, one moment avoiding Raskolnikov's suspicious glance, then again standing still and looking him straight in the face.

His fat round little figure looked very strange, like a ball rolling from one side to the other and rebounding back.

"We've plenty of time. Do you smoke? Have you got your own? Here, a cigarette!" he went on, offering his visitor a cigarette. "You know I am receiving you here, but my own quarters are through there, you know, my government quarters. But I am living outside for the time being, I had to have some repairs done here. It's almost finished now . . . Government quarters, you know, are a wonderful thing. Eh, what do you think?"

"Yes, a wonderful thing," answered Raskolnikov, looking at him almost ironically.

"A wonderful thing, a wonderful thing," repeated Porfiry Petrovich, as though he had just thought of something quite different. "Yes, a wonderful thing," he almost shouted at last, suddenly staring at Raskolnikov and stopping short two steps from him.

This stupid repetition was too inept for the serious, brooding and enigmatic glance he turned upon his visitor.

But this stirred Raskolnikov's anger more than ever and he could not resist an ironical and somewhat incautious challenge.

"Tell me, please," he asked suddenly, looking almost insolently at him and taking a kind of pleasure in his own insolence. "I believe it's a sort of legal rule, a sort of legal tradition—for all investigating lawyers—to begin their attack from afar, with a trivial, or at least an irrelevant subject, so as to encourage, or rather, to divert the man they are cross-examining, to disarm his caution and then all at once to give him an unexpected knockdown blow with some fatal question. Isn't that so? It's a sacred tradition, mentioned, I fancy, in all the manuals of the art?"

"Yes, yes . . . Why, do you imagine that was why I spoke about government quarters . . . eh?"

And as he said this Porfiry Petrovich screwed up his eyes and winked; a good-humored, crafty look passed over his face. The wrinkles on his forehead were smoothed out, his eyes contracted, his features broadened and he suddenly went off into a nervous prolonged laugh, shaking all over and looking Raskolnikov straight in the face. The latter forced himself to laugh, too, but when Porfiry, seeing that he was laughing, broke into such a guffaw that he turned almost crimson, Raskolnikov's repulsion overcame all precaution; he left off laughing, scowled and stared with hatred at Porfiry, keeping his eyes fixed on him while his intentionally prolonged laughter lasted. There was lack of precaution on both sides, however, for Porfiry Petrovich seemed to be laughing in his visitor's face and to be almost undisturbed by the annoyance with which the visitor received it. The latter fact was very significant in Raskolnikov's eyes: he saw that Porfiry Petrovich had not been embarrassed just before either, but that he, Raskolnikov, had perhaps fallen into a trap; that there must be something, some motive here unknown to him; that, perhaps, everything was ready and in another moment would break upon him . . .

He came straight to the point, rose from his seat and took his cap.

"Porfiry Petrovich," he began resolutely, though with considerable irritation, "yesterday you expressed a desire that I should come to you for some inquiries" (he laid special stress on the word "inquiries"). "I have come and, if you have anything to ask me, ask it, and if not, allow me to withdraw. I have no time to spare . . . I have to be at the funeral of that man who was run over, of whom you . . . know also," he added, feeling angry at once at having made this addition and more irritated at his anger, "I am sick of it all, do you hear, and I have long been. It's partly what made me ill. In short," he shouted, feeling that the phrase about his illness was still more out of place, "in short, kindly examine me or let me go, at once. And if you must examine me, do so properly! I will not allow you to do so otherwise, and so meanwhile, goodbye, as we have evidently nothing to keep us now."

"Good heavens! What do you mean? What shall I question you about?" cackled Porfiry Petrovich with a change of tone, instantly cutting his laughter short. "Please don't disturb yourself," he began fidgeting from place to place and fussily making Raskolnikov sit down. "There's no hurry, there's no hurry, it's all nonsense. Oh, no, I'm very glad you've come to see me at last . . . I look on you simply as a visitor. And as for my accursed laughter, please excuse it, Rodion Romanovich. Rodion Romanovich? That is your name? . . . It's my nerves, you tickled me so much with your witty observation; I assure you, sometimes I shake with laughter like an India-rubber ball for half an hour at a time . . . I'm often afraid of an attack of paralysis. Do sit down. Please do, or I shall think you are angry . . . "

Raskolnikov did not speak; he listened, watching him, still frowning angrily. He did sit down, but still held his cap.

"I must tell you one thing about myself, my dear Rodion Romanovich," Porfiry Petrovich continued, moving about the room and again avoiding his visitor's eyes. "You see, I'm a bachelor, a man of no consequence and not used to company; besides, I have nothing before me, I'm set, I'm running to seed and . . . and have you noticed, Rodion Romanovich, that in our Petersburg circles, if two clever men meet who are not intimate, but respect each other, like you and me, it takes them half an hour before they can find a subject for conversation—they cannot speak, they sit opposite each other and feel awkward. Everyone has subjects of conversation, ladies for instance . . . people in high society always have their subjects of conversation, it's *de rigueur*,* but people of the middle sort like us, thinking people that is, are always tongue-tied and awkward. What's the reason for it? Whether it is a lack of public interest, or whether it is that we are so honest we don't want to deceive one another, I don't know. What do you think? Please put down your cap, it looks as if you were just going, it makes me uncomfortable . . . I am so delighted . . . "

Raskolnikov put down his cap and continued listening in silence with a serious frowning face to the vague and empty chatter of Porfiry Petrovich. "Does he really want to distract my attention with his silly babble?"

"I can't offer you coffee here; but why not spend five minutes with a friend," Porfiry pattered on, "and you know all these official duties . . . please don't mind my running up and down, forgive me, my dear fellow, I am very much afraid of offending you, but exercise is absolutely indispensable for me. I'm always sitting and so glad to be moving about for five minutes . . . I suffer from my sedentary life . . . I always intend to join a gymnasium; they say that officials of

---

*Compulsory (French).

all ranks, even Privy Councilors may be seen skipping gaily there; there you have it, modern science . . . yes, yes . . . But as for my duties here, inquiries and all such formalities . . . you mentioned inquiries yourself just now . . . I assure you these interrogations are sometimes more embarrassing for the interrogator than for the interrogated . . . You made the observation yourself just now very aptly and wittily." (Raskolnikov had made no observation of the kind.) "People get into a muddle! A real muddle! They keep harping on the same note, like a drum! There will be a reform and we shall be called by a different name, at least, he-he-he! And as for our legal tradition, as you so wittily called it, I thoroughly agree with you. Every prisoner on trial, even the simplest peasant, knows that they begin by disarming him with irrelevant questions (as you so happily put it) and then deal him a knock-down blow, he-he-he!—your beautiful expressions, my boy, he-he! So you really imagined that I meant by government quarters . . . he-he! You are truly ironic. So, come. I won't go on! Ah, by the way, yes! One word leads to another. You spoke of formality just now, apropos of the inquiry, you know. But what's the use of formality? In many cases it's nonsense. Sometimes you have a friendly chat and get a good deal more out of it. You can always fall back on formality, may I assure you. And, after all, what does it amount to? An examining lawyer cannot be bounded by formality at every step. The work of investigation is, so to speak, a free art in its own way, he-he-he!"

Porfiry Petrovich paused for breath. He had simply babbled on uttering empty phrases, letting slip a few enigmatic words and again reverting to incoherence. He was almost running around the room, moving his fat little legs quicker and quicker, looking at the ground, with his right hand behind his back, while with his left making gestures that bore extraordinarily little relation to his words. Raskolnikov suddenly noticed that as he ran about the room he seemed twice to stop for a moment near the door, as though he were listening.

"Is he expecting anything?"

"You are certainly quite right about it," Porfiry began gaily, looking with extraordinary simplicity at Raskolnikov (which startled him and instantly put him on his guard), "certainly quite right in laughing so wittily at our legal forms, he-he! Some of these elaborate psychological methods are extremely ridiculous and perhaps useless, if you follow the forms too closely. Yes . . . I am talking about forms again. Well, if I recognize, or more strictly speaking, if I suspect someone or other to be a criminal in any case entrusted to me . . . you're a law student, of course, Rodion Romanovich?"

"Yes, I was . . . "

"Well, then it is a precedent for you for the future—though don't suppose I should venture to instruct you after the articles you publish about crime! No, I simply make bold to state it by way of fact, if I took this man or that for a criminal, why, I ask, should I worry him prematurely, even if I had evidence against him? In one case I may be bound, for instance, to arrest a man at once, but another may be in quite a different position, you know, so why shouldn't I let him walk about the town a bit, he-he-he! But I see you don't quite understand, so I'll give you a clearer example. If I put him in prison too soon, I may very likely give him, so to speak, moral support, he-he! You're laughing?"

Raskolnikov had no intention of laughing. He was sitting with compressed lips, his feverish eyes fixed on Porfiry Petrovich's.

"Yes, that is the case, with some types especially, for men are so different. You say evidence. Well, there may be evidence. But evidence, you know, can generally be taken two ways. I am an examining lawyer and a weak man, I confess it. I should like to make a proof, so to say, mathematically clear, I should like to make a chain of evidence such as twice two is four, it ought to be a direct, irrefutable proof! And if I shut him up too soon—even though I might be convinced he was the man, I should very likely be depriving myself of the means of getting further evidence against him. And how? By giving him, so to speak, a definite position, I shall put him out of suspense and set his mind at rest, so that he will retreat into his shell. They say that at Sevastopol, soon after Alma,* the clever people were in a terrible fright that the enemy would attack openly and take Sevastopol at once. But when they saw that the enemy preferred a regular siege, they were delighted, I am told and reassured, for the thing would drag on for two months at least. You're laughing, you don't believe me again? Of course, you're right, too. You're right, you're right.

---

*During the Crimean War, the French and the English defeated the Russians at the Alma River in 1854 before attacking Sevastopol.

These are special cases, I admit. But you must observe this, my dear Rodion Romanovich, the general case, the case for which all legal forms and rules are intended, for which they are calculated and laid down in books, does not exist at all, for the reason that every case, every crime for instance, as soon as it actually occurs, at once becomes a thoroughly special case and sometimes a case unlike any that's gone before. Very comic cases of that sort sometimes occur. If I leave one man completely alone, if I don't touch him and don't worry him, but let him know or at least suspect every moment that I know all about it and am watching him day and night, and if he is in continual suspicion and terror, he'll be bound to lose his head. He'll come forward of his own accord, or maybe do something which will make it as plain as twice two is four—it's delightful. It may be so with a simple peasant, but with one of our sort, an intelligent man cultivated on a certain side, it's a dead certainty. For, my dear fellow, it's a very important matter to know on what side a man is cultivated. And then there are nerves, there are nerves, you have overlooked them! Why, they are all sick, nervous and irritable! . . . And then how angry they all are! That I assure you is a regular gold mine for us. And it's no anxiety to me, him running about the town free! Let him, let him walk about for a bit! I know well enough that I've caught him and that he won't escape me. Where could he escape to, he-he? Abroad, perhaps? A Pole will escape abroad, but not here, especially as I am watching and have taken measures. Will he escape into the depths of the country? But you know, peasants live there, real rude Russian peasants. A modern cultivated man would prefer prison to living with such strangers as our peasants. He-he! But that's all nonsense, and on the surface. It's not merely that he has nowhere to run to, he is psychologically unable to escape me, he-he! What an expression! Through a law of nature he can't escape me if he had anywhere to go. Have you seen a butterfly round a candle? That's how he will keep circling and circling round me. Freedom will lose its attractions. He'll begin to brood, he'll weave a tangle round himself, he'll worry himself to death! What's more he will provide me with a mathematical proof—if I only give him a long enough interval . . . And he'll keep circling round me, getting nearer and nearer and then—flop! He'll fly straight into my mouth and I'll swallow him, and that will be very amusing, he-he-he! You don't believe me?"

Raskolnikov made no reply; he sat pale and motionless, still gazing with the same intensity into Porfiry's face.

"It's a lesson," he thought, turning cold. "This is beyond the cat playing with a mouse, like yesterday. He can't be showing off his power with no motive . . . prompting me; he is far too clever for that . . . he must have another object. What is it? It's all nonsense, my friend, you are pretending, to scare me! You've no proofs and the man I saw had no real existence. You simply want to make me lose my head, to work me up beforehand and crush me. But you are wrong, you won't do it! But why give me such a hint? Is he reckoning on my shattered nerves? No, my friend, you are wrong, you won't do it even though you have some trap for me . . . let us see what you have in store for me."

And he braced himself to face a terrible and unknown ordeal. At times he longed to fall on Porfiry and strangle him. This anger was what he had dreaded from the beginning. He felt that his parched lips were flecked with foam, his heart was throbbing. But he was still determined not to speak till the right moment. He realized that this was the best policy in his position, because instead of saying too much he would be irritating his enemy by his silence and provoking him into speaking too freely. Anyhow, this was what he hoped for.

"No, I see you don't believe me, you think I am playing a harmless joke on you," Porfiry began again, getting more and more lively, chuckling at every instant and again pacing round the room. "And, to be sure, you're right: God has given me a figure that can awaken none but comic ideas in other people; a buffoon; but let me tell you and I repeat it, excuse an old man, my dear Rodion Romanovich, you are still a young man, in your first youth, so to speak, and so you put intellect above everything, like all young people. Playful wit and abstract arguments fascinate you and that's for all the world like the old Austrian Hofkriegsrat,* as far as I am any judge of military matters, that is: on paper they'd beaten Napoleon and taken him prisoner, and there in their study they worked it all out in the cleverest fashion, but then General Mack† surrendered with all his army, he-he-he! I see, I see, Rodion Romanovich, you are laughing at a civilian like me, tak-

---

*Royal Austrian military council.
†Austrian general Karl Mack lost to Napoleon at Ulm in 1805.

ing examples out of military history! But I can't help it, it's my weakness. I am fond of military science. And I'm ever so fond of reading
all the military histories. I've certainly missed my proper career. I
should have been in the army, I swear I should have been. I wouldn't
have been a Napoleon, but I might have been a major, he-he-he! Well,
I'll tell you the whole truth, my friend, about this special case, I
mean: actual fact and a man's temperament are weighty matters and
it's astonishing how they sometimes deceive the sharpest calculation!
I—listen to an old man—am speaking seriously, Rodion Romanovich" (as he said this Porfiry Petrovich, who was scarcely thirty-
five, actually seemed to have grown old; even his voice changed and
he seemed to shrink together), "moreover, I'm a candid man . . . am
I a candid man or not? What do you say? I think I must be: I tell you
these things for nothing and don't even expect a reward for it, he-he!
Well, to proceed, cleverness in my opinion is a splendid thing, it is,
so to say, an adornment of nature and a consolation of life, and what
tricks it can play! So that it sometimes is hard for a poor examining
lawyer to know where he is, especially when he's liable to be carried
away by his own imagination, too, for you know he is a man after all.
But the poor fellow is saved by the criminal's temperament, worse
luck for him! But young people carried away by their own wit don't
think of that 'when they overstep all obstacles' as you wittily and
cleverly expressed it yesterday. He will lie—that is, the man who is a
special case, the incognito, and he will lie well, in the cleverest fashion; you might think he would triumph and enjoy the fruits of his
cleverness, but at the most interesting, the most flagrant moment he
will faint. Of course there may be illness and a stuffy room as well,
but anyway! Anyway he's given us the idea! He lied incomparably, but
he didn't reckon on his temperament. That's what betrays him! Another time he will be carried away by his playful wit into making fun
of the man who suspects him, he will turn pale as it were on purpose
to mislead, but his paleness will be too natural, too much like the real
thing, again he has given us an idea! Though his questioner may be
deceived at first, he will think differently next day if he is not a fool,
and, of course, it is like that at every step! He puts himself forward
where he is not wanted, speaks continually when he ought to keep
silent, brings in all sorts of allegorical allusions, he-he! Comes and
asks why didn't you take me long ago, he-he-he! And that can hap-

pen, you know, with the cleverest man, the psychologist, the literary man. The temperament reflects everything like a mirror! Gaze into it and admire what you see! But why are you so pale, Rodion Romanovich? Is the room stuffy? Shall I open the window?"

"Oh, don't trouble yourself, please," cried Raskolnikov and he suddenly broke into a laugh. "Please don't trouble yourself."

Porfiry stood facing him, paused a moment and suddenly he too laughed. Raskolnikov got up from the sofa, abruptly checking his hysterical laughter.

"Porfiry Petrovich," he began, speaking loudly and distinctly, though his legs trembled and he could scarcely stand. "I see clearly at last that you actually suspect me of murdering that old woman and her sister Lizaveta. Let me tell you for my part that I am sick of this. If you find that you have a right to prosecute me legally, to arrest me, then prosecute me, arrest me. But I will not let myself be jeered at to my face and worried . . . "

His lips trembled, his eyes glowed with fury and he could not restrain his voice.

"I won't allow it!" he shouted, bringing his fist down on the table. "Do you hear that, Porfiry Petrovich? I won't allow it."

"Good heavens! What does it mean?" cried Porfiry Petrovich, apparently quite frightened. "Rodion Romanovich, my dear fellow, what is the matter with you?"

"I won't allow it," Raskolnikov shouted again.

"Hush, my dear man! They'll hear and come in. Just think, what could we say to them?" Porfiry Petrovich whispered in horror, bringing his face close to Raskolnikov's.

"I won't allow it, I won't allow it," Raskolnikov repeated mechanically, but he too spoke in a sudden whisper.

Porfiry turned quickly and ran to open the window.

"Some fresh air! And you must have some water, my dear friend. You're ill!" and he was running to the door to call for some when he found a decanter of water in the corner. "Come, drink a little," he whispered, rushing up to him with the decanter. "It will be sure to do you good."

Porfiry Petrovich's alarm and sympathy were so natural that Raskolnikov was silent and began looking at him with wild curiosity. He did not take the water, however.

"Rodion Romanovich, my dear friend, you'll drive yourself out of your mind, I assure you, my goodness! Have some water, do drink a little."

He forced him to take the glass. Raskolnikov raised it mechanically to his lips, but set it on the table again with disgust.

"Yes, you've had a little attack! You'll bring back your illness again, my dear fellow," Porfiry Petrovich cackled with friendly sympathy, though he still looked rather disconcerted. "Goodness, you must take more care of yourself! Dmitri Prokofich was here, came to see me yesterday—I know, I know, I've a nasty ironic temper, but what they made of it! . . . Goodness, he came yesterday after you'd been. We dined and he talked and talked away, and I could only throw up my hands in despair! Did he come from you? But do sit down, for mercy's sake, sit down!"

"No, not from me, but I knew he went to you and why he went," Raskolnikov answered sharply.

"You knew?"

"I knew. What of it?"

"Because, Rodion Romanovich, I know more than that about you; I know about everything. I know how you went to take an apartment at night when it was dark and how you rang the bell and asked about the blood, and the workmen and the porter did not know what to make of it. Yes, I understand your state of mind at that time . . . but you'll drive yourself mad like that, I swear it! You'll lose your head! You're full of generous indignation at the wrongs you've received, first from destiny, and then from the police officers, and so you rush from one thing to another to force them to speak out and make an end of it all, because you are sick of all this suspicion and foolishness. That's so, isn't it? I have guessed how you feel, haven't I? Only in that way you'll lose your head and Razumikhin's, too; he's too good a man for such a position, you must know that. You are ill and he is good and your illness is infectious for him . . . I'll tell you about it when you are more yourself . . . But do sit down, for goodness' sake. Please rest, you look shocking, do sit down."

Raskolnikov sat down; he no longer shivered, he was hot all over. In amazement he listened with strained attention to Porfiry Petrovich who still seemed frightened as he looked after him with friendly solicitude. But he did not believe a word he said, though he felt a strange inclination to believe. Porfiry's unexpected words about the apartment had utterly overwhelmed him. "How can it be, he knows about the apartment then," he thought suddenly, "and he tells me so himself!"

"Yes, in our legal practice there was a case which was almost exactly identical, a case of morbid psychology," Porfiry went on quickly. "A man confessed to murder and how he kept it up! It was a regular hallucination; he brought forward facts, he imposed upon every one and why? He had been partly, but only partly, unintentionally the cause of a murder and when he knew that he had given the murderers the opportunity, he sank into dejection, it got on his mind and turned his brain, he began imagining things and he persuaded himself that he was the murderer. But at last the appeal court went into it and the poor man was acquitted and given proper care. Thanks to the appeal court! Tut-tut-tut! Why, my dear friend, you may drive yourself into delirium if you have the impulse to work upon your nerves, to go ringing bells at night and asking about blood! I've studied all this morbid psychology in my practice. A man is sometimes tempted to jump out of a window or from a belfry. Just the same with bell-ringing . . . It's all illness, Rodion Romanovich! You have begun to neglect your illness. You should consult an experienced doctor, what's the good of that fat friend of yours? You are lightheaded! You were delirious when you did all this!"

For a moment Raskolnikov felt everything turning.

"Is it possible, is it possible," flashed through his mind, "that he is still lying? He can't be, he can't be." He rejected that idea, feeling to what a degree of fury it might drive him, feeling that that fury might drive him mad.

"I was not delirious. I knew what I was doing," he cried, straining every faculty to penetrate Porfiry's game, "I was quite myself, do you hear?"

"Yes, I hear and understand. You said yesterday you were not delirious, you were particularly emphatic about it! I understand all you can tell me! A-ach! . . . Listen, Rodion Romanovich, my dear fellow. If you were actually a criminal, or were somehow mixed up in this damnable business, would you insist that you were not delirious but in full possession of your faculties? And so emphatically and persistently? Would it be possible? Absolutely impossible, the way I see it. If you had anything on your conscience, you would certainly insist that you were delirious. That's so, isn't it?"

There was a note of slyness in this inquiry. Raskolnikov drew back on the sofa as Porfiry bent over him and stared in silent perplexity at him.

"Another thing about Razumikhin—you certainly ought to have said that he came of his own accord, to have concealed your part in it! But you don't conceal it! You lay stress on the fact that he came at your instigation."

Raskolnikov had not done so. A chill went down his back.

"You keep telling lies," he said slowly and weakly, twisting his lips into a sickly smile, "you are trying again to show that you know all my game, that you know all I shall say beforehand," he said, conscious himself that he was not weighing his words as he should. "You want to frighten me . . . or you are just laughing at me . . . "

He still stared at him as he said this and again there was a light of intense hatred in his eyes.

"You keep lying," he said. "You know perfectly well that the best policy for the criminal is to tell the truth as nearly as possible . . . to conceal as little as possible. I don't believe you!"

"What a cunning person you are!" Porfiry tittered, "You can't be caught out; you have a real monomania. So you don't believe me? But still you do believe me, you believe a quarter; I'll soon make you believe the whole, because I have a sincere liking for you and genuinely wish you good."

Raskolnikov's lips trembled.

"Yes, I do," went on Porfiry, touching Raskolnikov's arm genially, "you must take care of your illness. Besides, your mother and sister are here now; you must think of them. You must soothe and comfort them and you do nothing but frighten them . . . "

"What has that to do with you? How do you know anything about it? What concern is it of yours? You are keeping watch on me and want to let me know it?"

"Goodness! Why, I learnt it all from you yourself! You don't notice that in your excitement you tell me and others everything. From Razumikhin, too, I learnt a number of interesting details yesterday. No, you interrupted me, but I must tell you that, for all your cleverness, your suspiciousness makes you lose the common-sense view of things. To return to bell-ringing, for instance. I, an examining lawyer, have betrayed a precious thing like that, a real fact (for it is a fact worth having), and you see nothing in it! Why, if I had the slightest suspicion of you, should I have acted like that? No, I should first have disarmed your suspicions and not let you see I knew of that fact, should have diverted your attention and suddenly have dealt you a knock-down blow (your expression) saying: 'And what were you doing, sir, pray, at ten or nearly eleven at the murdered woman's apartment and why did you ring the bell and why did you ask about blood? And why did you invite the porters to go with you to the police station, to the lieutenant?' That's how I ought to have acted if I had a grain of suspicion about you. I ought to have taken your evidence in due form, searched your apartment and perhaps have arrested you, too . . . so I have no suspicion about you, since I have not done that! But you can't look at it normally and you see nothing, I say again."

Raskolnikov started so that Porfiry Petrovich could not fail to perceive it.

"You are lying all the time," he cried, "I don't know what you're aiming at, but you are lying. You did not speak like that just now and I cannot be mistaken!"

"I am lying?" Porfiry repeated, apparently incensed, but preserving a good-humored and ironical face, as though he were not in the least concerned at Raskolnikov's opinion of him. "I am lying . . . but how did I treat you just now, I, the examining lawyer? Prompting you and giving you every means for your defense; illness, I said, delirium, injury, melancholy and the police officers and all the rest of it? Ah! He-he-he! Though in fact all those psychological means of defense are not very reliable and cut both ways: illness, delirium, I don't remember—that's all right, but why, my friend, in your illness and in your delirium were you haunted by just those delusions and not by any others? There may have been others, eh? He-he-he!"

Raskolnikov looked haughtily and contemptuously at him.

"Briefly," he said loudly and imperiously, rising to his feet and in so doing pushing Porfiry back a little, "briefly, I want to know, do you acknowledge me perfectly free from suspicion or not? Tell me, Porfiry Petrovich, hurry up and tell me once and for all!"

"What trouble I'm having with you!" cried Porfiry with a perfectly good-humored, sly and composed face. "And why do you want to know, why do you want to know so much, since they haven't begun to worry you? You are like a child asking for matches! And why are you so uneasy? Why do you force yourself upon us, eh? He-he-he!"

"I repeat," Raskolnikov cried furiously, "that I can't put up with it!"

"With what? Uncertainty?" interrupted Porfiry.

"Don't jeer at me! I won't have it! I tell you I won't have it. I can't and I won't, do you hear, do you hear?" he shouted, bringing his fist down on the table again.

"Hush! Hush! They'll overhear! I warn you seriously, take care of yourself. I am not joking," Porfiry whispered, but this time there was not the look of old womanish good nature and alarm in his face. Now he was peremptory, stern, frowning, and for once laying aside all mystification.

But this was only for an instant. Raskolnikov, bewildered, suddenly fell into actual frenzy, but, strange to say, he again obeyed the command to speak quietly, though he was at the height of his fury.

"I will not allow myself to be tortured," he whispered, instantly recognizing with hatred that he could not help obeying the command and driven to even greater fury by the thought. "Arrest me, search me, but please act in due form and don't play with me! Don't you dare!"

"Don't worry about the form," Porfiry interrupted with the same sly smile, as it were, gloating with enjoyment over Raskolnikov. "I invited you to see me quite in a friendly way."

"I don't want your friendship and I spit on it! Do you hear? Look—I'm taking my cap and I'm going. What will you say now if you intend to arrest me?"

He took up his cap and went to the door.

"And won't you see my little surprise?" chuckled Porfiry, again taking him by the arm and stopping him at the door.

He seemed to become more playful and good-humored which maddened Raskolnikov.

"What surprise?" he asked, standing still and looking at Porfiry in alarm.

"My little surprise, it's sitting there behind the door, he-he-he!" (He pointed to the locked door.) "I locked him in so that he would not escape."

"What is it? Where? What? . . . "

Raskolnikov walked to the door and would have opened it, but it was locked.

"It's locked, here is the key!"

And he brought a key out of his pocket.

"You are lying," roared Raskolnikov without restraint, "you are lying, you damned *punchinello*!" and he rushed at Porfiry who retreated to the other door, not at all alarmed.

"I understand it all! You are lying and mocking so I will betray myself to you . . . "

"Why, you could not betray yourself any further, my dear Rodion Romanovich. You are in a passion. Don't shout, I shall call the clerks."

"You are lying! Call the clerks! You knew I was ill and tried to work me into a frenzy to make me betray myself, that was your aim! Produce your facts! I understand it all. You've no evidence, you have only wretched trashy suspicions like Zametov's! You knew my character, you wanted to drive me to fury and then to knock me down with priests and deputies . . . Are you waiting for them? eh! What are you waiting for? Where are they? Produce them?"

"Why deputies, my good man? What things people will imagine! And to do so would not be acting in form as you say, you don't know the business, my dear fellow . . . And there's no escaping form, as you see," Porfiry muttered, listening at the door through which a noise could be heard.

"Ah, they're coming," cried Raskolnikov. "You've sent for them! You expected them! Well, produce them all: your deputies, your witnesses, what you like! . . . I am ready!"

But at this moment a strange incident occurred, something so unexpected that neither Raskolnikov nor Porfiry Petrovich could have imagined that their interview would come to such a conclusion.

CHAPTER SIX

WHEN HE REMEMBERED THE scene afterwards, this is how Raskolnikov saw it.

The noise behind the door increased, and suddenly the door was opened a little.

"What is it?" cried Porfiry Petrovich, annoyed. "I gave instructions . . . "

For an instant there was no answer, but it was evident that there were several persons at the door, and that they were apparently pushing somebody back.

"What is it?" Porfiry Petrovich repeated, uneasily.

"The prisoner Nikolai has been brought," someone answered.

"He is not wanted! Take him away! Let him wait! What's he doing here? This is entirely out of order!" cried Porfiry, rushing to the door.

"But he . . . " began the same voice, and suddenly ceased.

Two seconds, not more, were spent in actual struggle, then someone gave a violent shove, and then a man, very pale, strode into the room.

This man's appearance was at first sight very strange. He stared straight before him, as though seeing nothing. There was a determined gleam in his eyes; at the same time there was a deathly pallor in his face, as though he were being led to the scaffold. His white lips were faintly twitching.

He was dressed like a workman and was of medium height, very young, slim, with a round haircut and thin spare features. The man whom he had thrust back followed him into the room and succeeded in seizing him by the shoulder; he was a warder. Nikolai pulled his arm away.

Several people crowded inquisitively into the doorway. Some of them tried to get in. All this took place almost instantaneously.

"Go away, it's too soon! Wait until you are sent for! . . . Why have you brought him so soon?" Porfiry Petrovich muttered, extremely annoyed, as if his plans had been upset.

But Nikolai suddenly knelt down.

"What's the matter?" cried Porfiry, surprised.

"I am guilty! The sin is mine! I am the murderer," Nikolai articulated suddenly, rather breathless, but speaking fairly loudly.

For ten seconds there was a silence as though everyone had been struck dumb; even the warder stepped back, mechanically retreated to the door, and stood motionless.

"What is it?" cried Porfiry Petrovich, recovering from his momentary disbelief.

"I am the murderer," repeated Nikolai, after a brief pause.

"What . . . you . . . what . . . who did you kill?" Porfiry Petrovich was obviously bewildered.

Nikolai again was silent for a moment.

"Aliona Ivanovna and her sister Lizaveta Ivanovna, I . . . killed . . . with an axe. Darkness came over me," he added suddenly, and fell silent again.

He remained on his knees. Porfiry Petrovich stood for some moments as though meditating, but suddenly roused himself and waved back the uninvited spectators. They instantly vanished and closed the door. Then he looked towards Raskolnikov, who was standing in the corner, staring wildly at Nikolai, and moved towards him, but stopped short, looked from Nikolai to Raskolnikov and then again at Nikolai, and seeming unable to restrain himself darted at the latter.

"You're in too great a hurry," he shouted at him, almost angrily. "I didn't ask you what came over you . . . Tell me, did you kill them?"

"I am the murderer . . . I want to give evidence," Nikolai pronounced.

"Ah! What did you kill them with?"

"An axe. I had it ready."

"Ah, he is in a hurry! Alone?"

Nikolai did not understand the question.

"Did you do it alone?"

"Yes, alone. And Mitka is not guilty and had no share in it."

"Don't be in a hurry about Mitka! A-ah! How was it you ran downstairs like that at the time? The porters met you both!"

"It was to put them off the scent . . . I ran after Mitka," Nikolai replied hurriedly, as though he had prepared the answer.

"I knew it!" cried Porfiry, with vexation. "It's not his own tale he is telling," he muttered as though to himself, and suddenly his eyes rested on Raskolnikov again.

He was apparently so taken up with Nikolai that for a moment he had forgotten Raskolnikov. He was a little taken aback.

"My dear Rodion Romanovich, excuse me!" he flew up to him, "this shouldn't have happened; I'm afraid you must go . . . it'll be no good if you stay . . . I will . . . you see, what a surprise! . . . Goodbye!"

And taking him by the arm, he showed him to the door.

"I suppose you didn't expect it?" said Raskolnikov who, though he had not yet fully grasped the situation, had regained his courage.

"You did not expect it either, my friend. See how your hand is trembling! He-he!"

"You're trembling, too, Porfiry Petrovich!"

"Yes, I am; I didn't expect it."

They were already at the door; Porfiry was impatient for Raskolnikov to be gone.

"And your little surprise, aren't you going to show it to me?" Raskolnikov said, sarcastically.

"Why, his teeth are chattering as he asks, he-he! You have a real sense of irony! Come on, until we meet!"

"I believe we can say goodbye!"

"That's in God's hands," muttered Porfiry, with an unnatural smile.

As he walked through the office, Raskolnikov noticed that many people were looking at him. Among them he saw the two porters from the house, whom he had invited that night to the police station. They stood there waiting. But he was no sooner on the stairs than he heard the voice of Porfiry Petrovich behind him. Turning round, he saw the latter running after him, out of breath.

"One word, Rodion Romanovich; as for the rest of it, it's in God's hands, but as a matter of form there are some questions I shall have to ask you . . . so we shall meet again, shan't we?"

And Porfiry stood still, facing him with a smile.

"Shan't we?" he added again.

He seemed to want to say something more, but could not speak out.

"You must forgive me, Porfiry Petrovich, for what has just passed . . . I lost my temper," began Raskolnikov, who had regained his courage to such an extent that he felt irresistibly inclined to display his coolness.

"Don't mention it, don't mention it," Porfiry replied, almost gleefully. "I myself, too . . . I have a wicked temper, I admit it! But we shall meet again. If it's God's will, we may see a great deal of one another."

"And will get to know each other properly?" added Raskolnikov.

"Yes; know each other properly," assented Porfiry Petrovich, and he screwed up his eyes, looking earnestly at Raskolnikov. "Now you're going to a birthday party?"

"To a funeral."

"Of course, the funeral! Take care of yourself, and get well."

"I don't know what to wish you," said Raskolnikov, who had begun to descend the stairs, but looked back again. "I would like to wish you success, but your office is such a comical one."

"Why comical?" Porfiry Petrovich had turned to go, but he seemed to prick up his ears at this.

"How you must have been torturing and harassing that poor Nikolai psychologically, in that way of yours, until he confessed! You must have been at him day and night, proving to him that he was the murderer, and now that he has confessed, you'll begin vivisecting him again. 'You are lying,' you'll say. 'You are not the murderer! You can't be! It's not your own tale you are telling!' You must admit it's a comical business!"

"He-he-he! You noticed then that I said to Nikolai just now that it was not his own tale he was telling?"

"How could I help noticing it!"

"He-he! You are quick-witted. You notice everything! You've really a playful mind! And you always fasten on the comic side . . . he-he! They say that was the marked characteristic of Gogol,* among the writers."

"Yes, of Gogol."

"Yes, of Gogol . . . I shall look forward to meeting you."

"So shall I."

Raskolnikov walked straight home. He was so muddled and bewildered that when he got home he sat for a quarter of an hour on the sofa, trying to collect his thoughts. He did not attempt to think about Nikolai; he was stupefied; he felt that his confession was something inexplicable, amazing—something beyond his understanding. But Nikolai's confession was an actual fact. The consequences of this fact were clear to him at once, its falsehood could not fail to be discovered, and then they would be after him again. Until then, at least,

---

*Nikolai Gogol (1809–1852), a favorite author of Dostoevsky's who had a particular gift for grotesque humor.

he was free and must do something for himself, for the danger was imminent.

But how imminent? His position gradually became clear to him. Remembering, sketchily, the main outlines of his recent scene with Porfiry, he could not help shuddering again with horror. Of course, he did not yet know all Porfiry's aims, he could not see into all his calculations. But he had already partly shown his hand, and no-one knew better than Raskolnikov how terrible Porfiry's "lead" had been for him. A little more and he might have given himself away completely, circumstantially. Knowing his nervous temperament and seeing through him from the first, Porfiry, though playing a bold game, was bound to win. There's no denying that Raskolnikov had compromised himself seriously, but no facts had come to light as yet; there was nothing positive. But was he taking a true view of the position? Wasn't he mistaken? What had Porfiry been trying to get at? Had he really some surprise prepared for him? And what was it? Had he really been expecting something or not? How would they have parted if it had not been for the unexpected appearance of Nikolai?

Porfiry had shown almost all his cards—of course, he had risked something in showing them—and if he had really had anything up his sleeve (Raskolnikov reflected), he would have shown that, too. What was that "surprise"? Was it a joke? Had it meant anything? Could it have concealed anything like a fact, a piece of positive evidence? His yesterday's visitor? What had become of him? Where was he today? If Porfiry really had any evidence, it must be connected with him . . .

He sat on the sofa with his elbows on his knees and his face hidden in his hands. He was still shivering nervously. At last he got up, took his cap, thought a minute, and went to the door.

He had a sort of presentiment that for today, at least, he might consider himself out of danger. He had a sudden sense almost of joy; he wanted to hurry to Katerina Ivanovna's. He would be too late for the funeral, of course, but he would be in time for the memorial dinner, and there at once he would see Sonia.

He stood still, thought a moment, and a suffering smile came for a moment on to his lips.

"Today! Today," he repeated to himself. "Yes, today! So it must be . . . "

But as he was about to open the door, it began opening of itself. He started and moved back. The door opened gently and slowly, and suddenly a figure appeared—yesterday's visitor from under the ground.

The man stood in the doorway, looked at Raskolnikov without speaking, and took a step forward into the room. He was exactly the same as yesterday; the same figure, the same dress, but there was a great change in his face; he looked dejected and sighed deeply. If he had only put his hand up to his cheek and leaned his head on one side he would have looked exactly like a peasant woman.

"What do you want?" asked Raskolnikov, numb with terror. The man was still silent, but suddenly he bowed down almost to the ground, touching it with his finger.

"What is it?" cried Raskolnikov.

"I have sinned," the man articulated softly. "I have had evil thoughts."

They looked at one another.

"I was worried. When you came—maybe you were drunk—and told the porters to go to the police station and asked about the blood, I was worried that they let you go and thought you were drunk. I was so worried I lost my sleep. And remembering the address we came here yesterday and asked for you . . . "

"Who came?" Raskolnikov interrupted, instantly beginning to remember.

"I did, I've wronged you."

"Then you came from that house?"

"I was standing at the gate with them . . . don't you remember? We have carried on our trade in that house for many years. We cure and prepare hides, we take work home . . . most of all I was worried . . . "

And the whole scene of the day before yesterday in the gateway came clearly into Raskolnikov's mind; he recalled that there had been several people there besides the porters, women among them. He remembered one voice had suggested taking him straight to the police station. He could not recall the face of the speaker, and even now he did not recognize it, but he remembered that he had turned round and made him some answer . . .

So this was the solution of yesterday's horror. The most awful thought was that he had been actually almost lost, had almost done for himself on account of such a trivial circumstance. So this man could tell nothing except the fact that he asked about the apartment and the blood stains. So Porfiry, too, had nothing but that delirium, no facts but this psychology which cuts both ways, nothing positive. So if no more facts come to light (and they must not, they must not!) then . . . then what can they do to him? How can they convict him, even if they arrest him? And Porfiry then had only just heard about the apartment and had not known about it before.

"Was it you who told Porfiry . . . that I'd been there?" he cried, struck by a sudden idea.

"What Porfiry?"

"The head of the detective department?"

"Yes. The porters did not go there, but I went."

"Today?"

"I got there two minutes before you. And I heard, I heard it all, how he worried you."

"Where? What? When?"

"In the next room. I was sitting there all the time."

"What? So you were the surprise? But how could that happen? It's unbelievable!"

"I saw that the porters did not want to do what I said," began the man; "because it's too late, they said, and maybe he'll be angry that we didn't come at the time. I was anxious and I lost sleep over it, so I began making inquiries. And when I found out yesterday where to go, I went there today. The first time I went he wasn't there; when I came an hour later he couldn't see me. So I went a third time, and they showed me in. I told him everything, just as it happened, and he started skipping around the room and punching himself on the chest. 'Why did you horrors not tell me? If I'd known about it I should have arrested him!' The he ran out, called somebody and began talking to him in the corner, then he turned to me, reprimanding and questioning me. He criticized me a great deal; and I told him everything, and I told him that you didn't dare to say a word in answer to me yesterday and that you didn't recognize me. And he started running around again and kept on hitting himself on the chest, and getting angry and running around, and when they announced that you were here he told me to go into the next room. 'Sit there for a bit,' he said. 'Don't move, whatever you hear.' And he put a chair there for me and locked me in. 'I may call you,' he said, 'perhaps.' And when Nikolai had been brought he let me out as soon as you were gone. 'I'll send for you and question you again,' he said."

"And did he question Nikolai while you were there?"

"He got rid of me like he got rid of you, before he spoke to Nikolai."

The man stood still, and again suddenly bowed down, touching the ground with his finger.

"Forgive me for my evil thoughts, and my slander."

"May God forgive you," answered Raskolnikov.

And as he said this, the man bowed down again, but not to the ground, turned slowly and went out of the room.

"It all cuts both ways, now it all cuts both ways," repeated Raskolnikov, and he went out more confident than ever.

"Now we'll make a fight of it," he said, with a malicious smile, as he went down the stairs. His malice was aimed at himself; with shame and contempt he recalled his "cowardice."

PART FIVE

CHAPTER ONE

THE MORNING THAT FOLLOWED the fateful interview with Dunia and her mother brought sobering influences to bear on Peter Petrovich. Intensely unpleasant as it was, he was forced little by little to accept as an unshakeable fact what had seemed to him only the day before to be fantastic and incredible. The black snake of wounded vanity had been gnawing at his heart all night. When he got out of bed, Peter Petrovich immediately looked in the looking-glass. He was afraid that he had jaundice. However his health seemed unimpaired so far, and looking at his noble, clear-skinned face which had recently grown fattish, Peter Petrovich for an instant was positively comforted in the conviction that he would find another bride, and perhaps even a better one. But coming back to the sense of his present position, he turned aside and spat vigorously, which provoked a sarcastic smile in Andrei Semionovich Lebeziatnikov, the young friend with whom he was staying. Peter Petrovich noticed that smile, and held it against his young friend at once. He had recently held many things against him. His anger was doubled when he reflected that he ought not to have told Andrei Semionovich about the result of yesterday's interview. That was the second mistake he had made in his temper, through impulsiveness and irritability . . . Moreover, all morning one unpleasantness followed another. He even found a hitch awaiting him in his legal case in the Senate. He was particularly irritated by the owner of the apartment which had been taken due to his approaching marriage and was being redecorated at his own expense; the owner, a rich German tradesman, would not entertain the idea of breaking the contract which had just been signed and insisted on the full forfeit money, though Peter Petrovich would be giving him back the apartment practically redecorated. In the same way the upholsterers refused to return a single ruble of the installment paid for the furniture purchased but not yet removed to the apartment.

"Am I to get married simply for the sake of the furniture?" Peter Petrovich ground his teeth and at the same time once more he had a gleam of desperate hope. "Can it all really be over so irrevocably? Is it no use to make another effort?" The thought of Dunia sent a voluptuous pang through his heart. He went through agonies at that moment, and if it had been possible to kill Raskolnikov instantly by wishing it, Peter Petrovich would promptly have uttered the wish.

"It was my mistake, too, not to have given them money," he thought, as he returned dejectedly to Lebeziatnikov's room, "and why on earth was I such a Jew? It was false economy! I meant to keep them without a penny so that they would turn to me as their providence, and look at them! Foo! If I'd spent about fifteen hundred rubles on them for the trunk and presents, on knick-knacks, dressing-cases, jewelry, materials, and all that sort of trash from Knopp's* and the English store, my position would have been better and . . . stronger! They could not have refused me so easily! They are the sort of people that would feel bound to return money and presents if they broke it off; and they would find it hard to do it! And their consciences would prick them: how can we dismiss a man who has hitherto been so generous and delicate? . . . Hm! I've made a blunder."

And grinding his teeth again, Peter Petrovich called himself a fool—but not aloud, of course.

He returned home, twice as irritated and angry as before. The preparations for the funeral dinner at Katerina Ivanovna's aroused his curiosity as he passed. He had heard about it the day before; he imagined, in fact, that he had been invited, but absorbed in his own worries he had paid no attention. When he asked Madame Lippewechsel, who was busy laying the table while Katerina Ivanovna was away at the cemetery, he heard that the entertainment was going to be substantial, that all the tenants had been invited, some of whom had not known the dead man, that even Andrei Semionovich Lebeziatnikov was invited despite his previous quarrel with Katerina Ivanovna, that he, Peter Petrovich, was not only invited, but was eagerly expected as he was the most important of the tenants. Amalia Ivanovna herself had been invited with great ceremony despite all the recent unpleasantness, and so she was very busy with preparations and was taking real pleasure in them; she was moreover dressed up to the nines, in new black silk, and she was proud of it. All this gave Peter Petrovich an idea and he went into his room, or rather Lebeziatnikov's, somewhat thoughtful. He had learnt that Raskolnikov was to be one of the guests.

Andrei Semionovich had been at home all morning. Peter Petro-

---

*Fashionable toiletries store in St. Petersburg.

vich's attitude to this gentleman was strange, though perhaps natural. Peter Petrovich had despised and hated him from the day he came to stay with him and at the same time he seemed somewhat afraid of him. He had not come to stay with him on his arrival in Petersburg solely due to his own tightfistedness, though that had been perhaps his chief object. He had heard that Andrei Semionovich, who had once been his protégé, was a leading young progressive who was playing an important part in certain interesting circles, the doings of which were a legend in the provinces. It had impressed Peter Petrovich. These powerful, omniscient circles, which despised everyone and showed everyone up for what they really were, had long been for him a peculiar but wholly vague cause for concern. He had not, of course, been able to form even an approximate notion of what they meant. He, like everyone, had heard that there were, especially in Petersburg, progressives of some sort, nihilists and so on, and, like many people, he exaggerated and distorted the significance of those words to an absurd degree. What for many years past he had feared more than anything was being shown up for what he really was and this was the chief ground for his continual uneasiness at the thought of transferring his business to Petersburg. He was afraid of this in the same way as little children are sometimes panic-stricken. Some years previously, when he was just embarking on his own career, he had come upon two cases in which rather important people in the province, patrons of his, had been cruelly shown up. One instance had ended in great scandal for the person attacked and the other had very nearly ended in serious trouble. For this reason Peter Petrovich intended to go into the subject as soon as he reached Petersburg and, if necessary, to anticipate contingencies by seeking the favor of "our younger generation." He relied on Andrei Semionovich for this and before his visit to Raskolnikov he had succeeded in picking up some current phrases. He soon discovered that Andrei Semionovich was a commonplace simpleton, but that by no means reassured Peter Petrovich. Even if he had been certain that all the progressives were fools like him, it would not have allayed his uneasiness. All the doctrines, the ideas, the systems with which Andrei Semionovich pestered him had no interest for him. He had his own object—he simply wanted to find out at once what was happening here. Did these people have any power or not? Had he anything to fear from them? Would they expose any enterprise of his? And what precisely was now the object of their attacks? Could he somehow make up to them and get round them if they really were powerful? Was this the thing to do or not? Couldn't he gain something through them? In fact hundreds of questions presented themselves.

Andrei Semionovich was an anemic, scrofulous little man, with strangely flaxen mutton-chop whiskers of which he was very proud. He was a clerk and had almost always something wrong with his eyes. He was rather soft-hearted, but self-confident and sometimes extremely conceited in speech, which had an absurd effect, incongruous with his little figure. He was one of the tenants whom Amalia Ivanovna most respected because he did not get drunk and paid regularly for his lodgings. Andrei Semionovich was in fact rather stupid; he attached himself to the cause of progress and "our younger generation" out of his own enthusiasm. He was one of the numerous and varied legion of dullards, of half-animate abortions, conceited, half-educated idiots, who attach themselves to the idea most in fashion only to vulgarize it and who caricature every cause they serve, however sincerely.

Though Lebeziatnikov was so good-natured, he, too, was beginning to dislike Peter Petrovich. This happened on both sides unconsciously. However simple Andrei Semionovich might be, he began to see that Peter Petrovich was duping him and secretly despising him, and that "he was not the right sort of man." He had tried expounding to him the system of Fourier and the Darwinian theory, but of late Peter Petrovich began to listen too sarcastically and even to be rude. The fact was he had begun instinctively to guess that Lebeziatnikov was not merely a commonplace simpleton, but perhaps a liar too, and that he had no connections of any consequence even in his own circle, but had simply picked things up third-hand; and that very likely he did not even know much about his own work of propaganda, for he was in too great a muddle. A fine person he would be to show anyone up! It must be noted, by the way, that Peter Petrovich had during those ten days eagerly accepted the strangest praise from Andrei Semionovich; he had not protested, for instance, when Andrei Semionovich congratulated him for being ready to contribute to the establishment of the new "commune," or to abstain from christening his future children, or to acquiesce if Dunia were to take a lover a month after marriage, and so on. Peter Petrovich took such pleasure in hearing his praises sung that he did not even look down upon such virtues when they were attributed to him.

That morning, Peter Petrovich happened to have cashed some five per cent bonds and now he sat down to the table and counted up bundles of notes. Andrei Semionovich, who hardly ever had any money, walked around the room, pretending to himself that he could look at all those bank notes with indifference and even contempt. Nothing would have convinced Peter Petrovich that Andrei Semionovich could really look on the money unmoved, and the latter kept thinking bitterly that Peter Petrovich was capable of entertaining such an idea about him and was, perhaps, glad to get a chance tease his young friend by reminding him of his inferiority and the great difference between them.

He found him incredibly inattentive and irritable, though he, Andrei Semionovich, began enlarging on his favorite subject, the foundation of a new special "commune." The brief remarks that dropped from Peter Petrovich between the clicking of the beads on the abacus betrayed an impolite and unmistakable irony. But the "humane" Andrei Semionovich ascribed Peter Petrovich's ill-humor to his recent breach with Dunia and he was burning with impatience to talk about it. He had something progressive to say on the subject which might comfort his eminent friend and "could not fail" to promote his development.

"There is some sort of entertainment being prepared at that . . . at the widow's, isn't there?" Peter Petrovich asked suddenly, interrupting Andrei Semionovich at the most interesting passage.

"Do you really not know? But I was telling you last night what I think about all those ceremonies. And she invited you too, I heard. You were talking to her yesterday . . . "

"I would never have expected that foolish beggar to have spent on this feast all the money she got from that other fool, Raskolnikov. I was surprised just now when I went to take a look at the preparations there—the wines! Several people have been invited. It's beyond anything!" continued Peter Petrovich, who seemed to have some purpose in pursuing the conversation. "What? Did you say I was invited as well? When was that? I don't remember. But I shan't go. Why should I? I only said a word to her in passing yesterday about the possibility of her obtaining a year's salary as a destitute widow of a government clerk. I suppose that's why she's invited me, isn't it? He-he-he!"

"I don't intend to go either," said Lebeziatnikov.

"I should think not, after giving her a thrashing! You might well hesitate, he-he!"

"Who thrashed? Whom?" cried Lebeziatnikov, flustered and blushing.

"You thrashed Katerina Ivanovna a month ago. I heard so yester-day . . . so that's what your convictions amount to . . . and the question of women, too, wasn't an entirely sound one, he-he-he!" and Peter Petrovich, as though he were comforted, went back to clicking his beads.

"It's all slander and nonsense!" cried Lebeziatnikov, who was always afraid of references to the subject. "It was not like that at all, it was completely different. You've heard it wrong; it's a false rumor. I was simply defending myself. She rushed at me first with her nails, she pulled out all my whiskers . . . It's permissible for anyone, I should hope, to defend themselves; I never allow anyone to use violence against me on principle, it's an act of despotism. What should I have done? I just pushed her back."

"He-he-he!" Luzhin went on laughing maliciously.

"You keep on like that because you are in a bad mood yourself . . . But that's nonsense and it has nothing, nothing whatsoever to do with the question of women! You don't understand; I used to think, in fact, that if women are equal to men in all respects, even in strength (as is maintained now), there ought to be equality in that, too. Of course, I reflected afterwards that a question like that really shouldn't arise, because there shouldn't be any fighting and, in the future society, fighting is unthinkable . . . and that it would be strange to try to find a principle of equality in fighting. I am not so stupid . . . though, of course, there is fighting . . . there won't be later, but at the moment there is . . . damn it! How muddled I get with you! That's not why I'm not going. I'm not going on principle, in order not to take part in the revolting convention of memorial dinners, that's why! Though, of course, I might go to laugh at it . . . I am sorry there won't be any priests at it. I would certainly go if there were."

"Then you would sit down at another man's table and insult it and those who invited you. Eh?"

"Certainly not insult, but protest. I would do it with a good purpose in mind. I might indirectly assist the cause of enlightenment and propaganda. It's every man's duty to work for enlightenment and propaganda and the more harshly, perhaps, the better. I might drop a seed, an idea . . . And something might grow up from that seed. How should I be insulting them? They might be offended at first, but afterwards they'd see I'd done them a service. You know, Terebyeva (who is in the commune now) was blamed because when she left her family and . . . devoted . . . herself, she wrote to her father and mother that she wouldn't go on living conventionally and was embarking on a free marriage and people said that it was too harsh, that she might have spared them and written more kindly. I think that's all nonsense; there's no need to be soft. On the contrary—what's needed is protest. Varents had been married seven years, she abandoned her two children, she told her husband straight out in a letter: 'I have realized that I cannot be happy with you. I can never forgive you that you have deceived me by concealing from me that there is another means of organizing society—through communes. I have only recently learned this from a very magnanimous man to whom I have given myself and with whom I am establishing a commune. I am speaking to you frankly because I consider it dishonest to deceive you. Do as you think best. Do not hope to win me back—you will be too late. I hope you will be happy.' That's how letters like that ought to be written!"

"Is that Terebyeva the one you said had made a third free marriage?"

"No, it's only the second, really! But what if it were the fourth, what if it were the fifteenth, that's all nonsense! And if ever I regretted the death of my father and mother, it is now, and I sometimes think if my parents were living what a protest I would have aimed at them! I would have done something on purpose . . . I would have shown them! I would have astonished them! I am really sorry there is no-one!"

"To surprise! He-he! Well, be that as it may," Peter Petrovich interrupted, "but tell me this; do you know the dead man's daughter, the delicate-looking little thing? It's true what they say about her, isn't it?"

"What of it? I think, that is, it is my own personal conviction, that this is the normal condition of women. Why not? I mean, let us distinguish. In our present society, it is not altogether normal, because it is compulsory, but in the future society, it will be perfectly normal, because it will be voluntary. Even as it is, she was quite right: she was suffering and that was her asset, so to speak, her capital which she had a perfect right to dispose of. Of course, in the future society, there will be no need of assets, but her part will have another significance, which will be rational and in accordance with her environment. As for Sofia Semionovna personally, I regard her action as a vigorous protest against the organization of society, and I respect her deeply for it; I rejoice, in fact, when I look at her!"

"I was told that you got her turned out of these rooms."

Lebeziatnikov was enraged.

"That's another slander," he yelled. "That's not true at all! That was all Katerina Ivanovna's invention, she didn't understand! And I never flirted with Sofia Semionovna! I was simply developing her, entirely disinterestedly, trying to rouse her to protest . . . All I wanted was her protest and Sofia Semionovna could not have remained here anyway!"

"Have you asked her to join your commune?"

"You keep on laughing and very inappropriately, may I add. You don't understand! There is no such role in a commune. The commune is established so that there should be no such roles. In a commune, such roles are essentially transformed and what is stupid here is sensible there, what, under present conditions, is unnatural becomes perfectly natural in the commune. It all depends on the environment. It's all the environment and man himself is nothing. And I am on good terms with Sofia Semionovna to this day, which is a proof that she never regarded me as having wronged her. I am trying now to attract her to the commune, but on a completely different level. What are you laughing at? We are trying to establish a commune of our own, a special one, on a broader basis. We have gone further in our convictions. We reject more! And meanwhile I'm still developing Sofia Semionovna. She has a beautiful, beautiful character!"

"And you take advantage of her fine character, eh? He-he!"

"No, no! Oh, no! On the contrary."

"Oh, on the contrary! He-he-he! A strange thing to say!"

"Believe me! Why should I disguise it? In fact, I feel strange myself that she is so timid, chaste and modern with me!"

"And you, of course, are developing her . . . he-he! Trying to prove to her that all that modesty is nonsense?"

"Not at all, not at all! How coarsely, how stupidly—excuse me for saying so—you misunderstand the word 'development'! Goodness, how . . . crude you still are! We are striving for the freedom of women and you have only one idea in your head . . . Setting aside the general question of chastity and feminine modesty as useless in themselves and indeed prejudicial, I fully accept her chastity with me, because that's for her to decide. Of course if she were to tell me herself that she wanted me, I should consider myself very lucky, because I like the girl very much; but as it is, no-one has ever treated her more courteously than I, with more respect for her dignity . . . I wait in hope, that's all!"

"You had much better give her some kind of present. I bet you never thought of that."

"You don't understand, I've told you already! Of course, she is in just that kind of a position, but that's another question. Another question entirely! You simply despise her. Seeing a fact which, you mistakenly consider, is worthy of contempt, you refuse to take a humane view of a fellow creature. You don't know what a character she is! I am only sorry that recently she has completely given up reading and borrowing books. I used to lend them to her. I am sorry, too, that with all the energy and resolution in protesting— which she has already shown once—she has too little self-reliance, too little independence, so to speak, to break free from certain prejudices and certain foolish ideas. Yet she thoroughly understands some questions, for instance about kissing hands, that is, that it's an insult to a woman for a man to kiss her hand, because it's a sign of inequality. We had a debate about it and I described it to her. She listened attentively to an account of the workers' associations in France, too. Now I am explaining the question of coming into the room in the future society."

"And what's that, pray?"

"We had a debate recently about the question: Has any member of the commune the right to enter another member's room, be they a man or a woman, at any time . . . and we decided that they have!"

"It might be at an inconvenient moment, he-he!"

Lebeziatnikov was furious.

"You are always thinking of something unpleasant," he cried

with aversion. "Pah! How irritated I am that when I was expounding our system, I referred prematurely to the question of personal privacy! It's always a stumbling-block to people like you, they ridicule it before they understand it. And how proud they are of it, too! Pah! I've often maintained that that question should not be approached by a novice until he has firm faith in the system. And tell me, please, what do you find so shameful even about cesspools? I would be the first to be ready to clean out any cesspool you like. And it's not a question of self-sacrifice, it's simply work, honorable, useful work which is as good as any other and much better than the work of a Raphael and a Pushkin, because it is more useful."

"And more honorable, more honorable, he-he-he!"

"What do you mean by 'more honorable'? I don't understand such expressions to describe human activity. 'More honorable,' 'nobler'—all those are old-fashioned prejudices which I reject. Everything which is of use to mankind is honorable. I only understand one word: useful! You can snigger as much as you like, but that's the truth!"

Peter Petrovich laughed heartily. He had finished counting the money and was putting it away. But some of the notes he left on the table. The "cesspool question" had already been a subject of dispute between them. What was absurd was that it made Lebeziatnikov really angry, while it amused Luzhin and at that moment he particularly wanted to anger his young friend.

"It's your bad luck yesterday that has made you so bad-tempered and annoying," blurted out Lebeziatnikov, who in spite of his "independence" and his "protests" did not attempt to oppose Peter Petrovich and still behaved to him with some of the respect which had been habitual to him in earlier years.

"You'd better tell me this," Peter Petrovich interrupted with haughty displeasure, "can you . . . or, rather, are you really friendly enough with that young lady to ask her to step in here for a minute? I think they've all come back from the cemetery . . . I hear the sound of steps . . . I want to see her, that young lady."

"What for?" Lebeziatnikov asked with surprise.

"Oh, I want to. I am leaving here today or tomorrow and therefore I wanted to speak to her about . . . But you can stay while we talk. It would be better if you did, in fact. There's no knowing what you might imagine."

"I shan't imagine anything. I only asked and, if you've anything to say to her, nothing would be easier than to call her in. I'll leave immediately and you can be sure I won't be in your way."

Five minutes later Lebeziatnikov came in with Sonia. She came in very surprised and overwhelmed with shyness as usual. She was always shy in such circumstances and was always afraid of new people; she had been as a child and was even more so now . . . Peter Petrovich met her "politely and affably," but with a certain shade of bantering informality which in his opinion was suitable for a man of his respectability and weight in dealing with a creature as young and as interesting as she. He swiftly "reassured" her and made her sit down facing him at the table. Sonia sat down, looked around her—at Lebeziatnikov, at the notes lying on the table and then again at Peter Petrovich and her eyes remained riveted to his face. Lebeziatnikov was moving towards the door. Peter Petrovich indicated to Sonia that she should remain seated and stopped Lebeziatnikov.

"Is Raskolnikov in there? Has he come?" he asked him in a whisper.

"Raskolnikov? Yes. Why? Yes, he is there. I saw him just come in . . . Why?"

"Well, I particularly beg you to remain here with us and not to leave me alone with this . . . young woman. I only want a few words with her, but God knows what they will make of it. I wouldn't like Raskolnikov to repeat anything . . . You understand what I mean?"

"I understand!" Lebeziatnikov saw the point. "Yes, you are right . . . Of course, I am convinced personally that you have no reason to be uneasy, but . . . still, you are right. I'll definitely stay. I'll stand here at the window and get out of your way . . . I think you are right . . . "

Peter Petrovich returned to the sofa, sat down opposite Sonia, looked attentively at her and made his face look extremely dignified, even severe, as if to say, "Don't you make any mistake, my girl." Sonia was overwhelmed with embarrassment.

"Firstly, Sofia Semionovna, will you send my excuses to your dear mother . . . That's right? Katerina Ivanovna is like a mother to you, isn't she?" Peter Petrovich began with great dignity, though affably.

It was evident that his intentions were friendly.

"Quite right, yes; like a mother," Sonia answered, timidly and hurriedly.

"Then will you make my apologies to her? Due to inevitable circumstances I am forced to be absent and shall not be at the dinner, despite your mother's kind invitation."

"Yes . . . I'll tell her . . . at once."

And Sonia hastily jumped up from her seat.

"Wait, that's not all," Peter Petrovich detained her, smiling at her simplicity and ignorance of good manners, "and you know me little, my dear Sofia Semionovna, if you think I would have bothered to trouble a person like you about a matter of such little importance which affects only myself. I have another purpose."

Sonia sat down hurriedly. Her eyes rested again for an instant on the gray and rainbow-colored notes that remained on the table, but she quickly looked away and fixed her eyes on Peter Petrovich. She felt that it was horribly impolite, especially for her, to look at another person's money. She stared at the gold eyeglass which Peter Petrovich held in his left hand and at the massive and extremely handsome ring with a yellow stone on his middle finger. But suddenly she looked away and, not knowing where to turn, ended up staring Peter Petrovich straight in the face again. After a pause of even greater dignity he continued.

"I happened yesterday in passing to exchange a couple of words with Katerina Ivanovna, poor woman. It was enough to enable me to realize that she is in a—preternatural position, if it can expressed like that."

"Yes . . . preternatural . . . " Sonia hurriedly agreed.

"Or it would be simpler and more comprehensible to say, ill."

"Yes, simpler and more comprehen . . . yes, ill."

"Absolutely. So then, out of my human feelings and compassion, so to speak, I would be glad to be of service to her in any way, foreseeing her unfortunate position. I believe the whole of this poverty-stricken family depends now entirely on you?"

"Allow me to ask," Sonia rose to her feet, "did you say something to her yesterday about the possibility of a pension? Because she told me you had agreed to get her one. Was that true?"

"Not in the slightest, and in fact it's an absurdity! I merely hinted that she might obtain temporary assistance as the widow of an official who had died in service—if only she had patronage . . . but apparently your late father had not served his full term and recently, in fact, had not been in service at all. In fact, if there were any hope, it would be completely accidental, because there would be no claim for assistance in his case, far from it . . . And she is dreaming of a pension already, he-he-he! . . . A forward-thinking lady!"

"Yes, she is. Because she is too trusting and she has a good heart, and she believes everything because of the goodness of her heart and . . . and . . . and she is like that . . . yes . . . You must excuse her," said Sonia, and again she got up to go.

"But you haven't heard what I have to say."

"No, I haven't heard," muttered Sonia.

"Then sit down." She was terribly confused; she sat down again a third time.

"Seeing her position with her unfortunate little ones, I should be glad, as I have said before, as far as it lies within my power, to be of service, that is, as far as it lies within my power to be, not more. One might for instance get up a subscription for her, or a lottery, something of the sort, such as is always arranged in such cases by friends or even outsiders who wish to assist people. It was of that I intended to speak to you; it might be done."

"Yes, yes . . . God will repay you for it," faltered Sonia, gazing intently at Peter Petrovich.

"It might be, but we will talk about that later. We might start today, we will talk it over this evening and lay the foundation, so to speak. Come to me at seven o'clock. Mr. Lebeziatnikov, I hope, will assist us. But there is one circumstance of which I ought to warn you beforehand and for which I would like to trouble you, Sofia Semionovna, to come here. In my opinion money cannot be . . . in fact, it's unsafe to put it into Katerina Ivanovna's own hands. The dinner today proves that. Though she has not, so to speak, even got a crust of bread for tomorrow and . . . well, boots or shoes, or anything; she has bought Jamaica rum today, and even, I believe, Madeira and . . . and coffee. I saw it as I passed through. Tomorrow it will all fall upon you again, they won't have a crust of bread. It's absurd, really, and so, the way I see it, a subscription should be raised so that the unhappy widow would not know of the money's existence—only you would, for instance. Am I right?"

"I don't know . . . this is only today, once in her life . . . She was so anxious to do him some kind of honor, to celebrate his memory . . . And she is very sensible . . . but just as you think and I shall be very, very . . . they will all be . . . and God will reward . . . and the orphans . . . "

Sonia burst into tears.

"Very well, then, keep it in mind; and now will you accept for the benefit of your relation the small sum that I am able to spare, from me personally. I am very anxious that my name should not be mentioned in connection with it. Here . . . having so to speak anxieties of my own, I cannot do more . . . "

And Peter Petrovich held out to Sonia a ten-ruble note carefully unfolded. Sonia took it, flushed crimson, jumped up, muttered something and began to leave. Peter Petrovich accompanied her ceremoniously to the door. She got out of the room at last, agitated and distressed, and returned to Katerina Ivanovna, overwhelmed with confusion.

All this time Lebeziatnikov had stood at the window or walked around the room, anxious not to interrupt the conversation; when Sonia had gone he walked up to Peter Petrovich and solemnly held out his hand.

"I heard and saw everything," he said, laying stress on the last verb. "That is honorable, I mean to say, it's humane! You wanted to avoid gratitude, I saw! And although I cannot, I confess, in principle sympathize with private charity, for it not only fails to eradicate the evil but even promotes it, yet I must admit that I witnessed your action with pleasure—yes, yes, I like it."

"That's all nonsense," muttered Peter Petrovich, somewhat disconcerted, looking carefully at Lebeziatnikov.

"No, it's not nonsense! A man who has suffered distress and annoyance as you did yesterday and who can still sympathize with the misery of others, such a man . . . even though he is making a social mistake—is still deserving of respect! In fact, I did not expect it of you, Peter Petrovich, especially as according to your ideas . . . oh, what a drawback your ideas are to you! How distressed you are for instance by your bad luck yesterday," cried the simple-hearted Lebeziatnikov, who felt his affection for Peter Petrovich return. "And, what do you want with marriage, with legal marriage, my dear, noble Peter Petrovich? Why do you cling to this legality of marriage? Well, you may beat me if you like, but I am glad, truly glad it hasn't succeeded, that you are free, that you are not quite lost for humanity . . . you see, I've spoken my mind!"

"Because I don't want in your free marriage to be made a fool of and to bring up another man's children, that's why I want a legal marriage," Luzhin replied in order to make some answer.

He seemed preoccupied by something.

"Children? You referred to children," Lebeziatnikov started off like a warhorse at the trumpet call. "Children are a social question and a question of the utmost importance, I agree; but the question of children has another solution. Some refuse to have children altogether, because they suggest the institution of the family. We'll talk about children later, but now, as for the question of honor, I confess that's my weak point. That horrid, military, Pushkinian expression is unthinkable in the dictionary of the future. What does it mean? It's nonsense, there will be no deception in a free marriage! That is only the natural consequence of a legal marriage, so to say, its corrective, a protest. So that in fact it's not humiliating . . . and if I ever, to suppose an absurdity, were to be legally married, I would be truly glad of it. I should say to my wife: 'My dear, up until now I have loved you, now I respect you, because you've shown you can protest!' You laugh! That's because you are of incapable of getting away from prejudices. Damn it all! I understand now why being deceived in a legal marriage is unpleasant, but it's simply a despicable consequence of a despicable position in which both people are humiliated. When the deception is open, as in a free marriage, then it does not exist, it's unthinkable. Your wife will only prove how she respects you by considering you incapable of opposing her happiness and avenging yourself on her for her new husband. Damn it all! I sometimes dream if I were to get married, foo! I mean if I were to get married, legally or not, it's all the same, I should present my wife with a lover if she had not found one for herself. 'My dear,' I should say, 'I love you, but even more than that I desire you to respect me. See!' Am I not right?"

Peter Petrovich sniggered as he listened, but without much merriment. In fact, he hardly heard it. He was preoccupied with something else and at last even Lebeziatnikov noticed it. Peter Petrovich seemed excited and rubbed his hands. Lebeziatnikov remembered all this and reflected upon it afterwards.

CHAPTER TWO

IT WOULD BE DIFFICULT to explain exactly what could have put the idea of that senseless dinner into Katerina Ivanovna's disordered brain. Nearly ten of the twenty rubles which Raskolnikov gave for Marmeladov's funeral were wasted on it. Perhaps Katerina Ivanovna felt obliged to honor the memory of her late husband "suitably," so that all the tenants, Amalia Ivanovna in particular, might know "that he was in no way their inferior, and perhaps very much their superior," and that no-one had the right "to turn up his nose at him." Perhaps the chief element was that peculiar "poor man's pride," which compels many poor people to spend their last savings on some traditional social ceremony, simply in order to do it "like other people," and not to "be looked down upon." It is very probable, too, that Katerina Ivanovna longed on this occasion, at the very moment when she seemed to be abandoned by everyone, to show those "wretched contemptible lodgers" that she knew "how to do things, how to entertain" and that she had been brought up "in a genteel, she might almost say aristocratic colonel's family" and had not been meant for sweeping floors and washing the children's rags at night. Even the poorest and most broken-spirited people are sometimes liable to these spasms of pride and vanity which take the form of an irresistible nervous craving. And Katerina Ivanovna was not broken-spirited; she might have been killed by the circumstances in which she found herself, but her spirit could not have been broken, that is, she could not have been intimidated, her will could not be crushed. Moreover, Sonia had said with good reason that her mind was unhinged. No-one could call her insane, but for a year now she had been so harassed that her mind might well be overstrained. The later stages of tuberculosis are apt, doctors tell us, to affect the intellect.

There was not a large selection of wines, nor was there Madeira; but wine there was nevertheless. There was vodka, rum and Lisbon wine, all of the poorest quality but in sufficient quantity. Besides the traditional rice and honey, there were three or four dishes, one of which consisted of pancakes, all prepared in Amalia Ivanovna's kitchen. Two samovars were boiling in order that tea and punch might be offered after dinner. Katerina Ivanovna had herself seen to purchasing the provisions, with the help of one of the lodgers, an unfortunate little Pole who had somehow been stranded at Madame Lippewechsel's. He promptly put himself at Katerina Ivanovna's disposal and had been running around all day as fast as his legs could carry him, and was very anxious that everyone should be aware of it. For every minor problem he ran to Katerina Ivanovna, even hunting her out at the market, at every instant called her "Pani." She was thoroughly sick of him before the end of it, though she had declared at first that she could not have got on without this "serviceable and magnanimous man." It was one of Katerina Ivanovna's characteristics to paint everyone she met in the most glowing colors. Her praises were so exaggerated as to be embarrassing on occasion; she would invent various circumstances to the credit of her new acquaintance and quite genuinely believe in their reality. Then all of a sudden she would be disillusioned and would rudely and contemptuously repulse the person she had been literally adoring only a few hours previously. She had a naturally merry, lively and peace-loving disposition, but due to her continual failures and misfortunes she had come to desire so keenly that everyone should live in peace and joy and should not dare to break the peace that the slightest problem, the smallest disaster reduced her almost to a frenzy, and she would pass in an instant from the brightest hopes and fancies to cursing her fate and raving and knocking her head against the wall.

Amalia Ivanovna, too, suddenly acquired extraordinary importance in Katerina Ivanovna's eyes and was treated by her with extraordinary respect, probably only because Amalia Ivanovna had thrown herself heart and soul into the preparations. She had undertaken to lay the table, to provide the linen, crockery, etc., and to cook the dishes in her kitchen, and Katerina Ivanovna had left it all in her hands and gone off to the cemetery. Everything had been well done. Even the tablecloth was nearly clean; the crockery, knives, forks and glasses had been lent by different lodgers and were naturally of all shapes and patterns, but the table was properly laid at the time fixed, and Amalia Ivanovna, feeling she had done her work well, had put on a black silk dress and a cap with new mourning ribbons and met the returning party with some pride. This pride, though justifiable, displeased Katerina Ivanovna for some reason: "as though the table could not have been laid except by Amalia Ivanovna!" She disliked the cap with its new ribbons, too. "Could she be so dismissive, the stupid German, because she was the mistress of the house and had agreed as a favor to help her poor tenants! As a favor! Imagine! Katerina Ivanovna's father, who had been a colonel and almost a governor, had sometimes had the table set for forty people, and anyone like Amalia Ivanovna, or rather Ludwigovna, would not have been allowed into the kitchen."

Katerina Ivanovna, however, put off expressing her feelings for the time being and contented herself with treating her coldly, though she decided inwardly that she would certainly have to put Amalia Ivanovna down and set her in her place, for goodness only knew how highly she thought of herself. Katerina Ivanovna was irritated too by the fact that hardly any of the tenants whom she had invited had come to the funeral, except the Pole who had just managed to run into the cemetery, while to the memorial dinner the poorest and most insignificant of them had turned up, the wretched creatures, many of them not quite sober. The older and more respectable ones among them stayed away, as if by common consent. Peter Petrovich Luzhin, for instance, who could be described as the most respectable of all the tenants, did not appear, though Katerina Ivanovna had the evening before told the whole world, that is Amalia Ivanovna, Polenka, Sonia and the Pole, that he was the most generous, noble-hearted man with a large property and vast connections, who had been a friend of her first husband's, and a guest in her father's house, and that he had promised to use all his influence to secure her a considerable pension. It must be noted that when Katerina Ivanovna praised anyone's connections and fortune, it was without any ulterior motive, entirely disinterestedly, for the mere pleasure of increasing the importance of the person praised. Probably "taking his cue" from Luzhin, "that contemptible wretch Lebeziatnikov had not turned up either. Why did he think so highly of himself? He was only invited out of kindness and because he was sharing the same room with Peter Petrovich and was a friend of his: it would have been awkward not to invite him."

Among those who failed to appear were "the genteel lady and her old-maidish daughter," who had only been lodgers in the house for the last fortnight, but had several times complained of the noise and uproar in Katerina Ivanovna's room, especially when Marmeladov had come back drunk. Katerina Ivanovna heard this from Amalia Ivanovna who, quarrelling with Katerina Ivanovna, and threatening to turn the whole family out of doors, had shouted at her that they "were not worth the foot" of the honorable lodgers whom they were disturbing. Katerina Ivanovna determined now to invite this lady and her daughter, "whose foot she was not worth," and who had turned away haughtily when she met them casually, so that they might know that "she was more noble in her thoughts and feelings and did not harbor malice," and might see that she was not accustomed to her way of living. She had proposed to make this clear to them at dinner with allusions to her late father's governorship, and also at the same time to hint that it was extremely stupid of them to turn away on meeting her. The fat colonel-major (he was really a discharged officer of low rank) was also absent, but it appeared that he had "not been himself" for the last two days. The party consisted of the Pole, a wretched looking clerk with a spotty face and a greasy coat, who had not a word to say for himself and smelt abominably, and a deaf and almost blind old man who had once been in the post office and who had been maintained by someone at Amalia Ivanovna's for as long as anyone could remember.

A retired clerk of the commissariat department came, too; he was drunk, had a loud and extremely indecent laugh and, just imagine— he came without a waistcoat! One of the visitors sat straight down at the table without even greeting Katerina Ivanovna. Finally, one person with no suit on appeared in his dressing gown, but this was too much, and the efforts of Amalia Ivanovna and the Pole succeeded in removing him. The Pole brought with him, however, two other Poles who did not live at Amalia Ivanovna's and whom no-one had seen here before. All this irritated Katerina Ivanovna intensely. "For whom had they made all these preparations then?" To make room for the visitors the children had not even had places laid for them at the table; but the two little ones were sitting on a bench in the furthest corner with their dinner laid on a box, while Polenka, as the biggest girl, had to look after them, feed them, and keep their noses wiped like well-bred children's.

Katerina Ivanovna, in fact, could hardly help meeting her guests with increased dignity, and even arrogance. She stared at some of them with particular severity, and loftily invited them to take their seats. Rushing to the conclusion that Amalia Ivanovna must be responsible for those who were absent, she began treating her with extreme indifference, which the latter promptly observed and resented. Such a beginning was not a good omen for the end. All were seated at last.

Raskolnikov came in almost at the moment of their return from the cemetery. Katerina Ivanovna was greatly delighted to see him, firstly, because he was the one "educated visitor, and, as everyone knew, was to take a professorship at the university in two years' time," and secondly because he immediately and respectfully apologized for the fact that he had been unable to be present at the funeral. She absolutely pounced on him, and made him sit at her left (Amalia Ivanovna was at her right). Despite her continual anxiety that the dishes should be passed round correctly and that everyone should taste them, in spite of the agonizing cough which interrupted her every minute and seemed to have grown worse during the last few days, she hastened to pour out in a half whisper to Raskolnikov all her suppressed feelings and her just indignation at the failure of the dinner, interspersing her remarks with lively and uncontrollable laughter at the expense of her visitors and especially of her landlady.

"It's all that cuckoo's fault! You know who I mean? Her, her!" Katerina Ivanovna nodded towards the landlady. "Look at her, she's making round eyes, she feels that we are talking about her and can't understand. Foo, the owl! Ha-ha! (Cough-cough-cough.) And what does she put on that cap for? (Cough-cough-cough.) Have you noticed that she wants everyone to consider that she is patronizing me and doing me an honor by being here? I asked her like a sensible woman to invite people, especially people who knew my late husband, and look at the set of fools she has brought! The sweeps! Look at that one with the spotty face. And those wretched Poles, ha-ha-ha! (Cough-cough-cough.) Not one of them has ever poked his nose in here, I've never set eyes on them. What have they come here for, I ask you? There they sit in a row. Hey, Pan!" she cried suddenly to one of them, "have you tasted the pancakes? Take some more! Have some beer! Won't you have some vodka? Look, he's jumping up and making his bows, they must be absolutely starved, poor people. Never mind, let them eat! They don't make a noise, anyway, though I'm really afraid for our landlady's silver spoons . . . Amalia Ivanovna!" she addressed her suddenly, almost aloud, "if your spoons should happen to be stolen, I won't be responsible, I warn you! Ha-ha-ha!" She laughed turning to Raskolnikov, and again nodding towards the landlady, very pleased with her attack. "She didn't understand, she didn't understand again! Look how she sits with her mouth open! An owl, a real owl! An owl in new ribbons, ha-ha-ha!"

Here her laugh turned again to an insufferable fit of coughing that lasted five minutes. Drops of perspiration stood out on her forehead and her handkerchief was stained with blood. She showed Raskolnikov the blood in silence, and as soon as she could get her breath began whispering to him again with extreme animation and a hectic flush on her cheeks.

"Do you know, I gave her the most delicate instructions, so to speak, for inviting that lady and her daughter, you understand who I am talking about? It needed the utmost delicacy, the greatest nicety, but she has managed things so that that fool, that conceited baggage, that provincial nonentity, simply because she is the widow of a major, and has come to try and get a pension and fray out her skirts in the government offices, because at fifty she paints her face (everybody knows it) . . . a creature like that did not think fit to come, and has not even answered the invitation, which the most ordinary good manners required! I can't understand why Peter Petrovich has not come! But where's Sonia? Where has she gone? Ah, there she is at last! What is it, Sonia, where have you been? It's odd that even at your father's funeral you should be so unpunctual. Rodion Romanovich, make room for her beside you. That's your place, Sonia . . . take what you like. Have some of the cold entrée with the jelly, that's the best. They'll bring the pancakes in a few minutes. Have they given the children some? Polenka, have you got everything? (Cough-cough-cough.) That's all right. Be a good girl, Lida, and, Kolia, don't fidget with your feet; sit like a little gentleman. What are you saying, Sonia?"

Sonia hurriedly gave her Peter Petrovich's apologies, trying to speak loud enough for everyone to hear and carefully choosing the most respectful phrases which she attributed to Peter Petrovich. She added that Peter Petrovich had particularly told her to say that, as soon as he possibly could, he would come immediately to discuss business alone with her and to consider what could be done for her, etc., etc.

Sonia knew that this would comfort Katerina Ivanovna, flatter her and satisfy her pride. She sat down beside Raskolnikov; she made him a hurried bow, glancing curiously at him. But for the rest of the time she seemed to avoid looking at him or speaking to him. She seemed absent-minded, though she kept looking at Katerina Ivanovna, trying to please her. Neither she nor Katerina Ivanovna had been able to get mourning clothes; Sonia was wearing dark brown, and Katerina Ivanovna was in her only dress, a dark striped cotton one.

The message from Peter Petrovich was very successful. Listening to Sonia with dignity, Katerina Ivanovna inquired with equal dignity how Peter Petrovich was, then at once whispered almost aloud to Raskolnikov that it certainly would have been strange for a man of Peter Petrovich's position and standing to find himself in such "extraordinary company," in spite of his devotion to her family and his old friendship with her father.

"That's why I am so grateful to you, Rodion Romanovich, that you have not disdained my hospitality, even in such surroundings," she added almost aloud. "But I am sure that it was only your special affection for my poor husband that has made you keep your promise."

Then once more with pride and dignity she scanned her visitors, and suddenly inquired aloud across the table of the deaf man: "wouldn't he have some more meat, and had he been given some wine?" The old man did not answer and for a long time could not understand what he was asked, though his neighbors amused themselves by poking and shaking him. He simply gazed about him with his mouth open, which only increased the general amusement.

"What an imbecile! Look, look! Why was he brought? But as for Peter Petrovich, I always had confidence in him," Katerina Ivanovna continued, "and, of course, he is not like . . . " with an extremely stern face she addressed Amalia Ivanovna so sharply and loudly that the latter was entirely disconcerted, "not like your dressed up floozies who my father would not have taken as cooks into his kitchen. My late husband would have done them the honor of taking them in if he had invited them in the goodness of his heart."

"Yes, he was fond of drink, he was fond of it, he did drink!" shouted the commissariat clerk, gulping down his twelfth glass of vodka.

"My late husband certainly had that weakness, and everyone

knows it," Katerina Ivanovna attacked him at once, "but he was a kind and honorable man, who loved and respected his family. The worst of it was that his good nature made him trust all sorts of disreputable people, and he drank with people who were not worth the sole of his shoe. Would you believe it, Rodion Romanovich, they found a gingerbread cockerel in his pocket; he was dead drunk, but he did not forget the children!"

"A cockerel? Did you say a cockerel?" shouted the commissariat clerk.

Katerina Ivanovna did not vouchsafe a reply. She sighed, lost in thought.

"No doubt you think, like everyone, that I was too severe with him," she went on, addressing Raskolnikov. "But that's not true! He respected me, he respected me very much! He was a kind-hearted man! And how sorry I was for him sometimes! He would sit in a corner and look at me, I used to feel so sorry for him, I used to want to be kind to him and then I would think to myself: 'Be kind to him and he will drink again,' it was only through severity that you could keep him within bounds."

"Yes, he used to get his hair pulled pretty often," roared the commissariat clerk again, swallowing another glass of vodka.

"Some fools would be the better for a real beating, as well as having their hair pulled. I am not talking about my late husband now!" Katerina Ivanovna snapped at him.

The flush on her cheeks grew more and more marked, her chest heaved. In another minute she would have been ready to make a scene. Many of the visitors were sniggering, evidently delighted. They began poking the commissariat clerk and whispering something to him. They were evidently trying to egg him on.

"Allow me to ask what are you referring to," began the clerk, "that is to say, whose . . . about whom . . . did you say just now . . . But I don't care! That's nonsense! Widow! I forgive you . . . Pass!"

And he took another drink of vodka.

Raskolnikov sat in silence, listening with disgust. He only ate out of politeness, just tasting the food that Katerina Ivanovna was continually putting on his plate, to avoid hurting her feelings. He watched Sonia intently. But Sonia became more and more anxious and distressed; she, too, foresaw that the dinner would not end peaceably, and saw with terror Katerina Ivanovna's growing irritation. She knew that she, Sonia, was the chief reason for the "genteel" ladies' contemptuous treatment of Katerina Ivanovna's invitation. She had heard from Amalia Ivanovna that the mother was positively offended at the invitation and had asked the question: "How could she let her daughter sit down beside that young person?" Sonia had a feeling that Katerina Ivanovna had already heard this and an insult to Sonia meant more to Katerina Ivanovna than an insult to herself, her children, or her father. Sonia knew that Katerina Ivanovna would not be satisfied now, "till she had shown those floozies that they were both . . ." To make matters worse someone passed Sonia, from the other end of the table, a plate with two hearts pierced with an arrow, cut out of black bread. Katerina Ivanovna flushed crimson and at once said aloud across the table that the man who sent it was "a drunken ass!"

Amalia Ivanovna was foreseeing that something would go wrong, and at the same time she was deeply wounded by Katerina Ivanovna's dismissiveness, so to restore the good mood at the party and raise herself in their esteem she began, entirely at random, to tell a story about an acquaintance of hers, "Karl from the chemist's", who was driving one night in a cab, and that "the cabman wanted him to kill, and Karl very much begged him not to kill, and wept and clasped hands, and frightened and from fear pierced his heart." Though Katerina Ivanovna smiled, she observed at once that Amalia Ivanovna ought not to tell anecdotes in Russian; the latter was even more offended, and she retorted that her *"Vater aus Berlin* was a very important man, and always went with his hands in pockets." Katerina Ivanovna could not restrain herself and laughed so much that Amalia Ivanovna lost patience and could scarcely control herself.

"Listen to the owl!" Katerina Ivanovna whispered at once, her good-humor almost restored, "she meant to say he kept his hands in his pockets, but she said he put his hands in people's pockets. (Cough-cough.) And have you noticed, Rodion Romanovich, that all these Petersburg foreigners, the Germans especially, are all stupider than we are! Can you fancy anyone of us telling how 'Karl from the chemist's pierced his heart from fear' and that the idiot instead of punishing the cabman, 'clasped his hands and wept, and much begged.' Ah, the fool! And you know she thinks it's very touching and does not suspect how stupid she is! The way I see it, that drunken commissariat clerk is a great deal cleverer, anyway one can see that he has addled his brains with drink, but you know, these foreigners are always so well behaved and serious . . . Look how she sits glaring! She is angry, ha-ha! (Cough-cough-cough.)"

Regaining her temper, Katerina Ivanovna began to tell Raskolnikov that when she had obtained her pension, she intended to open a school for gentlemen's daughters in her native town, T____. This was the first time she had spoken to him about the project, and she launched out into the most alluring details. It suddenly appeared that Katerina Ivanovna had in her hands the same certificate of honour which Marmeladov had told Raskolnikov about in the tavern, when he told him that Katerina Ivanovna, his wife, had danced the shawl dance before the governor and other important people when she left school. This certificate of honour was obviously intended now to prove Katerina Ivanovna's right to open a boarding-school; but she had armed herself with it chiefly with the purpose of overwhelming "those two stuck-up floozies" if they came to the dinner, and proving incontestably that Katerina Ivanovna was of the most noble, "she might even say aristocratic family, a colonel's daughter and was far superior to certain adventuresses who have been so much to the fore recently." The certificate of honor immediately passed into the hands of the drunken guests, and Katerina Ivanovna did not try to retain it, for it actually contained the statement *en toutes lettres** that her father was a major, and also a companion of an order, so that she really was almost the daughter of a colonel.

Warming up, Katerina Ivanovna proceeded to enlarge on the peaceful and happy life they would lead in T____, on the gymnasium teachers whom she would engage to give lessons in her boarding-school, one a highly respectable old Frenchman called Mangot, who had taught Katerina Ivanovna herself in the old days and was still living in T____, and would no doubt teach in her school on moderate terms. Next she spoke of Sonia who would go with her to T____ and help her in all her plans. At this someone at the further end of the table suddenly chuckled.

Though Katerina Ivanovna tried to appear to be disdainfully unaware of it, she raised her voice and began at once speaking with con-

---

*In black and white (French).

viction of Sonia's undoubted ability to assist her, of "her gentleness, patience, devotion, generosity and good education," tapping Sonia on the cheek and kissing her warmly twice. Sonia flushed crimson, and Katerina Ivanovna suddenly burst into tears, immediately observing that she was "nervous and silly, that she was too upset, that it was time to finish, and as the dinner was over, it was time to hand round the tea."

At that moment, Amalia Ivanovna, deeply aggrieved that she had played no part in the conversation and that no-one was listening to her, made one last effort, and with secret misgivings ventured on an extremely deep and weighty observation, that "in the future boarding-school she would have to pay particular attention to *die Wasche*, and that there certainly must be a good *Dame* to look after the linen, and secondly that the young ladies must not novels at night read."

Katerina Ivanovna, who was certainly upset and very tired, as well as heartily sick of the dinner, at once cut short Amalia Ivanovna, saying "she knew nothing about it and was talking nonsense, that it was the business of the laundry maid, and not of the directress of a high-class boarding-school to look after *die Wasche*, and as for novel reading, that was simply rude, and she begged her to be silent." Amalia Ivanovna was enraged and observed that she only "meant her good," and that "she had meant her very good," and that "it was long since she had paid her gold for the lodgings."

Katerina Ivanovna at once put her down, saying that it was a lie to say she wished her good, because only yesterday, when her dead husband was lying on the table, she had bothered her about the lodgings. To this Amalia Ivanovna very appropriately retorted that she had invited those ladies, but "those ladies had not come, because those ladies are ladies and cannot come to a lady who is not a lady." Katerina Ivanovna at once pointed out to her, that as she was a slut she could not judge what made one really a lady. Amalia Ivanovna at once declared that her "*Vater aus Berlin* was a very, very important man, and both hands in pockets went, and always used to say: poof! poof!" and she leapt up from the table to represent her father, sticking her hands in her pockets, puffing her cheeks, and uttering vague sounds resembling "poof! poof!" amid loud laughter from all the lodgers, who deliberately encouraged Amalia Ivanovna, hoping for a fight.

But this was too much for Katerina Ivanovna, and she at once declared, so all could hear, that Amalia Ivanovna probably never had a father, but was just a drunken Petersburg Finn, and had certainly once been a cook and probably something worse. Amalia Ivanovna turned red as a lobster and squealed that perhaps Katerina Ivanovna never had a father, "but she had a *Vater aus Berlin* and that he wore a long coat and always said poof-poof-poof!"

Katerina Ivanovna observed contemptuously that everyone knew who her family was and that on that very certificate of honour it was stated in print that her father was a colonel, while Amalia Ivanovna's father—if she really had one—was probably some Finnish milkman, but that probably she never had a father at all, since it was still uncertain whether her name was Amalia Ivanovna or Amalia Ludwigovna.

At this Amalia Ivanovna, lashed to fury, struck the table with her fist, and shrieked that she was Amalia Ivanovna, and not Ludwigovna, "that her *Vater* was named Johann and that he was a burgomeister, and that Katerina Ivanovna's *Vater* was quite never a burgomeister." Katerina Ivanovna rose from her chair, and with a stern and apparently calm voice (though she was pale and her chest was heaving) observed that "if she dared for one moment to set her contemptible wretch of a father on a level with her papa, she, Katerina Ivanovna, would tear her cap off her head and trample it under foot." Amalia Ivanovna ran about the room, shouting at the top of her voice, that she was mistress of the house and that Katerina Ivanovna should leave the lodgings that minute; then she rushed for some reason to collect the silver spoons from the table. There was a great outcry and uproar, the children began crying. Sonia ran to restrain Katerina Ivanovna, but when Amalia Ivanovna shouted something about "the yellow ticket," Katerina Ivanovna pushed Sonia away, and rushed at the landlady to carry out her threat.

At that minute the door opened, and Peter Petrovich Luzhin appeared on the threshold. He stood scanning the party with severe and vigilant eyes. Katerina Ivanovna rushed towards him.

CHAPTER THREE

"PETER PETROVICH," SHE CRIED, "protect me . . . you at least! Make this foolish woman understand that she can't behave like this to a lady in misfortune . . . that there is a law for such things . . . I'll go to the governor-general himself . . . She shall answer for it . . . Remember my father's hospitality; protect these orphans."

"Allow me, madam . . . Allow me." Peter Petrovich waved her off. "Your father, as you are well aware, I did not have the honor of knowing" (someone laughed aloud) "and I do not intend to take part in your everlasting squabbles with Amalia Ivanovna . . . I have come here to speak of my own affairs . . . and I want to have a word with your stepdaughter, Sofia . . . Ivanovna, I think it is? Allow me to pass."

Peter Petrovich, edging by her, went to the opposite corner where Sonia was.

Katerina Ivanovna remained standing where she was, as though thunderstruck. She could not understand how Peter Petrovich could deny having enjoyed her father's hospitality. Though she had invented it herself, she believed in it firmly by this time. She was struck too by the businesslike, dry and even contemptuously menacing tone of Peter Petrovich. All the clamor gradually died away when he came in. Not only was this "serious business man" strikingly incongruous with the rest of the party, but it was evident, too, that he had come about some matter of importance, that some exceptional cause must have brought him and that therefore something was going to happen. Raskolnikov, standing beside Sonia, moved aside to let him pass; Peter Petrovich did not seem to notice him. A minute later Lebeziatnikov, too, appeared in the doorway; he did not come in, but stood still, listening with marked interest, almost amazement, and seemed to be temporarily perplexed.

"Excuse me for possibly interrupting you, but it's a matter of some importance," Peter Petrovich observed, addressing the company generally. "I am glad, in fact, to find other people present. Amalia Ivanovna, I humbly beg you as mistress of the house to pay careful attention to what I have to say to Sofia Ivanovna. Sofia Ivanovna," he went on, addressing Sonia, who was very much surprised and already alarmed, "immediately after your visit I found that a hundred-ruble note was missing from my table, in the room of my friend Mr. Lebeziatnikov. If in any way whatever you know and will tell us where it is now, I assure you on my word of honor and call all present to witness that the matter shall end there. In the opposite case

I shall be compelled to have recourse to very serious measures and then . . . you must blame yourself."

Complete silence reigned in the room. Even the crying children were still. Sonia stood deadly pale, staring at Luzhin and unable to say a word. She seemed not to understand. Some seconds passed.

"Well, how is it to be then?" asked Luzhin, looking intently at her.

"I don't know . . . I know nothing about it," Sonia articulated faintly at last.

"No, you know nothing?" Luzhin repeated and again he paused for some seconds. "Think for a moment, young lady," he began severely, but still, as it were, reprimanding her. "Think it over, I am prepared to give you time for consideration. Please observe: if I were not so entirely convinced I would not, you may be sure, with my experience attempt to accuse you so directly. I am aware that for such direct accusation before witnesses, if false or even mistaken, I should myself in a certain sense be made responsible. This morning I changed for my own purposes several five per cent. securities for the sum of approximately three thousand rubles. The account is noted down in my pocket-book. On my return home I proceeded to count the money, as Mr. Lebeziatnikov will testify, and after counting two thousand three hundred rubles I put the rest in my pocket-book in my coat pocket. About five hundred rubles remained on the table and among them three notes of a hundred rubles each. At that moment you entered (at my invitation) and all the time you were present you were extremely embarrassed; three times you jumped up in the middle of the conversation and tried to leave. Mr. Lebeziatnikov can bear witness to this. You yourself, young lady, will probably not refuse to confirm my statement that I invited you through Mr. Lebeziatnikov, solely in order to discuss with you the hopeless and destitute position of your relative, Katerina Ivanovna (whose dinner I was unable to attend), and the advisability of starting something like a subscription or a lottery for her benefit. You thanked me and even shed tears. I describe all this as it took place, primarily to recall it to your mind and secondly to show you that not the slightest detail has escaped my recollection. Then I took a ten-ruble note from the table and handed it to you as a first installment on my part for the benefit of your relative. Mr. Lebeziatnikov saw all this. Then I accompanied you to the

door, during which you were still in the same state of embarrassment, after which I was left alone with Mr. Lebeziatnikov and talked
to him for ten minutes; then Mr. Lebeziatnikov went out and I returned to the table with the money lying on it, intending to count
it and to put it aside, as I proposed doing before. To my surprise
one hundred-ruble note had disappeared. Please consider my position. Mr. Lebeziatnikov I cannot suspect. I am ashamed even to
refer to any such suspicion. I cannot have made a mistake in my
calculations, because the minute before you came in I had finished
my accounts and found the total to be correct. You will admit that
when I recalled your embarrassment, your eagerness to leave and
the fact that you kept your hands for some time on the table, and
taking into consideration your social position and the habits associated with it, I was, so to say, horrified and compelled to entertain
a suspicion entirely against my will—a cruel, but justifiable suspicion! I will go further and repeat that despite my positive conviction, I realize that I run a certain risk in making this accusation, but
as you see, I could not let it pass. I have taken action and I will tell
you why: solely, madam, solely because of your blackest ingratitude! How is this? I invite you for the benefit of your destitute relative, I present you with my donation of ten rubles and you, on the
spot, repay me with an action like that. It is too bad! You need to
learn a lesson. Think about it! Moreover, as a true friend I beg
you—and you could have no better friend at the moment—think
about what you are doing, otherwise I will refuse to alter my position! Well, what do you say?"

"I have taken nothing," Sonia whispered in terror, "you gave me
ten rubles, here it is, take it."

Sonia pulled her handkerchief out of her pocket, untied a corner
of it, took out the ten-ruble note and gave it to Luzhin.

"And the hundred rubles you do not confess to taking?" he insisted reproachfully, not taking the note.

Sonia looked about her. All were looking at her with such awful,
stern, ironic, hostile eyes. She looked at Raskolnikov . . . he stood
against the wall, with his arms crossed, looking at her with glowing
eyes.

"Good God!" broke from Sonia.

"Amalia Ivanovna, we shall have to send for the police and therefore I humbly beg you meanwhile to send for the house porter," Luzhin said softly and even kindly.

"*Gott der barmherzige!* I knew she was the thief," cried Amalia Ivanovna, throwing up her hands.

"You knew it?" Luzhin caught her up, "then I suppose you had some reason before this for thinking so. I beg you, my dear Amalia Ivanovna, to remember your words which have been uttered before witnesses."

There was a buzz of loud conversation on all sides. All were in movement.

"What!" cried Katerina Ivanovna, suddenly realizing the position, and she rushed at Luzhin. "What! You accuse her of stealing? Sonia? Ah, the wretches, the wretches!"

And running to Sonia she flung her wasted arms round her and held her as if in a vice.

"Sonia! How dared you take ten rubles from him? Foolish girl! Give it to me! Give me the ten rubles at once—here!"

And snatching the note from Sonia, Katerina Ivanovna crumpled it up and flung it straight into Luzhin's face. It hit him in the eye and fell on the ground. Amalia Ivanovna swiftly picked it up. Peter Petrovich lost his temper.

"Hold that mad woman!" he shouted.

At that moment several other persons, besides Lebeziatnikov, appeared in the doorway, among them the two ladies.

"What! Mad? Am I mad? Idiot!" shrieked Katerina Ivanovna. "You are an idiot yourself, pettifogging lawyer, base man! Sonia, Sonia take his money! Sonia a thief! She'd give away her last penny!" and Katerina Ivanovna broke into hysterical laughter. "Did you ever see such an idiot?" she turned from side to side. "And you too?" she suddenly saw the landlady, "and you too, sausage eater, you declare that she is a thief, you trashy Prussian hen's leg in a crinoline! She hasn't been out of this room: she came straight from you, you wretch, and sat down beside me, everyone saw her. She sat here, by Rodion Romanovich. Search her! Since she's not left the room, the money would have to be on her! Search her, search her! But if you don't find it, then excuse me, my dear fellow, you'll answer for it! I'll go to our Sovereign, to our Sovereign, to our gracious Tsar himself, and throw myself at his feet, today, this minute! I am alone in the world! They would let me in! Do you think they wouldn't? You're wrong, I will get in! I will get in! You counted on her meekness! You relied upon that! But I am not so submissive, let me tell you! You've gone too far yourself. Search her, search her!"

And Katerina Ivanovna in a frenzy shook Luzhin and dragged him towards Sonia.

"I am ready, I'll be responsible . . . but calm yourself, madam, calm yourself. I see that you are not so submissive! . . . Well, well, but as to that . . . " Luzhin muttered, "that ought to be before the police . . . though in fact there are enough witnesses as it is . . . I am ready . . . But in any case it's difficult for a man . . . on account of her sex . . . But with the help of Amalia Ivanovna . . . though, of course, it's not the way to do things . . . How is it to be done?"

"As you will! Let anyone who likes search her!" cried Katerina Ivanovna. "Sonia, turn out your pockets! See. Look, monster, the pocket is empty, here was her handkerchief! Here is the other pocket, look! Do you see, do you see?"

And Katerina Ivanovna turned—or rather snatched—both pockets inside out. But from the right pocket a piece of paper flew out, traced a parabola in the air and fell at Luzhin's feet. Everyone saw it, several cried out. Peter Petrovich stooped down, picked up the paper in two fingers, lifted it where all could see it and opened it. It was a hundred-ruble note folded in eight. Peter Petrovich held up the note, showing it to everyone.

"Thief! Out of my lodging. Police, police!" yelled Amalia Ivanovna. "They must to Siberia be sent! Away!"

Exclamations arose on all sides. Raskolnikov was silent, keeping his eyes fixed on Sonia, except for an occasional rapid glance at Luzhin. Sonia stood still, as though unconscious. She was hardly able to feel surprise. Suddenly the color rushed to her cheeks; she uttered a cry and hid her face in her hands.

"No, it wasn't I! I didn't take it! I know nothing about it," she cried with a heartrending wail, and she ran to Katerina Ivanovna, who clasped her tightly in her arms, as though she would shelter her from the whole world.

"Sonia! Sonia! I don't believe it! You see, I don't believe it!" she cried in the face of the obvious fact, swaying her to and fro in her arms like a baby, kissing her face continually, then snatching at her hands and kissing them, too. "You took it! How stupid these people are! Oh dear! You are fools, fools," she cried, addressing the whole room, "you don't know, you don't know what a heart she has, what a girl she is! She take it, she? She'd sell her last rag, she'd go barefoot to help you if you needed it, that's what she is! She has the yellow passport because my children were starving, she sold herself for us! Ah, husband, husband! Do you see? Do you see? What a memorial dinner for you! Merciful heavens! Defend her, why are you all standing still? Rodion Romanovich, why don't you stand up for her? Do you believe it, too? You are not worth her little finger, all of you together! Good God! Defend her now, at least!"

The wail of the poor, consumptive, helpless woman seemed to produce a great effect on her audience. The agonized, wasted, tubercular face, the parched, blood-stained lips, the hoarse voice, the tears unrestrained as a child's, the trustful, childish and yet despairing prayer for help were so piteous that every one seemed to feel for her. Peter Petrovich at any rate was at once moved to compassion.

"Madam, madam, this incident does not reflect upon you!" he cried impressively, "no-one would take upon himself to accuse you of being an instigator or even an accomplice in it, especially as you have proved her guilt by turning out her pockets, showing that you had no previous idea of it. I am most ready, most ready to show compassion, if poverty, so to speak, drove Sofia Semionovna to it, but why did you refuse to confess, mademoiselle? Were you afraid of the disgrace? The first step? You lost your head, perhaps? One can quite understand it . . . But how could you have lowered yourself to such an action? Gentlemen," he addressed the whole company, "gentlemen! Compassionate and so to say commiserating with these people, I am ready to overlook it even now in spite of the personal insult lavished upon me! And may this disgrace be a lesson to you for the future," he said, addressing Sonia, "and I will carry the matter no further. Enough!"

Peter Petrovich stole a glance at Raskolnikov. Their eyes met, and the fire in Raskolnikov's seemed ready to reduce him to ashes. Meanwhile Katerina Ivanovna apparently heard nothing. She was kissing and hugging Sonia like a madwoman. The children, too, were embracing Sonia on all sides, and Polenka—though she did not fully understand what was wrong—was drowned in tears and shaking with sobs, as she hid her pretty little face, swollen with weeping, on Sonia's shoulder.

"How vile!" a loud voice cried suddenly in the doorway.

Peter Petrovich looked round quickly.

"What vileness!" Lebeziatnikov repeated, staring him straight in the face.

Peter Petrovich practically shuddered—everyone noticed it and recalled it afterwards. Lebeziatnikov strode into the room.

"And you dared to call me as a witness?" he said, going up to Peter Petrovich.

"What do you mean? What are you talking about?" muttered Luzhin.

"I mean that you . . . are a slanderer, that's what my words mean!" Lebeziatnikov said hotly, looking sternly at him with his shortsighted eyes.

He was extremely angry. Raskolnikov gazed intently at him, as though seizing and weighing each word. Again there was a silence. Peter Petrovich seemed almost dumbstruck at first.

"If you mean that for me, . . . " he began, stammering. "But what's the matter with you? Are you out of your mind?"

"I'm in my mind, but you are a scoundrel! Ah, how vile! I have heard everything. I kept waiting on purpose to understand it, for I must admit even now it is not quite logical . . . What you have done it all for I can't understand."

"Why, what have I done then? Stop talking in your nonsensical riddles! Or maybe you are drunk!"

"You may be a drunkard, perhaps, you disgusting individual, but I am not! I never touch vodka, because it's against my convictions. Would you believe it, he, he himself, with his own hands gave Sofia Semionovna that hundred-ruble note—I saw it, I was a witness, I'll take my oath! He did it, he!" repeated Lebeziatnikov, addressing all.

"Are you crazy, you milksop?" squealed Luzhin. "She is in front of you herself—she herself here declared just now in front of everyone that I gave her only ten rubles. How could I have given it to her?"

"I saw it, I saw it," Lebeziatnikov repeated, "and although it is against my principles, I am ready this very minute to take any oath you like before the court, because I saw how you slipped it in her pocket. Only like a fool I thought you did it out of kindness! When you were saying goodbye to her at the door, while you held her hand in one hand, with the other, the left, you slipped the note into her pocket. I saw it, I saw it!"

Luzhin turned pale.

"What lies!" he cried insolently, "why, how could you, standing by the window, see the note! You imagined it with your shortsighted eyes. You are raving!"

"No, I didn't imagine it. And though I was standing some way off, I saw it all. And though it certainly would be hard to distinguish a note from the window—that's true—I knew for certain that it was a hundred-ruble note, because, when you were going to give Sofia Semionovna ten rubles, you picked up from the table a hundred-ruble note (I saw it because I was standing nearby at the time, and an idea struck me at once, so I did not forget you had it in your hand). You folded it and kept it in your hand all the time. I didn't think of it again until, when you were getting up, you changed it from your right hand to your left and nearly dropped it! I noticed it because the same idea struck me again, that you meant to do her a kindness without me seeing anything. You can imagine how I watched you and I saw how you succeeded in slipping it into her pocket. I saw it, I saw it, I'd swear an oath on it."

Lebeziatnikov was almost breathless. Exclamations arose on all sides, chiefly expressing amazement, but some were menacing in tone. They all crowded round Peter Petrovich. Katerina Ivanovna flew to Lebeziatnikov.

"I was mistaken about you! Protect her! You are the only one to take her side! She is an orphan. God has sent you!"

Katerina Ivanovna, hardly knowing what she was doing, sank on her knees before him.

"A pack of nonsense!" yelled Luzhin, infuriated. "It's all nonsense you've been talking! 'An idea struck you, you didn't think, you noticed'—what does it amount to? So I gave it to her on the sly on purpose? What for? With what aim? What do I have to do with this . . . ?"

"What for? That's what I can't understand, but that what I am telling you is the fact, that's certain! Far from being mistaken, you infamous, criminal man, I remember how, because of it, a question occurred to me at once, just when I was thanking you and pressing your hand. What made you put it secretly in her pocket? Why did you do it secretly, I mean? Could it be simply to conceal it from me, knowing that my convictions are opposed to yours and that I do not approve of private benevolence, which brings about no radical cure? Well, I decided that you really were ashamed of giving such a large sum in front of me. Perhaps, too, I thought, he wants to give her a surprise, when she finds a whole hundred-ruble note in her pocket. (For I know some benevolent people are very fond of decking out their charitable actions in that way.) Then the idea struck me, too, that you wanted to test her, to see whether, when she found it, she would come to thank you. Then, too, that you wanted to avoid thanks and that, as the saying is, your right hand should not know . . . something of that sort, in fact. I thought of so many possibilities that I put off considering it, but still thought it indelicate to show you I knew your secret. But another idea struck me again that Sofia Semionovna might easily lose the money before she noticed it, which was why I decided to come in here to call her out of the room and to tell her that you put a hundred rubles in her pocket. But on my way I went first to Madame Kobilatnikov's to take them the 'General Treatise on the Positive Method'* and especially to recommend Piderit's article (and also Wagner's); then I come on here and what a state of things I find! Now could I, could I, have all these ideas and reflections, if I had not seen you put the hundred-ruble note in her pocket?"

When Lebeziatnikov finished his long-winded assault with the logical deduction at the end, he was quite tired, and the perspiration streamed from his face. He could not, alas, even express himself correctly in Russian, though he knew no other language, and so he was totally exhausted, almost emaciated after this heroic exploit. But his speech produced a powerful effect. He had spoken with such passion, with such conviction that everyone obviously believed him. Peter Petrovich felt that things were going badly for him.

"What is it to do with me if silly ideas did occur to you?" he shouted, "that's no evidence. You may have dreamt it, that's all! And I tell you, you are lying, sir. You are lying and slandering from some spite against me, simply because you were somehow offended that I

---

*Anthology of articles on natural science edited by Nikolai Neklyudov and published in St. Petersburg in 1866.

did not agree with your freethinking, godless, social propositions!"

But this retort did not benefit Peter Petrovich. Murmurs of disapproval were heard on all sides.

"Ah, that's your line now, is it!" cried Lebeziatnikov, "that's nonsense! Call the police and I'll take my oath! There's only one thing I can't understand: what made him risk such a contemptible action. Oh, pitiful, despicable man!"

"I can explain why he risked such an action, and if necessary, I, too, will swear to it," Raskolnikov said at last in a firm voice, and he stepped forward.

He appeared to be firm and composed. Everyone felt clearly, just from way he looked, that he really knew something about it and that the mystery would be solved.

"Now I can explain it all to myself," said Raskolnikov, addressing Lebeziatnikov. "From the very beginning of this whole business, I suspected that there was some terrible plot behind it. I began to suspect this due to some special circumstances known only to myself, which I will explain at once to everyone: they account for everything. Your valuable evidence has finally made everything clear to me. I beg everyone to listen. This gentleman" (he pointed to Luzhin) "was recently engaged to be married to a young lady—my sister, Avdotia Romanovna Raskolnikov. But when he came to Petersburg he quarreled with me, the day before yesterday, at our first meeting and I drove him out of my room—I have two witnesses to prove it. He is a very spiteful man . . . The day before yesterday I did not know that he was staying here, in your room, and that consequently on the day we quarreled—the day before yesterday—he saw me give Katerina Ivanovna some money for the funeral, as a friend of the late Mr. Marmeladov. He at once wrote a note to my mother and informed her that I had given away all my money, not to Katerina Ivanovna, but to Sofia Semionovna, and referred in a most contemptible way to the . . . character of Sofia Semionovna, that is, hinted at the nature of my attitude to Sofia Semionovna. All this, you understand, was carried out with the purpose of dividing me from my mother and sister, by insinuating that I was squandering on unworthy objects the money which they had sent me and which was all they had. Yesterday evening, before my mother and sister and in his presence, I declared that I had given the money to Katerina Ivanovna for the funeral

and not to Sofia Semionovna and that I had no acquaintance with
Sofia Semionovna and had never seen her before, indeed. At the same
time I added that he, Peter Petrovich Luzhin, with all his virtues was
not worth Sofia Semionovna's little finger, though he spoke so badly
of her. To his question—would I let Sofia Semionovna sit down beside my sister—I answered that I had already done so that day. Irritated that my mother and sister were unwilling to quarrel with me at
his insinuations, he gradually began to be unforgivably rude to them.
A final rupture took place and he was turned out of the house. All this
happened yesterday evening. Now I beg you to pay close attention:
consider: if he had succeeded now in proving that Sofia Semionovna
was a thief, he would have shown to my mother and sister that he
was almost right in his suspicions, that he had reason to be angry at
my putting my sister on a level with Sofia Semionovna, that, in attacking me, he was protecting and preserving the honor of my sister,
his betrothed. In fact he might even, through all this, have been able
to estrange me from my family, and no doubt he hoped to be restored
to favor with them; to say nothing of avenging himself on me personally, for he has grounds for supposing that the honour and happiness of Sofia Semionovna are very precious to me. That was what he
was working for! That's how I understand it. That's the whole reason
for it and there can be no other!"

It was like this, or somewhat like this, that Raskolnikov wound up
his speech which was followed very attentively, though often interrupted by exclamations from his audience. But in spite of interruptions
he spoke clearly, calmly, exactly, firmly. His decisive voice, his tone of
conviction and his stern face made a great impression on everyone.

"Yes, yes, that's it," Lebeziatnikov assented joyfully, "that must
be it, for he asked me, as soon as Sofia Semionovna came into our
room, whether you were here, whether I had seen you among Katerina Ivanovna's guests. He called me aside to the window and
asked me in secret. It was essential for him that you should be here!
That's it, that's it!"

Luzhin smiled contemptuously and did not speak. But he was
very pale. He seemed to be considering the best means of escape. Perhaps he would have been glad to give up everything and get away, but
at the moment this was scarcely possible. It would have implied admitting the truth of the accusations brought against him. Moreover,

the guests, who had already been excited by drink, were now too emotional to allow it. The commissariat clerk, though indeed he had not grasped the whole position, was shouting louder than anyone and was making some suggestions which were very unpleasant to Luzhin. But not everyone there was drunk; tenants came in from all the rooms. The three Poles were tremendously excited and were continually shouting at him: "The *Pan* is a *lajdak!*"* and muttering threats in Polish. Sonia had been listening with strained attention, though she too seemed unable to grasp it all; she seemed as though she had just returned to consciousness. She did not take her eyes off Raskolnikov, feeling that in him lay her personal safety. Katerina Ivanovna breathed hard and painfully and seemed horribly exhausted. Amalia Ivanovna stood looking more stupid than anyone, with her mouth wide open, unable to make out what had happened. She only saw that Peter Petrovich had somehow come to grief.

Raskolnikov was attempting to speak again, but they did not let him. Everyone was crowding round Luzhin with threats and shouts of abuse. But Peter Petrovich was not intimidated. Seeing that his accusation of Sonia had completely failed, he reverted to insolence:

"Allow me, gentlemen, allow me! Don't squeeze, let me pass!" he said, making his way through the crowd. "And no threats if you please! I assure you it will be useless, you will gain nothing by it. On the contrary, you'll have to answer, gentlemen, for violently obstructing the course of justice. The thief has been more than unmasked, and I shall prosecute. Our judges are not so blind and . . . not so drunk, and will not believe the testimony of two notorious infidels, agitators, and atheists, whose accusations are motivated by a desire for personal revenge which they are foolish enough to admit . . . Yes, allow me to pass!"

"Don't let me find a trace of you in my room! You will kindly leave at once, and everything between us will be at an end! When I think of the trouble I've been taking, the way I've been expounding . . . all fortnight!"

"I told you myself today that I was going, when you tried to keep me; now I will simply add that you are a fool. I advise you to see a doctor for your brains and your short sight. Let me pass, gentlemen!"

---

*The gentleman is a scoundrel (Polish)!

He forced his way through. But the commissariat clerk was unwilling to let him off so easily: he picked up a glass from the table, brandished it in the air and flung it at Peter Petrovich; but the glass flew straight at Amalia Ivanovna. She screamed, and the clerk, overbalancing, fell heavily under the table. Peter Petrovich made his way to his room and half an hour later had left the house. Sonia, timid by nature, had felt before that day that she could be ill-treated more easily than anyone, and that she could be wronged with impunity. Yet until that moment she had imagined that she might escape misfortune by care, gentleness and submissiveness before everyone. Her disappointment was too great. She could, of course, bear with patience and almost without murmur anything, even this. But at first she felt it was too bitter. Despite her triumph and her justification—when her first terror and astonishment had passed and she could understand it all clearly—the feeling of her helplessness and of the wrong done to her made her heart throb with anguish and she was overcome with hysterical weeping. At last, unable to bear any more, she rushed out of the room and ran home, almost immediately after Luzhin's departure. When amidst loud laughter the glass flew at Amalia Ivanovna, it was more than the landlady could endure. With a shriek she rushed like a fury at Katerina Ivanovna, considering her to blame for everything.

"Out of my lodgings! At once! Quick march!"

And with these words she began snatching up everything she could lay her hands on that belonged to Katerina Ivanovna, and throwing it on the floor, Katerina Ivanovna, pale, almost fainting, and gasping for breath, jumped up from the bed where she had sunk in exhaustion and darted at Amalia Ivanovna. But the battle was too unequal: the landlady waved her away like a feather.

"What! As though that godless calumny was not enough—this vile creature attacks me! What! On the day of my husband's funeral I am turned out of my lodgings! After eating my bread and salt she turns me into the street, with my orphans! Where am I to go?" wailed the poor woman, sobbing and gasping. "Good God!" she cried with flashing eyes, "is there no justice on earth? Whom should you protect if not us orphans? We shall see! There is law and justice on earth, there is, I will find it! Wait a minute, you godless creature! Polenka, stay with the children, I'll come back. Wait for me, if you have to wait in the street. We will see whether there is justice on earth!"

And throwing over her head that green shawl which Marmeladov had mentioned to Raskolnikov, Katerina Ivanovna squeezed her
way through the disorderly and drunken crowd of lodgers who still
filled the room, and, wailing and tearful, she ran into the street—
with a vague intention of going somewhere at once to find justice.
Polenka with the two little ones in her arms crouched, terrified, on
the trunk in the corner of the room, where she waited trembling for
her mother to come back. Amalia Ivanovna raged about the room,
shrieking, lamenting and throwing everything she came across on
the floor. The lodgers talked incoherently, some commented to the
best of their ability on what had happened, others quarreled and
swore at one another, while others struck up a song . . .

"Now it's time for me to go," thought Raskolnikov. "Well, Sofia
Semionovna, we shall see what you'll say now!"

And he set off in the direction of Sonia's lodgings.

CHAPTER FOUR

Raskolnikov had been a vigorous and active champion of Sonia
against Luzhin, although he had such a load of horror and anguish in
his own heart. But having gone through so much in the morning, he
found a sort of relief in a change of sensations, apart from the strong
personal feeling which impelled him to defend Sonia. He was agitated too, especially at some moments, by the thought of his approaching interview with Sonia: he had to tell her who had killed
Lizaveta. He knew the terrible suffering it would be to him and, as it
were, brushed away the thought of it. So when he cried as he left Katerina Ivanovna's, "Well, Sofia Semionovna, we shall see what you'll
say now!" he was still superficially excited, still vigorous and defiant
from his triumph over Luzhin. But, strange to say, by the time he
reached Sonia's lodging, he felt a sudden impotence and fear. He
stood still in hesitation at the door, asking himself the strange question: "Must I tell her who killed Lizaveta?" It was a strange question
because he felt at the very time not only that he could not help telling
her, but also that he could not put it off. He did not yet know why it

must be so, he only felt it, and the agonizing sense of his impotence before the inevitable almost crushed him. To cut short his hesitation and suffering, he quickly opened the door and looked at Sonia from the doorway. She was sitting with her elbows on the table and her face in her hands, but seeing Raskolnikov she got up at once and came to meet him as though she were expecting him.

"What would have become of me but for you!" she said quickly, meeting him in the middle of the room.

She had evidently wanted say this to him as soon as she could. It was what she had been waiting for.

Raskolnikov went to the table and sat down on the chair from which she had only just risen. She stood facing him, two steps away, just as she had done the day before.

"Well, Sonia?" he said, and felt that his voice was trembling, "it was all due to 'your social position and the habits associated with it.' Did you understand that just now?"

Her face showed her distress.

"Only don't talk to me as you did yesterday," she interrupted him. "Please don't start. There is misery enough without that."

She quickly smiled, afraid that he might not like the reproach.

"I was silly to come away from there. What is happening there now? I wanted to go back straightaway, but I kept thinking that . . . you would come."

He told her that Amalia Ivanovna was turning them out of their lodging and that Katerina Ivanovna had run off somewhere "to seek justice."

"My God!" cried Sonia, "let's go at once . . . "

And she snatched up her cape.

"It's always the same thing!" said Raskolnikov, irritably. "You've no thought except for them! Stay a little with me."

"But . . . Katerina Ivanovna?"

"You won't lose Katerina Ivanovna, you may be sure, she'll come to you herself if she's run out," he added peevishly. "If she doesn't find you here, you'll be blamed for it . . . "

Sonia sat down in painful suspense. Raskolnikov was silent, gazing at the floor and deliberating.

"This time Luzhin did not want to prosecute you," he began, not looking at Sonia, "but if he had wanted to, if it had suited his plans, he would have sent you to prison if it had not been for Lebeziatnikov and me. Ah?"

"Yes," she assented in a faint voice. "Yes," she repeated, preoccupied and distressed.

"But I might easily not have been there. And it was quite an accident that Lebeziatnikov turned up."

Sonia was silent.

"And if you'd have gone to prison, what then? Do you remember what I said yesterday?"

Again she did not answer. He waited.

"I thought you would shout again, 'don't talk about it, leave off.'" Raskolnikov laughed, but in a rather forced way. "What, silence again?" he asked a minute later. "We must talk about something, you know. It would be interesting for me to know how you would solve a certain 'problem,' as Lebeziatnikov would say." (He was beginning to lose the thread.) "No, really, I am serious. Imagine, Sonia, that you had known all of Luzhin's intentions beforehand. Known, that is, for a fact, that they would be the ruin of Katerina Ivanovna and the children and yourself all in one—since you don't count yourself for anything—Polenka, too . . . she'll go the same way. Well, if suddenly it all depended on your decision whether he or they should go on living, that is whether Luzhin should go on living and doing wicked things, or Katerina Ivanovna should die? How would you decide which of them was to die? I ask you?"

Sonia looked uneasily at him. There was something peculiar in this hesitating question, which seemed to be approaching something in a roundabout way.

"I felt that you were going to ask some question like that," she said, looking inquisitively at him.

"I dare say you did. But how should it be answered?"

"Why do you ask about what could not happen?" said Sonia reluctantly.

"Then it would be better for Luzhin to go on living and doing wicked things? You haven't dared to decide even that!"

"But I can't know the Divine Providence . . . And why do you ask what can't be answered? What's the use of such foolish questions? How could it depend on my decision? Who has made me a judge to decide who ought to live and who ought not to live?"

"Oh, if the Divine Providence is going to be mixed up in it, no-one can do anything," Raskolnikov grumbled morosely.

"You'd better say straight out what you want!" Sonia cried in distress. "You are leading up to something again . . . Can you have come just to torture me?"

She could not control herself and began crying bitterly. He looked at her in gloomy misery. Five minutes passed.

"Of course you're right, Sonia," he said softly at last. He changed suddenly. His tone of assumed arrogance and helpless defiance was gone. Even his voice was suddenly weak. "I told you yesterday that I was not coming to ask for your forgiveness and almost the first thing I've said is to ask for your forgiveness . . . I said that about Luzhin and Providence for my own sake. I was asking for your forgiveness, Sonia . . ."

He tried to smile, but there was something helpless and incomplete in his pale smile. He bowed his head and hid his face in his hands.

And suddenly a strange, surprising sensation of a sort of bitter hatred for Sonia passed through his heart. As it were wondering and frightened of this sensation, he raised his head and looked intently at her; but he met her uneasy and painfully anxious eyes fixed on him; there was love in them; his hatred vanished like a phantom. It was not the real feeling; he had mistaken one feeling for the other. It only meant that the time had come.

He hid his face in his hands again and bowed his head. Suddenly he turned pale, got up from his chair, looked at Sonia, and without uttering a word sat down mechanically on her bed.

His sensations that moment were terribly like the moment when he had stood over the old woman with the axe in his hand and felt that "he must not lose another minute."

"What's the matter?" asked Sonia, dreadfully frightened.

He could not utter a word. This was not at all, not at all the way he had intended to "tell" and he did not understand what was happening to him now. She went up to him, softly, sat down on the bed beside him and waited, not taking her eyes off him. Her heart throbbed and sank. It was unendurable; he turned his deadly pale face to her. His lips worked, helplessly struggling to utter something. A pang of terror passed through Sonia's heart.

"What's the matter?" she repeated, drawing a little away from him.

"Nothing, Sonia, don't be frightened . . . It's nonsense. It really is nonsense, if you think of it," he muttered, like a man in delirium. "Why have I come to torture you?" he added suddenly, looking at her. "Why, really? I keep asking myself that question, Sonia . . . "

He had perhaps been asking himself that question a quarter of an hour before, but now he spoke helplessly, hardly knowing what he said and feeling a continual tremor all over.

"Oh, how you are suffering!" she muttered in distress, looking intently at him.

"It's all nonsense . . . Listen, Sonia." He suddenly smiled, a pale helpless smile for two seconds. "You remember what I meant to tell you yesterday?"

Sonia waited uneasily.

"I said as I went away that perhaps I was saying goodbye for ever, but that if I came today I would tell you who . . . who killed Lizaveta."

She began trembling all over.

"Well, here I've come to tell you."

"Then you really meant it yesterday?" she whispered with difficulty. "How do you know?" she asked quickly, as though she were suddenly regaining her reason.

Sonia's face grew paler and paler, and she breathed painfully.

"I know."

She paused a minute.

"Have they found him?" she asked timidly.

"No."

"Then how do you know about it?" she asked again, hardly audibly and again after a minute's pause.

He turned to her and looked very intently at her.

"Guess," he said, with the same distorted helpless smile.

A shudder passed over her.

"But you . . . why do you frighten me like this?" she said, smiling like a child.

"I must be a great friend of his . . . since I know," Raskolnikov went on, still gazing into her face, as though he could not turn his eyes away. "He . . . did not mean to kill that Lizaveta . . . he . . . killed her accidentally . . . He meant to kill the old woman when she was alone and he went there . . . and then Lizaveta came in . . . he killed her too."

Another awful moment passed. Both still gazed at one another.

"You can't guess, then?" he asked suddenly, feeling as though he were flinging himself down from a steeple.

"N-no . . . " whispered Sonia.

"Take a good look."

As soon as he had said this again, the same familiar sensation froze his heart. He looked at her and all at once seemed to see in her face the face of Lizaveta. He remembered clearly the expression in Lizaveta's face, when he approached her with the axe and she stepped back to the wall, putting out her hand, with childish terror in her face, looking like little children do when they begin to be frightened of something, looking intently and uneasily at what frightens them, shrinking back and holding out their little hands on the verge of tears. Almost the same thing happened now to Sonia. With the same helplessness and the same terror, she looked at him for a while and, suddenly putting out her left hand, pressed her fingers faintly against his breast and slowly began to get up from the bed, moving further from him and keeping her eyes fixed even more immovably on him. Her terror infected him. The same fear showed itself on his face. In the same way he stared at her and almost with the same childish smile.

"Have you guessed?" he whispered at last.

"Good God!" broke in an awful wail from her chest.

She sank helplessly on the bed with her face in the pillows, but a moment later she got up, moved quickly to him, seized both his hands and, gripping them tight in her thin fingers, began looking into his face again with the same intent stare. In this last desperate look she tried to look into him and catch some last hope. But there was no hope; there was no doubt remaining; it was all true! Later on, indeed, when she recalled that moment, she thought it was strange and wondered why she had seen at once that there was no doubt. She could not have said, for instance, that she had foreseen something of the sort—and yet now, as soon as he told her, she suddenly imagined that she had really foreseen this very thing.

"Stop, Sonia, enough! Don't torture me," he begged her miserably.

It was not at all, not at all like this that he had thought of telling her, but this is how it happened.

She jumped up, seeming not to know what she was doing, and, wringing her hands, walked into the middle of the room; but quickly went back and sat down again beside him, her shoulder almost touching his. All of a sudden she started as though she had been stabbed, uttered a cry and fell on her knees before him, she did not know why.

"What have you done—what have you done to yourself!" she said in despair, and, jumping up, she flung herself on his neck, threw her arms round him, and held him tight.

Raskolnikov drew back and looked at her with a mournful smile.

"You are a strange girl, Sonia—you kiss me and hug me when I tell you about that . . . You're not thinking about what you're doing."

"There is no-one, no-one in the whole world now who is as unhappy as you!" she cried in a frenzy, not hearing what he said, and she suddenly broke into violent hysterical weeping.

A feeling long unfamiliar to him flooded his heart and softened it at once. He did not struggle against it. Two tears started into his eyes and hung on his eyelashes.

"Then you won't leave me, Sonia?" he said, looking at her almost with hope.

"No, no, never, nowhere!" cried Sonia. "I will follow you, I will follow you everywhere. Oh, my God! Oh, how miserable I am! . . . Why, why didn't I know you before! Why didn't you come before? Oh, dear!"

"And now I have come."

"Yes, now! What's to be done now! . . . Together, together!" she repeated as it were unconsciously, and she hugged him again. "I'll follow you to Siberia!"

He recoiled at this, and the same hostile, almost haughty smile came to his lips.

"Perhaps I don't want to go to Siberia yet, Sonia," he said.

Sonia looked at him quickly.

Again after her first passionate, agonizing sympathy for the unhappy man the terrible idea of the murder overwhelmed her. In his changed tone she seemed to hear the murderer speaking. She looked at him bewildered. She knew nothing as yet, why, how, with what aim the crime had been committed. Now all these questions rushed at once into her mind. And again she could not believe it: "He, he is a murderer! Could it be true?"

"What's the meaning of it? Where am I?" she asked in complete bewilderment, as though still unable to recover herself. "How could you, you, a man like you . . . How could you bring yourself to it? . . . What does it mean?"

"To plunder, perhaps? Leave off, Sonia," he answered wearily, almost with vexation.

Sonia stood as though she had been struck dumb, but suddenly she cried:

"You were hungry! It was . . . to help your mother? Yes?"

"No, Sonia, no," he muttered, turning away and hanging his head. "I was not as hungry as that . . . I certainly did want to help my mother, but . . . that's not the real reason either . . . Don't torture me, Sonia."

Sonia clasped her hands.

"Could it, could it all be true? Good God, what a truth! Who could believe it? And how could you give away your last penny and still rob and murder! Ah," she cried suddenly, "that money you gave Katerina Ivanovna . . . that money . . . Can that money . . . "

"No, Sonia," he broke in hurriedly, "that money was not it. Don't worry yourself! That money my mother sent me and it came when I was ill, the day I gave it to you . . . Razumikhin saw it . . . he took it for me . . . That money was mine—my own."

Sonia listened to him in bewilderment and did her utmost to understand him.

"And that money . . . I don't even really know whether there was any money," he added softly, as though reflecting. "I took a purse off her neck, made of chamois leather . . . a purse stuffed full of something . . . but I didn't look in it; I suppose I didn't have time . . . And the things—chains and trinkets—I buried under a stone with the purse next morning in a yard off the V____ Prospect. They are all there now . . . "

Sonia strained every nerve to listen.

"Then why . . . why, you said you did it to rob, but you took nothing?" she asked quickly, catching at a straw.

"I don't know . . . I haven't yet decided whether to take that money or not," he said, musing again; and, seeming to wake up with a start, he gave a brief ironic smile. "Ah, what nonsense I'm talking, eh?"

The thought flashed through Sonia's mind: wasn't he mad? But she dismissed it at once. "No, it was something else." She could make nothing of it, nothing.

"Do you know, Sonia," he said suddenly with conviction, "let me tell you something: if I'd simply killed someone because I was hungry," laying stress on every word and looking enigmatically but sincerely at her, "I would be happy now. You must believe that! What would it matter to you," he cried a moment later with a sort of despair, "what would it matter to you if I were to confess that I did wrong! What do you gain by such a stupid triumph over me? Ah, Sonia, was it for that I've come to you today?"

Again Sonia tried to say something, but did not speak.

"I asked you to go with me yesterday because you are all I have left."

"Go where?" asked Sonia timidly.

"Not to steal and not to murder, don't be anxious," he smiled bitterly. "We are so different . . . And you know, Sonia, it's only now, only at this moment that I understand where I asked you to go with me yesterday! Yesterday when I said it I did not know where. I asked you for one thing, I came to you for one thing—not to leave me. You won't leave me, Sonia?"

She squeezed his hand.

"And why, why did I tell her? Why did I let her know?" he cried a minute later in despair, looking with infinite anguish at her. "Here you expect an explanation from me, Sonia; you are sitting and waiting for it, I can see that. But what can I tell you? You won't understand and will only suffer misery . . . on my account! Well, you are crying and embracing me again. Why do you do it? Because I couldn't bear my burden and have come to throw it on another: you suffer too, and I shall feel better! And can you love such a mean wretch?"

"But aren't you suffering, too?" cried Sonia.

Again a wave of the same feeling surged into his heart, and again for an instant softened it.

"Sonia, I have a bad heart, take note of that. It may explain a great deal. I have come because I am bad. There are people who wouldn't have come. But I am a coward and . . . an evil wretch. But . . . never mind! That's not the point. I must speak now, but I don't know how to begin."

He paused and sank into thought.

"Ah, we are so different," he cried again, "we are not alike. And why, why did I come? I shall never forgive myself for that."

"No, no, it was a good thing you came," cried Sonia. "It's better I should know, far better!"

He looked at her with anguish.

"What if it were really that?" he said, as though reaching a conclusion. "Yes, that's what it was! I wanted to become a Napoleon, that is why I killed her . . . Do you understand now?"

"N-no," Sonia whispered naively and timidly. "Just tell me, tell me, I shall understand, I shall understand it myself!" she kept begging him.

"You'll understand? Very well, we shall see!" He paused and was for some time lost in meditation.

"It was like this: I asked myself this question one day—what if Napoleon, for instance, had happened to be in my place, and if he had not had Toulon or Egypt or the passage of Mont Blanc to start his career, but instead of all those picturesque and monumental things, there had simply been some ridiculous old hag, a pawnbroker, who had to be murdered too to get money from her trunk (for his career, you understand). Well, would he have brought himself to that, if there had been no other means? Wouldn't he have felt a pang at its being so far from monumental and . . . and sinful, too? Well, I must tell you that I worried myself so terribly over that 'question' that I was extremely ashamed when I guessed at last (all of a sudden, somehow) that it would not have given him the least pang, that it would not even have struck him that it was not monumental . . . that he would not have seen that there was anything in it to pause over, and that, if he had had no other way, he would have strangled her in a minute without thinking about it! Well, I too . . . left off thinking about it . . . murdered her, following his example. And that's exactly how it was! Do you think it's funny? Yes, Sonia, the funniest thing of all is that perhaps that's just how it was."

Sonia did not think it at all funny.

"You had better tell me straight out . . . without examples," she begged, even more timidly and scarcely audibly.

He turned to her, looked sadly at her and took her hands.

"You are right again, Sonia. Of course that's all nonsense, it's almost all just talk! You see, you know of course that my mother has scarcely anything, my sister happened to have a good education and

was condemned to slave away as a governess. All their hopes were centered on me. I was a student, but I couldn't keep myself at the university and was forced for a time to leave it. Even if I had lingered on like
that, in ten or twelve years I might (with luck) hope to be some sort
of teacher or clerk with a salary of a thousand rubles" (he repeated it
as though it were a lesson) "and by that time my mother would be
worn out with grief and anxiety and I could not succeed in keeping
her in comfort while my sister . . . well, my sister might well have
fared worse! And it's a hard thing to pass everything by all your life,
to turn your back upon everything, to forget your mother and politely
accept the insults inflicted on your sister. Why should you? When you
have buried them to burden yourself with others—wife and children—and to leave them again without a penny? So I resolved to gain
possession of the old woman's money and to use it for my first years
without worrying my mother, to keep myself at the university and for
a little while after leaving it—and to do this all on a broad, thorough
scale, so as to build up a completely new career and enter upon a new
life of independence . . . Well . . . that's all . . . Well, of course in killing
the old woman I did wrong . . . Well, that's enough."

He struggled to the end of his speech in exhaustion and let his
head sink.

"Oh, that's not it, that's not it," Sonia cried in distress. "How
could one . . . no, that's not right, not right."

"You see yourself that it's not right. But I've spoken truly, it's the
truth."

"As though that could be the truth! Good God!"

"I've only killed a louse, Sonia, a useless, loathsome, harmful
creature."

"A human being—a louse!"

"I know too that it wasn't a louse," he answered, looking
strangely at her. "But I am talking nonsense, Sonia," he added. "I've
been talking nonsense for a long time . . . That's not it, you are right
there. There were quite, quite different causes for it! I haven't talked
to anyone for so long, Sonia . . . My head aches dreadfully now."

His eyes shone with feverish brilliance. He was almost delirious;
an uneasy smile strayed on his lips. His terrible exhaustion could be
seen through his excitement. Sonia saw how he was suffering. She too
was growing dizzy. And he talked so strangely; it seemed somehow

comprehensible, but yet . . . "But how, how! Good God!" And she wrung her hands in despair.

"No, Sonia, that's not it," he began again suddenly, raising his head, as though a new and sudden train of thought had struck and as it were roused him—"that's not it! Better . . . imagine—yes, it's certainly better—imagine that I am vain, envious, malicious, base, vindictive and . . . well, perhaps with a tendency to insanity. (Let's have it all out at once! They've talked of madness already, I noticed.) I told you just now I could not keep myself at the university. But do you know that perhaps I might have done? My mother would have sent me what I needed for the fees and I could have earned enough for clothes, boots and food, no doubt. Lessons had turned up at half a ruble. Razumikhin works! But I turned sulky and wouldn't. (Yes, sulkiness, that's the right word for it!) I sat in my room like a spider. You've been in my den, you've seen it . . . And do you know, Sonia, that low ceilings and tiny rooms cramp the soul and the mind? Ah, how I hated that closet! And yet I wouldn't leave it! I wouldn't on purpose! I didn't go out for days on end, and I wouldn't work, I wouldn't even eat, I just lay there doing nothing. If Nastasia brought me anything, I ate it, if she didn't, I went all day without food; I wouldn't ask, on purpose, because of my sulkiness! At night I had no light, I lay in the dark and I wouldn't earn money for candles. I ought to have studied, but I sold my books; and the dust is lying an inch thick on the notebooks on my table. I preferred lying still and thinking. And I kept thinking . . . And I had dreams all the time, strange dreams of all sorts, no need to describe them! Only then I began to imagine that . . . No, that's not it! Again I'm getting it wrong! You see, I kept asking myself then: why am I so stupid that if others are stupid—and I know they are—I still won't be any wiser? Then I saw, Sonia, that if you wait for everyone to get wiser it'll take too long . . . Afterwards I understood that that would never happen, that people won't change and that nobody can alter it and that it's not worth wasting effort over it. Yes, that's true. That's the law of their nature, Sonia . . . that's true! . . . And I know now, Sonia, that whoever is strong in mind and spirit will have power over them. Anyone who is very daring is right in their eyes. He who despises most things will be a lawgiver among them and he who dares most of all will be most in the right! That's how it has been until now and that's how it will always be. A person has to be blind not to see it!"

Though Raskolnikov looked at Sonia as he said this, he no longer cared whether she understood or not. The fever had complete hold of him; he was in a sort of gloomy ecstasy (he certainly had gone too long without talking to anyone). Sonia felt that his gloomy creed had become his faith and code.

"Then I understood, Sonia," he went on eagerly, "that power is only entrusted to the person who dares to bend down and pick it up. There is only one thing, one thing which is required: you just have to dare! Then for the first time in my life an idea took shape in my mind which no-one had ever thought of before me, no-one! I saw clear as day how strange it is that not a single person living in this mad world has had the daring to go straight for it all and send it flying to the devil! I . . . I wanted to have the daring . . . and I killed her. I only wanted to have the daring, Sonia! That was the whole cause of it!"

"Oh hush, hush," cried Sonia, clasping her hands. "You turned away from God and God has smitten you, has given you over to the devil!"

"Then Sonia, when I used to lie there in the dark and all this became clear to me, was it a temptation of the devil, eh?"

"Hush, don't laugh, you blasphemer! You don't understand, you don't understand! Oh God! He won't understand!"

"Hush, Sonia! I am not laughing. I know myself that it was the devil leading me. Hush, Sonia, hush!" he repeated with gloomy insistence. "I know it all, I have thought it all over and over and whispered it all over to myself, lying there in the dark . . . I've argued it all over with myself, every point of it, and I know it all, all! And how sick, how sick I was then of going over it all! I've kept wanting to forget it and make a fresh start, Sonia, and leave off thinking. And you don't suppose that I went into it headlong like a fool? I went into it like a wise man, and that was just my destruction. And you mustn't think I didn't know, for instance, that if I began to question myself as to whether I had the right to gain power—I certainly didn't have the right—or that, if I asked myself whether a human being is a louse, it proved that it wasn't true for me, though it might be for a man who would go straight to his goal without asking ques-

tions . . . If I worried myself all day long, wondering whether
Napoleon would have done it or not, I felt clearly of course that I
wasn't Napoleon. I had to endure all the agony of that battle of ideas,
Sonia, and I longed to throw it off: I wanted to murder without casuistry, to murder for my own sake, for myself alone! I didn't want
to lie about it even to myself. It wasn't to help my mother I did the
murder—that's nonsense—I didn't do the murder to gain wealth
and power and to become a benefactor of mankind. Nonsense! I just
did it; I did the murder for myself, for myself alone, and whether I
became a benefactor to others, or spent my life like a spider catching
men in my web and sucking the life out of men, I couldn't have cared
at that moment . . . And it was not the money I wanted, Sonia, when
I did it. It was not so much the money I wanted, but something else
. . . I know it all now . . . Understand me! Perhaps I should never have
committed a murder again. I wanted to find out something else; it
was something else which led me on. I wanted to find out then and
there whether I was a louse like everybody else or a man. Whether I
can overstep barriers or not, whether I dare bend down to pick up or
not, whether I am a trembling creature or whether I have the
right . . . "

"To kill? Have the right to kill?" Sonia clasped her hands.

"Ah, Sonia!" he cried irritably and seemed about to make some
retort, but was contemptuously silent. "Don't interrupt me, Sonia. I
want to prove one thing only, that the devil led me on then and he
has shown me since that I did not have the right to take that path, because I am just a louse like all the rest. He was mocking me and, look,
I've come to you now! Welcome your guest! If I weren't a louse,
would I have come to you? Listen: when I went then to the old
woman's I only went to try . . . You may be sure of that!"

"And you murdered her!"

"But how did I murder her? Is that how men do murders? Do
men go to commit a murder as I went then? I'll tell you some day
how I went! Did I murder the old woman? I murdered myself, not
her! I crushed myself once and for all, forever . . . But it was the devil
that killed that old woman, not I. Enough, enough, Sonia, enough!
Let me be!" he cried in a sudden spasm of agony, "let me be!"

He leaned his elbows on his knees and squeezed his head in his
hands as if in a vice.

"What suffering!" A wail of anguish broke from Sonia.

"Well, what should I do now?" he asked, suddenly raising his head and looking at her with a face hideously distorted by despair.

"What should you do?" she cried, jumping up, and her eyes that had been full of tears suddenly began to shine. "Stand up!" (She seized him by the shoulder, he got up, looking at her almost bewildered.) "Go at once, this minute, stand at the crossroads, bow down, first kiss the earth which you have defiled and then bow down to all the world and say to all men aloud, 'I am a murderer!' Then God will send you life again. Will you go, will you go?" she asked him, trembling all over, snatching his two hands, squeezing them tight in hers and gazing at him with eyes full of fire.

He was amazed at her sudden ecstasy.

"You mean Siberia, Sonia? I must give myself up?" he asked gloomily.

"Suffer and atone for your sin by it, that's what you must do."

"No! I am not going to them, Sonia!"

"But how will you go on living? What will you live for?" cried Sonia, "how is it possible now? Why, how can you talk to your mother? (Oh, what will become of them now!) But what am I saying? You have abandoned your mother and your sister already. He has abandoned them already! Oh, God!" she cried, "why, he knows it all himself. How, how can he live by himself! What will become of you now?"

"Don't be a child, Sonia," he said softly. "What wrong have I done them? Why should I go to them? What should I say to them? That's only a phantom . . . They destroy millions themselves and look on it as a virtue. They are crooks and scoundrels, Sonia! I am not going to them. And what should I say to them—that I murdered her, but did not dare to take the money and hid it under a stone?" he added with a bitter smile. "They would laugh at me, and would call me a fool for not getting it. A coward and a fool! They wouldn't understand and they don't deserve to understand. Why should I go to them? I won't. Don't be a child, Sonia . . . "

"It will be too much for you to bear, too much!" she repeated, holding out her hands in despairing supplication.

"Perhaps I've been unfair to myself," he observed gloomily, pondering, "perhaps after all I am a man and not a louse and I've been in too great a hurry to condemn myself. I'll make another fight for it."

A haughty smile appeared on his lips.

"What a burden to bear! And your whole life, your whole life!"

"I shall get used to it," he said grimly and thoughtfully. "Listen," he began a minute later, "stop crying, it's time to discuss the facts: I've come to tell you that the police are after me, on my trail . . . "

"Ah!" Sonia cried in terror.

"Well, why are you upset? You want me to go to Siberia and now you are frightened? But let me tell you: I shan't give myself up. I shall make a struggle for it and they won't do anything to me. They've no real evidence. Yesterday I was in great danger and believed I was lost; but today things are going better. All the facts they know can be explained two ways, that's to say I can turn their accusations to my credit, do you understand? And I shall, for I've learnt my lesson. But they will certainly arrest me. If it had not been for something that happened, they would have done so today for certain; perhaps even now they will arrest me today . . . But it doesn't matter, Sonia; they'll let me out again . . . because there isn't any real proof against me, and there won't be, I give you my word for it. And they can't convict a man on what they have against me. Enough . . . I only tell you that you may know . . . I will try to manage somehow to put it to my mother and sister so that they won't be frightened . . . My sister's future is secure, however, now, I believe . . . and my mother's must be too . . . Well, that's all. Be careful, though. Will you come and see me in prison when I am there?"

"Oh, I will, I will."

They sat side by side, both mournful and dejected, as though they had been cast up by the tempest alone on some deserted shore. He looked at Sonia and felt how great her love was for him, and strange to say he felt it suddenly burdensome and painful to be loved so much. Yes, it was a strange and awful sensation! On his way to see Sonia he had felt that all his hopes rested on her; he expected to be rid of at least part of his suffering, and now, when all her heart turned towards him, he suddenly felt that he was immeasurably unhappier than before.

"Sonia," he said, "you'd better not come and see me when I am in prison."

Sonia did not answer; she was crying. Several minutes passed.

"Do you have you a cross on you?" she asked, as though she was suddenly thinking of it.

He did not at first understand the question.

"No, of course not. Here, take this one, of cypress wood. I have another, a copper one that belonged to Lizaveta. I changed with Lizaveta: she gave me her cross and I gave her my little icon. I will wear Lizaveta's now and give you this. Take it . . . it's mine! It's mine, you know," she begged him. "We will go to suffer together, and together we will bear our cross!"

"Give it to me," said Raskolnikov.

He did not want to hurt her feelings. But immediately he drew back the hand he held out for the cross.

"Not now, Sonia. Better later," he added to comfort her.

"Yes, yes, better," she repeated with conviction, "when you go to meet your suffering, then put it on. You will come to me, I'll put it on you, we will pray and go together."

At that moment someone knocked three times at the door.

"Sofia Semionovna, may I come in?" they heard in a very familiar and polite voice.

Sonia rushed to the door in a fright. The flaxen head of Mr. Lebeziatnikov appeared at the door.

CHAPTER FIVE

Lebeziatnikov looked anxious.

"I've come to you, Sofia Semionovna," he began. "Excuse me . . . I thought I would find you," he said, addressing Raskolnikov suddenly, "that is, I didn't mean anything . . . of that sort . . . But I just thought . . . Katerina Ivanovna has gone out of her mind," he blurted out suddenly, turning from Raskolnikov to Sonia.

Sonia screamed.

"At least it seems so. But . . . we don't know what to do, you see! She came back—she seems to have been turned out somewhere, perhaps even beaten . . . So it seems at least, . . . She had run to your father's former boss, she didn't find him at home: he was dining at some other general's . . . Only imagine this, she rushed off there, to the other general's, and she was so persistent that she managed to get the chief to see her, had him fetched out in the middle of his dinner, it seems. You can imagine what happened. She was turned out, of course; but, according to her own story, she abused him and threw something at him. You could well believe it . . . How she wasn't arrested, I can't understand! Now she's telling everyone, including Amalia Ivanovna; but it's difficult to understand her, she is screaming and flinging herself about . . . Oh yes, she is shouting that since everyone has abandoned her, she will take the children and go into the street with a barrel-organ, and the children will sing and dance, and she too, and collect money, and will go every day under the general's window . . . 'to let everyone see well-born children, whose father was an official, begging in the street.' She keeps beating the children and they are all crying. She is teaching Lida to sing 'My Village,' the boy to dance, Polenka the same. She is tearing up all the clothes, and making them little caps like actors; she intends to carry a tin basin and make it tinkle, instead of music . . . She won't listen to anything . . . Imagine the state of things! It's beyond anything!"

Lebeziatnikov would have gone on, but Sonia, who had heard him almost breathless, snatched up her cloak and hat, and ran out of the room, putting on her things as she went. Raskolnikov followed her and Lebeziatnikov came after him.

"She's gone mad for sure!" he said to Raskolnikov, as they went out into the street. "I didn't want to frighten Sofia Semionovna, so I said 'it seemed like it,' but there isn't a doubt. They say that in tuberculosis, the tubercles sometimes occur in the brain; it's a pity I know nothing about medicine. I did try to persuade her, but she wouldn't listen."

"Did you talk to her about the tubercles?"

"Not precisely. Besides, she wouldn't have understood! But what I say is that if you convince a person logically that they have nothing to cry about, they'll stop crying. That's clear. Is it your conviction that they won't?"

"Life would be too easy if that were so," answered Raskolnikov.

"Excuse me, excuse me; of course it would be rather difficult for Katerina Ivanovna to understand, but do you know that in Paris they have been conducting serious experiments as to the possibility of curing the insane, simply by logical argument? One professor there, a scientific man of standing who died recently, believed in the possibility of such treatment. His idea was that there's nothing really wrong with the physical organism of the insane, and that insanity is, so to say, a logical mistake, an error of judgment, an incorrect view of things. He gradually showed the madman his error and, would you believe it, they say he was successful? But as he made use of douches too; how far his success was due to that treatment remains uncertain . . . So it seems, at least."

Raskolnikov had stopped listening long ago. Reaching the house where he lived, he nodded to Lebeziatnikov and went in at the gate. Lebeziatnikov woke up with a start, looked around him and hurried on.

Raskolnikov went into his little room and stood still in the middle of it. Why had he come back here? He looked at the yellow, tattered paper, at the dust, at his sofa . . . From the yard came a loud continuous knocking; someone seemed to be hammering . . . He went to the window, rose on tiptoe and looked out into the yard for a long time with an air of absorbed attention. But the yard was empty and he could not see who was hammering. In the house on the left he saw some open windows; on the window-sills were pots of sickly-looking geraniums. Linen was hanging out of the windows . . . He knew it all by heart. He turned away and sat down on the sofa.

Never, never had he felt so terribly alone!

Yes, he felt once more that he would perhaps come to hate Sonia, now that he had made her more miserable.

"Why had he gone to her to beg for her tears? What need had he to poison her life? Oh, the meanness of it!"

"I'll remain alone," he said resolutely, "and she won't come to the prison!"

Five minutes later he raised his head with a strange smile. That was a strange thought.

"Perhaps it really would be better in Siberia," he thought suddenly.

He could not have said how long he sat there with vague thoughts surging through his mind. All at once the door opened and Dunia came in. At first she stood still and looked at him from the doorway, just as he had done at Sonia; then she came in and sat down in the same place as yesterday, on the chair facing him. He looked silently and almost vacantly at her.

"Don't be angry, brother; I've only come for a minute," said Dunia.

Her face looked thoughtful but not stern. Her eyes were bright and soft. He saw that she too had come to him with love.

"Rodia, now I know everything, everything. Dmitri Prokofich has explained and told me about all of it. They are worrying and persecuting you with a stupid and contemptible suspicion . . . Dmitri Prokofich told me that there is no danger, and that you are wrong in looking at it with such horror. I don't think so, and I fully understand how indignant you must be, and that that indignation may have a permanent effect on you. That's what I am afraid of. As for your proposal to cut yourself off from us, I'm not judging you, I'm not going to judge you, and forgive me for having blamed you for it. I feel that, if I had a difficulty as great as that, I too would keep away from everyone. I shall tell mother nothing of this, but I shall talk about you continually and shall tell her from you that you will come very soon. Don't worry about her; I will set her mind at rest; but don't you try her too much—come once at least; remember that she is your mother. And now I have come simply to say" (Dunia began to get up) "that if you should need me or should need . . . all my life or anything . . . call me, and I'll come. Goodbye!"

She turned abruptly and went towards the door.

"Dunia!" Raskolnikov stopped her and went towards her. "That Razumikhin, Dmitri Prokofich, is a very good person."

Dunia flushed slightly.

"Well?" she asked, waiting a moment.

"He is competent, hardworking, honest and capable of real love . . . Goodbye, Dunia."

Dunia flushed crimson, then suddenly became alarmed.

"But what does that mean, Rodia? Are we really parting for ever so you . . . can give me such a parting message?"

"Never mind . . . Goodbye."

He turned away, and walked to the window. She stood for a moment, looked at him uneasily, and went out troubled.

No, he was not cold to her. There was an instant (the very last one) when he had longed to take her in his arms and say goodbye to her, and even to tell her, but he had not dared even to touch her hand.

"Afterwards she may shudder when she remembers that I embraced her, and will feel that I stole her kiss."

"And would she stand that test?" he went on a few minutes later to himself. "No, she wouldn't; girls like that can't stand things! They never do."

And he thought of Sonia.

There was a breath of fresh air from the window. The daylight was fading. He took up his cap and went out.

He could not, of course, and would not consider how ill he was. But all this continual anxiety and agony of mind could not but affect him. And if he were not lying in high fever it was perhaps just because this continual inner strain helped to keep him on his legs and in possession of his faculties. But this artificial excitement could not last long.

He wandered aimlessly. The sun was setting. A special form of misery had begun to oppress him recently. There was nothing poignant, nothing acute about it; but there was a feeling of permanence, of eternity about it; it brought a foretaste of hopeless years of this cold leaden misery, a foretaste of an eternity "on a square yard of space." Towards evening this sensation usually began to weigh on him more heavily.

"With this idiotic, purely physical weakness, depending on the sunset or something, you can't help doing something stupid! You'll go to Dunia's, as well as Sonia's," he muttered bitterly.

He heard his name called. He looked round. Lebeziatnikov rushed up to him.

"Just imagine, I've been to your room looking for you. Imagine, she's carried out her plan and taken away the children. Sofia Semionovna and I have had a difficult time finding them. She is rapping on a frying-pan and making the children dance. The children are crying. They keep stopping at the crossroads and in front of the stores; there's a crowd of fools running after them. Come along!"

"And Sonia?" Raskolnikov asked anxiously, hurrying after Lebeziatnikov.

"Just frantic. That is, it's not Sofia Semionovna who's frantic, but Katerina Ivanovna, though Sofia Semionovna's frantic too. But Katerina Ivanovna is absolutely frantic. I'm telling you, she's completely mad. They'll be taken to the police. You can imagine what an effect that'll have . . . They are on the canal bank, near the bridge now, not far from Sofia Semionovna's, quite close."

On the canal bank near the bridge and not even two houses away from the one where Sonia lodged, there was a crowd of people, consisting principally of street urchins. The hoarse broken voice of Katerina Ivanovna could be heard from the bridge, and it certainly was a strange spectacle likely to attract a street crowd. Katerina Ivanovna in her old dress with the green shawl, wearing a torn straw hat, crushed in a hideous way on one side, was really frantic. She was exhausted and breathless. Her wasted tubercular face looked more long-suffering than ever, and in fact out of doors in the sunshine a tubercular person always looks worse than at home. But her excitement did not flag, and every moment her irritation grew more intense. She rushed at the children, shouted at them, coaxed them, told them in front of the crowd how to dance and what to sing, began explaining to them why it was necessary and, driven to desperation by their lack of understanding, beat them . . . Then she would make a rush at the crowd; if she noticed any decently dressed person stopping to look, she immediately appealed to them to see what these children "from a genteel, one may say aristocratic, house" had been brought to. If she heard laughter or jeering in the crowd, she would rush at once at the scoffers and begin squabbling with them. Some people laughed, others shook their heads, but everyone felt curious at the sight of the madwoman with the frightened children. The frying-pan which Lebeziatnikov had mentioned was not there; at least, Raskolnikov did not see it. But instead of rapping on the pan, Katerina Ivanovna began clapping her wasted hands, when she made Lida and Kolia dance and Polenka sing. She too joined in the singing, but broke down at the second note with a terrible cough, which made her curse in despair and even shed tears. What made her most furious was the weeping and terror of Kolia and Lida. Some effort had been made to dress the children up as street singers are dressed. The boy had on a turban made of something red and white to make him look like a Turk. There had been no costume for Lida; she just had a red knitted cap, or rather a night cap that had belonged to Marmeladov, decorated with a broken piece of white ostrich feather, which had been Katerina Ivanovna's grandmother's and had been preserved as a family possession. Polenka was in her everyday dress; she looked in timid perplexity at her mother, and kept at her side, hiding her tears. She dimly realized her mother's condition, and looked uneasily about her. She was extremely frightened of the street and the crowd. Sonia followed Katerina Ivanovna, weeping and beseeching her to return home, but Katerina Ivanovna was not to be persuaded.

"Leave off, Sonia, leave off," she shouted, speaking fast, panting and coughing. "You don't know what you're asking me to do; you're like a child! I've told you before that I am not going back to that drunken German. Let everyone, let all of Petersburg see the children begging in the streets, though their father was an honorable man who served all his life in truth and fidelity and, you might say, died in service." (Katerina Ivanovna had by now invented this fantastic story and thoroughly believed it.) "Let that wretch of a general see it! And, Sonia, you're being silly: what do we have to eat? Tell me that. We have worried you enough, I won't go on! Ah, Rodion Romanovich, is that you?" she cried, seeing Raskolnikov and rushing up to him. "Explain to this silly girl, please, that nothing better could be done! Even organ-grinders earn their living, and everyone will see at once that we are different, that we are an honorable and bereaved family reduced to beggary. And that general will lose his post, you'll see! We shall perform under his windows every day, and if the Tsar drives by, I'll fall on my knees, put the children before me, show them to him, and say 'Defend us, father.' He is the father of the fatherless, he is merciful, he'll protect us, you'll see, and that wretch of a general . . . Lida, *tenez-vous droite!** Kolia, you'll be dancing again. Why are you whimpering? Whimpering again! What are you afraid of, stupid? Goodness, what should I do with them, Rodion Romanovich? If you only knew how stupid they are! What can you do with such children?"

And she, almost crying herself—which did not stop her uninterrupted, rapid flow of talk—pointed to the crying children. Raskolnikov tried to persuade her to go home and even said, hoping to work on her vanity, that it was unseemly for her to be wandering about the streets like an organ-grinder, as she was intending to become the principal of a boarding-school.

"A boarding-school, ha-ha-ha! A castle in the air," cried Katerina

---

*Stand up straight (French)!

Ivanovna, her laugh ending in a cough. "No, Rodion Romanovich, that dream is over! Everyone has abandoned us! . . . And that general . . . You know, Rodion Romanovich, I threw an ink spot at him—it happened to be standing in the waiting-room by the paper where you sign your name. I wrote my name, threw it at him and ran away. Oh the scoundrels, the scoundrels! But enough of them, now I'll provide for the children myself, I won't bow down to anybody! She has had to bear enough for us!" she pointed to Sonia. "Polenka, how much have you got? Show me! What, only two farthings! Oh, the mean wretches! They give us nothing, only run after us, putting their tongues out. There, what is that blockhead laughing at?" (She pointed to a man in the crowd.) "It's all because Kolia here is so stupid; I have such problems with him. What do you want, Polenka? Tell me in French, *parlez-moi français*.* But I've taught you, you know some phrases. How else are you going to show that you are from a good family, that you're well-bred children, and not at all like other organ-grinders? We aren't going to have a Punch and Judy show in the street, we're going to sing a genteel song . . . Ah, yes, . . . What are we going to sing? You keep putting me out, but we . . . you see, we are standing here, Rodion Romanovich, to find something to sing and get money, something Kolia can dance to . . . Because, as you can imagine, our performance is all improvised . . . We must talk it over and rehearse it all thoroughly, and then we shall go to Nevsky, where there are far more people from fine society, and we shall be noticed at once. Lida only knows 'My Village,' nothing apart from 'My Village,' and everyone sings that. We must sing something far more genteel . . . Well, have you thought of anything, Polenka? If only you'd help your mother! My memory's completely gone, or I would have thought of something. We really can't sing 'An Hussar.' Ah, let's sing in French, '*Cinq sous*,'† I have taught it to you, I have taught it you. And as it is in French, people will see at once that you are children from a good family, and that will be much more touching . . . You might sing '*Marlborough s'en va-t-en guerre*,'§ for that's quite a child's song and is sung as a lullaby in all the aristocratic houses.—

---

*Talk to me in French (French).

†Five pennies (French).

§"Marlborough is off to war" (French)-a popular song. In 1704 the first Duke of Marlborough, John Churchill, defeated the French at the Battle of Blenheim.

Marlborough s'en va-t-en guerre
Ne sait quand reviendra . . . "—*

she began singing. "But no, better sing 'Cinq sous.' Now, Kolia, your hands on your hips, make haste, and you, Lida, keep turning the other way, and Polenka and I will sing and clap our hands!—

Cinq sous, cinq sous
Pour monter notre ménage.—†

(Cough-cough-cough!) Put your dress straight, Polenka, it's slipped down on your shoulders," she observed, panting from coughing. "Now it's particularly necessary to behave nicely and genteelly, so that everyone will see that you are well-born children. I said at the time that the bodice should be cut longer, and made of two widths. It was your fault, Sonia, with your advice to make it shorter, and now you see the child is seriously deformed by it . . . Why, you're all crying again! What's the matter, stupids? Come, Kolia, begin. Hurry up, hurry up! Oh, what an unbearable child!—

Cinq sous, cinq sous.—

A policeman again! What do you want?"

A policeman was indeed forcing his way through the crowd. But at that moment a gentleman in civilian uniform and an overcoat—a solid-looking official of about fifty with a decoration on his neck (which delighted Katerina Ivanovna and had its effect on the policeman)—approached and wordlessly handed her a green three-ruble note. His face wore a look of genuine sympathy. Katerina Ivanovna took it and gave him a polite, even ceremonious, bow.

"I thank you, honored sir," she began loftily. "The causes that have induced us (take the money, Polenka: you see there are generous and honorable people who are ready to help a poor gentlewoman in distress). You see, honored sir, these orphans of good family—I might even say of aristocratic connections—and that wretch of a gen-

---

*Doesn't know when he'll be back (French).
†To repair our house (French).

eral sat eating grouse . . . and stamped at my disturbing him. 'Your excellency,' I said, 'protect the orphans: you knew my late husband, Semion Zakharovich, and on the very day of his death the basest of scoundrels slandered his only daughter.' . . . That policeman again! Protect me," she cried to the official. "Why is that policeman edging up to me? We have only just run away from one of them. What do you want, fool?"

"It's forbidden in the streets. You mustn't make a disturbance."

"It's you who are making a disturbance. It's just as if I were grinding an organ. What business is it of yours?"

"You have to get a license for an organ, and you haven't got one, and that way you collect a crowd. Where do you live?"

"What, a license?" wailed Katerina Ivanovna. "I buried my husband today. Why do I need a license?"

"Calm yourself, madam, calm yourself," began the official. "Come along; I will escort you . . . This is no place for you in the crowd. You are ill."

"Honored sir, honored sir, you don't know," screamed Katerina Ivanovna. "We are going to the Nevsky . . . Sonia, Sonia! Where is she? She is crying too! What's the matter with you all? Kolia, Lida, where are you going?" she cried suddenly in alarm. "Oh, silly children! Kolia, Lida, where are they off to? . . . "

Kolia and Lida, scared out of their wits by the crowd, and their mother's mad pranks, suddenly seized each other by the hand, and ran off at the sight of the policeman who wanted to take them away somewhere. Weeping and wailing, poor Katerina Ivanovna ran after them. She was a pitiful and indecent spectacle when she ran, weeping and panting for breath. Sonia and Polenka rushed after them.

"Bring them back, bring them back, Sonia! Oh stupid, ungrateful children! . . . Polenka! catch them . . . It's for your sakes I . . . "

She stumbled as she ran and fell down.

"She's cut herself, she's bleeding! Oh, dear!" cried Sonia, bending over her.

All ran up and crowded round. Raskolnikov and Lebeziatnikov were the first at her side, the official too hastened up, and behind him the policeman who muttered, "Bother!" with a gesture of impatience, feeling that the job was going to be a troublesome one.

"Pass on! Pass on!" he said to the crowd that pressed forward.

"She's dying," someone shouted.

"She's gone out of her mind," said another.

"Lord have mercy on us," said a woman, crossing herself. "Have they caught the little girl and the boy? They're being brought back, the elder one's got them . . . Ah, the wicked little things!"

When they examined Katerina Ivanovna carefully, they saw that she had not cut herself against a stone, as Sonia thought, but that the blood that stained the pavement red was from her chest.

"I've seen that before," muttered the official to Raskolnikov and Lebeziatnikov; "that's tuberculosis; the blood flows and chokes the patient. I saw the same thing with a relative of my own not long ago . . . nearly a pint of blood, all in a minute . . . What's to be done though? She is dying."

"This way, this way, to my room!" Sonia implored. "I live here! . . . See, that house, the second from here . . . Come to me, make haste," she turned from one to the other. "Send for the doctor! Oh, dear!"

Thanks to the official's efforts, this plan was adopted, the policeman even helping to carry Katerina Ivanovna. She was carried to Sonia's room, almost unconscious, and laid on the bed. The blood was still flowing, but she seemed to be coming round. Raskolnikov, Lebeziatnikov, and the official accompanied Sonia into the room and were followed by the policeman, who first drove back the crowd which followed right up to the door. Polenka came in holding Kolia and Lida, who were trembling and weeping. Several people came in too from the Kapernaumovs' room; the landlord, a lame one-eyed man of strange appearance with whiskers and hair that stood up like a brush, his wife, a woman with a constantly scared expression, and several open-mouthed children with wonder-struck faces. Among these, Svidrigailov suddenly made his appearance. Raskolnikov looked at him with surprise, not understanding where he had come from and not having noticed him in the crowd. A doctor and priest wore spoken of. The official whispered to Raskolnikov that he thought it was too late now for the doctor, but he ordered him to be sent for. Kapernaumov ran himself.

Meanwhile Katerina Ivanovna had regained her breath. The bleeding ceased for a time. She looked with sick but intent and penetrating eyes at Sonia, who stood pale and trembling, wiping the sweat from her brow with a handkerchief. At last she asked to be raised. They sat her up on the bed, supporting her on both sides.

"Where are the children?" she said in a faint voice. "You've brought them, Polenka? Oh the silly idiots! Why did you run away . . . Oh!"

Once more her parched lips were covered with blood. She moved her eyes, looking around her.

"So that's how you live, Sonia! Never once have I been in your room." She looked at her with a face of suffering.

"We have been your ruin, Sonia. Polenka, Lida, Kolia, come here! Well, here they are, Sonia, take them all! I hand them over to you, I've had enough! The ball is over. (Cough!) Lay me down, let me die in peace."

They laid her back on the pillow.

"What, the priest? I don't want him. You haven't got a ruble to spare. I have no sins. God must forgive me without that. He knows how I have suffered . . . And if He won't forgive me, I don't care!"

She sank more and more into uneasy delirium. At times she shuddered, turned her eyes from side to side, recognized everyone for a minute, but at once sank into delirium again. Her breathing was hoarse and difficult, and there was a sort of a rattle in her throat.

"I said to him, your excellency," she forced out, gasping after each word. "That Amalia Ludwigovna, ah! Lida, Kolia, hands on your hips, hurry up! *Glissez, glissez!** Pas de basque! Tap with your heels, be a graceful child!—

> Du hast Diamanten und Perlen—[†]

"What next? That's what we should sing.—

> Du hast die schönsten Augen
> Mädchen, was willst du mehr?—[§]

"What an idea! *Was willst du mehr.* What things the fool invents! Ah, yes!—

> In the heat of midday in the vale of Dagestan.—

---

*Slide into it, slide into it! (French).
†You have diamonds and pearls (German).
§You have the most beautiful eyes. / My girl, what more do you want? (German).

"Ah, how I loved it! I loved that song to distraction, Polenka! Your father, you know, used to sing it when we were engaged . . . Oh those days! Oh that's the thing for us to sing! How does it go? I've forgotten. Remind me! How was it?"

She was violently excited and tried to sit up. At last, in a horribly hoarse, broken voice, she began, shrieking and gasping at every word, with a look of growing terror.

> "In the heat of midday! . . . in the vale! . . . of Dagestan! . . .
> With lead in my breast! . . . "*

"Your excellency!" she wailed suddenly with a heartrending scream and a flood of tears, "protect the orphans! You have been their father's guest . . . aristocratic, you might say . . . " She started, regaining consciousness, and gazed at everyone with a sort of terror, but at once recognized Sonia.

"Sonia, Sonia!" she articulated softly and caressingly, as though surprised to find her there. "Sonia darling, are you here, too?"

They lifted her up again.

"Enough! It's over! Farewell, poor thing! I am done for! I am broken!" she cried with vindictive despair, and her head fell heavily back on the pillow.

She sank into unconsciousness again, but this time it did not last long. Her pale, yellow, wasted face dropped back, her mouth fell open, her leg moved convulsively, she gave a deep, deep sigh and died.

Sonia fell upon her, flung her arms around her, and remained motionless with her head pressed to the dead woman's wasted chest. Polenka threw herself at her mother's feet, kissing them and weeping violently. Though Kolia and Lida did not understand what had happened, they had a feeling that it was something terrible; they put their hands on each other's little shoulders, stared straight at one another and both at once opened their mouths and began screaming. They were both still in their fancy dress; one in a turban, the other in the cap with the ostrich feather.

---

*The opening of "Dream," a poem by Russian writer Mikhail Lermontov (1814–1841) that describes a fatal duel similar to the one in which he would soon perish.

And how did "the certificate of merit" come to be on the bed beside Katerina Ivanovna? It lay there by the pillow; Raskolnikov saw it.

He walked away to the window. Lebeziatnikov skipped up to him.

"She is dead," he said.

"Rodion Romanovich, I must have a word with you," said Svidrigailov, coming up to them.

Lebeziatnikov at once made room for him and delicately withdrew. Svidrigailov drew Raskolnikov further away.

"I will undertake all the arrangements, the funeral and all that. You know it's a question of money and, as I told you, I have plenty to spare. I will put those two little ones and Polenka into some good orphanage, and I will settle fifteen hundred rubles to be paid to each on coming of age, so that Sofia Semionovna need not worry about them. And I will pull her out of the mud too, for she is a good girl, isn't she? So tell Avdotia Romanovna that that is how I am spending her ten thousand."

"What is your motive for such benevolence?" asked Raskolnikov.

"Ah! You skeptical person!" laughed Svidrigailov. "I told you I had no need of that money. Won't you admit that I'm just doing it for the sake of human kindness? She wasn't 'a louse,' you know" (he pointed to the corner where the dead woman lay), "was she, like some old pawnbroker woman? Come, you'll agree, is Luzhin to go on living, and doing wicked things or is she to die? And if I didn't help them, Polenka would go the same way."

He said this with an air of a sort of gay winking slyness, keeping his eyes fixed on Raskolnikov, who turned white and cold, hearing the phrases which he had used with Sonia. He quickly stepped back and looked wildly at Svidrigailov.

"How do you know?" he whispered, hardly able to breathe.

"I live here at Madame Resslich's, the other side of the wall. Here is Kapernaumov, and there lives Madame Resslich, an old and devoted friend of mine. I am a neighbor."

"You?"

"Yes," continued Svidrigailov, shaking with laughter. "I assure you on my honor, dear Rodion Romanovich, that you have interested me enormously. I told you we'd become friends, I predicted it. Well, here we have. And you will see what an accommodating person I am. You'll see you can get on with me!"

PART SIX

CHAPTER ONE

A STRANGE PERIOD BEGAN for Raskolnikov: it was as though a fog had fallen upon him and wrapped him in a dreary solitude from which there was no escape. Recalling that period long afterwards, he believed that his mind had been clouded at times, and that it had continued so, with intervals, until the final catastrophe. He was convinced that he had been mistaken about many things at that time, for instance about the date of certain events. Anyway, when he tried later on to piece his recollections together, he learnt a great deal about himself from what other people told him. He had mixed up incidents and had explained events as due to circumstances which existed only in his imagination. At times he was a prey to agonies of morbid uneasiness, amounting sometimes to panic. But he remembered, too, moments, hours, perhaps whole days, of complete apathy, which came upon him as a reaction to his previous terror and might be compared with the abnormal insensibility which is sometimes seen in the dying. He seemed to be trying in that latter stage to escape from a full and clear understanding of his position. Certain essential facts which required immediate consideration were particularly irritating to him. How glad he would have been to be free from some of his worries which, if he had neglected them, would have threatened him with complete, inevitable ruin.

He was particularly worried about Svidrigailov, he might be said to be permanently thinking of Svidrigailov. From the time of Svidrigailov's excessively menacing and unmistakable words in Sonia's room at the moment of Katerina Ivanovna's death, the normal working of his mind seemed to break down. But although this new fact caused him extreme uneasiness, Raskolnikov was in no hurry to explain it. At times, finding himself in a solitary and remote part of the town, in some wretched eating-house, sitting alone lost in thought, hardly knowing how he had come there, he suddenly thought of Svidrigailov. He recognized suddenly, clearly, and with dismay that he ought at once to come to an understanding with that man and to make what terms he could. Walking outside the city gates one day, he actually imagined that they had fixed a meeting there, that he was waiting for Svidrigailov. Another time he woke up before daybreak lying on the ground under some bushes and could not at first understand how he had come there.

But during the two or three days after Katerina Ivanovna's death, he had two or three times met Svidrigailov in the building where Sonia lived, to which he had gone aimlessly for a moment. They exchanged a few words and made no reference to the vital subject, as though they had tacitly agreed not to speak of it for a period.

Katerina Ivanovna's body was still lying in the coffin, Svidrigailov was busy making arrangements for the funeral. Sonia too was very busy. At their last meeting Svidrigailov informed Raskolnikov that he had made an arrangement, and a very satisfactory one, for Katerina Ivanovna's children; that he had, through certain connections, succeeded in getting hold of certain people with whose help the three orphans could be at once placed in very suitable institutions; that the money he had given them had been of great assistance, as it is much easier to place orphans who have some kind of property than destitute ones. He said something too about Sonia and promised to come himself in a day or two to see Raskolnikov, mentioning that "he would like to consult with him, that there were things they must talk over . . . "

This conversation took place in the passage on the stairs. Svidrigailov looked intently at Raskolnikov and suddenly, after a brief pause, dropping his voice, asked: "But how is it, Rodion Romanovich; you don't seem yourself? You look and you listen, but you don't seem to understand. Cheer up! We'll talk things over; I'm just sorry, I've so much of my own business and of other people's to do. Ah, Rodion Romanovich," he added suddenly, "what everyone needs is fresh air, fresh air . . . more than anything!"

He moved to one side to make way for the priest and server, who were coming up the stairs. They had come for the requiem service. On Svidrigailov's orders it was sung twice a day, punctually. Svidrigailov went his way. Raskolnikov stood still for a moment, thought, and followed the priest into Sonia's room. He stood at the door. They began to sing the service quietly, slowly and mournfully. From his childhood the thought of death and the presence of death had been something oppressive and mysteriously awful; and it was a long time since he had heard the requiem service. And there was something else here as well, too awful and disturbing. He looked at the children:

they were all kneeling by the coffin; Polenka was weeping. Behind them Sonia prayed, softly, and, as it were, timidly weeping.

"For the last two days she hasn't said a word to me, she hasn't glanced at me," Raskolnikov thought suddenly. The sunlight was bright in the room; the incense rose in clouds; the priest read, "Give rest, oh Lord . . . " Raskolnikov stayed throughout the service. As he blessed them and took his leave, the priest looked round strangely. After the service, Raskolnikov went up to Sonia. She took both his hands and let her head sink on his shoulder. This slight friendly gesture bewildered Raskolnikov. It seemed strange to him that there was no trace of repugnance, no trace of disgust, no tremor in her hand. It was the furthest limit of self-abnegation, at least so he interpreted it.

Sonia said nothing. Raskolnikov pressed her hand and went out. He felt very miserable. If it had been possible to escape to some solitude, he would have considered himself lucky, even if he had to spend his whole life there. But although he had almost always been by himself recently, he had never been able to feel alone. Sometimes he walked out of the town onto the high road, once he had even reached a little wood, but the lonelier the place was, the more he seemed to be aware of an uneasy presence near him. It did not frighten him, but greatly annoyed him, so he made haste to return to the town, to mingle with the crowd, to go into restaurants and taverns, to walk in busy streets. There he felt easier and even more solitary. One day at dusk he sat for an hour listening to songs in a tavern and he remembered that he actually enjoyed it. But at last he had suddenly felt the same uneasiness again, as though his conscience was smiting him. "Here I sit listening to singing, is that what I ought to be doing?" he thought. Yet he felt at once that that was not the only cause of his uneasiness; there was something requiring immediate decision, but it was something he could not clearly understand or put into words. It was a hopeless tangle. "No, better have the struggle again! Better have Porfiry again . . . or Svidrigailov . . . Better have some challenge again . . . some attack. Yes, yes!" he thought. He went out of the tavern and rushed away almost at a run. The thought of Dunia and his mother suddenly reduced him almost to a panic. That night he woke up before morning among some bushes in Krestovsky Island, trembling all over with fever; he walked home, and it was early morning when he arrived. After some hours' sleep the fever left him, but he woke up late, at two o'clock in the afternoon.

He remembered that Katerina Ivanovna's funeral had been fixed for that day, and was glad that he was not present at it. Nastasia brought him some food; he ate and drank with appetite, almost with greediness. His head was fresher and he was calmer than he had been for the last three days. He even felt a passing sense of amazement at his previous panic attacks.

The door opened and Razumikhin came in.

"Ah, he's eating; then he's not ill," said Razumikhin. He took a chair and sat down at the table opposite Raskolnikov.

He was troubled and did not attempt to conceal it. He spoke with evident annoyance, but without hurrying or raising his voice. He looked as though he had some special fixed determination.

"Listen," he began resolutely. "As far as I'm concerned, you can all go to hell, but from what I see, it's clear to me that I can't make head or tail of it; please don't think I've come to ask you questions. I don't want to know, damn it! If you begin telling me your secrets, I don't think I'd stay to listen, I'd go away cursing. I have only come to find out once for all whether it's a fact that you are mad? There is a conviction in the air that you are mad or very nearly so. I admit I've been disposed to that opinion myself, judging from your stupid, repulsive and quite inexplicable actions, and from your recent behavior to your mother and sister. Only a monster or a madman could treat them as you have; so you must be mad."

"When did you see them last?"

"Just now. Haven't you seen them since then? What have you been doing with yourself? Tell me, please. I've been to see you three times already. Your mother has been seriously ill since yesterday. She had made up her mind to come to you; Avdotia Romanovna tried to prevent her; she wouldn't hear a word. 'If he is ill, if his mind is giving way, who can look after him like his mother can?' she said. We all came here together, we couldn't let her come alone all the way. We kept begging her to be calm. We came in, you weren't here; she sat down, and stayed ten minutes, while we stood waiting in silence. She got up and said: 'If he's gone out, that is, if he is well, and has forgotten his mother, it's humiliating and unseemly for his mother to stand at his door begging for kindness.' She returned home and took to her bed; now she is in a fever. 'I see,' she said, 'that he has time for his girl.' She means by your girl Sofia Semionovna, your betrothed or your mistress, I don't know. I went at once to Sofia Semionovna's because I wanted to know what was going on. I looked round, I saw the coffin, the children crying, and Sofia Semionovna getting them to try on mourning dresses. No sign of you. I apologized, went away, and reported it all to Avdotia Romanovna. So that's all nonsense and you haven't got a girl; the most likely thing is that you are mad. But here you sit, guzzling boiled beef as though you'd not had a bite for three days. Though as far as that goes, madmen eat too, but though you have not said a word to me yet . . . you are not mad! That I'd swear! Above all, you are not mad. So you can go to hell, all of you, because there's some mystery, some secret about it, and I don't intend to worry my brains over your secrets. So I've just come to swear at you," he finished, getting up, "to relieve my mind. And I know what to do now."

"What do you intend to do now?"

"What business is it of yours what I intend to do?"

"You are going out for a drinking bout."

"How . . . how did you know?"

"Well, it's pretty clear."

Razumikhin paused for a minute.

"You've always been a very rational person and you've never been mad, never," he observed suddenly with warmth. "You're right: I shall drink. Goodbye!"

And he moved to go out.

"I was talking with my sister—the day before yesterday I think it was—about you, Razumikhin."

"About me! But . . . where can you have seen her the day before yesterday?" Razumikhin stopped short and even turned a little pale.

His heart was throbbing slowly and violently.

"She came here by herself, sat there and talked to me."

"She did!"

"Yes."

"What did you say to her . . . I mean, about me?"

"I told her you were a very good, honest, and industrious man. I didn't tell her you love her, because she knows that herself."

"She knows that herself?"

"Well, it's pretty clear. Wherever I go, whatever happens to me, you will remain to look after them. I, so to speak, give them into your keeping, Razumikhin. I say this because I know quite well how you love her, and am convinced of the purity of your heart. I know that she too may love you and perhaps does love you already. Now decide for yourself, as you know best, whether you need go in for a drinking bout or not."

"Rodia! You see . . . well . . . Ah, damn it! But where do you intend to go? Of course, if it's all a secret, never mind . . . But I . . . I shall find out the secret . . . and I am sure that it must be some ridiculous nonsense and that you've made it all up. Anyway you are a wonderful person, a wonderful person!" . . .

"That was just what I wanted to add, only you interrupted, that that was a very good decision of yours not to find out these secrets. Leave it to time, don't worry about it. You'll know it all in time when it's all revealed. Yesterday a man said to me that what a man needs is fresh air, fresh air, fresh air. I intend to go to him directly to find out what he meant by that."

Razumikhin stood lost in thought and excitement, making a silent conclusion.

"He's a political conspirator! He must be. And he's on the eve of some desperate step, that's certain. It can only be that! And . . . and Dunia knows," he thought suddenly.

"So Avdotia Romanovna comes to see you," he said, weighing each syllable, "and you're going to see a man who says we need more air, and so of course that letter . . . that too must have something to do with it," he concluded to himself.

"What letter?"

"She got a letter today. It upset her very much—very much indeed. Too much so. I started talking about you, she begged me not to. Then . . . then she said that perhaps we should very soon have to part . . . then she began warmly thanking me for something; then she went to her room and locked herself in."

"She got a letter?" Raskolnikov asked thoughtfully.

"Yes, and you didn't know? Hm . . . "

They were both silent.

"Goodbye, Rodion. There was a time, my friend, when I . . . Never mind, goodbye. You see, there was a time . . . Well, goodbye! I

must be off too. I am not going to drink. There's no need now . . .
That's all stupid!"

He hurried out; but when he had almost closed the door behind
him, he suddenly opened it again, and said, looking away:

"Oh, by the way, do you remember that murder, you know Porfiry's, that old woman? Do you know the murderer has been found,
he has confessed and given the proofs. It's one of those workmen, the
painter, just imagine! Do you remember I defended them here?
Would you believe it, that whole scene of fighting and laughing with
his companion on the stairs while the porter and the two witnesses
were going up, he put on deliberately to disarm suspicion. The cunning, the presence of mind that little dog had! It can hardly be cred-
ited; but it's his own explanation, he has confessed it all. And what a
fool I was about it! Well, he's simply a genius of hypocrisy and re-
sourcefulness in disarming the suspicions of the lawyers—so there's
nothing much to wonder at, I suppose! Of course, people like that are
always possible. And the fact that he couldn't keep up the character,
but confessed, makes him easier to believe in. But what a fool I was!
I was frantically supporting them!"

"Tell me, please, who did you hear that from, and why does it interest you so much?" Raskolnikov asked with unmistakable agitation.

"What next? You ask me why it interests me! . . . Well, I heard it
from Porfiry, among others . . . It was from him I heard almost everything about it."

"From Porfiry?"

"From Porfiry."

"What . . . what did he say?" Raskolnikov asked in dismay.

"He gave me a brilliant explanation of it. Psychologically, after
his fashion."

"He explained it? Explained it himself?"

"Yes, yes; goodbye. I'll tell you all about it another time, but now
I'm busy. There was a time when I imagined . . . But no matter, another time! . . . What need is there for me to drink now? You have
made me drunk without wine. I am drunk, Rodia! Goodbye, I'm
going. I'll come again very soon."

He went out.

"He's a political conspirator, there's no doubt about it," Razumikhin decided, as he slowly descended the stairs. "And he's drawn

his sister in; that's entirely, entirely in keeping with Avdotia Romanovna's character. There are meetings between them! . . . She hinted at it too . . . So many of her words . . . and hints . . . have implied that! And how else can this whole tangle be explained? Hm! And I was almost thinking . . . Goodness, what was I thinking! Yes, I took leave of my senses and I wronged him! It was his doing, under the lamp in the corridor that day. Foo! What a crude, nasty, vile idea on my part! Nikolai is a real godsend, for confessing . . . And how clear everything is now! His illness then, all his strange actions . . . before this, in the university, how pessimistic he used to be, how gloomy . . . But what's the meaning now of that letter? There's something in that, too, perhaps. Who was it from? I suspect . . . ! No, I must find out!"

He thought of Dunia, realizing everything he had heard and his heart throbbed, and he suddenly broke into a run.

As soon as Razumikhin went out, Raskolnikov got up, turned to the window, walked from one corner to another, as though forgetting the smallness of his room, and sat down again on the sofa. He felt, so to speak, renewed; again the struggle, so a means of escape had come.

"Yes, a means of escape had come! It had been too stifling, too cramping, the burden had been too agonizing. A lethargy had come upon him at times. From the moment of the scene with Nikolai at Porfiry's he had been suffocating, penned in without any hope of escape. After Nikolai's confession, on that very day had come the scene with Sonia; his behavior and his last words had been utterly unlike anything he could have imagined beforehand; he had grown feebler, instantly and fundamentally! And he had agreed at the time with Sonia, he had agreed in his heart he could not go on living alone with such a thing on his mind!

"And Svidrigailov was a riddle . . . He worried him, that was true, but somehow not on the same point. He might still have a struggle to come with Svidrigailov. Svidrigailov, too, might be a means of escape; but Porfiry was a different matter.

"And so Porfiry himself had explained it to Razumikhin, had explained it psychologically. He had started bringing in his damned psychology again! Porfiry? But to think that Porfiry should for a moment believe that Nikolai was guilty, after what had passed between them before Nikolai's appearance, after that one-on-one interview, which could have only one explanation? (During those days Raskolnikov had often recalled passages in that scene with Porfiry; he could not bear to let his mind rest on it.) Such words, such gestures had passed between them, they had exchanged such glances, things had been said in such a tone and had reached such a pass, that Nikolai, whom Porfiry had seen through at the first word, at the first gesture, could not have shaken his conviction.

"And to think that even Razumikhin had begun to suspect! The scene in the corridor under the lamp had produced its effect then. He had rushed to Porfiry . . . But what had induced the latter to receive him like that? What had been his aim in putting Razumikhin off with Nikolai? He must have some plan; there was some design, but what was it? It was true that a long time had passed since that morning—too long a time—and no sight or sound of Porfiry. Well, that was a bad sign . . . "

Raskolnikov took his cap and went out of the room, still pondering. It was the first time for a long while that he had felt clear in his mind, at least. "I must settle Svidrigailov," he thought, "and as soon as possible; he, too, seems to be waiting for me to come to him of my own accord." And at that moment there was such a rush of hate in his weary heart that he might have killed either of those two—Porfiry or Svidrigailov. At least he felt that he would be capable of doing it later, if not now.

"We shall see, we shall see," he repeated to himself.

But no sooner had he opened the door than he stumbled upon Porfiry himself in the passage. He was coming in to see him. Raskolnikov was dumbfounded for a minute, but only for a minute. Strange to say, he was not very astonished to see Porfiry and was scarcely even afraid of him. He was simply startled, but was quickly, instantly, on his guard. "Perhaps this will mean the end? But how could Porfiry have approached so quietly, like a cat, so he would hear nothing? Could he have been listening at the door?"

"You didn't expect a visitor, Rodion Romanovich," Porfiry explained, laughing. "I've been meaning to look in for a long time; I was passing by and thought—why not go in for five minutes! Are you going out? I won't keep you long. Just let me have one cigarette."

"Sit down, Porfiry Petrovich, sit down." Raskolnikov gave his visitor a seat with so pleased and friendly an expression that he would have marveled at himself if he could have seen it.

The final moment had come, the last drops had to be drained! So a man will sometimes go through half an hour of mortal terror with a brigand, yet when the knife is at his throat at last, he feels no fear.

Raskolnikov seated himself directly facing Porfiry, and looked at him without flinching. Porfiry screwed up his eyes and began lighting a cigarette.

"Say something, say something," seemed as though it would burst from Raskolnikov's heart. "Come on, why aren't you saying anything?"

CHAPTER TWO

"AH THESE CIGARETTES!" PORFIRY Petrovich said at last, having lit one. "They are pernicious, absolutely pernicious, and yet I can't give them up! I cough, I begin to have a tickle in my throat and difficulty breathing. You know I am a coward, I went recently to Dr. B___n;* he always gives at least half an hour to each patient. He really laughed looking at me; he gave me an inspection: 'Tobacco's bad for you,' he said, 'your lungs are affected.' But how am I going to give it up? What is there to take its place? I don't drink, that's the problem, he-he-he, that I don't. Everything is relative, Rodion Romanovich, everything is relative!"

"He's playing his professional tricks again," Raskolnikov thought with disgust. All the circumstances of their last interview suddenly came back to him, and he felt a rush of the feeling that had come upon him then.

"I came to see you the day before yesterday, in the evening; you didn't know?" Porfiry Petrovich went on, looking round the room. "I came into this very room. I was passing by, just as I did today, and I thought I'd return your call. I walked in as your door was wide open,

---

*Dr. Botkin, personal doctor of Tsar Alexander II and a renowned professor of medicine.

I looked round, waited and went out without leaving my name with your servant. Don't you lock your door?"

Raskolnikov's face grew more and more gloomy. Porfiry seemed to guess his state of mind.

"I've come to have it out with you, Rodion Romanovich, my dear friend! I owe you an explanation and I must give it to you," he continued with a slight smile, just patting Raskolnikov's knee.

But almost at the same instant a serious and careworn look came into his face; to his surprise Raskolnikov saw a touch of sadness in it. He had never seen and never suspected such an expression on his face.

"A strange scene passed between us last time we met, Rodion Romanovich. Our first interview, too, was a strange one; but then . . . and one thing after another! This is the point: I have perhaps acted unfairly to you; I feel it. Do you remember how we parted? Your nerves were unhinged and your knees were shaking and so were mine. And, you know, our behavior was indecent, even ungentle-manly. And yet we are gentlemen, above all, in any case, gentlemen; that must be understood. Do you remember what we came to? . . . It was absolutely indecent."

"What is he up to, what does he take me for?" Raskolnikov asked himself in amazement, raising his head and looking with open eyes at Porfiry.

"I've decided openness is better between us," Porfiry Petrovich went on, turning his head away and dropping his eyes, as though un-willing to disconcert his former victim and as though he were setting aside his former cunning. "Yes, such suspicions and such scenes can-not continue for long. Nikolai put a stop to it, or I don't know what we might not have come to. That damned workman was sitting at the time in the next room—do you realize that? You know that, of course; and I am aware that he came to see you afterwards. But what you supposed then was not true: I had not sent for anyone, I had made no kind of arrangements. You ask why I hadn't? What shall I say to you: it had all come to me so suddenly. I had scarcely sent for the porters (you noticed them as you went out, I dare say). An idea flashed upon me; I was firmly convinced at the time, you see, Rodion Romanovich. Come on, I thought—even if I let one thing slip for a period, I shall get hold of something else—I shan't lose what I want, anyway. You are nervous and irritable, Rodion Romanovich, by tem-

perament; it's out of proportion to the other qualities of your heart
and character, and I flatter myself to think I have to some extent divined them. Of course I did reflect even then that it does not always
happen that a man gets up and blurts out his whole story. It does happen sometimes, if you make a man lose all his patience, though even
then it's rare. I was capable of realizing that. If I only had a fact, I
thought, the least little fact to go upon, something I could lay hold
of, something tangible, not merely psychological. For if a man is
guilty, you must be able to get something substantial out of him; you
can count upon the most surprising results. I was counting on your
temperament, Rodion Romanovich, on your temperament above all!
I had great hopes of you at that time."

"But what are you driving at now?" Raskolnikov muttered at last,
asking the question without thinking.

"What is he talking about?" he wondered distractedly, "does he
really take me to be innocent?"

"What am I driving at? I've come to explain myself, I consider it
my duty, so to speak. I want to make clear to you how the whole
business, the whole misunderstanding arose. I've caused you a great
deal of suffering, Rodion Romanovich. I am not a monster. I understand what it must mean for a man who has been unfortunate, but
who is proud, imperious and above all, impatient, to have to bear
such treatment! I regard you in any case as a man of noble character
and not without elements of magnanimity, though I don't agree with
all your convictions. I wanted to tell you this first, frankly and quite
sincerely, for above all I don't want to deceive you. When I made your
acquaintance, I felt attracted by you. Perhaps you will laugh at my
saying so. You have a right to. I know you disliked me from the first
and in fact you've no reason to like me. You may think what you like,
but I now wish to do all I can to erase that impression and to show
that I have a heart and a conscience. I am saying this sincerely."

Porfiry Petrovich made a dignified pause. Raskolnikov felt a rush
of renewed alarm. The thought that Porfiry believed him to be innocent began to make him uneasy.

"It's scarcely necessary to go over everything in detail," Porfiry
Petrovich went on. "Indeed I could scarcely attempt it. To begin with
there were rumors. Through whom, how, and when those rumors
came to me . . . and how they affected you, I need not explain. My

suspicions were aroused by a complete accident, which might just as easily not have happened. What was it? Hm! I believe there is no need to go into that either. Those rumors and that accident led to one idea in my mind. I admit it openly—for one may as well be clear about it—I was the first to pitch on you. The old woman's notes on the pledges and the rest of it—that all came to nothing. Yours was one of a hundred. I happened, too, to hear of the scene at the office, from a man who described it excellently, unconsciously reproducing the scene with great vividness. It was just one thing after another, Rodion Romanovich, my dear fellow! How could I avoid being brought to certain ideas? From a hundred rabbits you can't make a horse, a hundred suspicions don't make a proof, as the English proverb says, but that's only from the rational point of view—you can't help being partial, for after all a lawyer is only human. I thought, too, of your article in that journal, do you remember, during your first visit we talked about it? I jeered at you at the time, but that was only to lead you on. I repeat, Rodion Romanovich, you are ill and impatient. That you were bold, headstrong, in earnest and . . . had felt a great deal I recognized long before. I, too, have felt the same, so your article seemed familiar to me. It was conceived on sleepless nights, with a throbbing heart, in ecstasy and with suppressed enthusiasm. And that proud suppressed enthusiasm in young people is dangerous! I jeered at you then, but let me tell you that, as a literary amateur, I am awfully fond of such first essays, full of the heat of youth. There is a mistiness and a chord vibrating in the mist. Your article is absurd and fantastic, but there's a transparent sincerity, a youthful incorruptible pride and the daring of despair in it. It's a gloomy article, but that's what's good about it. I read your article and put it aside, thinking as I did so 'that man won't go the common way.' Well, I ask you, after that as a preliminary, how could I help being carried away by what followed? Oh, dear, I am not saying anything, I am not making any statement now. I simply noted it at the time. What is there in it? I reflected. There's nothing in it: that is, really nothing and perhaps absolutely nothing. And it's not at all the thing for the prosecutor to let himself be carried away by notions: here I have Nikolai on my hands with actual evidence against him—you may think what you like of it, but it's evidence. He brings in his psychology, too; you have to consider him, too, because it's a matter of life and death. Why am I explaining this to you? So that you will understand, and not blame my malicious behavior on that occasion. It was not malicious, I assure you, he-he! Do you suppose I didn't come to search your room at the time? I did, I did, he-he! I was here when you were lying ill in bed, not officially, not in person, but I was here. Your room was searched to the last thread at the first suspicion; but *umsonst!* I thought to myself, now that man will come, will come of his own accord and quickly, too; if he's guilty, he's sure to come. Another man wouldn't but he will. And you remember how Mr. Razumikhin began discussing the subject with you? We arranged that to excite you, so we spread rumors on purpose, so that he might discuss the case with you, and Razumikhin is not a man to restrain his indignation. Mr. Zametov was tremendously struck by your anger and your open daring. Think of blurting out in a restaurant: 'I killed her.' It was too daring, too reckless. I thought so myself: if he is guilty, he will be a formidable opponent. That was what I thought at the time. I was expecting you. But you simply bowled Zametov over and . . . well, you see, this is where it all lies—this damnable psychology can be taken two ways! Well, I kept expecting you, and that was how it was, you came! My heart was really throbbing. Ah!

"Now, why need you have come? Your laughter, too, as you came in, do you remember? I saw it all plain as day, but if I hadn't expected you so specially, I should not have noticed anything in your laughter. You see what influence a mood has! Mr. Razumikhin then—ah, that stone, that stone under which the things were hidden! I seem to see it somewhere in a kitchen garden. It was in a kitchen garden, you told Zametov and afterwards you repeated that in my office? And when we began picking your article to pieces, how you explained it! One could take every word of yours in two senses, as though there were another meaning hidden.

"So in this way, Rodion Romanovich, I reached the furthest limit, and knocking my head against a post, I pulled myself up, asking myself what I was about. After all, I said, you can take it all in another sense if you like, and it's more natural to take it that way, in fact. I couldn't help admitting it was more natural. I was bothered! 'No, I'd better get hold of some little fact,' I said. So when I heard of the bell-ringing, I held my breath and was all in a tremor. 'Here is my little fact,' I thought, and I didn't think it over, I simply wouldn't. I would have given a thousand rubles at that minute to have seen you with my own eyes, when you walked a hundred paces beside that workman, after he had called you murderer to your face, and you did not dare to ask him a question all the way. And then what about your trembling, what about your bell-ringing in your illness, in semi-delirium?

"And so, Rodion Romanovich, can you wonder that I played such pranks on you? And what made you come at that very minute? Someone seemed to have sent you, by Jove! And if Nikolai had not parted us . . . and do you remember Nikolai at the time? Do you remember him clearly? It was a thunderbolt, a regular thunderbolt! And how I met him! I didn't believe in the thunderbolt, not for a minute. You could see it for yourself; and how could I? Even afterwards, when you had gone and he began making very, very plausible answers on certain points, so plausible that I was surprised at him myself, even then I didn't believe his story! You see what it is to be as firm as a rock! No, thought I, *morgen früh*. What has Nikolai got to do with it!"

"Razumikhin told me just now that you think Nikolai is guilty and had assured him of it yourself . . . "

His voice failed him, and he broke off. He had been listening in indescribable agitation, as this man who had seen through him went back upon himself. He was afraid of believing it and did not believe it. In those words, which were still ambiguous, he kept eagerly looking for something more definite and conclusive.

"Mr. Razumikhin!" cried Porfiry Petrovich, seeming glad of a question from Raskolnikov, who had until then been silent. "He-he-he! But I had to put Mr. Razumikhin off; two is company, three is none. Mr. Razumikhin is not the right man; besides, he is an outsider. He came running to me with a pale face . . . But never mind him, why bring him into it! To return to Nikolai, would you like to know what sort of a type he is, how I understand him, that is? To begin with, he is still a child and not exactly a coward, but something of an artist. Really, don't laugh at my describing him like that. He is innocent and open to influence. He has a heart, he is a fantastic fellow. He sings and dances, he tells stories, they say, so well that people come from other villages to hear him. He attends school too, and laughs until he cries if you hold up a finger to him; he will drink himself senseless—not

as a regular vice, but at times when people treat him like a child. And
he stole, too, then, without knowing it himself, for 'How can it be
stealing, if you pick it up?' And do you know he is an Old Believer,*
or rather a dissenter? There have been Wanderers† in his family, and
for two years in his village he was under the spiritual guidance of an
elder. I learnt all this from Nikolai and his fellow villagers. And what's
more, he wanted to run into the wilderness! He was full of fervor,
prayed at night, read the old books, 'the true' ones, and read himself
crazy."—

"Petersburg had a great effect upon him, especially the women
and the wine. He responds to everything and he forgot the elder and
all that. I learnt that an artist here took a fancy to him, and used to go
and see him, and now this business came along.

"Well, he was frightened, he tried to hang himself! He ran away!
How can you get over the idea the people have of Russian legal proceedings! The very word 'trial' frightens some of them. Whose fault
is it? We shall see what the new juries will do. God grant they do
good! Well, in prison, it seems, he remembered the venerable elder,
the Bible, too, made its appearance again. Do you know, Rodion Romanovich, the force of the word 'suffering' among some of these
people! It's not a question of suffering for someone's benefit, but
simply, 'you must suffer.' If they suffer at the hands of the authorities,
so much the better. In my time there was a very meek and mild prisoner who spent a whole year in prison always reading his Bible on
the stove at night and he read himself crazy, and so crazy, do you
know, that one day, apropos of nothing, he seized a brick and flung
it at the governor, though he had done him no harm. And the way he
threw it too: aimed it a yard on one side on purpose, for fear of hurting him. Well, we know what happens to a prisoner who assaults an
officer with a weapon. So 'he took his suffering.'

"So I suspect now that Nikolai wants to take his suffering or
something of the sort. I even know it for certain from the facts. Only
he doesn't know that I know. What, you don't admit that there are
such fantastic people among the peasants? Lots of them. The elder

*A religious dissenter who did not accept the reforms of the Russian Orthodox
Church introduced by the patriarch Nikon in the mid-seventeenth century.
†Christian sect whose members refused to recognize official authority and wan-
dered from village to village without any priests.

now has begun influencing him, especially since he tried to hang himself. But he'll come and tell me everything himself. You think he'll hold out? Wait a bit, he'll take his words back. I am waiting hour by hour for him to come and swear in his evidence. I have come to like that Nikolai and am studying him in detail. And what do you think? He-he! He answered me very plausibly on some points, he obviously had collected some evidence and prepared himself cleverly. But on other points he is simply at sea, knows nothing and doesn't even suspect that he doesn't know!

"No, Rodion Romanovich, Nikolai doesn't come into it! This is a fantastic, gloomy business, a modern case, an incident of our time, when the heart of man is troubled, when the phrase is quoted that blood 'renews,' when comfort is preached as the aim of life. Here we have bookish dreams, a heart unhinged by theories. Here we see resolution in the first stage, but resolution of a special kind: he resolved to do it like jumping over a precipice or from a bell tower and his legs shook as he went to the crime. He forgot to shut the door after him, and murdered two people for a theory. He committed the murder and couldn't take the money, and what he did manage to snatch up he hid under a stone. It wasn't enough for him to suffer agony behind the door while they battered at the door and rung the bell, no, he had to go to the empty lodging, half delirious, to recall the bell-ringing, he wanted to feel the cold shiver over again . . . Well, that we grant, was through illness, but consider this: he is a murderer, but looks upon himself as an honest man, despises others, poses as an injured innocent. No, that's not the work of a Nikolai, my dear Rodion Romanovich!"

All that had been said before had sounded so like a recantation that these words were too great a shock. Raskolnikov shuddered as though he had been stabbed.

"Then . . . who then . . . is the murderer?" he asked in a breathless voice, unable to restrain himself.

Porfiry Petrovich sank back in his chair, as though he were amazed at the question.

"Who is the murderer?" he repeated, as though unable to believe his ears. "You, Rodion Romanovich! You are the murderer," he added almost in a whisper, in a voice of genuine conviction.

Raskolnikov leapt from the sofa, stood up for a few seconds and sat down again without uttering a word. His face twitched convulsively.

"Your lip is twitching just as it did before," Porfiry Petrovich observed almost sympathetically. "You've been misunderstanding me, I think, Rodion Romanovich," he added after a brief pause, "that's why you are so surprised. I came on purpose to tell you everything and deal openly with you."

"It was not me who murdered her," Raskolnikov whispered like a frightened child caught in the act.

"No, it was you, you, Rodion Romanovich, and no-one else," Porfiry whispered sternly, with conviction.

They were both silent and the silence lasted strangely long, about ten minutes. Raskolnikov put his elbow on the table and passed his fingers through his hair. Porfiry Petrovich sat quietly waiting. Suddenly Raskolnikov looked scornfully at Porfiry.

"You are at your old tricks again, Porfiry Petrovich! Your old method again. I'm amazed you don't get sick of it!"

"Oh, stop that, what does that matter now? It would be a different matter if there were witnesses present, but we are whispering alone. You see yourself that I have not come to chase and capture you like a hare. Whether you confess it or not is nothing to me now; as far as I am concerned, I am convinced without it."

"If so, what did you come for?" Raskolnikov asked irritably. "I ask you the same question again: if you consider me guilty, why don't you take me to prison?"

"Oh, that's your question! I will answer you, point for point. Firstly, to arrest you so directly is not in my interest."

"How so? If you are convinced you ought . . . "

"Ah, what if I am convinced? That's only my dream for the time being. Why should I put you in safety? You know that's it, since you ask me to do it. If I confront you with that workman for instance and you say to him 'were you drunk or not? Who saw me with you? I simply thought you were drunk, and you were drunk, too.' Well, what could I answer, especially as your story is a more likely one than his, for there's nothing but psychology to support his evidence— that's almost unseemly with his ugly mug, while you hit the mark exactly, because that rascal is an inveterate drunkard, and notoriously so. And I myself have frankly admitted several times already that that psychology can be taken in two ways and that the second way is stronger and looks far more probable, and that apart from that I have as yet nothing against you. And though I shall put you in prison and indeed have come—quite contrary to etiquette—to inform you of it beforehand, yet I tell you frankly, also contrary to etiquette, that it won't be to my advantage. Well, secondly, I've come to you because . . . "

"Yes, yes, secondly?" Raskolnikov was listening breathless.

"Because, as I told you just now, I consider I owe you an explanation. I don't want you to look upon me as a monster, as I have a genuine liking for you, you may believe me or not. And in the third place I've come to you with a direct and open proposition—that you should surrender and confess. It will be infinitely more to your advantage and to my advantage too, for my task will be done. Well, is this open on my part or not?"

Raskolnikov thought a minute. "Listen, Porfiry Petrovich. You said just now you have nothing but psychology to go on, yet now you've gone on mathematics. Well, what if you are mistaken yourself, now?"

"No, Rodion Romanovich, I am not mistaken. I have a little fact even then; Providence sent it to me."

"What little fact?"

"I won't tell you what, Rodion Romanovich. And in any case, I haven't got the right to put it off any longer, I must arrest you. So think it over: it makes no difference to me now and so I speak only for your sake. Believe me, it will be better, Rodion Romanovich."

Raskolnikov smiled malignantly.

"That's not just ridiculous, it's absolutely shameless. Why, even if I were guilty, which I don't admit, what reason would I have to confess, when you tell me yourself that I shall be in greater safety in prison?"

"Ah, Rodion Romanovich, don't put too much faith in words, perhaps prison will not be an entirely restful place. That's only theory and my theory, and what authority am I for you? Perhaps even now I am hiding something from you? I can't lay everything bare, he-he! And how can you ask what advantage? Don't you know how it would lessen your sentence? You would be confessing at a moment when another man has taken the crime on himself and has therefore muddled the whole case. Consider that! I swear before God that I will so arrange for your confession to come as a complete surprise. We will make a clean sweep of all these psychological points, of any suspicion against you, so that your crime will appear to have been something like an aberration, for in truth it was an aberration. I am an honest man, Rodion Romanovich, and I will keep my word."

Raskolnikov maintained a mournful silence and let his head sink dejectedly. He pondered a long while and at last smiled again, but his smile was sad and gentle.

"No!" he said, apparently abandoning all attempt to keep up appearances with Porfiry. "It's not worth it. I don't care about lessening the sentence!"

"That's just what I was afraid of!" Porfiry cried warmly and, as it seemed, involuntarily. "That's just what I feared, that you wouldn't care about the mitigation of your sentence."

Raskolnikov looked sadly and expressively at him.

"Ah, don't disdain life!" Porfiry went on. "You have a great deal of it in front of you. How can you say you don't want a mitigation of your sentence? You are an impatient person!"

"A great deal of what lies before me?"

"Of life. What sort of prophet are you, do you know much about it? Seek and ye shall find. This may be God's means for bringing you to Him. And it's not forever, the bondage . . . "

"The time will be shortened," laughed Raskolnikov.

"Why, is it the bourgeois disgrace you are afraid of? It may be that you are afraid of it without knowing it, because you are young! But anyway you shouldn't be afraid of giving yourself up and confessing."

"Oh, damn it!" Raskolnikov whispered with loathing and contempt, as though he did not want to speak aloud.

He got up again as though he meant to go away, but sat down again in evident despair.

"Damn it, if you like! You've lost faith and you think that I am grossly flattering you; but how long has your life been? How much do you understand? You made up a theory and then you were ashamed that it broke down and turned out to be not at all original! It turned out to be something base, that's true, but you are not hopelessly base! By no means so base! At least you didn't deceive yourself for long, you went straight to the furthest point in one leap. How do I see you? I see you as one of those men who would stand and smile at their torturer while he cuts their entrails out, if only they have found faith or God. Find it and you will live. You have long needed a change of air. Suffering, too, is a good thing. Suffer! Maybe Nikolai is right in wanting to suffer. I know you don't believe in it—but don't be over-wise; fling yourself straight into life, without deliberation; don't be afraid—the flood will bring you to the bank and set you safe on your feet again. What bank? How can I tell? I only believe that you have a long life before you. I know that you think all my words now are a set speech prepared beforehand, but maybe you will remember them afterwards. They may be of use some time. That's why I speak. It's as well that you only killed the old woman. If you'd invented another theory you might perhaps have done something a thousand times more hideous. You ought to thank God, perhaps. How do you know? Perhaps God is saving you for something. But keep your good heart and have less fear! Are you afraid of the great atonement before you? No, it would be shameful to be afraid of it. Since you have taken such a step, you must harden your heart. There is justice in it. You must fulfill the demands of justice. I know that you don't believe it, but life, in fact, will bring you through. You will live it down in time. What you need now is fresh air, fresh air, fresh air!"

Raskolnikov shuddered.

"But who are you? What prophet are you? From the height of what majestic serenity do you proclaim these words of wisdom?"

"Who am I? I am a man with nothing to hope for, that's all. A man perhaps of feeling and sympathy, maybe of some knowledge too, but my day is over. But you are a different matter, there is life awaiting you. Though who knows, maybe your life, too, will pass off in smoke and come to nothing. Come on, what does it matter, that you will leave this class of men for another? It's not comfort you regret, with your heart! What of it that perhaps no-one will see you for so long? It's not time, it's you that will decide that. Be the sun and everyone will see you. The sun, above all, has to be the sun. Why are you smiling again? Because I'm such a Schiller? I bet you're thinking I'm trying to get round you by flattery. Well, perhaps I am, he-he-he! Perhaps you'd better not take my word for it, perhaps you'd better never believe it altogether; I'm made that way, I confess. But let me add, you can judge for yourself, I think, to what extent I am base and to what extent I am honest."

"When do you intend to arrest me?"

"Well, I can let you walk about another day or two. Think it over, my dear fellow, and pray to God. It's more in your interest, believe me."

"And what if I run away?" asked Raskolnikov with a strange smile.

"No, you won't run away. A peasant would run away, a fashionable dissenter would run away, the flunkey of another man's thought, for you've only to show him the end of your little finger and he'll be ready to believe in anything for the rest of his life. But you've ceased to believe in your theory already, what will you run away with? And what would you do in hiding? It would be hateful and difficult for you, and what you need more than anything in life is a definite position, an atmosphere to suit you. And what sort of atmosphere would you have? If you ran away, you'd come back to yourself. You can't get along without us. And if I put you in prison—say you've been there a month, or two, or three—remember my word, you'll confess of your own accord and perhaps to your own surprise. You won't know an hour beforehand that you are coming to confess. I am convinced that you will decide 'to take your suffering.' You don't believe my words now, but you'll come to the same realization by yourself. For suffering, Rodion Romanovich, is a great thing. Never mind the fact that I've got fat, I know it anyway. Don't laugh at it, there's a fine idea in suffering; Nikolai is right. No, you won't run away, Rodion Romanovich."

Raskolnikov got up and took his cap. Porfiry Petrovich also rose.

"Are you going for a walk? The evening will be beautiful as long as we don't have a storm. Though it would be a good thing to freshen the air."

He too took his cap.

"Porfiry Petrovich, please don't think I've confessed to you today," Raskolnikov pronounced with sullen insistence. "You're a strange man and I have listened to you just from curiosity. But I've admitted nothing, remember that!"

"Oh, I know that, I'll remember. Look at him, he's trembling! Don't be uneasy, my dear fellow, have it your own way. Walk about a bit, you won't be able to walk too far. If anything happens, I have one request to make of you," he added, dropping his voice. "It's an awkward one, but it's important. If anything were to happen (though I don't believe it would and I consider you utterly incapable of it), in case you became fascinated during these forty or fifty hours with the notion of putting an end to the business in some other way, in some fantastic way—laying hands on yourself—(it's an absurd proposition, but you must forgive me for it), do leave a brief but precise note—two lines only—and mention the stone. It will be more generous. Come, until we meet! I wish you good thoughts and sound decisions!"

Porfiry went out, stooping and avoiding Raskolnikov's gaze. The latter went to the window and waited with irritable impatience until he calculated that Porfiry had reached the street and moved away. Then he too went hurriedly out of the room.

CHAPTER THREE

HE HURRIED TO SVIDRIGAILOV'S. What he had to hope from that man he did not know. But Svidrigailov had some hidden power over him. Having recognized this once, he could not rest, and now the time had come.

On the way, one question worried him in particular: had Svidrigailov been to Porfiry's?

As far as he could judge, he would swear that he had not. He pondered again and again, went over Porfiry's visit; no, he hadn't been, of course he hadn't.

But if he had not been there yet, would he go? Meanwhile, for the present he fancied he couldn't. Why? He could not have explained, but if he could, he would not have wasted much thought over it at the moment. It all worried him and at the same time he could not attend to it. Strange to say, no-one would have believed it perhaps, but only he felt a faint vague anxiety about his immediate future. Another, much more important anxiety tormented him—it concerned himself, but in a different, more vital way. Moreover, he was conscious of immense moral fatigue, though his mind was working better that morning than it had done of late.

And was it worthwhile, after all that had happened, to contend with these new trivial difficulties? Was it worthwhile, for instance, to perform some maneuver so that Svidrigailov would not go to Porfiry's? Was it worthwhile to investigate, to establish the facts, to waste time over anyone like Svidrigailov?

Oh how sick he was of it all!

And yet he was hastening to Svidrigailov's; could he be expecting something new from him, information, or means of escape? People do clutch at straws! Was it destiny or some instinct bringing them together? Perhaps it was only fatigue, despair; perhaps it was not Svidrigailov but some other person whom he needed, and Svidrigailov had simply presented himself by chance. Sonia? But what should he go to Sonia for now? To beg for her tears again? He was afraid of Sonia, too. Sonia stood before him like an irrevocable sentence. He must go his own way or hers. At that moment especially he did not feel strong enough to see her. No, would it not be better to try Svidrigailov? And he could not help inwardly admitting that he had long felt that he must see him for some reason.

But what could they have in common? Even their evil-doing could not be of the same kind. The man, moreover, was very unpleasant, evidently depraved, undoubtedly cunning and deceitful, possibly malignant. Such stories were told about him. It is true he was befriending Katerina Ivanovna's children, but who could tell with what motive and what it meant? The man always had some scheme, some project.

There was another thought which had been continually hovering around Raskolnikov's mind recently, and which was causing him great uneasiness. It was so painful that he made evident efforts to get rid of it. He sometimes thought that Svidrigailov was shadowing him. Svidrigailov had found out his secret and had had intentions towards Dunia. What if he had them still? Wasn't it practically certain that he had? And what if, having learnt his secret and gained power over him, he were to use it as a weapon against Dunia?

This idea sometimes even tormented his dreams, but it had never presented itself so vividly to him as on his way to Svidrigailov. Even the thought of it moved him to gloomy rage. To begin with, this would transform everything, even his own position; he would have to confess his secret at once to Dunia. Would he have to give himself up, perhaps, to prevent Dunia from taking some rash step? The letter? This morning Dunia had received a letter. From whom could she get letters in Petersburg? Luzhin, perhaps? It's true Razumikhin was there to protect her, but Razumikhin knew nothing of her position. Perhaps it was his duty to tell Razumikhin? The thought of it repulsed him.

In any case he must see Svidrigailov as soon as possible, he decided finally. Thank God, the details of the interview would not have many consequences, if only he could get to the root of the matter; but if Svidrigailov were capable . . . if he were plotting against Dunia, then . . .

Raskolnikov was so exhausted by what he had been through that month that he could only decide this type of question in one way. "Then I shall kill him," he thought in cold despair.

A sudden anguish oppressed his heart; he stood still in the middle of the street and began looking around to see where he was and which way he was going. He found himself in X. Prospect thirty or forty yards from the Haymarket, through which he had come. The whole second storey of the house on the left was used as a tavern. All the windows were wide open; judging from the figures moving at the windows, the rooms were full to overflowing. There were sounds of singing, of clarinets and violins, and the boom of a Turkish drum. He could hear women shrieking. He was about to turn back wondering why he had come to X. Prospect, when suddenly at one of the end windows he saw Svidrigailov, sitting at a tea-table right in the open window with a pipe in his mouth. Raskolnikov was completely taken aback, almost terrified. Svidrigailov was silently watching and scrutinizing him, and what struck Raskolnikov at once was that he seemed to be intending to get up and slip away unobserved. Raskolnikov at once pretended not to have seen him, but to be looking absentmindedly away, while he watched him out of the corner of his eye. His heart was beating violently. Yet it was evident that Svidrigailov did not want to be seen. He took the pipe out of his mouth and was about to hide himself, but as he got up and moved his chair back, he seemed to have become suddenly aware that Raskolnikov had seen him and was watching him. What had passed between them was much the same as what happened at their first meeting in Raskolnikov's room. A sly smile came into Svidrigailov's face and grew broader and broader. Both of them knew that they had been seen and were being watched by the other. At last Svidrigailov broke into a loud laugh.

"Well, well, come in if you want me; I am here!" he shouted from the window.

Raskolnikov went up into the tavern. He found Svidrigailov in a tiny back room next to the saloon in which merchants, clerks and people of all sorts were drinking tea at twenty little tables to the desperate bawling of a chorus of singers. The click of billiard balls could be heard in the distance. On the table in front of Svidrigailov stood an open bottle, and a glass half full of champagne. In the room he also found a boy with a little hand organ, a healthy-looking, red-cheeked, eighteen-year-old girl, wearing a tucked-up striped skirt and a Tyrolese hat with ribbons. In spite of the chorus in the other room, she was singing some servants' hall song in a rather husky contralto, to the accompaniment of the organ.

"Come on, that's enough," Svidrigailov stopped her at Raskolnikov's entrance. The girl at once broke off and stood waiting respectfully. She had sung her guttural rhymes, too, with a serious and respectful expression on her face.

"Hey, Philip, a glass!" shouted Svidrigailov.

"I don't want anything to drink," said Raskolnikov.

"As you wish, I didn't intend it to be for you. Drink, Katia! I don't want anything else today, you can go." He poured her a full glass, and laid out a yellow note.

Katia drank up her glass of wine, as women do, without putting it down, in twenty gulps, took the note and kissed Svidrigailov's hand, which he allowed her to do quite seriously. She went out of the room and the boy trailed after her with the organ. Both of them had been brought in from the street. Svidrigailov had not even been in Petersburg a week, but everything about him was already, so to speak, in patriarchal mode; the waiter, Philip, was by now an old friend and had fallen right under his thumb.

The door leading to the saloon had a lock on it. Svidrigailov was at home in this room and perhaps spent whole days in it. The tavern was dirty and wretched, not even second rate.

"I was going to see you, I started looking for you," Raskolnikov began, "but I don't know what made me turn out of the Haymarket into X. Prospect just now. I never take this turning. I turn right out of the Haymarket. And this isn't the way to your house. I just turned and here you are. Strange!"

"Why don't you say straight off, 'It's a miracle'?"

"Because it may be only chance."

"Oh, that's the way with all you people," laughed Svidrigailov. "You won't admit it, even if you inwardly believe it's a miracle! Here you say that it may only be chance. And what cowards they all are here, about having an opinion of their own, you can't imagine, Rodion Romanovich. I don't mean you, you have an opinion of your own and you aren't afraid to have it. That's how you attracted my curiosity."

"Nothing else?"

"Well, that's enough, as you know," Svidrigailov was obviously exhilarated, but only slightly; he had not had more than half a glass of wine.

"I think you came to see me before you knew that I was capable of having what you call an opinion of my own," observed Raskolnikov.

"Oh, well, that was a different matter. Everyone has his own plans. And as for the miracle, let me tell you, I think you have been asleep for the last two or three days. I told you about this tavern myself, there is no miracle in your coming straight here. I explained the way myself, told you where it was, and the hours you could find me here. Do you remember?"

"I don't remember," answered Raskolnikov with surprise.

"I believe you. I told you twice. The address has been stamped mechanically on your memory. You turned this way mechanically and yet precisely according to the directions, though you aren't aware of it. When I told you then, I hardly hoped you understood me. You give yourself away too much, Rodion Romanovich. And another thing— I'm convinced there are lots of people in Petersburg who talk to themselves as they walk. This is a town of crazy people. If only we had scientists, doctors, lawyers and philosophers might make some highly valuable investigations in Petersburg. There are few places where there are so many gloomy, strong and strange influences on the human soul as in Petersburg. The influence of the climate alone means so much. And it's the administrative center of all Russia and its character must be reflected on the whole country. But that is neither here nor there now. The point is that I have watched you several times. You walk out of your house—holding your head high—twenty paces from home you let it sink, and fold your hands behind your back. You look and evidently see nothing in front of you or beside you. At last you begin moving your lips and talking to yourself, and sometimes you wave one hand and declaim, and at last stand still in the middle of the road. That's definitely not the thing to do. Someone may be watching you apart from me, and it won't do you any good. It's nothing really to do with me and I can't cure you, but, of course, you understand me."

"Do you know that I am being followed?" asked Raskolnikov, looking inquisitively at him.

"No, I know nothing about it," said Svidrigailov, seeming surprised.

"Well, then, let's leave me out of it," Raskolnikov muttered, frowning.

"Very well, let's leave you out of it."

"You had better tell me, if you come here to drink, and directed me twice to come here to see you, why did you hide and try to get away just now when I looked at the window from the street? I saw it."

"He-he! And why was it you lay on your sofa with closed eyes and pretended to be asleep, though you were wide awake while I stood in your doorway? I saw it."

"I may have had . . . reasons. You know that yourself."

"And I may have had my reasons, though you don't know them."

Raskolnikov dropped his right elbow on the table, leaned his chin in the fingers of his right hand, and stared intently at Svidrigailov. For a full minute he scrutinized his face, which had impressed him before. It was a strange face, like a mask; white and red, with bright red lips, with a flaxen beard, and flaxen hair which was still thick. His eyes were somehow too blue and their expression somehow too heavy and fixed. There was something extremely unpleasant in that handsome face, which looked so wonderfully young for its age. Svidrigailov was smartly dressed in light summer clothes and looked particularly refined in his linen. He wore a huge ring with a precious stone in it.

"Have I got to bother myself now with you too?" said Raskolnikov suddenly, coming straight to the point with nervous impatience. "Even though you might be the most dangerous if you wanted to hurt me, I don't want to put myself out anymore. I will show you at once that I don't prize myself as much as you probably think I do. I've come to tell you at once that if you keep to your former intentions with regard to my sister and if you wish to derive any benefit in that direction from what has been discovered of late, I will kill you before you get me locked up. You can count on my word. You know that I can keep it. And, secondly, if you want to tell me anything—because I keep thinking all the time that you have something to tell me—hurry up and tell it, because time is precious and very likely it will soon be too late."

"Why in such haste?" asked Svidrigailov, looking at him curiously.

"Everyone has his plans," Raskolnikov answered gloomily and impatiently.

"You urged me yourself to be frank just now, and you refuse to answer the first question I put to you," Svidrigailov observed with a smile. "You keep imagining that I have aims of my own and so you look at me with suspicion. Of course it's perfectly natural in your position. But though I would like to be friends with you, I shan't trouble myself to convince you of the opposite. The game isn't worth the candle and I wasn't intending to talk to you about anything special."

"What did you want me, for, then? It was you who came hanging around me."

"Just as an interesting subject for observation. I liked the fantastic nature of your position—that's what it was! Besides, you are the brother of a person who greatly interested me, and from that person I had in the past heard a very great deal about you, from which I gathered that you had a great influence over her; isn't that enough? Ha-ha-ha! Still I must admit that your question is rather complex; it is difficult for me to answer. Here, you, for instance, have come to me not only with a definite purpose, but also for the sake of hearing something new. Isn't so? Isn't that so?" persisted Svidrigailov with a sly smile. "Well, can't you imagine then that on my way here in the train I too was counting on you, on the fact that you would tell me something new, and on the fact that I would make some profit out of you! You see what rich men we are!"

"What profit could you make?"

"How can I tell you? How do I know? You see the tavern in which I spend all my time and it's my enjoyment, that's to say it's no great enjoyment, but I have to sit somewhere; that poor Katia now—you saw her? . . . If only I had been a glutton now, a club gourmand, but you see I can eat this."

He pointed to a little table in the corner where the remnants of a terrible looking beef-steak and potatoes lay on a tin dish.

"Have you had dinner, by the way? I've had something and I don't want anything else. I don't drink, for instance, at all. Except for champagne I never touch anything, and not more than a glass of that all evening, and even that is enough to make my head ache. I ordered it just now to wind myself up: I am just going off somewhere and you see I am in a strange state of mind. That was why I hid myself just now like a schoolboy, because I was afraid you would get in my way. But I believe," he pulled out his watch, "I can spend an hour with you. It's half-past four now. If only I'd been something, a landowner, a father, a cavalry officer, a photographer, a journalist . . . I am nothing, no specialty, and sometimes I am positively bored. I really thought you would tell me something new."

"But what are you, and why have you come here?"

"What am I? You know, a gentleman, I served for two years in the cavalry, then I knocked about here in Petersburg, then I married Marfa Petrovna and lived in the country. There you have my biography!"

"You're a gambler, I believe?"

"No, a poor sort of gambler. A card-cheat—not a gambler."

"You've been a card-cheat then?"

"Yes, I've been a card-cheat too."

"Didn't you get thrashed sometimes?"

"It did happen. Why?"

"Because you might have challenged them . . . all in all, it must have been lively."

"I won't contradict you and, besides, I am no good at philosophy. I confess that I hurried here because of the women."

"As soon as you buried Marfa Petrovna?"

"Quite so," Svidrigailov smiled with engaging candor. "What does it matter? You seem to find something wrong in my speaking like that about women?"

"Are you asking whether I find anything wrong in vice?"

"Vice! Oh, that's what you're after! But I'll answer you in order, first about women in general; you know I am fond of talking. Tell me, what should I restrain myself for? Why should I give up women, since I have a passion for them? It's an occupation, anyway."

"So you hope for nothing here but vice?"

"Oh, very well, for vice then. You insist that it's vice. But anyway I like a direct question. In this vice at least there is something permanent, founded upon nature and not dependent on fantasy, something present in the blood like an ever-burning ember, forever setting one on fire and possibly not to be quickly extinguished, even with years. You'll agree it's an occupation of a sort."

"That's nothing to rejoice at, it's a disease and a dangerous one."

"Oh, that's what you think, is it? I agree that it is a disease like everything that exceeds moderation. And, of course, in this you must exceed moderation. But firstly, everybody does so in one way or another, and secondly, of course, you ought to be moderate and prudent, however mean it may be, but what am I to do? If I hadn't got this, I might have to shoot myself. I am ready to admit that a decent man ought to put up with being bored, but yet . . . "

"And could you shoot yourself?"

"Oh, come on!" Svidrigailov parried with disgust. "Please don't talk about it," he added hurriedly and with none of the bragging tone he had shown in the whole of the previous conversation. His face changed completely. "I admit it's an unforgivable weakness, but I can't help it. I am afraid of death and I don't like it when people talk about it. Do you know that I am to a certain extent a mystic?"

"Ah, the apparitions of Marfa Petrovna! Do they still go on visiting you?"

"Oh, don't talk of them; there have been no more in Petersburg, damn them!" he cried with an air of irritation. "Let's talk about that instead . . . though . . . Hm! I haven't got much time, and I can't stay long with you, it's a pity! I would have found plenty to tell you."

"What's your engagement, a woman?"

"Yes, a woman, a casual incident . . . No, that's not what I want to talk of."

"And the hideousness, the filthiness of all your surroundings, doesn't that affect you? Have you lost the strength to stop yourself?"

"And do you pretend to have strength, too? He-he-he! You surprised me just now, Rodion Romanovich, though I knew beforehand it would be so. You preach to me about vice and aesthetics! You—a Schiller, you—an idealist! Of course that's all as it should be and it would be surprising if it were not so, yet it is strange in reality . . . Ah, what a pity I have no time, you're an extremely interesting type! And, by the way, are you fond of Schiller? I am extremely fond of him."

"But what a braggart you are," Raskolnikov said with some disgust.

"I'm not, I swear it," answered Svidrigailov laughing. "However, I won't dispute it, let me be a braggart, why not brag, if it doesn't hurt anyone? I spent seven years in the country with Marfa Petrovna, so now when I come across an intelligent person like you—intelligent and highly interesting—I am simply glad to talk and, besides, I've drunk that half-glass of champagne and it's gone to my head a little. And, besides, there's a certain fact that has wound me up tremendously, but about that I . . . will keep quiet. Where are you off to?" he asked in alarm.

Raskolnikov had begun getting up. He felt oppressed and stifled and, as it were, ill at ease at having come here. He felt convinced that Svidrigailov was the most worthless scoundrel on the face of the earth.

"A-ah! Sit down, stay a little!" Svidrigailov begged. "Let them bring you some tea, anyway. Stay a little, I won't talk nonsense, about myself, I mean. I'll tell you something. If you like I'll tell you how a woman tried 'to save' me, as you'd put it? It'll be an answer to your first question, in fact, because the woman was your sister. May I tell you? It will help to pass the time."

"Tell me, but I trust that you . . . "

"Oh, don't be uneasy. Besides, even in a worthless low person like me, Avdotia Romanovna can only arouse the deepest respect."

CHAPTER FOUR

"You know perhaps—yes, I told you myself," began Svidrigailov, "that I was in the debtors' prison here, for an immense sum of money, and had no expectation of being able to pay it. There's no need to go into the particulars of how Marfa Petrovna bought me out; do you know how insanely a woman can sometimes love? She was an honest woman, and very sensible, although completely uneducated. Would you believe that this honest and jealous woman, after many scenes of hysterics and reproaches, condescended to enter into a kind of contract with me which she kept throughout our married life? She was considerably older than I was, and, besides, she always kept a clove or something in her mouth. There was so much swinishness in my soul and honesty too, of a sort, that I told her straight out I couldn't be absolutely faithful to her. This confession drove her to frenzy, but yet she seems in a way to have liked my brutal frankness. She thought it showed I was unwilling to deceive her if I warned her like this beforehand and for a jealous woman, you know, that's the first consideration. After many tears an unwritten contract was drawn up between us: first, that I would never leave Marfa Petrovna and would always be her husband; secondly, that I would never go off without her permission; thirdly, that I would never have a permanent mistress; fourthly, in return for this, Marfa Petrovna gave me a free hand with the maids, but only with her secret knowledge; fifthly, God forbid my falling in love with a woman of our class; sixthly, in case I—God forbid—should have a serious passion I was obliged to reveal it to Marfa Petrovna. On this last score, however, Marfa Petrovna was fairly at ease. She was a sensible woman and so she could not help looking upon me as a dissolute womanizer incapable of real love. But a sensible woman and a jealous woman are two very different things, and that's where the trouble came in. But to judge some people impartially we must renounce certain preconceived opinions and our habitual attitude to the ordinary people about us. I have reason to have faith in your judgment rather than in anyone else's. Perhaps you have already heard a great deal that was ridiculous and absurd about Marfa Petrovna. She certainly had some very ridiculous ways, but I tell you frankly that I feel really sorry for the innumerable sufferings which I caused. Well, that's enough, I think, for a decorous *oraison funèbre** for the most tender wife of a most tender husband. When we quarreled, I usually held my tongue and did not irritate her and that gentlemanly conduct rarely failed to ful-

---

*Funeral speech (French).

fill its aim: it influenced her, it pleased her, in fact. These were times
when she was truly proud of me. But your sister she couldn't put up
with anyway. And how she came to risk taking such a beautiful creature into her house as a governess! My explanation is that Marfa
Petrovna was an ardent and impressionable woman and simply fell in
love herself—literally fell in love—with your sister. Well, little wonder—look at Avdotia Romanovna! I saw the danger at first sight and,
what do you know, I resolved not to look at her even. But Avdotia Romanovna herself made the first step, would you believe it? Would you
believe it too that Marfa Petrovna was actually angry with me at first
for my persistent silence about your sister, for my careless reception
of her continual adoring praises of Avdotia Romanovna. I don't know
what it was she wanted! Well, of course, Marfa Petrovna told Avdotia
Romanovna every detail about me. She had the unfortunate habit of
telling literally everyone all our family secrets and continually complaining about me; how could she fail to confide in such a delightful
new friend? I expect they talked of nothing else but me and no doubt
Avdotia Romanovna heard all those dark mysterious rumors that
were current about me . . . I don't mind betting that you too have
heard something of the sort already?"

"I have. Luzhin charged you with having caused the death of a
child. Is that true?"

"Don't refer to those vulgar tales, I beg you," said Svidrigailov
with disgust and annoyance. "If you insist on wanting to know about
all that idiocy, I will tell you one day, but now . . . "

"I was told too about some footman of yours in the country
whom you treated badly."

"I beg you to drop the subject," Svidrigailov interrupted again
with obvious impatience.

"Was that the footman who came to you after death to fill your
pipe? . . . you told me about it yourself," Raskolnikov felt more and
more irritated.

Svidrigailov looked at him attentively and Raskolnikov thought
he caught a flash of spiteful mockery in that look. But Svidrigailov restrained himself and answered very civilly.

"Yes, it was. I see that you, too, are extremely interested, and I
shall feel it my duty to satisfy your curiosity at the first opportunity.
Upon my soul! I see that I really might pass for a romantic figure with

some people. Judge how grateful I must be to Marfa Petrovna for having repeated to Avdotia Romanovna such mysterious and interesting gossip about me. I dare not guess what impression it made on her, but in any case it worked in my interests. With all Avdotia Romanovna's natural aversion and in spite of my invariably gloomy and repellent aspect—she did at least feel pity for me, pity for a lost soul. And once a girl's heart is moved to pity, it's more dangerous than anything. She is bound to want to 'save him,' to bring him to his senses, and lift him up and draw him to nobler aims, and restore him to new life and usefulness—well, we all know how far such dreams can go. I saw at once that the bird was flying into the cage of her own accord. And I too prepared myself. I think you're frowning, Rodion Romanovich? There's no need. As you know, it all ended in smoke. (Damn it all, what a lot I am drinking!) Do you know, I always, from the very beginning, regretted that it wasn't your sister's fate to be born in the second or third century A.D., as the daughter of a reigning prince or some governor or proconsul in Asia Minor. She would undoubtedly have been one of those who would endure martyrdom and would have smiled when they branded her bosom with hot pincers. And she would have gone to it of her own accord. And in the fourth or fifth century she would have walked away into the Egyptian desert* and would have stayed there thirty years living on roots and ecstasies and visions. She is simply thirsting to face some torture for someone, and if she can't get her torture, she'll throw herself out of a window. I've heard something of a Mr. Razumikhin—he's said to be a sensible fellow; his surname suggests it, in fact. He's probably a divinity student. Well, he'd better look after your sister! I believe I understand her, and I am proud of it. But at the beginning of an acquaintance, as you know, people tend to be more careless and stupid. They don't see clearly. Damn it all, why is she so beautiful? It's not my fault. In fact, it began on my side with a most irresistible physical desire. Avdotia Romanovna is awfully chaste, incredibly and phenomenally so. Take note, I tell you this about your sister as a fact. She is almost morbidly chaste, in spite of her broad intelligence, and it will stand in her way. There happened to be a girl in the house then,

---

*Reference to the sixth-century saint Mary of Egypt, who is said to have spent more than forty years in a desert close to the River Jordan.

Parasha, a black-eyed wench, whom I had never seen before—she
had just come from another village—very pretty, but incredibly stupid: she burst into tears, wailed so that she could be heard all over
the place and caused scandal. One day after dinner Avdotia Romanovna followed me into an avenue in the garden and with flashing eyes insisted that I left poor Parasha alone. It was almost our first
conversation by ourselves. I, of course, was only too pleased to obey
her wishes, tried to appear disconcerted, embarrassed, in fact played
my part not badly. Then came interviews, mysterious conversations,
exhortations, entreaties, supplications, even tears—would you believe it, even tears? Think what the passion for propaganda will
bring some girls to! I, of course, threw it all on my destiny, posed as
hungering and thirsting for light, and finally resorted to the most
powerful weapon in the subjection of the female heart, a weapon
which never fails. It's the well-known resource—flattery. Nothing in
the world is harder than speaking the truth and nothing easier than
flattery. If there's the hundredth part of a false note in speaking the
truth, it leads to a discord, and that leads to trouble. But if everything, to the last note, is false in flattery, it is just as agreeable, and is
heard not without satisfaction. It may be a coarse satisfaction, but
still a satisfaction. And however coarse the flattery, at least half will
be sure to seem true. That's so for all stages of development and
classes of society. A vestal virgin might be seduced by flattery. I can
never remember without laughter how I once seduced a lady who
was devoted to her husband, her children, and her principles. What
fun it was and how little trouble! And the lady really had principles,
of her own, anyway. All my tactics lay in simply being utterly annihilated and prostrate before her purity. I flattered her shamelessly,
and as soon as I succeeded in getting a pressure of the hand, even a
glance from her, I would reproach myself for having snatched it by
force, and would declare that she had resisted, so that I could never
have gained anything but for the fact that I was so unprincipled. I
maintained that she was so innocent that she could not foresee my
treachery, and yielded to me unconsciously, unawares, and so on. In
fact, I triumphed, while my lady remained firmly convinced that she
was innocent, chaste, and faithful to all her duties and obligations
and had succumbed quite by accident. And how angry she was with
me when I explained to her at last that it was my sincere conviction

that she was just as eager as I. Poor Marfa Petrovna was extremely susceptible to flattery, and if I had wanted to, I might have had all her property settled on me during her lifetime. (I am drinking an awful lot of wine now and talking too much.) I hope you won't be angry if I mention now that I was beginning to produce the same effect on Avdotia Romanovna. But I was stupid and impatient and spoiled it all. Avdotia Romanovna had several times—and one time in particular—been greatly displeased by the expression of my eyes, would you believe it? There was sometimes a light in them which frightened her and grew stronger and stronger and more unguarded until it was hateful to her. No need to go into detail, but we parted. There I acted stupidly again. I started jeering in the coarsest way at all such propaganda and efforts to convert me; Parasha came on to the scene again, and not she alone; in fact, there was a serious incident. Ah, Rodion Romanovich, if you could only see how your sister's eyes can flash sometimes! Never mind the fact that I'm drunk at the moment and have had a whole glass of wine. I am speaking the truth. I assure you that this glance has haunted my dreams; the very rustle of her dress was more than I could eventually stand. I really began to think that I might become epileptic. I could never have believed that I could be moved to such a frenzy. It was essential, indeed, to be reconciled, but by then it was impossible. And imagine what I did then! To what a pitch of stupidity a man can be brought by frenzy! Never undertake anything in a frenzy, Rodion Romanovich. I reflected that Avdotia Romanovna was after all a beggar (ah, excuse me, that's not the word . . . but does it matter if it expresses the meaning?), that she lived by her work, that she had her mother and you to keep (ah, damn it, you are frowning again), and I resolved to offer her all my money—thirty thousand rubles I could have made available then—if she would run away with me here, to Petersburg. Of course I should have vowed eternal love, rapture, and so on. Do you know, I was so wild about her at that time that if she had told me to poison Marfa Petrovna or to cut her throat and to marry her, I would have done it at once! But it ended in the catastrophe which you know about already. You can imagine how frantic I was when I heard that Marfa Petrovna had got hold of that ghastly attorney, Luzhin, and had almost made a match between them—which would really have been just the same thing as I was proposing. Wouldn't it? Wouldn't it? I notice that you've begun to be very attentive . . . you interesting young man . . . "

Svidrigailov struck the table with his fist impatiently. He was flushed. Raskolnikov saw clearly that the glass or glass and a half of champagne that he had sipped almost unconsciously was affecting him—and he resolved to take advantage of the opportunity. He felt very suspicious of Svidrigailov.

"Well, after what you have said, I am fully convinced that you have come to Petersburg with designs on my sister," he said directly to Svidrigailov, in order to irritate him further.

"Oh, nonsense," said Svidrigailov, seeming to rouse himself. "Why, I told you . . . besides your sister can't endure me."

"Yes, I am certain that she can't, but that's not the point."

"Are you so sure that she can't?" Svidrigailov screwed up his eyes and smiled mockingly. "You are right, she doesn't love me, but you can never be sure of what has passed between husband and wife or lover and mistress. There's always a little corner which remains a secret to the world and is only known to those two. Will you answer for it that Avdotia Romanovna regarded me with aversion?"

"From some words you've dropped, I notice that you still have designs—and of course evil ones—on Dunia and intend to carry them out promptly."

"What, have I dropped words like that?" Svidrigailov asked in naive dismay, taking not the slightest notice of the epithet bestowed on his designs.

"But you're dropping them even now. Why are you so frightened? What are you so afraid of now?"

"Me—afraid? Afraid of you? You should rather be afraid of me, *cher ami*.* But what nonsense . . . I've drunk too much though, I see that. I was almost saying too much again. Damn the wine! Hi there, water!"

He snatched up the champagne bottle and flung it without ceremony out of the window. Philip brought the water.

"That's all nonsense!" said Svidrigailov, wetting a towel and putting it to his head. "But I can answer you in one word and annihilate all your suspicions. Do you know that I am going to get married?"

---

*Dear friend (French).

"You told me so before."

"Did I? I've forgotten. But I couldn't have told you so for certain because I hadn't even seen my fiancée; I only meant to. But now I really have a fiancée and it's been settled, and if it weren't that I have business that can't be put off, I would have taken you to see them at once, because I would like to ask your advice. Ah, damn it, only ten minutes left! See, look at the watch. But I must tell you, it's an interesting story, my marriage, in its own way. Where are you off to? Going again?"

"No, I'm not going away now."

"Not at all? We shall see. I'll take you there, I'll show you my betrothed, only not now. Soon you'll have to be off. You have to go right and I have to go left. Do you know that Madame Resslich, the woman I am lodging with now, eh? I know what you're thinking, that she's the woman whose girl they say drowned herself in the winter. Come on, are you listening? She arranged it all for me. You're bored, she said, you want something to fill up your time. Since, as you know, I am a depressed, gloomy person. Do you think I'm light-hearted? No, I'm gloomy. I do no harm and sit in a corner without speaking a word for three days at a time. And that Resslich is a sly one, I tell you. I know what she's got on her mind; she thinks I'll get sick of it, abandon my wife and leave, and she'll get hold of her and make a profit out of her—in our class, of course, or higher. She told me the father was a broken-down retired official, who has been sitting in a chair for the last three years with his legs paralyzed. The mamma, she said, was a sensible woman. There is a son serving in the provinces, but he doesn't help; there is a daughter, who is married, but she doesn't visit them. And they've got two little nephews on their hands, as though their own children were not enough, and they've taken their youngest daughter out of school, a girl who'll be sixteen in another month, so that she can be married. She was for me. We went there. How funny it was! I present myself—a landowner, a widower, with a well-known name, with connections, with a fortune. What if I am fifty and she is not yet sixteen? Who thinks about that? But it's fascinating, isn't it? It's fascinating, ha-ha! You should have seen how I talked to the papa and mamma. It was worth paying to have seen me at that moment. She comes in, curtsys, you can imagine, still in a short frock—an unopened bud! Blushing like a sunset—she had been told, no doubt. I don't know how you feel about female faces, but to my mind these sixteen years, these childish eyes, shyness and tears of bashfulness are better than beauty; and she is a perfect little picture, too. Fair hair in little curls, like a lamb's, full little rosy lips, tiny feet, a charmer! . . . Well, we made friends. I told them I was in a hurry because of domestic circumstances, and the next day, that is the day before yesterday, we were engaged. When I go now I take her on my knee at once and keep her there . . . Well, she blushes like a sunset and I kiss her every minute. Her mamma of course impresses on her that this is her husband and that this is how it must be. It's just delicious! The present condition of being engaged is perhaps better than marriage. Here you have what is called *la nature et la vérité*,* ha-ha! I've talked to her twice, she is far from a fool. Sometimes she steals a look at me that absolutely scorches me. Her face is like Raphael's Madonna. You know, the Sistine Madonna's face has something fantastic in it, the face of mournful religious ecstasy. Haven't you noticed it? Well, she's something in that line. The day after we'd been engaged, I bought her presents worth fifteen hundred rubles—a set of diamonds and another of pearls and a silver dressing-case as large as this, with all sorts of things in it, so that even my Madonna's face glowed. I sat her on my knee, yesterday, and I suppose rather too unceremoniously—she flushed crimson and the tears started, but she didn't want to show it. We were left alone, she suddenly flung herself on my neck (for the first time of her own accord), put her little arms round me, kissed me, and vowed that she would be an obedient, faithful, and good wife, would make me happy, would devote all her life, every minute of her life, would sacrifice everything, everything, and that all she asks in return is my respect, and that she wants 'nothing, nothing more from me, no presents.' You'll admit that to hear such a confession, alone, from an angel of sixteen in a muslin frock, with little curls, with a flush of maiden shyness in her cheeks and tears of enthusiasm in her eyes is rather fascinating! Isn't it fascinating? It's worth paying for, isn't it? Well . . . listen, we'll go to see my fiancée, only not just now!"

"The fact is that this monstrous difference in age and development excites your sensuality! Will you really make such a marriage?"

---

*Nature and truth (French).

"But of course. Everyone thinks of himself, and the man who lives most gaily knows best how to deceive himself. Ha-ha! But why are you so keen on virtue? Have mercy on me, my good friend. I am a sinful man. Ha-ha-ha!"

"But you have provided for the children of Katerina Ivanovna. Though . . . though you had your own reasons . . . I understand it all now."

"I am always fond of children, very fond of them," laughed Svidrigailov. "I can tell you one curious example of this. The first day I came here I visited various places, after seven years I just rushed at them. You probably notice that I am not in a hurry to renew my acquaintance with my old friends. I shall do without them as long as I can. Do you know, when I was with Marfa Petrovna in the country, I was haunted by the thought of these places where anyone who knows his way around can find a great deal. Yes, I swear on my soul! The peasants have vodka, the educated young people, shut out from activity, waste themselves in impossible dreams and visions and are crippled by theories; Jews have sprung up and are amassing money, and all the rest give themselves up to debauchery. From the first hour the town reeked of its familiar odors. I happened to be in a terrible den—I like my dens dirty—it was a dance, so called, and there was a cancan such as I never saw in my day. Yes, there you have progress. All of a sudden I saw a little girl of thirteen, nicely dressed, dancing with a specialist in that line, with another one vis-à-vis. Her mother was sitting on a chair by the wall. You can't fancy what a cancan that was! The girl was ashamed, blushed, at last felt insulted, and began to cry. Her partner seized her and began whirling her round and performing before her; everyone laughed and—I like the public, even the cancan public—they laughed and shouted, 'Serves her right—serves her right! Shouldn't bring children!' Well, it's not my business whether that consoling reflection was logical or not. I at once fixed on my plan, sat down by her mother, and began by saying that I too was a stranger and that people here were ill-bred and that they couldn't recognize decent people and treat them with respect, let her know that I had plenty of money and offered to take them home in my carriage. I took them home and got to know them. They were staying in a miserable little hole and had only just arrived from the country. She told me that she and her daughter could only regard my acquaintance as an honor. I found out that they had nothing of their own and had come to town on some legal business. I offered my services and money. I learnt that they had gone to the dancing saloon by mistake, believing that it was a genuine dancing class. I offered to assist in the young girl's education in French and dancing. My offer was accepted with enthusiasm as an honor—and we are still friendly . . . If you like, we'll go and see them, only not just now."

"Stop! Enough of your disgusting, nasty anecdotes, you vile, depraved man!"

"Schiller, you are a regular Schiller! *Où la vertu va-t-elle se nicher?**
But you know I shall tell you these things on purpose, for the pleasure of hearing your outcries!"

"I dare say. I can see I'm ridiculous myself," muttered Raskolnikov angrily.

Svidrigailov laughed heartily; finally he called Philip, paid his bill, and began getting up.

"Goodness, I am drunk, *assez causé*,"[†] he said. "It's been a pleasure."

"I should think it must be a pleasure!" cried Raskolnikov, getting up. "No doubt it is a pleasure for a worn-out profligate to describe such adventures with a monstrous project of the same sort in his mind—especially under such circumstances and to a person like me . . . It's stimulating!"

"Well, if you come to that," Svidrigailov answered, scrutinizing Raskolnikov with some surprise, "if you come to that, you are a thorough cynic yourself. You've plenty to make you so, anyway. You can understand a great deal . . . and you can do a great deal too. But enough. I sincerely regret not having talked to you more, but I shan't lose sight of you . . . Just wait a bit."

Svidrigailov walked out of the restaurant. Raskolnikov walked out after him. Svidrigailov, however, was not very drunk, the wine had affected him for a moment, but it was wearing off every minute. He was preoccupied with something of importance and was frowning. He was apparently excited and uneasily anticipating something. His behavior towards Raskolnikov had changed during the last few minutes, and he was ruder and more sneering every moment. Raskol-

---

*Where will virtue find its nest? (French).
†Enough of this chatter (French).

nikov noticed all this, and he too was uneasy. He became very ṣ
cious of Svidrigailov and resolved to follow him.

They came out on to the pavement.

"You go right, and I go left, or if you like, the other way. Only
*adieu, mon plaisir,** may we meet again."

And he walked right towards the Haymarket.

CHAPTER FIVE

RASKOLNIKOV WALKED AFTER HIM.

"What's this?" cried Svidrigailov turning round, "I thought I
said . . ."

"It means that I am not going to lose sight of you now."

"What?"

Both stood still and gazed at one another, as though measuring
their strength.

"From all your half tipsy stories," Raskolnikov observed harshly,
"I am convinced that you have not given up your designs on my sister, but are pursuing them more actively than ever. I have learnt that
my sister received a letter this morning. You have hardly been able to
sit still all this time . . . You may have unearthed a wife on the way,
but that means nothing. I should like to make certain myself."

Raskolnikov could hardly have said himself what he wanted and
what he wished to make certain of.

"My goodness! I'll call the police!"

"Call away!"

Again they stood for a minute facing each other. At last Svidrigailov's face changed. Having satisfied himself that Raskolnikov was
not frightened at his threat, he assumed a mirthful and friendly air.

"What a person! I purposely avoided referring to your affair,
though I am devoured by curiosity. It's fantastic. I've put it off until
another time, but you're enough to rouse the dead . . . Well, let us go,
only I warn you beforehand I am only going home for a moment, to

---

*Farewell, my dear (French).

get some money; then I shall lock up the apartment, take a cab and go to spend the evening at the Islands. Now, now are you going to follow me?"

"I'm coming to your house, not to see you but Sofia Semionovna, to say I'm sorry not to have been at the funeral."

"That's as you like, but Sofia Semionovna is not at home. She has taken the three children to an old lady of high rank, the patroness of some orphan asylums, whom I used to know years ago. I charmed the old lady by depositing a sum of money with her to provide for the three children of Katerina Ivanovna and subscribing to the institution as well. I also told her the story of Sofia Semionovna in full detail, suppressing nothing. It produced an indescribable effect on her. That's why Sofia Semionovna has been invited to call today at the X. Hotel where the lady is staying for the time."

"It doesn't matter; I'll come all the same."

"As you like, it's nothing to me, but I won't come with you; here we are at home. By the way, I am convinced that you regard me with suspicion just because I have shown such delicacy and have not troubled you with questions so far . . . you understand? It struck you as extraordinary; I don't mind betting it's that. Well, it teaches people to show delicacy!"

"And to listen at doors!"

"Ah, that's it, is it?" laughed Svidrigailov. "Yes, I would have been surprised if you had let that pass after all that has happened. Ha-ha! Though I did understand something of the pranks you had been up to and were telling Sofia Semionovna about, what was the meaning of it? Perhaps I am quite behind the times and can't understand. For goodness' sake, explain it, my dear boy. Expound the latest theories!"

"You couldn't have heard anything. You're making it all up!"

"But I'm not talking about that (though I did hear something). No, I'm talking of the way you keep sighing and groaning now. The Schiller in you is in revolt every moment, and now you tell me not to listen at doors. If that's how you feel, go and inform the police that you had this mischance; you made a little mistake in your theory. But if you are convinced that people shouldn't listen at doors but that they may murder old women at their pleasure, you'd better hurry off to America. Run, young man! There may still be time. I'm being sincere. Haven't you got the money? I'll give you the fare."

"I'm not thinking of that at all," Raskolnikov interrupted with disgust.

"I understand (but don't put yourself out, don't discuss it if you don't want to). I understand the questions you are worrying over— moral ones, aren't they? Duties of citizen and man? Lay them all aside. They are nothing to you now, ha-ha! You'll say you are still a man and a citizen. If so you ought not to have got into this coil. It's no use taking up a job you are not fit for. Well, you'd better shoot yourself, or don't you want to?"

"You seem to be trying to enrage me, to make me leave you alone."

"What a strange person! But here we are. Welcome to the staircase. You see, that's the way to Sofia Semionovna. Look, there is noone at home. Don't you believe me? Ask Kapernaumov. She leaves the key with him. Here is Madame de Kapernaumov herself. Hey, what? She is rather deaf. Has she gone out? Where? Did you hear? She is not in and won't be until late in the evening probably. Well, come to my room; you wanted to come and see me, didn't you? Here we are. Madame Resslich's not at home. She is always busy, an excellent woman, I assure you . . . She might have been of use to you if you had been a little more sensible. Now, look! I'm taking this five per cent bond out of the bureau—see what a lot I've got of them still— this one will be turned into cash today. I mustn't waste any more time. The bureau is locked, the apartment is locked, and here we are again on the stairs. Shall we take a cab? I'm going to the Islands. Would you like a lift? I'll take this carriage. Ah, so you refuse? You are tired of it! Come for a drive! I believe it will rain. Never mind, we'll put down the hood . . . "

Svidrigailov was already in the carriage. Raskolnikov decided that his suspicions were unjust, at least for the moment. Without answering a word he turned and walked back towards the Haymarket. If he had only turned round on his way he might have seen Svidrigailov get out not even a hundred paces away, dismiss the cab and walk along the pavement. But he had turned the corner and could see nothing. Intense disgust drew him away from Svidrigailov.

"To think that I could for one instant have looked for help from that coarse brute, that depraved sensualist and blackguard!" he cried.

Raskolnikov's judgment was uttered too lightly and hastily: there was something about Svidrigailov which gave him a certain original, even a mysterious character. As concerned his sister, Raskolnikov was convinced that Svidrigailov would not leave her in peace. But it was too tiresome and unbearable to go on thinking and thinking about this.

When he was alone, he had not gone twenty paces before he sank, as usual, into deep thought. On the bridge he stood by the railing and began gazing at the water. And his sister was standing close by him.

He met her at the entrance to the bridge, but passed by without seeing her. Dunia had never met him like this in the street before and was struck with dismay. She stood still and did not know whether to call to him or not. Suddenly she saw Svidrigailov coming quickly from the direction of the Haymarket.

He seemed to be approaching cautiously. He did not go on to the bridge, but stood aside on the pavement, doing all he could to avoid Raskolnikov seeing him. He had been observing Dunia for some time and had been making signs to her. She thought he was signaling to beg her not to speak to her brother, but to come towards him.

That was what Dunia did. She stole past her brother and went up to Svidrigailov.

"Let us hurry away," Svidrigailov whispered to her, "I don't want Rodion Romanovich to know about our meeting. I must tell you I've been sitting with him in the restaurant close by, where he looked me up, and I had great difficulty in getting rid of him. He has somehow heard of my letter to you and suspects something. It wasn't you who told him, of course, but if not you, who then?"

"Well, we've turned the corner now," Dunia interrupted, "and my brother won't see us. I should tell you now that I am going no further with you. Speak to me here. You can tell me everything in the street."

"In the first place, I can't say it in the street; secondly, you must hear Sofia Semionovna too; and, thirdly, I will show you some papers . . . Oh well, if you won't agree to come with me, I shall refuse to give any explanation and go away at once. But I beg you not to forget that a very curious secret of your beloved brother's is entirely in my keeping."

Dunia stood still, hesitating, and looked at Svidrigailov with searching eyes.

"What are you afraid of?" he observed quietly. "The town is not the country. And even in the country you did me more harm than I did you."

"Have you prepared Sofia Semionovna?"

"No, I have not said a word to her and I am not quite certain whether she is at home now. But most likely she is. She has buried her stepmother today: she is not likely to go out visiting people on a day like that. For the time being I don't want to speak to anyone about it and I half regret having spoken to you. The slightest indiscretion is as bad as betrayal in a thing like this. I live there in that house, we are coming to it. That's the porter of our house—he knows me very well; you see, he's bowing; he sees I'm coming with a lady and no doubt he has noticed your face already and you will be glad of that if you are afraid of me and suspicious. Excuse the fact that I'm putting things so coarsely. I haven't got an apartment to myself; Sofia Semionovna's room is next to mine—she lodges in the next apartment. The whole floor is let out to tenants. Why are you frightened? You look like a child. Am I really so terrible?"

Svidrigailov's lips were twisted in a condescending smile; but he was in no smiling mood. His heart was throbbing and he could scarcely breathe. He spoke rather loud to cover his growing excitement. But Dunia did not notice this curious excitement, she was so irritated by his remark that she was frightened of him, that she looked like a child and that he was so terrible to her.

"Though I know that you are not a man . . . of honor, I am not in the least bit afraid of you. Lead the way," she said with apparent composure, but her face was very pale.

Svidrigailov stopped at Sonia's room.

"Allow me to ask whether she is at home . . . She is not. How unfortunate! But I know she may come quite soon. If she's gone out, it can only be to see a lady about the orphans. Their mother is dead . . . I've been meddling and making arrangements for them. If Sofia Semionovna does not come back in ten minutes, I will send her to you, today if you like. This is my apartment. These are my two rooms. Madame Resslich, my landlady, has the next room. Now, look this way. I will show you my chief piece of evidence: this door from my bedroom leads into two totally empty rooms, which are available for rent. Here they are . . . You must look into them with some attention."

Svidrigailov occupied two fairly large furnished rooms. Dunia was looking around her mistrustfully, but saw nothing special in the furniture or in the position of the rooms. Yet there was something to observe, for instance, that Svidrigailov's apartment was exactly between two sets of almost uninhabited apartments. His rooms were not entered directly from the passage, but through the landlady's two almost empty rooms. Unlocking a door leading out of his bedroom, Svidrigailov showed Dunia the two empty rooms that were to let. Dunia stopped in the doorway, not knowing what she was being asked to look at, but Svidrigailov swiftly explained.

"Look here, at this second large room. Notice that door, it's locked. By the door stands a chair, the only one in the two rooms. I brought it from my rooms in order to listen more conveniently. Just the other side of the door is Sofia Semionovna's table; she sat there talking to Rodion Romanovich. And I sat here listening on two successive evenings, for two hours at a time—and of course I was able to learn something, what do you think?"

"You listened?"

"Yes, I did. Now come back to my room; we can't sit down here."

He brought Avdotia Romanovna back into his sitting-room and offered her a chair. He sat down at the opposite side of the table, at least seven feet from her, but there was probably the same glow in his eyes which had once frightened Dunia so much. She shuddered and once more looked about her distrustfully. It was an involuntary gesture; she evidently did not wish to betray her uneasiness. But the secluded position of Svidrigailov's lodging had suddenly struck her. She wanted to ask whether his landlady at least were at home, but pride kept her from asking. Moreover, she had another worry in her heart incomparably greater than fear for herself. She was in great distress.

"Here is your letter," she said, laying it on the table. "Can it be true what you write? You hint at a crime committed, you say, by my brother. You hint at it too clearly; you daren't deny it now. I must tell you that I'd heard of this stupid story before you wrote and don't believe a word of it. It's a disgusting and ridiculous suspicion. I know the story and why and how it was invented. You can't have any proof. You promised to prove it. Speak! But let me warn you that I don't believe you! I don't believe you!"

Dunia said this, speaking hurriedly, and for an instant the color rushed to her face.

"If you didn't believe it, how could you risk coming alone to my rooms? Why have you come? Just out of curiosity?"

"Don't torment me. Speak, speak!"

"There's no denying that you are a brave girl. In all honesty, I thought you would have asked Mr. Razumikhin to escort you here. But he was not with you nor anywhere near. I was on the look-out. It's courageous of you, it proves you wanted to spare Rodion Romanovich. But everything is divine in you . . . About your brother, what should I tell you? You've just seen him yourself. What did you think of him?"

"Surely that's not the only thing you are building on?"

"No, not on that, but on his own words. He came here on two successive evenings to see Sofia Semionovna. I've shown you where they sat. He made a full confession to her. He is a murderer. He killed an old woman, a pawnbroker, with whom he had pawned things himself. He killed her sister too, a saleswoman called Lizaveta, who happened to come in while he was murdering her sister. He killed them with an axe he brought with him. He murdered them to rob them and he did rob them. He took money and various things . . . He told all this, word for word, to Sofia Semionovna, the only person who knows his secret. But she has had no share by word or deed in the murder; she was as horrified at it as you are now. Don't be anxious, she won't betray him."

"It cannot be," muttered Dunia, with white lips. She gasped for breath. "It cannot be. There was not the slightest cause, no sort of ground . . . It's a lie, a lie!"

"He robbed her, that was the cause, he took money and various things. It's true that by his own admission he made no use of the money or the things and hid them under a stone, where they are now. But that was because he did not dare make use of them."

"But how could he steal, rob? How could he dream of it?" cried Dunia, and she jumped up from the chair. "But you know him, you've seen him, can he be a thief?"

She seemed to be imploring Svidrigailov; she had entirely forgotten her fear.

"There are thousands and millions of combinations and possibilities, Avdotia Romanovna. A thief steals and knows he is a scoundrel, but I've heard of a gentleman who broke open the mail. Who knows, very likely he thought he was doing a gentlemanly thing! Of course I should not have believed it myself if I'd been told of it as you have, but I believe my own ears. He explained all the causes of it to Sofia Semionovna too, but she did not believe her ears at first, yet she believed her own eyes at last."

"What . . . were the causes?"

"It's a long story, Avdotia Romanovna. Here's . . . how shall I tell you?—A theory of a sort, the same one by which I for instance consider that a single misdeed is permissible if the principal aim is right, a solitary wrongdoing and hundreds of good deeds! It's galling too, of course, for a young man of gifts and overweening pride to know that if he had, for instance, a paltry three thousand, his whole career, his whole future would be differently shaped and yet not to have that three thousand. Add to that, nervous irritability from hunger, from lodging in a hole, from rags, from a vivid sense of the charm of his social position and his sister's and mother's position too. Above all, vanity, pride and vanity, though goodness knows he may have good qualities too . . . I am not blaming him, please don't think it; besides, it's not my business. A special little theory came in too—a theory of a sort—dividing mankind, you see, into material and superior people, that is people to whom the law does not apply owing to their superiority, who make laws for the rest of mankind, the material, that is. It's all right as a theory, une théorie comme une autre.* Napoleon attracted him tremendously, that is, what affected him was that a great many men of genius have not hesitated at wrongdoing, but have overstepped the law without thinking about it. He seems to have fancied that he was a genius too—that is, he was convinced of it for a time. He has suffered a great deal and is still suffering from the idea that he could make a theory, but was incapable of boldly overstepping the law, and so he is not a man of genius. And that's humiliating for a young man of any pride, in our day especially . . . "

"But remorse? You deny him any moral feeling then? Is he like that?"

"Ah, Avdotia Romanovna, everything is in a muddle now; not

---

*A theory like any other (French).

that it was ever in very good order. Russians in general are broad in their ideas, Avdotia Romanovna, broad like their land and extremely disposed to the fantastic, the chaotic. But it's a misfortune to be broad without a special genius. Do you remember what a lot of talk we had together on this subject, sitting in the evenings on the terrace after supper? Why, you used to reproach me with breadth! Who knows, perhaps we were talking at the very time when he was lying here thinking over his plan. There are no sacred traditions amongst us, especially in the educated class, Avdotia Romanovna. At best someone will make them up somehow for himself from books or from scme old chronicle. But those are for the most part the learned and all of them are old, so that it would be almost ill-bred in a man of society. You know my opinions in general, though. I never blame anyone. I do nothing at all, I persevere in that. But we've talked of this more than once before. I was so happy indeed as to interest you in my opinions . . . You are very pale, Avdotia Romanovna."

"I know his theory. I read that article of his about men for whom everything is permissible. Razumikhin brought it to me."

"Mr. Razumikhin? Your brother's article? In a magazine? Is there such an article? I didn't know. It must be interesting. But where are you going, Avdotia Romanovna?"

"I want to see Sofia Semionovna," Dunia articulated faintly. "How can I see her? Maybe she has come back. I must see her at once. Perhaps she . . . "

Avdotia Romanovna could not finish. Her breath literally failed her.

"Sofia Semionovna will not be back until nightfall, at least I believe not. She was going to come back at once, but if not, then she will not be in until pretty late."

"Ah, then you are lying! I see . . . you were lying . . . lying all the time . . . I don't believe you! I don't believe you!" cried Dunia, completely losing her head.

Almost fainting, she sank on to a chair which Svidrigailov hastily gave her.

"Avdotia Romanovna, what is it? Control yourself! Here is some water. Drink a little . . . "

He sprinkled some water over her. Dunia shuddered and came to herself.

"It has acted violently," Svidrigailov muttered to himself, frowning. "Avdotia Romanovna, calm yourself! Believe me, he has friends. We will save him. Would you like me to take him abroad? I have money, I can get a ticket in three days. And as for the murder, he will do all sorts of good deeds yet, to atone for it. Calm yourself. He may become a great man yet. Well, how are you? How do you feel?"

"You cruel man! How can you jeer at it! Let me go . . . "

"Where are you going?"

"To see him. Where is he? Do you know? Why is this door locked? We came in through that door and now it is locked. When did you manage to lock it?"

"We couldn't be shouting all over the apartment about such a subject. I am far from jeering; it's simply that I'm sick of talking like this. But how can you go in such a state? Do you want to betray him? You will drive him to fury, and he will give himself up. Let me tell you, he is already being watched; they are already on his trail. You will simply be giving him away. Wait a little: I saw him and was talking to him just now. He can still be saved. Wait a bit, sit down; let us think it over together. I asked you to come in order to discuss it alone with you and to consider it thoroughly. Sit down!"

"How can you save him? Can he really be saved?"

Dunia sat down. Svidrigailov sat down beside her.

"It all depends on you, on you, on you alone," he began with glowing eyes, almost in a whisper and hardly able to utter the words for emotion.

Dunia drew back from him in alarm. He too was trembling all over.

"You . . . one word from you, and he is saved. I . . . I'll save him. I have money and friends. I'll send him away at once. I'll get a passport, two passports, one for him and one for me. I have friends . . . capable people . . . If you like, I'll take a passport for you . . . for your mother . . . What do you want with Razumikhin? I love you too . . . I love you beyond everything . . . Let me kiss the hem of your dress, let me, let me . . . The very rustle of it is too much for me. Tell me, 'do that,' and I'll do it. I'll do everything. I will do the impossible. What you believe, I will believe. I'll do anything—anything! Don't, don't look at me like that. Do you know that you are killing me? . . . "

He was almost beginning to rave . . . Something seemed suddenly to go to his head. Dunia jumped up and rushed to the door.

"Open it! Open it!" she called, shaking the door. "Open it! Is there no-one there?"

Svidrigailov got up and regained his composure. His still trembling lips slowly broke into an angry mocking smile.

"There is no-one at home," he said quietly and emphatically. "The landlady has gone out, and it's a waste of time to shout like that. You are only exciting yourself uselessly."

"Where is the key? Open the door at once, at once, base man!"

"I have lost the key and cannot find it."

"This is an outrage," cried Dunia, turning pale as death. She rushed to the furthest corner, where she hurriedly barricaded herself with a little table.

She did not scream, but fixed her eyes on her tormentor and watched every movement he made.

Svidrigailov remained standing at the other end of the room facing her. He really was composed, at least in appearance, but his face was pale as before. The mocking smile did not leave his face.

"You spoke of outrage just now, Avdotia Romanovna. In that case you may be sure I've taken measures. Sofia Semionovna is not at home. The Kapernaumovs are far away—there are five locked rooms between. I am at least twice as strong as you are and I have nothing to fear, besides. For you could not complain afterwards. You surely would not be willing actually to betray your brother? Besides, no-one would believe you. Why would a girl have come alone to visit a solitary man in his lodgings? So that even if you do sacrifice your brother, you could prove nothing. It is very difficult to prove an assault, Avdotia Romanovna."

"Scoundrel!" whispered Dunia indignantly.

"As you like, but observe I was only speaking by way of a general proposition. It's my personal conviction that you are perfectly right—violence is hateful. I only spoke to show you that you need have no remorse even if . . . you were willing to save your brother of your own accord, as I have suggested to you. You would be simply submitting to circumstances, to violence, in fact, if we must use that word. Think about it. Your brother's and your mother's fate are in your hands. I will be your slave . . . all my life . . . I will wait here."

Svidrigailov sat down on the sofa about eight steps from Dunia. She had not the slightest doubt now of his unbending determination. Besides, she knew him. Suddenly she pulled out of her pocket a revolver, cocked it and laid it in her hand on the table. Svidrigailov jumped up.

"Aha! So that's it, is it?" he cried, surprised but smiling maliciously. "Well, that completely alters the way we look at things. You've made things much easier for me, Avdotia Romanovna. But where did you get the revolver? Was it Mr. Razumikhin? Why, it's my revolver, an old friend! And how I've hunted for it! The shooting lessons I've given you in the country have not been thrown away."

"It's not your revolver, it belonged to Marfa Petrovna, whom you killed, wretch! There was nothing of yours in her house. I took it when I began to suspect what you were capable of. If you dare to advance one step, I swear I'll kill you." She was frantic.

"But your brother? I ask out of curiosity," said Svidrigailov, still standing where he was.

"Inform on him, if you want to! Don't move! Don't come closer! I'll shoot! You poisoned your wife, I know; you are a murderer yourself!" She held the revolver ready.

"Are you so positive I poisoned Marfa Petrovna?"

"You did! You hinted it yourself! You spoke to me about poison . . . I know you went to get it . . . you had it ready . . . It was your doing . . . It must have been your doing . . . Blackguard!"

"Even if that were true, it would have been for your sake . . . you would have been the cause."

"You are lying! I hated you, always, always . . . "

"Oh, Avdotia Romanovna! You seem to have forgotten how you softened to me in the heat of propaganda. I saw it in your eyes. Do you remember that moonlight night, when the nightingale was singing?"

"That's a lie," there was a flash of fury in Dunia's eyes, "that's a lie and a libel!"

"A lie? Well, if you like, it's a lie. I made it up. Women ought not to be reminded of such things," he smiled. "I know you will shoot, you pretty, wild creature. Well, shoot away!"

Dunia raised the revolver, and deadly pale, gazed at him, measuring the distance and awaiting the first movement on his part. Her lower lip was white and quivering and her big black eyes flashed like fire. He had never seen her so beautiful. The fire glowing in her eyes at the moment she raised the revolver seemed to kindle him and there was a pang of anguish in his heart. He took a step forward and a shot rang out. The bullet grazed his hair and flew into the wall behind. He stood still and laughed softly.

"The wasp has stung me. She aimed straight at my head. What's this? Blood?" he pulled out his handkerchief to wipe the blood, which flowed in a thin stream down his right temple. The bullet seemed to have just grazed the skin.

Dunia lowered the revolver and looked at Svidrigailov not so much in terror as in a sort of wild amazement. She seemed not to understand what she was doing and what was going on.

"Well, you missed! Fire again, I'll wait," said Svidrigailov softly, still smiling, but gloomily. "If you go on like that, I shall have time to seize you before you cock again."

Dunia started, quickly cocked the pistol and again raised it.

"Let me be," she cried in despair. "I swear I'll shoot again. I . . . I'll kill you."

"Well . . . at three paces you can hardly help it. But if you don't . . . then." His eyes flashed and he took two steps forward. Dunia shot again: it misfired.

"You haven't loaded it properly. Never mind, you have another bullet there. Get it ready, I'll wait."

He stood facing her, two paces away, waiting and gazing at her with wild determination, with feverishly passionate, stubborn, set eyes. Dunia saw that he would sooner die than let her go. "And . . . now, of course she would kill him, at two paces!" Suddenly she flung away the revolver.

"She's dropped it!" said Svidrigailov with surprise, and he drew a deep breath. A weight seemed to have rolled from his heart—perhaps not only the fear of death; indeed, he may scarcely have felt it at that moment. It was the deliverance from another feeling, darker and more bitter, which he could not himself have defined.

He went to Dunia and gently put his arm round her waist. She did not resist, but, trembling like a leaf, looked at him with imploring eyes. He tried to say something, but his lips moved without being able to utter a sound.

"Let me go," Dunia implored. Svidrigailov shuddered. Her voice now was quite different.

"Then you don't love me?" he asked softly. Dunia shook her head.

"And . . . and you can't? Never?" he whispered in despair.

"Never!"

There followed a moment of terrible, dumb struggle in the heart of Svidrigailov. He looked at her with an indescribable gaze. Suddenly he withdrew his arm, turned quickly to the window and stood facing it. Another moment passed.

"Here's the key."

He took it out of the left pocket of his coat and laid it on the table behind him, without turning or looking at Dunia.

"Take it! Hurry!"

He looked stubbornly out of the window. Dunia went up to the table to take the key.

"Hurry! Hurry!" repeated Svidrigailov, still without turning or moving. But there seemed a terrible significance in the tone of that "hurry."

Dunia understood it, snatched up the key, flew to the door, unlocked it quickly and rushed out of the room. A minute later, beside herself, she ran out on to the canal bank in the direction of X. Bridge.

Svidrigailov spent three minutes standing at the window. At last he slowly turned, looked about him and passed his hand over his forehead. A strange smile contorted his face, a pitiful, sad, weak smile, a smile of despair. The blood, which was already getting dry, smeared his hand. He looked angrily at it, then wetted a towel and washed his temple. The revolver which Dunia had flung away lay near the door and suddenly caught his eye. He picked it up and examined it. It was a little pocket three-barrel revolver of old-fashioned construction. There were still two charges and one capsule left in it. It could be fired again. He thought a little, put the revolver in his pocket, took his hat and went out.

CHAPTER SIX

HE SPENT THAT EVENING until ten o'clock going from one low haunt to another. Katia too turned up and sang another gutter song, about how a certain "villain and tyrant"—"began kissing Katia."—

Svidrigailov treated Katia and the organ-grinder and some singers and the waiters and two little clerks. He was particularly drawn to these clerks by the fact that they both had crooked noses, one bent to the left and the other to the right. They took him finally to a pleasure garden, where he paid for their entrance. There was one lanky three-year-old pine tree and three bushes in the garden, besides a "Vauxhall,"* which was in reality a drinking-bar where tea too was served, and there were a few green tables and chairs standing round it. A chorus of wretched singers and a drunken, but extremely depressed German clown from Munich with a red nose entertained the public. The clerks quarrelled with some other clerks and a fight seemed imminent. Svidrigailov was chosen to decide the dispute. He listened to them for a quarter of an hour, but they shouted so loud that there was no possibility of understanding them. The only fact that seemed certain was that one of them had stolen something and had even succeeded in selling it on the spot to a Jew, but would not share the spoil with his companion. Finally it appeared that the stolen object was a teaspoon belonging to the Vauxhall. It was missed and the affair began to seem troublesome. Svidrigailov paid for the spoon, got up, and walked out of the garden. It was about six o'clock. He had not drunk a drop of wine all this time and had ordered tea more for the sake of appearances than anything.

It was a dark and stifling evening. Threatening storm-clouds came over the sky at about ten o'clock. There was a clap of thunder, and the rain came down like a waterfall. The water did not fall in drops, but beat on the earth in streams. There were flashes of lightning every minute and each flash lasted while one could count five.

Drenched to the skin, he went home, locked himself in, opened the bureau, took out all his money and tore up two or three papers. Then, putting the money in his pocket, he was about to change his clothes, but, looking out of the window and listening to the thunder and the rain, he gave up the idea, took up his hat and went out of the room without locking the door. He went straight to Sonia. She was at home.

She was not alone: the four Kapernaumov children were with her. She was giving them tea. She received Svidrigailov in respectful

---

*Small park with a theater modeled on Vauxhall Gardens in London.

silence, looking wonderingly at his soaking clothes. The children all ran away at once in indescribable terror.

Svidrigailov sat down at the table and asked Sonia to sit beside him. She timidly prepared to listen.

"I may be going to America, Sofia Semionovna," said Svidrigailov," and as I am probably seeing you for the last time, I have come to make some arrangements. Well, did you see the lady today? I know what she said to you, you need not tell me." (Sonia made a movement and blushed.) "Those people have their own way of doing things. As to your sisters and your brother, they are really provided for and the money assigned to them I've put into safe keeping and have received acknowledgments. You had better take charge of the receipts, in case anything happens. Here, take them! Well, now that's settled. Here are three 5 per cent bonds to the value of three thousand rubles. Take those for yourself, entirely for yourself, and let that be strictly between ourselves, so that no-one knows of it, whatever you hear. You will need the money, because to go on living in the old way, Sofia Semionovna, is bad, and besides there is no need for it now."

"I am so obliged to you, and so are the children and my stepmother," said Sonia hurriedly, "and if I've said so little . . . please don't consider . . . "

"That's enough! That's enough!"

"But as for the money, Arkady Ivanovich, I am very grateful to you, but I don't need it now. I can always earn my own living. Don't think me ungrateful. If you are so charitable, that money . . . "

"It's for you, for you, Sofia Semionovna, and please don't waste words over it. I haven't got the time for it. You will want it. Rodion Romanovich has two alternatives: a bullet in the brain or Siberia." (Sonia looked wildly at him, and started.) "Don't be uneasy, I know all about it from his own lips and I am not a gossip; I won't tell anyone. It was good advice when you told him to give himself up and confess. It would be much better for him. Well, if it turns out to be Siberia, he will go and you will follow him. That's so, isn't it? And if so, you'll need money. You'll need it for him, do you understand? Giving it to you is the same as my giving it to him. Besides, you promised Amalia Ivanovna to pay what you owe. I heard you. How can you undertake such obligations so carelessly, Sofia Semionovna? It was Katerina Ivanovna's debt and not yours, so you ought not to have taken any notice of the German woman. You can't get through the world like that. If you are ever questioned about me—tomorrow or the day after you will be asked—don't say anything about the fact that I am coming to see you now and don't show the money to anyone or say a word about it. Well, now, goodbye." (He got up.) "My greetings to Rodion Romanovich. By the way, you'd better put the money for the present in Mr. Razumikhin's keeping. You know Mr. Razumikhin? Of course you do. He's not a bad man. Take it to him tomorrow or . . . when the time comes. And until then, hide it carefully."

Sonia, too, jumped up from her chair and looked in dismay at Svidrigailov. She longed to speak, to ask a question, but for the first moments she did not dare and did not know how to begin.

"How can you . . . how can you be going now, in rain like this?"

"What, set off for America, and get stopped by the rain! Ha, ha! goodbye, Sofia Semionovna, my dear! Live and live long, you will be of use to others. By the way . . . tell Mr. Razumikhin I send my greetings to him. Tell him Arkady Ivanovich Svidrigailov sends his greetings. Be sure to."

He went out, leaving Sonia in a state of wondering anxiety and vague apprehension.

It appeared afterwards that on the same evening, at twenty past eleven, he made another very eccentric and unexpected visit. The rain still persisted. Drenched to the skin, he walked into the little apartment where the parents of his fiancée lived, in Third Street on Vassilyevsky Island. He knocked for some time before he was admitted, and his visit at first caused a great disturbance; but Svidrigailov could be very fascinating when he liked, so that the first and in fact very intelligent surmise of the sensible parents—that Svidrigailov had probably had so much to drink that he did not know what he was doing—vanished immediately. The decrepit father was wheeled in to see Svidrigailov by the tender and sensible mother, who as usual began the conversation with various irrelevant questions. She never asked a direct question, but began by smiling and rubbing her hands and then, if she had to ask about some detail—for instance, when Svidrigailov would like to have the wedding—she would start with interested and almost eager questions about Paris and the court life there, and only by degrees brought the conversation round to Third Street. On other occasions this had of course been very impressive, but this time Arkady Ivanovich seemed particularly impatient, and insisted on seeing his betrothed at once, though he had been informed to begin with that she had already gone to bed. The girl of course appeared.

Svidrigailov informed her at once that very important affairs obliged him to leave Petersburg for a time, that he had therefore brought her fifteen thousand rubles and that he begged her accept them as a present from him, as he had long been intending to make her this trifling present before their wedding. The logical connection of the present with his immediate departure and the absolute necessity of visiting them for that purpose in pouring rain at midnight was not made clear. But it all came off very well; even the inevitable questions, the inevitable expressions of wonder and regret were extraordinarily few and restrained. On the other hand, the gratitude expressed was remarkably glowing and was reinforced by tears from this most sensible of mothers. Svidrigailov got up, laughed, kissed his fiancée, patted her cheek, declared he would soon come back, and noticing in her eyes, along with childish curiosity, a sort of earnest, dumb inquiry, reflected and kissed her again, though he felt sincere anger inwardly at the thought that his present would be immediately locked up in the keeping of the most sensible of mothers. He went away, leaving them all in a state of extraordinary excitement, but the tender mamma, speaking quietly in a half whisper, settled some of the most important of their doubts, concluding that Svidrigailov was a great man, a man of great affairs and connections and of great wealth—there was no knowing what he had in his mind. He would start off on a journey and give away money just as his fancy took him, so there was nothing surprising about it. Of course it was strange that he was wet through, but Englishmen, for instance, are even more eccentric, and all these people of high society didn't think about what people said and didn't stand on ceremony. In fact, he may have come like that on purpose to show that he was not afraid of anyone. Above all, not a word should be said about it, because God knows what might come of it, and the money must be locked up, and it was extremely fortunate that Fedosia, the cook, had not left the kitchen. And above all not a word must be said to that old cat, Madame Resslich, and so on and so on. They sat up whispering until two o'clock, but the girl went to bed much earlier, amazed and rather sorrowful.

Meanwhile, at midnight exactly, Svidrigailov crossed the bridge on the way back to the mainland. The rain had ceased and there was a roaring wind. He began shivering, and for one moment he gazed at the black waters of the Little Neva with a look of special interest, even inquiry. But he soon felt it very cold, standing by the water; he turned and went towards Y____ Prospect. He walked along that endless street for a long time, almost half an hour, more than once stumbling in the dark on the wooden pavement, but continually looking for something on the right side of the street. He had noticed passing through this street recently that there was a hotel somewhere near the end, built of wood, but fairly large, and its name, he remembered, was something like Adrianople. He was not mistaken: the hotel was so conspicuous in that God-forsaken place that he could not fail to see it even in the dark. It was a long, blackened wooden building, and although it was late there were lights in the windows and signs of life within. He went in and asked a ragged fellow who met him in the corridor for a room. The latter, scanning Svidrigailov, pulled himself together and led him at once to a tiny, stuffy room in the distance, at the end of the corridor, under the stairs. There was no other room; all of them were occupied. The ragged fellow looked inquiringly.

"Is there tea?" asked Svidrigailov.

"Yes, sir."

"What else is there?"

"Veal, vodka, savories."

"Bring me tea and veal."

"And you don't want anything else?" he asked with apparent surprise.

"Nothing, nothing."

The ragged man went away, completely disillusioned.

"It must be a nice place," thought Svidrigailov. "How was it I didn't know it? I expect I look as if I came from a *café chantant* and had some adventure on the way. It would be interesting to know who stayed here."

He lit the candle and looked at the room more carefully. It was so low-pitched that Svidrigailov could only just stand up in it; it had one window; the bed, which was very dirty, and the plain stained chair and table almost filled it up. The walls looked as though they were made of planks, covered with shabby paper, so torn and dusty

that the pattern was indistinguishable, though the general color—
yellow—could still be made out. One of the walls was cut short by
the sloping ceiling, though the room was not an attic, but just under
the stairs.

Svidrigailov put down the candle, sat down on the bed and sank
into thought. But a strange persistent murmur which sometimes rose
to a shout in the next room attracted his attention. The murmur had
not ceased from the moment he entered the room. He listened:
someone was upbraiding and almost tearfully scolding, but he heard
only one voice.

Svidrigailov got up, shaded the light with his hand and at once
he saw light through a crack in the wall; he went up and peeped
through. The room, which was somewhat larger than his, had two
occupants. One of them, a very curly-headed man with a red in-
flamed face, was standing like an orator, without his coat, with his
legs wide apart to keep his balance, and smiting himself on the chest.
He reproached the other with being a beggar, with having no standing whatsoever. He declared that he had taken the other one out of
the gutter and he could turn him out when he liked, and that only
the finger of Providence sees it all. The object of his reproaches was
sitting in a chair, and had the air of a man who desperately wants to
sneeze, but can't. He sometimes turned sheepish and misty eyes on
the speaker, but obviously had not the slightest idea what he was talking about and scarcely heard it. A candle was burning down on the
table; there were wine glasses, a nearly empty bottle of vodka, bread
and cucumber, and glasses with the dregs of stale tea. After gazing attentively at this, Svidrigailov turned away indifferently and sat down
on the bed.

The ragged attendant, returning with the tea, could not resist
asking him again whether he didn't want anything more, and again
receiving a negative reply, finally withdrew. Svidrigailov swiftly drank
a glass of tea to warm himself, but could not eat anything. He began
to feel feverish. He took off his coat and, wrapping himself in the
blanket, lay down on the bed. He was annoyed. "It would have been
better to be well for the occasion," he thought with a smile. The
room was close, the candle burnt dimly, the wind was roaring outside, he heard a mouse scratching in the corner and the room smelt
of mice and of leather. He lay in a sort of reverie: one thought fol-

lowed another. He felt a longing to fix his imagination on something. "It must be a garden under the window," he thought. "There's a sound of trees. How I dislike the sound of trees on a stormy night, in the dark! They give me a horrible feeling." He remembered how he had disliked it when he passed Petrovsky Park just now. This reminded him of the bridge over the Little Neva and he felt cold again as he had when standing there. "I never have liked water," he thought, "even in a landscape," and he suddenly smiled again at a strange idea: "Surely now all these questions of taste and comfort ought not to matter, but I've become more particular, like an animal that picks out a special place . . . for such an occasion. I ought to have gone into Petrovsky Park! I suppose it seemed dark, cold, ha-ha! As though I were looking for pleasant sensations! . . . By the way, why haven't I put out the candle?" he blew it out. "They've gone to bed next door," he thought, not seeing the light at the crack. "Well, now, Marfa Petrovna, now is the time for you to turn up; it's dark, and the very time and place for you. But now you won't come!"

He suddenly recalled how, an hour before carrying out his plan involving Dunia, he had recommended Raskolnikov to trust her to Razumikhin's keeping. "I suppose I really did say it, as Raskolnikov guessed, to tease myself. But what a rogue that Raskolnikov is! He's gone through a good deal. He may be a successful rogue in time when he's got over his nonsense. But now he's too eager for life. These young men are contemptible on that point. But damn him! Let him please himself, it's nothing to do with me."

He could not get to sleep. By degrees Dunia's image rose before him, and a shudder ran over him. "No, I must give up all that now," he thought, rousing himself. "I must think of something else. It's strange. I never had any great hatred for anyone, I never particularly wanted to revenge myself even, and that's a bad sign, a bad sign, a bad sign. I never liked quarrelling either, and never lost my temper—that's a bad sign too. And the promises I made her just now, too—Damnation! But—who knows?—perhaps she would have made a new man of me somehow . . . "

He ground his teeth and sank into silence again. Again Dunia's image rose before him, just as she was when, after shooting the first time, she had lowered the revolver in terror and gazed blankly at him, so that he might have seized her twice over and she would not have lifted a hand to defend herself if he had not reminded her. He recalled how at that instant he felt almost sorry for her, how he had felt a pang at his heart . . .

"Ah! God, these thoughts again! I must put them away!"

He was dozing off; the feverish shiver had stopped, when suddenly something seemed to run over his arm and leg under the bedclothes. He started. "Ugh! Damn it! I think it's a mouse," he thought, "that's the veal I left on the table." He was extremely unwilling to pull off the blanket, get up, get cold, but suddenly something unpleasant ran over his leg again. He pulled off the blanket and lighted the candle. Shaking in a feverish chill, he bent down to examine the bed: there was nothing. He shook the blanket and suddenly a mouse jumped out on the sheet. He tried to catch it, but the mouse ran to and fro in zigzags without leaving the bed, slipped between his fingers, ran over his hand and suddenly darted under the pillow. He threw down the pillow, but in one instant felt something leap on his chest and dart over his body and down his back under his shirt. He trembled nervously and woke up.

The room was dark. He was lying on the bed and wrapped up in the blanket as before. The wind was howling under the window. "How disgusting," he thought with annoyance.

He got up and sat on the edge of the bedstead with his back to the window. "It's better not to sleep at all," he decided. There was a cold damp draught from the window, however; without getting up he drew the blanket over him and wrapped himself in it. He was not thinking of anything and did not want to think. But one image rose after another, incoherent scraps of thought without beginning or end passed through his mind. He sank into drowsiness. Perhaps the cold, or the dampness, or the dark, or the wind that howled under the window and tossed the trees roused a sort of persistent craving for the fantastic. He kept dwelling on images of flowers, he imagined a charming flower garden, a bright, warm, almost hot day, a holiday—Trinity Sunday. A fine, sumptuous country cottage in the English taste overgrown with fragrant flowers, with flower beds going round the house; the porch, wreathed in climbers, was surrounded with beds of roses. A light, cool staircase, carpeted with rich rugs, was decorated with rare plants in china pots. He noticed particularly in the windows nosegays of tender, white, heavily fragrant narcissus bending over their bright, green, thick long stalks. He was reluctant to move away from them, but he went up the stairs and came into a large, high drawing-room and again everywhere—at the windows, the doors onto the balcony, and on the balcony itself—were flowers. The floors were strewn with fragrant, freshly-cut hay, the windows were open, a fresh, cool, light air came into the room. The birds were chirruping under the window, and in the middle of the room, on a table covered with a white satin shroud, stood a coffin. The coffin was covered with white silk and edged with a thick white frill; wreaths of flowers surrounded it on all sides. Among the flowers lay a girl in a white muslin dress, with her arms crossed and pressed on her bosom, as though carved out of marble. But her loose fair hair was wet; there was a wreath of roses on her head. The stern and already rigid profile of her face looked as though it too was chiseled of marble, and the smile on her pale lips was full of an immense unchildish misery and sorrowful appeal. Svidrigailov knew that girl. There was no holy image, no burning candle beside the coffin, no sound of prayers; the girl had drowned herself. She was only fourteen, but her heart was broken. And she had destroyed herself, crushed by an insult that had appalled and amazed that childish soul, had corrupted that angel purity with unmerited disgrace and torn from her a last scream of despair, brutally disregarded, on a dark night in the cold and wet while the wind howled . . .

Svidrigailov came to, got up from the bed and went to the window. He felt for the latch and opened it. The wind lashed furiously into the little room and stung his face and his chest, only covered with his shirt, as though with frost. Under the window there must have been something like a garden, and apparently a pleasure garden. There, too, probably there were tea tables and singing in the daytime. Now drops of rain flew in at the window from the trees and bushes; it was as dark as in a cellar, so that he could only just make out some dark blurs of objects. Svidrigailov, bending down with elbows on the window-sill, gazed for five minutes into the darkness; the boom of a cannon, followed by a second one, resounded in the darkness of the night. "Ah, the signal! The river is overflowing," he thought. "By morning it will be swirling down the street in the lower parts, flooding the basements and cellars. The cellar rats will swim out, and men will curse in the rain and wind as they drag their rubbish to their upper floors. What time is it now?" And he had hardly thought it when, somewhere near, a clock on the wall, ticking away hurriedly, struck three.

"Aha! It will be light in an hour! Why wait? I'll go out at once, straight to the park. I'll choose a great bush there drenched with rain, so that as soon as one's shoulder touches it, millions of drops drip on one's head."

He moved away from the window, shut it, lit the candle, put on his waistcoat, his overcoat and his hat and went out, carrying the candle, into the passage to look for the ragged attendant who would be asleep somewhere in the midst of candle ends and all sorts of rubbish, to pay him for the room and leave the hotel. "It's the best moment; I couldn't choose a better one."

He walked for some time through a long narrow corridor without finding anyone and was just going to call out, when suddenly in a dark corner between an old cupboard and the door he caught sight of a strange object which seemed to be alive. He bent down with the candle and saw a little girl, not more than five years old, shivering and crying, with her clothes as wet as a soaking house-flannel. She did not seem afraid of Svidrigailov, but looked at him with blank amazement out of her big black eyes. Now and then she sobbed as children do when they have been crying a long time, but are starting to be comforted. The child's face was pale and tired, she was numb with cold. "How can she have come here? She must have hidden here and not slept all night." He began questioning her. The child suddenly became animated, chattered away in her baby language, something about "Mother" and that "Mother would beat her," and about some cup that she had "bwoken." The child chattered on without stopping. He could only guess from what she said that she was a neglected child, whose mother, probably a drunken cook, in the service of the hotel, whipped and frightened her; that the child had broken a cup of her mother's and was so frightened that she had run away the evening before, had hidden for a long while somewhere outside in the rain, at last had made her way in here, hidden behind the cupboard and spent the night there, crying and trembling from the damp, the darkness and the fear that she would be badly beaten for it. He took her in his arms, went back to his room, sat her on the bed, and began undressing her. The torn shoes which she had on her stockingless feet were as wet as if they had been standing in a puddle all night. When he had undressed her, he put her on the bed, covered her up and wrapped her in the blanket from her head downwards. She fell asleep at once. Then he sank into dreary musing again.

"How stupid it was to trouble myself," he decided suddenly with an oppressive feeling of annoyance. "What idiocy!" In vexation he picked up the candle to go and look for the ragged attendant again and leave. "Damn the child!" he thought as he opened the door, but he turned again to see whether the child was asleep. He raised the blanket carefully. The child was sleeping soundly, she had got warm under the blanket, and her pale cheeks were flushed. But strange to say that flush seemed brighter and coarser than the rosy cheeks of childhood. "It's a flush of fever," thought Svidrigailov. It was like the flush from drinking, as though she had been given a full glass to drink. Her crimson lips were hot and glowing; but what was this? He suddenly fancied that her long black eyelashes were quivering, as though the lids were opening and a sly crafty eye peeped out with an unchildlike wink, as though the little girl were not asleep, but pretending. Yes, it was so. Her lips parted in a smile. The corners of her mouth quivered, as though she were trying to control them. But now she quite gave up all effort, now it was a grin, a broad grin; there was something shameless, provocative in that quite unchildish face; it was depravity, it was the face of a harlot, the shameless face of a French harlot. Now both eyes opened wide; they turned a glowing, shameless glance upon him; they laughed, invited him . . . There was something infinitely hideous and shocking in that laugh, in those eyes, in such nastiness in the face of a child. "What, at five years old?" Svidrigailov muttered in genuine horror. "What does it mean?" And now she turned to him, her little face all aglow, holding out her arms . . . "Damned child!" Svidrigailov cried, raising his hand to strike her, but at that moment he woke up.

He was in the same bed, still wrapped in the blanket. The candle had not been lighted, and daylight was streaming in at the windows.

"I've been having bad dreams all night!" He got up angrily, feeling utterly shattered; his bones ached. There was a thick mist outside and he could see nothing. It was nearly five. He had overslept! He got up, put on his still damp jacket and overcoat. Feeling the revolver in his pocket, he took it out and then he sat down, took a notebook out of his pocket and in the most conspicuous place on the title page wrote a few lines in large letters. Reading them over, he sank into thought with his elbows on the table. The revolver and the notebook lay beside him. Some flies woke up and settled on the untouched veal, which was still on the table. He stared at them and at last with his free right hand began trying to catch one. He tried until he was tired, but could not catch it. At last, realizing that he was engaged in this interesting pursuit, he started, got up and walked resolutely out of the room. A minute later he was in the street.

A thick milky mist hung over the town. Svidrigailov walked along the slippery dirty wooden pavement towards the Little Neva. He was picturing the waters of the Little Neva swollen in the night, Petrovsky Island, the wet paths, the wet grass, the wet trees and bushes and at last the bush ... He began ill-humoredly staring at the houses, trying to think of something else. There was not a cabman or a passerby in the street. The bright yellow, wooden, little houses looked dirty and dejected with their closed shutters. The cold and damp penetrated his whole body and he began to shiver. From time to time he came across store signs and read each carefully. At last he reached the end of the wooden pavement and came to a big stone house. A dirty, shivering dog crossed his path with its tail between its legs. A man in an overcoat lay dead drunk, face downwards across the pavement. He looked at him and went on. A high tower stood up on the left. "Bah!" he shouted, "here is a place. Why should it be Petrovsky? It will be in the presence of an official witness anyway ... "

He almost smiled at this new thought and turned into the street where there was the big house with the tower. At the great closed gates of the house, a little man stood with his shoulder leaning against them, wrapped in a gray soldier's coat, with a copper Achilles helmet on his head. He cast a drowsy and indifferent glance at Svidrigailov. His face wore that perpetual look of peevish dejection, which is so sourly printed on all faces of Jewish race without exception. Both of them, Svidrigailov and Achilles, stared at each other for a few minutes without speaking. At last it struck Achilles that it was unusual for a man not drunk to be standing three steps from him, staring and not saying a word.

"What do you want here?" he said, without moving or changing his position.

"Nothing, my friend, good morning," answered Svidrigailov.

"This isn't the place."

"I am going to foreign lands, my friend."

"To foreign lands?"

"To America."

"America."

Svidrigailov took out the revolver and cocked it. Achilles raised his eyebrows.

"I told you, this is no place for jokes!"

"Why shouldn't it be the place?"

"Because it isn't."

"Well, my friend, I don't mind. It's a good place. When you are asked, you just say he was going, he said, to America."

He put the revolver to his right temple.

"You can't do it here, it's not the place," cried Achilles, rousing himself, his eyes growing bigger and bigger.

Svidrigailov pulled the trigger.

CHAPTER SEVEN

THE SAME DAY, ABOUT seven o'clock in the evening, Raskolnikov was on his way to his mother's and sister's lodging—the apartment in Bakaleyev's house which Razumikhin had found for them. The stairs went up from the street. Raskolnikov walked with lagging steps, as though still hesitating whether to go or not. But nothing would have turned him back: his decision was taken.

"Besides, it doesn't matter, they still know nothing," he thought, "and they are used to thinking of me as an eccentric."

He was appallingly dressed: his clothes torn and dirty, soaked with a night's rain. His face was almost distorted from fatigue, exposure, the inward conflict that had lasted for twenty-four hours. He had spent all the previous night alone, God knows where. But anyway he had reached a decision.

He knocked at the door which was opened by his mother. Dunia was not at home. Even the servant happened to be out. At first Pulcheria Alexandrovna was speechless with joy and surprise; then she took him by the hand and drew him into the room.

"Here you are!" she began, faltering with joy. "Don't be angry with me, Rodia, for welcoming you so foolishly with tears: I am laughing, not crying. Did you think I was crying? No, I am delighted, but I've got into such a stupid habit of shedding tears. I've been like that ever since your father's death. I cry for anything. Sit down, dear boy, you must be tired; I see you are. Ah, how muddy you are."

"I was in the rain yesterday, Mother . . . " Raskolnikov began.

"No, no," Pulcheria Alexandrovna hurriedly interrupted, "you thought I was going to question you in the womanish way I used to. Don't be anxious, I understand, I understand it all; now I've learned how things are here I can see for myself that they are better. I've made up my mind once for all: how could I understand your plans and expect you to give an account of them? God knows what concerns and plans you may have, or what ideas you are hatching; so it's not for me to keep nudging your elbow, asking you what you are thinking about. But, my goodness! Why am I running to and fro as though I were crazy . . . ? I am reading your article in the magazine for the third time, Rodia. Dmitri Prokofich brought it to me. When I saw it I cried out to myself, there you are, you foolish old thing, I thought, that's what he's busy about; that's the solution of the mystery! Learned people are always like that. He may have some new ideas in his head just now; he is thinking them over and I worry him and upset him. I read it, my dear, and of course there was a great deal I did not understand; but that's only natural—how should I?"

"Show me, Mother."

Raskolnikov took the magazine and glanced at his article. Incongruous as it was with his mood and his circumstances, he felt that strange and bitter sweet sensation that every author experiences the first time he sees himself in print; besides, he was only twenty-three. It lasted only a moment. After reading a few lines he frowned and his heart throbbed with anguish. He recalled all the inward conflict of the preceding months. He flung the article on the table with disgust and anger.

"But, however foolish I may be, Rodia, I can see for myself that you will very soon be one of the leading—if not the leading man— in the world of Russian thought. And they dared to think you were mad! You don't know, but they really thought that. Ah, the despicable creatures, how could they understand genius! And Dunia, Dunia was all but believing it—what do you say to that! Your father sent things twice to magazines—the first time, poems (I've got the manuscript, I'll show you), and the second time a whole novel (I begged him to let me copy it out) and how we prayed that they would be taken—they weren't! I was breaking my heart, Rodia, six or seven days ago over your food and your clothes and the way you are living. But now I see again how foolish I was, for you can attain any position you like by your intellect and talent. No doubt you don't care about that for the moment, and you are occupied with much more important matters . . . "

"Dunia's not at home, Mother?"

"No, Rodia. I often don't see her; she leaves me alone. Dmitri Prokofich comes to see me, it's so good of him, and he always talks about you. He loves you and respects you, my dear. I wouldn't say that Dunia was inconsiderate towards me. I am not complaining. She has her ways and I have mine; she seems to have got some secrets of late and I never have any secrets from you two. Of course, I am sure that Dunia has far too much sense, and besides she loves you and me . . . but I don't know what it will all lead to. You've made me so happy by coming now, Rodia, but she has missed you by going out; when she comes in I'll tell her, 'Your brother came in while you were out.' Where have you been all this time? You mustn't spoil me, Rodia, you know; come when you can, but if you can't, it doesn't matter, I can wait. I shall know, anyway, that you are fond of me, that will be enough for me. I shall read what you write, I shall hear about you from everyone, and sometimes you'll come yourself to see me. What could be better? Here you've come now to comfort your mother, I see that."

Here Pulcheria Alexandrovna began to cry.

"Here I am again! Don't mind my foolishness. My goodness, why am I sitting here?" she cried, jumping up. "There is coffee and I don't offer you any. Ah, that's the selfishness of old age. I'll get it at once!"

"Mother, don't trouble yourself, I am going now. I haven't come for that. Please listen to me."

Pulcheria Alexandrovna went up to him timidly.

"Mother, whatever happens, whatever you hear about me, whatever you are told about me, will you always love me as you do now?" he asked suddenly from the fullness of his heart, as though not thinking of his words and not weighing them.

"Rodia, Rodia, what is the matter? How can you ask me such a question? Why, who will tell me anything about you? Besides, I wouldn't believe anyone, I would refuse to listen."

"I've come to reassure you that I've always loved you and I am glad that we are alone, even glad Dunia is out," he went on with the same impulse. "I have come to tell you that though you will be unhappy, you must believe that your son loves you now more than himself, and that everything you thought about me, that I was cruel and didn't care about you, was all a mistake. I shall never stop loving you . . . Well, that's enough: I thought I must do this and start with this . . . "

Pulcheria Alexandrovna embraced him in silence, pressing him to her bosom and weeping gently.

"I don't know what is wrong with you, Rodia," she said at last. "I've been thinking all this time that we were simply boring you and now I see that there is great sorrow in store for you, and that's why you are miserable. I've seen it coming for a long time, Rodia. Forgive me for speaking about it. I keep thinking about it and lie awake at nights. Your sister lay talking in her sleep all last night, talking of nothing but you. I caught something, but I couldn't make it out. I felt all morning as though I were going to be hanged, waiting for something, expecting something, and now it has come! Rodia, Rodia, where are you going? You are going away somewhere?"

"Yes."

"That's what I thought! I can come with you, you know, if you need me. And Dunia, too; she loves you, she loves you dearly—and Sofia Semionovna may come with us if you like. You see, I am glad to look upon her as a daughter even . . . Dmitri Prokofich will help us to go together. But . . . where . . . are you going?"

"Goodbye, Mother."

"What, today?" she cried, as though she were losing him forever.

"I can't stay, I must go now . . . "

"And can't I come with you?"

"No, but kneel down and pray to God for me. Your prayer perhaps will reach Him."

"Let me bless you and sign you with the cross. That's right, that's right. Oh, God, what are we doing?"

Yes, he was glad, he was very glad that there was no-one there, that he was alone with his mother. For the first time after all those awful months his heart was softened. He fell down in front of her, he kissed her feet and both of them wept, embracing. And she was not surprised and did not question him this time. For some days she had realized that something awful was happening to her son and that now some terrible moment had come for him.

"Rodia, my darling, my firstborn," she said, sobbing, "now you are just as when you were little. You would run like this to me and hug me and kiss me. When your father was alive and we were poor, you comforted us simply by being with us and when I buried your father, how often we wept together at his grave and embraced, as now. And if I've been crying recently, it's because my mother's heart has had a foreboding of trouble. The first time I saw you, that evening you remember, as soon as we arrived here, I guessed it just from your eyes. My heart sank at once, and today when I opened the door and looked at you, I thought the fatal hour had come. Rodia, Rodia, you are not going away today?"

"No!"

"You'll come again?"

"Yes . . . I'll come."

"Rodia, don't be angry, I don't dare question you. I know I mustn't. Just tell me—is it far where you are going?"

"Very far."

"What is awaiting you there? Some post or career for you?"

"What God sends . . . just pray for me." Raskolnikov went to the door, but she clutched him and gazed despairingly into his eyes. Her face was gripped with terror.

"Enough, Mother," said Raskolnikov, deeply regretting that he had come.

"Not forever, it's not yet forever? You'll come, you'll come tomorrow?"

"I will, I will, goodbye." He tore himself away at last.

It was a warm, fresh, bright evening; it had cleared up in the morning. Raskolnikov went to his lodgings; he made haste. He wanted to finish everything before sunset. He did not want to meet anyone until then. Going up the stairs he noticed that Nastasia rushed from the samovar to watch him intently. "Can anyone have come to see me?" he wondered. He had a disgusted vision of Porfiry. But opening his door he saw Dunia. She was sitting alone, plunged in deep thought, and looked as though she had been waiting a long time. He stopped short in the doorway. She rose from the sofa in dismay and stood up facing him. Her eyes fixed upon him, betrayed horror and infinite grief. And from those eyes alone he saw at once that she knew.

"Should I come in or go away?" he asked uncertainly.

"I've been all day with Sofia Semionovna. We were both waiting for you. We thought that you would be sure to come here."

Raskolnikov went into the room and sank exhausted on a chair.

"I feel weak, Dunia, I am very tired; and I would have liked at this moment to be able to control myself."

He glanced at her mistrustfully.

"Where were you all night?"

"I don't remember clearly. You see, sister, I wanted to make up my mind once and for all, and several times I walked by the Neva, I remember that I wanted to end it all there, but . . . I couldn't make up my mind," he whispered, looking at her mistrustfully again.

"Thank God! That was just what we were afraid of, Sofia Semionovna and I. Then you still have faith in life? Thank God, thank God!"

Raskolnikov smiled bitterly.

"I haven't any faith, but I have just been weeping in our mother's arms; I haven't any faith, but I have just asked her to pray for me. I don't know how it is, Dunia, I don't understand it."

"Have you been to see her? Have you told her?" cried Dunia, horror-stricken. "Surely you haven't done that?"

"No, I didn't tell her . . . in words; but she understood a great deal. She heard you talking in your sleep. I am sure she half understands it already. Perhaps I was wrong to go and see her. I don't know why I did go. I am a contemptible person, Dunia."

"A contemptible person, but ready to face suffering! You are, aren't you?"

"Yes, I am going. At once. Yes, to escape the disgrace I thought of drowning myself, Dunia, but as I looked into the water, I thought that if I had considered myself strong until now I'd better not be afraid of disgrace," he said, hurrying on. "It's pride, Dunia."

"Pride, Rodia."

There was a gleam of fire in his lusterless eyes; he seemed to be glad to think that he was still proud.

"You don't think, sister, that I was simply afraid of the water?" he asked, looking into her face with a sinister smile.

"Oh, Rodia, hush!" cried Dunia bitterly. Silence lasted for two minutes. He sat with his eyes fixed on the floor; Dunia stood at the other end of the table and looked at him with anguish. Suddenly he got up.

"It's late, it's time to go! I am going at once to give myself up. But I don't know why I am going to give myself up."

Big tears fell down her cheeks.

"You are crying, sister, but can you hold out your hand to me?"

"You doubted it?"

She threw her arms round him.

"Aren't you half atoning for your crime by facing the suffering!" she cried, holding him close and kissing him.

"Crime? What crime?" he cried in sudden fury. "That I killed a vile noxious insect, an old pawnbroker woman, of no use to any-one! . . . Killing her was an atonement for forty sins. She was sucking the life out of poor people. Was that a crime? I am not thinking of it and I am not thinking of atoning for it, and why are you all rubbing it in on all sides? 'A crime! A crime!' Only now I see clearly the im-becility of my cowardice, now that I have decided to face this super-fluous disgrace. It's simply because I am contemptible and have nothing in me that I have decided to, perhaps too for my advantage, as that . . . Porfiry . . . suggested!"

"Rodia, Rodia, what are you saying! You have shed blood!" cried Dunia in despair.

"Which all men shed," he put in almost frantically, "which flows and has always flowed in streams, which is spilt like champagne, and for which men are crowned in the Capitol* and are later called bene-factors of mankind. Look into it more carefully and understand it! I

---

*Hill in Rome where generals thanked the gods for their victories.

too wanted to do good and would have done hundreds, thousands of good deeds to make up for that one piece of stupidity, not stupidity even, simply clumsiness, for the idea was by no means as stupid as it seems now that it has failed . . . (Everything seems stupid when it fails.) By that stupidity I only wanted to put myself into an independent position, to take the first step, to obtain means, and then everything would have been smoothed over by benefits immeasurable in comparison . . . But I . . . I couldn't carry out even the first step, because I am contemptible, that's what's the matter! And yet I won't look at it as you do. If I had succeeded I would have been crowned with glory, but now I'm trapped."

"But that's not so, not so! Rodia, what are you saying!"

"Ah, it's not picturesque, not esthetically attractive! I fail to understand why bombarding people by regular siege is more honorable. The fear of appearances is the first symptom of impotence. I've never, never recognized this more clearly than now, and I am further than ever from seeing that what I did was a crime. I've never, never been stronger and more convinced than now."

The color had rushed into his pale exhausted face, but as he uttered his last explanation, he happened to meet Dunia's eyes and he saw such anguish in them that he could not help being checked. He felt that he had any way made these two poor women miserable, that he was in any case the cause . . .

"Dunia darling, if I am guilty forgive me (though I cannot be forgiven if I am guilty). Goodbye! We won't argue. It's time, high time for me to go. Don't follow me, I have somewhere else to visit . . . But you go at once and sit with mother. I beg you! It's my last request of you. Don't leave her at all; I left her in a state of anxiety that she is not fit to bear; she will die or go out of her mind. Be with her! Razumikhin will be with you. I've been talking to him . . . Don't cry about me: I'll try to be honest and manly all my life, even if I am a murderer. Perhaps I shall some day make a name for myself. I won't disgrace you, you'll see; I'll still show . . . Now goodbye for the present," he concluded hurriedly, noticing again a strange expression in Dunia's eyes at his last words and promises. "Why are you crying? Don't cry, don't cry: we are not parting forever! Ah, yes! Wait a minute, I'd forgotten!"

He went to the table, took up a thick dusty book, opened it and took from between the pages a little water-color portrait on ivory. It was the portrait of his landlady's daughter, who had died of fever, that strange girl who had wanted to be a nun. For a minute he gazed at the delicate expressive face of his fiancée, kissed the portrait and gave it to Dunia.

"I used to talk a great deal about it to her, only to her," he said thoughtfully. "To her heart I confided much of what has since been so hideously realized. Don't be uneasy," he returned to Dunia, "she was as much opposed to it as you, and I am glad that she is gone. The great point is that everything now is going to be different, is going to be broken in two," he cried, suddenly returning to his dejection. "Everything, everything, and am I prepared for it? Do I want it myself? They say it is necessary for me to suffer! What's the object of these senseless sufferings? Shall I know any better what they are for, when I am crushed by hardships and idiocy, and weak as an old man after twenty years' penal servitude? And what shall I have to live for then? Why am I consenting to that life now? Oh, I knew I was contemptible when I stood looking at the Neva at daybreak today!"

At last they both went out. It was hard for Dunia, but she loved him. She walked away, but after going fifty paces she turned round to look at him again. He was still in sight. At the corner he too turned and for the last time their eyes met; but noticing that she was looking at him, he motioned her away with impatience and even vexation, and turned the corner abruptly.

"I am wicked, I see that," he thought to himself, feeling ashamed a moment later of his angry gesture to Dunia. "But why are they so fond of me if I don't deserve it? Oh, if only I were alone and no-one loved me and I too had never loved anyone! None of this would have happened. But, I wonder, shall I in those fifteen or twenty years grow so meek that I shall humble myself before people and whimper at every word that I am a criminal. Yes, that's it, that's it, that's what they are sending me there for, that's what they want. Look at them running to and fro about the streets, every one of them a scoundrel and a criminal at heart and, worse still, an idiot. But try to get me off and they'd be wild with righteous indignation. Oh, how I hate them all!"

He start imagining the process which would accomplish it, that he could be humbled before all of them, indiscriminately—humbled by conviction. And yet why not? It must be so. Would not twenty years of continual servitude crush him utterly? Water wears out a stone. And why, why should he live after that? Why should he go now when he knew that it would be so? It was the hundredth time perhaps that he had asked himself that question since the previous evening, but still he went.

CHAPTER EIGHT

WHEN HE ENTERED SONIA'S room, it was already getting dark. All day Sonia had been waiting for him in terrible anxiety. Dunia had been waiting with her. She had come to her that morning, remembering the words of Svidrigailov's which Sonia knew. We will not describe the conversation and the tears of the two girls, and how friendly they became. Dunia gained one comfort at least from that interview—that her brother would not be alone. He had gone to her, Sonia, first with his confession; he had gone to her for human companionship when he needed it; she would go with him wherever fate might send him. Dunia did not ask, but she knew it was true. She looked at Sonia almost with reverence and at first almost embarrassed her by it. Sonia was almost on the point of tears. She felt herself, on the contrary, hardly worthy to look at Dunia. Dunia's gracious image when she had bowed to her so attentively and respectfully at their first meeting in Raskolnikov's room had remained in her mind as one of the most beautiful visions of her life.

Dunia at last became impatient and, leaving Sonia, went to her brother's room to wait for him there; she kept thinking that he would come there first. When she had gone, Sonia began to be tortured by her dread that he would commit suicide, and Dunia feared it too. But they had spent the day trying to persuade each other that that could not happen, and both were less anxious while they were together. As soon as they parted, each thought of nothing else. Sonia remembered how Svidrigailov had said to her the day before that Raskolnikov had two alternatives—Siberia or . . . Besides she knew his vanity, his pride and his lack of faith.

"Is it possible that he has nothing but cowardice and fear of death to make him live?" she thought at last in despair.

Meanwhile the sun was setting. Sonia was standing in dejection, looking intently out of the window, but from it she could see nothing but the unwhitewashed blank wall of the next house. At last, when she began to feel sure that he was dead—he walked into the room.

She gave a cry of joy, but looking carefully into his face she turned pale.

"Yes," said Raskolnikov, smiling. "I have come for your cross, Sonia. It was you who told me to go to the crossroads; why is it you are frightened now it's come to that?"

Sonia gazed at him astonished. His tone seemed strange to her; a cold shiver ran over her, but in a moment she guessed that the tone and the words were a mask. He spoke to her looking away, as though to avoid meeting her eyes.

"You see, Sonia, I've decided that it will be better so. There is one fact . . . But it's a long story and there's no need to discuss it. But do you know what angers me? It annoys me that all those stupid brutish faces will be gaping at me directly, pestering me with their stupid questions, which I shall have to answer—they'll point their fingers at me . . . Pah! You know I am not going to Porfiry, I am sick of him. I'd rather go to my friend, the Explosive Lieutenant; how I shall surprise him, what a sensation I shall make! But I must be cooler; I've become too irritable recently. You know I was nearly shaking my fist at my sister just now because she turned to take a last look at me. It's a brutal state to be in! Ah! What am I coming to! Well, where are the crosses?"

He seemed hardly to know what he was doing. He could not stay still or concentrate on anything; his ideas seemed to gallop after one another; he talked incoherently; his hands trembled slightly.

Without a word Sonia took out of the drawer two crosses, one of cypress wood and one of copper. She made the sign of the cross over herself and over him, and put the wooden cross on his neck.

"It's the symbol of my taking up the cross," he laughed. "As though I had not suffered much until now! The wooden cross, that is the peasant one; the copper one, that is Lizaveta's—you will wear it yourself, show me! So she had it on . . . at that moment? I remember two things like these too, a silver one and a little icon. I threw them back on the old woman's neck. Those would be appropriate now, really, those are what I ought to put on now . . . But I'm talking nonsense and forgetting what matters; I'm forgetful somehow . . . You see I have come to warn you, Sonia, so you might know . . . that's all—that's all I came for. But I thought I had more to say. You wanted me to go yourself. Well, now I'm going to prison and you'll have your wish. Well, what are you crying for? You too? Don't. Leave off! Oh, how I hate it all!"

But his feeling was stirred; his heart ached, as he looked at her. "Why is she grieving too?" he thought to himself. "What am I to her? Why does she weep? Why is she looking after me, like my mother or Dunia? She'll be my nurse."

"Cross yourself, say at least one prayer," Sonia begged in a timid broken voice.

"Oh, certainly, as much as you like! And sincerely, Sonia, sincerely . . . "

But he wanted to say something quite different.

He crossed himself several times. Sonia took up her shawl and put it over her head. It was the green *drap de dames* shawl which Marmeladov had talked about, "the family shawl." Raskolnikov thought of that looking at it, but he did not ask. He began to feel himself that he was certainly forgetting things and was disgustingly agitated. He was frightened at this. He was suddenly struck too by the thought that Sonia intended to go with him.

"What are you doing? Where are you going? Stay here, stay! I'll go alone," he cried in cowardly vexation, and almost resentful, he moved towards the door. "What's the use of going in procession!" he muttered going out.

Sonia remained standing in the middle of the room. He had not even said goodbye to her; he had forgotten her. A poignant and rebellious doubt surged in his heart.

"Was it right, was it right, all this?" he thought again as he went down the stairs. "Couldn't he stop and retract it all . . . and not go?"

But still he went. He felt suddenly once for all that he mustn't ask himself questions. As he turned into the street he remembered that he had not said goodbye to Sonia, that he had left her in the middle of the room in her green shawl, not daring to stir after he had shouted at her, and he stopped short for a moment. At the same instant, another thought dawned upon him, as though it had been lying in wait to strike him then.

"Why, with what object did I go to her just now? I told her—on business; on what business? I had no sort of business! To tell her I was going; but where was the need? Do I love her? No, no, I drove her away just now like a dog. Did I want her crosses? Oh, how low I've sunk! No, I wanted her tears, I wanted to see her terror, to see how her heart ached! I had to have something to cling to, something to delay me, some friendly face to see! And I dared to believe in myself, to dream of what I would do! I am a beggarly contemptible wretch, contemptible!"

He walked along the canal bank; he had not much further to go. But on reaching the bridge he stopped and turning out of his way along it went to the Haymarket.

He looked eagerly to right and left, gazed intently at every object and could not fix his attention on anything; everything slipped away. "In another week, another month I shall be driven in a prison van over this bridge, how shall I look at the canal then? I should like to remember this!" slipped into his mind. "Look at this sign! How shall I read those letters then? It's written here 'Campany,' that's a thing to remember, that letter a, and to look at it again in a month—how shall I look at it then? What shall I be feeling and thinking then? . . . How trivial all of it must be, what I am worrying about now! Of course it must all be interesting . . . in its way . . . (Ha-ha-ha! What am I thinking about?) I am becoming a baby, I am showing off to myself; why am I ashamed? Foo, how people shove! That fat man—a German, he must be—who pushed against me, does he know who he pushed? There's a peasant woman with a baby, begging. It's curious that she thinks I am happier than she is. I might give her something, if only because it'd be so out of place. Here's a five kopeck piece left in my pocket, where did I get it? Here, here . . . take it, my dear!"

"God bless you," the beggar chanted in a tearful voice.

He went into the Haymarket. It was distasteful, very distasteful to be in a crowd, but he walked just where he saw the most people. He would have given anything in the world to be alone; but he knew himself that he would not have remained alone for a moment. There was a man drunk and disorderly in the crowd; he kept trying to dance and falling down. There was a ring round him. Raskolnikov squeezed his way through the crowd, stared for some minutes at the drunken man and suddenly gave a short jerky laugh. A minute later he had forgotten him and did not see him, though he still stared. He moved away at last, not remembering where he was; but when he got into the middle of the square an emotion suddenly came over him, overwhelming him body and mind.

He suddenly recalled Sonia's words, "Go to the crossroads, bow down to the people, kiss the earth, for you have sinned against it too, and say aloud to the whole world, 'I am a murderer.'" He trembled, remembering that. And the hopeless misery and anxiety of all that time, especially of the last few hours, had weighed so heavily upon him that he clutched passionately at the chance of this new unmixed, complete sensation. It came over him like a fit; it was like a single spark kindled in his soul and spreading fire through him. Everything in him softened at once and the tears started into his eyes. He fell to the earth on the spot . . .

He knelt down in the middle of the square, bowed down to the earth, and kissed that filthy earth with bliss and rapture. He got up and bowed down a second time.

"He's smashed," a youth near him observed.

There was a roar of laughter.

"He's going to Jerusalem, brothers, and saying goodbye to his children and his country. He's bowing down to the whole world and kissing the great city of St. Petersburg and its pavement," added a workman who was a little drunk.

"Quite a young man, too!" observed a third.

"And a gentleman," someone observed soberly.

"There's no knowing who's a gentleman and who isn't nowadays."

These exclamations and remarks checked Raskolnikov, and the words, "I am a murderer," which were perhaps on the point of dropping from his lips, died away. He bore these remarks quietly, however, and without looking round, he turned down a street leading to the police office. He had a glimpse of something on the way which did not surprise him; he had felt that it must be so. The second time he bowed down in the Haymarket, he saw Sonia standing fifty paces from him on the left. She was hiding from him behind one of the wooden shanties in the market-place. She had followed him then on his painful way! Raskolnikov at that moment felt and knew once for all that Sonia was with him forever and would follow him to the ends of the earth, wherever fate might take him. It wrung his heart . . . but he was just reaching the fatal place.

He went into the yard fairly resolutely. He had to go up to the third floor. "I shall be some time going up," he thought. He felt as though the fateful moment was still far away, as though he had plenty of time left for consideration.

Again the same rubbish, the same eggshells lying about on the spiral staircase, again the open doors of the apartments, again the same kitchens and the same fumes and stench coming from them. Raskolnikov had not been here since that day. His legs were numb and gave way under him, but still they moved forward. He stopped for a moment to take a breath, to collect himself, in order to go in like a man. "But why? What for?" he wondered, reflecting. "If I must drink the cup what difference does it make? The more revolting the better." He imagined for an instant the figure of the "explosive lieutenant," Ilia Petrovich. Was he actually going to him? Couldn't he go to someone else? To Nikodim Fomich? Couldn't he turn back and go straight to Nikodim Fomich's rooms? At least then it would be done privately . . . No, no! To the "explosive lieutenant"! If he must drink it, drink it off at once.

Turning cold and hardly conscious, he opened the door of the office. There were very few people in it this time—just a house porter and a peasant. The doorkeeper did not even peep out from behind his screen. Raskolnikov walked into the next room. "Perhaps even now I don't have to speak," passed through his mind. Some sort of clerk who was not in a uniform was settling himself at a bureau to write. In a corner another clerk was seating himself. Zametov wasn't there, nor, of course, Nikodim Fomich.

"No-one in?" Raskolnikov asked, addressing the person at the bureau.

"Who do you want?"

"A-ah! Not a sound was heard, not a sight was seen, but I sense the Russian . . . how does it go in the fairy tale . . . I've forgotten! At your service!" a familiar voice cried suddenly.

Raskolnikov shuddered. The Explosive Lieutenant stood before him. He had just come in from the third room. "It's the hand of fate," thought Raskolnikov. "Why's he here?"

"You've come to see us? What about?" cried Ilia Petrovich. He was obviously in an extremely good mood and perhaps a little exhilarated. "If it's on business you are rather early.* I'm only here by chance . . . however, I'll do what I can. I must admit, I . . . what is it, what is it? Excuse me . . . "—

"Raskolnikov."

"Of course, Raskolnikov. You didn't imagine I'd forgotten? Don't think I am like that . . . Rodion Ro—Ro—Rodionovich, that's it, isn't it?"

"Rodion Romanovich."

"Yes, yes, of course, Rodion Romanovich! I was just getting at it. I made many inquiries about you. I assure you I've been genuinely grieved since that . . . since I behaved like that . . . it was explained to me afterwards that you were a literary man . . . and a learned one too . . . and so to say the first steps . . . Mercy on us! What literary or scientific man does not begin his career with some originality of conduct! My wife and I have the greatest respect for literature, in my wife it's a genuine passion! Literature and art! If only a man is a gentleman, all the rest can be gained by talents, learning, good sense, genius. As for a hat—well, what does a hat matter? I can buy a hat as easily as I can a bun; but what's under the hat, what the hat covers, I can't buy that! I was even meaning to come and apologize to you, but thought maybe you'd . . . But I am forgetting to ask you, is there anything you want really? I hear your family have come?"

"Yes, my mother and sister."

"I've even had the honor and happiness of meeting your sister— a highly cultivated and charming person. I confess I was sorry I got so hot and bothered with you. There it is! But as for my looking suspiciously at your fainting fit—that's been cleared up splendidly! Bigotry and fanaticism! I understand your indignation. Perhaps you're changing your lodging because your family's arrived?"

"No, I only looked in . . . I came to ask . . . I thought that I might find Zametov here."

"Oh, yes! Of course, you've made friends, I heard. Well, no, Zametov is not here. Yes, we've lost Zametov. He's not been here since

---

*Dostoevsky appears to have forgotten that it is after sunset, and that the last time Raskolnikov visited the police office at two in the afternoon, he was reproached for coming too late [Garnett's note].

yesterday . . . he quarreled with everyone when he left . . . in the rudest way. He is a feather-headed youngster, that's all; you might have expected something from him, but there, you know what they are, our brilliant young men. He wanted to go in for some examination, but it's only to talk and boast about it, it'll go no further than that. Of course it's a very different matter with you or Mr. Razumikhin there, your friend. Your career is an intellectual one and you won't be deterred by failure. For you, one may say, all the attractions of life *nihil est** —you are an ascetic, a monk, a hermit! . . . A book, a pen behind your ear, a learned researcher—that's where your spirit soars! I am the same way myself . . . Have you read Livingstone's Travels?"[†]

"No."

"Oh, I have. There are a great many Nihilists about nowadays, you know, though it's nothing to be surprised at. What sort of days are they? I ask you. But we thought . . . you are not a Nihilist of course? Answer me openly, openly!"

"N-no . . . "

"Believe me, you can speak as openly to me as you would to yourself! Official duty is one thing but . . . you are thinking I meant to say friendship is quite another? No, you're wrong! It's not friendship, but the feeling of a man and a citizen, the feeling of humanity and of love for the Almighty. I may be an official, but I am always bound to feel myself a man and a citizen . . . You were asking about Zametov. Zametov will make a scandal in the French style in a house of bad reputation, over a glass of champagne . . . that's all your Zametov is good for! While I'm perhaps, so to speak, burning with devotion and lofty feelings, and besides I have rank, consequence, a post! I am married and have children, I fulfill the duties of a man and a citizen, but who is he, may I ask? I appeal to you as a man ennobled by education . . . Then these midwives, too, have become extraordinarily numerous."

Raskolnikov raised his eyebrows inquiringly. The words of Ilia Petrovich, who had obviously just been out for dinner, were for the most part a stream of empty sounds for him. But some of them he

---

*The Latin is loosely translated as "are nothing."
[†]*Narrative of an Expedition to the Zambesi and Its Tributaries* (1865), by English explorers David and Charles Livingstone.

understood. He looked at him inquiringly, not knowing how it would end.

"I mean those crop-headed wenches," the talkative Ilia Petrovich continued. "Midwives is my name for them. I think it's a very satisfactory one, ha-ha! They go to the Academy, study anatomy. If I fall ill, should I send for a young lady to treat me? What do you say? Ha-ha!" Ilia Petrovich laughed, quite pleased with his own wit. "It's a ravenous passion for education, but once you're educated, that's enough. Why abuse it? Why insult honorable people, like that scoundrel Zametov does? Why did he insult me, I ask you? Look at these suicides, too, how common they are, you can't imagine! People spend their last kopeck and kill themselves, boys and girls and old people. Only this morning we heard about a gentleman who had just come to town. Nil Pavlich, I say, what was the name of that man who shot himself?"

"Svidrigailov," someone answered from the other room with drowsy listlessness.

Raskolnikov started.

"Svidrigailov! Svidrigailov has shot himself!" he cried.

"What, do you know Svidrigailov?"

"Yes . . . I knew him . . . He hadn't been here long."

"Yes, that's true. He had lost his wife, was a man of reckless habits and all of a sudden shot himself, and in such a shocking way . . . He left in his notebook a few words; that he died in full possession of his faculties and that no-one is to blame for his death. He had money, they say. How did you come to know him?"

"I . . . was acquainted . . . my sister was a governess in his family."

"Bah-bah-bah! Then no doubt you can tell us something about him. You had no suspicion?"

"I saw him yesterday . . . he . . . was drinking wine; I knew nothing."

Raskolnikov felt as though something had fallen on him and was stifling him.

"You've turned pale again. It's so stuffy here . . . "

"Yes, I must go," muttered Raskolnikov. "Excuse me for troubling you . . . "

"Oh, not at all, as often as you like. It's a pleasure to see you and I am glad to say so."

Ilia Petrovich held out his hand.

"I only wanted . . . I came to see Zametov."

"I understand, I understand, and it's a pleasure to see you."

"I . . . am very glad . . . goodbye," Raskolnikov smiled.

He went out; he reeled, he was overcome with dizziness and did not know what he was doing. He began going down the stairs, supporting himself with his right hand against the wall. He fancied that a porter pushed past him on his way upstairs to the police office, that a dog in the lower floor kept up a shrill barking and that a woman flung a rolling-pin at it and shouted. He went down and out into the yard. There, not far from the entrance, stood Sonia, pale and horror-stricken. She looked wildly at him. He stood still before her. There was a look of poignant agony, of despair, in her face. She clasped her hands. His lips were contorted into an ugly, meaningless smile. He stood still a minute, grinned and went back to the police office.

Ilia Petrovich had sat down and was rummaging among some papers. Before him stood the same peasant who had pushed by on the stairs.

"Hello! Back again! Have you left something behind? What's the matter?"

Raskolnikov, with white lips and staring eyes, came slowly nearer. He walked right up to the table, leaned his hand on it, tried to say something, but could not; only incoherent sounds were audible.

"You are feeling ill, a chair! Here, sit down! Some water!"

Raskolnikov dropped onto a chair, but he kept his eyes fixed on the face of Ilia Petrovich which expressed unpleasant surprise. Both looked at one another for a minute and waited. Water was brought.

"It was I . . . " began Raskolnikov.

"Drink some water."

Raskolnikov refused the water with his hand, and softly and brokenly, but distinctly said:

"It was I who killed the old pawnbroker woman and her sister Lizaveta with an axe and robbed them."

Ilia Petrovich opened his mouth. People ran up on all sides.

Raskolnikov repeated his statement.

EPILOGUE

CHAPTER ONE

SIBERIA. ON THE BANKS of a broad solitary river stands a town, one of the administrative centers of Russia; in the town there is a fortress, and in the fortress there is a prison. In the prison the second-class* convict Rodion Raskolnikov has been confined for nine months. Almost a year and a half has passed since his crime.

There had been little difficulty about his trial. The criminal adhered exactly, firmly and clearly to his statement. He did not confuse or misrepresent the facts, or soften them in his own interest, or omit the smallest detail. He explained every incident of the murder, the secret of the pledge (the piece of wood with a strip of metal) which was found in the murdered woman's hand. He described minutely how he had taken her keys, what they were like, as well as the chest and its contents; he explained the mystery of Lizaveta's murder; described how Koch and, after him, the student knocked, and repeated all they had said to one another; how afterwards he had run downstairs and heard Nikolai and Dmitri shouting; how he had hidden in the empty apartment and afterwards gone home. He finished by indicating the stone in the yard off the Voznesensky Prospect under which the purse and the trinkets were found. The whole thing, in fact, was perfectly clear. The lawyers and the judges were very much struck, amongst other things, by the fact that he had hidden the trinkets and the purse under a stone, without making use of them, and that, what was more, he did not now remember what the trinkets were like, or even how many there were. The fact that he had never opened the purse and did not even know how much was in it seemed incredible. It turned out to hold three hundred and seventeen rubles and sixty kopecks. Because it had been lying under the stone for so long, some of the most valuable notes had suffered from the damp. They spent a long while trying to discover why the accused man should tell a lie about this when he had made a truthful and straightforward confession about everything else. Finally some of the lawyers more versed in psychology admitted that it was possible he had really not looked into the purse and so didn't know what was in it

---

*Second-class convicts served eight to twelve years in jail.

when he hid it under the stone. But they immediately deduced that
the crime could only have been committed through temporary mental derangement, through homicidal mania, without any purpose or
pursuit of gain. This fell in with the most recent fashionable theory
of temporary insanity, so often applied nowadays in criminal cases.
Moreover Raskolnikov's hypochondriac condition was proved by
many witnesses, by Dr. Zossimov, his former fellow students, his
landlady and her servant. All this pointed strongly to the conclusion
that Raskolnikov was not quite like an ordinary murderer and robber,
but that there was another element in the case.

To the intense annoyance of those who maintained this opinion, the criminal scarcely attempted to defend himself. To the decisive question as to what motive impelled him to the murder and the
robbery, he answered very clearly with the coarsest frankness that
the cause was his miserable position, his poverty and helplessness,
and his desire to provide for his first steps in life by the help of the
three thousand rubles he had reckoned on finding. He had been led
to the murder through his shallow and cowardly nature, exasperated
moreover by poverty and failure. To the question what led him to
confess, he answered that it was his heartfelt repentance. All this was
almost coarse . . .

The sentence however was more merciful than could have been
expected, perhaps partly because the criminal had not tried to justify
himself, but had rather shown a desire to exaggerate his guilt. All the
strange and peculiar circumstances of the crime were taken into consideration. There could be no doubt of the abnormal and poverty-
stricken condition of the criminal at the time. The fact that he had
made no use of what he had stolen was put down partly to the effect
of remorse, partly to his abnormal mental state at the time of the
crime. Incidentally, the murder of Lizaveta served in fact to confirm
the last hypothesis: a man commits two murders and forgets that the
door is open! Finally, the confession, at the very moment when the
case was hopelessly muddled by the false evidence given by Nikolai
through melancholy and fanaticism, and when, moreover, there were
no proofs against the real criminal, no suspicions even (Porfiry Petrovich fully kept his word)—all this did much to soften the sentence.
Other circumstances, too, in the prisoner's favor came out quite unexpectedly. Razumikhin somehow discovered and proved that while

Raskolnikov was at the university he had helped a poor consumptive fellow student and had spent his last penny on supporting him for six months, and when this student died, leaving a decrepit old father whom he had maintained almost from his thirteenth year, Raskolnikov had got the old man into a hospital and paid for his funeral when he died. Raskolnikov's landlady bore witness, too, that when they had lived in another house at Five Corners, Raskolnikov had rescued two little children from a house on fire and was burnt in doing so. This was investigated and fairly well confirmed by many witnesses. These facts made an impression in his favor.

And in the end the criminal was in consideration of extenuating circumstances condemned to penal servitude in the second class for a term of eight years only.

At the very beginning of the trial Raskolnikov's mother fell ill. Dunia and Razumikhin found it possible to get her out of Petersburg during the trial. Razumikhin chose a town on the railway not far from Petersburg, so as to be able to follow every step of the trial and at the same time to see Avdotia Romanovna as often as possible. Pulcheria Alexandrovna's illness was a strange nervous one and was accompanied by a partial derangement of her intellect.

When Dunia returned from her last interview with her brother, she had found her mother already ill, in feverish delirium. That evening Razumikhin and she agreed what answers they must make to her mother's questions about Raskolnikov and made up a complete story for her mother's benefit that he had to go away to a distant part of Russia on a business commission, which would eventually bring him money and renown.

But they were struck by the fact that Pulcheria Alexandrovna never asked them anything on the subject, neither then nor thereafter. On the contrary, she had her own version of her son's sudden departure; she told them with tears how he had come to say goodbye to her, hinting that she alone knew many mysterious and important facts, and that Rodia had many very powerful enemies, so that it was necessary for him to be in hiding. As for his future career, she had no doubt that it would be brilliant when certain sinister influences could be removed. She assured Razumikhin that her son would one day be a great statesman, that his article and brilliant literary talent proved it. She read this article continually, she even read it aloud, almost took it to bed with her, but scarcely asked where Rodia was, though the subject was obviously avoided by the others, which might have been enough to awaken her suspicions.

They began to be frightened at last at Pulcheria Alexandrovna's strange silence on certain subjects. She did not, for instance, complain that she never received any letters from him, though in previous years she had lived solely on the hope of letters from her beloved Rodia. This was a cause of great uneasiness to Dunia; the idea occurred to her that her mother suspected that there was something terrible in her son's fate and was afraid to ask, for fear of hearing something still more awful. In any case, Dunia saw clearly that her mother was not in full possession of her faculties.

Once or twice, however, Pulcheria Alexandrovna gave such a turn to the conversation that it was impossible to answer her without mentioning where Rodia was, and on receiving unsatisfactory and suspicious answers she immediately became gloomy and silent. Such moods would last for a long time. Dunia saw at last that it was hard to deceive her and came to the conclusion that it was better to be absolutely silent on certain points; but it became more and more evident that the poor mother suspected something terrible. Dunia remembered her brother telling her that her mother had overheard her talking in her sleep on the night after her interview with Svidrigailov and before the fatal day of the confession: had she not understood something from that? Sometimes days and even weeks of gloomy silence and tears would be followed by a period of hysterical animation, and the invalid would begin to talk almost incessantly of her son, of her hopes of his future . . . Her ideas were sometimes very strange. They humored her, pretended to agree with her (she saw perhaps that they were pretending), but she still went on talking.

Five months after Raskolnikov's confession, he was sentenced. Razumikhin and Sonia saw him in prison as often as possible. At last the moment of separation came. Dunia swore to her brother that the separation should not be for ever, Razumikhin did the same. Razumikhin, in his youthful ardor, had firmly resolved to lay the foundations at least of a secure livelihood during the next three or four years, save up a certain sum and emigrate to Siberia, a country rich in every natural resource and in need of workers, active men and capital. There they would settle in the town where Rodia would be living and begin a new life together. They all wept when they parted.

Raskolnikov had been very dreamy for a few days before. He asked a great deal about his mother and was constantly anxious about her. He worried so much about her that it alarmed Dunia. When he heard about his mother's illness he became very gloomy. With Sonia he was particularly reserved all the time. With the help of the money left to her by Svidrigailov, Sonia had long ago made her preparations to follow the party of convicts in which he was dispatched to Siberia. Not a word passed between Raskolnikov and her on the subject, but both knew that was how it would be. At their final parting he smiled strangely at his sister's and Razumikhin's fervent anticipations of their happy future together when he would come out of prison. He predicted that their mother's illness would soon end fatally. At last, Sonia and he set off.

Two months later Dunia was married to Razumikhin. It was a quiet and sorrowful wedding; Porfiry Petrovich and Zossimov, however, were invited. During this whole period Razumikhin wore an air of resolute determination. Dunia implicitly believed he would carry out his plans and indeed she could not but believe in him. He displayed a rare strength of will. Among other things he began attending university lectures again in order to take his degree. They were continually making plans for the future; both counted on settling in Siberia within five years at least. Until then they rested their hopes on Sonia.

Pulcheria Alexandrovna was delighted to give her blessing to Dunia's marriage with Razumikhin; but after the marriage she became even more melancholy and anxious. To give her pleasure Razumikhin told her how Raskolnikov had looked after the poor student and his decrepit father and how a year ago he had been burnt and injured in rescuing two little children from a fire. These two pieces of news excited Pulcheria Alexandrovna's disordered imagination almost to ecstasy. She talked about them continually, even entering into conversation with strangers in the street, though Dunia always accompanied her. In public conveyances and stores, wherever she could capture a listener, she would start talking about her son, his article, how he had helped the student, how he had been burnt in the fire, and so on. Dunia did not know how to restrain her. Apart from the

danger of her morbid excitement, there was the risk of someone recalling Raskolnikov's name and speaking of the recent trial. Pulcheria
Alexandrovna found out the address of the mother of the two children her son had saved and insisted on going to see her.

At last her restlessness reached an extreme point. She would
sometimes begin to cry suddenly and was often ill and feverishly
delirious. One morning she declared that by her reckoning Rodia
should soon be home, that she remembered when he said goodbye
to her he said that they must expect him back in nine months. She
began to prepare for his arrival, began to do up her room for him, to
clean the furniture, to wash and put up new hangings and so on.
Dunia was anxious, but said nothing and helped her to arrange the
room. After a fatiguing day spent in continual fantasies, in joyful day-
dreams and tears, Pulcheria Alexandrovna was taken ill in the night
and by morning she was feverish and delirious. It was brain fever. She
died within a fortnight. In her delirium she dropped hints which
showed that she knew a great deal more about her son's terrible fate
than they had supposed.

For a long time Raskolnikov did not know of his mother's death,
though a regular correspondence had been maintained from the time
he reached Siberia. It was carried on by means of Sonia, who wrote
every month to the Razumikhins and received replies with unfailing
regularity. At first they found Sonia's letters dry and unsatisfactory, but
later on they came to the conclusion that the letters could not be better, since from these letters they received a complete picture of their
unfortunate brother's life. Sonia's letters were full of the most matter
of fact detail, the simplest and clearest description of all Raskolnikov's
surroundings as a convict. There was no word of her own hopes, no
predictions for the future, no description of her feelings. Instead of
any attempt to interpret his state of mind and inner life, she gave the
simple facts—that is, his own words, an exact account of his health,
what he asked for at their interviews, what commission he gave her
and so on. All these facts she gave with extraordinary minuteness. The
picture of their unhappy brother stood out at last with great clarity
and precision.

There could be no mistake, because nothing was given but facts.

But Dunia and her husband could derive little comfort from the
news, especially at first. Sonia wrote that he was constantly sullen and

unready to talk, that he scarcely seemed interested in the news she gave him from their letters, that he sometimes asked after his mother and that when, seeing that he had guessed the truth, she told him at last of her death, she was surprised to find that he did not seem greatly affected by it, not externally at any rate. She told them that, although he seemed so wrapped up in himself and, as it were, shut himself off from everyone, he took a very direct and simple view of his new life; that he understood his position, expected nothing better for the time being, had no ill-founded hopes (as is so common in his position) and scarcely seemed surprised at anything in his surroundings, which were so unlike anything he had known before. She wrote that his health was satisfactory; he did his work without shirking or seeking to do more; he was almost indifferent about food, but, except on Sundays and holidays, the food was so bad that at last he had been glad to accept some money to have his own tea every day. He begged her not to trouble about anything else, declaring that all the fuss only annoyed him. Sonia wrote further that in prison he shared the same room with the rest, that she had not seen the inside of their barracks, but concluded that they were crowded, miserable and unhealthy; that he slept on a plank bed with a rug under him and was unwilling to make any other arrangement. But that he lived so poorly and roughly, not from any intention or plan, but simply from inattention and indifference.

Sonia wrote simply that he had at first shown no interest in her visits, had almost been irritated with her for coming; he had even been rude to her and unwilling to talk. But in the end these visits had become a habit and almost a necessity for him, and he was positively distressed when she was ill for several days and could not come to see him. She used to meet him on holidays at the prison gates or in the guard-room, to which he would be brought for a few minutes to be with her. On working days she would go to see him at work either at the workshops or at the brick kilns, or at the sheds on the banks of the Irtysh.*

About herself, Sonia wrote that she had succeeded in making some acquaintances in the town, that she sewed and, as there was scarcely a dressmaker in the vicinity, she was looked upon as an in-

---

*River close to the fort in the Siberian town of Omsk, where Dostoevsky spent part of his exile.

dispensable person in many houses. But she did not mention that the authorities were, through her, interested in Raskolnikov; that his task was lightened and so on.

At last the news came (Dunia had indeed noticed signs of alarm and uneasiness in the preceding letters) that he had remained aloof from everyone, that his fellow prisoners did not like him, that he kept silent for days at a time and was becoming very pale. In the last letter Sonia wrote that he had been taken very seriously ill and was in the convict ward of the hospital.

CHAPTER TWO

HE WAS ILL FOR a long time. But it was not the horrors of prison life, not the hard labor, the bad food, the shaven head, or the patched clothes that crushed him. What did he care for all those trials and hardships! He was even glad of the hard work. Physically exhausted, he could at least count on a few hours of quiet sleep. And what did the food matter to him, the thin cabbage soup with beetles floating in it? In the past as a student he had often not had even that. His clothes were warm and suited to his way of life. He did not even feel the chains. Was he ashamed of his shaven head and his prison coat? In whose presence? In Sonia's? Sonia was afraid of him, how could he feel ashamed in her presence? And yet he was even ashamed when he came to see Sonia, because of which he tortured her with his rough, contemptuous manner. But it was not his shaven head and his chains he was ashamed of: his pride had been stung to the quick. It was wounded pride that made him ill. Oh, how happy he would have been if he could have blamed himself! He could have endured anything then, even shame and disgrace. But he judged himself severely, and his exasperated conscience found no particularly terrible fault in his past, except a simple blunder which might happen to anyone. He was ashamed just because he, Raskolnikov, had so hopelessly, stupidly come to grief through some decree of blind fate, and must humble himself and submit to "the idiocy" of a sentence in order somehow to find peace.

Vague and aimless anxiety in the present, and in the future a continual sacrifice leading to nothing—that was all that lay before him.

And what comfort was it to him that at the end of eight years he would be only thirty-two and able to begin a new life! What did he have to live for? What did he have to look forward to? Why should he strive? To live in order to exist? He had been ready a thousand times before to give up existence for the sake of an idea, for a hope, even for a whim. Mere existence had always been too little for him; he had always wanted more. Perhaps it was just because of the strength of his desires that he had considered himself a man to whom more was permissible than to others.

And if only fate would have sent him repentance—burning repentance that would have torn his heart and robbed him of sleep, that repentance, the awful agony of which brings visions of hanging or drowning! Oh, he would have been glad of it! Tears and agonies would at least have been life. But he did not repent of his crime.

At least he might have found relief in raging at his stupidity, as he had raged at the grotesque blunders that had brought him to prison. But now in prison, in freedom, he thought over and criticized all his actions again and by no means found them as blundering and as grotesque as they had seemed at the fatal time.

"In what way," he asked himself, "was my theory more stupid than others that have swarmed and clashed from the beginning of the world? You only have to look at the thing entirely independently, broadly, and uninfluenced by commonplace ideas, and my idea will by no means seem so . . . strange. Oh, skeptics and halfpenny philosophers, why do you halt halfway!"

"Why does my action strike them as so horrible?" he said to himself. "Is it because it was a crime? What is meant by crime? My conscience is at rest. Of course, it was a legal crime, of course, the letter of the law was broken and blood was shed. Well, punish me for the letter of the law . . . and that's enough. Of course, in that case many of the benefactors of mankind who snatched power for themselves instead of inheriting it ought to have been punished at their first steps. But those men succeeded and so they were right, and I didn't, and so I had no right to have taken that step."

It was only in that that he recognized his criminality, only in the fact that he had been unsuccessful and had confessed it.

He suffered from another question: why had he not killed himself? Why had he stood looking at the river and preferred to confess?

Was the desire to live so strong and was it so hard to overcome it? Had not Svidrigailov overcome it, although he was afraid of death?

In his misery he asked himself this question and could not understand that, at the very time he had been standing looking into the river, he had perhaps been dimly conscious of the fundamental falsity in himself and his convictions. He didn't understand that that consciousness might be the promise of a future crisis, of a new view of life and of his future resurrection.

He preferred to attribute it to the dead weight of instinct which he could not step over, again through weakness and meanness. He looked at his fellow prisoners and was amazed to see how they all loved life and prized it. It seemed to him that they loved and valued life more in prison than in freedom. What terrible agonies and privations some of them, the tramps for instance, had endured! Could they care so much for a ray of sunshine, for the primeval forest, the cold spring hidden away in some unseen spot, which the tramp had marked three years before, and longed to see again, as he might to see his sweetheart, dreaming of the green grass round it and the bird singing in the bush? As he went on he saw even more inexplicable examples.

In prison, of course, there was a great deal he did not see and did not want to see; he lived as it were with downcast eyes. It was loathsome and unbearable for him to look. But in the end there was much that surprised him and he began, as it were involuntarily, to notice much that he had not suspected before. What surprised him most of all was the terrible, impossible gulf that lay between him and all the rest of them. They seemed to be a different species, and he looked at them and they at him with distrust and hostility. He recognized and understood the reasons for his isolation, but he would never have admitted until then that those reasons were so deep and strong. There were some Polish exiles, political prisoners, among them. They simply looked down upon everyone else and treated them like ignorant fools; but Raskolnikov could not look upon them like that. He saw that these ignorant men were in many respects far wiser than the Poles. There were some Russians who were just as contemptuous, a former officer and two seminarians.* Raskolnikov saw their mistake

---

*Some of the most notorious Russian radicals of the period were former seminarians, or trainee priests.

as clearly. He was disliked and avoided by everyone; they finally even began to hate him—why, he could not tell. Men who had been guilty of far greater offenses despised and laughed at his crime.

"You're a gentleman," they used to say. "You shouldn't hack about with an axe; that's not a gentleman's work."

The second week in Lent, his turn came to take the sacrament with his gang. He went to church and prayed with the others. A quarrel broke out one day, he did not know how. Everyone fell on him at once in a fury.

"You're an infidel! You don't believe in God," they shouted. "You ought to be killed."

He had never talked to them about God or his belief, but they wanted to kill him because he was an infidel. He said nothing. One of the prisoners rushed at him in an absolute frenzy. Raskolnikov awaited him calmly and silently; his eyebrows did not quiver, his face did not flinch. The guard succeeded in intervening between him and his assailant, or there would have been bloodshed.

There was another question he could not resolve: why were they all so fond of Sonia? She did not try to win their favor; she rarely met them, only occasionally coming to see him at work, and even then only for a moment. And yet everybody knew her, they knew that she had come out to follow him, knew how and where she lived. She never gave them money, did them no particular service. Only once, at Christmas, did she send them all presents of pies and rolls. But by degrees closer relations sprang up between them and Sonia. She would write and post letters for them to their relations. Relations of the prisoners who visited the town, at their instructions, left presents and money for them with Sonia. Their wives and sweethearts knew her and used to visit her. And when she visited Raskolnikov at work, or met a party of the prisoners on the road, they all took off their hats to her. "Little mother Sofia Semionovna, you are our dear, good little mother," coarse branded criminals said to that frail little creature. She would smile and bow to them and everyone was delighted when she smiled. They even admired her gait and turned round to watch her walking; they admired her too for being so little, and, in fact, did not know what to admire her most for. They even came to her for help with their illnesses.

He was in the hospital from the middle of Lent until after Easter.

When he was better, he remembered the dreams he had had while he was feverish and delirious. He dreamt that the whole world was condemned to a terrible strange new plague that had come to Europe from the depths of Asia. Everyone was to be destroyed except a few chosen ones. Some sort of new microbe was attacking people's bodies, but these microbes were endowed with intelligence and will. Men attacked by them became instantly furious and mad. But never had men considered themselves so intellectual and so completely in possession of the truth as these sufferers, never had they considered their decisions, their scientific conclusions, their moral convictions so infallible. Whole villages, whole towns and peoples were driven mad by the infection. Everyone was excited and did not understand one another. Each thought that he alone had the truth and was wretched looking at the others, beat himself on the breast, wept, and wrung his hands. They did not know how to judge and could not agree what to consider evil and what good; they did not know who to blame, who to justify. Men killed each other in a sort of senseless spite. They gathered together in armies against one another, but even on the march the armies would begin attacking each other, the ranks would be broken and the soldiers would fall on each other, stabbing and cutting, biting and devouring each other. The alarm bells kept ringing all day long in the towns; men rushed together, but why they were summoned and who was summoning them no-one knew. The most ordinary trades were abandoned, because everyone proposed their own ideas and their own improvements, and they could not agree. The land too was abandoned. Men met in groups, agreed on something, swore to keep together, but at once began on something quite different from what they had proposed. They accused one another, fought and killed each other. There were conflagrations and famine. All men and all things were involved in destruction. The plague spread and moved further and further. Only a few men could be saved in the whole world. They were a pure chosen people, destined to found a new race and a new life, to renew and purify the earth, but no-one had seen these men, no-one had heard their words and their voices.

Raskolnikov was worried that this senseless dream haunted his memory so miserably, that the impression of this feverish delirium persisted so long. The second week after Easter had come. There were warm bright spring days; in the prison ward the grating windows under which the sentinel paced were opened. Sonia had only been able to visit him twice during his illness; each time she had to obtain permission, and it was difficult. But she often used to come to the hospital yard, especially in the evening, sometimes only to stand a minute and look up at the windows of the ward.

One evening, when he was almost well again, Raskolnikov fell asleep. When he awoke he happened to go to the window, and at once saw Sonia in the distance at the hospital gate. She seemed to be waiting for someone. Something almost stabbed his heart at that moment. He shuddered and moved away from the window. The next day Sonia did not come, nor the day after; he noticed that he was expecting her uneasily. At last he was discharged. On reaching the prison he learnt from the convicts that Sofia Semionovna was lying ill at home and was unable to go out.

He was very uneasy and sent a message to inquire after her; he soon learnt that her illness was not dangerous. Hearing that he was anxious about her, Sonia sent him a penciled note, telling him that she was much better, that she had a slight cold and that she would come soon, very soon and see him at work. His heart throbbed painfully as he read it.

Again it was a warm bright day. Early in the morning, at six o'clock, he went off to work on the river bank, where they used to pound alabaster and had a kiln for baking it in a shed. There were only three of them who were sent. One of the convicts went with the guard to the fortress to fetch a tool; the other began getting the wood ready and laying it in the kiln. Raskolnikov came out of the shed on to the river bank, sat down on a heap of logs by the shed and began gazing at the wide deserted river. From the high bank a broad landscape opened before him, the sound of singing floated faintly audible from the other bank. In the vast steppe, bathed in sunshine, he could just see, like black specks, the nomads' tents. There there was freedom, there other men were living, utterly unlike those here; there time itself seemed to stand still, as though the age of Abraham and his flocks had not passed. Raskolnikov sat gazing, his thoughts passed into daydreams, into contemplation; he thought of nothing, but a vague restlessness excited and troubled him. Suddenly he found Sonia beside him; she had come up noiselessly and sat down at his side. It was still quite early; the morning chill was still sharp. She wore her threadbare old wrap and the green shawl; her face still showed signs of illness, and it was thinner and paler. She gave him a joyful, welcoming smile, but held out her hand with her usual timidity. She was always timid about holding out her hand to him and sometimes did not offer it at all, as though she were afraid he would repel it. He always took her hand as if with repugnance, always seemed irritated to meet her and was sometimes obstinately silent throughout her visit. Sometimes she trembled before him and went away deeply upset. But now their hands did not part. He stole a rapid glance at her and dropped his eyes on the ground without speaking. They were alone, no-one had seen them. The guard had turned away for the time being.

How it happened he did not know. But all at once something seemed to seize him and fling him at her feet. He wept and threw his arms round her knees. At first instant she was terribly frightened and she turned pale. She jumped up and looked at him trembling. But at the same moment she understood, and a light of infinite happiness came into her eyes. She knew and had no doubt that he loved her above everything else and that at last the moment had come . . .

They wanted to speak, but could not; tears stood in their eyes. They were both pale and thin; but those sick pale faces were bright with the dawn of a new future, of a full resurrection into a new life. They were renewed by love; the heart of each held infinite sources of life for the heart of the other.

They resolved to wait and be patient. They had another seven years to wait, and what terrible suffering and what infinite happiness before them! But he had risen again and he knew it and felt it in his whole being, while she—she lived through him alone.

On the evening of the same day, when the barracks were locked, Raskolnikov lay on his plank bed and thought of her. He had even imagined that day that all the convicts who had been his enemies looked at him differently; he had even started talking to them and they answered him in a friendly way. He remembered that now, and thought it was bound to be so. Wasn't everything now bound to be changed?

He thought of her. He remembered how continually he had tormented her and wounded her heart. He remembered her pale, thin little face. But these recollections scarcely troubled him now; he knew with what infinite love he would now repay all her sufferings. And what were all the agonies of the past! Everything, even his crime, his sentence and imprisonment, seemed to him now in the first rush of feeling an external, strange fact with which he had no concern. But he could not think of anything for long that evening, and he could not have analyzed anything consciously; he was simply feeling. Life had stepped into the place of theory and something quite different would work itself out in his mind.

Under his pillow lay the New Testament. He took it up mechanically. The book belonged to Sonia; it was the one from which she had read the raising of Lazarus to him. At first he was afraid that she would worry him about religion, would talk about the gospel and pester him with books. But to his great surprise she had not once approached the subject and had not even offered him the Testament. He had asked her for it himself not long before his illness and she brought him the book without a word. Until now he had not opened it.

He did not open it now, but one thought passed through his mind: "Can her convictions not be mine now? Her feelings, her aspirations at least . . . "

She too had been greatly agitated that day, and at night she was taken ill again. But she was so happy—and so unexpectedly happy—that she was almost frightened of her happiness. Seven years, only seven years! At the beginning of their happiness at some moments they were both ready to look on those seven years as though they were seven days. He did not know that the new life would not be given him for nothing, that he would have to pay dearly for it, that it would cost him great striving, great suffering.

But that is the beginning of a new story—the story of the gradual renewal of a man, the story of his gradual regeneration, of his transition from one world into another, of his initiation into a new, unknown life. That might be the subject of a new story, but our present story is over.——

THE END

F. M. Dostoevsky, 1868

F. M. Dostoevsky, 1880

INSPIRED BY CRIME AND PUNISHMENT

Sigmund Freud and Psychoanalysis

Sigmund Freud, the father of psychoanalysis, remarked in a letter to his friend, the writer Stefan Zweig, that "Dostoevsky cannot be understood without psychoanalysis . . . he illustrates it himself in every character and every sentence." Freud regarded Dostoevsky as one of the greatest literary psychologists in history, second only to Shakespeare. As a psychoanalyst, Freud attempted to unearth and identify the myriad submerged voices and desires in the unconscious of his patients. Crime and Punishment mirrors this process by probing the multiple and often contradictory motivations in the mind of Raskolnikov.

Rather than trying to discover who committed a crime, as a detective or mystery novel might do, Crime and Punishment asks a more complex question: Why did Raskolnikov commit murder? No previous novel had so relentlessly sought the motivation for a character's action. Raskolnikov identifies a number of possible reasons for the murder—he needed money; he wanted to rid the world of a "louse"; he wanted to prove he was above society's definitions of duty and conscience—noting as well that his act was prompted by pent-up rage, a response to his feelings of powerlessness, and his alienation from the community.

Porfiry Petrovich, the police official investigating the murders, takes an interest in easing Raskolnikov's tormented psyche. Rather than forcing a confession, which he believes would not be beneficial, Porfiry uses conversation to help the murderer discover some of his hidden motivations. The prototype of literary detectives who are fluent in criminal psychology, Porfiry is also the first counselor to offer another character a "talking cure"—a nickname for psychoanalysis.

Freud often said that "the poets" discovered the unconscious before he did. Like Freud, Dostoevsky saw tremendous significance in dreams as manifestations of the unconscious. When Raskolnikov murders the pawnbroker, it is not in a state of lucidity and rationality, but in a dream-like trance, demonstrating Freud's later premise that dreams contain desires too difficult to express in waking life.

Dostoevsky's *The Brothers Karamazov* was the subject of Freud's essay "Dostoevsky and Parricide" (1928), which analyzed the Russian writer's psychology. In this article, which many find deeply flawed, Freud attempts to locate the guilt Dostoevsky felt regarding the death-wish he held for his father, who was murdered by his serfs when Dostoevsky was eighteen. Freud believed that the Oedipus complex was the fundamental human drama, and saw it as no coincidence that three masterpieces of world literature—*Hamlet*, *Oedipus Rex*, and *The Brothers Karamazov*—each centered on the murder of a father.

The Übermensch

Raskolnikov is a familiar literary and philosophical type: the intellectually gifted but socially disconnected student who views himself as above society and its law. In creating Raskolnikov—neither the first nor the last such character, though perhaps the best known—Dostoevsky was influenced by novelist Ivan Turgenev and literary critic Dimitry Pisarev. In Turgenev's *Fathers and Sons* (1862), Bazarov, a student, espouses radical, nihilistic views about society and feels he is superior to those around him. Pisarev, in his essay "Bazarov," published the same year, exalts the character's disregard for the law and proposes that, for the most exceptional members of society, murder is always an option. This character type also forms the basis of *Rope*, Alfred Hitchcock's 1948 film about a "perfect" murder; the story is loosely based on a real-life slaying by two University of Chicago students, Nathan Leopold and Richard Loeb.

The concept of the *übermensch* (German for "overman") has frequently been used to explain the character of Raskolnikov. Friedrich Nietzsche first developed the idea in *Thus Spoke Zarathustra*, a highly influential philosophical work published in multiple parts in the 1880s. In it, the philosopher Zarathustra comes to earth to urge mankind to emulate the *übermensch*, a hypothetical individual Zarathustra sees as the pinnacle of human potential. The *übermensch* possesses a will so strong that he is completely self-determining. He ignores the morality and prejudices of society, overcomes disease, and disdains the false security of religion. He sublimates his baser human desires, such as the sex drive, to stronger, more creative outlets, such as art and philosophy.

Raskolnikov puts forward a similar idea of the "extraordinary man" in his article "On Crime," which Porfiry has read, and uses his "extraordinary man" theory to justify his murder of the pawnbroker during his conversations with Porfiry. However, Raskolnikov lacks the primary quality Nietzsche identifies in the übermensch: the superhuman will to power. Raskolnikov performs his societal transgression not as a powerful act of will, but with a monomania that makes the murder practically involuntary. Raskolnikov also lacks the independence from religion and unimpeachable health of the übermensch.

While Nietzsche had not read Crime and Punishment before writing Thus Spoke Zarathustra, he later came to admire the work greatly. In an odd convergence of art and real life, in 1889 he acted out one of Crime and Punishment's most memorable scenes. Incoherent and emotionally disabled, Nietzsche, witnessing the mistreatment of a horse in Turin, Italy, ran to the animal and took it in his arms. His action echoed Raskolnikov's dream (in chapter five of part one) in which a young boy kisses the lips and eyes of a bloody horse beaten by the drunken Mikolka. The episode in Turin was the dramatic beginning of the complete mental breakdown that defined the final decade of Nietzsche's life.

Existentialism

Jean-Paul Sartre and Albert Camus, French writers associated with the diverse philosophical movement known as existentialism, were heavily influenced by the work of Dostoevsky. An exploration of freedom from external laws and its incumbent angst connects the work of the three writers, and forms the basis of the existentialist discussion.

In his 1946 lecture "Existentialism Is a Humanism," Sartre calls a line spoken by Ivan Karamazov in The Brothers Karamazov—"If God does not exist, everything is permitted"—the "starting point" of all existentialist thought. Sartre insists that a person's actions can never be explained by human nature or determinism; rather, he posits, man is perpetually free to do what he likes and therefore is responsible for all his actions. Sartre's short novel Nausea (1938) and his philosophical work *Being and Nothingness* (1943) are central documents of existentialism.

    Crime and Punishment depicts Raskolnikov agonizing over questions of motive and responsibility that Sartre eventually addresses with existentialism: Why did he commit his murder? Should he be punished for it? Are some men more free than others? By the end of the novel, Raskolnikov has not found a good reason for having murdered the pawnbroker. Instead, he repents his crime, seeking solace in God. Raskolnikov does not discover the existential truth—that there was no good reason for killing her—which may have provided him some comfort.

    In his essay "The Myth of Sisyphus," published in 1942, Camus confronts the problems inherent in the discovery that life cannot be explained in terms of reason. He rejects both religion, such as that in which Raskolnikov believed, and suicide as responses to that terrible discovery. Instead, he believes that embracing the absurdity of human life is the key to finding happiness. He fleshes out this notion in his short novel *The Stranger* (1942), in which the main character lives as he pleases because the world refuses to provide him with meaning. Like Raskolnikov, Mersault commits a senseless murder; once on trial, he refuses to provide any motive for his deed, illustrating the existentialist argument that it is irrational to attempt to affix meaning to actions. Awaiting execution, he realizes that his life has meant nothing and neither will his death. The certainty of death and meaninglessness frees Mersault from the burden of hope, and he is happy.

    Dostoevsky's early novella *Notes from the Underground* also figures heavily in the history of existentialist thought, with some scholars calling it the founding document. In it, the solitary Underground Man attacks determinism and finds meaning in freedom, while also acknowledging the suffering freedom causes.

Crimes and Misdemeanors, by Woody Allen

Crimes and Misdemeanors (1989) is Woody Allen's most successful attempt at blending a dramatic plot with a comedic one. The serious or "crimes" storyline revolves around an upper-middle-class ophthalmologist, Judah Rosenthal, played masterfully by Martin Landau.

Publicly honored for his contributions to science and humanity, Judah is a fake, and he knows it. Not only has he rejected his father's Jewish faith; he has also managed hospital funds in a less-than-ethical way and is having an affair with Dolores, a flight attendant played with frantic pathos by Angelica Houston. It is possible to see Judah, who is possessed of a self-serving illusion of superiority and distance from the "real world," as a modern-day Raskolnikov. As his mistress becomes increasingly upset and threatens to expose Judah's indiscretions, Judah calls on his brother (Jerry Orbach), who has mob connections, to orchestrate a hit on her.

Judah avoids punishment, but in a way that comments on Dostoevsky's novel. In the coda, Judah meets the documentary film director Cliff (Allen's familiar on-screen persona, who has been at the heart of the comic or "misdemeanors" plot line) at a wedding party. Under the pretence of talking about a movie idea, the two have an existential discussion concerning the possible consequences—spiritual and punitive—of committing murder. Judah, now happy, relates his own real-life experience, framing it as idle conjecture: What if, he poses to Cliff, after the initial agonizing pangs of remorse the guilt "just went away"? In this intriguing film, Woody Allen reconceptualizes Dostoevsky's themes within the context of today's faithless, comfort-seeking world—and, in effect, turns *Crime and Punishment*'s outcome on its head. Without morality and a firm sense of God, ideas and processes like punishment, forgiveness, and redemption prove to be pointless.

COMMENTS & QUESTIONS

In this section, we aim to provide the reader with an array of perspectives on the text, as well as questions that challenge those perspectives. The commentary has been culled from sources as diverse as reviews contemporaneous with the work, letters written by the author, literary criticism of later generations, and appreciations written throughout the work's history. Following the commentary, a series of questions seeks to filter Fyodor Dostoevsky's Crime and Punishment through a variety of points of view and bring about a richer understanding of this enduring work.

Comments

LEO TOLSTOY

I wish I had the power to say all that I think of Dostoevsky! When you inscribed your thoughts, you partly expressed mine. I never saw the man, had no sort of direct relations with him; but when he died, I suddenly realized that he had been to me the most precious, the dearest, and the most necessary of beings. It never even entered my head to compare myself with him. Everything that he wrote (I mean only the good, the true things) was such that the more he did like that, the more I rejoiced. Artistic accomplishment and intellect can arouse my envy; but a work from the heart—only joy. I always regarded him as my friend, and reckoned most confidently on seeing him at some time. And suddenly I read that he is dead. At first I was utterly confounded, and when later I realized how I had valued him, I began to weep—I am weeping even now.

—from a letter to A. N. Strachov,
translated by Ethel Colburn Mayne (1881)

ROBERT LOUIS STEVENSON

"Raskolnikoff" is easily the greatest book I have read in ten years; I am glad you took to it. Many find it dull: Henry James could not finish it: all I can say is, it nearly finished me. It was like having an illness. James did not care for it because the character of Raskolnikoff was not objective; and at that I divined a great gulf between us, and, on further reflection, the existence of a certain impotence in many minds of to-day, which prevents them from living in a book or a character, and keeps them standing afar off, spectators of a puppet show. To such I suppose the book may seem empty in the centre; to the others it is a room, a house of life, into which they themselves enter, and are tortured and purified. The Juge d'Instruction I thought a wonderful, weird, touching, ingenious creation: the drunken father, and Sonia, and the student friend, and the uncircumscribed, protoplasmic humanity of Raskolnikoff, all upon a level that filled me with wonder: the execution also, superb in places. Another has been translated—"Humiliés et Offensés." It is even more incoherent than "Le Crime et le Châtiment," but breathes much of the same lovely goodness, and has passages of power, Dostoieffsky is a devil of a swell, to be sure.

—from a letter to J. A. Symonds (spring 1886)

FRIEDRICH NIETZSCHE

Dostoevsky [is] the only psychologist, incidentally, from whom I had something to learn; he ranks among the most beautiful strokes of fortune in my life.　　　　—from *Twilight of the Idols* (1889)

WILLIAM DEAN HOWELLS

It used to be one of the disadvantages of the practice of romance in America, which Hawthorne more or less whimsically lamented, that there were so few shadows and inequalities in our broad level of prosperity; and it is one of the reflections suggested by Dostoevsky's novel, *The Crime and the Punishment*, that whoever struck a note so profoundly tragic in American fiction would do a false and mistaken thing—as false and as mistaken in its way as dealing in American fiction with certain nudities which the Latin peoples seem to find edifying.

—from *Criticism and Fiction* (1891)

MAURICE BARING

In 1866 came "Crime and Punishment," which brought Dostoevsky fame. This book, Dostoevsky's "Macbeth," is so well known in the French and English translations that it hardly needs any comment. Dostoevsky never wrote anything more tremendous than the portrayal of the anguish that seethes in the soul of Raskolnikov, after he has killed the old woman, "mechanically forced," as Professor Brückner says, "into performing the act, as if he had gone too near machinery in motion, had been caught by a bit of his clothing and cut to pieces." And not only is one held spellbound by every shifting hope, fear, and doubt, and each new pang that Raskolnikov experiences, but the souls of all the subsidiary characters in the book are revealed to us just as clearly; the Marmeladov family, the honest Razumihin, the police inspector, and the atmosphere of the submerged tenth in St. Petersburg—the steaming smell of the city in the summer. There is an episode when Raskolnikov kneels before Sonia, the prostitute, and says to her: "It is not before you I am kneeling, but before all the suffering of mankind." That is what Dostoevsky does himself in this and in all his books; but in none of them is the suffering of all mankind conjured up before us in more living colours, and in none of them is his act of homage in kneeling before it more impressive.

—from *An Outline of Russian Literature* (1914)

JOHN COWPER POWYS

The first discovery of Dostoievsky is, for a spiritual adventurer, such a shock as is not likely to occur again. One is staggered, bewildered, insulted. It is like a hit in the face, at the end of a dark passage; a hit in the face, followed by the fumbling of strange hands at one's throat. Everything that has been *forbidden*, by discretion, by caution, by self-respect, by atavistic inhibition, seems suddenly to leap out of the darkness and seize upon one with fierce, indescribable caresses. All that one has *felt*, but has not dared to think; all that one has *thought*, but has not dared to say; all the terrible whispers from the unspeakable margins; all the horrible wreckage and silt from the unsounded depths, float in upon us and overpower us . . .

Dostoievsky's Russians are cruelly voluble, but their volubility taps the evil humour of the universal human disease. Their thoughts are *our* thoughts, their obsessions, *our* obsessions. Let no one think, in his vain security, that he has a right to say: "I have no part in this morbidity. I am different from these poor madmen."

The curious nervous relief we experience as we read these books is alone a sufficient vindication. They relieve us, as well as trouble us, because in these pages we all confess what we have never confessed to anyone. Our self-love is outraged, but outraged with that strange accompaniment of thrilling pleasure that means an expiation paid, a burden lightened. Use the word "degenerate," if you will. But in this sense we are all "degenerates," for thus and not otherwise is woven the stuff whereof men are made.

—from *Visions and Revisions: A Book of Literary Devotions* (1915)

PRINCE PETER KROPOTKIN
The favourite themes of Dostoyévskiy are the men who have been brought so low by the circumstances of their lives, that they have not even a conception of there being a possibility of rising above these conditions. You feel moreover that Dostoyévskiy finds a real pleasure in describing the sufferings, moral and physical, of the down-trod-den—that he revels in representing that misery of mind, that absolute hopelessness of redress, and that completely broken-down condition of human nature which is characteristic of neuro-pathological cases. By the side of such sufferers you find a few others who are so deeply human that all your sympathies go with them; but the favourite heroes of Dostoyévskiy are the man and the woman who consider themselves as not having either the force to compel respect, or even the right of being treated as human beings. They once have made some timid attempt at defending their personalities, but they have succumbed, and never will try it again. They will sink deeper and deeper in their wretchedness, and die, either from consumption or from exposure, or they will become the victims of some mental affection—a sort of half-lucid lunacy, during which man occasionally rises to the highest conceptions of human philosophy—while some will conceive an embitterment which will bring them to commit some crime, followed by repentance the very next instant after it has been done.

—from *Ideals and Realities in Russian Literature* (1915)

D. H. LAWRENCE
They are great parables, the novels, but false art. They are only parables. All the people are fallen angels—even the dirtiest scrubs. This I cannot stomach. People are not fallen angels, they are merely people.

—on Dostoevsky, from a letter to J. Middleton Murray
and Katherine Mansfield (February 17, 1916)

Questions

1. Is Raskolnikov's salvation by the saintly prostitute Sonia plausible? Could it be argued that Dostoevsky was so anxious to make a point that he moved from realism to parable at the end of the novel? If so, what motivates the shift in tone in the Epilogue?

2. *Raskol* means "schism" in Russian. Why then does Dostoevsky name the hero Raskolnikov?

3. Svidrigailov originally appears in the novel almost as Raskolnikov's dream double. Why does Svidrigailov commit suicide while Raskolnikov does not?

4. Have the issues debated in *Crime and Punishment* lost their relevance to us, or are they still alive? If so, what are contemporary examples of the questions he raises?

5. Henry James, speaking of Tolstoy and Dostoevsky, noted, "How great a vice is their lack of composition, their defiance of economy and architecture." Do you agree with James? Is there a defense of Dostoevsky against this charge?

6. Trace the recurring mentions of water, yellow, thresholds, bells, and blood throughout the book. What are they associated with and what meanings do they take on?

7. Writing in 1891, William Dean Howells said he believed that America, lacking "shadows and inequalities," could not produce a fiction like *Crime and Punishment*. Is Howells's premise sound? Did America then lack "shadows and inequalities"? Does it now? Can you cite examples of subsequent American novels that bear a kinship with *Crime and Punishment*?

8. If you read *Crime and Punishment* exclusively as a psychological novel, omitting the religious aspect, what does that leave out of Dostoevsky's view of human nature?

9. Why does Dostoevsky have Raskolnikov almost confess his crime in a tavern called the Crystal Palace? How is it connected to Dostoevsky's argument with Socialism?

FOR FURTHER READING

Works by Dostoevsky

Poor Folk (1846)

The Double (1846)

The Friend of the Family (1859)

The Insulted and the Injured (1861)

The House of the Dead (1862)

Notes from Underground (1864)

The Idiot (1868–1869)

The Possessed (1871–1872)

The Brothers Karamazov (1879–1880)

The Notebooks for Crime and Punishment. Edited and translated by Edward Wasiolek. Chicago: University of Chicago Press, 1967.

A Writer's Diary. Vol. 1: 1873–1876. Translated and annotated by Kenneth Lantz; introductory study by Gary Saul Morson. Evanston, IL: Northwestern University Press, 1993.

Biography and Criticism

Bakhtin, Mikhail. Problems of Dostoevsky's Poetics. Translated and edited by Caryl Emerson, with an introduction by Wayne C. Booth. Minneapolis: University of Minnesota Press, 1984.

Berlin, Isaiah. Russian Thinkers. Edited by Henry Hardy and Aileen Kelly. New York: Viking Press, 1978.

Blackmur, R. P. Eleven Essays in the European Novel. New York: Harcourt, Brace and World, 1964.

Fanger, Donald. Dostoevsky and Romantic Realism: A Study of Dostoevsky in Relation to Balzac, Dickens, and Gogol. Cambridge, MA: Harvard University Press, 1965.

Frank, Joseph. Dostoevsky: The Miraculous Years, 1865–1871. Princeton, NJ: Princeton University Press, 1995.

Holquist, Michael. *Dostoevsky and the Novel*. Princeton, NJ: Princeton University Press, 1977.

Jackson, Robert Louis. *Dialogues with Dostoevsky: The Overwhelming Questions*. Stanford, CA: Stanford University Press, 1993.

———, ed. *Dostoevsky: New Perspectives*. Englewood Cliffs, NJ: Prentice-Hall, 1984.

Miller, Robin Feuer. *Critical Essays on Dostoevsky*. Boston: G. K. Hall, 1986.

Mochulsky, Konstantin. *Dostoevsky: His Life and Work*. Translated by Michael A. Minihan. Princeton, NJ: Princeton University Press, 1967.

Rosenshield, Gary. *Crime and Punishment: The Techniques of the Omniscient Narrator*. Lisse: Peter de Ridder Press, 1976.

Steiner, George. *Tolstoy or Dostoevsky: An Essay in the Old Criticism*. Second edition. New Haven, CT: Yale University Press, 1996.

Wellek, René, ed. *Dostoevsky: A Collection of Critical Essays*. Twentieth Century Views. Englewood Cliffs, NJ: Prentice-Hall, 1962.

Other Works of Interest

Chernyshevsky, Nikolai. *What Is to Be Done?* Translated by Michael R. Katz. Ithaca, NY: Cornell University Press, 1989.

Balzac, Honoré de. *Père Goriot*. Translated by Henry Reed. Signet Classics. New York: New American Library, 1962.

Pushkin, Alexander. *The Queen of Spades and Other Stories*. Translated by Alan Myers. Oxford: Oxford University Press, 1997.

Look for the following titles, available now and forthcoming from
BARNES & NOBLE CLASSICS.

Visit your local bookstore for these fine titles.

Title	Author	ISBN	Price
Adventures of Huckleberry Finn	Mark Twain	1-59308-000-X	$4.95
The Adventures of Tom Sawyer	Mark Twain	1-59308-068-9	$4.95
The Age of Innocence	Edith Wharton	1-59308-143-X	$5.95
Alice's Adventures in Wonderland and Through the Looking-Glass	Lewis Carroll	1-59308-015-8	$5.95
Anna Karenina	Leo Tolstoy	1-59308-027-1	$8.95
The Art of War	Sun Tzu	1-59308-017-4	$7.95
The Awakening and Selected Short Fiction	Kate Chopin	1-59308-001-8	$4.95
The Brothers Karamazov	Fyodor Dostoevsky	1-59308-045-X	$9.95
The Call of the Wild and White Fang	Jack London	1-59308-200-2	$5.95
Candide	Voltaire	1-59308-028-X	$4.95
A Christmas Carol, The Chimes and The Cricket on the Hearth	Charles Dickens	1-59308-033-6	$5.95
The Collected Poems of Emily Dickinson		1-59308-050-6	$5.95
The Complete Sherlock Holmes, Vol. I	Sir Arthur Conan Doyle	1-59308-034-4	$7.95
The Complete Sherlock Holmes, Vol. II	Sir Arthur Conan Doyle	1-59308-040-9	$7.95
The Count of Monte Cristo	Alexandre Dumas	1-59308-151-0	$7.95
Daniel Deronda	George Eliot	1-59308-290-8	$8.95
David Copperfield	Charles Dickens	1-59308-063-8	$7.95
The Death of Ivan Ilych and Other Stories	Leo Tolstoy	1-59308-069-7	$7.95
Don Quixote	Miguel de Cervantes	1-59308-046-8	$9.95
Dracula	Bram Stoker	1-59308-114-6	$6.95
Emma	Jane Austen	1-59308-089-1	$4.95
Essays and Poems by Ralph Waldo Emerson		1-59308-076-X	$6.95
The Essential Tales and Poems of Edgar Allan Poe		1-59308-064-6	$7.95
Frankenstein	Mary Shelley	1-59308-115-4	$4.95
Great American Short Stories: from Hawthorne to Hemingway		1-59308-086-7	$7.95
Great Expectations	Charles Dickens	1-59308-006-9	$4.95
Gulliver's Travels	Jonathan Swift	1-59308-132-4	$5.95
Hard Times	Charles Dickens	1-59308-156-1	$5.95
Heart of Darkness and Selected Short Fiction	Joseph Conrad	1-59308-021-2	$4.95
The Histories	Herodotus	1-59308-102-2	$6.95
The House of Mirth	Edith Wharton	1-59308-153-7	$6.95
Howards End	E. M. Forster	1-59308-022-0	$6.95
The Hunchback of Notre Dame	Victor Hugo	1-59308-047-6	$5.95
The Idiot	Fyodor Dostoevsky	1-59308-058-1	$7.95
The Importance of Being Earnest and Four Other Plays	Oscar Wilde	1-59308-059-X	$6.95
The Inferno	Dante Alighieri	1-59308-051-4	$6.95
Jane Eyre	Charlotte Brontë	1-59308-007-7	$4.95
Jude the Obscure	Thomas Hardy	1-59308-035-2	$6.95
The Jungle Books	Rudyard Kipling	1-59308-109-X	$5.95
The Jungle	Upton Sinclair	1-59308-008-5	$4.95
The Last of the Mohicans	James Fenimore Cooper	1-59308-137-5	$5.95
Leaves of Grass: First and "Death-bed" Editions	Walt Whitman	1-59308-083-2	$9.95
Les Misérables	Victor Hugo	1-59308-066-2	$9.95
Little Women	Louisa May Alcott	1-59308-108-1	$6.95

(continued)

Main Street	Sinclair Lewis	1-59308-036-0	$5.95
Mansfield Park	Jane Austen	1-59308-154-5	$5.95
The Metamorphosis and Other Stories	Franz Kafka	1-59308-029-8	$6.95
Moby-Dick	Herman Melville	1-59308-018-2	$9.95
My Ántonia	Willa Cather	1-59308-202-9	$5.95
Narrative of the Life of Frederick Douglass, an American Slave		1-59308-041-7	$4.95
Notes From Underground, The Double and Other Stories	Fyodor Dostoevsky	1-59308-037-9	$4.95
O Pioneers!	Willa Cather	1-59308-205-3	$5.95
The Odyssey	Homer	1-59308-009-3	$5.95
Oliver Twist	Charles Dickens	1-59308-206-1	$6.95
The Origin of Species	Charles Darwin	1-59308-077-8	$7.95
Paradise Lost	John Milton	1-59308-095-6	$7.95
Persuasion	Jane Austen	1-59308-130-8	$5.95
The Picture of Dorian Gray	Oscar Wilde	1-59308-025-5	$4.95
The Portrait of a Lady	Henry James	1-59308-096-4	$7.95
A Portrait of the Artist as a Young Man and Dubliners	James Joyce	1-59308-031-X	$6.95
Pride and Prejudice	Jane Austen	1-59308-201-0	$5.95
The Prince and Other Writings	Niccolò Machiavelli	1-59308-060-3	$5.95
The Red Badge of Courage and Selected Short Fiction	Stephen Crane	1-59308-119-7	$4.95
Republic	Plato	1-59308-097-2	$6.95
Robinson Crusoe	Daniel Defoe	1-59308-360-2	$5.95
The Scarlet Letter	Nathaniel Hawthorne	1-59308-207-X	$4.95
Sense and Sensibility	Jane Austen	1-59308-125-1	$5.95
Sons and Lovers	D. H. Lawrence	1-59308-013-1	$7.95
The Souls of Black Folk	W. E. B. Du Bois	1-59308-014-X	$5.95
The Strange Case of Dr. Jekyll and Mr. Hyde and Other Stories	Robert Louis Stevenson	1-59308-131-6	$4.95
A Tale of Two Cities	Charles Dickens	1-59308-138-3	$5.95
Tao Te Ching	Lao Tzu	1-59308-256-8	$5.95
The Three Musketeers	Alexandre Dumas	1-59308-148-0	$8.95
The Time Machine and The Invisible Man	H. G. Wells	1-59308-032-8	$4.95
Tom Jones	Henry Fielding	1-59308-070-0	$8.95
Treasure Island	Robert Louis Stevenson	1-59308-247-9	$4.95
The Turn of the Screw, The Aspern Papers and Two Stories	Henry James	1-59308-043-3	$5.95
Twenty Thousand Leagues Under the Sea	Jules Verne	1-59308-302-5	$5.95
Uncle Tom's Cabin	Harriet Beecher Stowe	1-59308-121-9	$7.95
Vanity Fair	William Makepeace Thackeray	1-59308-071-9	$7.95
Villette	Charlotte Brontë	1-59308-316-5	$7.95
The Voyage Out	Virginia Woolf	1-59308-229-0	$6.95
Walden and Civil Disobedience	Henry David Thoreau	1-59308-208-8	$5.95
The War of the Worlds	H. G. Wells	1-59308-085-9	$3.95
Wuthering Heights	Emily Brontë	1-59308-044-1	$4.95

Ⓑ

BARNES & NOBLE CLASSICS

If you are an educator and would like to receive an
Examination or Desk Copy of a Barnes & Noble Classic edition,
please refer to Academic Resources on our website at
WWW.BN.COM/CLASSICS
or contact us at
B&NCLASSICS@BN.COM.

All prices are subject to change.